D1149990

THE JUMP

Also by Martina Cole

Dangerous Lady
The Lady Killer
Goodnight Lady

THE JUMP

Martina Cole

HEADLINE

Copyright © 1995 Martina Cole

The right of Martina Cole to be identified as the Author of
the Work has been asserted by her in accordance with the
Copyright, Designs and Patents Act 1988.

First published in 1995 by
HEADLINE BOOK PUBLISHING

10 9 8 7 6 5 4 3 2 1

British Library Cataloguing in Publication Data

Cole, Martina
The Jump
I. Title
823.914 [F]

ISBN 0-7472-1133-7 (hbk)
ISBN 0-7472-7795-8 (sbk)

Typeset by
Letterpart Limited, Reigate, Surrey

Printed and bound in Great Britain by
Mackays of Chatham PLC, Chatham, Kent

HEADLINE BOOK PUBLISHING
A division of Hodder Headline PLC
338 Euston Road
London NW1 3BH

For my big brothers Christopher and Anthony Whiteside (in the words of Horace, Par nobile fratrum.) With my love always and my thanks to you both for being there when I needed you.

In loving memory of: Patrick D'Arcy, Ellen Whiteside, Tommy Whiteside, Jack O'Loughlin and Christopher Lane.

Also Ronald Burt, Roy Burt and Bernie Steingold remembering our youth and long summer days.

Many thanks to: the twins and KC and the Sunshine Band for all the help, the stories and the laughter.

Prologue

'Georgio shouldn't be much longer now, Harry. Let me get you a refill.'

Donna Brunos took the Waterford crystal whisky glass from the small man in front of her and smiled at him tightly. He'd already had more than enough to drink; a few more whiskies and his nasty streak would surface.

She poured a hefty measure of ginger ale into the glass, topping it up with a small amount of Red Label whisky. She closed her eyes tightly for a few seconds, hoping to take away the ache behind them.

As she turned to face Harry Robertson, his wife Bunty gave one of her high-pitched laughs. Donna handed the drink to Harry and, using the excuse that she was wanted in the kitchen, moved through the lounge, stopping here and there to have a brief word with different people.

Donna was aware that they were all waiting for her husband, that they classed her a poor second as hostess. The only reason they were here, the men as well as the women, was because Georgio had invited them personally. Everyone was grateful for a little bit of attention from Georgio, she knew that, had always known that. Donna smiled ruefully; she felt that way herself and she was his wife. It was a knack he had. When Georgio looked at a person, he could make them feel as if there was no one else in the world and he used this to his advantage.

Inside the kitchen she leant against the wall and sighed.

'He's bloody cutting it fine,' said Dolly, her housekeeper and friend.

Donna nodded and, pushing herself away from the wall, she surveyed the work surfaces intently. 'How's the duck?'

'Drier than a nun's tits!'

Donna laughed gently, a laugh she didn't think she had inside her. 'You're crude, Dolly, but then you already know that.'

Dolly flicked the ash from her cigarette into the waste disposal and shrugged good-naturedly.

'It's nearly half-eight – why don't you sit down without him? The

1

sooner they eat, the sooner they'll go. When Georgio gets in, he'll be grateful most of it is over. He can get down to the business in hand over the brandy and we can all be in bed for twelve.'

Donna pushed her heavy dark hair off her face; it was a weary gesture and Dolly smiled at her sympathetically.

'You want to tear the arse off him when he gets home, love.'

Donna removed the cigarette from the older woman's hand and took a long drag, holding the smoke in before letting it out heavily in a thick grey cloud.

'I would, Dolly, if I thought he'd take any notice. Give him another half an hour then serve, all right?'

'Okey doke. Get yourself in and join the fray. Sixteen of the town's bigwigs to dinner and the golden boy doesn't turn up! That's him all over.'

This was said with a rough pride. Dolly Parkins loved her employers, and they loved her, and – more importantly – they trusted her. Dolly could be herself with them and she abused this shamelessly. Throwing the butt of the cigarette into the bin, she began putting the plates in the oven to warm.

Donna left the sanctuary of the kitchen and went once more into the lounge, where Betty Hawkins's loud braying voice immediately hit her with the force of a sledgehammer.

'Donna! Donna, get over here and tell this fool that your husband has a 911 Carerra with my name on it!'

'When's the delivery date, Betty? I've forgotten.'

Donna fixed a smile on her face and joined in the conversation. In her mind she decided she would take Dolly's advice. She would tear the arse off her husband when he finally arrived home.

The port and Stilton were on the table and Harry Robertson was holding forth on local government. Donna tried to look interested but her eyes were straying over the debris strewn across the table. Bunty Robertson had burned a cigarette hole in the Venetian lace tablecloth and it was like a magnet, drawing Donna's eyes. She had always hated the woman; in fact, she realised, she hated everyone sitting around the table. In different degrees, maybe, but it was a form of dislike for each and every one of them. Yet, as Georgio was always saying, they needed them; or more to the point, *he* needed them. It was Georgio who had arranged this dinner, had even told her the menu and ordered in the wine specially, and who had not turned up – not even had the decency to ring and make his excuses.

Harry Robertson was now on his favourite subject – the courts, his

2

role as magistrate, and the sentencing of juvenile offenders. With enough drink in him to knock out an Irish navvy, he began his monologue on the judicial system. One day, Donna promised herself, she was going to ask him how he felt about drunk drivers. She had lost count of the number of times he had wheelspinned out of her driveway, completely blotto, and gone zig-zagging down the lane towards the M25, his wife hiccuping beside him, both feeling they were a law unto themselves.

Donna heard the doorbell and sighed with relief. Georgio was home. He would take over in that easy way he had, and soon everyone would forget that he hadn't turned up for the meal, and would all vie with one another to assure him they didn't mind waiting for him in the least.

She stood up and Harry Robertson said snidely, 'Now then, Donna, don't you go giving him a hard time – at least not until we've all gone home.' Everyone laughed dutifully. It was on the tip of Donna's tongue to reply: 'Oh, you are going home, then? That's something to look forward to anyway.'

As she left the room she heard Bunty's voice, as she knew she was meant to, saying, 'Honestly – Donna!' in that maddening tone she had. Closing the door firmly behind her, she met Dolly in the hallway.

'It's all right, I'll answer the door.'

Dolly shrugged and went back into the kitchen.

Donna's heart sank as she saw four large outlines through the glass of the double front doors. Georgio had brought people home on top of everything else. Her headache was heavier now, a migraine in the making. Putting her shoulders back and pushing out her narrow chest, she plastered a big smile on her face and opened the door. Georgio always liked her to be in control, or at least look as if she was in control.

'Mrs Donna Brunos?'

The uniforms of two of the men registered in her mind and she felt the panic well up inside her chest.

'Yes . . . I'm Mrs Brunos. My husband, Georgio . . . What's happened?' In her imagination she saw him in the twisted wreckage of his Mercedes Sports. Remembered all her warnings to him to drive carefully. She was totally unprepared for what she heard next.

The bigger of the men in plain clothes was mouthing words at her, she was shaking her head in denial, then they were actually walking into her home.

'We have a warrant to search these premises.'

'A what?' She was aware that Dolly was beside her, and somewhere

3

in the recesses of her mind, she registered loud laughter coming from the dining room.

'Your husband was arrested today for armed robbery. He is being held at Chelmsford police station. I am Detective Inspector Frank Laughton from the Serious Crime Squad . . .'

The migraine was bearing down on her, jagged, probing. She heard the dining-room door open and Harry Robertson emerged, Council Planning Officer and pillar of the local community, asking in his strident voice what the hell was going on – and then, mercifully, she passed out.

As Donna sank down into oblivion, her mind flashed up images and memories to compensate for the shock just dealt to her. She saw herself as a child again, her face white and strained as she listened to her mother's strident voice. Covering her ears with her hands, she froze, waiting for the noise she knew was to come.

The soft thud came through the wall on cue. She knew her mother had fallen against the dressing table. She had to have fallen. Donna's father wouldn't hurt her, not deliberately.

The room was cold; the house was always cold. Even in the middle of summer it had a damp, clammy feel to it that was more to do with the occupants than the weather.

She could once more hear her mother's voice, goading her father on, telling him things about himself best left unsaid. She wished her brother Hamish was still at home, but Donna rarely saw him now he was married.

This was a strange household.

During the day, the almost clinical cleanliness could break a girl's heart. Anyone entering the house automatically spoke in whispers, as if in the presence of the dead. Donna's mother was pretty in an austere way, her face a beacon of righteousness. She and her husband were well respected; they 'kept themselves to themselves', a favourite saying of theirs, along with, 'It's nobody's business but ours'.

The child waited for her father to go to his room, and sighed heartily as she heard the door shut softly behind him. She took after her father, everyone said so. Self-effacing, self-contained, anything for a quiet life.

Tomorrow, the incident would be over – never, ever to be mentioned.

Especially by a little girl who knew exactly how to be seen and not heard.

Her face was flaming, burning as if the skin would melt off it. Mrs

4

Dowson was looking at her with a pitying expression on her normally dour face.

'You should have told someone, Donna! Why didn't you tell your mother?' Mrs Dowson knew why Donna Fenland had not imparted the news to her mother, but she had to ask the question anyway.

Monica Fenland stood like a hefty wedge between her daughter and the door. Her eyes scrutinised her child, bored into her with a pale grey ferocity. 'Come on, Donna, answer Mrs Dowson.'

Donna looked up into her mother's eyes – eyes that were saying, 'Keep in control, Donna. Don't show any emotion at all, and talk yourself out of this embarrassing situation.'

'My mother had already explained it all to me, and I didn't see the need to bother her with any of it. Today was the only time I have ever felt remotely ill since I . . .' She paused. 'Well, since they came.'

Mrs Dowson saw Monica Fenland smile grimly and wondered why the hell she'd bothered.

'I see. Now do you think you might be better off at home, just for today? Until the period calms itself down a mite, eh.' She was gratified to see the girl's obvious relief at the outcome.

Ten minutes later Donna and her mother drove home from the school in silence. Inside the house Donna was tucked into bed, given a hot water bottle and a copy of *Black Beauty* to read.

Then Monica Fenland sat on the side of the bed and smiled at her daughter before saying, 'You did well today, Donna. Your monthly visitor is private – Mrs Dowson had no right bringing it into the open like that. She should have popped you in a cab . . . But there, it's done now. I was called from work, I had to travel to your school, and now I have to return to my work. Not that Mrs Dowson would understand that, I suspect. So you just lie back and relax, and if you're feeling better later on, you can peel a few potatoes for me, eh?' Standing up, she smoothed out the creases in her plaid skirt.

'What happens now, Mum? Will it be like this every month?' But Monica Fenland was already walking from the bedroom, Donna's words falling on deaf ears.

As she started up her car, Monica glanced at the neat detached house, at her daughter's bedroom window, and sighed heavily. Not a natural mother, she cared for her daughter but knew she failed her. Monica had never experienced the rush of love other mothers talked about on first seeing their child after the delivery.

The birth of Hamish had been difficult and humiliating. It was an act she had refused to repeat. Then, just as she was convinced her childbearing days were over, along had come a baby girl. The

5

embarrassment of her late pregnancy still made her face go hot fourteen years later.

Pregnant at forty-three.

Leaning on the cool leather covering of her steering wheel she felt the tears, because no matter how hard she tried, she couldn't really love her daughter.

And she knew that Donna Fenland was a child who needed a great deal of love.

Pulling out of the drive, she felt the familiar urge for a drink.

'Donna, you're so bloody boring! Come on, girl.'

Donna followed Jackie's lead and together they looked through the motley collection of shoes displayed on the market stall.

'Your mum can't stop you doing anything now . . .' Jackie's voice trailed off. 'Oh, Donna, I'm so sorry. I didn't mean that how it came out.'

Donna looked into the honest blue eyes of her best friend and nodded.

'I know.' She shrugged lightly, her instinctive feeling that you had to be accommodating coming to the fore as she tried to pacify her friend. 'I know what you mean, Jackie. My parents weren't exactly hip, were they? Sometimes I wonder if they even realised I was in the house.'

The desolation in her voice, and the honesty of the answer, made Jackie's eyes water. 'Oh, Donna, I'm really, really sorry.'

Donna smiled widely. 'Don't be, they gave me a good life in their own way. Now they're gone, and I'm here on holiday with you so let's have some fun!'

'Do you miss them?' Jackie's voice was soft.

Donna nodded slowly. 'Yes, I do. They were all I ever knew. I loved them, and now they're gone I miss them.'

The Cockney stallholder grinned as he shouted at the two girls: 'You keeping that shoe, love, or waiting for Cinderella?'

Laughing at his raucous voice, Donna replaced the black patent shoe on the stall.

As they walked off, Donna saw an apparition of manhood so excitingly gorgeous it made her breath catch in her throat. And the most amazing thing of all was, he was smiling right at her. Looking over her shoulder in case it was someone else he was staring at, she turned back to find him planted firmly in her path.

'Hello, girls.'

His voice was rich and brown but Donna heard the cockney inflection in it.

'So what are your names then?'

6

Georgio Brunos always talked to pretty girls, and giving the two friends a once-over with his practised eye, decided the blonde one was a little raver, and the dark one a challenge. He concentrated on the dark one, and was amazed to find himself staring into a pair of eyes so startling, he was nearly lost for words.

And on closer inspection, the face before him was one of the most beautiful he had ever encountered.

Still smiling jauntily, he switched his gaze back to Jackie. He took in her lipsticked mouth, jutting breasts and short skirt. She was his usual armload. Yet this slim, flat-chested dark piece intrigued him . . .

And Georgio Brunos didn't know why.

He managed to get a firm date and her phone number, much to the chagrin of Blondie. The little dark piece's absolute shock and bewilderment made him feel good.

She had potential.

A lot of potential.

As he swaggered away, he knew she was still watching him.

Donna stood in the doorway of the cramped living room, her heart hammering in her chest. The flat was a confusion of smells, noise and bustle. The worn furniture was covered in people and Donna felt an urge to run away.

A heavy-set woman in her forties, with a beaming smile, false teeth and red work-worn hands, came towards her with surprising agility, shouting, 'Come away in. Oh Georgio, she's beautiful. Like a little flower!'

Georgio laughed in delight.

His elder sister Mary got up from the battered chair by the fireside and offered it to the thin pale girl her mother was practically dragging into the cramped room.

'Christ, child, your hands are like ice.'

Sitting Donna in the chair, she began chafing the slim fingers between her own, as if Donna was five instead of eighteen and a half.

'Jaysus save us, would one of yous shut your galloping traps and bring the child a cup of tea?'

Nuala, the youngest, tripped gaily from the room singing: 'Georgio's got a girlfriend, Georgio's got a girlfriend!' He chased her out and playfully slapped her bottom.

Ten minutes later, Donna had been introduced to everyone, had a cup of scalding tea balanced precariously on her lap and a plate of sandwiches and cake on the wide arm of the chair. In shocked silence she listened as everyone talked at once, shouting over each other to be

7

heard and arguing playfully about just about everything.

Then a tall man walked into the room with a large covered dish in his hands and everyone fell silent.

Placing the dish on the table he smiled at one and all, saying in broken English, 'My first-born son has brought home a girl at last! I have made a large pan of Stifado, and downstairs there's a beautiful crispy plate of Baklava, full of honey and nuts, to enjoy on this special occasion.'

Donna's eyes were drawn to the large handsome man before her, and as everyone in the room turned to look, Pa Brunos put his ample arms around her waist and kissed her gently on both cheeks. Always near to tears, an emotional man by nature, he then pulled out a large white handkerchief and wiped his eyes.

'Oh, Jesus save us!' snorted his wife. 'He'll be roaring after a few Ouzos, child. Ignore him!'

Donna laughed with everyone, and in those few seconds, amid the rich garlicky smell of the food and the chattering voices, Donna Fenland fell in love once more.

Georgio she already loved. She had loved him for six months, from the first day she had clapped eyes on him in the Roman Road market.

But now she realised she had fallen in love with a whole family.

A real family, full of real people.

Georgio winked at her and tapped his pocket, where he had a ring ready to place on her slim finger. They'd picked it that day. She was going to marry the tall handsome man with the deep brown eyes and the deep brown voice, and because of that, she would also gain this family.

This family who were enveloped in love, who were warm, spontaneously affectionate, and close.

It was something she would thank God for more than once over the next twenty years.

After her early experience of life without real love, she would thrive on the abundance of it, overflowing from her husband and from his family.

Especially his family.

As she looked around her at the smiling faces of the younger children, at the fond glances from his parents, and at the big handsome man she had somehow managed to capture, Donna Fenland felt as if, after a long and painful journey, she had finally and irrevocably come home.

'I'm sorry, but I think you must have made a very serious mistake.'

Donna's voice was high and breathless, her face a white strained

8

mask that made even the most hardened of the policemen present feel a tinge of pity for her.

Donna heard Bunty's refined tones and closed her eyes in consternation.

'Do you know who my husband is?' It was more of a shocked statement than a question, and even in her own distress, Donna felt a moment's smugness that Bunty wasn't getting it all her own way. The other dinner guests had left as soon as possible; only Bunty and Harry had stayed on.

'We're quite well aware of your husband's standing in the community, madam. We would advise you that we have a warrant to search these premises and that is what we intend to do.'

Harry stormed into the lounge, his face grey-tinged, the alcohol he'd consumed lying heavily on his fat stomach. 'Come along, Bunty, there's no more we can do here. I would advise you, Donna, to get your husband a solicitor as soon as possible. Bunty, shut your mouth and let's get home.'

She stared wide-eyed at her husband. 'But surely . . . surely there's been some mistake? I mean . . .'

'Get your coat, dear, we're leaving. I've been on the phone to the Chief Super and he informs me there is no mistake at all. Now can we please leave?' His eyes warned against any further objection and Bunty, having always prided herself on being quick on the uptake, moved silently from the room.

In the hallway, Harry helped his wife on with her wrap. As he picked up the keys to his BMW a voice said hoarsely, 'Going to call a cab for him, missus? I don't think *the local magistrate* would be happy being stopped for drunk driving.'

Bunty and Harry both looked at Frank Laughton. Replacing the keys in his pocket, Harry picked up the phone, a red tinge flooding his face as he dialled the number.

Laughton walked nonchalantly past them, a smile on his face. Going into the lounge, he shut the door noisily in Bunty's face.

Donna was sitting on a small leather stool, her face devoid of colour and her whole body trembling. Looking at her, so fine-boned, so feminine, Laughton felt the full force of the woman's attraction. Pushing her heavy dark hair from her face, she looked him in the eye. Tears were rolling down her cheeks, but she made no move to wipe them away.

'This is all a ghastly mistake. My husband is somehow caught up in a ghastly mistake.' She begged him with her eyes to tell her what she said was true. Laughton did not wish to witness her pain. Instead he said gruffly, 'Your housekeeper is making some tea. I

9

would advise you to put a drop of brandy in it.'

Helping her from the stool, he escorted her to the kitchen, ignoring Bunty and Harry as they passed in the hallway.

Dolly's cockney accent could be heard even before they reached the kitchen door. 'Get your ruddy feet off of my clean floor, and stop picking at the food! If you're not careful . . .'

As Donna and Laughton walked into the kitchen, she looked at them and said loudly, 'So! PC Plod has arrived back, has he? You've dropped the biggest bollock of your career tonight, I only hope you realise that . . .'

'Hello, Dolly, long time no see.'

She snorted. 'Not long enough for me, Laughton. Still fitting people up, I see.'

The three policemen in the kitchen smiled at the older woman's choice of words. Dolly nodded at them all, her small black eyes sharp.

'I know what I'm talking about. I had dealings with him when he was greener than the proverbial grass. Grass being the operative word with you, eh, Laughton?'

'Shut up, Dolly. You always was a mouthy bitch and you ain't improved with age.'

'How's the wife, Frank? Still turning a blind eye, is she? Mind you, looking at you now, I'd bet me last penny you don't get much luck from the blaggers' wives these days.' She nodded at the three policemen and grinned widely. 'Oh, that's true, all right. You could set your watch by him years ago. If the old man got a twelve at three in the afternoon, Laughton would be round the house by eight-thirty, suited and booted, fish and chips under one arm and a bottle of wine in the other. No prizes for guessing what else he had for them . . .'

'Shut up, Dolly, and give your arse a chance.' Laughton's voice was hard.

'Truth hurt, does it, Frankie? You ain't worn very well, but then your kind never do, do they?'

'You was an old boot then, and you're still one now. How's your old man? Grateful for getting banged up, I imagine. Anything has to be better than living with you. Now you're with another blagger. I might have guessed I'd find you here.'

Donna put her hands to her ears and said loudly, 'I can't believe this is happening!' She turned to face Frank Laughton. 'You come into my home – *my home*! – and try to tell me my husband is a criminal, and then you have the audacity to stand there and harangue my housekeeper! You call my husband a blagger? Well, Mr Laughton, you had better prove your allegations or I will see to it that

10

you pay for this night's work. Now do what the hell you have to then get out of my home. Do you hear me? Get out of my home!'

Dolly pulled the distraught woman into her arms, glaring at the policemen as they trooped out of the kitchen.

'Oh Dolly, what's going on? What on earth is going on? There's obviously been some kind of mistake. They won't even let me go and see Georgio.'

'It's all a big mistake, darlin'. Before you know it, everything will be sorted out and back to normal. Look on the bright side, love. It got rid of that load of ponces, eh?'

Donna smiled wanly. 'Oh, Dolly. I don't know what to do.' Her voice was thick with tears.

Dolly held her close. She could smell the expensive shampoo Donna always used.

'I'll pour you out a strong cup of tea. This'll all be over before you know it.'

Five minutes later they sat and listened as the house was systematically torn apart around them.

Detective Laughton was smiling widely. He was known as 'Arsehole Laughton' by criminals and his own men alike. He wasn't what would be termed a well-liked man and he knew this; accepted it. Revelled in it, in fact. He prided himself that his men might not love him, but at least they respected him. It would have pained him to know that, in reality, the men he worked with had more respect for the majority of the criminals they captured than for their Guv'nor.

Lighting one of the eighty cigarettes he smoked a day, Laughton coughed loudly, a phlegm-ridden, hacking cough that made the young DC's insides rise up in protest.

'Cigarette, Mr Brunos?' Laughton's face screwed up as he fought to hold back another wracking bout.

Georgio shook his head in distaste.

Laughton let the cough go, spraying Georgio and the younger man with spittle and mucus.

'Leave it out, for fuck's sake!' Georgio Brunos was disgusted and it showed in his face.

'Oh, what's the matter, Mr Brunos? Are we too, too sophisticated for all this, eh?' Laughton's voice was sarcastic and hard. 'Does living the life of fucking Riley in a big drum, with flash cars and plenty of booze and skirt, make you better than everyone else then?'

Georgio shook his head slowly, wiping his face with a large brown hand. 'Listen, Mr Laughton, with respect, a pig in shit has more sophistication than you!'

11

The young DC smiled, and hastily turned away from his boss.

Laughton stared down at the handsome man sitting before him, a wave of malice and temper washing through him. 'I'll have you, Brunos, you know that, don't you? I'll see me day with you, boyo, see if I don't.'

Georgio shook his head sadly. 'Why are you so determined to pin this on me, Laughton? Did I sell you a right steamer for the wife or something? Did I annoy you in another life and now you've been reborn to fucking haunt me in this one – is that it?'

Laughton took a rasping drag on his cigarette and smiled grimly. 'I hear the whispers, Brunos, I hear everything. I know you're not as white as you'd like everyone to believe. I know you was behind that blag, everyone knows . . .'

Georgio laughed out loud. 'Everyone knows, do they? Well, I wish they'd let *me* in on it, mate, because I don't even know what you're talking about.'

Laughton stubbed out his cigarette on a saucer and promptly lit another. 'Wilding, send in DC Masterson, please. And go and get yourself a cup of tea or something. I don't want to see you for about forty minutes, OK?'

The younger man hesitated for a split second before Laughton bellowed: 'You heard me, boy. Move it! Do you want it tattooed on your arse then?'

DC Wilding looked into Georgio's eyes briefly and left the room. The silence was tangible, heavy on the air like electricity before a summer storm.

Five minutes later, one of the biggest men Georgio had ever laid eyes on walked into the room.

'You wanted me, Mr Laughton?' The man's face was open, kind.

'Sit over there, son. I'll tell you what to do when the time comes.'

Georgio Brunos, a small tremor of fear inside him now, smiled at the man as nonchalantly as possible, then turning to Laughton he said quietly: 'You wouldn't dare, Laughton.'

The DI laughed loudly. 'Oh, I'd dare, Georgio. You ask Peter Wilson. Bless his little cotton socks, even as we speak he's nursing his wounds. Never the bravest of blokes Peter, but very eager to please. Does what he's told, does young Peter. You could learn from him, Brunos. Tell the truth and shame the devil.'

Georgio stood up abruptly. 'I want me brief, Laughton, and I want a break.'

Laughton's voice was low and cold now. 'Sit down, Brunos.'

Georgio stood firmly, facing the older man.

12

'Sit down, you Greek ponce, before I put you through the fucking wall!'

Georgio stood his ground, refusing to be intimidated.

Sighing heavily, Laughton said, 'Sit the man down, son, before we have a mutiny on our hands.'

Masterson stood up, his amiable face still half-smiling. Georgio couldn't believe it when he was forced back into his seat with such force his spine felt as if it had been crushed. Humiliated, stunned, and losing his temper, Georgio said menacingly, 'You'll pay for this, Laughton. The lot of you will pay for this one!'

The policeman smiled, displaying his tobacco-stained teeth. 'I don't like you, Brunos. I don't like your good looks, your charming manners, and your two-faced fucking way of life. I don't like your money, your business, or your pretty little wife. I don't like your family, or your friends. In short, as I said earlier, I'm going to have you, Brunos. I'm going to put you away. I'm going to put you away for so long, it'll make Nelson Mandela's sentence look like a stint in Borstal.'

Georgio stared into the manic face above him and felt real fear forming in his bowels.

'I ain't done nothing, Laughton. Three people saw me in my car lot today. Three people! What more do you want – a fucking signed statement from the Queen?'

'I want you, Brunos, because you're a piece of shite, you and Davey Jackson and the rest of them. You're the dog shit on my shoes. I've got you bang to rights, Brunos.'

Georgio shook his head in exasperation. 'You're talking bollocks and you know it. You must be hard up for a face to try and pin this one on me. I've got more witnesses than the ascension into heaven!'

Turning to the large DC, Laughton said in a friendly voice: 'Hurt him.'

The younger man stood up, and in stunned disbelief Georgio felt himself being dragged from the chair and forced onto the ground. He could smell the dirty floor and the polished leather of the man's boots as he was kicked viciously in the stomach five times.

Eventually, the DI pulled the larger man away, knelt down and said quietly: 'In a minute, I'm going to put on the nice tape recorder and read you your rights, because Peter Wilson gave us enough to put you away. No bail for you, Greek boy. You're off to Chelmsford nick tonight. But first I'm going to have a cuppa and a fag and watch you squirm on the floor for a while. I hate your guts, Brunos, but don't take it too personally – I hate everyone.'

Georgio held down the bile that was rising into his mouth, burning

13

his throat and tongue. This was a nightmare, a bona fide twenty-two-carat nightmare, and inside himself he knew that if Wilson was telling Laughton what he wanted to hear, the nightmare could go on for months. Looking up, Georgio felt the fight leave his body to be replaced by a calmness that surprised him.

'I never done nothing and you know it,' he said. 'I'm being fitted up and I'll prove it.'

Laughton laughed again. 'Yeah, course you will. Conspiracy to rob, conspiracy to murder, and aggravated assault on a police officer are only a few of the charges against you, but they'll grow, Brunos. Like a cancer, they'll grow – I'll see to that. God, I wish we still had hanging! A young man died today. You know about it and you know where the dosh is, or my name ain't Frank Laughton. You can deny it until the cows come home and the Second Coming arrives. I couldn't give a flying fuck. You're in this up to your neck, and for the widow of that boy, and for his kids, I'll see you go away for it. You might not have pulled the trigger, Brunos, but you was there in spirit. You set it up and I'll prove it. With the help of Wilson, I'll prove it.'

Georgio closed his eyes and coughed gently, a small trail of bile escaping from his lips. Looking up into Laughton's face he said loudly, 'Fuck you, Laughton. You can't prove nothing.'

Then the kicking really started.

14

BOOK ONE

Dilige et quod vis fac
Love, and do what you will—

St Augustine of Hippo, AD 354–430

All the privilege I claim for my own sex
is that of loving longest, when existence
or when hope is gone—

Persuasion Jane Austen, 1755–1817

Chapter One

Peter Wilson was frightened. As he looked into Frank Laughton's face he sensed the full force of the older man's determination and temper. Running his tongue around his teeth, he felt the looseness of two of them and the split on the inside of his cheek where he had bitten it.

'Please, Mr Laughton, I can't tell you nothing, see. I don't know nothing.'

Frank Laughton sighed heavily and stared up at the clock on the wall of the interview room. 'Did anyone ever tell you how dogs know you're frightened of them? They smell your fear, see – like I can smell yours now.' He took a deep drag on his cigarette and threw it to the floor, crushing it with his heavy boot.

'You see, Peter, I want what you've got. That is, I want you to tell me what I want to hear. Now it won't be the first time, will it, eh? Me and you go back a long way, don't we? Remember the tellies a while back? I let you walk that one, because you were helpful. I like helpful people. I can be nice to helpful people. Whereas, when people are like you are now, annoying me, I want to hurt them and lock them away. I enjoy locking people away. It's my job, and I get pats on the back and things like that, see? Now, at this moment in time, I am in a good mood, but I can feel that mood gradually slipping away and that ain't good news for you, because it means I might really take it on myself to hurt you. Do you get my drift, shitbag?'

The quiet sing-song voice was more frightening to Peter Wilson than anything else Laughton could have done. Peter had grown up in children's homes and foster homes, each worse than the last. He was used to the worst. Abused by his father and others over a fifteen-year period, Peter was a small-time hood, small-time husband and small-time father. He could barely read or write, and used words of only one or two syllables. He was a gofer, nothing more and nothing less. He had a haphazard sort of friendship with the people who used him to do the little jobs they couldn't be bothered with themselves. He was a drug user, an abuser of alcohol, and also a nonsense case,

17

having three convictions for tampering with neighbours' children and his own. He was a loser of the first water and inside himself he knew all this. Had first had it knocked into him as a child, then repeatedly since becoming a grown man. As he listened to Laughton he knew in his heart he would do as he was asked. Eventually.

'But what about me, Mr Laughton? What will happen to me?'

Laughton laughed. 'What usually happens to you, Peter? You get pissed on, of course, like always.'

'Is there any money in it?'

Frank smiled. In his heart of hearts he hated Wilson more than he hated Brunos and the others he put away. At least Brunos was going after the big rents.

'There might be.'

Seeing a quick few quid, Peter smiled craftily. 'I ain't got a very good memory, though. If it's difficult like, what I have to say . . .'

Frank wiped a hand across his face and sighed heavily. Glancing at the big electric clock once more, he realised it was three-fifteen in the morning and he hadn't eaten for over eight hours. He could taste the cigarettes and tannin on his tongue and suddenly, feeling a rush of temper, he crashed a huge fist into the boy's face, sending him flying back against the wall with tremendous force, and knocking over the plastic chairs.

Leaning over the trembling form, he said quietly: 'Don't annoy me tonight, Peter. I have one difficult customer already, and you're going to help me put him away, as and when I tell you to – get it?' Straightening up, he brushed down his suit jacket and tidied his hair.

Peter Wilson watched him from the floor. As Laughton reached the door, Peter said timidly, 'Who's the face, Mr Laughton? Tell me that at least.'

Laughton grinned, knowing the boy was his now, as he had known all along he would be. Turning, he said, 'An old friend of yours, Peter. Georgio Brunos.'

He walked from the room, grinning.

Peter lay on the floor, his hands protectively holding his wedding tackle, and two big fat tears rolled down his face.

He was a dead man, and he knew it.

'What do you fucking mean, what's going on? Do you think I'm here for the beer or something?'

Georgio's voice was high and indignant and Donna closed her eyes before answering him.

'Don't swear at me, Georgio, I'm not the enemy.'

18

He wiped a heavy hand across his face and sighed. 'It's a fucking setup, Donna, you know it is. What the fuck would I be doing at a blag, eh? Especially one with loaded guns and a fucking bunch of ice creams doing the actual blagging.'

Donna drew in a deep breath before speaking, trying to calm down the erratic beating of her heart. 'Look, Georgio, all I know is, they've turned the house over . . .'

He pounced on her then, grabbing her thin arms above the elbows and shaking her. 'Did they take anything? Say anything?'

'Georgio, for God's sake. Calm down! You're hurting me.'

He stared down into the beautiful strained face of his wife, then, pulling her into his arms, he crushed her against his body. Burying his face in her hair he breathed in her scent.

'Laughton's after me, Donna. He wants my face in the frame and I can't do a fucking thing about it.'

Donna hugged her husband to her, feeling for the first time ever a sense of unease about the man she had married.

'But why would this Laughton want you so badly? What have you ever done to him, Georgio, that he should do this to you?' She pulled herself from her husband's embrace and looked into his face. 'It just doesn't make any sense.'

Pushing her roughly away, he bellowed, 'What do you mean? Do you think I had a tickle then, is that it? Fuck me, my own wife thinks I'm a blagger now! That's all I need, ain't it? Where you been then? Round me mother's? I bet she's loving this, ain't she. Christ! I can't believe you fucking said that.'

He stormed around the small interview room, his shoulders tense, his face a mask of hard energy and rage.

'Will you calm down, Georgio, please? I am not trying to say anything. I just want to know what the hell is going on, why you should be blamed. That's all.'

He bit on his bottom lip. His pupils were like pinpoints in the harsh lights of the room. He was agitated and Donna realised then that he was really in trouble. Serious trouble.

'Get me a brief, love, a good brief. Phone that cunt Simpson – it's about time he earned his collar anyway. Then get on to Davey and the others at the lot, tell them the score. Tell Davey I'll be in touch whatever happens, all right?'

Donna nodded, then realised that she was being dismissed. He wanted her to leave! Standing straight, she pushed the strap of her bag over her shoulder.

'I'll go then. Leave you to sort this lot out, shall I? It's seven-thirty in the morning and I haven't slept all night, my home has been

19

ransacked, legally ransacked, and you have the audacity to dismiss me?'

Georgio looked at her in consternation. 'Leave it out, Donna. I've got enough on me plate without you crying and bawling. Laughton's hauling me up the court this morning to get an extension, the way things are going I ain't even going to get bail, so the last thing on my mind is you. I'm sorry if that upsets you, love, but that's the truth of it.'

He gazed into her face and sighed once more. 'I'm looking at a ten stretch here, don't you realise that, woman!'

Donna nodded. 'I do now, thank you, Georgio. Only I didn't think people got ten years for nothing. But there, you learn a new thing every day, don't you? Now I'll go and get you yet another brief, shall I? Only I got you one last night in case you didn't notice!'

Georgio stormed across the room and grabbed her arm. Twisting her round to face him, he hissed: 'This is the real world, Donna. I'm a builder, a used-car dealer, I'm fucking Essex Man, love. I ain't got to do nothing, I just need to be implicated. I ain't no angel, never pretended I was, but this is over my head, darlin'. Way over my head. I've never so much as nicked a penny sweet, but Laughton wants me. Yeah, Donna, come down into the real world. Think of the Guildford Four and the Birmingham Six. Think about the West Midlands Crime squad. Where do you suppose my black eye came from, eh? The dirt on my clothes? He'll tell people I was trying to do a runner, or that I attacked them. It's all part of the game, love. The filth fit people up all the time, and that's why I'm so frightened, because on the big ones, they always get away with it.'

She swallowed back the fear that what he said was true. She said quietly, 'But those people were released . . .'

Georgio hugged her to him, his laugh rich and deep and worried. 'After how long, sweetheart? Think on that one. How long were they banged up in some stinking nick before they were earholed out, eh? That's the frightener, love. That's what frightens me.'

Looking up at her husband's strained face, Donna felt the fight leaving her body. In his position she would be upset, she would be full of bitterness and agitation.

'Oh, Georgio . . .' The tears came then, hot and stinging, and she savoured her husband's tight embrace and the words of love whispered in the stale confines of the interview room that smelt of cigarettes and urine.

Georgio stroked her silky hair and said softly, 'You don't understand this world, Donna – you never did, that's why I picked you. You had a bit of class, a bit of savvy. But you have to be my girl now,

20

my clever girl, because I'm going to need you, more than ever before.'

He stared into her face, holding her head between his large, rough hands. 'I'm depending on you, Donna.'

He saw the depths of his wife's eyes, saw the perfect bow of her lips and the perfect arch of her eyebrows. He drank in her beauty then, wondering how long it was since he had really looked at her. Suddenly he saw her as another man might and the pain in his chest was brutal.

'I love you, girl. I've always loved you, and together we'll beat that bastard at his own game.'

Donna nodded, her lips trembling, unsure that she could actually speak the words he wanted to hear.

'See, darling, this is what I want. What I need. You and me against the world, eh?'

Donna nodded again, licking the salty tears from her lips.

'With you beside me, I'll walk away from this, and then Laughton will never come near or by me again.'

Donna rested her head on his chest, the tears coming faster now, needing the feel of his hands on her tiny waist. He was hers, and she loved him, and any disloyal thoughts she might have had, she forced from her mind.

For the first time in nineteen years, Georgio needed her. It was heady stuff indeed.

The car lot was deserted, as if everyone had heard what had happened and were keeping away. Donna locked up her Mercedes and stepped carefully across the forecourt. Davey Jackson watched her from the office window and swore softly under his breath. His eyes swept the small office and registered the mess everywhere. He broke into the conversation he was having on the phone.

'Yeah, all right, Paddy. I've got to go, her ladyship's just turned up. I'll ring you back.'

Donna walked into the office just as he replaced the receiver. 'Hello, Donna. All right, love?'

She nodded, smiling slightly, and Davey wondered just how Georgio had landed a stunner like her and kept her all these years.

'I suppose you've heard?'

Lighting a cigarette, he took a deep drag on it. 'Slags they are, especially Laughton. He prides himself on being the dog's gonads and everyone knows he's a prize prat. He came after me a few years ago. He's renowned for fitting people up.'

Donna sat on the edge of the desk. 'Dolly says the same thing.

21

Everyone does. But why Georgio?'

Davey shrugged nonchalantly. 'He's a face, Donna. He might have a little tickle now and again, nothing too elaborate like. It's par for the course in this game, we don't even entertain ringers. He's done well, he looks like he does well. That's enough for that ponce Laughton. Georgio knew it was only a matter of time before someone had a sniff, only we thought it would be the big boys, the Revenue. So there you go, love. What's the score anyway?'

'They've been to court and got the extension, another forty-eight hours, then they have to charge him or let him go.'

'He'll be home before you know it, love. Carol was only saying this morning, when he gets back we'll have a night out, eh? Just the four of us.'

Donna nodded, wishing she was as sure of everything as Carol and Davey Jackson.

'How's his mother took it?'

'I haven't told her yet,' Donna confessed. 'I don't know what to say. So far the News has only said they've pulled in two people for questioning. No names, nothing. I'll wait until he gets home before I start worrying them. After all, what's the point? If he comes home, we'll be all right.'

Davey smiled sadly. This woman in front of him wasn't geared up for all this. It was unfair.

'He'll be home, darlin'. Laughton's a prat. Everyone has a bit of hag off him at some time or another – it's par for the course.'

Donna smiled, a tiny restrained smile, and Davey felt his heart melt in his chest.

'So everyone keeps saying. Georgio told me to tell you to carry on as normal.'

Davey swept out his arms in a gesture of good will. 'That's exactly what I am doing, my lovely.'

'Can I do anything?'

Davey laughed then, a deep belly laugh. 'Go home and get yourself tarted up for the conquering hero. That's all you need to do, Donna love.'

She didn't smile back. Instead she slipped from the desk and nodded. 'Of course it is. Now why didn't I think of that?'

Turning abruptly, she walked from the tiny office and slammed the door behind her. Davey watched her walk stiff-backed towards her car, and he tapped his teeth reflectively with the end of a biro. There was more to Donna Brunos than met the eye. Now why had he never realised that before?

Thoughtfully, he picked up the phone and began dialling.

★ ★ ★

Maeve Brunos was reading the *Sun* and drinking a large mug of strong black coffee. It was a ritual she enjoyed every day. Her husband was at work in the restaurant downstairs, preparing the evening meals, and her children were out and about. Bringing up six kids in a small flat made you very aware of quality time. And this was her quality time, her time alone. 'Maeve's half-hour' they called it, and she loved every second of it.

She read the leader on the front page and tutted. A photograph of the young security man who had died the day before in an armed robbery was emblazoned across the front page. It had been taken on his wedding day; the caption read: FIND THE KILLERS.

Maeve sipped at the strong coffee and lit herself a Benson & Hedges Light. Drawing deep on the smoke she began to read the story, her eyes darting continually to the photo of the young man and his pretty, plump wife. Tragedy was always a decent seller of newspapers and Maeve lapped it up, getting her excitement in the comfort and security of her own home. When the doorbell rang she sighed and heaved herself out of her seat, and lumbered down the steep staircase. Recognising her daughter-in-law's outline, she smiled gently. Her heavily-lined face lit up at the prospect of a visit from Donna. Maeve pulled the door open clumsily, banging it against the wall.

'Come away in, darlin'. Let's see you. Jaysus, you're looking terrible! What's wrong?'

Donna silently followed her mother-in-law up the stairs, listening to her talk.

'Is that bugger playing up, eh? He might be a grown man, but a slap across the arse wouldn't do him any harm . . .' Then followed the usual ritual of Maeve's pretending her son was a nuisance to be put up with, when everyone knew she worshipped Georgio, as she did all her children.

'Maeve . . . sit down. I have to talk to you.'

But Maeve slapped a cup of coffee on to the small, scratched drop-leaf table and carried on talking as if Donna had not even spoken.

'Did you see the newspaper, about the robbery? What a crying shame. His wife was on Thames News last night, a pretty little girl, crying and bawling over her husband's murder. What's the world coming to, I ask meself? A young man shot down in his prime. For what, eh? Money. Always money. Have these people never heard of working for a living? Christ, I hope they hang the bastards by the balls, I do. Those tiny children left without a father . . .'

23

Donna closed her eyes as Maeve carried on, knowing in her heart that conversations similar to this one were going on all over the country at this very moment. It was a death to shock the nation, like that of PC Blakelock, the policeman from Muswell Hill who was killed in a riot on a North London housing estate. The papers were having a field day, and the case would undoubtedly be dragged up time and again whenever something similar happened. It was political. Law and Order. Death and Destruction. Everyone calling for the reintroduction of hanging, birching, and anything else they could think of – everyone including the mother of the man who was likely to be charged with the murder.

'MAEVE! Will you listen to me, please?'

Donna's loud, agitated voice halted Maeve in mid-sentence.

'What's the matter, child? What's happened?'

Donna hung her head, unable to look into the faded blue eyes of the woman in front of her. 'It's Georgio, Maeve. He's been arrested.'

Maeve's eyes opened to their utmost. 'What's he done now?' This was said in a flat voice and Donna felt a moment's anger, but it flickered and died. Maeve had loved her children wholeheartedly but she had never harboured any illusions about them.

'He hasn't done anything, Maeve.'

Mrs Brunos pushed her lank grey hair away from her face in a gesture of defeat. 'Then why has he been arrested?'

Donna looked up into the older woman's face. She pointed at the newspaper on the table and whispered, 'He's been accused of being behind all this.'

Maeve blinked a few times in consternation, then taking a deep breath, she said quietly, 'I don't think I grasp what you're saying, child. Behind all what?'

'Behind the robbery in Essex. The robbery yesterday where the security man died.'

Maeve sank down into her chair, her face pale and tightly closed like a nun's prayerbook.

'He's what?'

Her mouth was open and a thin line of spittle was hanging from her top lip. Then Donna heard a loud keening, a thin high-pitched wail that gradually became louder as the seconds wore on. Putting an arm around her mother-in-law's shoulder, Donna pulled her head to her own breast, glad of the warmth of Maeve's body against hers, glad to be doing something for someone else instead of waiting, waiting, and knowing that nothing she could do would change the situation.

Donna heard Pa Brunos's steps coming heavily up the stairs and a minute later she relinquished the hysterical woman to her husband.

24

Then, sitting back at the table she watched them both, dry-eyed. Unable to cry any more. Because the shock had worn off, and she was back again in what Georgio called 'the real world'.

Georgio stood in the courtroom listening to the charges against him being read out. His black eye was evident, as was his broken finger and his dirty clothes, yet no one mentioned them, or indeed seemed to take notice. He smiled grimly at his wife and shook his head in a gesture of denial.

He was being accused of providing cars, guns and plans. Of conspiracy to pervert the course of justice.

Georgio's solicitor, Henry Watkins, stood up and cleared his throat loudly.

'Your Honour, this man has never been in trouble with the law before. He is innocent of any crime and I would like to propose bail on his own recognisance . . .'

Judge Blatley interrupted: 'You will recall, Mr Watkins, that a young man died. That your client has been accused of conspiracy to murder because he allegedly told the perpetrators of the robbery to shoot to kill. I take it you *have* read the statements?'

Henry Watkins nodded and opened his mouth to speak, but was once more interrupted.

'You will realise then that I cannot be responsible for letting this man walk out of here on his own recognisance – or anyone else's, come to that. I assume you read the conspiracy to murder charge?' Blatley watched Georgio's solicitor redden and then said smoothly: 'The prisoner will be taken to Chelmsford prison. Bail denied.'

'*You what!*'

Georgio jumped from his seat and Watkins tried to restrain him.

'I never done nothing!' he shouted. 'You hear me? Nothing! This is a fucking fit up. I've heard better stories on *Jackanory*!'

Blatley peered over his pince-nez while Georgio was restrained by two officers of the court.

'Mr Brunos, don't you think you're in enough trouble as it is, without a contempt of court charge against you?'

Georgio's face was twisted in temper. Watching him, Donna felt her heart sink down to her boots.

'Bollocks to you, and to Laughton, and the rest of you! I'll prove my case, you just watch me. Call this British justice, eh? Three people saw me in my car lot – three people! You're going on the word of a smalltime hood. I'm a businessman, I pay me taxes, I'll see me day with the lot of you. When you're paying out my compensation you'll wish you'd never heard of Georgio Brunos . . .'

25

Judge Blatley bellowed across the courtroom, his face contorted, 'Have you *quite* finished, Mr Brunos?'

Georgio stared at the men around him, as if memorising their features, burning them into his brain.

'Yeah, I've finished.'

Peering at Georgio for a few moments, as if unable to believe what he was seeing, the judge said peremptorily: 'Take him down.'

Jimmy Crossley was well-built and blunt-featured. He looked what he was, and he made a point of acting the part: a smalltime villain with dreams of the bigtime.

As he stepped out of The Bull pub in Hornchurch, he pulled the keys to his Renault out of his pocket. The six pints of beer he had consumed were lying heavily on his belly and he belched loudly, putting a large hand up to his mouth as if he was a fastidious person, which he wasn't. As he lumbered towards his car, he saw a figure getting out of a dark blue Daimler.

Sighing loudly, he stood and waited for the figure to approach him before saying loudly, 'Hello, Mr Laughton, and what can't I do for you?'

Frank Laughton laughed gently, showing his brown-stained teeth and a yellow-coated tongue.

'How are you these days, Jimmy? Still taking it up the arse for the big boys, eh?'

Laughton grinned at the look of shock in Jimmy's face. 'You know why you'll never make the big time, don't you? You're too open, too trusting. Only you would park your car away from the entrance to a pub. A big villain would have a decent car, not a French tart's motor, and he'd leave it where he could keep an eye on it. See what I mean, eh? You got no class, Jimmy. Now put away your car keys and let's me and you go and have a little chat.'

Jimmy frowned. 'I ain't going nowhere, Mr Laughton. You got a warrant for me?'

Laughton shook his head. 'Course not. This is me, Laughton, not fucking Paul Condon, you prat. Since when did I need a warrant – or anything else, come to that?'

Jimmy took a step backwards, straight into the arms of two uniformed officers.

'Bollocks, Laughton! I ain't getting in no motor with you . . .'

Laughton spat noisily on to the tarmacadam. 'Get him in the car, lads. I ain't got all fucking night.'

Jimmy was sandwiched between the two officers inside the blue unmarked Daimler, while Laughton sat in the front seat. Leaning

26

nonchalantly back he smiled into Jimmy's frightened countenance.

'I want the score on Georgio Brunos,' he said. 'And before you begin, Jimmy, if push comes to shove I'll smash your face in without a thought for blood, AIDs, gristle or bone. Do you get my drift?'

Jimmy shook his head sadly. 'I don't know Brunos. I mean, I know *of* him, but not personally like. All I know is, he's a face. But I don't know anything about him. What's he supposed to have done?'

Laughton lit up another cigarette and looked out into the car park for a few moments, as if debating with himself over his answer.

'Never mind what he's done. I want *you* to tell me what he's done. You, James Crossley, Grass of the Year and prize prat. Now tell me all you know about Brunos because I'm beginning to get annoyed. I've collared Wilson, and according to him you're a bit of a face lately. So just open your fucking trap and we can all get home for a kip.'

Jimmy kept his eyes on the dashboard, not trusting himself to look at Laughton. The smell of the cigarette was making him feel ill. One of the uniformed men had been eating garlic, and the combination of odours was causing the beer to rise up in his stomach. He swallowed nervously.

'Look, Mr Laughton. If I knew anything . . .'

Laughton sighed. 'Belt him one, Stanley, the night's drawing on.'

The policeman to Jimmy's left jabbed him in the face with a short uppercut. Jimmy felt the man's knuckles jar on his teeth. He could taste blood, and knew his lip was split and probably swelling badly.

Putting his hand instinctively to his mouth, he mumbled, 'Fucking leave it out! I tell you, I don't know anything!'

Blows were rained on him by both men now. Jimmy, trapped between them, was helpless as the two officers pummelled his face and head.

Laughton leaned over the seat, and the two men resumed their earlier positions. Neither was even breathing heavily after his exertions.

'Don't wind me up, Jimmy. I'm on the verge of losing it, believe me.'

Jimmy was nearly in tears. Laughton watched the changing expressions on the man's face with a deep-felt glee. He hated this villain and all his counterparts.

'Now Brunos's arse is up for robbery, the big robbery that has even impressed the government. So you can imagine, I want as much as possible on our Georgio before I get him to court, and that is where you come in, Jimmy. I want you to tell me what I want to hear, see? Even you can manage that, surely?' Jimmy stared into the older man's face. 'You must be mad, Mr Laughton.'

27

Laughton laughed noisily. 'Mad? Oh yes, I'm as mad as a hatter, my son, and don't you ever forget it. Now, talk.'

Jimmy's eyes were burning bright with malice. 'With respect, Mr Laughton, if Brunos's face is in the frame for that robbery, then quite frankly you can kick the shit out of me and I'll just take it. Because I'm more inclined to be frightened of Brunos at this moment than I am of you. Do you get my drift? I ain't putting no one down for a long one. No fucking way. Especially not Georgio Brunos.'

Laughton smiled, a chilling little smile. 'Would you get up in a court of law and say that then? That you're too frightened to give information about Georgio Brunos?'

Jimmy closed his eyes. 'That's not fair, Mr Laughton, because I don't know anything, you know I don't. There probably ain't anything *to* know. That's why you're here.'

Laughton lit another cigarette and grinned. 'I just want a statement saying you refuse to give any evidence on Brunos, that's all.'

Jimmy shook his head sadly. 'You're an arsehole, Mr Laughton.'

'So I've been told, Jimmy. Many times, and by better men than you. Now let's get to the station, shall we?'

28

Chapter Two

Donna stared around her.

The jury were filing back into the room. Eight men and four women. They looked serious, as they were supposed to. Donna was reminded of long-forgotten courtroom dramas from America, in which the suspect's wife, knowing her husband is innocent, has to watch him being condemned. But now there was no amiable cop around to pip the jury to the post. She felt an insane urge to laugh, only knew it was not with humour but with hysteria. She fought the urge, and held her breath instead.

As she watched a reporter at work sketching Georgio, she expelled the breath in a long silent sigh. Six weeks ago at the start of the trial, Georgio had been jaunty, confident. He had sat upright, offering his profile to the young girl so she could draw him at his best. Smiling that engaging smile of his. Today, he sat slumped in his chair. He looked beaten. Donna felt her heart going out to him, this man of hers, this husband whom she missed so much, especially in the night.

'Jaysus, they're taking their time. Would they just get it all over with?'

Maeve Brunos's voice was loud, her face, semi-obscured by a large hat, looked ferocious. Donna took her hand and squeezed it tightly. Pa Brunos was wiping his forehead with a large handkerchief. His enormous bulk was squeezed into a dark blue suit, and he looked out of place – a peasant once more in the company of his betters.

Donna felt her heart constrict with love for these two kind people, both of whom were amazed and bewildered by the events of the last year. God-fearing, law-abiding citizens of their adopted country, they couldn't comprehend what had transpired. Their eldest son, their pride and joy, had been accused of masterminding a bank robbery, a robbery that had been violent in the extreme. During the execution of it, a guard had died – a young man with a pretty plump wife and two innocent children. Another guard had been shot in the leg, wounded badly enough to be confined to a desk, his permanent limp a painful legacy of doing his job. He had lain beside his dead colleague while

29

the masked raiders loaded up the money into a car, one that Georgio Brunos had reported stolen three months previously.

The evidence was all circumstantial. Georgio had been in the car lot the day of the robbery – three people had testified to that. Except that those three people were not reliable. One, a woman named Matilda Braithwaite, had been looking at cars; she had dropped in to inspect a small Mercedes Sports. A woman in the wrong place at the wrong time. Under oath she had been reduced to a quivering wreck, finally unsure if it had been on that day or the one before that she had called in at the lot; admitting that she often traipsed around car dealerships looking at different models. It was a kind of hobby with her, rather like those women who look at other people's houses. The other two witnesses had been swiftly discredited because one was a convicted criminal, the other a well-known layabout already convicted of perjury.

The prosecution had brought forward a battery of men who said they would not, under any circumstances, give evidence against Georgio. It had been a farce, but an elaborate farce. No one had been able to get a straight answer from any of them. Only that they refused to give evidence either way. One man, a Jimmy Something or other, had mumbled his lines as if rehearsed. Which Donna had a sneaking feeling they were. Well-rehearsed.

Then out had come the reliable, and oh so plausible Peter Wilson, dressed in a nice grey catalogue suit with his hair cut and blowdried. He told the court he was a wheelman, and had been approached by Georgio Brunos to drive the car on the day of the robbery. He said he had taken the car that was used for the job from the car lot three months previously, in order to get it 'tuned up'. He too refused to name the other men in the robbery – men who were supposedly now on the run – for fear of his life. He was only telling the truth about Georgio because he understood it was his duty. As for the others, he did not know them personally; they were 'outside' men brought in by Brunos and known only to Wilson by sight: he had first seen them on the actual day of the robbery. He understood they had travelled over from Marbella for the job, and supposed that was where they were now. He would receive a reduced sentence for his part in the robbery because of his help.

As all this travelled through her mind, Donna became aware that the judge was being handed a piece of paper. He opened it, deliberately taking his time. Pulling herself back to reality, she listened intently to his words.

'Has the jury reached a decision?'

A tall, emaciated man was standing up. He was wearing a dark

30

green suit and Donna thought he looked rather like a tally man or insurance salesman. His nose was long and thin, like his body, and his nostrils flared as he nodded his head.

'We have, Your Honour.'

'And is it a unanimous verdict?'

'It is, Your Honour.'

The judge's eyes swept the jury before he said loudly, 'How do you find the defendant?'

The man looked at the floor and said distinctly, 'Guilty as charged, sir.'

She saw her husband's head shake in denial.

In her mind's eye, she had pictured him at this moment jumping from his seat and screaming at Peter Wilson, calling him a liar and a grassing bastard. Saw him being restrained by two policemen, then escorted from the courtroom down into the depths of the Old Bailey to the holding cells, still protesting his innocence. She recalled his dignity and his calm demeanour during the first few days of the trial – a composure she had seen crushed as each witness that appeared helped put another nail into his already tightly closed coffin. Every day it had looked worse for him. He had stopped talking about how he was going to sue the police once it was all over, had stopped telling them all how he would be the victor in the end.

Now the moment of truth was at hand, her husband simply looked guilty, because all his credibility was gone . . . had vanished out of the door of the Old Bailey, along with Peter Wilson.

Peter Wilson, a man to whom Georgio had given generously, a man he had looked after, had set on his feet after a long term in prison. A man who had betrayed him without a second thought.

Donna was brought back to reality by Maeve's voice beside her reciting the 'Hail Mary' in a monotonous undertone.

'Hail Mary, full of grace, the Lord is with thee, blessed art thou amongst women . . .'

The clinking of the rosary beads was loud in the hushed quiet of the courtroom.

'Georgio Anthony Brunos, you have been found guilty.'

Donna gasped, holding her hand to her breast as if to stem her heart's erratic beating. Her eyes flew once more to Georgio. His face, normally so handsome and dark-skinned, was a sickly grey.

'You have been found guilty of conspiracy to murder and conspiracy to commit armed robbery.'

The judge paused to take off his glasses, polish and replace them. It was a theatrical gesture and Donna knew this, but the people in the

31

public gallery were leaning forward in their seats, enjoying the spectacle. Revelling in the tension.

'You masterminded a robbery in which an innocent man lost his life. Although you did not take part in the robbery, you were there in as much as you furnished the details to your cronies, as well as supplying them with cars and guns – guns which you told the men to use at the first sign of trouble.'

His voice rose then. 'Guns which were used to murder one guard and leave another incapacitated for the rest of his life. These were men with families, leading full and useful lives, which through your greed and viciousness were tragically cut short. As we have heard in this courtroom, you ruled your empire with terror, hiding behind the façade of a respectable building contractor and dealer in prestige cars. A man with a high profile in the community, an affluent man, a cunning man. You have refused to name those responsible for the robbery, insisting throughout this débâcle that you had no knowledge of it whatsoever, even though witnesses have sworn on oath that they are too terrified of you to give evidence against you. I can only hope that your conscience will trouble you in the future, when you think of Mr Thomas, who was a fine, upstanding and very brave man, and of his widow, who must now bring up two young children alone without the benefit of their father.'

The judge removed his spectacles once more.

'Georgio Anthony Brunos, I would be failing in my duty as a public servant if I did not impose the maximum penalty possible, under the present law. It is my solemn duty to remove you from society, which I feel most strongly has earned a respite from you. I sentence you to life imprisonment, with a recommendation that you serve at least eighteen years. I can only hope you use the time to reflect on your life and put right the many wrongs you have done. Have you anything to say for yourself?'

Georgio stood up unsteadily, his face a mask of fear and shock. Pointing to Inspector Laughton, he said weakly: 'This man has fitted me up and you fell for it, hook, line and sinker. You're all fucking mad!' Then leaning on the rail before him, he began to shout: 'You're all off your fucking heads! There's nothing to put me away for, nothing!'

As Georgio was dragged from the court, Donna could hear herself screaming his name. It was only as he disappeared down the stairs behind the holding box that she realised the voice was only inside her head. The tears escaped from her eyes; she felt a heavy hand drop on to her shoulder. Seeing the dark hairs on it, she recognised it as Pa Brunos's. He pulled her up gently and all she could say was: 'The

32

world's gone mad. The whole world's gone mad. He is innocent, Pa. Innocent!'

Donna's legs were trembling as the police officer opened the cell door.

'You can have ten minutes, love.'

She gave him a tired smile and walked into the cramped coolness of the cell. Georgio was sitting on the small bed, his head in his hands.

'Georgio . . . Oh, Georgio!' The crack in her voice seemed to make him spring from the bed. Then she was in his arms and he was whispering to her, his voice drenched with tears.

'I didn't do it, Don Don, I swear to you. That bastard Laughton fitted me up, Laughton and Wilson. I can't believe this is happening. Eighteen years, Don Don. Eighteen bastard years!'

Donna held him to her tightly, savouring the smell of him, the feel of him. He pushed his hands up under her skirt and caressed the flesh beneath. He was rough, urgent. All the time talking to her, at her. Needing to put into words what had happened as if that would make it real.

'Oh, Don Don, what am I going to do, eh? They've tucked me up. I'll see that Wilson dead! I'll hear him screaming! That bastard lied through his teeth. He lied, Don Don. You believe me, don't you? You believe me. If I didn't have you, I'd die. I'd die inside, Don Don.'

She held him, remembering back over the years to when they had first met. He had called her Don Don then. He hadn't called her that for years. In the still of the night, they had lain in bed together and he would whisper it to her, to make her laugh. Now it had an added significance. He was trying to hold on to the past, and it was breaking her heart. Tearing her up inside.

'You can appeal,' she said desperately. 'Everything is circumstantial. Once we know what's happening, we can appeal.'

He stood before her, looking down into her face. It hadn't changed much over twenty years. He saw the tears on her dark lashes, the pain buried deep at the back of her eyes, and pushing his hands into her thick brown hair, he pulled her face up to his, kissing her with a fervour, a deep passion. A mark of ownership.

'Don't leave me, Donna. I couldn't go on if I thought I didn't have you.'

She shook her head in denial, as if he had accused her of leaving him already.

'Promise me you'll stand by me, no matter what happens? Promise

33

me that, Donna. So I can take it with me, to keep me alive. Give me something to hold on to.'

'I'll never leave you, Georgio, never. We'll get you out of this. Home again. You'll be home again. Once we appeal . . .'

He cut off her words with his mouth, forcing his tongue between her lips. They heard the cell door open.

'Come on, love, your time's up.'

She held on to her husband tighter, unable to break the embrace. Frightened to stop holding him in case she never held him again.

Georgio pushed her away from him gently. 'Promise me, Donna? Promise you won't leave me.'

She smiled bravely. 'Never. I love you too much, Georgio.'

'You're a good girl. You were always a good girl.'

'Come on, love. I'm sorry but you have to go now.' The policeman's voice was kind.

Donna turned and felt her skirt bunched up over her thighs. Hastily tugging it down, she sniffed loudly. 'They're taking you to Wormwood Scrubs. I'll visit you as soon as I can.'

Georgio nodded, unable to speak.

Her head held high, Donna walked out of the cell. Georgio had always liked her to look as if she was in control. At the doorway she turned and smiled at him tremulously. Suddenly he looked much smaller, vulnerable, and that was the hardest thing to take. Her Georgio, her big strong husband, looked broken. Something she had never expected to see in her lifetime.

The officer closed the cell door gently, but the sound of it was like a thunderclap. She followed the man slowly out of the cell area, her head low now, tears raining down her face.

Inside his cell, Georgio Brunos threaded his hands through his hair and pulled it hard, then he began to groan low in the back of his throat, the desolate sound gaining in volume as he pulled harder and harder on his hair.

Detective Inspector Frank Laughton opened the small metal window in the cell door. He smiled grimly as he watched the antics of Georgio Brunos.

'Open the door.' His voice was clipped as he addressed the young policeman beside him.

Stepping into the cell, he smiled widely. 'Eighteen years, Brunos. Gutted or what, eh?'

Georgio stood staring at the man in front of him, his face hard. 'I'll see me day with you, Laughton, you see if I don't.'

Frank Laughton stopped grinning. It was as if a hand had wiped the expression from his face.

34

'I promised myself I'd give you a visit on the day you were sent down. It gave me something to look forward to. I've got you now, Brunos, and I won't ever let you go. I'm still investigating you. I know you could hold your hand up to a lot more robberies, and when I have the evidence I need, I'll haul your arse back into that court so fast you'll burn a fucking great hole in the carpet!'

'Tell Wilson he'll be seeing me.'

Laughton laughed. 'I think he's sussed that one out for himself. Well, I'm off home. I'm taking my wife out tonight to celebrate.'

'Did you book your trough in advance?'

Laughton chuckled gently again. 'Still the bravado. Still the hard man. Did you know you're to be Category A? You'll be in Maximum Security with the scum of the earth, so you should feel well at home. I'll be seeing you again soon, Georgio. Look after yourself for me. There's a Dover Sole with my name on it, so I'd better get off home. I'll be thinking about you tonight when I'm eating and drinking and making merry.'

'I hope you choke, you ponce!'

'I wouldn't have expected anything less from you. How about a little bet then, before I go?'

'Fuck off, Laughton. You've had your gloat, now piss off.'

The policeman carried on as if Georgio hadn't spoken. 'I'll bet you a oner your lovely little wife is taking on all comers by Christmas.'

Georgio launched himself at the man before him, his face twisted in hatred, but three uniformed men were on him before he could throw one punch. On the floor of the cell, with his hands pushed up his back and his cheek pressed on to the cold concrete, Georgio felt the rage explode uselessly inside him as he heard the Inspector's shoes clomping heavily along the corridor and his deep laugh reverberating around the cell walls.

Donna sat in the El Greco restaurant in Canning Town. The whole family was there. In the harsh daylight, the faded paintwork and scratched bar surfaces were mercilessly revealed. Pa Brunos looked on his restaurant as his life's work. His sons had all been waiters there at one time or another, his youngest daughter Nuala did the book-keeping, he and Maeve did the cooking. As he watched his family drinking Retsina and Ouzo, observed their different degrees of disbelief, he felt a tightening across his chest. Taking a small bottle of heart pills from his pocket, he unobtrusively slipped one into his hand and placed it under his tongue.

'Come on, Donna. Eat something, love.' Maeve's voice was tired, low.

35

Donna shook her head. 'I couldn't eat anything, thank you.' Her eyes were red with crying.

Maeve pulled her chair closer and placed a large meaty arm around her daughter-in-law. 'He's my son, God love him, but we have to keep our strength up. Tonight me and Pa will open up this restaurant, we'll smile at the customers and chat with them. Life must go on. You must tell yourself that once his appeal comes up, Georgio will be back home. That is what I keep telling myself.'

'I can't believe it happened, any of it.'

Nuala gave a loud snort as she shouted: 'It's the police, Donna. They wanted him – they got him. They needed someone and he fitted the bill.'

Mario, her elder brother, shook his head. 'Georgio was a fool; he mixed with the wrong people. I told him so. A few weeks before it all happened, I saw him with Jack Black. I mean, who in their right mind would cultivate him, eh? Jack Black, the biggest villain in Silvertown! But no, our Georgio wouldn't listen. He knew best.' Mario's voice was high, almost girlish, and full of anger towards his brother.

'What do you know, Mario?' Patrick Brunos spoke up. 'In his lines of business he had to mix with all sorts, surely you can see that? Jack Black has the ear on the building everywhere. He also has a haulage business. It was sound economics for our Georgio to deal with him.'

Nuala pushed back her short black hair. 'That's true. He's right, Mario. You're too hard on Georgio. You've always been hard on him, just because he's done better than you. He's done better than everyone.'

Nuala was upset and Donna closed her eyes. This family fought like other families loved. Yet they were closer than most families could ever hope to be.

'What do you know, Nuala? Running around with that no-hoper Dicky Barlow. If you're not careful, you'll be visiting him and your brother together . . .'

Pa Brunos banged his fist on the table in front of him, knocking over a glass of red wine in the process.

'Be quiet! You all hear me? No more of this! We have enough trouble as it is without you all arguing among yourselves. Where is my Mary? Why isn't she here?'

Nuala's voice was low now. 'She had to get back. Geoff has to open his own restaurant tonight.'

Pa Brunos nodded, his eyes closed. 'Of course. The businesses must be seen to. You will need to look into Georgio's businesses now,

36

Donna. We don't know when he will be home. Will you be keeping on that Mark Hancock or will you get someone else?'

'I don't know Pa. I haven't really thought about it. All the time I believed Georgio would be coming home.'

Maeve pulled her into her arms. 'And he will, darlin', I promise you. I could cheerfully smack his face for him, big as he is. Getting involved with all this . . .' Her voice trailed off.

Pa Brunos poked himself in the chest. 'If you need me, just call, Donna. I will personally see to anything you want me to. It is the least I can do for you.'

'Thank you.'

Nuala poured out more Ouzo and said, 'Why don't you run the business, Donna? If nothing else it would keep you occupied. Then, when you visit Georgio, it will give you something to talk about. He'll feel much better knowing you're looking after things.'

Maeve nodded. 'For once in your life, Nuala, you've opened that big galloping trap of yours and something intelligent has come out. After all the money your education cost, that bit of talk was like balm to me poor spirits.'

Everyone laughed at this. It broke the tension in the room. The second youngest Brunos son, Stephen, smiled at Donna.

'I have a business degree, as you know. I'm quite willing to help you out in any way. We all are. As I see it, the building business is best put into the hands of a competent manager, then you can learn from them. As for the cars, Georgio is in partnership with Davey Jackson. Davey will keep that sorted until you can get actively involved. He only has a twenty-five percent stake in the company so you have what's known as the controlling interest . . .'

'Jaysus, Stephen, what did you have for breakfast, a company report? Leave the girl alone. There's plenty of time for all that once the shock wears off.'

Stephen shook his head. Taking off gold-rimmed glasses, he began cleaning them on a table napkin. 'All I'm saying is, there's a lot of money involved, Mum. Our Georgio had many business interests; his accountant is a known face in the City. I don't think it would be a good idea to leave it too long. It's been left for nearly nine months as it is. The sooner someone starts sorting everything out, the better. Georgio can run his business from prison, through Donna.'

'I don't know if I could, Stephen . . .'

'Of course you can, Donna. Georgio would be over the moon to think you were looking after things for him,' Nuala said with finality. 'We'll all help in any way we can.'

'Then once he wins his appeal, everything can get back to normal.'

37

Patrick's voice was full of forced joviality.

'I'll drink to that.' Stephen held up his glass of milky Ouzo, and everyone followed suit.

'To Georgio's homecoming.'

Donna lifted her glass and forced back the tears once more. She had these people, they were her family. With all of them behind her, things couldn't really be that bad.

'Eighteen years? The dirty bastards!' Dolly's voice was low, shocked. 'I heard it on the local News. Nearly fainted away, I did. How's his mum taken it?'

Donna sipped her tea. 'Surprisingly well actually, Dolly. Maeve is strong. Stronger than people realise. Pa Brunos has taken it badly, but that is to be expected. Georgio was his pride and joy. Proof of all his adopted country has to offer. There've been a few phone calls from Rhodes. The papers there carried the story and, well, word gets round. I think he feels ashamed.'

Dolly shook her head. 'Georgio was fitted up – he said so himself. Once we prove that, everything will be fine once more. Do you want a drop of scotch in that tea, love? You're looking very white.'

She poured a good measure of cheap Tesco whisky into Donna's cup. 'You get that down your neck, girl. It's going to be a hard few months. Before I forget, Davey Jackson rang. He'll be round on Sunday morning.'

Donna sipped the warm tea, the bite of the scotch burning her tongue.

'What am I going to do, Dolly?' she asked hopelessly. 'I feel as if my life is on hold without him. I hadn't thought of him being sent to prison, I only thought of him coming home. How could they believe Wilson? Everyone knows what he is. Yet in a suit, with his hair all washed and cut, he looked so respectable. The things he was saying about Georgio! That Georgio had told them to shoot to kill, and threatened them all that if they botched up the job he would kill them. It was all kill, kill kill. I know Georgio, he wouldn't hurt a fly. Christ Almighty, he cried when we had old Sam put down. He loved that dog.' Her voice broke again, and she swallowed back her tears.

'Wilson was saving his own arse, love. I expect Laughton did a deal with him for a reduced sentence. He'll get his comeuppance in the nick. No one likes a grass.'

Donna smiled through her tears. 'You sound so knowledgeable, Dolly, like an old jailbird yourself!'

'After years with my old man, I know all the jargon, my love. Now

38

if *he* had got eighteen years, I'd be celebrating me drawers off. How about I run you a nice bath, put in some Radox, and while you're soaking, I'll cook you a light meal? An omelette, say. You've got to eat, to keep your strength up. The appeal will take up all your time, and the businesses. Come on, I'll run the bath while you get stripped off.'

As they stood up Donna grabbed at the older woman's hand. 'I'm so glad I've got you, Dolly. This house is so empty without him.'

'I know my little love. Believe me, I know.'

Davey Jackson turned up at eight-thirty on Sunday morning. Donna was in her conservatory, drinking coffee and smoking a cigarette, when she heard Carol Jackson's strident voice. She closed her eyes wearily. Davey Jackson was all right, she could cope with him, but Carol Jackson was a different kettle of fish. Donna loathed her and she loathed Donna.

'How you feeling, Donna? Gutted, I bet. Bags of shit, the lot of them, bags of stinking shit!'

Donna was surprised to see genuine concern in Carol's face.

'Sit down, Davey, you make me nervous looming over us like that. I tell you something, Donna, me and you have never seen eye to eye, but if ever you need a shoulder, girl, well, mine's always there for the taking.'

Donna was inordinately grateful. Over the last nine months she had been gradually dropped by most of her friends. Bunty and Harry Robertson had looked right through her only a week previously when she had met them in the village. She had said hello and they had ignored her, leaving her deep red with embarrassment and hurt. Over the years they had both courted Georgio's friendship. Now they wanted nothing to do with him or anyone connected to him. Even Donna's neighbours had stopped waving if they drove past and she was on her driveway.

'Thanks, Carol, I appreciate it.' The truth of the statement came over in her voice and Carol smiled.

'You find out who your mates are at times like this, girl. I remember when me brother got a big one. Twelve years. Mind you, he had done the robbery – got caught red-handed with the guns and the money. But all that aside, his wife really took some stick. Mind you, for saying that, she was batting away from home within six months. Takes some of the wives like that. Lonely, see. You keep your mind occupied and your legs crossed, girl. The filth will come out of the woodwork now. A few of Georgio's mates would have liked a crack at you. Now he's banged up they'll think the field is clear. So be careful when men start offering you a bit of help. When is the appeal? I take it he is appealing?'

'Oh, yes. As soon as we get a date I'll let you know. Can I offer you some refreshment?'

Carol Jackson laughed her loud, cackling laugh. ' "Can I offer you some refreshment"! You're a riot, Donna, if you only knew it. I'll have a cup of Rosie. I'll just pop in and see old Dolly for a bit. Leave you and Davey to sort out your business.'

Donna watched her plump frame, encased in skintight leather, wobble from the conservatory on impossibly high heels. Her long bleached-blonde hair, screaming with split ends, was backcombed into a mass of knots visible from behind.

Davey finally spoke. 'She ain't a bad girl really, my Carol. You've just got to know how to take her. She's a good wife and an excellent mother.'

Donna nodded. 'I realised that a long time ago. You don't have to defend her to me, Davey. In fact, she's one of the few people who actually seem concerned about me and Georgio.'

'She's right in what she says, you know, Donna. You're an attractive woman, so be careful. Even Georgio's mates are now suspect, remember that. That's why I brought Carol with me this morning. Georgio will hear everything, who's in here and who ain't. Don't ask me *how* he'll know, but believe me when I say that he will.'

Davey paused for breath and drew on his cigarette before continuing. 'If any of his business associates come round, make sure you're not alone, or that they bring their wives. If possible, meet them in a pub or a restaurant. It's the rules you live by when your old man's banged up. Be especially wary of blokes who turn up on spec. Don't let them over the doorstep. Georgio's brothers will keep an eye on you, so don't be too worried, just wary. You understand?'

Donna was stunned. Davey was talking as if she was some kind of gangster's moll. As if Georgio really was a villain.

Carol tripped back into the conservatory with two mugs of tea. She gave one to Davey and sat down at the table. Lighting herself a cigarette, she picked up Donna's *Sunday Times* and began turning the pages.

'What's happening with the car lot, Donna?'

She shook her head. 'I really don't know, Davey. Stephen wants to look over the books and that. He thinks I should run it.'

Davey looked at Donna as she spoke. Her face was heart-shaped, her cheekbones prominent. Her thick brown hair fell loosely across

40

her shoulders, and her deep-set blue eyes were framed with thick black lashes. Her full mouth moved gently. Economical with words and movement was Donna Brunos, and as Davey looked into her beautiful face he felt a stirring in his guts.

Carol Jackson watched her husband as he looked at Donna and sighed inwardly. She didn't blame him one bit. She had always resented Donna's looks, her poise, her natural grace. That's why they had never hit it off. Now, though, poor old Donna was on her own, and she was as green as the proverbial grass. Carol would keep an eye on her, and at the same time keep an eye on Davey boy. He wasn't much, she admitted that to herself, but he was all hers. Women were vulnerable when the old man was banged up for a long stretch, and Donna had never had to look after herself before.

'I think you should learn the business, Donna,' she said now. 'We sell at least one car a month, that's when business is bad, but with the cheapest car coming out at nearly twenty grand, that ain't a bad living. You'll need something to keep you occupied. Believe me, I know from experience. If I can grasp the business, I'm bleeding sure you can.'

'Everyone keeps telling me I should take over where Georgio left off. But I don't think I'm cut out for all that . . .'

Carol waved a hand at her. 'No one knows that they're capable of until they try. Your trouble is you never had to do a day's collar in your life. Well, now you can have a go. Might find you surprise yourself. I mean, do you honestly want to spend the next twelve months looking at this house, as nice as it is? You'll soon go stir crazy. I'll expect you at the car lot tomorrow morning at nine. Then, once you've had a look-see, I'd advise you to get on to a few of the building sites, show your face like. Georgio will be much happier finding out the state of play from the horse's mouth. Think about that. You could run everything through him. If I know Georgio, he'll want someone he can trust in the driving seat.'

Donna looked into the face opposite hers. It was a harsh face, yet at this moment Donna was also seeing it as a kind face.

'I'll see you in the morning then.'

With those few words, Donna immediately felt better. The decision had been made. She would look into the businesses. Georgio would be proud of her. At the end of the day, that was the important thing.

She would do anything for Georgio, and as everyone kept saying, he would feel much better if he had someone he could trust in the driving seat.

41

A decision, once made, makes everything seem much easier. For the first time in days Donna felt a stirring of life inside her. She would work for Georgio until his appeal was over. Then, when he got home, she could go back to being just plain Donna Brunos, wife.

Her biggest regret was that she couldn't add the accolade of mother.

Chapter Three

Georgio stood under the cold water of the shower, and rubbed his body vigorously with a sliver of dark green soap. He gritted his teeth together in an effort to force away the goose pimples covering the whole of his skin. The white tiles were cracked and broken, the small crevices between them black from years of dirt and neglect. He closed his eyes for a few seconds and imagined that he was in his ensuite bathroom at home. He would leap out of bed for a hot shower, then downstairs to Dolly for coffee and croissants. If he told the blokes in here what he ate for breakfast they would assume he was a shirtlifter, a homosexual.

He was brought back to reality by the voice of Peter Pearson saying: 'Crying shame, Georgio, eighteen bloody long ones. A crying shame. Should have shot the blooming lot of them.' His voice was lost in a bubbling sound as he stuck his head under his shower nozzle, words still coming thick and fast. Georgio didn't answer; there was nothing to say.

Turning off the shower, he wiped the excess liquid from his body and, pulling a towel around his waist, walked out into the toilet area. He was bending over the sink and cleaning his teeth when he felt a stinging sensation across his buttocks. Straightening up, he put his hand to his behind. When he looked at his fingers a second later they were red with blood. Clenching his fists, he turned and pulled off the towel, looking into the plastic-framed mirror above the washstands. He had a stripe about ten inches long across both buttocks. It was a fairly deep wound, but he knew it wouldn't require stitches. It would be sore for a while; he would not enjoy sitting down. That was the whole idea of it.

Mr Gantry the warder smiled and shook his head slowly. 'I get the impression they don't like you in here, Georgio. Now I wonder why that is?' He turned to a young boy of eighteen who was shaving but watching the commotion, and shouted: 'Want to kiss it better for him, do you?'

The boy shook his head in fright.

43

'Then finish your shave and piss off!'

Georgio was holding the towel to the wound to stem the bleeding. When the boy picked up his shaving gear and rushed out, Gantry said through gritted teeth, 'That's a taster from Lewis. He asked me to tell you he don't like you, and when they ship you to the Island, he wants a word.'

Georgio looked into the man's face and said directly, 'You know, a lot of accidents happen in these places, and not just to the cons either. You tell whoever striped my harris that I'll be seeing them. And you can also lay money on the fact that sometime, in some place, Mr Gantry, I'll also be seeing you.'

Gantry laughed loudly, showing expensive false teeth. 'You're finished, Georgio, the word's already out.'

Now it was Georgio's turn to laugh, and he gave one of his handsome grins. 'Finished – me? I ain't even fucking started.'

Gantry grinned back. 'I'd say you've started. Eighteen years sentence, that's what you've started. And you'll have to look over your shoulder for the whole time.'

Georgio's face was serious now, hard-looking. 'In that case, Mr Gantry, then so will you. Tell Lewis it will take a bit more than a kid with a razor to scare me. If I'd been in his shoes I'd have had the razor wiped clean across my throat. In fact, I'd have done it myself.'

Pushing past Gantry, he went back into the shower room and took another towel from the rail. Tying it around his waist, he returned to his cell. He knew that everyone was waiting for his reaction, so he whistled nonchalantly, smiling in a carefree way.

Once inside the privacy of his cell, he wiped a hand over his face in agitation. Lewis had come straight out into the open. His arm was long. He was doing a twenty in Parkhurst yet he'd arranged this welcome in the Scrubs within twenty-four hours of Georgio's sentencing.

One thing was imperative: he had to get out. Whatever happened, *he had to get out*. Once he hit the Island he was as good as dead.

Petey Pearson walked into the cell and grinned. When Georgio didn't grin back, Petey slapped his shoulder and said jovially, 'Cheer up, Georgio. You're like a con with a sore arse!'

Worried as he was, Georgio had to laugh.

The laughter was heard along the wing, noted and commented on. Lewis knew about the aftermath within an hour of the attack taking place.

He wasn't in the least amused.

Donna dressed herself in a dark grey suit, low-heeled black shoes,

44

and tied her hair back with a piece of black velvet ribbon. When she walked into the car lot, she was whistled at by a passing motorist and Davey shook his head. He was already regretting asking her here; she would be like an albatross around his neck. Even done up like this, all businesslike and covered up, she looked what she was: vulnerable. Her open face was the last thing he needed when selling cars. Especially the special cars, the ringers, which he supplied to bank robbers or even kidnappers on some occasions. He saw the crew in the workshop smiling at her and sighed again. The silly mare had smiled back and waved.

As she walked into the small office he commented: 'You got here, then?'

Donna smiled widely, her innocent face devoid of make-up, and his heart ached for her.

'Yes, I got here, Davey. Though what I'm supposed to do now I'm actually here, I don't really know.'

'I've just made a coffee, you want one?'

She nodded. Then, putting her bag on the floor, she sat at the desk, looking around her in bewilderment. The place was a shambles.

Ten minutes later, Davey was still trying to make conversation with her when the phone rang. After a mumbled discussion he said awkwardly, 'I have to go out for a while. You can answer the phone and make appointments. If anyone asks something, just say you're a temp – that's what Carol does. They'll call back if they're interested.'

Donna fixed a large smile on her face and tried to look in control. She failed dismally. As she watched Davey drive off her heart sank.

The office was a pit. There were papers everywhere, folders full to overflowing on the chairs, on the floor, even under the desk. Letters were stuffed into drawers that no longer shut, they were so full up. Walking into the small kitchen area to wash up the cups, she shuddered. Tea bags were piled in the sink and on the draining board, old milk cartons lay scattered everywhere. The smell was ripe. Going back into the office she nearly cried. Then, taking off her jacket, she hung it on a hook on the door and rolled up the sleeves of her blouse. She gritted her teeth. Her natural tidiness coming to the fore, she began clearing up, starting with the kitchen.

Two hours later when Davey came back she was in the office. He walked through the door and nearly passed out.

'What on earth are you doing?'

After taking four calls from people who demanded to speak to Davey and had put the phone down on her in mid-conversation, then experiencing the fright of her life when she touched an old black bag in the kitchen and saw it move of its own accord, courtesy of a

45

maggot-ridden sandwich, she turned on Davey. With two high pink spots on her cheeks she snapped. 'What the hell does it look like?'

Davey, taken aback at her sharp tone, said gently, 'I know where everything is. Carol never touches anything, Donna. You should have left it.'

Near to tears and upset by his attitude she said, 'This pile of letters here is for answering, this pile is for filing. These are bills – and incidentally they're cutting the phone off tomorrow if that bill's not paid. In the filing cabinet there are now files instead of old pizza boxes, and the notepaper and envelopes are all in this top drawer here. I found them under a pile of old brochures behind the door to the kitchen. Also, I have taken three appointments and actually put them in the diary. In addition I also took four calls from a man called Briggley, and I have ordered new binders and invoices from the wholesalers. On top of all that, I have cleaned out the kitchen, which was practically on the verge of being condemned by the health people. That, Davey, is what I have been doing. And, I might add, not before bloody time!'

Looking at her grubby face, her broken nails and white blouse covered in ink from the carbon paper he had stuffed into the bottom drawer of the filing cabinet, Davey began to laugh. Donna, to her surprise, began to join in. Only her laugh was high-pitched, on the verge of hysteria.

'I'm sorry, Donna, I should have got Carol to have a sort-out here. She does that, now and again.'

'Now and again being the operative words. It wasn't like this when Georgio was here.'

'I meant to employ someone, full-time like, but I never got round to it. You know what my Carol's like.'

Donna wiped her eyes and grinned. 'Well, I think now I've sorted this place out, I can keep it under control. To be honest it's the first time in ages I haven't been brooding over Georgio. I'll take on the job of secretary, it might do me a bit of good.'

'Whatever you say, Donna. You and Georgio own more of this place than I do.'

'Don't be like that, Davey.' She put a hand gently on his arm. 'Georgio respects you a lot. He's over the moon at how you've kept the place running since he's been away.'

Davey nodded. 'You'll soon learn the ropes.'

Donna walked through to the kitchen and began washing her hands. She shouted over her shoulder, 'By the way, what's a goer? A bloke rang up for an XJS. I told him I was a temp and he put the phone down on me.'

46

In the now tidy office Davey closed his eyes in distress and said lightly, 'One thing at a time, Donna. You'll learn it all soon enough.'

And that, he remarked to himself, was just what he was frightened of. He had envisaged her coming in and doing a bit of typing, maybe a bit of the legit book-keeping, but no way had he thought she would start to look through everything. If she had bothered to read the files under the desk . . . It did not bear thinking about. He would stay late tonight, and move them to the inner office. Thank God she had not gone in there; he kept it locked. Now he would have to keep a few more things locked up.

Donna stood up as Georgio was brought into the visiting room. She was smiling widely but as he kissed her, felt the familiar sting of tears in the back of her throat.

'Hello, darlin'.' His voice was gruff with emotion.

'Oh, Georgio, it's so lovely to see you!'

While he went and got them both a coffee and a KitKat, Donna looked surreptitiously around the visiting room. Women with children were sitting chatting to their husbands as if this was normal, and to the majority it was. They lived an 'outside life', their own lives. As Dolly always had. A small half-caste child of about two was running up and down between the tables, playing peek-a-boo with a huge Rastafarian, her father. He was grinning at his little girl's antics.

As Georgio came back with the coffees he said casually, 'That's Big Black Joe, he murdered three men. He was a drug dealer – nice bloke actually, once you get to know him. Shot them in their house, three brothers, the McBains. Scum of the earth.'

Donna bit her lip at what Georgio was saying, and how he was saying it. He smiled at her. 'My old mum used to say, "Show me the company you keep and I'll tell you what you are." I shouldn't have told you that, Donna, I've shocked you.' He smiled disarmingly at her.

'I hate the thought of you in here, Georgio, with these people. People like him, and sex offenders. Murderers.' She was dangerously close to tears.

Gripping her small hand hard in his he said, 'It won't be for long, love. I'll be home before you can say knife.'

'The appeal will sort everything out, won't it, Georgio?'

He grinned again. 'Course it will. Now, shall I tell you my news first?'

Donna nodded; she didn't trust herself to speak just yet.

'I'm off to the Island in the next few days. As you know, I'm Category A, so there will be a three-ring circus to take me there. Even

47

a helicopter following the prison van. I dunno. They squander the taxpayers' money away.'

'Why do you need all that? It was bad enough at the trial, all those men on motorbikes and everything.'

'It's to make you look bad as possible.' Georgio sipped his coffee and shrugged. 'When the Old Bill want to send you down, they pull out all the stops. If that piece of scum Wilson hadn't done a deal, I'd be home with you. He's in Camp Hill on the Island, in with the nonces and the gas-meter bandits, the slag! He fitted me up, Donna. They had nothing, it was all on his hearsay. Gordon Bennett, I can't believe the jury fell for all that old fanny. Wilson's a lying toerag if ever there was one. I could kill him with me bare hands. I could throttle the bastard!'

Donna shook her head in distress. 'Stop it, Georgio, stop talking like that. Swearing and carrying on. It frightens me. I don't like it.'

Georgio grabbed her hand again, gently this time. 'I'm sorry, Don Don. It's being in here, with all these.' He swept his hand out dramatically. 'It makes you like them. It makes you full of hate inside. I shouldn't be here, you know that as well as I do. When they bang us up of a night, I could scream the place down.'

His face was like a little boy's, bewildered, unable to take in what was going on. It was a painfully handsome face, one that had captured her heart when she was a young girl, and her love and adoration of him had increased over the years. Until now, he'd been the very air she breathed. Without him, she felt she was nothing. With him, she was a somebody, Donna Brunos, wife of Georgio, the man everyone liked, wanted to be with, vied with each other to befriend. At least, they had until all this had happened . . .

As if reading her mind, Georgio asked: 'Have you heard anything from the honourable town planner or the magistrate? My so-called friends.'

'Not a word. Bunty and Harry cut me dead in the village.' Donna shook her head sadly.

Georgio's eyes narrowed. 'Oh, they did, did they? I might open my trap about him yet – do what Wilson did. You ring him and tell him I want me stuff back. Say I have a buyer. Do that for me, will you? Say just that. Georgio wants his stuff, he's got a buyer. Do that for me, Donna, promise?' His face was dark, earnest.

'What stuff? What are you talking about?'

Georgio waved a hand at her. 'Never mind what stuff. When he tells you he's got it, send Davey for it. He knows the score.'

Donna pushed her hair back off her face, a gesture she always used when agitated. 'What on earth are you talking about?'

48

Georgio took a deep breath and held it, then kissed her on the cheek. 'Forget what I said. It was temper talking. We had a few scams, nothing serious, but I was annoyed that he cut you dead like that. He has no right to judge me, he's more crooked than a corkscrew. They all are. They make me sick.'

Donna watched her husband as he opened his KitKat. His big hands ripped the packaging apart.

'Calm down,' she said nervously. 'Once we get to appeal, this will all be sorted out.'

Georgio laughed gently. 'Oh, yeah, course it will.'

His attitude scared her; this new Georgio scared her. Never before had she seen him like this – beaten, out of control. It was a shock, a revelation. For the first time she admitted to herself that Georgio didn't hold out much hope now the trial was over. He had depended on an acquittal; Wilson had seen that he didn't get one. She was aware now, fully and irrevocably, that Georgio was in an even more dangerous situation than she had thought. He had lost heart. She pushed these worries from her mind and attempted to change the subject.

'I started work at the car lot . . .' She was interrupted by Georgio choking on his KitKat.

'*You what!*'

Donna smiled at his incredulity and said, 'I started work at the car lot. Davey and Carol, everyone, even your family, said I ought to take an interest in the businesses. So that's what I'm going to do. It was really funny. I tidied up the office and Davey nearly had a heart attack. I must have made an impression, though, because he cleared out the storeroom last night. It was all spick and span when I went in this morning.'

She was smiling at him, aware the smile was sticking to her face, frozen there with the need to have done the right thing. Then Georgio laughed out loud.

Shaking his head, he said jocularly, 'Poor old Davey, I bet he didn't know what was going on.'

On the defensive now, Donna said quickly, without thinking, 'Look, Georgio, I am a part-owner of the businesses, as everyone keeps telling me. I thought you'd be pleased I was trying to help out. You can still run the businesses through me. I don't know why you and Davey think it's so funny.' Her voice was hurt, she felt a fool.

Georgio hugged her tightly. 'I'm sorry, but it seems – I don't know, funny, to think of you in the car lot. I know you're only trying to help, but forget it. I can run the businesses through my brothers.

49

Patrick is coming in tomorrow, and Mario. I'll sort it out with them. You forget all about it, love.'

Donna pursed her lips and said in a low voice, 'Look, Georgio, I'm not being funny, but on the headed notepaper at the car lot, I'm down as Managing Director, and the same thing with the building business. I looked through your desk at home last night. I'm on an awful lot of headed notepaper. If Carol can be trusted to work in the car lot, I don't see why I am judged too stupid to be there. I didn't even want to go but everyone was saying how I should take an interest, even your mum and dad . . .' She was upset. Very upset. Over the years she had taken a back seat to Georgio, always had. It was expected of her. Now his cavalier attitude to her trying to help hit a sore spot inside her. A spot she had just realised had been with her for years.

Georgio closed his eyes and wiped a hand across his face. 'I'm sorry, angel. Honestly, I'm deeply sorry. It's not that I don't think you're capable, it's just that you've never worked, you never had to work, and you certainly don't need any money. Every penny we have in the bank was earned fair and square. They couldn't prove the houses, the cars, or anything else was ever bought with stolen money. That's the big joke of this situation. Every year I do will be on the say-so of Wilson. They couldn't prove I had ever done a dodgy deal in my life. All my businesses were legit. So you just carry on as you have always done. Leave the businesses to me.'

Donna's head was down now, and as Georgio looked at the glossy brown of her hair he sighed. She was such a child in a lot of ways. It was this vulnerability that had attracted him.

'But what about me, Georgio?' she said in a low voice. 'What do I do all day while you're in here? Our friends treat us as if we have contracted the plague. I'll rephrase that – your friends. I never liked any of them. I keep getting lectures about men coming out of the woodwork – Davey's expression, not mine. I am told by all and sundry to look out for my husband's interests. So you tell me, Georgio, what do I do, eh? Do I sit at home like Cinderella, all dressed up and nowhere to go, or what? I realised yesterday that I need a job of some kind. I can't sit in that house every day waiting for you to write to me or to come up here for a visit. You don't come home any more, remember? I am alone, completely alone, except for Dolly. I don't even have a child to occupy me. Now I try and take an interest in the businesses and you laugh me off like I'm a silly girl. So you tell me, my love, what do I do?'

In twenty years Georgio had never heard his wife talk like this. Before, she had always told him what he wanted to hear. He realised that the nine months leading up to the trial had been a testing time for

50

her. He suddenly saw how beautiful she was, how poised, saw her as others did: the lovely wife of Georgio Brunos. She was an ornament to him, the passion he'd felt, the real passion, having been smothered by familiarity. She had stood by him, and he was grateful to her for that. Other wives of her ilk would have lined their pockets and been batting away from home before the case had even come to trial.

He took a deep breath. His soft brown eyes boring into hers, he said gently, 'I'm sorry, Donna. You're right. I am so full of myself. I was always too full of myself. It's a bad habit I picked up when I was a child. I know my faults, no one better. Forgive me. You do whatever you think you need to. I just didn't want you to knock yourself out when there's no need.'

She swallowed heavily, her throat full of tears. She seemed to spend her whole life crying lately.

'I need to do something,' she told him. 'The house is so big, so empty without you. Before all this, I knew you were coming home, and I kept your home for you – not me. Now I feel like I'm in prison – a different kind of prison perhaps, but a prison just the same. I walk around the house, touching things. Dolly keeps the place like an operating theatre it's so clean. I do a bit of gardening, maybe read a magazine or a book. I go to bed at nine, accompanied by a sleeping tablet and a glass of scotch. Is that what you want for me, Georgio? I'll die slowly of boredom, worry and regret. For the first time in twenty years I'm on my own, really on my own, and I don't like it. I hate it! But it's how things are. Once you come home, we'll get back on our old footing, but now I want to work. I think it would probably be the best thing for both of us.'

He nodded. 'I'm sorry, girl, I open me mouth without putting my brain in gear. You do what you have to. In fact, once you get a bit more involved I'll probably be glad. If I can't trust you, then who can I trust?'

Donna smiled. She had a feeling she had won something. Just what, she wasn't sure. All she knew was that her husband's attitude had cut her to the quick. And another thing she'd realised was that she had power now. Power over Georgio. For the first time ever she was more or less her own woman. Even though the way it had come about hurt her deeply, another little part of her was secretly pleased. She would become expert at running the businesses if that's what it took to get that look on his face once more. For the first time in years she had surprised him, he had really taken notice of her. He pampered her, petted her, but very rarely took a deep interest in her. Now he was looking at her with surprise, a grudging respect lighting up his deep brown eyes.

That alone was heady stuff.

51

★ ★ ★

Maeve drove into the driveway and screeched to a halt. She looked at the imposing residence belonging to her eldest son and sighed. Nearly a million the house was worth, though Georgio had had it built for next to nothing ten years before. Unlike most new houses, it had been constructed with character. A brick-built mock Georgian mansion, it sported a tennis court and swimming pool in the three-acre grounds. The house had six bedrooms, three bathrooms and a self-contained granny flat where Dolly lived. The conservatory on the back was fifty feet by twenty. That alone had cost more than her place in Canning Town.

She got out of her Lada and slammed the door. The car was full of rubbish – old ice-cream wrappers from the grandchildren, and cigarette ends overflowing from the ashtrays. It was tatty, rusting, and she loved it. Georgio had hated her driving it, offering to buy her a new car. She had always got a wicked pleasure from screeching up his drive in it. The pleasure was gone now, gone with Georgio.

Slinging her worn leather bag on to her shoulder, Maeve crunched across the gravel, past the garage block towards the front door. Dolly was waiting for her and the two women embraced.

'Hello, Dolly love, where's your woman?'

Dolly's face crinkled into a smile. 'She'll be in soon. I told her you were coming. I made us a nice casserole.'

They wandered through to the kitchen and the appetising smell made Maeve's mouth water. Like most cooks, any food presented to her that she had not had to prepare was like ambrosia. Also, she grudgingly admitted, Dolly could cook.

'How is she, Dolly?'

'She seems better now. When he was first sentenced she was terrible, God love her. But this last couple of weeks, she's picked up quite a bit. She works in the car lot during the day, though she has been seeing the fella who's running the building sites. Everyone's had word from Georgio to humour her. That's the expression he used, Carol told me. But she seems all right. If it gets her out and about, then it can only be a good thing.'

Maeve nodded. 'He's me son and I love him, but Dolly, he never deserved that girl. Humour her, my eye! And him stuck in Parkhurst like a big galoot. He told Mario not to let on to her about too much. The girl's a fool where my son is concerned. If he's so clever, what's he doing rotting in that prison, I ask meself?'

Dolly didn't answer, just carried on making the tea. Maeve needed to sound off about Georgio and the only place she could do so in peace was here, provided her daughter-in-law was out.

52

'You know it's a terrible thing to say, and if my old man heard me he'd go mad, but I'm not so sure my Georgio was as innocent as he said. Over the years he came along in leaps and bounds, and even though the police could prove nothing much, I still feel in me gut there was more to it all than anyone knows or guesses. Donna told me the other day that this house was in her name. Solely in her name. Now why would he have done that? That's the puzzler. And she had known nothing about it! He gave her papers to sign and she signed them. She said that's how it had always been.'

Dolly sighed heavily and said, 'Look, Maeve, we both know Georgio was a ducker and diver. Whatever he's done, he's more than paying for it now.'

Maeve was stopped from answering by the front door opening and Donna's cheery hello as she came in. She walked into the kitchen with a stack of books held against her chest.

'Hello, Donna love. What's all those?'

'Hello, Maeve. Oh, these are the books from the car lot. I'm going to look them over, see if I can make head or tail of them. Hello, Dolly, how about a nice cup of tea? I couldn't half do with one.'

Dolly poured her out a cup and listened to her chattering on.

'I'm getting to like working there. I think it's because I'm getting the hang of it. Even Carol's started leaving me alone now to get on with it. I still don't understand a lot of stuff, but I'm getting there. Also Carol has started taking calls at home, which takes the pressure off. Davey can concentrate on the buyers, and travelling round looking at motors. So really, I think it's working out well!'

Maeve smiled. 'What kind of calls is Carol taking? Surely there's no reason for that if you're there all day?'

Donna shrugged and sat at the scrubbed pine table. 'I don't know. I think it's the regular customers – they think I might bodge it up or something. Once I get more experience I expect everything will be much easier for all concerned. I had a lovely letter from Georgio this morning. He's settled in at Parkhurst and his appeal should be in about eight months. He sounded much happier than he has for ages.'

She smiled widely at the two older women and they smiled back at her. Maeve sipped her tea, all the while wondering what kind of calls Carol could take at home, that couldn't come into the office any more?

'Look at her! What's she doing here?' Mark Hancock's voice was loud. The men all looked at the woman walking towards them in a white hard hat and designer Wellingtons. Her legs encased in tight black ski pants, with a heavy rib white jumper over them, made her

53

look as if she should be at a race meeting at the very least. Not on a building site in Ilford.

'What can I do for you, Mrs Brunos?' Mark said aggressively, and the men nearby sniggered.

Donna picked up the tone and smiled tightly, embarrassed already. 'I understand from my husband that the footings should have been in six weeks ago. So the contract is behind schedule—'

Mark interrupted her, his voice impatient. 'I assume your husband can see what the weather's like from his new abode? It's been raining. The planning officer wouldn't let us sink the concrete until the footings had been bailed out. Anyway, we're not over schedule. The work's picked up now the warmer weather's here. The houses will be built on time, I can assure you of that. Now, if that's all?' He raised thick red eyebrows and Donna felt her stomach lurch at his rude attitude.

Pulling herself up to her full height, she said with as much dignity as she could muster, 'Actually, that's *not* all. I received the invoices for the cement and it seems we ordered three hundred yards more than anticipated. As we are building four detached three-bedroomed houses and not a whole council estate, perhaps you would be so kind as to enlighten me as to exactly where the other concrete has gone? Also, I would like the names and addresses of the so-called lumpers employed. Two plastering firms have already been paid and the brickies aren't even up to the damp course yet, so I assume they have been paid in advance? Would you like me to carry on, or shall we go to your office and finish this conversation there?'

Mark stared into her face, his eyes bright with malice. He stormed past her and Donna had to run to keep up as she followed him. But she was aware of the workmen's laughter, and knew that this time it wasn't directed at her.

Her heart was in her mouth at her own audacity, her daring. Mario had pointed out discrepancies in the invoicing, and explained everything to her as he saw it. There was an inordinate amount of ripping off going on at the different sites. Donna had told him she would sort it out. She was supposed to be looking out for her husband's interests and she was determined that she would. It was this that gave her the courage needed to take on men like Mark Hancock. Also, the knowledge that Mario was ready to back her up whenever she needed it. In the last six weeks her life had been turned upside down, yet there was an up side too. She had actually started looking forward to getting out of bed.

Inside the office she smiled sweetly at Hancock, and was gratified to see he was looking decidedly worried.

54

Chapter Four

Paddy Donovon was enormous, over eighteen stone, but as his height was nearer seven feet than six, he could carry it. His huge leonine head was covered in reddish curls, with a liberal sprinkling of grey. His beard was long, bushy, and also going grey. His eyes were slate-blue, steely, and surrounded by sandy lashes.

His hands were like shovels, his shoulders broad and muscular. He was nearly fifty-five years old. There was nothing anyone could tell Paddy about the running of a building site. He had come to England in the early 1950s, established himself in Kilburn, reared a family and lost his wife to cancer, all the while working on different sites around the country. The only thing in his life that had stayed the same was the *Irish Post*, even though he only bought it these days for the obituaries.

He had offered a tearful Donna his expertise along with Mario's, and she had gratefully accepted. Now he told her exactly what to say, and what not to say on the sites. If the site manager didn't give her what Paddy called 'her due', then Paddy would make it quite plain that they would answer to him. Mark Hancock was the first to find this out and now, seething with indignation, he was once more trying to pacify not only Donna Brunos, a bitch of a woman, but also Big Paddy Donovon, ex-fistfighter and champion of anyone smaller than him – which in Mark's estimation took in ninety-five percent of the population.

'The damp course is up, we're starting the bricklaying in the next two days, the plasterers will be in afterwards. I don't know what else I can tell you.'

'How about where the money's gone? Also who the fecking eejit was who ordered the cement.'

Mark felt himself come over faint. Paddy's voice was low, but the menace in it was evident nonetheless.

Donna picked up a file to disguise the shaking of her hands. She fiddled with the papers inside while she waited for Hancock to answer.

55

'Look, Mr Hancock . . .' Her voice was shaking along with her whole body and she swallowed deeply before going on. 'My husband has handed over the running of all his businesses to me. I really need to have these questions answered. The fact that the cement has already been paid for, and that three hundred yards has gone astray, is obviously of paramount importance.'

Mark Hancock wiped a dirty hand across his face. 'It's the perk of the job normally that cement would go to another site, but as it didn't, I sold it off myself.'

'Huh!' Paddy's exclamation was like a gunshot in the small Portakabin. 'If I know you, Hancock, you already had the buyer when you made the order. It's the old story. When the cat's away . . . Especially as this cat is away for a long stretch. Well, you listen to me, and you listen good, boy. I'm personally employed by this young lady to look out for her businesses and I intend to do just that. You get word around the sites that all the paperwork had better be in good shape or I'll rip the head off the first bastard to try and do her down. Georgio gave us all jobs, even when we'd been in stir, and now you try and have her over. Well, the buck stops here and now. As for the plasterers . . . paying them up front! I've heard fairy stories in the Old Country with more credence than that one! But as the money's been paid then they have to do the work, no matter whose pocket it comes out of. And believe me when I say I want that plastering to shine like glass, the job's that good. So you'd better bring a good firm in. Now get out of me sight before I brain ye!'

Mark Hancock left the Portakabin as fast as his dignity would allow.

'Thanks, Paddy. I don't know what I'd do without you,' Donna told him.

He grinned, showing surprisingly white teeth.

'Listen, me little pickaheen, by the time I've finished educating you, you'd be able to run fecking Wimpey's!'

Donna grinned back, but she wished desperately that she had as much faith in herself as Big Paddy did. Just talking to the likes of Mark Hancock terrified her, more so in case she forgot what Paddy had told her to say. But as the big fella had pointed out, if she wanted the men's respect, the only way she would get it was to do the talking herself. He would back her up afterwards, but the men had to think she had a working knowledge of the sites.

Well, if she kept this up, that's exactly what she would have. Whether she wanted it or not!

Georgio listened, his whole body alert and tense. In the darkness, he could hear the irregular breathing of Timmy Lambert. He knew Timmy was awake. Georgio forced his breath to come out in regular small snores. His eyes were wide open as he tried to refine his night vision. Finally, after what seemed an age, he felt Timmy move in the bunk above him, then as he clenched his fists, was amazed to see a match flare as Timmy lit himself a roll-up.

'You awake, Georgio?'

'Well, I am now, Timmy.'

'I think we should have a little chat.'

'What about?' Georgio's voice was low now; he was on his guard.

Timmy slipped off the bunk and sat beside him, his big moon face visible as he pulled deeply on his match-thin roll-up. 'Lewis is back on the Wing tomorrow, I heard the whisper. He's only been on a laydown, twenty-eight days, that's all. I also hear he's after you, boyo, because of that robbery. Now there's two camps in this dump. One is Lewis's and the other is Lewis's. Do you understand what I'm saying?'

Georgio didn't answer. He wanted desperately to move his head away from the man's breath, and the stench of his body odour.

'The thing is, I heard another little whisper that Wilson is for the out. Now there's something not quite kosher going on here, and I'd love to know what it is.'

Georgio rubbed his eyes roughly with his fingers. 'So would I, Timmy. All I know is, my face was put in the frame by Wilson. That slag tucked me up. Now Lewis is jumping on the bandwagon and all. Well, he don't scare me, we go back a long time.'

Timmy laughed softly, the sound eerie in the dimness. 'I don't particularly like you, Brunos, but I have to admire you. If Lewis was after me, even I'd be worried.'

Georgio laughed again. 'Even you? What's that supposed to mean?'

Timmy's voice lost its friendliness. 'What that means, arsehole, is I know Lewis and I know his clout in here. He's got most of the cons on A Wing up his khyber, and the majority of the screws. I know he got you striped up in the Scrubs. His arm's long, Georgio, his temper's short, and every year he does in here it's getting shorter. That robbery had his stamp on it, and as you already said, you two go back a long way. Now it don't take a contender for *Mastermind* to suss out you've been a naughty boy, and Lewis has found that out. While you're in his bad books, you ain't safe and your family ain't safe. It also means I ain't safe, because we share a peter, and if he decides to burn you out, then the chances are I get burned with you. So if you have any dealings with him, I want to know.'

Georgio could understand the man's concern. In a small part of

57

him he was terrified of what was going to happen, but he had a plan up his sleeve, and after tomorrow he would know whether or not it was going to work.

'Listen, Timmy, I'm tired. I'll see Lewis tomorrow, so stop fretting your ugly head over it. All right?'

Timmy wiped a hand across his face, the scraping of his stubble loud in the silent cell.

'I'm fucking warning you, Georgio. I know you're a heavy-weight, I respect that. But at the end of the day, we're all hard nuts in here, one way or another, even the nancies. A few years A-Grade soon sorts out the men from the boys, and let's face it, you ain't ever done any bird before. So you keep me informed of what's going on. If you go down the pan, boy, you ain't taking me with you. Got that?'

Georgio turned over on his side. Tucking his hands under his head he said casually, 'Loud and clear. Goodnight, Timmy.'

Timmy sat for a few seconds longer before returning to his bunk. Georgio heard the springs groan as the man's huge bulk lay down above him.

Closing his eyes, he shuddered inwardly. He hadn't slept properly in a month. The thought of Lewis scared him shitless. But tomorrow, if he played his cards right, everything could be hunky-dory.

For the first time in years, Georgio actually prayed.

Donna awoke to weak sunshine and a lifting of her spirits. If someone had told her a few months ago that she would enjoy doing Georgio's job she would have laughed in their face. Yet, as she was his wife, and as everyone expected her to 'see to' things for him, she had felt pressured into taking everything on. Now she was glad she had. Even the paperwork for the building business was beginning to make sense to her. She needed guidance, she knew, but the day-to-day running was not as difficult as she had feared. In fact, once she had managed to sort through the offices, and had thrown out the rubbish, it was surprisingly straightforward.

When Georgio came home he would be so proud of her. She hugged this thought to herself.

Big Paddy had seen to it that she was given more than 'her due'. Now on the sites she was treated with respect, even with awe. But that could be due to Paddy's watchful presence, she admitted to herself.

Getting out of bed, she saw her reflection in the mirrored wardrobes. Holding her thick chestnut hair back from her face, she surveyed herself. She was thinner than ever since the trial, her

58

ribcage visible through her skin. Pulling back her narrow shoulders she sighed heavily. No amount of thrusting out would ever make her breasts look full. She was still a thirty AA cup, the same as she had been when she was fourteen. All her friends had blossomed, but not Donna. She had hoped that the advent of children would have given her at least a small cleavage. But it wasn't to be. She liked her legs though, she had always liked them. They were long, slim, and nicely shaped. She looked good in shorts, though she rarely wore them. Georgio always said her breasts were lovely, juicy he had called them, and she had always blushed at this. His rough words had embarrassed her even as she had loved hearing them.

She wrapped her arms around herself in despair. If only things were as they had been . . . Georgio would be getting up now, coughing and spluttering his way to the bathroom, his long muscly body naked. She had always watched him dress, even when she was really tired she had watched him, drinking him in with her eyes. She had never once, in all the years with him, grown bored of looking at him. In fact, she had loved him more as the years had gone on.

She admitted to herself that he had taken her for granted, but that was men, apparently. Dolly said that *her* husband wouldn't have noticed if she had fandangoed across the front room in the nude. Unless she had stood in front of the TV, then there would have been hell to pay.

Georgio, though, had always treated Donna with respect, had respected her feelings. Had never let her know when he was unfaithful. Though with the intuition of women, she had known, she had known immediately. It hadn't happened that often over the years, but when it had it had grieved her. Hurt her deeply. Yet, in a funny way, she had understood why Georgio had done it. He was a man who needed people, needed adoration, and he was a man who got what he wanted.

She had always thanked God for Georgio, thanked Him because He had seen fit to give him to her, little Donna Fenland. A nobody. Georgio had even stood by her when she had lost the babies, and she knew he had dearly wanted children. Being a mixture of Greek and Irish Catholic, it was a certainty he would want children. Yet he had not discarded her in favour of a fertile woman, had never once brought the subject up, even when they had rowed. Which wasn't often. She was scared to row with Georgio, scared to give him any excuse not to want her.

Now she was deprived of him as she had always feared she would be. But it was the police and the courts who had taken him away, not some large-breasted, blonde model type with hormones bursting out

59

of her every orifice. That had been Donna's biggest fear all her married life. Yet she almost wished he had left her now; in a funny way, she wished he had gone off with another woman. That would be preferable to thinking of him stuck in that prison on the Isle of Wight. Her Georgio, her free agent. Georgio who had a boat, Georgio who always liked to travel, Georgio who walked across the fields every Sunday after his dinner because he liked being in the air, liked his freedom.

She bit back the tears, their hot saltiness making her cough. Walking to the mirrored wardrobes, she stared into her own face. The eyes were black-rimmed, but still a deep blue. Her cheekbones were prominent, more so now she had lost so much weight. Her lips were dry and cracked from where she cried in the night, and chewed on them to stem the heartwrenching sobs of loneliness. Leaning her forehead on the cool glass, she took a deep breath. Georgio would be home once his appeal was over with; he would be home. She said it over and over like a mantra. She had to believe that, she had to.

If she ever stopped believing it, she would take a length of rope and hang herself. It was no idle threat; it was the truth, a deep inalterable truth.

Without Georgio Brunos, she was nothing.

She was hanging on by a minute thread. If Georgio lost his appeal the thread would snap and with it her reason. Her earlier joy on waking was gone now. The thought of her husband's pleasure in her work, in the businesses, gone also. Because if he didn't come home, the businesses, the house, the cars, all they possessed, were nothing.

All she had ever wanted in her life was him.

Donald Lewis was fifty-two years old. He wasn't a big man in stature, but what he lacked in size he made up for in reputation, and his reputation was one of the hardest. It had taken the Sweeney, the Flying Squad and the Serious Crime Squad eleven years of intensive work before they had brought him in. He was involved in every racket known to man, and a few that were as yet unknown to the police and public in general. He was an international villain, having seen the action over the Pond as a viable proposition before most of his contemporaries. He dealt in anything and everything, from women, to drugs, to boys, to guns. He was noted for his almost surgical cleanliness, and also his dry sense of humour. He liked young men, handsome young men, and his stint in Parkhurst had been likened to a busman's holiday by the screws.

Lewis's sheer force of personality gave him the edge over bigger, more violent men; that and his sadistic mind. He was dapper, almost feminine in his dress. He was also shrewd. Donald Lewis had been unable to write his own name before going into Hollandsy Bay Borstal at fifteen; there he had had the three Rs beaten into him, and had never looked back since. He had a natural hatred of any kind of authority, a hatred of women, and also a hatred of most of his contemporaries. Diagnosed as a psychotic, he had spent a lot of money to make sure he wasn't transferred to Broadmoor. Though the regime was much more relaxed there, you had next to no chance of either escape or, more importantly, parole.

He was a Double A Category prisoner, Maximum Security, which only left four prisons in England which could hold him. He had decided that he would have a stint in Durham in a few years, for a change of scene. Other than that he had no plans for the future except to keep himself alive, run his nefarious businesses, and stay on top of everything going on around him. Lewis was the Baron of Parkhurst, controlling the trade in drugs and tobacco. He also controlled his wing.

He was sitting at his small table now, waiting for his breakfast which was always cooked to perfection in the wing kitchen by a prisoner called Roberts. He was doing a ten stretch and had taken up cookery as a pastime. Being Double A Grade, Lewis could order in food, and the screws bought it for him in Sainsbury's. It was a joke among them but they accepted it as part of their job. If it kept the lifers happy, they were happy, and the world was an easier place.

As Lewis sipped his tea he smiled.

The laydown had been a pain but he had managed to get a lot of work done. Section 43, which dealt with A and Double A Category prisoners, stated that they could be moved for twenty-eight days at the discretion of the prison governor to a stipulated prison of their choice. Hence the laydown. They were taken away and put in solitary, generally in Wandsworth, which satisfied the governors that they could never plan an escape. The reasoning behind this was that they could be taken at any time of the day or night, with no advance warning. Section 43 was brought in ostensibly for terrorists, but any Maximum Security prisoner was liable to the rule.

His laydowns were a joy to Lewis; he had already bought himself enough staff in the prison service to assure himself an easy stay. His radio was left with him, as were his writing materials and his books. His food was decent and he drank tea and whisky by the gallon. It was the mark of his situation, his reputation, and his considerable bank balance, that he was allowed to live in relative ease.

Having taken to reading in his first year of prison, he was now a knowledgeable man who saw his lack of education as the reason

61

behind his criminal career. Now he craved knowledge as a thirsty man craves water, and used it to further his own ends. It had never occurred to him that with an education he could have been a legitimate businessman; he saw his lack of education as the reason to work doubly hard to be a success in his illegal businesses. Such was the temperament and mentality of Donald Lewis.

'Here's your breakfast, Mr Lewis.' The younger man placed a plate of bacon, eggs, tomatoes and mushrooms on the table.

Lewis smiled up at him and without a word picked up his knife and fork and tucked in.

The other man stood watching until he had started eating then, sighing with relief, left the cell and made his way back to his own breakfast. It was always a toss up whether Lewis would eat the breakfast or decorate the cell walls with it. Walking into the small kitchen, the cook cursed loudly; his sausage was gone as was his bacon.

'Thieving bastards!'

He smiled briefly as he heard laughter coming from the other cells. He inspected the rest of his food before beginning to eat. They were capable of anything in here in the name of a joke, from spitting on the food to putting LSD in your baked beans. He was just nervous at having Lewis back from his laydown. Everything was topsy-turvy this morning.

Lewis was mopping up the egg yolk with a slice of bread when he turned to see his minder, Harry Clarkson, standing in the doorway.

'I've brought Brunos, Mr Lewis. Shall I tell him to wait out here?'

Lewis laughed. Putting the bread delicately down he said, 'No, Harry. Why don't you ask him to wait in the governor's office?'

Harry stood still, blinking nervously.

Lewis sighed. Harry was all brawn and no brains but he was a good old stick and would murder for a packet of fags. So he smiled and said, 'Bring him in, Harry mate, and wait at the door.'

'Yes, Mr Lewis.'

Georgio walked through the door with an air of confidence he did not feel. 'All right, Donald? Long time no see.'

Lewis wiped his tongue across his teeth and said, 'Sit down, Georgio. Me and you need to have a few words.'

Georgio sat down and stared at the small man in front of him. The air of menace was practically tangible, it was so strong. It emanated from Lewis in invisible waves. The complete lack of expression in his voice was enough to make the hair on Georgio's arms stand up and bristle.

'Do you know Harry at all? He's in here because he murdered a

62

bloke he didn't like much. In fact, Harry would murder someone who looked like the bloke he didn't like much. He's that type of bloke, see. Now me and Harry have a little arrangement. I tell him what to do and he does it. Do you get my drift, Brunos, or do you want me to give you an example of my power over him? He'll crush your hands, break your jaw, or strangle you if I ask him nicely.'

Georgio swallowed down his fear and said lightly, 'Me and you go back a long way, Donald. You had me striped up in the Scrubs, and we was always mates. Always. You don't need to show me your performing gorilla.'

Lewis pushed his plate away and smiled again. 'How is your harris, by the way? I told them not to cut too deep. Not yet anyway. And I got your message about cutting my throat. Gave me a good laugh, that did.'

Georgio closed his eyes. 'I had to say that, Donald. I wouldn't have lasted five minutes if I'd have swallowed that striping without a word and you know it.'

Lewis picked up the knife from his plate and wiped it clean with a napkin. 'I am going to push this into your eye-socket in about five minutes, Georgio, unless you tell me where my dough is.' He looked at his watch. 'Start talking now.'

Georgio swallowed again. This time it was more difficult. His mouth was as dry as the Gobi Desert.

'Four minutes to go, Georgio. Your time's running out, my son.'

'I've got the money, don't worry about that. It's safe, and it will only stay safe while I'm alive and kicking. I had to have some insurance and hiding the money was it. I wouldn't tuck you up, Donald, and I'm deeply offended that you think I would.'

Lewis grinned. 'Deeply offended, are we? I'll rip your fucking heart out, Brunos, if you don't tell me where my dosh is stashed.'

Georgio smiled. 'It's in a place so safe, the Old Bill would need a message from St Bernadette before they'd believe it was even there.'

Lewis laughed then, excited. 'Where is it, Georgio?'

He put out his hands in a gesture of supplication.

'You know I can't tell you that, Donald. The minute I open me mouth I'm as good as dead. Only one person knows where that money's hidden, and that's me. Until I get me appeal, and I'm outside, you will never know where it is. But I take an oath, I would not tuck you up. Not in a month of Sundays. Your half is safe, as safe as the proverbial houses. While I'm safe, the dough is safe.'

Lewis smashed his fist on the table, making the plate and cutlery clatter on the wooden surface.

'Fucking safe? *Safe*? What do you think this is – kindergarten?

63

Cross me heart and hope to die? You have access to my dough, and I fucking want it. I set that robbery up. I set it up, you hear me! All you had to do was provide the cars and the guns, nothing else, not a fucking brass razoo. Just the guns and the cars. But you took it on yourself to fucking stick your big Greek conk into things that don't concern you. Now I don't know if you're aware of this, but Wilson will be found hanging in his cell at Camp Hill this morning. In fact, they should have found him in the last hour or so. Unless you want the same fate, or worse, you had better start talking to me.'

Georgio didn't flinch, didn't move. He took out his cigarettes and lit one slowly, aware of the man in front of him breathing in quick, sharp bursts. Lewis's temper was phenomenal.

'I'm sorry, but I ain't saying nothing. All I can guarantee you is that I have it all stashed away safe as houses. You listen to this. Wilson was going to take your cut, he was. It was only the Old Bill turning up like they did, and my quick thinking, that even saved the dough. I'd had it on me toes with it within minutes of the robbery. I had a feeling something was going down. Wilson was like a cat with a rat hanging on its arse, and the driver was practically a fucking geriatric. I oversaw that blag, and I oversaw it for you! Because you was me mate. And now I have to keep information from you in case you top me, so no one but me knows where the fuck the money is. I ain't enjoying all this, you know,' Georgio said hotly. 'I got eighteen fucking years, remember – eighteen years on the say-so of fucking Wilson. The same Wilson who had help this morning to top himself. So knowing you like I do, I have to have a bit of insurance. If you torture me and I talk, you still won't know if what I tell you is correct. And the way I feel, you could torture me till the cows come home and you'll get nothing out of me. Even Big Harry outside don't scare me. Eighteen years scares me, Lewis. I don't want to do it and if I don't get parole I might top meself anyway!'

Lewis sat back in his seat. He acknowledged that Georgio was trying to save himself; he accepted that. He also knew Georgio had had every intention of keeping a large portion of Lewis's money himself. What riled him was that Georgio now had the whole pack of cards, even the jokers. Because Lewis knew, in his heart of hearts, that everything Georgio said was true. Only he knew where the money was, and that was his insurance.

Donald Lewis, his eyes alight with malice, smiled and said: 'Georgio, we're friends. Friends shouldn't argue, especially not over money. I admit I've been a bit hard on you. I'm overwrought. But I'm sure that me and you can sort something out. You keep your peace, I accept your logic. But if, and I mean if, you get your parole and leave here, you'll be accompanied by a friend of mine until what I own is in a safe place. If you lose your appeal,' he laughed gently, 'then I'm afraid we'll have to reassess the situation.'

Georgio breathed a heavy sigh of relief. 'That's fair enough, Donald, but then you was always fair-minded. I accept what you say. I admire you, you know. You're a big man, a man with a reputation, yet you've got scruples. I know from experience that I can trust you implicitly. I only wish you afforded me the same consideration.'

Lewis grinned again, less hostile this time. 'Oh, but I do, Georgio, I do.'

He stood up and held out his hand. Georgio knew he was being dismissed.

Getting up, he shook the cold hand before him and left the cell.

As he reached the door Lewis said, 'By the way, Georgio, how's your wife? Lovely-looking girl that. I hear she's been a good little lass while you've been banged up. Not a lot of women like that these days. Pretty girl, if I remember rightly. Nice legs.'

Georgio turned and looked into Donald Lewis's laughing countenance.

'Be a shame if anything was to happen to her, wouldn't it?'

As Georgio marched back to his own cell his head was reeling. One thing was paramount: he had to get out of this place, and he had to get out of it as soon as possible.

His appeal could take up to three years. It was this thought that frightened him so much.

Three days with Lewis breathing down his neck was a nightmare. How would he cope as the days stretched into months then years? One thing was certain: he was not going to give Lewis one iota of the money from the robbery. It was his, he was entitled to it, and it came to nearly three-quarters of a million pounds. If his plan came off, he would be sitting pretty for the rest of his life. No more robbing Peter to pay Paul on the building sites, no more worrying. He was waiting to see how long it took Donna to realise that the only real money they had was invested in the house. He didn't even own the cars; they were on lease-hire. His credit was nearly up with the building suppliers and the money from the car lot was like pocket money. He had been living beyond his means for years.

But then, didn't everyone? It was the dream of the young Tory government in the early eighties.

Borrow now, pay back later.

Well, the paying was always the hardest part, and all his life Georgio Brunos had avoided doing anything he didn't like.

★ ★ ★

65

Donna sat in the restaurant in Canning Town, watching as Pa Brunos prepared Kleftiko, his large, chubby hands moving around the worktop deftly. He was singing softly to himself. Donna breathed in the smells of the kitchen, the oregano, basil and red wine which were always present.

She sipped at her own white wine and sighed gently. 'Pa, can I ask you something?'

'Of course you can, my little angel. Anything you like.'

Donna licked her lips. 'Do you think Georgio will get his appeal? Only when I spoke to the barrister today, he sounded, well, a bit offish . . .' Her voice trailed away.

Pa Brunos wiped his hands on his apron and hugged her to him hard, kissing the glossy brown hair with a smacking sound. 'Don't you be a-worrying. My Georgio is an innocent man. The laws of this country will make sure he is released. You probably caught the man when he was busy. We're all short when we're busy.'

Donna smiled gently. 'You're not.'

Pa laughed, a deep chuckle. 'I'm not with you, but with Maeve I shout like a lion! I scream at her to leave me in peace.'

'What does Maeve do?' Donna responded to the twinkling eyes.

'What does she do? She gets that Irish temper of hers out of her pocket and she screams into my lughole and I am sorry I ever said one word!'

Donna laughed.

Pa Brunos hugged her again. 'Don't you be a-worrying, you hear? Before you can say Jack Robinson my Georgio will be home and this restaurant will be having the biggest party in the world.'

'Of course it will, Pa. I just wish it was soon.'

Pa Brunos went back to his work and shrugged. 'I think sometimes that this will do Georgio a bit of good, eh? I think he is a bit too cocky as the Londoners say.'

Donna slipped off the stool and went to her father-in-law. 'What makes you say that, Pa? What do you mean?'

Pa smiled at her, an ear-splitting smile, showing off his teeth. 'Never mind, my little Donna. Forget I spoke. Sometimes I say things to the air that I should leave inside my head.'

Donna looked into the big, open, honest face and felt an urge to weep. Not because of what Pa had said, but because he had put into words what she had been thinking on and off since Georgio had been sentenced.

Only, until this moment, she had not admitted it to herself.

66

Chapter Five

Stephen Brunos was with his close friend Hattie Jacobs. She was fifty-five, big, voluptuous and jolly. When Stephen looked at her he felt happy. Hattie had a way of smiling all over; her eyes smiled even when her mouth was still. She exuded camaraderie, happiness and kindness. It was the last that attracted Stephen to her. Hattie never badmouthed anyone. He knew that his mother would class her as a big blowsy tart – most people would who didn't know her – the main reason being that Hattie *was* a tart. Though she no longer walked the pavements of Shepherd's Market, and only reminisced about the days she strolled along Park Lane; she worked now as a telephone tart.

All day long, she sat on her big double bed talking to strange men over the phone. The men were faceless, they paid by credit card and they explained exactly what kind of call they wanted. Hattie always obliged. She could be a nervous virgin, breathless and frightened, or she could be a mature woman who told her callers off, threatening them with corporal punishment and sighing happily when they promised to be good boys. Hattie was also adept at being a naughty housewife, a tantalising *femme fatale*, or in extreme cases a transvestite. The only thing Hattie would not be was a child. She drew the line at child sex even over a telephone line.

Stephen watched as Hattie 'finished off' the caller. Picking up a Mars bar, she pushed it into her mouth and sucked on it, making slapping, slurping noises, talking into the phone with her mouth full of chocolate about how big and hard it was. She saw Stephen watching her and rolled her eyes at the ceiling. She held the phone away from her ear, disgusted with the noises emanating from the receiver.

When she put the phone back to her ear the line was dead.

'I thought he was never going to come!' she told Stephen. 'I've been through about six Mars bars this morning! Put the kettle on and I'll take me phone off the hook. I've more than had enough, I can tell you.'

Stephen plugged in the small white kettle and grinned. 'That was

67

excellent, Hattie. You nearly had me going then.'

She pushed her huge bulk from the bed and waddled over to him. 'Listen, sunshine, twenty years ago I could have had you going all night and into the next afternoon.'

Stephen kissed the florid cheek and said gently, 'I believe you, Hattie. You know I do. You're still a good girl, my lovely.'

Hattie grinned with pleasure at the pretence. Stephen still treated her with respect; he kept up the fiction that she was someone worthwhile, even though she knew in her heart she was no one, a nobody. The only thing was, Stephen *did* believe everything he said. He loved Hattie Jacobs in a strange, unaccountable way. Since he had taken her on to the books, he had felt an affinity with her. He looked at her fat jowly face and saw radiant beauty. In her huge cumbersome body he saw warmth and comfort. Twice he had shared her bed; neither attempt had been satisfactory, but the feeling he had for her was still there.

'What can I do for you, Stephen? Or is this a social visit?'

He laughed gently. 'A bit of both actually, Hats. I want you to take on a couple of learners. One's nineteen, got a little baby so she'll bring it with her. The other's in her forties, out to make a few bob while the old man's out at work. She knits, I understand. So she'll be knitting her head off while spouting filth over the trombone. It never ceased to amaze me what the girls get up to while they're working. What I want is for you to learn them the "Starting ups" and "finishing offs". Both girls have an aptitude for this kind of work. They just need to learn the tricks of the trade.'

Hattie made the tea and nodded. 'Okey doke, Steve. I've got some oranges in, I'll show them the lot. Oral sex, anal sex, whatever. I hope they're not easily shocked though. They do realise this is one of the more exotic call lines, don't they?'

He nodded. Taking out his wallet, he extracted three fifty-pound notes.

'This is for your trouble, Hats.'

Hattie took the money and slid it into her slipper, a habit she had acquired on the streets. Even if a punter ripped off your gear, providing you kept your shoes on you didn't lose your dosh along with everything else.

'I ain't teaching them the baby talk though, you can get someone else to do that. You know how I feel about that, don't you?' Her big moon face was troubled.

Stephen pulled her into his arms and cuddled her, breathing in the scent of 4711 and sweat. 'Don't worry, Hats, you know I'd never ask you to do something you didn't want to.'

68

Hattie cuddled him back, her strong arms gripping his waist like a vice. 'Fair enough, Steve. They'll be experts in twenty-four hours.'

'That, Hats, is what I'm counting on. Now then, let's have our tea. How's your boys?'

Hattie turned back to the little table and sugared the two mugs of tea. 'My Brian's on the Island. Says your brother's there, Georgio. Someone striped his arse by all accounts – that slag Lewis. Never liked him, even when he was a boy. Weird, he was. I remember when we was all kids, about thirteen, he killed all his mum's kittens, drowned them, he did, in a puddle of all things. His mother nearly murdered him. Pity she didn't, she'd have saved herself a lot of grief.'

Stephen nodded absentmindedly. Georgio had mentioned nothing to him of a striping. He took the tea from Hattie and said, 'You sure it was my brother?'

Hattie nodded vigorously. 'Oh yeah, it was him all right. My Brian was shipped to the Island from the Scrubs with him. It might have happened in the Scrubs, now I come to think of it.'

'Oh, well. It'll all come out in the wash, Hats.'

'How's the phone business going then, Steve?'

Stephen grinned again. 'Going like the clappers, Hats. Can't get enough lines, in fact. The demand is phenomenal.'

'All this safe sex, I suppose. Better a wank over the trombone than a shag and a dose. That's the logic behind it.'

Stephen laughed out loud at her resigned voice. 'I expect you're right, Hattie, old girl. I expect you're dead right.'

Hattie punched him playfully on the arm. 'Not so much of the bleedin' old, if you don't mind.'

Stephen was back in his office in Soho within the hour. He walked past his secretary and told her to hold any calls until he said otherwise. Then he locked his office door and picked up his private line. He dialled and lit himself a cigarette while he waited for the connection.

'Hello, Hinckley? This is Stephen Brunos. I want a bit of information and I want it soon. It concerns my brother Georgio and Donald Lewis.'

He stubbed out the cigarette and listened carefully, his face growing redder by the second.

Nuala and Donna were going over the invoicing for the building sites. The two women worked in silence. Nuala glanced at the clock every few minutes.

'He'll ring, Nuala, don't worry.'

69

Nuala smiled wryly. 'He'd better.'

Donna picked up the folder she was working on and passed it over the table. 'What do you make of this?'

Nuala opened the file and stared at the columns of figures, then she looked at the front of the file once more, scanning the writing as if it might tell her something.

'I don't know what this is about, to be honest. What site is the Armageddon site? Never heard of it.'

Donna frowned. 'Neither have I. Look at the figures, Nuala – they're running into millions.'

Nuala scanned the closely-typed figures once more in silence. 'I can't make head nor tail of them. It seems to me to be one of those projection tables. Maybe it's something Georgio was working out on paper. I mean, Armageddon site – that sounds fanciful in itself. It's probably just a projection table he made up. You know, if I build so many houses, I can double up. Treble up. Build the last thirty houses for next to nothing. Builders do this sort of thing all the time.'

Donna nodded impatiently. 'I understand that, Nuala, but this starts with single pounds – look.' She pointed to the first table of figures.

Nuala sighed heavily. 'That definitely goes to show it's only pretend then, doesn't it? How many houses do you know get sold for a quid?'

'Maybe it's not houses. Maybe it's something else?'

Nuala looked into her sister-in-law's face and shook her head. 'Well, whatever it is, we'll never know about it. I'll sling it in the bin.'

Donna took the file and put it into her large shoulder bag. 'No, I'll take it home with me. You never know with Georgio, he might want it one day.'

Nuala smiled sadly. 'Yeah, you never know. You're missing him, aren't you? I mean, *really* missing him.'

Donna nodded. 'More each day, if that's possible.'

Nuala grasped her hand gently. 'I know my brother wasn't strictly on the level with a lot of things, but he wouldn't have hurt anyone, anyone at all. Duck and dive a bit with the businesses, yeah. But nothing like they've accused him of. Before you know it, he'll be home.'

'You know what really hurts, Nuala? The way that judge said he ruled his empire with fear. What empire? It was all on the say-so of Wilson.'

'Well, Wilson's paid the price for his skulduggery now.'

Donna frowned. 'In what way?'

70

'Didn't you know, Donna? He committed suicide in Camp Hill prison about two weeks ago.'

Donna's eyes widened. 'He killed himself?'

Nuala nodded. 'Stephen told me. I assumed he'd told you.'

Donna shook her head. 'He never said a word to me about it.'

'Maybe he didn't want you to worry, like. I mean, I shouldn't have said anything.'

'How the hell is Georgio going to get his parole if the only person who can prove he's innocent is dead?' Donna's voice was rising dangerously.

'Calm down, love. This isn't going to help him, is it? You getting in a state.'

'But if Wilson's dead . . . Did he leave a note of any kind?'

'I don't know. Stephen never mentioned it if he did.'

Donna put her hands up to her face, her distress visible. 'They'll never believe him now,' she whispered. 'The only chance he had – Wilson was the only chance that he had. If he had decided to tell the truth, or if we could have proved that Wilson was lying . . .'

Nuala went to her sister-in-law's side and stroked the thick brown hair. 'We'll prove it. In fact, it might even be easier now he's dead. I know that sounds hard, but he's not around to call us liars now, is he?'

Donna saw the logic in what Nuala was saying. 'How did he die?'

The young woman shrugged. 'Hanged himself, I think. Yeah, he was found hanging in his cell.'

Donna was running her fingers through her hair in agitation. 'I hope you're right. Maybe now they might believe Georgio. I'll go and see his lawyer. I mean, he would have been informed about Wilson. He should have told me! He'll know if Wilson left any kind of letter, won't he?'

'Well, if he don't he'll be able to find out anyway.'

'I think you might be right, Nuala.' Donna felt her spirits lift. 'Maybe now this Wilson's dead, it might be easier to prove he was lying.'

Nuala smiled. 'We can only try, darlin'. We can only try.'

Maeve and Donna sat before Mr William Booth, QC. His pinched face was devoid of any expression whatsoever. He wiped his beaked nose with a tissue and tossed it carelessly in the direction of a bin.

'I am quite aware that Peter Wilson committed suicide, Mrs Brunos, but it has no bearing on your husband's appeal. It seems that it was suicide while the balance of his mind was disturbed.

71

The sentence and the prison he was in contributed largely to his depression.'

'But he only got five years.' Maeve's voice was loud in the small chamber.

'Five years is five years too long for most people, Mrs Brunos. You have to understand, the man was suffering from clinical depression. It was an unfortunate thing to happen, granted, but unavoidable. If a man wants to kill himself he will. In fact, according to the coroner's report, Wilson had to hold his legs up in the air until he was unconscious. He was very determined by all accounts. The ceiling of the cell had nothing which he could use for his act. He had to use the iron coat-peg on the back of his cell door. Wilson was five ten, the door a standard six-foot-six. He couldn't actually hang, if you see what I mean, so in order to maximise his weight, he had literally to hold his legs up a foot or eighteen inches from the floor. Once unconscious, he slumped down – and this action actually finished off the strangulation. His own weight finally crushed his windpipe.'

Maeve closed her eyes in horror. 'What did he hang himself with?' she said faintly.

'A child's skipping rope of all things. Taken from the visiting room – probably when his wife and children had come to visit. As I say, he was very determined.'

'So how will this affect my husband's appeal?' Donna asked breathlessly.

Booth sighed heavily. 'Your husband's appeal is in hand, Mrs Brunos. Once we have collated the statements again, gone into the actual robbery once more and collected more statements, we shall be ready to proceed.'

'Do you hold out much hope for his acquittal?' Maeve's voice was low.

William Booth gave her a pained smile. 'I never make promises unless I can keep them, Mrs Brunos. I can only do my utmost, nothing more.'

'But surely with Wilson being dead and everything . . . Maybe he killed himself because he lied?'

'With respect, Mrs Brunos, without the aid of a medium I doubt very much we could prove that. Hint at it certainly, but we could not use that as the basis for the appeal. What we need are strong hard facts. Evidence. The evidence the police have is all circumstantial, and of course the statements from Wilson. Without him, it would seem our case is stronger, I grant you. But, as I said, I don't make promises, and I never give people false hope.'

72

Maeve and Donna rose from their seats.

'Well, thanks for your time, Mr Booth. By the way, are you still on a retainer?' This time, Maeve's voice was loud.

'I am.'

Donna watched the man's confusion.

'Then I suggest you start earning it. Good day, Mr Booth.'

Maeve bustled to the door of the office. Donna, scarlet-faced, nodded at the man and followed her mother-in-law out of the room.

As she shut the door behind her, she heard the hearty sigh of a man relieved of a great burden.

Donald Lewis watched as Georgio played football. He was now on the five-a-side team and they were practising for their Saturday afternoon match against B Wing. The score was a forgone conclusion; the A grade prisoners always won, even against the screws.

'Is it my imagination or is Brunos getting cocky?' Wally Wagstaff spoke out of the side of his mouth; only Lewis was aware of what he was saying.

'He *is* cocky, Wally. That's his problem. It'll always be his problem. He don't know when to shut his great big trap.'

Wally scratched his large beer belly. 'Want me to have a little reception committee waiting for him in his cell?'

'Nah. That's something I'm saving for when the time is more appropriate. Then I'm going to break his balls with my bare hands.' Lewis's voice became confidential. 'You see, Wally, the thing with Brunos is, he's big, handsome and clever. Three things guaranteed to get on my tits, so to speak. I have a little fright lined up for his nearest and dearest. That should guarantee our Georgie boy a loosening of the tongue, because if I don't find out what I need to know, and soon, he's going to be in big trouble. I can afford to write off the money, easy as pie. It's pennies and halfpennies to me. It's the principle of the thing, see? Georgio took the piss. I don't like people who take the piss out of me.'

Wally nodded his bald head sagely. 'I get your drift, Mr Lewis.'

Lewis turned on the man and sneered into his face. 'I couldn't give two fucks whether you get it or not, mate. You're like Georgio, you're just another ponce.' His tone was becoming agitated and Wally began to feel nervous.

'Shall I fuck off, Mr Lewis?'

Donald grinned. 'Nah! You stay put. I often get a little annoyed, you know. I don't mean nothing by it.'

Wally relaxed in his seat. 'I don't mind, Mr Lewis. I know you don't mean it.' He smiled widely at the man beside him.

73

Lewis frowned. 'Oh I meant what I said, Wally. You *are* a ponce. But at the moment that fact isn't bothering me. I'll let you know when it does.'

He turned his attention back to the pitch. Georgio scored a goal and everyone cheered. Lewis bit his lip in consternation. Trust Brunos to be the one to do that.

Lewis's posse was silent at the goal and that pleased him. He liked being in control of things. At the moment he wasn't in control of Georgio Brunos, and that fact dismayed and aggrieved him. But after his little wife had had a visit from a mutual friend, he was sure Georgio would open up. Once he told Lewis where the money was, and once the money had been recovered, it would be goodbye Georgio.

Lewis smiled at the thought.

Timmy Lambert watched the conversation between Lewis and Wally with interest. He sat across the football pitch from them, but could see them both clearly. Beside him sat Sadie Gold, real name Albert Moore. Sadie was wearing blue eyeshadow, brown mascara and bright red lipstick. His prison shirt was tied under his chest and his jeans were decorated with embroidered flowers. His dark hair was showing an inch of white roots, but it was backcombed out and lacquered.

Timmy and Sadie were an item in the prison. Sadie kept herself to herself and didn't run around on Timmy, and everyone kept out of their way. Lewis had countenanced the relationship. Being homosexual himself, he wasn't shocked by it. Some of the younger men were disgusted, shocked, or found it highly amusing. In different circumstances they might have taken pleasure in baiting Sadie. But this was Lewis's wing and so it was accepted and the two were left in peace. Not many would have taken on Timmy Lambert anyway; Sadie, however, was a different ballgame. They might have approached her for oral or anal sex when the need grew strong, but as it was she was left in relative peace.

Sadie enjoyed being looked after by Timmy; it helped her to do her time, allowed her a modicum of respect and guaranteed her a bit of peace. Sadie had murdered a customer while under the influence of barbiturates and alcohol. Her plea of self-defence might have been taken seriously had not the punter been a famous playwright noted for stunning dialogue and lovingly crafted screenplays about heterosexual relationships and the trials of adolescent first love. Sadie had been sentenced amid a blaze of public outcry and media attention.

What no one knew about Sadie though was that until the age of

74

sixteen she had been deaf. After an operation that gave her back fifty per cent of her hearing, Sadie still lipread when talking to people. She was now taking in Lewis's conversation with Wally and relaying it back to Timmy, word for word.

Timmy's attitude was that Lewis was a man you'd best be a jump ahead of – two jumps if possible. He had no intention of warning Brunos about the attack intended for his wife – that was between him and Lewis – but if the latter had any intention of firing the cell, smoking it, or leaving a welcoming committee, then Timmy wanted to know. It was hard enough doing your time without the added hag of someone else's troubles landing on your doorstep, so to speak.

He gently put his arm across Sadie's shoulders. 'Well done, Sadie, me old meat pie. You keep your eye out and about for any titbits you think might be of interest to me.'

She smiled up into Timmy's moon face. 'Fancy going back to my cell for a while? We'll have a bit of time to ourselves before the others come in.'

Timmy nodded and the two strolled back inside arm in arm. The screws watched them with amusement. In all truth they should cell them up together, but it was much more fun watching their furtive attempts at sex in odd places and at odd times.

It took the monotony out of the days, and God knew, that in itself was enough of a reason to keep the lovers apart for a while longer.

Georgio was reading a letter from Donna. He smiled to himself as she filled him in on her days. He felt much more relaxed now that Davey and Stephen had taken over the running of the main businesses. He was amazed, though, at how effectively Donna had slipped on the mantle of boss on the sites. Davey had told him how well she was doing. Even Big Paddy Donovon had been impressed with how quickly she had caught on. Georgio looked once more at the photographs Donna had sent in. They were from a holiday they had taken in Barbados a few years previously. Donna, tanned and lithe in a yellow bikini, looked good enough to eat. Another taken in St Tropez showed her topless, eating a large French gâteau. He had expressly asked for that photo. It had really turned him on that day, watching the fresh cream melting on her little breasts. He felt a stirring inside himself and put the photographs on the table.

Timmy laughed. 'Got the horn, Brunos? Tell them to put more bromide in your tea, mate!'

Georgio laughed back good-naturedly. 'You're a dirty-minded swine, Timmy. Not everyone's got your taste in women so some of us have to do without.'

75

'Gissa look at the photos then. I promise I won't get the horn. I'm interested to see what your old woman looks like.'

Georgio sorted through the photos and found one of Donna in a sundress in their garden, her face glowing with good health and happiness. He passed it to Timmy who took it in his meaty paw and smiled widely.

'Crikey, she's a lovely little thing, ain't she?' His voice held genuine admiration.

Georgio was pleased at the other man's reaction. 'Yes she is, Timmy, and I'm not just saying that either. She's a decent type of woman, you know. Respectable. Well-spoken, well-educated and everything. She took an Open University degree, got it and all. In Sociology.'

Timmy was doubly impressed. 'Brains as well as beauty, eh? Lucky bastard. My wife looks like the back of a number nine bus. Her arse is so big she wouldn't get in the cell door! Mind you, she's never done the dirty on me to my knowledge, and even though she's ugly as sin there's blokes out there who'd fuck their own grandmothers if it was dark enough.'

Georgio nodded at the truth of the statement. Most men's biggest fear in prison was who was in their bed at home. A majority of them knew that someone was keeping the old woman company. It was whether or not the wife would want that man permanently that bothered them. If you lost the wife, you lost access to the kids. A love poem in a prison was eagerly bought for precious cigarettes and lovingly copied out in the next letter home. Most of the prisoners' wives were courted only when their husbands were inside. Their idea of romance was a poem, a promise of love everlasting, and an oath that the old man was reformed. Most took this for what it was worth; others lived their whole married life in hope.

'My Donna's a quiet type, you know. Not one of these chatty women. She was an asset to me, in my business and that. She could arrange a dinner party as good as anything you'd get in Kensington Palace. Knew what to wear, what to say, how to conduct herself. An all-rounder, was my Donna.'

Timmy studied the photograph again as Sadie walked into the cell.

'I just came to say goodnight, lads. Oh, photos! Let's have a butchers.'

Timmy handed her the photograph and she smiled happily.

'Now that's what I call a beautiful woman.' This was spoken with a friendly envy. 'Look at that hair and those eyes! Who is it?'

'That's Georgio's little wife,' Timmy muttered.

'I thought it was your daughter, Georgio – no offence meant, like.'

76

Georgio grinned. 'None taken, Sadie. She looks young in that one. I'd better get meself down to the bathroom and clean me teeth before lockup. Do me a favour, Sadie, talk this bloke of yours into having a bath, would you? He don't half pen and ink.'

Sadie chuckled. 'Tell me about it!'

Timmy laughed good-naturedly. 'I smell like a man, you cheeky beggars.'

'Yeah, a man that's been dead a fortnight.' Sadie rolled her eyes.

Georgio was still laughing as he entered the shower-room. As he turned on the tap Sadie sidled up to him.

'Listen, Georgio, don't ask me how I know this, and don't repeat it to a living soul or we'll all live to regret it, but I heard a whisper today that your wife has a little surprise waiting for her, courtesy of Lewis. Warn her well.'

Georgio felt faint at the words. He grabbed at Sadie's nightdress. 'You what? How do you know this?'

Sadie looked into his worried eyes and shook her head. 'I heard it through the grapevine. She looks a nice little body and I don't want to see her get hurt. Just remember to warn her, or get someone to watch out for her. But whatever you do, don't let on I told you or I won't be able to get any more information on anything. Most of all, don't tell Timmy I said anything, OK?'

'When is this surprise?'

Sadie shrugged. 'That I don't know, mate, I swear. I'm only telling you because, for all my faults, I like people to play fair, know what I mean?' She left the shower room as quietly as she had entered it.

Georgio stood under the freezing shower and felt the prickle of tears. The surprise could be tonight. As he stood under the shower his Donna could be getting a hiding, being raped or tortured. He felt panic welling up inside and he willed it to subside, leave him in peace. But the pictures in his head grew stronger and more vivid.

He was stuck in Maximum Security and his wife, his little Donna, could be gasping her last breath. The futility of his situation was the hardest to bear – that he could do nothing, nothing at all. He clenched his hands into fists and began beating the tiled wall, blood soon running from his knuckles and mixing with the water, trickling in crimson rivulets down the drain.

One word was going over and over in his mind: *Donna. Donna. Donna.*

If only he could reach out to her with his mind, could warn her in some way.

Two wardens pulled him from the shower and Georgio began fighting with them. Between them they eventually overpowered him

77

and marched him to the Punishment Block. Thrown into the damp cell, naked, he slid down the wall and cried bitter tears into his hands.

He was still only capable of one word, and that was whispered brokenly in the gloom.

'*Donna..*'

If anything happened to her he would kill Lewis with his bare hands. Georgio stared around the cell like a caged animal. Lewis was a big man – the biggest, in fact – but he, Georgio Brunos, would outwit the bastard. If it was the last thing he did, he'd outwit him.

This was personal now.

It didn't cross Georgio's mind to inform the police about Lewis because he knew it would gain him nothing. He had no proof, only the word of a transvestite murderer.

But he swore he would get the better of Lewis. Somehow, someday, he would get the better of him. He sat up all night with pictures in his head of Donna and what could be happening to her even as he was slumped there.

He walked out of the cell the next day a changed man.

More than one person remarked on it.

78

Chapter Six

Like Donald Lewis, Frankie White was a big man in personality, and in reputation. His first prison sentence had been when he was twenty-one; he had received ten years for attempted murder and aggravated assault. Frankie had beaten his wife's boyfriend half to death and was in the process of doing the same thing to her when the police had interrupted him. One punch to his wife's boyfriend had been so hard it had forced his ribs through his heart. Only the intervention of a skilled surgeon had saved the man, who now lived in a one-bedroomed council flat in Poplar, unable to climb stairs or couple with a woman, as the jealous husband had also stamped repeatedly on his groin. Frankie's first wife had disappeared without a trace.

Frankie had gone to prison a hero, and left it seven years later a villain. Since then he had been involved in many nefarious dealings: had financed a night club, a building consortium, and betting shops. He was married now, aged forty-three, to a twenty-six-year-old woman who had produced three children in rapid succession. His children were his life, his reason for living. At an age when most of his contemporaries were looking forward to grandchildren, and were still financing their own children, Frankie White had only just realised the real depth of feeling that fatherhood gave him.

A known 'face', he could put up his hand to many illegal acts: armed robbery, GBH, and extortion to name but a few . . .

As he walked in his garden with his small son, Frankie Junior, he smiled at the antics of his daughters. Liselle at five was a real live wire. Unfortunately she had inherited his hooked nose, but Frankie was determined to disguise his mother's Jewish ancestry the moment the girl was old enough for plastic surgery. Desdemona, his three year old, was her mother's double, a blonde bimbette with a face like an angel and a voice like a navvy. He watched the two of them running towards the swimming pool and grinned. Frankie Junior, all of ten months, grinned with him. A large-boned amiable child, Frankie adored him.

79

As the girls slipped off their robes, Frankie saw the masked man in the bushes to the left side of the pool. His mind registered the gun, and his arms tightened on his son instinctively. Liselle screamed loudly in the quiet of the day as the man opened fire, and in stunned disbelief Frankie felt the cold heat of the bullets as they rained across his body and that of his infant son. Even as he fell to the ground, in the throes of death, he was still trying to protect his son. As he hit the earth with a heavy thud, his last sight was of his son's staring face. The cheerful, gummy smile still intact. But all trace of life gone.

Tracey White was shopping in East Ham market with her sister Sandra when the police found her. She listened in stunned disbelief to what her mother and the policeman were telling her.

Her only words were: 'But we live in Surrey. How could that happen in Surrey?'

No one as yet had the nerve to tell her about the death of her baby son.

Chapter Seven

Dolly placed a poached egg on toast in front of Donna. 'Get that down you, love, it'll set you up for the day.'

Donna sipped her Earl Grey and smiled. 'You and your breakfasts, Dolly.'

The housekeeper tucked into her own plate of bubble and squeak and bacon. 'My old mum used to say that breakfast was the most important meal of the day and she was right. Now eat that up.'

Donna stared at the white and yellow mass on the piece of brown toast and sighed. Food was becoming less and less enjoyable these days.

'I wonder what Georgio's having for breakfast?' she mused.

Dolly snorted through a mouthful of food. 'A lot more than you, love. My old man said they fed 'em plenty in nick. Porridge, eggs, toast and marmalade. Gallons of tea or coffee, fruit juice, the lot.'

Donna immediately brightened. 'Really? I was under the impression the food wasn't all that good.'

Dolly chewed on a large mouthful and shook her head. 'They eat all right. Now will you get that down you?'

Donna began eating. Dolly asked God to forgive her for her lies about prison food. But it was for Donna's own good; the girl was wasting away.

The shrill ringing of the phone on the kitchen wall broke their reveries. Donna got to her feet and picked it up.

'Hello?'

'Is that you, Don Don?'

'Georgio! Where are you?'

'Calm down, love. I'm still in nick. The prison chaplain got me a call to you. I've been feeling a bit down. Missing you, like.'

His voice trailed off. Donna felt her heart bursting with love for this man who would get a call to her because he missed her so much.

'It's so lovely to hear your voice, Georgio.' Her own voice was scratchy with emotion. 'I miss you too, love. More every day, in fact. I can't believe I'm talking to you.'

81

Georgio sighed heavily. 'Listen, Donna, do me a favour. Put Dolly on for a second, would you?'

'Of course. Dolly, come and talk. It's Georgio!'

Dolly took the phone in shock. 'Hello, Georgio?' The words came out high-pitched in disbelief.

'Listen to me, Dolly, and listen good. Someone might be sending someone to see Donna, and it won't be a friendly visit. Don't say a word, just tell Big Paddy what I told you. Say that Lewis is out to get me.'

Dolly's face blanched. 'I'll do that, mate. Here's Donna back. She's champing at the bit to talk to you.'

'Thanks, Dolly.'

'Georgio, is everything all right?'

He laughed down the phone. 'I tried it on with the chaplain love, told him I was depressed and wanted to top meself. He arranged for me to make this call.'

Donna's voice was small as she answered, 'Don't talk about killing yourself, Georgio. Especially after what happened to Wilson.'

The line went quiet and Donna wished fervently she could take back those few words.

'You know about him then?'

Donna nodded, forgetting he couldn't see her.

'I miss you, Don Don. I love you, darlin'. You're my life, don't ever forget that. You're my whole life.'

'And you're mine, Georgio. Always have been. I went to see your barrister with Maeve and he's got the appeal in hand. So try not to worry, all right?'

'All right, Donna love. Look, I've got to go, the chaplain's back in the office with me. Come and visit soon, and bring Big Paddy with you. I'd love to see him, all right? Promise me you'll bring Big Paddy?'

Donna wiped her eyes with her fingers. 'I'll bring him, Georgio. Don't worry.'

'Good girl. I've got to run. I love you, darlin'.'

'I love you too.' Before she finished talking the line was dead.

Dolly took the crying woman into her arms. 'Come on now, Donna. Pull yourself together, love. I'll make us another cuppa, eh?'

She walked Donna back to her chair and sat her down. Then, taking away the plate of poached egg, she placed it in the sink and poured Donna a fresh cup of tea. All the time her mind was racing. Someone was out to get Georgio – Donald Lewis to be exact. His name had never come up before, either during the trial or afterwards . . . so why the big deal now?

82

She would tell Stephen as soon as she could.

Dolly knew Lewis well. Not personally, but in the same way everyone knew the name of Donald Lewis. He was a big-time villain. He ran the East End of London and the West, in between running both North and South London. Lewis was bad news. And Lewis was after their Georgio . . .

A sudden heaviness settled on Dolly's heart.

Georgio was in big trouble.

Paddy Donovon was in the Portakabin with his friends, drinking tea. It was five minutes to ten and the tea-break was early. Men sat around on the benches reading the *Sun*, the *Sport* or in extreme cases the *Independent*. Paddy himself was listening to little Milton Hardcastle's version of a fight the previous Friday night in The Dean Swift public house.

'Jaysus, Paddy, the man was huge, with arms like a side of beef! I saw the first one coming at me, and I blocked it.' He held up his arm to demonstrate. 'Then I shoved me boot in his groin. As God is me witness, I nearly put his balls up on to the back of his neck!'

Paddy grinned at the blatant lying. 'Did you now? And who was this Hercules you were fighting with? Did he have a name at all?' Paddy winked at Del Boy Bryant as he spoke and the Cockney choked on his tea.

Milton shook his head sadly. 'No, I never got to find out who he was. The police were there before the ambulance and I didn't stick around to find out anything.'

Paddy made a deep obeisance of his head. 'Ah, sure, you did the right thing there, Milton. The buggers would have crucified you if they'd caught up with you.'

They would that, Paddy, and no mistaking.'

Milton shook his head again and sipped at his tea, deep in thought. He really believed his lies; after the first five minutes he was there, in among the action and reliving it, so to speak. He was the joke of the building trade. One of his most spectacular stories was how he had been out in the Falklands as a mercenary. An Irish mercenary, of course. The men accepted him and played along with him and he lightened many a dull dinner-hour or tea-break. One thing in Milton's favour, he was a demon of a worker, knew all there was to know about building and could have been a foreman if he hadn't such a reputation as a joker. Like most liars, Milton never gave himself credit for what he did achieve, only what he wished he could achieve.

Paddy's mobile phone rang and he took it out of his shirt pocket nonchalantly. His initial embarrassment at using it in front of the men was long gone.

'Hello, Paddy Donovon here.'

He listened for a while and the men all stared at him as he swore under his breath.

'Jesus fucking cross of Christ! Are you sure?'

He listened once more and then, shutting the phone off, got up quickly.

'Everything all right, Paddy?' Milton voiced everyone's thoughts.

'Yeah, fine, fine. Listen, can you lot get on with the work without me for a while? I have to go somewhere.'

The men all nodded.

'What's up, Paddy? You look in a right two and eight.' Del Boy's voice was concerned.

Paddy waved a hand at them. 'I have to go see Mrs Brunos. Listen, if she comes back here, make her wait for me. And if she arrives while I'm gone, ring me on me mobile. It's important, very important I speak to her, all right? Del Boy, get in the main office and sit by the phone. If she rings in, tell her to sit tight until I get to her . . . On second thoughts, tell her to come here. *Make* her come here. Then ring me. Make sure you ring only me or Stephen.'

'All right, Paddy, keep your hair on.'

Paddy practically ran from the Portakabin across the site to his car.

'What was all that about then?' Tommy Gibbons's voice was amazed.

Milton nodded his head sagely. 'I know, but I can't say.'

Del Boy, worried by Paddy's obvious confusion, said nastily: 'Why don't you go and lie on another site, Milton? Ain't we had enough porkies from you for one day?'

Milton sipped his tea in silence, looking for all the world like a man with a secret. To his chagrin, no one asked him what it was.

Donna was at the building suppliers in Bow, trying her hardest to raise their credit. After finding out that the money in her joint account with Georgio was all they possessed, she had been hard put to finance any more building work. After she'd paid over seven thousand pounds to the supplier, he had then informed her that unless another ten was forthcoming in the next few days, all their credit would be cut off.

It didn't take Donna long to realise that this scenario was nothing new. It seemed Georgio owed money left, right and centre. Stephen had explained that it was the recession and most big builders were feeling the pinch, if not leaving half-built houses to complete at

84

another time, when demand was once more the name of the game. Donna had left two sites with houses built only up to the damp course, laying off men or putting them on other sites. Now she had to see Mr Francis Pemberton and convince him to allow her more credit to finish some of the houses or he'd be paid nothing at all.

As she pulled up at the building suppliers, she rested her head on the steering wheel for a few seconds, savouring the sound of Georgio's voice once more. He had rung her. She had spoken to him. Those few words had meant the world to her.

She had turned off her car phone earlier, sick of the constant calls while she was driving, wanting a few hours' peace to think about Georgio and his words.

Finally getting out of the car, she smoothed her suede trousers and tidied her hair before walking into Francis Pemberton's yard. She passed through the main warehouse and walked over to the small office at the back.

Francis Pemberton was smoking a large Cuban cigar, the reek from it pervading the whole atmosphere. Donna knocked on the door and walked inside, smiling widely.

'Hello, darlin', and what can I do you for?' Francis Pemberton was forty-eight years old, tall, good-looking, and with a permanent smile that never touched his eyes. He wore handmade suits, Freeman, Hardy & Willis shoes, and white towelling socks. His head was big, his features heavy, his hair a curly salt and pepper halo that enhanced his rugged looks.

'Good morning, Mr Pemberton. I trust I'm not inconveniencing you, calling like this?'

Francis Pemberton laughed out loud. 'My old woman could do with a few lessons from you, love. She would give her eyeteeth, not to mention her right arm, for your voice. No matter how I dress her up, once she opens that big trap she's a typical Cockney. Still, she's my old woman so I have to swallow it, don't I?'

Donna smiled nervously at the man before her. Francis Pemberton talked to everyone as if they were his close friends or family. No topic was taboo, nothing shocking enough to be kept private. If it was in his head, it came out of his mouth. As simple as that.

Donna sat down opposite him and smiled once more. 'I'm here because . . .'

Francis held up his hand. 'Oh, I know why you're here, love. You want me to extend your credit. Well, I told you the other day – no way. You've got more chance of having Princess Di to tea than you've got of me giving your old man another cent.'

Donna lowered her eyes and took a deep breath. 'I thought you

85

were a businessman, Mr Pemberton. I was under the impression you knew all there was to know about the building trade. If I can't finish the work on my sites then I can't pay you a cent, as you so nicely put it. In fact, I will come clean with you. If I don't finish those houses then I am afraid my business will go to the wall. Now, I have been looking over old invoices and my husband has dealt with you for many years. Why are you being stubborn now? You always advanced him before.'

Francis took a deep drag on his impossibly large cigar and blew the offending smoke across the desk straight into Donna's face. 'You just hit the nail on the proverbial head, love. I dealt with your husband, Georgio. Now I know you're a nice little lady and all that, but at the end of the day, love, you're a bird, a woman, and women don't run building sites.'

'This one does.' Donna's voice came out curt and clipped.

Francis Pemberton laughed out loud at her audacity.

'In fact,' she went on, 'with the help of Big Paddy Donovon I run the sites every bit as well as Georgio did. I see my husband regularly and he still has a large input into the businesses. All of them. I didn't think you were the kind of man to spout sexist tripe, Mr Pemberton. You've always seemed rather intelligent to me.'

'Oh, I have, have I?' Francis' voice was barely audible.

'Yes, you have. I know you have a very good reputation around these parts and I will be quite frank with you. I don't have to pay any more invoices for three months – the seven thousand I just paid you guarantees that. I have been to see the Murphy brothers and they have offered me – me alone, not my husband – twenty thousand pounds credit. I am not going to lose my husband's business, Mr Pemberton. In fact, I shall labour twenty-four-hours a day if need be to keep it all going for him. I am willing to go to the Murphys if you give me no joy, but I thought it only fair to let you know exactly where you stood. I would be more inclined to pay the Murphys if that's who's supplying me. You, I am afraid, would have to wait.'

Francis Pemberton stared at Donna with new eyes. 'You're threatening me.'

She shook her head emphatically. 'I am not threatening you, Mr Pemberton, I am merely stating my case clearly and succinctly. Either you extend my credit or I go elsewhere. It's sound business sense. I have no interest in closing any more of the sites. If I finish off the main site in Ilford, I come out with close on one hundred thousand pounds clear. That's after everyone and everything has been paid. I will finish those houses, Mr Pemberton. That, as my husband would say, is a promise.'

86

Francis put his cigar in a large cut-glass ashtray. Linking his fingers together, he placed them on top of his desk. His face was closed, his eyes hooded. Donna felt her heart beating like a military tattoo inside her blouse. She hoped she hadn't gone too far. The Murphys had in fact laughed her out of their offices, both men being enemies of Georgio's from years gone by. But she hoped Pemberton didn't know that.

Francis smiled once more, his pretend smile. 'So Seamus Murphy offered you twenty grand, did he?'

Donna nodded, her mouth dry.

'You sure it was twenty grand, love?'

'Yes, I'm sure. It was twenty thousand. Even I can count, Mr Pemberton.'

He whistled softly. 'I thought they didn't get along with Georgio?'

Donna swallowed deeply. 'They don't. This is business, Mr Pemberton. I'm sure you do business with people you don't like, all the time. It doesn't make their money worth any less.'

'True, good point. But I know for a fact Seamus would see Georgio in the gutter before he'd lift a boot to help him – and then he'd only kick him up the arse to help him on his way.

'Please don't speak crudely to me, Mr Pemberton. It offends me. I have come here as a business associate, not a barmaid. I would appreciate your giving me your respect if not your money.'

Francis picked up his cigar and re-lit it with a gold Dunhill lighter, puffing on it furiously to keep it alight.

'All right then, you've got it.'

'Got what exactly, Mr Pemberton?'

'The money for starters. We'll see about the respect in a few months when you pay me back.'

'I'll pay you back, don't worry about that.'

Francis smiled then, a real smile. 'You're a spunky little lady. I hope Georgio gives you your due, love.'

Donna closed her eyes with happiness. 'He does, Mr Pemberton. I make sure of that.'

She shook hands with him and, nodding at him once more, walked from his office.

Outside in the fresh air she took a deep breath. She was pleased with herself, very pleased. Gradually, she was sorting out the mess that Georgio had left her in.

It said a lot for the distance Donna had travelled already that she now admitted her husband had left her in a mess. For no matter how she looked at it, that's exactly what his building business was: a mess.

And the act of sorting through it all was what kept her going from

87

one day to the next. The business would be booming when Georgio came home, she promised herself that night and morning.

She got into her car and decided to leave the phone turned off. She wanted to think, and God Himself knew, she had plenty to think about.

As she pulled away from Pemberton's she didn't see the navy-blue Jag pull out behind her.

It followed her back to the car lot.

Davey was like a cat on hot bricks. He chewed his thumbnail, gnawing at it as if he hadn't eaten in a month.

Carol Jackson snapped at him: 'For Christ's sake, will you relax! She's probably shopping!'

Davey stared at his wife and shook his head gravely. 'We're dealing with Lewis here, not fucking Boy Wonder. If he's after giving her a little surprise, the chances are she'll put the key in her motor and be blown sky high!'

Carol dismissed that idea with a shake of her head. 'Look, think about it, Davey. The last thing he wants is Donna dead. If he did, she'd have been a gonner by now, mate. He just wants to scare old Georgio into opening his trap, so he'll frighten her in some way then tell Georgio that next time he'll annihilate her. Stop worrying.'

Davey stared out of the window at the car lot, his face tight. Carol rubbed his shoulders, trying to ease the tension.

'I think she should be told the truth. The poor cow's labouring under the illusion he's as white as the driven snow. I mean, suppose she'd gone through the back office, eh? What would we have done then? Plus she has a bit more savvy than you or Georgio ever gave her credit for. Look at how she's sorted out the building sites! She'll click on eventually and then Georgio had better watch out. Her type can be very vindictive, mate.'

'Give it a rest, Carol, for fuck's sake. You're doing my head in.'

Carol shrugged. 'Listen to me, mate, I don't have to take this shit any more. I am entitled to my opinion such as it is. I know women's logic, Davey, and I know more about it than you do. She ain't never had a real worry in the last twenty years as Georgio looked after her, but she's still waters, is our Donna. She runs deep and cold, you mark my words.'

Davey listened to his wife's strident voice and admitted the truth of her words to himself.

Who would have thought Donna Brunos could have done as much as she had on the sites? Admittedly, she had Big Paddy Donovon, but even without him, Davey had a feeling she'd still have come out on

88

top. Still waters was the right expression for Donna Brunos. She'd been the little wife, and now she was the driven wife. Driven like a demon to see all her husband's assets safely looked after. Everyone had admired her, everyone had taken a step back and added respect to their liking. Because it was a fact, everyone liked her. You couldn't help it; even he admitted he liked her, more than he should in fact. He'd fantasised about having her in his bed more than once. She affected men like that. So calm, so cool, she was the proverbial ice maiden. Yet women liked her, too. Carol liked her, which was a shock in itself. Carol disliked most women heartily. Now he wondered if Carol liked her or admired her – there was a difference.

'I think she's been a bleeding saint since that Georgio got sent down. I can't help it, Davey, she's vulnerable in some ways, yet hard as nails in others. I hope that Greek shit appreciates her, I really do.'

'He does, Carol. Any man would.' He realised immediately he had said the wrong thing. The temperature in the office dropped below zero.

'I hope you appreciate me, Davey Jackson.'

Davey grabbed at her hand. 'I do, Carol,' he said urgently. 'More than you realise at times.'

Carol smiled half-heartedly and Davey breathed a sigh of relief. The last thing he needed today was a big punch-up with Carol, and with Carol, a big punch-up was what you got. She didn't know how to argue, only how to fight.

'Here she is!' Carol sounded relieved.

Davey stood up and breathed a deep, heartfelt sigh of relief.

As Donna walked across the forecourt she studied the cars intently. Five Mercedes, one a Sports, two BMWs and a Rolls-Royce Corniche shone in the weak sunshine.

She entered the office with a spring in her step. 'I got Pemberton to extend the credit!' Then she looked askance at the two people in front of her. 'Is everything all right?'

Carol grinned. ''Course it is, you just caught us having a barney!'

'Shall I go out and come back in again?' Donna joked.

'Nah,' Carol laughed. 'Just sit yourself down there and I'll make us all a cuppa.'

As she disappeared into the tiny kitchen Davey sat on the edge of the desk and looked at Donna as she took off her jacket.

'How'd you swing it with Pemberton?'

Donna shook her head. 'That man! He should be locked up. I talked rings round him – logically, as your Carol would say. Actually, he gave in quite quickly. I told him the Murphys had offered us the money.'

89

'And he believed that!'

Donna grinned. 'Not for a second. But he played the game. I told him that if I didn't get the houses finished he would not get a penny if the bank foreclosed. It was sound economics.'

'Anything else happen today?'

Donna sat behind the desk. 'Such as?'

Davey shrugged. 'I don't know, anything unusual?'

Donna shook her head. 'No. Has anyone rung here for me? I've had my car phone turned off. I hate taking calls while I'm driving.'

'Only Big Paddy. I'm just going to the workshop. I'll be back for my coffee in two shakes.'

Davey strode from the office and across the forecourt to the garage area, dialling Big Paddy's number as he walked. He had to let him know that Donna was safe and at the car lot.

Carol brought the cups of coffee through and placed one in front of Donna.

'What a day, eh? I tell you, Donna love, I'll be glad when it's over.'

Donna sipped her coffee without answering.

Lewis was watching *Fifteen to One* in the rec room and as usual you could hear a pin drop. It was Lewis's only concession to TV, that and *Mastermind*. He answered the majority of the general knowledge questions with ease, a sneaking feeling of pleasure at each right answer enveloping him.

He glanced over to where Georgio stood watching him, and grinned. 'Terrible news about Frankie White, ain't it? Gunned down with his little boy in his arms. What a ruthless bastard he must have been. The gunman, not Frankie. Frankie's trouble was, he thought he was a hard man.' Lewis shook his head in mock disgust. 'But all the same, a little baby. What is the world coming to? Still, good job his wife wasn't there, they might have topped her and all. It's a vicious world out there, Georgio, absolutely vicious. How's your little wife by the way?'

Georgio bit on his lip and watched Lewis like a mouse watches a snake. Warily and with a grudging respect.

'What's the matter, Georgio? Cat got your tongue? Answer Mr Lewis.'

Derek Marchant was one of Lewis's lesser henchmen and he wanted to rise in the ranks. Baiting Brunos looked like the way to do it. Everyone knew Lewis had it in for the Greek git.

Georgio turned his gaze on Derek and the man felt the force of Georgio's wrath then. A prickle of fear ran up his spine.

Georgio stood up. 'What did you say?'

90

Marchant was in a quandary. If he backed down now Lewis would disown him. Lewis only went for people who could look out for themselves, and for him. But one look at Brunos told him he had made a fatal mistake. He glanced around and noticed that Lewis's men were all waiting for his word before they moved.

Marchant shrugged, trying to look relaxed. 'You fucking heard.'

Georgio walked over to where Marchant was sitting down and peered into his face. The atmosphere was electric now. Men stopped playing cards and chatting quietly to watch Georgio front up Marchant.

'You trying to say I'm fucking Mutton and Jeff now, eh? Just what are you trying to do, Derek? Want a fucking row with me, do you? Come on then, get up and I'll row with you. Come on . . . don't sit there, get up!' Georgio's voice ended on a loud bellow.

Then, dragging Marchant from the chair, he punched him to the ground. Holding the man's hair in a vice-like grip, he smashed his face into the metal arm of the chair. He repeated the action five times, savouring the running blood and the release of his pent-up energy. Then he let go and watched Marchant slump to the floor. Turning round, he let his gaze roam over all the occupants in the room.

'Anyone else up for it then? Come on, I'm in the mood. Who else wants a go then?'

No one spoke. Lewis watched him warily. Bringing back his foot, Georgio kicked Marchant repeatedly in the groin. Finally spent, he stared down at the man on the floor for a few moments before looking around him once more.

'I am on a short fuse, and you'd better all get that in your heads.' Then he straightened his shoulders and marched out of the room.

Lewis held up his hand to stop two of his men following. 'Leave him be. This is what I wanted. Exactly what I wanted. Brunos needs to be put under pressure. I want him to blow.'

Turning up the TV, Lewis went back to watching *Fifteen to One*. No one took any notice of Marchant, who pulled himself to his feet and slowly staggered out of the room.

Dolly was making a cake, a cigarette dangling precariously from her lips as usual. Georgio used to joke that the ash from her fags enhanced her recipes.

Putting down the mixing bowl and spoon she flicked her cigarette butt into the waste disposal unit. She was about to pick up the bowl once more when she heard a car on the drive. Turning to the young man at her side, she pushed him unceremoniously out of the back door.

91

Donna had pulled up outside the house. Picking up her handbag, she got out of the car, pressed the automatic lock on her keyring and waited as the lights on the car flashed. She heard the soft clicking noise as the car locked itself.

Opening the front door, she walked through the large entrance hall to the kitchen.

Dolly greeted her with a smile. 'Hello, love, I'm making a nice cinnamon cake for us. There's a goulash that's only got to be popped into the oven to warm, and coffee on the stove. Why not go away up and have a shower, while I finish here.'

Donna put the kettle on and waved her hand dismissively. 'I need a strong cup of tea, Dolly. Do you want one?'

Dolly replaced the bowl and spoon on the worktop and, walking over to Donna, took the two china mugs from her hands. 'Go on up and have a shower,' she repeated, 'and I'll make you that cup of tea.'

Donna felt a moment's irritation; she quickly suppressed it. Taking the mugs back from Dolly, she said firmly, 'No thanks. I don't want a shower yet, Dolly, I want to make a cup of tea.'

Seeing the hurt look on the older woman's face she softened and said gently, 'I don't want to be rude, but sometimes you treat me like a little child. "Go and do this, go and do that." Honestly, it gets a bit wearing at times.'

Dolly bit on her lip for a few seconds. 'I'm sorry, Donna love. I'm only trying to help . . .'

Donna hugged the woman to her, smelling the cigarettes and cooking smells that always surrounded Dolly.

'I know that! But seriously, Dolly, Georgio was the same. I never really realised it before, but you all treat me like I'm fifteen, yet I'm nearly forty years old. Even Davey and Carol wanted to run me home from the car lot today! I mean, Dolly, I'm quite capable of making a cup of tea, for Christ's sake!'

Dolly was flabbergasted. Never before had she heard Donna talk like that. Not once in all the years she'd worked for the Brunoses. She felt the real threat of tears and turning abruptly away, went back to her cake mixture.

Donna closed her eyes so tightly it hurt. 'I'm sorry, Dolly, you didn't deserve that.'

The housekeeper lifted her shoulders and said, 'I deserved it. You're right, I do treat you like a child. You're like me own flesh and blood, Donna. I don't mean anything by it. I like looking after you. Gawd knows, I'd work here for free. I love you, girl. I always have.'

Donna went to the woman and put her arms around the ample waist. 'And I like being looked after, most of the time. I'm just an old

92

crosspatch today. Forgive me, Dolly?'

Dolly sniffed loudly and sighed. 'Of course I forgive you. Now are you making that tea or not? Me throat's as dry as a buzzard's crutch!'

'Oh, Dolly, that's gross!'

Dolly laughed good-naturedly. 'My old dad used to say his mouth felt like the inside of a Turkish wrestler's jockstrap. Now *that's* gross!' Her voice was stronger now, like the old Dolly.

Donna chuckled as she prepared the tea, and felt as if she had won a small victory. She loved Dolly with all her heart and soul but lately it had occurred to her that they all treated her like she was made of fine china. It had never bothered her before, or had it?

Georgio had always made the decisions, down to what cars they drove and what colours to decorate the house. He even insisted on planning the menus and ordering in the wines when they had people to dinner. Over the years she had come to resent his decision-making, especially when he organised a holiday, the destination, hotel and flights, without once consulting her. He even told her how her hair should be cut. She had suppressed these feelings but now they were surfacing. Donna had the distinct feeling that she was emerging from a cocoon, and smiled to herself at the metaphor. *Donna Brunos, wife of Georgio Brunos, Testosterone King and Essex Man, is gradually turning into a person in her own right. Now for the rest of the News . . .*

She laughed at her thoughts and Dolly grinned at her.

'A penny for 'em?'

Donna put the mugs of tea on to the table and smiled. 'They're not worth a penny. Come and drink your tea.'

Lighting yet another cigarette, Dolly sat down. Taking off her slippers, she waggled her toes.

'You were right, you know, Donna, with what you said just now. I know I treat you like a baby, but it's the effect you have on people. You make them want to look after you.'

The smoke from her cigarette was making her eyes screw up and for a split second Donna saw Dolly as others must: a large-boned, blowsy woman, with ill-fitting false teeth and a permanent wave. She saw the short stubby fingers and the chipped nails. The lined face with heavy jowls, and the rolls of fat underneath her spotlessly clean apron. Donna felt a surge of affection for her.

'Well, don't look after me too much, Dolly. From now on me and you are equal in this house, OK?'

Dolly nodded and took a deep drag on her cigarette. 'OK.'

She sipped her tea and grimaced as there wasn't any sugar in it. As she added three large heaped teaspoonsful, she smiled at the thought of the men hidden in the grounds outside at this very moment.

Me and you might be equal, Donna my love, she thought, but as for looking after you – someone's got to do it. Your old man's left you in a position where you'd need looking after if you was the Devil himself.

The two women chatted amiably while Big Paddy Donovon and his henchmen watched the house from every angle.

When Lewis's little mates struck, they'd be ready for them.

Chapter Eight

Georgio was watching Lewis as he played chess with one of his posse. Ricardo laBrett, known as Ricky, was a large Afro-Caribbean man, noted on the Wing for his big muscles and even bigger intellect. If anyone wanted to know anything, it was Ricky they went to. It was strange that Lewis, a known racist, courted Ricky's company. Georgio surmised that Lewis, fancying himself as an intellectual, hoped that his friendship with Ricky would put the seal of approval on it. Why he would want to impress the average lifer was beyond Georgio, but then Lewis had never done anything logical in his life so why should he start now?

Sadie waltzed into the recreation room and Georgio winked at her. After giving him the warning, Sadie had gone up in his estimation, though he was careful not to let it show. The News came on TV and there was a story about the Queen being slighted by a foreign president.

The men watching the news became aggressive.

'Fucking Australian cunt! I'll give him fucking snubbing the bleeding Queen! Who's he think he is anyway! Arseholes the bleeding Aussies are.'

'Lager-swilling wankers the lot of them. My sister emigrated there and she was home quick smart, I can tell you. Spiders bigger than Thatcher's gob crawling all over the place there is!'

The men in the rec room were getting excited now. It didn't take a lot to get them going. Normally it was a child sex case or a rape case on the television that really sent them over the edge.

One of the men got up and shook his fist at Paul Keating's picture on the television screen. 'You ugly bastard! The Queen should tell him and all the Australians to fuck off out of it. We don't need them anyway. Load of ponces they are!'

Sadie joined in the argument. 'I don't know what they've got to shout about out there – they've got a bigger gay population per capita than America even.'

'What's bleeding shitstabbers got to do with it? You should have

95

been put down at birth, you and that Aussie ponce!' As soon as Arnold Da Silva had opened his mouth he regretted it.

Lewis's voice came out in a thin hiss. 'What's that you just said, Arnold?'

The whole room went quiet. Even the two screws took a step towards the door.

Da Silva licked his lips nervously. 'I never said nothing, Mr Lewis, only a load of old crap.'

Lewis smiled menacingly. 'If you stopped to think once in a while instead of spending your days wanking you might get an insight into a bit of real life. We are all detained here at Her Majesty's pleasure. She owns this nick so to speak; we have all allegedly broken her laws. On your court documents it had "So and So versus the Crown". The Queen, I hasten to add, wears that crown. The Crown Prosecution Service put us all behind bars. If I met the fucking Queen I would not only snub her, I'd nut her.'

Devlin O'Grady, an Irish terrorist awaiting shipment to the Maze, clapped gently. 'Well said, Mr Lewis.'

Lewis smiled and resumed his game.

'As all our briefs said before we got sent down, "I rest my case"!'

Sadie's words brought laughter even from Lewis, and the atmosphere lightened once more. The screws laughed along with the cons and peace was thankfully restored.

Georgio left the room and went to his cell, glad to find it empty. Lying down, he put his arms under his head and stared at the wooden slats of the bunk above him. He had to get out of this place. Lewis was baiting him with every word, with every movement. Knowing he wanted to hurt Donna was killing Georgio, especially since he couldn't do anything about it. Only wait.

It was the waiting that was the worst.

At five o'clock in the morning, just as the dawn was breaking, Donna awoke abruptly. She lay in bed for a second listening. Turning over once more, she let sleep envelop her and was soon back in a dream with her and Georgio and their child. It was a fabulous dream she had dreamt on and off for over fifteen years.

As Donna snuggled down in her bed, Big Paddy Donovon and his henchmen were dragging two men off Donna's drive and out into the lane. They bundled them into a black Transit van parked on the grassy verge twenty-five yards from Donna's driveway.

Paddy relieved one of the men of a large brown holdall. Opening it, he took out a small package with a tiny LCD display travel clock attached to it. The men were both wearing ski masks. As they were removed, Paddy and the other men were shocked to see that the men were Chinese.

The one who had had the holdall spoke then. His voice had a thick cockney twang.

'If I were you I'd let us go now, before this gets out of hand. You have no idea who we're working for, and believe me when I say, you don't want to know.'

The words were said matter-of-factly, without emotion. When Paddy crushed the man's nose with a meaty fist, the other man blanched. Even under his sallow skin, they could all see him whiten.

'You were sent here by Donald Lewis,' Paddy snarled. 'Well, Lewis doesn't fecking scare me, meladdos. In fact, the man hasn't been born yet who could scare me, or even make me little heart race.'

Paddy stared at the man who was bleeding profusely everywhere. 'Was this device for the car?'

The man nodded, holding his hand under his dripping nose.

'Was it to kill?'

The other man shook his head. 'There's only enough there to give a good bang. It'd frighten her, not kill her. Maybe she'd get a few cuts off the windscreen, that's all.'

Paddy screwed up his eyes in consternation. 'You said *her*! You knew this was for a woman, didn't you? You knew this was for Donna Brunos!'

The men looked at their feet.

Paddy took a deep breath. 'Get moving, Padraic, we're off to Manor Park and a little firm I know to teach these two a lesson they won't forget.'

As the Transit pulled away in the early-morning light, the youngest of the Chinese men began to sweat. Everyone knew what was at Manor Park, East London – the crematorium – and when people like Paddy Donovon took you there you rarely, if ever, came out again.

More than a few bodies had gone in with the legitimate stock, never to be seen again.

While the transit made its way up the A13 and through the early-morning traffic with its two terrified passengers, Donna was turning in her sleep, murmuring her husband's name.

Outside in the grounds of Donna's house were five men; three watched the back and two the front. They kept in contact with small walkie-talkie radios. This time they'd had the element of surprise. Once Lewis realised his bombers had gone on the missing list, the next lot would come back prepared for resistance.

John O'Grady lit himself a small Cafe Crème cigar and savoured the burnt taste of the tobacco. This reminded him of the old days, in the fifties and sixties, when villains were villains and all this poncing around with computers was far in the future.

Later that morning, as Donna pulled out of her drive, John slipped onto a motorbike and followed her at a distance. She was a nice little thing who didn't deserve the flak over her old man. Unlike most of his contemporaries, John didn't really like Georgio Brunos. Even with that bit of Irish in him, John still found it hard to actually like the geezer. Georgio was a nice enough bloke, but in John's opinion, most of the time he was out of his league, as his nicking should have shown everyone. Lewis was a man to fear. Georgio's greed had put his little wife in a dangerous situation and John found that hard to credit, or indeed forgive.

As Donna slipped on to the M25 on her way towards Romford, he sighed. It was going to be a long day.

Georgio ate his breakfast slowly, forcing the food down his throat. He had just finished his last piece of bread when Ricky summoned him to Lewis's presence.

Walking nonchalantly, he followed the black man, his heart racing in his chest.

Lewis was picking at his teeth with a silver toothpick, the action making Georgio's stomach heave.

'Hello, Georgio, how are we then?' Lewis's voice was cold.

'I'm all right, thanks. Yourself?' Georgio was amazed at how relaxed his voice sounded.

Lewis seemed amazed too because he said abruptly, 'Sit down, I want to have a little chat.'

Georgio sat down opposite him and glanced around the cell. Unlike most cells Lewis's walls were not adorned with pictures of blonde bimbos in various states of undress. He didn't have The Chippendales either, like other homosexuals. On the walls were nice bright prints of flowers, cottages in the country, and one large picture of a tiger. On a table by his lone bunk was a silver-framed photograph of his mother, a small woman who glowered at the camera in a bright red pill-box hat, her grey hair scraped tidily into a small bun, her lips a bright orange slash. Looking at the photograph, Georgio shuddered.

There was a black and gold continental quilt on the bunk itself, and a small, state-of-the-art CD stack unit on the table. There was also a tiny television set, and a vase containing one fresh rose.

'Nice little place this, ain't it? Do you like me curtains? I got one of

98

the boys to run them up for me in the workshop. They go with the quilt set, don't you think?' Lewis's voice was begging for approval and Georgio was once more surprised by the different facets to his character.

'It looks very nice.'

Lewis smiled, pleased. 'Once you get your appeal over, you can start thinking about decorating your cell yourself. Only I have it on good authority that you're not going anywhere.' This was said with a smile.

'Don't tell me you now run the criminal justice system, Mr Lewis? I find it hard to believe that even you could have such a long arm.'

Lewis stared coldly at Georgio, the insult taken on board and filed away for future reference.

'How's your wife, Georgio? Well, is she?' The smugness of the voice made Georgio feel sick with apprehension. He was convinced Lewis knew something he didn't and struggled to keep his voice under control.

'You tell me, Mr Lewis. You seem to know everything else.'

Lewis sipped at his fresh Colombia coffee and sighed. 'Be a right shame if anything was to happen to her, wouldn't it? I mean you hear of these things, don't you? Did you read in the paper the other day about that bird who had a bomb under her car? Her old man made it, it was a nail bomb. She didn't die but she was pretty badly cut up. It went off right under her seat. Ripped her to pieces. The things people do, eh?'

Lewis shook his head at the malice of other people. 'Makes you sick to your stomach, don't it? I'd hate anything to happen to little Donna. You live out in Essex, don't you? A nice drum, I heard, tennis court, the lot. Must have cost a few bob, your family pile. No children though, shame that. I'd have liked you to have had children at this point.'

Lewis knew that the thought of a child being hurt brought most people round to his way of thinking.

'Remember Danny Simmonds?' Georgio nodded, dreading what he was going to hear. 'Terrible about his boy, wasn't it? Only sixteen, got knocked down by a hit-and-run driver while doing his paper round. No one ever found out who did it either. Tragic that. The boy would have been better off dead really. He's a vegetable, waiting out his days in hospital. I hear that Danny's old woman flipped her lid. Poor cow. Only child and all, weren't he? What was the kid's name?' Lewis made a show of thinking.

'That's it – Eric. What a bleeding name, eh? Eric.'

Georgio closed his eyes for a few seconds then stood up. 'Look,

99

Lewis, is there any point in this conversation? Only I don't know about you but it's beginning to bore me rigid.'

Lewis stared at him with a tight frown. 'Sit down and shut your trap. When I want you to leave I'll tell you to, all right? Until then, button your mutton and listen to what I'm telling you.'

Georgio sat down heavily. 'Let's get this over with, Mr Lewis, only I ain't got time for all these fun and games.'

Lewis grinned. 'You got eighteen years to listen to them, sonny boy, and listen you will, if I tell you to.' He called out over his shoulder: 'Harry, bring us in some fresh coffee, and a cup for Mr Brunos.'

Harry popped his head round the door. 'Righto, Mr Lewis.'

Lewis grinned again. There, let's have a nice cup of coffee and resume our little chat. Have you had any more thoughts on where the money is?'

Georgio grimaced. 'I told you before. I know where the money is and I'll get it for you once I'm out of here.'

Lewis nodded, as if this was what he expected to hear. He observed Georgio's expression and smiled inwardly. The strain was beginning to tell.

'I was talking about you the other day to an old crony of mine – he came up on a visit. He was telling me all about how your wife's running the car lot with that prat Jackson and his bleached-blonde wife. How she's running the sites with Big Paddy Donovon. I never liked Paddy, you know, too full of himself. The site in Ilford's going on well, I hear. Your old woman's doing a smashing job. Brains as well as beauty, eh? A winning combination. There's men out there, on the outside, who'd like a sniff round her, I bet. And how's your brother Stephen? Still in the sex game, is he? I hear he's the Telephone King of Soho. Good scam that. The Old Bill can't touch you, I hear. No legislation for it.' He paused before adding, 'Yet!'

Georgio sat watching Lewis's mouth move.

'My old mum saw your mum the other day – Maeve. They knew each other years back, when all us kids were small. She was saying the restaurant is doing very well. Be a shame if anything happened there, wouldn't it? Your old man was a nice bloke for a bubble. Gave my brother Frankie a job when he got out of the Scrubs. So don't you worry, your mum and dad's place is all right – for the moment. I remember people who've done me a good turn. It would pay you to remember that.'

Harry came in with the cafetière and crystallised sugar and fresh cream. Two bone-china cups sat daintily on the tray with silver teaspoons in the saucers.

100

'Your coffee, Mr Lewis.'

'Thank you, Harry, you can fuck off again now.'

Harry hurried from the cell.

'You're not saying much, Georgio. What's the matter, cat got your tongue?'

Georgio shrugged. 'Nothing to say. You seem to be doing all right on your own.'

Lewis picked up the cafetière and Georgio watched him battle with himself whether to throw the contents in his face or whether to pour it into the cups. The cups won.

'You're getting very flash, Georgio. I don't like flash people. I heard a whisper on the wing that Big Ricky quite fancies you. I'd watch yourself there. A few years ago him and a few other blokes lay in wait for one fella in the shower. Took him in turns they did. He was in the hospital wing for a month. They're big old boys, 'specially that Ricky. He's well-endowed, or so I hear anyway. Ricky likes them dark-skinned and handsome. Mr Hendry the screw likes to watch. Bet you didn't know that. Mr Hendry also pays good money to the rapists for transcripts of their trials. It's all there in black and white, witness statements, exactly what happened to them. Bit sick if you ask me but whatever turns you on, eh? Funny man he is, Mr Hendry. A good friend of mine. You're not drinking your coffee, Georgio. I hope our little chat ain't put you off?'

Georgio picked up two lumps of sugar and plopped them into his coffee before adding the cream. 'No, I'm just listening to you. There's not a lot I can say really, is there?'

Lewis laughed, a real laugh. 'I admire you, Georgio, in a funny way. Listen to me. Whatever happens in the future, it's not really personal, you know. Just business.'

Georgio sipped his lukewarm coffee. Lewis being friendly was even more intimidating than his attempts at frightening him.

So far he had threatened Georgio's wife, his brother, his parents and his businesses – to say nothing of Georgio's own skin. The pressure was beginning to tell on him, and Lewis knew it. That was the worst of it: he knew it.

Lewis's voice broke into his thoughts. 'Would you like a Garibaldi to go with your coffee?'

Georgio shook his head in despair.

He had to get out of here, he couldn't take much more.

Two days had passed since Paddy had shown the two Chinese men off Donna's property. He had placed people strategically all over the

101

sites, the car lot, and anywhere else Lewis might decide to get even with Georgio. It was all low key; Stephen Brunos was paying everyone double bubble, double time.

A pair of young brothers, Colin and Charlie Webster, were watching the car lot. They were armed with baseball bats and handguns. They both sat in the Rolls-Royce Corniche, happy to be doing their little job, even happier to be doing it inside such a nice motor. They were aged twenty and twenty-one respectively. Colin was talking about his girlfriend Lila, a pretty half-caste girl from Notting Hill.

'I tell you, Charlie, the bird's phenomenal. I'm bringing her round to meet the old woman this week.'

Charlie, the elder of the two, laughed. 'Love at first fright, was it?'

Colin grinned in the dimness of the car. 'You could say that.' He picked up a half-smoked joint from the ashtray and lit it with a bright green clipper lighter. Taking a heavy hit on it, he held the smoke in his lungs for a while before expelling it slowly. 'Lovely puff this, where'd you get it?'

Charlie took the proffered joint and sucked on it, blowing on the end as he expelled the smoke, lighting up his face with the embers. 'Up on the Railton Road, there's this Rasta who sells home-grown. Brixton, home of marijuana.'

Both boys laughed as if this was really funny. They finished the joint and Colin began to build another, his fingers rolling the three cigarette papers expertly. As he licked along the side to seal it, they were both aware of a set of headlights coming up the road. The vehicle stopped outside the forecourt and both boys were shocked into silence.

The vehicle was a Range-Rover, but the grille at the front had two large pieces of metal butting out of it.

The Range-Rover mounted the pavement and crashed into a G-reg, top-of-the-range Mercedes, sending it crashing into the BMW beside it. The cars were then pushed along, the screeching noise deafening as metal scraped metal. The Mercedes was now on its side, looking like something prehistoric in the dim moonlight.

Colin and Charlie, grabbing their scattered wits, jumped from the Rolls-Royce Cornice. Both unused to handguns, they immediately forgot them in the heat of the moment. They stood, Colin with the half-built joint still in his fingers, as the Range-Rover smashed up the cars in front of them. The car lot was a wasteground in five minutes and the Range-Rover, used previously for ram raiding, drove sedately along the road, the occupants

102

giving the boys a two-fingered salute as they passed them.

Five more minutes went by and the police arrived, alerted by a woman in the flats along from the car lot who could hear eight car alarms going off at once. Colin and Charlie were already gone.

Paddy heard the news fifteen minutes after it happened and blew what was known in the building trade as a gasket.

Stephen Brunos answered the phone and listened in amazement to what Paddy was telling him. Quickly getting dressed, he left his flat in Tobacco Dock, taking his car keys and his wallet. It wasn't until he was driving towards Essex that he realised he didn't have any socks on.

He arrived at Donna's at three thirty-five in the morning. Davey and Carol Jackson were already there, as were the police. Donna was sitting in her kitchen in shock, Dolly was making tea, and Carol Jackson was calling the police, the perpetrators of the offence, and anyone else she could lay her tongue on, whoresons.

Detective Inspector Richie Richardson was already sick to death of her.

'Mrs Brunos, have you any idea who would do this to your car lot?'

Donna shook her head for what seemed the millionth time. 'No idea whatsoever. I'm just glad we're insured.'

She looked at Davey as she said this and he had the grace to drop his eyes. The car lot, as well as all the sites, had all been hopelessly under-insured. It was one of the first things Donna had sorted out. In fact, it wasn't unusual for a car dealer to under-insure, because some of their cars were ringers, or cut and shunts. No one in their right mind insured them, that was up to the purchaser. Donna, in ignorance of this, got the insurance increased.

Dolly had made yet another cup of tea and everyone was sitting subdued around the large antique scrubbed pine table.

The DI spoke to Davey. 'Have you had any trouble with a customer recently? Maybe someone who bought a beast off you? It happens all the time.'

Davey straightened up and said nastily, 'None of our motors are beasts, mate, we deal in prestige cars. You saw them for yourself, didn't you? Mercs, BMWs, Rollers. We ain't talking Dagenham dustbins here, an odd Sierra or fucking Metro! They were decent motors!'

Richie Richardson waved a hand to calm him down. 'How about part-exchange motors, any pigs there? You sell them off, I take it?'

Davey shook his head. 'Go straight through the auctions at Chelmsford. Anything under a D-reg Jag is useless to us. We shove them straight through at Chelmsford as I keep telling you. You don't

103

part-ex on a forty grand motor with a fucking Reliant Robin, do you get my drift?'

'All right, all right, keep your hair on. I have to ask these questions. Any suspicious characters around the car lot lately?'

Carol Jackson pulled on her cigarette and said, 'They're all weird, mate. We get all sorts – daydreamers who want to sit and smell the leather upholstery and imagine pulling a bird in a nice motor, to old boys who can afford the cars but go back to their Granadas. We don't keep tabs on the people who look, for Christ's sake. Most of our working day is spent with people who do just that – look!'

The DI finished his tea. 'I'll be off then. Listen, if you get any thoughts, give me a bell, OK?'

As he got to the kitchen door he turned back. 'By the way, has anyone got it in for your old man, Mrs Brunos? I hear he's doing a long stretch.'

Donna looked up with frightened eyes. 'Not that I know of. Everyone liked my Georgio. But I could ask him, I suppose, when I go to see him.'

The DI smiled at her kindly. 'You do that, love.' He nodded once more and walked from the room followed by his sidekick, DC Lines.

Ricky Richardson felt sorry for Donna Brunos. It had come as a shock to her, a genuine shock. This wasn't an insurance scam as he had first suspected; there was more to it than met the eye. As he passed through the large entrance hall and took in the antique clock, he shook his head in disbelief.

Crime, it seemed, certainly did pay, and bloody well by the looks of it. He himself had a seventy grand mortgage and his house was worth less than he had paid for it, he had a wife and three kids, and was lucky if he got a week in Bournemouth once every two years.

He banged the front door with a satisfying slam on his way out.

Stephen saw out Davey and Carol and sent Dolly up to bed. In the kitchen he covered Donna's hand with his own.

'It sounds to me like vandals, love. Don't let it get to you.'

Donna sniffed loudly. 'Why, though? Why would vandals want to do something like that? I know a few years ago we had paint thrown over the motors, that's kids' idea of vandalism. This seems . . . Oh, I don't know, more sinister somehow.'

Stephen smiled a smile he would have sworn he didn't have in him. 'Kids are much more aggressive nowadays,' he told her. 'From what that woman said it sounded like a ram-raiding vehicle. They're out-and-out fuckers now, you've only got to read the papers.'

104

Donna was quiet as she listened to him. The silence was getting heavy when she finally spoke.

'Ram-raiders, as I understand it Stephen, go after electrical goods, or clothing, Reeboks and stuff like that. Why would you just smash up a car lot? There's no logic in that. If you had a vehicle with the capacity to smash through Dixons' window, why use it on a car front? There's more to this than meets the eye.'

'Now why would you think that, Donna?'

She wiped her nose with a tissue. Even this action was performed gracefully.

'I think there's a lot I'm not being told. By you, Davey, and everyone.'

Stephen laughed heartily. 'Don't be silly, Donna.'

'You sounded just like Georgio then. He would say that to me. Those exact words, in fact. Listen, Stephen, I have realised in the few months he's been away that we were living way beyond our means, that everything was hopelessly under-insured: the car lot, the sites, even this house. If this place had gone up in flames one night, we'd have been lucky to buy a three-bedroomed semi on the money we would have got off the insurance. The land would have been worth more. There was hardly any money in the business accounts, I had to talk that arsehole Pemberton into extending our credit to finish the building work, yet Georgio and I were taking holidays all over the globe. Our cars, I have also found out, are lease-hired. Georgio's is being repossessed, while mine is now paid up, courtesy of some jewellery I had. So please, Stephen, don't ever tell me not to be silly again. I love Georgio with all my heart, with my very breath, and I am going to visit him tomorrow and get this all straightened out, once and for all.'

She stood up unsteadily and walked to the kitchen door. 'You are welcome to one of the guest rooms, there's four of them. I'll see you in the morning.'

Donna went out and Stephen heard her footsteps as she padded up to bed in her slippers.

Of everything she had said, the most shocking thing of all was the word 'arsehole'. In twenty years he had never heard Donna mutter a single obscenity. She was really upset, that much was obvious, and more so was the fact that they had all underestimated her, Georgio most of all.

Stephen lit himself a cigarette and sat in the quiet kitchen. Maybe it was best for her to find out the truth of everything now, before it all got too involved. But how would Donna react to knowing that a man like Lewis was on her tail?

105

The thought of Lewis frightened even him shitless, Stephen admitted. What on earth would it do to a gentle creature like Donna?

He hoped that his brother had some answers for her, because he sure as hell didn't, whether true, made up, or induced by drugs. He had nothing to say to her at all.

Donna got back into bed, her mind numb now. The car lot had been destroyed by vandals . . . She shook her head in the darkness. She didn't believe that.

Whoever had destroyed the car lot had a reason, and the reason had something to do with Georgio. She wasn't sure of this because she had no proof; it was purely gut instinct.

She had found out so much over the last few months, and now she had to face Georgio with her knowledge, or lack of knowledge as the case may be. But on one thing she was determined. Tomorrow she would find out exactly what was going on. Georgio owed it to her.

More importantly, she owed it to herself to find out.

She was still awake when the first fingers of light crept in at her bedroom windows.

106

Chapter Nine

The prison environment was already getting to Georgio. He wondered, at times, if without the presence of Lewis, he might have found it easier to bear. Many of the inmates shared a rough camaraderie. If a man's wife had sent him a Dear John, there was always someone to advise him.

The sound of a young inmate on a ten-stretch, crying his heart out, was rarely mentioned the next day by the other men. The futility of their situation was often the hardest thing to bear. Lock-up every night at seven-thirty was hard; even a ten-year-old child was allowed the freedom of an evening to watch TV or write a letter, read a book or go for some air in the garden. For the men sharing a cell it was either easier to bear, because you could chat for a while, or harder because you were locked in a small space with someone you detested, and to add insult to injury, you were also forced to share their toilet facilities. Nothing was private. Opening your bowels was done before an audience.

A few of the other cons were quite intelligent. Those were a bonus, as far as Georgio was concerned. Many were not exactly bright. Most men used up hours of their day in the gym. Pumping iron was an escape, a way to get rid of excess energy or sexual desire. A way to keep in shape, hang on to a bit of self-respect. All the men had hard bodies; even the older ones had physiques a younger man, living an easy live on the outside, would have envied. Pumping iron was also a defence mechanism. The bigger you were, the less chance of a confrontation. In an environment where a fight could ensue over a matchstick-thin roll-up, it was only common sense to at least look as if you could take care of yourself.

Georgio had the added worry of living on a Wing that consisted of lifers. Long sentences were the norm here; they were all either A Grade, or Double A Grade. This included murderers and terrorists as well as run-of-the-mill hard men and bank robbers. This in itself wouldn't have been so bad if the Wing had not been the domain of Lewis. He was making it as hard as possible for Georgio. The only

107

redress Georgio had was never, by word or deed, to let on that Lewis was getting to him.

Georgio knew that once Lewis found out where his money was, that would be the end of him. The real end of him. Death was cheap in Parkhurst, whether by your own hand or someone else's. Rape was more prevalent on B Wing. It seemed that the shorter the sentence, the harder men found it to be without their wives. Georgio wondered if a really hefty sentence shut down your libido. As if it was a subliminal way of helping you through your sentence. Most of the men plastered their walls with naked women, and the more exotic magazines were like gold dust, hardcore porn being the main desire of most of them. Yet once the magazine was read, once the desire was again prominent in their minds, they seemed to lose the urge for the pictures and the magazine was sold on to the next bloke. Ribald comments were much safer and funnier. They broke the gloom and some of the men were natural comedians. It was therefore safer to joke about sex than think of it constantly. The women on daytime television were particularly good for a bit of fun.

As Georgio lay on the bench press, forcing the weights up over his head, his mind strayed to Donna, as it did more and more lately. Donna was his lifeline, his only definite friend. She was there for him, he knew that without a shadow of a doubt. Most of the men on the Wing were terrified of their wives finding an alternative pay cheque or a longtime bed partner. The biggest fear was that their wives or girlfriends would get pregnant. You could forgive the old woman an indiscretion, even make a joke of it. Be the big understanding man who took her back, after she had begged for a while; none of your friends would think any the worse of you. But a big bouncing baby was another kettle of fish altogether. That could not, and would not, be forgiven. Even if they wanted to. The other men would soon have something to say about that. You lost face, and losing face was tantamount to dying in this kind of set up. Georgio was glad he didn't have those kind of worries on top of everything else. It was hard enough to get through the day as it was without the added torture of thinking of Donna with her long slim legs wrapped around someone else's waist.

Many of the men were in for killing their wives or girlfriends. It amazed Georgio that they could bother to kill for the kind of women he saw in the visiting rooms. Most were typical blaggers' wives, with bleached blonde or dyed black hair, leather jackets and tight ski pants, their bra-less chests encased in tiny crop tops underneath the jackets. It was like the blaggers' wives' school uniform.

A few of the men had decent sorts, women they loved and

108

respected, but these were few and far between. The average lifer had maybe three marriages under his belt by the time he was thirty-five. After each sentence he would be released and would marry a young girl, fresh-faced, well-used, and loving the notoriety of being married to an armed robber. Both the girl and the man knew it was doomed to failure, that the man would move on, the girl would move on, or the Old Bill would intervene in the happy relationship. Knowing all this, Georgio thanked God for his Donna, even though he admitted he had not been the husband she thought he was. But that was all to the good.

What Donna didn't know, couldn't hurt her.

Donna walked through the automatic doors and stood in front of a female warder. She held her arms outstretched while the woman felt under her bra line, along her body, and inside the waistband of her skirt. She tidied herself up while the woman went through her shoulder bag. She gave Donna a numbered key, allowed her time to take her purse from the bag and then shut it and its contents into a small locker. Opening the next set of doors, Donna was finally allowed through to the visiting area.

Parkhurst's visiting area was quite large. It held a small canteen rather like the lock-up fastfood shops you might see on any British Rail station. This sold tea, coffee, soft drinks and sweets. As you walked through the large doors, on your right-hand side was a play area for the children, containing everything from small rocking horses to a Wendy House. Children were already happily playing there, unaware of their environment. Fathers and mothers watched them with delight.

Donna walked over to the left and the table area. The tables were spread as far apart as possible and women sat alone waiting for their spouses or sons to be brought through. Donna took a seat and placed her purse on the table. She smiled at an old woman waiting patiently at the table next to hers. The woman dropped her eyes back to her knitting and Donna sighed.

Already the buzz of conversation was quite loud. When the doors at the back of the room opened, Donna breathed a sigh of relief as she watched Georgio bound through them. He was wearing black jogging bottoms and a Lacoste shirt. He looked fit and healthy, only the lines on his face denoting the strain he was under. She stood up and he kissed her hard.

'Hello, darlin'. Am I pleased to see you!' He took her purse off the table and removed a five-pound note from it.

'What do you want? Coffee?'

109

Donna nodded and watched him as he purchased two coffees, five Mars bars and one KitKat. The KitKat, she knew already, was for her.

As he sat down once more and gave her the change, looking for all the world like a little boy, she felt a pang of sorrow for him.

'So what's been happening, Donna? How's everything?'

She took a deep breath and said calmly, much more calmly than she felt, 'Someone trashed the car lot last night. All the cars on the front were destroyed.'

She watched the incredulity on her husband's face and forced herself to carry on.

'The police think it was vandals, out in a large Range-Rover with nothing else to do. I don't think so myself.'

Georgio sipped his coffee, to give himself time to sort out in his mind what his wife was saying.

'I hope you'll have some answers for me today, Georgio, because I really feel that after last night, you owe me an explanation.'

He wiped his hand over his face in agitation.

'Look, love, you had better tell me what happened last night, from the beginning.'

It was Donna's turn now to sip at her coffee. She swallowed the bitter liquid, shuddering inwardly at what she was about to do. In nearly twenty years of marriage she had never once questioned her husband about anything; she had never questioned where their money went, what he did with it, how the credit cards were paid. She bought clothes as and when she wanted them; her American Express card was like her third hand, always there no matter what. She had never even had to take money out of the bank because there was always ample cash in the small safe in Georgio's office. Their bills were paid by standing order, she had never had to balance a cheque book, ask for a statement, or even think about money at all, except when she was spending it.

Now, she had to confront her husband not only about money, but about many other things she had been unaware of for years. She wished fervently that she was still unaware of them. This was the hardest thing she had ever had to do, mainly because Georgio was now a captive audience, being forced into listening to her talk about something they would never normally discuss. She felt the sensation of being in charge once more, being the one in control, and all because she could walk out of this prison and he couldn't.

'Last night the car lot was destroyed – at least, the cars were destroyed,' she began. 'When you were first sentenced, I took an interest in your businesses. The car lot, and the sites, were all

110

hopelessly under-insured.' Her voice faltered as she saw Georgio's face harden. She cleared her throat before continuing, telling herself that this was her husband, not a stranger she was talking to. This was the man she had slept with, loved and partnered for a long time. She had no need to be frightened of him, yet she knew that for some unaccountable reason she was.

'The money we had in our joint account I have used to bring the insurances up to date. I also used it to pay off the building suppliers, as they were not going to allow us any more credit. I also know that for the car lot, you and Davey have two sets of books. One I assume for yourselves, and one for the taxman. Davey doesn't know I found this out, so please don't blame him. I had to shut down some of the sites. The houses on the Essex site were up to the damp-proof level – they will be finished once we have the money. I am depending on the Ilford site to get us out of this mess. We stand to make a little over one hundred thousand off that. But then, you already know all this, don't you?'

She sipped her coffee once more as she looked into his stony face. 'The XJS you owned has been taken back. We couldn't meet the payments. I might add that the separate bank account you paid the leasehire from is now closed. I explained your circumstances to the bank, paid off your overdraft, and after talking to the leasehire company, everything was OK. My car I paid for by taking some of my jewellery, including my gold Rolex, to pawn. I now own the car.'

Georgio laughed nastily. 'All right, so you found out about my business practices. They're no better or worse than anyone else's in this recession, Donna. So don't make snap judgements.'

It was Donna's turn to lose her temper. 'Snap judgements! In four months you make a bit more than a snap judgement. I have been gradually finding all this out. I am your wife, Georgio, not some silly harebrained little girl who isn't capable of taking the simplest thing on board. I have been effectively running your businesses, have got you out of the shit, and all the while I've been working in the dark! Everyone kept saying to me "You should look after his interests, he's your husband." Well, that's exactly what I've been doing, in case it's escaped your notice. And quite frankly, it would have been a lot easier if I had known the score from day one. For instance, I own the house outright – well, I never knew that. I also own the sites outright – you're only a director. I own the car lot as well, and you're a director again. What the hell is going on, Georgio? I'm dragged out of bed by two policemen in the middle of the night to be told that vandals have wrecked the motors on a whim! Do I look that stupid? Also, who the hell rang your brother Stephen up? He arrived all

111

knowing and it didn't occur to me until I was sitting on the blasted ferry today that no one from the police could have got in touch with him. I asked Davey last night if he had contacted anyone and he said no. So what I want to know now is, what else am I in the dark about?'

Georgio was stunned. Donna watched the different expressions flitting across his face and felt the urge to take him in her arms and love him until everything was forgotten. Instead she sat fast in her seat, knowing that this was make or break time.

Georgio dropped his eyes to the table in front of him and finally spoke.

'Look, love, I never wanted you to know about the trouble with the businesses. It's been a hard old slog the last few years. The building craze died overnight, house prices dropped. I don't need to paint a picture, do I? I had invested in a lot of land and property, and when I realised I was overreaching myself I placed everything in your name in case they ever foreclosed on me. Lots of blokes did it. If they bankrupted me, they couldn't touch your assets. You didn't own the sites or the car lot until I was near my court date. Then I was hoping that somehow Stephen would run the businesses and bring them back out on top. When you began running them, I was frightened of this happening, but you were so happy to do it, my love, you were so pleased to be helping me, helping us, I couldn't deny you that pleasure. Also, I must admit you have done a fine job. I never realised what a good brain you had in that pretty little head, I suppose. I'm sorry you had to find out like this, but it was bound to come out at some time.'

Georgio's voice was broken, his whole demeanour crushed. Donna felt her heart break for him, knowing what it had taken for him to have to tell her that. Big Georgio Brunos whose wife had never had to worry about anything from the day they married. She knew he was proud of that fact. Georgio Brunos's wife had never worked and never wanted. He was so chauvinistic in that way, and she had gone along with it. Even when she had taken her OU degree, he had treated it like her little hobby.

She had deliberately played up to his ego, had acted how he wanted her to act. It occurred to Donna now that she had been living a lie for so long it had almost become a truth. She pushed that thought from her mind. She had wanted Georgio desperately, and had taken him on his terms. This was all her fault in a way. If she had spoken up before now she would have been more aware of what was going on and it wouldn't have been such a shock finding it all out. Carol Jackson and Davey had more of a partnership than she had ever had with Georgio. This knowledge hurt her deeply. Suddenly she knew that Carol

112

Jackson would have insisted on knowing exactly what was going on. Her respect for the woman went up one hundredfold in that split second.

'It still doesn't explain away what happened at the car lot. That seemed to me to be more sinister than everyone's making out. If I hadn't sorted the insurance we would have been in big trouble. As it stands, thank God, we'll be pounds better off. Did you and Davey arrange for that to happen, Georgio? Did you arrange for the car lot to be destroyed? I want to know the truth and I swear before God, I won't hold it against you if you did.'

Georgio felt an urge to laugh; he relaxed instantly. She thought *he* had trashed the car lot! She was willing to stand by him if he had. It was laughable. All the things she had found out, and guessed, she wasn't holding against him. She was telling him that it didn't matter, that she would sort it out. All she wanted was the truth. She had saved all their bacon by reinsuring the lot and the sites. It was his biggest nightmare that something would happen, a man would have an accident on the site and his insurance would barely cover the costs. Now his little wife, his little Donna, had taken his businesses and in four months had straightened them out. But before he got sentenced he had had other fish to fry, bigger fish, and he knew instinctively that he couldn't ever tell her about those. He had stopped worrying about the sites, the lot, everything legit, because the other businesses would have given him the earth. He had ploughed a lot of money into them, which was why he'd wanted Lewis's money. He had stripped his own assets to the bone. But then Stephen had helped him, good old Stephen, so there was no way Donna would find out about that.

He stared into her trusting face and felt a flicker of sorrow. It was so long since he had really looked at her. The strain was beginning to tell on her face. Little lines were appearing around her eyes. Her cheeks were not as firm and rounded as they had once been. Even her hair didn't look quite as lustrous. She looked good, though, as good as a woman nearing forty could look.

Georgio's tastes had always been for youth. It was her youth that had attracted him to her. She had stayed a child in his eyes for many years. Now the changes were becoming apparent. He was sorry to have been responsible for those changes. Even sorrier that she loved him more than he could ever love her. She always had: his ego had needed her to, and Donna had always done exactly what he wanted. He was sure enough of himself to know that she still would.

Her eyes stayed on him, the message in them clear.

Georgio ran his fingers through his thick black hair then, taking a deep breath, he said: 'I'm sorry, Donna.' He paused for a few seconds. 'What do you want me to say? That I'm sorry? Well, I am, believe me, I'm heart sorry. All my life I spent building up those businesses, and I made them work, you know that yourself. But, Donna, I made a few mistakes.'

She ran her tongue over her lips to moisten them. 'What kind of mistakes, Georgio? I know you stripped the businesses of money, I guessed that much. What I want to know is where it went.'

Georgio had the grace to look ashamed and Donna felt the pull of him as his dark eyes searched hers for a glimmer of understanding.

'I suppose I had better start at the beginning. Remember a few years ago when I was seeing a lot of Joseph Bronski?'

Donna shook her head. 'I can't say I do.'

Georgio was impatient. 'Remember when I went to Thailand? I was over there on and off for a year, you must remember that!'

Donna smiled faintly. 'I remember that all right.'

'Well, while I was out there, I did a few deals. I effectively bought a half share in two hotels. One in Bangkok, one in Sri Lanka. The hotels were built, I saw to that myself, albeit from a distance. It was a good move at the time. Thailand was ripe for me, it was full of tourists, people were killing themselves to get out there. The same with Sri Lanka, though that was more for the German and American market. Still, the point is I stripped everything here, took from everywhere I could, to finance this operation.'

Donna was puzzled. 'So what went wrong?'

Georgio smiled sadly. 'What went wrong? I'll tell you what went wrong. Bronski tucked me up. Not just me either but a few others. The hotels were built all right, I can't deny that, but they were worthless. The Thai government wouldn't give us house room. The hotels are sitting out there derelict, we can't even sell them.'

Donna shook her head in consternation. 'I don't understand.'

Georgio smiled once more. 'Bronski bought the land off an agent, or so he told us anyway. We had to believe him; he had always come up trumps before so we had no reason to doubt him. We were furnished with copies of the plans, I even went out there as you know to look at the progress on the building. Everything was going fine. Except the guy Bronski bought the land from was arrested for a large-scale land fraud. The government took back everything he owned, and it turned out he still owned fifty percent of the hotels. The one in Sri Lanka was only at the foundation stage. All our money was still in Bangkok. We were wiped out, Donna. Every one of us.'

She was dumbstruck. 'But surely our government can help . . .'

At this, Georgio laughed outright. 'Sure they can, and pigs can fly and little fairies live at the bottom of our garden! We could only build

114

providing we were in partnership with a Thai, and we were. Only he was a risky bugger but we didn't know that at the time. The guy had milked the money from us, we were giving him hundreds of thousands of pounds at a time. The worst of it all is, I helped to recruit the partners, and that's why the car lot was vandalised last night.'

Donna wasn't sure she had heard right. 'What has all this got to do with what happened last night?'

Georgio opened a Mars bar and bit into it. He chewed for a while before he carried on with his story.

'I encouraged a partnership with a man called Lewis. Ask anyone about Lewis, and they'll tell you all about him. He is one of the most dangerous men in England – in the British Isles, in fact. He is at the moment residing here with me on fraud charges, though he could be held accountable for more murders than the Third Reich. I never dreamt we were into a dodgy situation, I swear that to you. I heard through the grapevine that Lewis wanted to sink money into legitimate businesses. A lot of money. I approached him and he was very interested in the deal. I set it all up for him, and well, you know the rest now.'

Donna swallowed the lump in her throat. 'No, I don't. Tell me the rest, Georgio. I think I have a right to know.'

Georgio looked into his wife's face; it was a beautiful face even now, when it was drawn with worry. Weighed down with troubles.

'In short, Lewis thinks I ticked him up. He then decided to make sure I was out of the ball-game. Wilson gave evidence against me, and now I'm stuck in here. I have it on good authority that Lewis will make sure I never get parole. Wilson died a while ago . . .'

'I know that. He hanged himself.'

Georgio laughed low. 'I knew he was going to hang himself before he did. Lewis told me. The only person who could have got me out of here is dead.'

'But Wilson committed suicide – your barrister told me that himself!'

Georgio shook his head slowly. 'Wilson was helped on his way, my love. Take it from me, I know. Lewis told me he was going to commit suicide, hours before he was found. Lewis was behind it all, I know that for a fact. Now Lewis wants me, or to get to me. He thinks I can give him his money back, and nothing I say will convince him I can't. He owns the Wing I'm on, he also owns the screws who are supposed to be looking after us. He even had me striped across the arse in the Scrubs. Sort of a taster before I arrived here.'

Georgio looked her straight in the eyes. 'I know all about Lewis

115

and about why I'm here. I'm only sorry I never told you all this before. I have to get out of here, my darling, and I have to get out soon, or I'll be coming home to you in a box. Lewis saw to it that the car lot was trashed; it was a small warning to me. I didn't want to tell you any of this because I felt I had got us into it and I had to get us out. Well, I can't. I've tried, and I just can't.'

Georgio's voice broke and Donna grasped his hand across the table. They resembled any other prisoner and his wife; both had the aching look of loneliness on their face, both had the hopeless look of people separated too long. Both loved each other from a distance, and it was getting harder with each passing day.

'Oh, Georgio. What are we going to do? How the hell did you get involved with all this? What on earth possessed you to get caught up with people like Lewis?'

Georgio stared into her white face and said simply, 'Greed, Donna. Pure and simple greed.'

He kissed the hand that held his so tightly.

'If I had pulled it off, I would have been as rich as Croesus. We would have had everything we ever wanted in the world . . .'

Donna pulled her hand from his, an expression of utter contempt on her face.

'We *had* everything, Georgio, remember? I mean, how much do you want, eh? We had a home, money in the bank, and we had each other. What more could we really have wanted? Or, more precisely, what more could *you* have wanted? It's always been about what *you* want, hasn't it? Everything was always what you wanted, needed, cared about. I just came along for the ride. God! I must have been so stupid. So bloody stupid.'

Georgio was amazed at Donna's words. His Donna who had always been so pliant – that was the exact word to describe her, pliant. She had fitted in with whatever he wanted, and now she was sitting across the table from him, telling him exactly what she should have told him years before. He was honest enough to admit that to himself.

'Don't be upset, Don Don.'

Donna flinched. 'Don't call me Don Don! It sounds puerile. Nothing you can do at this moment in time will make me feel any better. Christ Almighty, Georgio, can't you see what you've done? You used everything we had to further your own aims and now where are we? You are stuck in here, a man is dead, and our last chance of earning a livelihood is in danger. Well, I hope you're pleased with yourself, I really do, because you've pulled some bloody stunts in your time but this one takes the biscuit!'

116

Georgio was shocked at her voice, at the contempt in it. At the utter frustration.

'I suppose I am in danger as well, am I?' she went on furiously. 'Is that why Big Paddy seems to be joined to my hip these days? Is that how your brother Stephen knew about the car lot so quickly? Is that why I am being treated like a child by all and sundry? I suppose even Carol Jackson was brought in on the big secret! Georgio has pulled a fast one again. This time it's all blown up in his face and now he's got a maniac after him. What do you want me to do about all this trouble now you've told me? I assume that's why I've been invited into your confidence, only you never deigned to tell me anything before.'

Georgio had waited for that last question. He answered her immediately. 'I want you to help me get out of here.'

Donna licked her dry lips twice before she could summon the strength to reply. 'I beg your pardon!'

Georgio smiled, that little grin that had always made her heart lurch inside her breast. 'I want you to get me out of here.'

Donna stared at her husband's face. It was full of hope, full of longing, and she saw his mouth quiver slightly as he watched her. She noticed for the first time the lines around his mouth, the grey in his thick hair, and the worry etched deeply across his forehead as he frowned.

Georgio looked suddenly old and this knowledge shocked her.

Then, as she thought about what he had said, she began to laugh. It was a low laugh at first, gradually building into a high-pitched giggle. People at tables near them turned and watched the pretty woman guffawing loudly. They smiled at her, joining in with the non-existent joke.

Donna could hear the laughter emanating from her body. It worked its way up and exploded from her mouth in long waves and she couldn't do anything to stop it. Helplessly she roared, the laughter painful now, her ribs and stomach aching from the force of it.

Georgio watched her in disbelief, his face a comic study in dismay as she screeched with laughter at him.

'Come on, Donna, give over. Calm down.'

Gradually the laughter left her body. She sat back in her seat and wiped her eyes with the back of her hands, leaving black lines from her mascara across her fingers.

'After all I heard here today, I never thought I'd laugh again. But there, you could always shock me, Georgio. It seems you haven't lost the knack.'

She picked up her purse from the table and stood up. 'I'm going

117

now, I have to get back. It's a long journey here, you know. I really don't know how the women with children manage it.' She kissed her husband's cheek and straightened up.

Georgio was flabbergasted. 'You're going? Visiting time's not up yet, we have another hour at least.'

'Your visit is up, Georgio. I need some good clean air in my lungs. I need time to think. I need time for me now.'

'Don't go, Donna. Please don't go yet.'

She stared down into her husband's face and grinned. 'If only you knew, Georgio, the number of times I've said that to you in my mind. Unlike you, though, I never had the guts to say it out loud. Maybe if I hadn't been such a coward, you might be at home with me now. Tell this Lewis he did us a favour with the car lot by the way – we're quids in.'

Georgio watched with amazement as his wife, his little Donna, left the visiting room.

He felt as if he had just lost something precious.

Chapter Ten

On the ferry back to the mainland, Donna sat beside a young girl with two children, a boy of about three and his big sister. The mother herself didn't look much older than twenty.

'Do you mind if I smoke?'

Donna shook her head. 'Not at all.'

The young woman lit a cigarette and drew the smoke down into her lungs. 'I should give up really, but I can't.'

Donna looked at her properly, taking in the light blonde hair and the expertly applied make-up.

'They're not very good for one's health.'

The woman roared with laughter. 'Sod me health, love. It's just that I can't really afford them!'

Donna found herself laughing with her as if what she had said was hilarious.

The young mother sat her son on her lap and wiped his face with a grubby handkerchief. 'What's your old man in for?'

Donna looked out of the window at the passing water and sighed. The girl carried on talking as if she had answered.

'My Wayne's on a twelve-stretch. I could have killed him. Robbed our local Tesco. Course, it was summertime, so he only had a T-shirt on and his tattoos, my name in a heart and the kids' underneath, were on show. One of me neighbours grassed him up. Not exactly Brain of Britain, know what I mean? Still, as I said to his mum, at least we know where he is!'

She laughed again, a good-natured infectious laugh, and suddenly Donna felt a great urge to cry for this beautiful young woman and her children.

'Your children are lovely. What are their names?'

The girl pulled her son's head around and kissed him hard on the mouth. 'This is Michael Joseph and she's Chivonne Maria, otherwise known as Micky and 'Vonne. He's three and she's six.' The little girl smiled shyly at Donna, displaying gapped front teeth. It made her look very endearing and vulnerable.

119

'They're gorgeous, and very good. They've hardly moved an inch since we boarded.'

The mother winked. 'That's because I threatened them with death, pain, torture and destruction before we set out today. But we've been doing this once a fortnight for nearly a year now, so they're quite used to it. They get more attention from their dad when he's banged up. My name's Caroline, by the way. What's yours?'

'Donna, Donna Brunos. Pleased to meet you.'

Caroline shook Donna's hand. 'I saw you today. Your old man's a bit of all right, ain't he? Very good-looking. Have you got any kids?'

The question was asked in innocence and Donna, looking into the girl's open, trusting face, felt once more an urge to cry her eyes out. The ferry docked and Donna stood up, taking Chivonne's hand and helping Caroline off the ferry with her pushchair and bags.

Outside it was overcast, and a wind was picking up off the sea.

'I'd better get a cab to the station,' Caroline said. 'Nice meeting you anyway, Donna. Probably see you again.'

Donna watched her struggling with the children and the bags, wheeling the pushchair with difficulty while she staggered on impossibly high heels, her narrow back making her look very young.

'Caroline,' she called out, 'where exactly are you going?'

'East Ham. Want to travel with me?'

Donna walked over to her. 'No. Let me give you a lift home. We can stop on the way, break the journey for the children, eh? I'm going to Canning Town anyway.'

Caroline's face was animated with pleasure. 'You sure now, 'cos these two can be a bit noisy?'

Donna grinned, taking Chivonne's hand. 'I'm sure. I don't have any children myself so consequently, I rather like them. Even if they are noisy!'

She led the little group over the road and into the car park opposite the ferry terminal. She opened up her Mercedes and Caroline was impressed.

'What a lovely motor! Your old man must have done you proud.'

Donna smiled tightly and helped her to belt the children into the back of the car. Michael Joseph was falling asleep on his feet, and Chivonne settled him back on the seat as if she was his mother.

Ten minutes later they had stowed the pushchair in the boot with the bags and were driving along the road. Caroline chattered her thanks and Donna was pleased she had her there, was glad of the company. While she had them in the car she didn't have to think.

'I'd love a car, Donna. Nothing expensive – a little runaround would do me. But I ain't got the money. It's a pain in the arse getting

120

down to visit Wayne. I could get the coach, but there's some right ones on there, you know. Right sorts. All talking about how hard their husbands are. Oh, you know the scenario. I can't handle it myself. So Wayne's mum and me come down by train. It's more expensive but it's worth it for the peace. How long is your old man doing?'

Donna said quietly, 'Eighteen years.'

Caroline's face spoke volumes. 'What's he done? Murder or something?' It was said with interest, no judgement whatsoever. Donna sighed. 'It's a long story.'

Caroline grinned. 'Well, I ain't going nowhere, love. But if you want to keep stumm about it, that's fine by me.'

She turned around in the car and checked on her children. 'All right, 'Vonne? Lovely to get a lift, ain't it?'

'I'm hungry, Mum. Me belly thinks me throat's been cut.'

Donna laughed at the child's words.

Caroline rolled her eyes. 'She picks all that up from me. Everything I say she copies. I have to watch me language, I can tell you!' She turned back to the child. 'When we get home I'll make you something. It won't be that long now, love, I promise.'

Ten minutes later Donna pulled into a Happy Eater on the motorway. She stopped the car and turned to Caroline.

'Let's all have something.' Caroline's face was sombre, her eyes blank. Donna frowned. 'What's wrong?'

Caroline looked out of the car window in distress. 'Look, I ain't got the money . . .'

Donna interrupted her and squeezed her arm. 'Well, I have. They do a lovely hamburger, I hear.'

'Vonne whooped with delight. 'Can I have French fries with mine? Not chips, I want French fries.'

Donna smiled at her. 'You can have anything you want, it's my treat.' Before Caroline could argue she was out of the car and opening the door. 'Come on then, kids. Let's get going!'

Chivonne was already unbuckling her brother's seat belt. Michael Joseph was awake and smiling.

Inside, Donna ordered the children a large meal and milkshakes; a hamburger and coffee for herself and when Caroline only asked for coffee, she ordered her a hamburger as well.

Sitting at the table, Caroline said, 'Thanks ever so much. They get so hungry, and they ate their sandwiches ages ago.'

Donna flicked a hand at her. 'Forget it. How long have you been married?'

Caroline shrugged. 'I'm not married. Wayne didn't want to be tied

121

down. I had the kids and he lived with me and still had his freedom. Or so he thought anyway. He never saw us without, not once. He always ducked and dived like, this was his first big one and he got caught. I could have murdered him when the Old Bill turned up. Smug bastards they were and all, but then you'd know that already. So he was nicked and eventually he got his sentence. No bail, nothing beforehand. I mean, we ain't got the money for anything like that. Michael was six months old when he got the capture. Wayne was twenty-three. We're the same age.'

Donna said, 'You must have been very young when you had Chivonne.'

'Just seventeen. I went out with Wayne from when I was fourteen. Never had another bloke in all me life. He was over the moon when Michael Joseph was born. I think that's why he done the blag. We was rock bottom, see. Couldn't pay the bills, nothing. He'd been out of work a good while. Couldn't even go clipping because he was a known face and he knew if he got caught he'd be in for a four at least. Then the silly bastard goes and does the blag at Tesco with his mate, and now he's away for eight years at least. Unless he pushes his luck, then he'll do the whole twelve.'

Chivonne was listening to her mother intently as she was speaking.

'He'll be good, Mum, he told me he would.'

Donna dropped her eyes to her plate. Her throat was thick with tears again. The child's acceptance of her plight was heartrending.

'Come on, 'Vonne, eat your grub. You shouldn't be listening to me talk.'

'Vonne, a beautiful child with long blonde hair and large green eyes, said impatiently, 'I can't help hearing you, Mum, because I ain't deaf!'

Even Donna smiled at the child's exasperated words.

'So, what happened with your old man?' Caroline enquired.

Donna found herself telling Caroline everything about Georgio's trial and subsequent sentence. It was an unburdening. She described how she had taken over all his businesses and the mess she had found them in, and then she told Caroline how she had confronted him. Everything.

Caroline shook her head and frowned. 'How long was you married?'

'Twenty years this year.'

'Didn't you want any children or anything?'

'I couldn't have any. We tried for a long time. Every month I thought, this is it. A baby. But it never happened. Eventually we went to see a specialist and I found that I can't conceive properly. It's

122

long and complicated. I had three miscarriages while on fertility drugs. It's funny, you know, but when I heard of people giving birth to six children at once, or five, it reminded me of an animal, like having a litter of puppies or something. Yet I would gladly have given birth to twenty in the end, I wanted a baby so desperately. I wanted a child for Georgio, because he wanted a child so much. I used to worry myself sick in case he left me for some fertile beauty with big breasts and child-bearing hips!'

Caroline laughed with her, but the girl's face was filled with sorrow for her newfound friend.

'Then, as the years went on, we talked about it less and less. In the end it was a self-defence thing. Our friends' children started growing up, and we were getting older, and then I tried having a test-tube baby. I lost it at four months, a perfectly formed little boy. I lost heart after that, and so did Georgio. I was depressed, so very depressed. Georgio was like a child himself in many respects. I looked after him, our home, everything. I never had to do a day's work. I even have a live-in housekeeper. My idea of a heavy day was doing the gardening – and I have a man who comes twice a week to cut the lawns and roll the tennis court. Another young man comes to clean the pool once a month. Outwardly I have everything, inside I'm empty. I have no children, and my husband is doing eighteen years, and now he wants me to do something I'm not sure I can do. Not even sure I want to do. It's all a mess, a terrible mess.'

Caroline was dumbstruck, unable to think of any words of comfort. She liked this woman enormously, liked everything about her, from the way she dressed to her lovely voice and kind nature. She felt as though Donna was centuries older than her, not in years but in experience of life. Listening to her loneliness was like a knife-thrust in the heart. She glanced at her own children, little Michael Joseph with a face covered in tomato sauce and a mouthful of hamburger, and her daughter, her Chivonne, with her blonde pigtails and gappy front teeth. She thought of her high-rise flat in East Ham and suddenly felt grateful for all she had. Being a natural mother herself, she recognised a kindred spirit in the well-dressed woman sitting opposite.

'What does he want you to do?'

Donna shook her head slowly. 'I can't tell you that, I'm sorry. I'm not even sure I heard him properly, it's so outrageous. I worshipped Georgio from the first time I saw him, I have lived my life to please him, I was frightened that if I argued with him he'd leave me high and dry. Especially as I couldn't give him a child. Consequently, he has lived his life as he wanted to, and I've allowed him to. He had affairs over the years and I never said a word, only lived for the day

123

when I knew instinctively it was over. Now I am in control, he needs me more than I need him, and I feel pleasure in that fact, even though I know it's wrong. It's evil.'

Caroline made a noise with her lips. 'I don't see why. He sounds a selfish bastard if you ask me. My mum says they're all selfish bastards, men. Twenty years you've given him; you've looked after him, his home, the works. It might do him good to see you showing a bit of strength. I know Wayne is proud of me and the way I cope. I'll tell you something else: I give him a bit of lip now, something I would never have done before he got sentenced. I like me bit of independence. I've been with him since I was a kid, he's called the tune and I've done the dance he wanted, same as you.'

Caroline paused and took a swig of her coffee. 'It's time for you to save your own life, girl,' she went on. 'Whatever he's asked, think about it long and hard before you make a decision. Do what your head tells you and not what your heart does. That's the only real advice I can offer. You're a good-looking woman, a nice woman, so don't sell yourself short. There's plenty of people around to do that for you. If you want him then have him, but on *your* terms. That's what I've done with my Wayne. I've got that poor git on his knees, and oh, it don't half feel good. I ain't stepped foot outside the house since he's been banged up, but I let him think I'm out and about. Not having it off or nothing, but out with me mates and that. In fact, I go to Bingo with me mum on a Friday at the Mecca, it's her treat, and me dad babysits! I've realised that a lot of life is not what you say, see, it's what you don't say. People have to make up their own minds then. It's like a game, and only we know the rules.'

Donna smiled at the simplicity of the words, and at the truth in them. This young girl, with a life harder than she could even imagine, had more knowledge of men than she did. Whether it came with the bearing of children she didn't know. Maybe, like a lioness, you lived your life for children with only their protection in mind. You took second place. Or maybe it was because Donna had been sheltered too much. She had met Georgio six months after her parents had died in that multiple car crash. He had come and taken her life over.

Her only other living relative was Hamish, her brother, twelve years older and with his own life in Liverpool. Austere Hamish, the graduate, the respectable man whose children were like characters from an old 1940s film. They called him and Annabel Mother and Father, not Mum and Dad. They were grown now, both leading exemplary lives, never having once roared with laughter naturally, or played anything more rowdy than Monopoly.

124

'Can I get you another coffee?' The waitress's voice broke into Donna's thoughts.

'Would you like another coffee, Caroline?'

'I'll have one if you're having one.'

Donna nodded at the young waitress, marvelling at how easy she felt inside herself.

'Penny for your thoughts? I was worried we'd lost you there, Donna. I was gonna put a sign on you saying, "Normal service will be resumed as soon as possible".'

Donna threw back her head and laughed out loud. 'You're funny, Caroline, do you know that? You're also like a dose of medicine. I'm so glad I met you today, I really am.'

Caroline smiled, her face half-sad. 'I'm glad I met you too, and thanks for treating the kids and that.'

'Can I have some ice cream, please?'

Donna smiled at the little boy and said, 'Today, Michael Joseph, you can have anything you want!'

He clapped his chubby hands with glee.

Georgio lay in his cell worrying. His eyes strayed to the photos of Donna on the wall by his bunk. He couldn't believe that she had walked out on him; never in all their lives together had she done a thing like that. It was a shock to realise just how much he really needed her. Especially now, when she had the house and the businesses in her name. Everything he had worked for and built up was in her name. The house was worth a small fortune and he wanted it. It had never occurred to him that she would be rebellious; she had always done exactly what he wanted. But he had never been banged up before doing eighteen years . . .

Timmy crashed into the cell full of good humour. 'All right, Georgio, my son? I had a lovely visit from the old woman and two of me girls. One of them's pregnant, but it's all right because the bloke's gonna marry her, my brothers have seen to that. Family, eh? What would we do without them? Look at this.'

Timmy pushed under his nose a photograph of a girl of about twenty-one with a child in her arms. The child was a little girl about two years old and you could see they were mother and daughter.

'That's my Tracy. Her little girl's called Corinne. Lovely little thing, ain't she?'

Georgio nodded. 'Very pretty, they both are.' Timmy kissed the photograph and grinned. 'Have a guess what my old woman told me. You know that young fella that just come on the Wing, Broomfield?

125

Well, he's a nonsense. He's in here for interfering with little kids, the piece of shite! Seems he raped a five-year-old girl. I thought he was funny, because unlike most cons he never says a word about his blag. I'll give him fucking blag! I thought he was a nice kid, you know, quiet type. I gave him a fucking roll-up the other night. You wait until I tell Lewis. He'll have the screws' guts for garters for not telling him. I bet they're waiting to segregate him somewhere. He's even got his own cell, ain't he! By Christ we were all dense, we should have smelt that rat before it was stinking.'

'He's really a nonsense?' Georgio's voice was disgusted.

Timmy nodded. 'Fucking real, ain't it? Imagine putting him in here with us. But apparently, he's a bit schiz, like – not all the ticket. He'll be even worse when I've finished with him, the ponce! He raped a little girl, a little baby. Not even at school yet. She had to have thirty stitches after he'd finished with her. No wonder he likes watching the kids' programmes, eh? Probably gets off on them.' And Timmy stamped from the cell to regale everyone on the Wing with the news.

Georgio was stunned. The boy was as good as dead, or at least in for a serious injury. Georgio could not find it in his heart to feel any compassion. Most of the men on the wing had children or nieces and nephews. Even the gays hated nonces. Paedophiles were the scum of the earth in this place and that was how it should be. No one had any time for the 'social worker syndrome'; the argument that these men had been abused themselves as children. A lot of the cons came from bad homes where they'd been abused, beaten, whatever. But they worshipped their children like gods. Could not understand a mentality that said, forgive them. Even the devout Catholics couldn't find an ounce of mercy for them.

Everyone was of the same opinion: get rid of them. Get them on the hospital wing and out of this environment. The murderer of a man in a fight was given his due; a man who murdered a girl down a lonely lane or whatever was given grief. It was how the prison set-up worked and the screws accepted this, even agreed with it. They must have been hard-pushed to put Broomfield on A Wing.

Georgio put the nonsense and his troubles out of his mind. He wasn't worth the energy or the time.

He walked slowly to the recreation room, which was nearly empty, and sat at a small table shuffling a pack of cards aimlessly, trying to work out what to write to Donna to make her come round to his way of thinking.

He had to get out – and she was the one person no one would ever suspect of helping him. He had already decided how it was to be

126

done. All he needed was her co-operation and he would be home and dry.

Samuel Broomfield walked into the room and smiled at Georgio, who dropped his eyes quickly, observing the boy surreptitiously as he flicked through the TV screen until he found a children's programme. Georgio watched Broomfield watch the children, who were running round a TV studio playing a game.

Three hours of heavy traffic later, Donna pulled up outside the high-rise block of flats in East Ham.

'Got time to come up for a quick coffee, Donna?'

'OK then.' She helped Caroline and the children from the car. Locking up, she followed them inside the building.

The entrance hall was full of litter, old newspapers, Coke cans and circulars. As the lift doors opened she was assailed with the stench of urine, human as well as canine.

On the seventh floor they disembarked, all giving a hearty sigh of relief and taking in a deep gulp of air. Donna was surprised to see Caroline unlock two mortice locks as well as a Chubb lock on the front door. It was dark in the lobby. Walking into the flat, Caroline turned on the hallway light.

'We have to use the lights all year round here. Come on in, Donna. Michael Joseph, take your coat off and put it on your bed. 'Vonne, go and put the pushchair in the cupboard. I'll put the kettle on.'

Donna followed her down the hallway into the lounge. The kitchen led off it and Donna looked around her at the neat home. The walls of the lounge were painted pale green; a deep green Dralon-covered Chesterfield and two chairs were strategically positioned to give maximum space, and the TV was in a dark wood cabinet. The large windows had deep green, swagged velvet curtains. A small coffee table held a few ornaments and a leadlight cabinet contained books and cut glass. The total effect was delightful.

'It's lovely in here!'

'Well, don't sound so surprised about it!' Caroline grinned. 'Me and Wayne done this place up just before he was nicked. I emulsioned the walls again a few weeks ago – keeps it looking fresh and clean.' She disappeared into the kitchen and put on the kettle.

'I bet your house is nice,' she called, 'what with the swimming pool and everything.'

Donna followed her into the kitchen and sat at the small table under the window.

'It's all right. Big is the best description. But it's not homey like this place.'

127

Caroline was surprised at the honesty of the words. 'Have you made up your mind yet what you're gonna do?'

Donna shook her head and lit a cigarette. 'I've got a lot of thinking to do about it all.'

Caroline sat opposite her. 'He ain't asked for a divorce, has he? Only a lot of the long-timers go through that. It's a self-defence mechanism. Before you give him the big E, he gives it to you, like.'

Donna grinned. 'No, it's nothing like that, Caroline. I wish I could tell you about it, but I daren't.'

Caroline shrugged. 'You keep your own counsel, girl. But if ever you need an ear, you know where I am. I appreciated what you done today. It was very good of you.'

'Believe it or not, Caroline, I enjoyed it.'

Michael Joseph came into the room, divested of his coat and also his trousers. He pulled himself up on to Donna's lap and she kissed the top of his head.

'Why don't you stay for supper? It's only ham and eggs but you're welcome to it.'

Donna smiled. 'All right then, Caroline, I will!'

She sat with the children and kept them amused while Caroline prepared the meal. She didn't want to have to think just yet about what her husband had said, and Michael Joseph and Chivonne were the perfect excuse.

She enjoyed herself enormously.

Dolly heard Donna's key in the lock at nine-thirty and she rushed out into the hallway.

'I've been worried out of me brains about you!'

Donna kissed the woman's cheek and said, 'I met a girl, gave her a lift home to East Ham and stayed on at her place for me tea!'

'You what! Come away in and I'll make you a drink and then you can tell me all about it.'

Donna sat at her scrubbed pine table and looked around the kitchen while Dolly made the coffee. She had never really had fun in this room, not like the fun she had experienced in East Ham this evening. The children had regaled her with stories of their doings, of their trips to the park and their nana's house. About their little wants and dreams. She had envied Caroline so much as she had made them get into the bath and then their pyjamas. Her own home seemed sterile by comparison, overclean and without a crease anywhere. She knew that if she walked into her lounge, her drawing room, dining room or conservatory, there wouldn't be a thing out of place. No evidence that people actually lived in this house . . .

128

For the first time in years she saw in her mind's eye the baby she had lost. Its perfectly formed body lying in the bed. The deep red of the blood as it seeped from her body on to the white sheets, surrounding the small foetus like a crimson blanket. Georgio picking it up gently with kitchen roll and placing it in a small shoebox, then holding her hand as they waited for the ambulance.

The strain of the day came over her. She took a deep breath to stem the tears, but they came nonetheless. Big wracking sobs that made her ribs ache and her heart sore. She felt the hot saltiness as they ran down her face and into her mouth. Felt Dolly's arms go around her, hold her to her big bosom and murmur endearments to her.

'What happened love? Is it Georgio – did he upset you?'

She cried harder, remembering the hospital, the lights and the operating theatre. The knowledge that all her chances were now gone, that it was all over. Sadness mingled with a kind of relief. Georgio's disappointed face, his tears as he had held his son's small body. She saw her parents' funeral, and her own wedding day, all inexplicably linked somehow. Then she saw the smiling faces of Michael Joseph and Chivonne, covered in ketchup and smelling of baby sweat and the dirt from the floor of the visiting room in Parkhurst.

Finally she saw Georgio saying to her, 'Get me out of here.'

And then she knew she would do whatever he asked.

She owed him that much.

129

Chapter Eleven

Junie Dent was thirty-two, looked thirty-five and fancied herself as nineteen. Five foot two and ten stone, she had inordinately small hands and feet. Her hair was long, permed and shiny, her breasts were huge, and all her own. She suffered from a large belly, but in a nice tight girdle she thought she looked very good. She had been Danny Simmonds's mistress for five years. Since Danny's son had been knocked off his bike by a hit-and-run driver, she had gradually come to realise that she could finally get him off his wife. Lorraine was now off her shopping trolley, as Danny so succinctly put it.

As she was pushed up against the wall of her tiny hallway, holding in her belly as best she could, feeling Danny's hands pulling open her dressing gown and grabbing at her breasts, she resigned herself to the inevitable. Danny was six two, and seventeen stone. He held her up against the wall with his hips, and she bit on her lip as he thrust his erect member inside her.

Rubbing her large breasts, he talked filth into her ear for two minutes before he said throatily, 'I'm coming, girl, I'm fucking nearly there.'

She looked into his face and went into her usual routine. 'Come on, Danny boy, give it to me. Go on, Danny, really shove it up me, hurt me!' Interspersed with little moans.

Danny shuddered inside her, and for a split second Junie was frightened that he'd let her fall down on to the hall carpet, but Danny kept his grip on her as his legs gave way under him.

'Fuck me, June, that's what I call emptying the old chain locker!'

Junie smiled. 'Put me down, Danny boy, before you drop me.'

He lowered her gently to the ground. Walking to the bathroom, he smiled at her. 'I'll just wash me tackle and then I'd better be off. Not bad, eh? Twice in two hours.'

Junie followed him into the bathroom. Putting her small hands on to his shoulders, she ironed out imaginary creases with the palms.

'I love you, Danny. You know that, don't you?'

Turning from the sink, he zipped up his trousers. The funny thing

130

was, he knew she really did love him. In her own way – the same way that he loved her. Her large blue eyes were bright with unshed tears, and for the first time in months Danny felt a flicker of real emotion.

'Come here, girl, give us a cuddle.'

As he held her against him he marvelled at how short she was. Even though, in the eyes of the world, she was a hefty bird. To him she was still petite. After all, he had seven stone on her.

Kissing the top of her silky head he said sadly, 'I've got to go, love, the old woman's expecting me home. I told her I'd gone to a Masons' do.'

Junie smiled and followed him to the front door. 'I'll watch you from the balcony, all right?'

He kissed her quickly and went down in the lift whistling to himself. Junie was his lifeline. He made the trip from his home in Silvertown to Plaistow four times a week, sometimes more. Since his son's accident, he was relying on her increasingly. Stricken with guilt, he had grown apart from his wife, knowing in his heart that his son's accident was his fault. Like most men of his ilk, he couldn't live with that, so he blamed his wife.

It was much easier.

Leaving the block of flats he walked across the small concrete car park and got into his dark green Cosworth. He could see Junie's outline on the balcony and smiled to himself. She was so uncomplicated, was Junie. You shagged her and you had a laugh, and that was it. No long drawn-out conversations, no recriminations. No nothing. Not like his wife, who had known all along about Junie and didn't have the decency to keep her trap shut about it.

What the fuck did these women want? he asked himself.

He flashed his lights so Junie would smile to herself in the darkness. He knew how to be romantic – whatever that mad cow at home thought.

As he put the key in the ignition he heard a noise behind him, and as he turned to look, he felt a rope going around his neck. Next thing, the passenger door was opening and he smelt petrol. Trying to pull at the rope, he felt the coldness of the petrol as it hit his face and shoulders, and soaked into his pure wool jacket.

Half-fainting with fright and lack of breath, he felt the pressure on his throat ease. As he tried to straighten himself up in the car he saw the naked flame of the lighter.

'Tata, Danny.'

Junie watched in wonderment as she saw the man opening the passenger door of the car. She couldn't see exactly what he was doing because the lights outside the flats very rarely worked. The little

131

bastard muggers saw to that. It was only when she heard the screams and saw the flames that she realised something had gone very wrong. She wasn't to know that the men had rigged up the car earlier in the evening, while she and Danny had been drinking Blue Nun and bonking away in bed as if their lives depended on it. The deafening bang as the car exploded made her sink weakly to her knees.

Lights were going on all over the tower block, and all that Junie Dent could do was cry bitter tears, because all she had ever really wanted was gone.

Chapter Twelve

Georgio lay on his bunk thinking about Donna and the events of the day before. He had hardly slept in the night and consequently felt ill. He had not bothered to shave or shower and he could smell himself. The sweat was sickly sweet; he had been weight-training the day before, waiting for Donna's visit. He had gone out to her full of himself. Pleased to see her. And she had thrown him with her words.

It was like reliving a nightmare every time he thought about what had happened.

If she stopped seeing him now, he would have lost everything. The house was his main concern. He had placed it in her name, she owned it outright. If she divorced him he would have to make a claim on it. But then she could divorce him for desertion, lifers' wives were given that privilege, and he wouldn't have the heart to fight for half of everything. After giving it to her, it would look strange if he suddenly wanted it back. Anyway, he wanted it all; the house, the businesses and the money. He had sweated blood for it and he was entitled to it.

The noise around him was lessening. Men had slopped out, were waiting for their breakfast. He could hear Sadie's voice above the others, laughing and joking as usual. Though what she found to laugh about he couldn't tell. Georgio abhorred the whole prison setup. He hated being confined, being inside this cement box. Having every door locked behind him; not even having the privilege of turning a light switch on and off. He hated looking over his shoulder all the time, in case Lewis sent out a welcome party either to the showers or the gym. He had heard about a man who had had two immense weights dropped on his chest 'by accident'. Accidents happened easily in here; he could never allow himself to forget that.

It was enemy territory, and he was at war. Except that his enemy was now trying to be his friend and Georgio found that harder to cope with. He stared at the photos of Donna on his cell wall. Her shiny hair . . . Closing his eyes, he imagined he could smell her perfume, the particular scent of her as they made love. He saw himself parting her legs gently, waiting until he saw the redness between them. He

133

felt himself stirring. Wanted more than anything to be inside her, pumping away all his frustration and needs. How many mornings had she placed her arm across him and caressed him, and how many mornings had he kissed her and leapt from the bed, ready for the day and all it had to bring? He had wasted so much of her, had always known she was there, had taken her for granted. Good old Donna, his little wife, his hostess. He knew many men gave her a second glance and he had enjoyed that knowledge then, aware that she was wholly his. Now the thought tortured him, even though he knew she loved him.

Donna had been a good lover, a juicy lover. A woman who enjoyed being taken. But his tastes had begun to run to younger women who took the initiative, who took him while he lay back and watched. He told himself he made love to Donna and he fucked them. But the fucking was more exciting than anything he had ever experienced with Donna.

Timmy came into the cell smelling sharply of carbolic soap and Wash & Go.

'All right, Georgio? That's some bonk on you've got there. Thinking about home, are we?'

Georgio stood up, unembarrassed by Timmy's observations. 'It's a piss proud actually. What's the occasion? Should I wish you Happy Birthday?'

Timmy laughed amiably. 'Broomfield gets it this morning. Cheek though, ain't it, putting him in here with us? Ricky was like a fucking lunatic by all accounts. The boys are gonna have him first, in the showers. That's what got me down there. Big Ricky's gonna run his arse ragged! If you want a shower this morning, you'd better get down there quick smart, before the cabaret starts. No prizes for guessing which screws will be taking a front row seat, eh?'

Georgio picked up his shower gel and walked towards the shower, taking a clean towel from the pile at the bathroom doors. Standing under the freezing cold water he soaped himself all over quickly, then as he was rinsing off he saw Broomfield. The boy was standing uncertainly in the shower entrance.

'What you looking at?' Georgio's voice was harsh.

The boy shook his head. 'Nothing.'

Georgio turned off the shower and pulled a towel around his waist. Going towards the boy, he stood in front of him. 'Had your look?'

The boy was terrified and Georgio got a small kick out of this fact. 'You're scared of me, aren't you?'

Broomfield nodded.

'Enjoy raping that little girl, did you? Give you a big thrill that, did it? Want to go back for some more, do you?'

134

Broomfield's face was white with shock and distress.

Georgio poked him hard in the chest. 'Come on, big man, answer me! Scream, did she, when you was giving her one? Frightened out of her life I should think, a bit like you are now, I suppose. Horrible to be scared of someone bigger than you, ain't it? Knowing that they can beat your head in and you can't do a thing about it.'

Taking back his fist, Georgio slammed it into the boy's face. Broomfield started crying, big gasping sobs. Grabbing the younger man by his hair, Georgio forced him into a shower cubicle and slammed him into the wall. Pulling the boy's head back, he hissed, 'Shit scared, aren't you? Tell me what it was like with the little girl, Broomfield. Tell me what you did to her.'

He found his voice. It shook. 'I never meant it. I swear I never meant it! She wanted me to do it. I wouldn't have done it otherwise. Honestly, you've got to believe me . . .' He was hysterical now, his face an ugly mask of fear, blood and tears.

Ricky laBrett came into the shower room with three other men. He smiled at Georgio. 'You want some, Brunos, you can have him after me.'

Georgio shook his head. 'He's all yours. By the way, Ricky, according to him the little girl wanted it, he wouldn't have done it otherwise.'

Ricky laughed, and tightened the belt strap around his hand. 'Of course she did, like he wants it now, don't you, white boy?'

Georgio watched as the boy was pushed to the ground. He lay spreadeagled on the tiled floor, too frightened now to do anything but give out low moans.

As Georgio walked back to his cell he heard the high-pitched scream as Ricky entered him. Sometimes the queerboys came in handy, very handy indeed.

He sat in his cell chatting to Timmy while anguished cries from the shower room carried all over the block.

No one, warden or prisoner, lifted a finger to help Broomfield.

Lewis's radio was tuned to Classic FM as usual; Mozart's Horn Concerto provided the accompaniment to the multiple rape in the showers.

'You're looking better today, Donna.'

'I feel better actually, much better. I slept very well last night. Don't bother with any breakfast today, just tea, I think.'

Dolly nodded, cursing Donna under her breath. In the oven was eggs and bacon. She knew Donna must have smelled it while it was cooking.

135

'If anyone wants me, I'll be over at Maeve's, OK?'

Dolly nodded and watched Donna slip from the room. She listened out for the car's engine before going to the back door. Outside was Terry Rawlings. He was smoking a roll-up and sipping a mug of tea.

'She's gone to her mother-in-law's, and will you stop coming so close to the bloody house! She'll suss something out. Come in, I've got a plate of breakfast for you.' Terry grinned. Taking out his mobile, he rang through to Big Paddy to inform him of Donna's destination and then sat down to a large plate of bacon and eggs.

'Everything all right last night?'

Terry nodded, his mouth full of bacon. 'Not a whisper, Mrs Parkins. I think that Lewis has made his point now, with the car lot like. I reckon she's safe as houses.'

Dolly made a snorting sound. 'I don't trust that bugger as far as I can throw him!'

Terry grinned. 'Neither do we, Mrs Parkins, so stop worrying.'

Dolly made herself another cup of tea and lit her fifth cigarette of the morning. She wished to Christ she had as much faith as this lot.

'Well, you tell Paddy that she's cute, my Donna, and she'll suss you lot out sooner or later.'

Terry didn't bother answering, he just carried on eating his breakfast.

Maeve was happy. Her sons were all out, Pa Brunos was at the wholesalers, and she could sit down and read the paper in relative peace. In the middle of the problem page, her favourite part of the paper and the only reason she bought the *Sun*, there was a loud banging on her front door.

Annoyed, she got up to answer it, clumping down the stairs of the flat in a huff. Seeing Donna's outline her spirits soared. Flinging the door open, she shrieked, 'Hello, darling! Come away in. I wasn't expecting you today!'

Donna smiled. 'I thought I'd give you a visit before I went into work.'

She followed Maeve up the steep flight of stairs to the flat. While Maeve busied herself making another pot of tea, Donna took off her jacket and settled herself at the kitchen table.

The flat as usual was a mess, but a homely mess. Not dirty, untidy. Georgio had always hated his mother's haphazard housework. Maeve's attitude was, a house is for living in. Georgio wanted a showplace, a magazine advert home. Donna had argued over the years with him about this. His mother had brought up a large family, four boys and two girls, in a three-bedroomed flat – not an easy task.

136

Every penny Pa and Maeve had accumulated had gone on the children's clothing or education or back into the business. Their restaurant was well known in Canning Town, and both Maeve and her husband worked there from early afternoon until late in the evening. Georgio, like all the boys, had had to work as a waiter there, but unlike the others, Georgio had hated it. He looked back on those days with pain.

In a strange way Donna could understand his feelings. Georgio was a person who cared deeply what impression he made. Donna herself had helped out when she was younger, and sometimes she missed it. The rushing around, the laughter, the smell of Kleftiko and Retsina. The large brandies after a hard night's work and the long discussions about the evening and the different diners. Yet Georgio liked to eat there, liked to be seen in his parents' restaurant, as if he was saying to people: 'Look how far I've come. Look at the boy who ran ragged-arsed around Canning Town flats with his friends.'

Unlike Georgio, Donna had hated his mother having to wait on her, feeling all the time it was wrong.

'So what brings you here bright and early in the morning?' Maeve's voice was jocular but Donna knew that the older woman was aware she was there for a specific reason.

'Actually, Maeve, I'm after your Visiting Order. I know my name's on it, and I want to ask you a favour really. Do you mind if I use it and visit Georgio by myself? I need to talk to him.'

Maeve shrugged. 'It's yours, darlin'. I'll root it out for you in a moment. Everything all right, is it? Between you and him?' Maeve sipped her steaming tea nonchalantly, and Donna felt an urge to laugh.

'Yes, I suppose so.'

Maeve was surprised at her daughter-in-law's answer. 'Listen, Donna, I know my son's failings better than anyone. All my children have faults, and being a mother I'd be a fool if I didn't know about them. With Stephen it's gambling, with Nuala it's a penchant for the wrong kind of men. With Mary – well, you know Mary. She's a snob. Now Patrick, he's a ladies' man, and Mario . . . well, I wonder at times whether Mario likes the men too much, you know. Seems he spends more time with his friends than with women if you get my meaning. But Georgio, my Georgio, my firstborn, the apple of my eye and his father's namesake – Georgio always had his eye on the main chance.'

She gave Donna a wry grin. 'When he married you I sighed with relief, child. I'd always expected him to come home with some tall blonde eejit, with more between her legs than between her ears.

137

That's the type he favoured until you came along. But for all that, I know my Georgio better than anyone else. He thinks Mary's a snob, they fight like cat and dog, and I know for a fact she hasn't even dropped him a line all the time he's been inside, but in his own way he's a bigger snob than her. Because Georgio always had the idea he was better than everyone. Too good for this place, too good to be a Brunos. In fact, I think he wished Pa had taken my name, Sullivan. I think he'd feel more English then. He always hated being Greek, or half-Greek anyway. Always at pains to tell everyone he was English. They used to call the kids "Bubbles" when they were small. You know the rhyming slang, Bubble and Squeak, Greek. If he's giving you any grief now, I'll lather the arse off him, big as he is. You just tell me and I'll be up that prison and slapping his face before you can say knife! No matter how hard he thinks he is, I can still frighten the life out of him with a look!'

Donna laughed at the incongruity of Maeve telling Georgio off in Parkhurst's visiting room.

'Everything is fine, Maeve. I just want to see him again, on my own. We don't get much chance for visits, you know, and nine times out of ten someone else is there. I had a fight with Big Paddy yesterday because he wanted to accompany me, even though he wasn't even on the VO! I just want to see my husband again, that's all.'

Maeve smiled. 'You're a good girl, Donna. I hope that big eejit of mine realises that.'

'He does, Maeve.'

'You're a beautiful girl, a credit to him. Has he told you yet what really happened?'

Donna was taken back by her mother-in-law's words. 'I beg your pardon?'

Maeve laughed gently. 'I'm not so green as I'm cabbage-looking. I know that more went on there than meets the eye. You don't get accused of all sorts like my Georgio did unless you was on the fringes at least. Did he take the fall for someone bigger than him? It wouldn't surprise me if he was in it up to his neck! After all, he admitted supplying the cars, didn't he? So he knew more than he was letting on.'

Donna stared down at the grubby white tablecloth. 'He never admitted that, Maeve. He admitted selling the cars to Wilson, that's a different thing altogether.'

'Wilson had on a posh suit in court. Did he look the type to you to be able to buy two expensive cars for cash? I mean, it seemed fishy to me and I'm Georgio's mother.'

138

'Georgio and Davey sell to anyone with the money, and I myself have dealt with car dealers who look like they're on the dole and yet have wads of money in their pockets. So, no, it doesn't seem strange to me at all.' Donna could hear her voice rising and fought to keep it at an even level.

'All right, love, calm down, it was just a thought. You're his wife, and I'm his mother. We're the two women closest to him. We both know him inside out, but maybe in different ways. Stephen says he stripped the businesses, do you know why?'

Donna stood up and went to her handbag for cigarettes. 'Look, what is this, Maeve? Am I on trial now along with Georgio? You missed your vocation, you should have joined the CPS.'

Maeve was flabbergasted. Never once, in all the years she had known Donna, had the girl spoken to her like that. But she wasn't a girl anymore, and Maeve admitted this to herself. She was a woman, a woman of nearly forty who only looked like a girl because she had never been scarred by the trials of childrearing. Only the want of them. They had all looked after Donna and now, after five months without her husband, it seemed she could look after herself.

'I'm sorry, Donna, I don't know what's wrong with me lately. I apologise for interrogating you like that!'

Donna turned to face her and smiled. 'I'm sorry too, Maeve. Maybe I'm too touchy. If I could just have the VO . . .'

Maeve jumped from her seat and left the kitchen to find the Visiting Order. 'Of course, I'll get it for you.'

Donna closed her eyes and lit herself a cigarette. Never had she had cross words with Maeve before. But her saying all those things about Georgio hurt Donna, because deep down she knew they were all true. Now Georgio wanted to drag her into the mire with him, and after yesterday she knew in her heart she was going to let him.

Stephen was in his office when Donna turned up there. He was interviewing two girls from Manchester who had decided to take on TS, as it was known, as a sideline. Telephone Sex brought Stephen in nearly eight thousand pounds a week. He was forever buying new airtime and changing numbers, because Oftel caught up with him, but the legislation was no problem. It was only a warning and maybe the threat of a fine. Within twenty-four hours they were up and running once more. The regular clients had a landline phone number where they called, gave their credit card number, explained what they wanted and then were given a number to ring. A lot of the girls had phones at home; others had mobiles. It depended on the girl's situation. Some worked from their local park, chatting into the

139

phone while they watched their kids on the swings. Others worked from pubs and clubs. That was the best thing about it: you could do this work anywhere. One thing all the girls had in common was that they despised the customers and joked about them shamelessly.

Della Markham and Josie Whalley were both young prostitutes who wanted to take on TS as a way of making extra money. They could average ten pounds from each call, which meant up to a hundred pounds a day tax free.

Donna sat outside Stephen's office and waited while he finished his interview. His secretary Carmel was an austere woman in her forties who took her job seriously. She made Donna a coffee and then went into the office to announce her arrival. Donna was amazed to see the two girls who were interviewed. They didn't look like escorts any sane man would want to be seen with. She picked up a magazine and flicked through it. Stephen's offices were white, almost clinical. Two large prints were on the wall, both of women in high-fashion poses. Carmel's desk was practically clear with only two phones and a large ledger. A fax machine stood inside Stephen's room. It seemed very sparse to Donna but she didn't really give it much thought.

This was only her second visit here, and the constant ringing of the phones amazed her. She had never realised escorts were in such demand. Georgio had gone to great pains to assure her this wasn't anything to do with call girls, but after looking at the two young women in Stephen's office, she was beginning to wonder.

Since the revelations from Georgio she was beginning to wonder lots of things: it seemed she had been just a bit too naive to be true. She heard a high-pitched laugh and stared at the office door. It opened and Stephen was seeing the two girls out.

'You can rely on us, Mr Brunos, we know all the tricks, believe me!'

He smiled tightly. 'If you could leave your details with my secretary, I'll get back to you.' He turned to Donna, obviously embarrassed. 'Donna, do come in. Carmel, a pot of coffee when you're ready.'

Carmel was looking at the two girls with distaste. She nodded almost imperceptibly at his words.

Donna stepped into the office and sat down. 'I can't see them escorting anyone, Stephen.'

He grinned. 'Neither can I, Donna! One of my friends sent them. I had to see them as a favour really. They'll never get any work from me, I can tell you. My girls are all like Miss Jean Brodie's!'

Donna smiled as she said: 'The *crème de la crème*!'

'Precisely. Now what can I do for you?'

140

'I want some help from you actually. I was wondering if you could give me some advice.'

'Of course.'

'I want to pass over the main work on the sites to Paddy. I've done all that I can there now, and there's no real reason any longer for me to be constantly on the sites. Everyone knows I can do it, so if I delegate to Paddy I think I'll probably have more time for the office work, which is what I do best.'

'So what do you want from me? You seem to have everything sorted out OK.'

'What I want from you is advice on how much I should pay him for the extra work. I was thinking of bringing him in on a percentage, like a bonus scheme, you know. Say two percent?'

Stephen raised his eyebrows and shook his head. 'I don't know what Georgio will have to say about that.'

'With respect,' Donna told him, 'Georgio isn't running the businesses – I am. I feel that Paddy has put in an awful lot of time and energy and should be rewarded.'

'Well, yes, I can see what you're getting at . . .'

'Good,' she said briskly. 'I always find it helps to talk things through, don't you? By the way, I was unaware until last night that Georgio has a twenty-five percent interest in this place. Or should I say, *I* have a twenty-five percent interest? I was going through Georgio's papers and wondered exactly what Talkto Enterprises was. Then I finally found an address for it in Georgio's phone book, and it was here. I thought this was called Brunos Escort Agency? I assume you changed the name at some point. What I am really interested in, Stephen, is where my twenty-five percent of the profits is going?'

The atmosphere in the room was electric. Stephen's dark handsome face looked amazed. Donna relaxed in her leather chair and smiled at him charmingly.

He regained his composure. 'The profits for Talkto are being ploughed back into the business for the first two years, Donna. Georgio will tell you that much himself. You should start realising a profit in the next few months. I will get my accountant to have the books ready for your perusal by the weekend. That's if you insist on seeing them?' His voice was stiff.

'I do insist, Stephen. I insist because it seems you and my husband have a habit of starting up businesses and putting my name on them. Now the money from this enterprise would come in very handy at the moment – I need capital and I hope you are going to tell me that I have some. Because these premises in Soho can't be cheap, the escort agency must be doing a roaring trade, and

141

Talkto – whatever that is – must be doing OK or I would have thought the partnership would have been dissolved. So how well is it doing and what exactly is it?'

Stephen was saved from answering by Carmel arriving with the coffee. When she had left the room, Donna sugared her own coffee in silence.

'Talkto is a phone line. You see them all the time in papers and magazines. You know the ones. "How to cope with bereavement" or "How to cope with arthritis". We have been gradually setting up a small library of different lines; they are going quite well in fact. We also do sex lines. You know: "How to achieve orgasm", "What to do if your husband's impotent". They are the bigger moneyspinners, I admit, but they are perfectly legal and they provide a service.'

Donna smiled. 'So that's what Talkto is. How does the setup work?'

Stephen shrugged. 'You phone an 0898 number, you listen to a recorded message. The calls can last anything up to ten minutes. They supply leaflets etc, you leave your phone number and we send them on.'

Donna sipped her coffee. 'I see.'

Stephen picked up his own coffee and said acidly, 'Nothing illegal about that, is there?'

Donna frowned. 'I never suggested there was, Stephen. I just wanted to know exactly what my name is being used for. I don't think you or Georgio give me credit for even a few brains in my head. I find my name is being used for all sorts and neither of you thinks I have a right to be informed. I have already had this out with Georgio and now I'm having it out with you. If I am to run these businesses properly then I need to know what's going on.'

Stephen interrupted her. 'You're not running this business! You're nothing but a sleeping partner. Georgio put up an amount of money in your name. You have no say in running it, Donna.'

'I have the right to see the paperwork though, and I want to see it this weekend, as arranged.'

'You'll get all the relevant information, Donna, don't worry.'

'But I'm *not* worried, Stephen. It's you who seems worried.'

He stood up. 'If you'll excuse me, I'm very busy, Donna.'

She stood up too and walked to the door. Opening it, she saw another girl sitting outside waiting to be interviewed. The girl was small, with backcombed black hair and heavy make-up. She wore a tight red Lycra dress and high heels. She was chewing gum loudly.

'Another favour for a friend, Stephen?' Donna's eyebrows rose as she spoke.

142

He watched her as she walked from the office. His breath was coming fitfully, so great was his temper.

Carmel carried on with her phone call, seemingly unaware of the atmosphere around her.

Donna drove out of London and on to the A13 bound for home. She was going to go through Georgio's office with a fine-tooth comb, and then tomorrow she would visit him fully primed. Before she agreed to his newest scheme she wanted to know everything that was going on. It seemed she had been a fool over the years, and in a way she didn't blame Georgio for keeping her in the dark.

She had been like a child in a lot of respects. He looked after her, patted her on the head when she'd been a good girl, and gave her a present when the fancy took him. For her part she had allowed this treatment of herself and now she was wondering why.

Why the hell had she allowed herself to be treated so shabbily? Why hadn't she done something about it – asserted herself before now? Her husband was in prison doing eighteen years, their lives were destroyed, his businesses were going down the pan, and she had known nothing, nothing at all. She had not even guessed that something was wrong.

Was it because she was so frightened of him casting her aside if she pried? She knew he had cultivated Harry Robertson and the others because they were on the Council, and Harry dealt with Planning. But somehow that didn't really seem illegal because everyone they knew was doing it and they paid their taxes. What was the difference?

Now she was finding out so much about her husband, and none of it was good.

Stephen's offices in Soho were for prostitutes, but hadn't she known that deep down long ago? Hadn't she guessed that, and shrugged it off? Stephen's business was his business.

That had always been the way. Donna had never pried and now she was sorry. Sorry because she was finding it out all at once and it was killing a little bit of her every day.

All she wanted was Georgio home, back in her bed, his arms around her and the knowledge that he'd be there all the time.

She would do anything to gain that end. Anything.

In a way she felt responsible for Georgio and what happened to him. If she had stood beside him as a wife should, as Carol Jackson did with Davey, maybe he wouldn't have got so deeply involved in everything. The hotels that died a death in Asia, and the Talkto business. She wasn't stupid, she knew exactly what those phone lines were for. She had known as soon as she saw Stephen's name alongside

143

her own, because he had always dealt in women, his mother knew that and she knew that, though it was never actually discussed.

It was the old story. If you didn't talk about it then it had never happened.

Like her life with Georgio, in fact.

Don't ask your husband what he's been doing because he just might tell you, then you'd have to do something about it. Well, she was going to do something about it. Twenty years too late maybe, but she'd do something anyway.

Because the one thing she wanted now, more than anything, was to have her husband back beside her.

Tomorrow she would talk to him properly, and then give him her final answer. She had a feeling she was going to do whatever he asked. After all, why break the habit of a lifetime?

She had given him twenty years of her life, and could not imagine giving herself to anyone else. He was hers, right or wrong. *Hers.*

He was all she had, and she loved him with a ferocity that startled her it was so strong.

She knew now that no matter what he did, she would forgive him, as she had over the years forgiven him his women, his separate lifestyle, and his periodic neglect of her.

He was the only man she had ever really wanted, the only man to share her bed, and the only man she could love.

No matter what he did, he was hers, and she would move heaven and earth to keep it that way.

144

Chapter Thirteen

Paddy watched as the girl gyrated around the stage. Her cosmetically-enlarged breasts looked even more false in the harsh lights. As she bent towards him they hung down from her ribcage like two lumps of cement. Paddy sighed in boredom. Her face was angelic and he wondered if her father knew what she did for a living, and if he knew, whether he cared.

He glanced at his watch and frowned. Stephen was cutting it fine. Sipping his scotch he watched the girl once more, her swivelling hips making him want to laugh. Instead he looked around him at the men in the club. All were middle-aged, all had the shining expectant eyes of perverts, and all had half of bitter in front of them. He saw Stephen walk in at the club doorway and sat back in his seat. He hated these places; they were depressing and the odour of cheap perfume and male sweat made him feel queasy.

Stephen slipped into the seat beside him. Ignoring the girl on the stage, he said peremptorily: 'Did you know Danny Simmonds was murdered last night?' He was gratified at Paddy's look of shock.

'You're joking!'

'I'm not, Paddy. He was burnt alive in his car outside his bird's flat. You know his boy was run over, don't you?'

Paddy nodded. 'A crying shame that. I never had much time for Simmonds meself as you know, but the lad was nothing to do with any of it. Lewis is getting out of hand.'

Stephen sighed. 'That's Frankie White, Peter Wilson and Danny Simmonds. All brown bread. All that's left of the blaggers now is Georgio, and unlike the others he wasn't there. Lewis wants all the dosh, and you know the worst of it, don't you? Frankie and Danny are only dead because Georgio wouldn't tell Lewis where he hid it.'

Paddy sipped at his drink and shrugged. 'Well, I'm sorry, Stephen, but I'm not going to lose any sleep over them. What's done is done.'

'Well, don't you think my brother should tell that bastard Lewis where the dosh is?'

145

Paddy laughed harshly. 'No, actually, I don't. It's his only insurance, isn't it? Once he opens his mouth about it, then he follows them to hell.'

Stephen watched the girl as she picked up her few scraps of clothing and left the stage.

'I wish I knew where Georgio had stashed the money, don't you?' He looked straight into Paddy's eyes and Paddy returned his gaze without blinking.

'No, I don't. And I'll give you a bit of advice, Stephen. You're Georgio's brother and he loves you, but like me, he can see right through you.' And Paddy watched as Stephen's face hardened.

A plump woman came on to the stage in a tight red satin basque. She would never see forty-five again, and as the strains of 'Ma, He's Making Eyes at Me' blared out of the loudspeaker, Paddy stood up to leave. Leaning closer to Stephen, he winked and said, 'Now this one is much more your cup of tea, eh? Old enough to be your mother.'

Laughing loudly, he walked from the smoky club, leaving Stephen fuming, not because of what Paddy had said about the stripper but because he had been foolish enough to come out into the open.

Settling back in his seat he watched the woman's act until the end. Then he left the club as unobtrusively as possible.

Chapter Fourteen

Dolly looked into the room Georgio used as his office and tutted loudly. 'Did you find what you were looking for last night?'

Donna was walking down the stairs. 'I'll clear it all up when I get back later,' she promised.

Dolly flapped a hand. 'Don't worry, I'll clear it up for you after breakfast.'

'I'd really rather you left it alone, Dolly. I want to put the stuff back myself so I can make some rhyme and reason out of it, all right? Thanks anyway for offering.'

Dolly nodded, bewildered. 'Whatever you like, love. My, you look beautiful. You'll knock your man's eyes out. New, is it?'

Donna smiled. 'I bought it a while ago and never wore it. I thought I'd give it an airing today. How did you know I was going to see Georgio again?'

Dolly walked through to the kitchen. 'Oh, Maeve mentioned it when she rang. Why? Is it a big secret or something?'

Donna found herself getting annoyed. 'No, it's just I wondered how you knew, that's all. It seems to me lately that everyone knows everything about me before I do.'

Dolly faced her and said gently, 'You need a rest, darlin', to get away for a bit. You're getting paranoid about everything.'

'And where do you suggest I go, Dolly?' Donna sighed. 'Or haven't you and Maeve sorted that out yet?' Even as she spoke, Donna was aware how unfair she was being. She put her arms around Dolly's waist and said, 'Oh, I'm sorry. But I've got a lot on my mind lately. I hate all this constant questioning, you see. You never wanted to know so much before.'

Dolly hugged her back, thinking: *You never had Lewis hanging over you before* – but she kept her own counsel.

'I worry about you, ducks.'

'I know you do, but I'm a grown woman and I can look after myself. Now I must go – I'll see you later. If Davey rings or Paddy, tell them they can get me on my mobile.'

147

'Okey doke. Give your man all my love, won't you?'

Donna smiled. 'Of course I will.'

Five minutes later she pulled out of her drive, unaware of the black Sierra that followed her.

Donna noted the looks she gathered as she walked into the visiting room at Parkhurst. Taking a seat at a small table, she observed the families around her. Children played with their fathers while their mothers looked on. Women visiting sons stared around them in bewilderment, as if wondering what they were doing there. Prisoners watched their wives with interest, drinking in the sights and sounds of their families. A man nearby bounced a young child on his knee as he chatted to his family; he could have been anywhere, the casual way he was acting. As if being in this prison environment was natural. Which she supposed it was, to a majority of the men.

A slim young man, effeminate-looking, walked over to her.

'Hello, my name's Albert but they call me Sadie. You're Donna Brunos, aren't you?'

She nodded. 'How do you do.'

'I know your husband Georgio. He shares a cell with a friend of mine, Timmy. I expect he's mentioned him?'

Donna nodded, unable to decide how to treat the young man before her.

'I just wanted to say I love your suit, dear. The blue colour brings out your eyes. You should always wear suede. You can carry it off, love, you're so thin, see, and that short skirt shows off your legs perfectly. What is it? Italian?'

Donna nodded wordlessly.

'I thought so. Lovely hand with suede and leather, the Eyeties. Well, I'd better get back to me visitor. Nice meeting you anyway.'

'Nice meeting you as well.' She smiled at him as he sat back down with his visitor, an elderly man in a business suit.

She was grateful to see Georgio being led in, and stood up and waved.

Georgio's face was a study in pleasure as he saw who his visitor was. Rushing over to Donna, he kissed her hard on the lips for two minutes until a screw called out: 'All right, Brunos, that's enough. You ain't got conjugal visits yet, mate.'

Donna felt her face go scarlet at his words.

'It's so good to see you, darling. I've missed you so much.' As they sat down he grasped her hand tightly. 'You're the only woman I know who still blushes. Nowadays the girls are too knowing by half. It's one of your most endearing qualities. You look fantastic, Donna.

148

That suit's a bit near the mark though, ain't it?'

Donna was pleased to see the jealous look on his face. 'I rather like it myself.'

Georgio grinned. 'So does every old lag in here, by the looks of it! You're beautiful, Donna. I know I never told you that often enough but I always thought it, Donna, I swear.'

She felt her lips trembling as she looked into his face. He was so handsome, this husband of hers.

'I'm sorry about the other day,' he went on. 'You were right in all you said. But I never wanted you to worry, you've got to believe that. I always only wanted you to have the best. I was foolish, I know, getting involved with everything. But I never dreamt it would all go sour, not for a moment.'

Donna smiled sadly. 'I know about Talkto, Georgio, I know about everything.'

He stared into her face. 'I never actually had anything to do with Talkto . . .'

Donna cut him off. 'I know that, Stephen explained it all to me. If, and it's a big if, I am going to help you, Georgio, you must be honest with me.'

He felt his heart lift at her words.

'I always knew inside that you were not exactly kosher, as you would put it. Over the years I guessed a lot, even if I never actually put my thoughts into words. You're my husband, and I love you. I've always loved you, Georgio. Even after all this.' She held out her arms in supplication. 'I still love you.'

Georgio's eyes were filled with tears. 'I've always loved you, baby, you know that.'

Donna nodded. 'This Lewis, how much danger are you in from him?'

Georgio shrugged. 'A lot. As I told you, he wasted Wilson. He owns everyone in here – the screws, the cons, everyone. He sank a lot of money abroad with me, and now he thinks I've tucked him up. I tell you, Donna, no one could get me out of here legally. He's already told me that I have no chance of appeal. He thinks it's all a big joke. I've told him some old cock and bull story about locating his money and paying it back, which is keeping him sweet for the moment, but I'll never be able to raise the kind of sum he wants. Even if we sold the house and all we own.'

'Has he really got that much sway?'

Georgio laughed bitterly. 'Look, Donna, most people have no idea about what's going on in this country. Lewis can get a motion tabled in the Commons if he wants to. It seems everyone is for sale one way

149

or another and he knows exactly how much they cost. He has been running his different businesses for years. They only got him on fraud charges. They can't prove nothing else as he's got powerful friends. In fact, I wouldn't be surprised if he upped and walked out of here one day with a pardon. If you can buy one, then Lewis can afford it.

'Everyone is afraid of him here,' he went on, 'everyone. And it's nothing to be ashamed of either, because hardened criminals are scared of him. You don't know what it's like in here, love. It's the pits, believe me. Lewis even has his food specially cooked for him. He has more privileges than the bloody governor!

'Yesterday they gang-raped a young lad who was in on a child-sex case. He'd raped a five-year-old girl. Lewis saw to it that he was hurt. The men respect him for that. These are the kind of people you're dealing with. The lad's cell will be burnt out later on tonight when he comes back from the hospital wing. These men are the scum of the earth and Lewis is in charge of them. He has henchmen who'd torture you just for a laugh, for something to do. Lewis himself is a violent personality who enjoys inflicting pain. It's like living in a nightmare, Don Don. I have to escape from it. That is the only way I'll ever get out of here, short of being carried out in a box.'

Donna licked her dry lips, her face a mask of disbelief. 'But how will we get you out?'

Georgio grinned. 'I have an old mate, Alan Cox, who owes me a favour. We go back a long time. Alan was once like Lewis, although he didn't do things for fun. If Alan hurt someone, it was for a reason, and they were all in the game. Like an occupational hazard, if you like. If you go to see him, he'll help us, I know he will. But you must keep it to yourself. Don't even tell Stephen – don't tell *anyone* what you're doing. That's the best way. The fewer people who know the better. Lewis has a long arm and big ears, darlin', and he's dangerous. I don't want you to get hurt.'

'What does this Alan do now?'

'He runs a nightclub up West,' Georgio told her, 'and a couple of restaurants. He was put away for murder, did his time, kept his head down and got out. He didn't want to go back to the hag of the life so he retired.'

Donna's eyes widened. 'Who did he murder?'

'That's the funny thing. Alan kicked to death a small-time hustler called Tang. He was from Chinatown. It was penny halfpenny stuff – a bit of drugs, he ran a few girls, nothing too elaborate. No one knows why he did it. Alan never said and I've never asked.'

'How come you know all these people, Georgio?'

150

He shrugged. 'I thought we'd already established that I have been a naughty boy. In my game, building and motors, you meet all sorts, love. I never judged them, just took their money – money that kept us in the manner we had become accustomed to.'

'It also got you in a lot of trouble.' This was said with some bitterness.

'I was small-time, Donna,' he objected. 'I was on the fringes. How was I to know it would all blow up in me boat? It never had before.'

She sighed heavily. 'No, I suppose it didn't. So where do I find this Alan?'

'You'll find him any night of the week at his restaurant in Greek Street. Don't worry about talking to him, you can tell him anything, absolutely anything. Explain about Lewis, he'll need to know all about that. His restaurant is called Amigo's. Make sure you mention you're Georgio's wife, OK? Let him know you're my wife before you do any talking.'

'All right then. I'll go tonight.'

Georgio grabbed her hand. 'You're a good girl, Donna. I knew I could trust you.'

'Do you really think he can get you out of here?'

'If anyone can, Alan can.'

'Say he does, what then?'

Georgio kissed her fingers. 'One thing at a time, baby. Let's concentrate on getting me out first, then we'll start making plans. Now, how about a cup of coffee?'

Donna handed him her purse and watched as he bounded over to the snack bar.

She had a feeling that she was mad, that the whole thing was mad.

She lit herself a cigarette and wasn't surprised to see that her hands were shaking.

Donna parked in Frith Street and walked slowly to Greek Street. It was early evening to the people in Soho on a Friday night, just gone ten o'clock. Donna took in her surroundings with interest. As she had driven around looking for a parking space she had been amazed at the women in the stripjoint kiosks. Some walked out on to the pavement scantily clad, shouting their wares and the delights to be found inside the small cinemas and clubs.

One young girl was pear-shaped with enormous legs and tiny breasts encased in a tight Lurex shorts suit, her black tights sporting large ladders and holes in them. Another in Old Compton Street was arguing with a passer by who had shouted something obscene at her,

151

her loud voice, with its disgusting language, shocking Donna to the core. As she had crawled along behind a black cab full of businessmen in suits, she had been amazed to see that the girl was only about sixteen, her face plastered in make-up and her eyes unnaturally bright. Donna's last sight of the girl was of her giving a particularly rude sign to the man's back and laughing uproariously as she did so. The black cab discharged its customers outside a delicatessen and Donna was pleased to be able to drive on, frightened for a moment that the girl might turn her attention to her.

As she approached Amigo's, she could smell a delicious aroma of fresh baked bread. The smell led her into the doorway of the small restaurant, lifting her spirits with its homely associations.

A young man dressed in a dinner suit walked towards her, smiling pleasantly. 'Can I help you, madam?' His voice had a real Italian accent and Donna found herself smiling back at him.

'I am here to see Mr Alan Cox. I am Mrs Georgio Brunos.'

The man looked at her long and hard before answering. 'Mr Cox does not see people without an appointment.'

Donna swallowed heavily. 'If you would be so kind as to tell Mr Cox I am here, I am sure he will see me. Tell him it's Georgio Brunos's wife, make sure you emphasise that fact.'

Without waiting for an answer she settled herself on a stool at the bar and ordered a drink. 'Could I have a white wine and soda, please?'

The young man behind the bar looked at the maître d' before he served her. Donna watched in the mirrors behind the bar as the man nodded his acquiescence. She glanced around the empty restaurant in distress. She felt as if she had gatecrashed an audience with the Pope.

'While you have your drink, I'll see if Mr Cox is available.' The words were spoken with an air of indifference.

Donna nodded and took the proffered glass. She gulped at her drink to hide her embarrassment. Not for the first time that day, she wondered if she was indeed mad even to consider doing what Georgio had asked her.

Ricardo walked up the steep staircase that took him to Alan Cox's office. The restaurant was quiet. Once it livened up Alan would come down for an hour and preside over it, chatting to the customers and making sure everyone was enjoying themselves.

The clientèle of Amigo's was very select, from publishing and advertising to television executives who preferred the muted luxury of Amigo's to the shabbiness of the Groucho. It also catered to a select community of villains, men who wore handmade suits

152

and discussed business there with their bankers and accountants, hoping to impress. They gave the place an air of danger. Unlike Langan's, where anyone could book a table, or Del'Ugo, your face had to fit at Amigo's. It did a roaring if subdued trade. More than one star had been unobtrusively shown the door; Alan Cox had ejected more than a few himself. Amigo's was a place where you could bring your wife, your mother, your mistress or your business associates. The main restaurant was for smoking, the more select part was situated down in the basement. To get into the basement you had to have clout, and plenty of it.

Alan Cox sat in his office preparing the menus for the coming week while his chef, David Smalls, stood waiting patiently for his boss's decisions.

Cox perused the menus and made notes on the typewritten sheets. Amigo's always had a set menu. It was usually so delicious people chose it immediately. At forty-five pounds a head it was the cheapest way to eat in Amigo's. There were no house wines here, the least expensive started at seventeen pounds a bottle. In Amigo's you ate and drank and you expected to drop at least one hundred and fifty pounds a couple for that pleasure. It frequently amazed Alan Cox that people fought to patronise his establishment.

David watched his employer smile slightly, and relaxed. 'These are good. You can use them from tomorrow. I have changed only two, Monday's and Friday's. How many times do I have to tell you I like fish on the menu on Fridays?'

'Sorry, Mr Cox.'

The older man sighed and puffed on a large cigar. 'And how many times must I tell you that as well, David? The name's Alan or Al, take your pick, but please stop calling me Mr Cox. I'm not in my dotage yet!'

David grinned. 'I'll get these down to the kitchens. I thought the pâté was particularly good last night, didn't you?'

Alan Cox nodded. 'Is it the work of that young kid again?'

David nodded. 'He's certainly got a gift, Alan.'

'Well, look after him, Davey boy.'

There was a discreet knock on his office door and he called out, 'Enter.' As David left with the menus, Alan greeted his maître d'.

'Ricardo, what can I do for you?'

'There's a lady downstairs to see you, Mr Cox.'

He frowned. 'Did she give a name?'

'She certainly did. It's Mrs Georgio Brunos.'

Alan's eyebrows rose a fraction. 'What's she look like?'

'Late-thirties, well-dressed – I'd say she was wearing an original.

153

Slim, not too tall, and she has good legs. Very good bone structure, classic beauty, light makeup. And she is very determined.'

Alan grinned. 'Then send her up!' As Ricardo walked to the door, Alan added, 'What size shoe do you reckon she wears?'

Ricardo paused and thought. 'A tenner says she wears a size four.'

Alan laughed. 'You're on!'

Five minutes later, Donna was on her way up the thickly-carpeted stairs, her drink carried on a small salver by Ricardo, who ushered her courteously into the large office.

Donna's first reaction to Alan Cox was one of absolute astonishment. He was so big he seemed to fill the entire room with his presence. His hair was gold, a dirty-sovereign colour, thick and luxurious, and cut into a college boy style that suited his tanned face beautifully. His eyes were a deepsea blue that was practically violet. His mouth was full. Only his Roman nose was at variance with his other features, a lasting reminder of his years as a bareknuckle boxer.

Alan Cox had earned his first real stake, five hundred pounds, at the back of a shoe factory warehouse in East Tilbury. Twenty-six fights later, he had made himself a small fortune, had travelled abroad to fight, and had lost only twice, once in Los Angeles to a huge Irishman called Rourke, and once in France, in a barn outside Toulouse, to a Frenchman called Pardou. He could not remember the name of any of the men he had beaten in the other twenty-four fights.

When he smiled at Donna, she saw white teeth, the only flaw being that his two front teeth overlapped slightly, but far from taking away from his general handsomeness, it seemed to enhance it.

'So you're Georgio's wife, then. Pleased to meet you, Mrs Brunos.' His voice was deep, clear, and although not pronounced, an East London inflection was there nonetheless. He made no attempt to disguise it. Donna felt her hand being shaken firmly but gently by a large meaty fist.

'How do you do, Mr Cox.'

Alan Cox smiled with delight. Brunos's old woman, he thought to himself, weren't a bad little piece.

'Sit yourself down, love. You can refresh our drinks, Ricardo, and hold the calls.'

The waiter bent slightly from the waist and Alan saw the smirk on his face and grinned to himself. Ricardo knew him better than he knew himself.

Donna sat down in a deep leather chair and crossed her legs. She noticed Alan Cox's interest and cursed under her breath. She should

154

have worn trousers. Alan Cox looked the type of man who ate women for breakfast, broke their hearts by lunchtime, and was thoroughly bored with them by supper.

He sat behind his large leather-topped desk, picked up a fresh cigar, cut off the top, and then proceeded to place it in a large glass of beer. Donna watched him in amazement.

'Give it a better taste, my love.' He wiped off the excess beer with his fingers then lit the cigar slowly, completely unconscious of his actions. For some reason Donna felt as if she had witnessed something personal and erotic. She hastily lit herself a cigarette to overcome her shyness.

'So what's your proper name? Mine's Alan as you probably know.'

'It's Donna, Donna Brunos.'

Alan smiled again, once more looking her over from head to foot. 'How's old Georgio getting on then? I heard he got the big one. He's on the Island, ain't he?'

Donna nodded. 'It was Georgio who asked me to come and see you, Mr Cox.'

'Well, I didn't think it was Mother Theresa who asked you to drop in, love.'

Donna was saved from answering by Ricardo's tap on the office door and his serving of the drinks.

When he had left them alone once more Alan said, 'So, what does Georgio want?'

Donna watched him puffing on his cigar for a while before she answered.

'Georgio asked me to tell you that he felt you owed him one. That's his terminology, not mine.'

'I'd never have guessed.'

She smiled at his quick retort. 'He needs help, Mr Cox, which is why I'm here.'

'I ain't got a lot of sway inside, not now I'm out anyway. I can get him a few little bits and bobs like. No drugs though . . .'

Donna's eyes widened. 'I most certainly would not ask for anything like that, Mr Cox, and I am sure Georgio wouldn't either.'

Alan grinned. 'All right, all right, keep your hair on, love. I never meant any harm. A lot of people sell a bit of whizz or a bit of puff inside. It helps you to do your time, and gives you a modicum of prestige. A lot of lags wouldn't touch it out here, but a long one, well, that puts a different complexion on it.'

Donna sighed in despair. This man was one of the most irritating people she had ever come across. He pre-empted all her moves and then proceeded to lecture her afterwards.

155

'If you would let me finish, Mr Cox . . .'

Alan laughed. 'Oh, am I getting on your nerves? My old mum used to say to me: "Alan, you could talk the hind legs off a table, my son!" ' He roared with laughter at his own wit. 'I lost her a year ago, bless her. I still miss the old bat.'

Donna smiled, while her insides twisted with nerves.

'Anyway, love, you carry on and I'll shut up.'

She took another deep breath. 'Georgio said that you would help him. There's something important he needs . . .' Her voice trailed off.

Alan held out his arms, waving the cigar around, its thick blue smoke spiralling all over the place.

'Well? What's he want then?'

Donna stared at the big amiable man in front of her, remembering that he was a murderer. She leaned forward and stubbed out her cigarette.

'He said before I asked you, to remind you that you and him went back a long time together. That you ran the streets as children, that you were very close.'

Alan grinned. 'We were. Me and Georgio were like that.' He crossed his fingers to emphasise the point. 'He did me a very big favour once, a long time ago. I will never forget that.'

He smiled at her in a friendly way before speaking again. 'Look, can I ask you something?'

Donna nodded.

'Do I make you nervous?'

She shook her head and said in a strong voice, 'No, Mr Cox, you don't make me nervous at all, why?'

Alan smirked as he pointed out, 'You just put your cigarette out in my bowl of peanuts.'

Donna looked into the small ceramic bowl and felt her heart sink down to her boots. Among the cashews and other nuts was the glowing ember of her St Moritz cigarette.

She stared at the bowl, her face scarlet with embarrassment. 'I am so sorry.'

Alan realised that she was near to tears and felt sympathy wash over him. He had assumed she would see the funny side of what she had done. Instead she was lighting yet another cigarette with shaking hands.

He watched her tightly drawn face as she pulled the smoke into her lungs, saw the faint circles under her eyes and the chipped nail varnish on the third finger of her right hand.

He saw the way she was sitting bolt upright in the seat, as if she had

156

a poker stuffed down the back of her very expensive suit, and the way her left eye twitched at the corner every now and then.

This was one very uptight lady, yet he had heard through the grapevine that she was running the whole shooting match for Georgio while he was banged up and, more startling, that she was making a bloody good job of it.

She was an anomaly all right, and he decided that he liked her a lot. She was too good for Georgio, he knew that. Much as he liked Georgio, he also knew him very well and this little lady was probably unaware of the half of it where her husband was concerned.

Alan stood up and walked around the desk. 'Look, calm yourself down and I'll pour you a nice brandy. Take a few deep breaths. It was only a few nuts, Donna, nothing major. I'm not going to bite your head off or anything, no matter what you've heard about me. I draw the line at killing women or children.'

He watched her face pale at the words and knew immediately that his reputation had preceded him. He was sorry, because he hated to intimidate anyone he didn't need to. His murder charge was what made his restaurant select; people whispered about it, and he played the part of the bad man gone straight. He was a perfect example of the villain gone legit. In fact he *was* legit. The fact amazed even him at times. He had no qualms about what he had done, rarely thought about it now, though there had been a time when it was on his mind constantly. But he had paid his so-called debt to society and now was free and clear. It was a long time ago and unless he was reminded of it, like now, he didn't think about it for weeks at a time. He went to his globe drinks cabinet and poured out a large brandy. He took it back to Donna and placed it in her hand.

'Look, love, I don't know what you've heard, but divide it by four and then halve it. I am a legitimate businessman, I am seeing you even though you didn't have an appointment, and I promise faithfully, cross me heart and hope to die, not to murder you or anyone else tonight. Now I can't say fairer than that, can I?'

Donna looked up into his face and felt a flush of shame roll over her. He knew what was wrong with her, the man could read her like a book.

'Drink your brandy,' he said kindly, 'and then just come out and say what it is Georgio wants. Whatever it is, I'll give it to him. I owe him one, as he so succinctly put it.' He smiled at her disarmingly.

Donna took a large gulp of the brandy, feeling it burn her throat as she swallowed. Looking into his face, she gathered up her courage and blurted out: 'Georgio wants you to get him out.'

157

She saw Alan's face drop, and it was his turn to go white. Donna sat watching for long moments before she spoke up. 'Did you hear what I said, Mr Cox?'

Alan Cox nodded. 'I heard, and there's only one thing I can say.'

Donna swallowed hard. 'What's that?'

'I think I'll join you in that brandy.'

Chapter Fifteen

Alan sipped his brandy and stared at the woman opposite him. She was smoking nervously. He got up and once more replenished her glass.

'I'm driving.'

Alan nodded. 'Don't worry. If push comes to shove, love, I'll get you driven home by one of my lads. They'll deliver your car for you at the same time. I do it for a lot of my customers. Why does Georgio want out so badly? I mean, he ain't asking me a small favour, is he? He's asking me to risk everything for him.'

Donna shrugged. 'All I can say is, Georgio said to remind you exactly what he did for you, though I can't because I don't know what it was.'

Alan smiled faintly. 'Then I'll tell you, shall I?'

He relit his cigar and settled himself once more in his seat. 'Your husband and I grew up together in Canning Town. Unlike Georgio's, my family weren't exactly respectable. My old man was a drunk, spent more time in the pub than he did in the house. I don't have to paint a picture, you look the type to watch Channel Four!' He smiled at her again. 'Well, old Pa Brunos, he took me under his wing, like. He used to take me and Georgio boxing together. I could have gone professional, but I didn't. Instead I became a street-fighter. A bareknuckle man. I'm a big bloke and I attracted a good crowd of people. You'd be amazed at the types who turn up to see two blokes punching the fuck out of each other.

'Well, me and Georgio, we still kept in touch. He got into his building lark and I got into the boxing scene. So professionally we were worlds apart, though Georgio used to come and see me fight, and we'd have the odd drink together in The Bridge House. Twelve years ago, I beat a man to death not five minutes from where we're sitting now. It was in Chinatown, actually. I did it in full view of a lot of people and I got life imprisonment. I am not going to tell you why I did it, that's a secret known only to me and a couple of other people.

While I was inside Georgio looked after my family. My wife

159

divorced me. I accepted that, we'd grown apart anyway. But Georgio looked after them all. My son was at Ampleforth, Georgio paid his fees, and my daughter was at home with her mum. She went to a convent nearby. Georgio made sure she had enough money. You see, when I got life, a certain person I was in partnership with did a runner with all our money. My wife would have had to sell the house, everything, to make ends meet. I wrote to Georgio and he came up trumps for me. He also sorted out the slag who'd tucked me up. I did seven years before I was eligible for parole and I was out after eight years and five days. Georgio did a lot for me.

'I'll never forget him for that. I also told him that I owed him one, and I stand by that statement now. So you can tell him that I will move heaven and earth to help him, but I can't make any promises. What he's asked me is a biggy. But if it's at all possible, I will make it happen. Now I can't say fairer than that, can I?'

Donna shook her head, unable to take in what the man had said.

Georgio had done all that and he had never once mentioned it to her. And though she admired and respected him for helping this man's family, another part of her was grievously wounded that he could have done all that without giving her so much as an inkling of it. He had never once mentioned it to her. She did not even know this man or his family had existed until today.

'How's he bearing up?' Alan asked now.

Donna sipped her drink to wash down the tears that had welled up inside her.

'Very well under the circumstances. He hates it in there, though. He was fitted up. A man called Wilson pointed the finger at him.'

'I heard about that. Shame he's brown bread, ain't it? No chance of making him change his statement now, is there?'

Donna shook her head again. 'None. There's a man called Lewis involved. Georgio got into something with him, and now Lewis is on the Island with him. He's making things very difficult for Georgio. He got in with the big boys, I'm afraid, right over his head. Now this is the upshot.'

'I know Lewis of old,' Alan said. 'Georgio should have had a bit more savvy than to have done any kind of business with him. He's an arsehole, if you'll pardon my French. A ginger beer and all. I heard Lewis loves it in there, like a holiday for him. I also heard he bought himself out of Broadmoor. The man's a psychopath. I can understand why Georgio wants out. If Lewis is on his tail, he's better off as far away as possible. Has he decided where he wants to go?'

Donna shook her head.

'Well, I've got a villa in Spain. He could hole up there for a while. I

160

own a timeshare complex out there. Nothing fishy, all my places are top class. I don't rip anyone off, never have. I got into the timeshare there a few years back. I have a large place myself I use to take me kids on their holidays. My little grandson is four now. You'd love him. Right little hard man he is.'

Donna found herself smiling at his proud voice. 'How old are your children?'

'My Lisa is twenty-five and my son Alan Junior is twenty-one. I am forty-nine years old, before you ask.'

'I never knew Georgio had done so much for you. He never said anything.'

Alan smiled. 'Well, he wouldn't, would he? It's between me and him, the same way all this will be between me and you. I ain't making any promises. I'll look into this thoroughly, and if there's a chance, then we'll be off.'

Donna finished her brandy in one gulp, grateful for its burn. She had never felt so misused in all her life. Georgio could be cruel at times, so cruel. He'd lived a completely separate life from her and she had never realised it until now.

Another part of her mind was telling her that the things she had found out about him, had she known them at the time, would only have caused her sleepless nights. Georgio had probably guessed this, which was why he'd never told her, but had looked after her according to his lights. As far as her husband was concerned, he had done well by her. She had to hold on to that thought.

Anything he had done, had been for her as well as himself. She had lived a good life with him, she had had everything she'd wanted, more than anyone could want in fact. They had travelled the world, lived like kings, she had accounts at Harrods and Fortnum's to name but a few. She had never questioned where all the money came from, she had just spent it. If she had known, she would have been worried and Georgio had always been at pains to stop her worrying about anything.

Alan watched the different expressions flickering across her face and sighed. She seemed a nice woman, a respectable type, definitely too good for Georgio.

'Come on, let's go down and get something to eat,' he suggested. 'All this drink is making me hungry.'

Donna stood up unsteadily. She felt much better after she had consumed a large plate of spaghetti marinara, the clams still having the salty tang of the sea. It had been cooked to perfection. She wiped her mouth daintily with her napkin and Alan poured out a glass of sparkling water for her.

161

'Drink that, it'll dilute the brandy.'

Donna did as she was told. 'That was excellent!'

Alan smiled. 'I've always liked me grub. Banged up, the food is terrible – unless you cook your own. Lots of old lags become quite good cooks on a long stretch. Sex and food are the two most important things to men – and not necessarily in that order!'

Donna laughed with him. He was an attractive personality. Big enough to win attention wherever he went, Alan Cox was also gentle and kind. The kindness shone through his rough exterior, especially when talking about his children or his grandson.

'I'm going to start putting feelers out in the morning,' he promised her. 'I take it Georgio wants you as the go-between?'

Donna nodded. 'I suppose so.'

Alan grinned. 'You don't sound too sure.'

She finished the glass of water and said seriously, 'I don't know anything any more, Alan. I thought I knew a lot once. About my husband, my life. I thought I was settled. I thought I would carry on as I was until I died. I felt safe. Now, I have a husband who's doing eighteen years, I am sitting in a restaurant with a man who, if you'll forgive my saying it, murdered someone in cold blood not far from where we're sitting, and I am planning the escape from prison of someone who didn't even have the decency to tell me he kept your family for years. I am beginning to wonder if I actually know him. In fact, I'm beginning to wonder exactly what Georgio is capable of.'

Alan heard the loneliness and the hurt in her voice. Realised that Georgio, as usual, had ridden roughshod over the little woman in front of him. She was out of her depth, way out of her depth. She was frightened, intimidated and worried, deeply worried. She wasn't the usual villain's wife. That sort, even if they didn't know for sure, could take a shrewd guess what the score was. This girl, or woman, was as green as the proverbial grass.

He clicked his fingers together and a waiter came over. 'Bring a bottle of my good brandy, will you? And two glasses.'

Donna snapped, 'I don't want any more to drink.'

Alan frowned and snapped back: 'Well, you're having some. You need a livener, girl. We've got a lot of work ahead of us, dangerous work. You could end up in clink, love. So if I was you I'd think long and hard about how deep you get in all this shit. Talk it over with Georgio, tell him to find someone else to do his running around. He will, he's a known face. You've done your bit by coming here.'

Donna stared down at the tablecloth, biting back the retort that was on the tip of her tongue.

'He can't trust anyone but me. I already know that.'

162

Alan sighed. 'Then he's a lucky man, and you're an unlucky woman. If we're to plan this thing together I need someone who won't cry their eyes out at the first sign of trouble, do you get what I'm saying?'

Donna nodded.

'It's going to be dangerous, and it's going to be hair-raising. It's going to cost the earth and it's going to take a lot of our time. The Old Bill will be sniffing round, the Serious Crime Squad will be yapping at our heels, and the Sweeny will know something's afoot within twenty-four hours of me putting out feelers. There's enough grasses in Soho alone to turf Wembley stadium. Do you think you can handle all this?'

Donna kept her head down, frightened to look at the big man opposite her.

'You will be dragged through places you didn't even know existed, with people you can only imagine in your wildest nightmares. I ain't trying to frighten you, just letting you know the score. If you're going to shit out, I'd rather it was now, before you know too much about what's going on.'

The waiter came to the table with the brandy and glasses. While he served them, Donna was grateful for the respite, and forced herself to appear calm.

Alan gave her a balloon glass half-full of brandy. She took it gratefully.

'So, what are you going to do, love? See Georgio and tell him to get someone else?'

Donna took a gulp of brandy, wincing at the burning in her throat. 'I think I will be all right, Mr Cox.'

'The name's Alan,' the big man grinned, 'and I'll take your word for the other. But I warn you now, love, one sign of you cracking and you're out. Georgio can give me a back up in case I need it. I can't visit, so everything has to be done with a go-between. Now I don't care who it is as long as they're reliable. I'd prefer a geezer, but I expect you know that already.'

'Don't worry, I'll be fine.'

She took a cigarette from her pack and Alan lit it for her. Donna's hands were shaking so much he had to steady her fingers with his free hand.

'Oh, you'll be all right, will you? You're shaking like a leaf now, and we ain't even started planning anything!'

Donna leaned across the table and hissed, 'Why don't you shut up!'

Alan laughed out loud. 'I like a bit of spunk. I only hope you've got

163

a big reserve of it, Donna, because believe me, my little love, you're going to need it.'

Alan had arranged for Donna to be taken home. As he watched the car disappear around the corner he sighed. He began a leisurely walk around to Dean Street where he entered a doorway. The small drinking club had been there since he had been a boy. The man who owned it was called Fido. No one knew his full name or anything about him. Alan was a welcome customer. He was rich, well-dressed and well-respected, and he could have a row: the perfect credentials for Fido's place.

Fido sat in a small booth and Alan joined him without being invited. Fido was thin to the point of emaciation; he was also chalk white with sparse grey hair, and he looked like a gangling civil servant.

'Hello, Alan, long time no see. What can I do you for?'

'I need a message delivered on to the Island. Private. I don't want it to get to the ears of a man called Lewis.'

Fido laughed softly. 'I can arrange that. I deal with Lewis's messengers anyway. He's a slag, but he pays well. Who's the message for?'

'Georgio Brunos. Just tell him Alan said, find a number two. He'll know what I'm talking about.'

'It's as good as done, my son,' Fido assured him.

A woman in her forties walked over to the booth and Fido ignored her as she spoke to him, not even glancing in her direction.

'Come on, Fido, where's Jerry? I know he's been in. Jack told me he has.'

Fido carried on ignoring her as he spoke. 'Don't you ever ask me anything about anyone again, Vera. If you do, I'll stripe your face till the cows come home, all right?'

Vera, a large redhead, turned and walked away, her back ramrod straight with temper.

Fido sighed softly. 'I wish these toms would get a handle on their pimps, Alan. In my young days they stuck to their mark like shit to a blanket. She's looking for him to give him his wedge and the fucker's nowhere to be seen.'

He shook his head sadly. 'Today it's all different. No finesse any more. I yearn for the good old days meself. Soho died in the sixties, you know. Once they legalised everything, the fun went out of it.'

'You're still here though, Fido.'

He grinned. 'They'll take me out of here in a box, mate.' He

164

paused for a few seconds before saying: 'Brunos is doing an eighteen and Lewis is riding his back. Sent two blokes to rough up his old woman, I heard. They've disappeared and now Lewis is like a monkey with a red-hot poker up his arse. I took the messages. I don't like him so you're lucky. I take his money and do me job, but that's it. I owe him no allegiance, so I'll give you a bit of advice *gratis*.

'Lewis wants his poke, Alan, and Georgio knows where it's hidden. The sooner that man opens his mouth, the sooner he gets buried. I'll waive any money for this first message. That way you know I'm not on anyone's take. No one will know about it, I can guarantee that. Afterwards each message is a grand, OK?'

'You're a mate, Fido.'

'I'm your mate, Alan, because me and you go back to the old days. God knows, I do miss them.'

'So do I, Fido. So do I.'

The other man shook his head wearily. 'They're arming the Old Bill now. I never thought I'd see the day. Once they carry a piece it'll be open season for the villains. Every likely lad with a oner will be carrying a gun. Old Teddy Black's in on it already. You know if you have handguns, each one must be registered, right? Well, with shotguns you only need one licence and you can have as many as you like. He's putting out scores of sawn-offs. Like a fucking armoury his drum is, and it's legal. Well, semi-legal, and that's enough for old Teddy. It's the drugs, see. Drugs and guns go hand in hand.'

Alan nodded in agreement. 'Never liked drugs meself. But then, you already know that. When will the message be given?'

'Tomorrow, by noon. I have a few screws on me payroll, I won't send this one through a lag.'

'You're a diamond. I'd better get back and cash up. They'll all think I've been nicked if I don't show me face soon.'

'I hear Amigo's is doing well.'

'It's a living, Fido. I owe you one, all right?'

Fido nodded. 'I'll send someone round tomorrow to let you know the message has been delivered.'

'I'll be there.'

Alan left the club and walked slowly back to Greek Street. He looked at the debris-strewn pavements, the McDonald's boxes, the circulars and flyers in the gutter, and sighed. Fido was right. The West End was changing, and he wasn't sure whether it was for the good.

Donna arrived home at ten past three. She thanked the driver of her car and watched as he was then picked up by another man in a

165

Mercedes. She stood on her driveway, dishevelled and half-drunk. The heat sensor lights were blazing and she looked around her as if for the first time.

The front garden was about seventy-five feet. It was neatly laid to lawn, with conifers screening each side and a large willow by the front gates. The gravel crunched under her feet as she wearily made her way to her front door.

As she selected the doorkey from the bunch in her hand she saw a movement out of the corner of her eye. Willing herself not to look, she stepped into her home, shutting the door firmly behind her.

Someone had been standing in between the conifers by the side of the house. She shuddered.

Walking up the stairs, she went into her bedroom and turned on the light. Then she crept back down the stairs in darkness, making her way slowly to the conservatory at the rear of the house. The conservatory ran along the whole back wall; it was huge, her pride and joy. It housed her swimming pool, the marble-tiled floor of which was a decorative feat in itself. This was also her reading room, having two large sofas, three chairs, a large table where she would eat in the summer, and a small bar area. From the far end she could see to the side of the house.

Donna groped her way along in the darkness, wishing she had not drunk so much brandy. Finally, she was there, and she pushed her face close to the window. The heat sensor lights would be going out at any moment then she wouldn't see anything.

She watched in amazement as her back gate opened gently and a large man slipped through. She was even more amazed to see that it was Paddy Donovon.

The drink making her bold now, she waited until he was level with the window. She was just about to knock on it, to attract his attention, when she saw he was carrying a handgun. Then the lights went out and left the whole place once more in darkness.

Donna sat down on the cane chair by her side, her hands trembling. In the dimness she turned over the thoughts in her head.

Paddy definitely had a gun.

Was he here to harm her? She immediately dismissed this idea. She trusted Paddy with her life.

She closed her eyes.

Was her life in danger then? Was that why Paddy was creeping around her grounds in the middle of the night?

She tried to remember what the gun had looked like and failed. All she was sure of was that Paddy had a gun, and he was creeping

166

around her house like Wee Willy Winky at half-past three in the morning.

She stood up and stared out into her garden, the water in the pool making gentle lapping sounds in the darkness. Then, as if making a decision, she opened one of the patio doors, grateful that she had not yet turned on the burglar alarm. Stepping out into the night, she followed the path along the garden towards the tennis court. She saw Paddy and knew instinctively he had sensed her.

'It's me, Paddy. You can lower your gun.'

'Donna?' It was a question, as if he couldn't quite believe his eyes.

'Yes, Donna. I think it's about time you and me had a talk, don't you?' Her voice was stronger than she would have believed possible. She put this down to the brandy.

'Let's go inside and have a cup of coffee.'

As he followed her back to the house she was amazed that someone so big could make no sound at all as he walked behind her.

Inside the conservatory, she turned on the pool lights. They gave off a red glow that made the conservatory look friendly. She immediately felt more in control.

'I'd rather a drop of hard, Donna, if you don't mind.'

She went to the bar and poured him a large Bushmill's, then she sat down on one of the large settees, and Paddy sat beside her. The gun was gone from view now.

'What's going on, Paddy? Why are you sneaking around my house? In the middle of the night, with a gun?'

He gulped at his drink and shook his head. 'I can't tell you that, Donna love.'

He looked into her deep blue eyes, saw the strain on her face, and felt the pull of her inside him. She didn't deserve all this; she had never asked for any of it. Not for the first time since Georgio had been nicked, Paddy felt an urge to beat him. To let him know exactly what he had done through his greed.

Donna's back stiffened and she hissed through clenched teeth, 'You can't tell me what you're doing on *my* property? You have the gall to sit in my home, drinking my drink, and tell me that you can't say why you're here? Wait until Georgio hears this one! Or are you here because of him – is that it? Has Wonderboy decided I need nursing now or is he just worried I might be batting away from home, as Carol Jackson so eloquently puts it? What were you going to do, shoot the man for your boss or just maim him?'

Paddy shook his head, ashamed now. 'Look, Donna, all we're here for is to protect you, that's all.'

Donna's eyes narrowed. 'We? How many are there of you? A

167

battalion, a platoon, a gang of you – what?'

Paddy finished his drink. 'There's five of us here at any given time. Now listen to me, this is the exact reason why we never told you anything about it. You'd worry. Look how you're reacting now . . .'

Donna interrupted him. 'Excuse me, Mr Donovon, but I am incensed because I have been covertly watched for God knows how long. I come home and find you tripping around my garden with a firearm no less, and then you say you didn't tell me anything about it because I would have been upset. That's the understatement of the year! I am bloody well livid. If my life is in danger, as this would seem to confirm, I think I am the first person who should have been informed, not the last.'

Paddy reached for her hand but she pulled it from his grasp. 'Your life is not in danger, at least not that we know of anyway. This is just insurance, Donna. Nothing more. You know that Lewis is up to a lot of tricks? Well, we didn't want him getting to Georgio through you. We didn't want anything happening to you, that's all.'

Donna shook her head again, completely sober now. The shock had done that. She wished she was still half-drunk; maybe it would have numbed the blow.

'So I'm in danger from this Lewis, am I? He's not content with wrecking my life and my husband's, getting him put into prison, but now he wants to harm me as well, does he? This is like a bloody nightmare!'

She bit on her lip. 'Tell me something truthfully, Paddy.'

He looked into her face. 'Anything.'

'Has Georgio done something to this man? Why is Lewis so against him? I want the truth.'

'Fetch me another drink, Donna love, and get one for yourself. I think you might need it.'

As she refilled his glass and poured a drink for herself, Paddy battled with himself as to whether or not to tell her the truth. One half of him wanted to desperately, but he was frightened of the effect it might have on her. As she walked back towards him, he made a decision. She deserved the truth. At least half of it anyway.

Donna sat beside him and sipped at her Rémy Martin. Her face was open, earnest, and Paddy was undone.

'Georgio provided motors for villains. He had a ringing business. Ringing a motor is getting two cars, say two Cosworths, one of which is smashed at the back, the other at the front. They're insurance writeoffs. We'd collect them from different breakers' yards all over the country. Then we would buy in a new car, a lovely motor, and we'd ring the other two cars. That involves welding the two halves of

168

the cars together. We'd then give it the number plate of the good motor, see? It's pukka stuff. If it ever came back to us, we bought it sold as seen; the ringing had been done at an earlier date.

'Well, the original car is now worth a small fortune to a blagger. I mean real blaggers here, not penny-halfpenny robbers. I mean blaggers who are looking at netting anything around a million – like Brink's-Mat for example. That car is clean, in perfect condition, it can outrun an Old Bill motor without even gunning it, and it can fetch forty-five thousand pounds or above. Bearing in mind the ringer can also fetch eighteen thousand or above, you're looking at a nice little earner, see.

'Well, Georgio provided the cars for a robbery in East London earlier this year, the robbery he was given eighteen years for. The security guard died, that's what caused all the hag. Georgio provided the cars, and through a friend of ours, the guns also, though we thought they wouldn't be loaded. We never supplied any ammunition with them – they did that off their own bat. Normally a sawn-off shotgun is enough to calm everyone down. You don't have to fire it, see. People are just plain scared anyway.

'Well, Wilson's gun *was* loaded. He shot the guard. It all went up the wall.' Paddy shook his head in disgust. 'Wilson went to one of the sites with the money. It was his job to stash it and the jewellery. Georgio took the stuff and stashed it again. He also hid out Wilson, then the prat went walkabout to his wife and kids and got a capture. If he'd have stayed put for a while we'd all have been home and dry. All he had to do was keep a low profile for a few months. His wife and kids would have been looked after.

'Now Wilson's dead – topped himself in nick, so we're led to believe . . . and Danny Simmonds and Frankie White have both copped it too. Now Donald Lewis was the man behind the blag. He knew everything about the security van down to what it would be carrying, the names of the guards – everything. The guard who got shot was in on it. I think Wilson was maybe told to waste him . . . I'm not sure of that, but it's an idea I have. So now Georgio is the only one with access to the money. He didn't want to rip Lewis off, he still doesn't, but you see how strange it all looks? Wilson's dead, the other two blaggers both murdered, and once Georgio lets on where the money is, he's dead meat as well. It's a big balls-up from start to finish.

'Georgio should have kept right out of it,' the big man concluded. 'Just supplied the cars and nothing else. But he needed cash, his businesses were in trouble. It seemed like a good way out at the time.'

Donna sat very still, staring down at her hands. The last few

169

months had been such a revelation to her; her whole life, it seemed, was based on lies. But not lies exactly, because Georgio had simply never told her anything.

In a way she felt that was worse. Could she really have lived with, slept with, eaten with, made love with a man she didn't know?

She was surprised to find she was crying and felt herself being pulled into the large strong arms of Paddy. She lay against him, breathing in the smell of Capstan cigarettes and Old Spice aftershave, and she wept like a baby. This long night had been a time for revelations. First from Alan Cox, about Georgio looking after his family, and now from Paddy.

How could she never have guessed what was going on all these years?

Then a little voice inside her head said gently: *Because you didn't want to know*. And somehow she knew that those few words were true.

Her mother used to say, 'What you don't know, can't hurt you.' Well, that was a lie, as big a lie as Mrs Donna Brunos had been living for twenty years.

170

Chapter Sixteen

'Do you know something, Paddy? Georgio has been a bastard to me. I never thought I'd say that, but he has.'

Paddy tried to calm her. 'Stop your crying, Donna love. Georgio did what he thought was best. This is why he never told you anything. You'd worry. You'd be scared. Can't you see, little love, that he was protecting you?'

Donna pulled herself from the older man's arms.

'He wasn't protecting me, Paddy, and you know it! He just didn't think I warranted telling, that's the truth of it. I saw a man earlier on who told me Georgio had looked after his wife and children while he was in prison for murder. I suppose he didn't tell me about *that* either in case I might have worried!'

Paddy sighed, his craggy face soft in the red glow from the pool lights.

'You're wrong, Donna. So wrong. Georgio Brunos worshipped the ground you walked on. He thought you were the greatest thing he had ever achieved in his life. To him, Donna, you were class. A bit of class. He bragged about you constantly to everyone. My Donna, he'd say, could cook a meal fit for the Queen. "She graces the table," was his expression. He thought of you all the time. He didn't tell you things because he didn't want you worrying. You're not of the calibre of, say, Carol Jackson or even Dolly. You've never been brought up in this environment.

'Coming from Canning Town, Georgio knew old lags before he knew how to walk. Pa Brunos was a lad in his day. All the Greeks stick together. Oh, he's respectable enough now, but in his younger days he was a right tearaway. The Greeks ran the cabbing in Piccadilly for years. That's how old man Brunos got the money for his restaurant. Admittedly, he wasn't in the league of Georgio or even Stephen, but he did his share of ducking and diving.

'For all Georgio's faults, he never robbed anyone, never hurt anyone. He supplied cars, that's all, and if he hadn't then someone else would have. He supplied guns once, and even then they were

171

without ammunition. It's as simple as that. As for not telling you . . . be fair, Donna. Put yourself in his position. Your brother is a bloody lawyer, you come from a good middle-class home. You couldn't have coped with it all. I only hope you can cope with it now, because now, you know the lot. Everything.

'One thing I will say before I shut me mouth. That man couldn't live without you. Everything he wanted, he wanted for you. Seeing you dressed in the best, driving the best car, living in a beautiful home – it was for you alone. He told me that himself. He felt you deserved it all. He was only sorry you couldn't have a child. It was the one thing he felt he couldn't give you – a child. I know you're not able to have babies, Georgio told me everything, and be fair, Donna, he never stepped away from you because of that, even though a child was what he wanted dearly. He accepted it as he accepted you, whole-heartedly. You were his wife for better or worse. He's a Catholic, and although he might not be wearing a pathway to the church, he still believes in its values. If he can love you, why can't you still love him, even knowing what you know now?'

It was the longest speech she had ever heard Paddy Donovon make. It was as if he was her father or an elder brother talking some sense into her. The mention of a child had hurt, it had hurt a lot. It was the one thing she had regretted all her married life, not being able to give Georgio a child. She felt once more that sensation of being second best, as she always did when reminded of her failure to produce a living, breathing child. She saw that Georgio had always tried to protect her, always. Had made a point of never mentioning children in any context. Maybe that's why he didn't tell her about Alan Cox's children. Maybe he'd thought it would have broken her, as the knowledge was breaking her now. It was unfair for Paddy to say all this to her. It was grossly unfair, because she had no argument to give him in her own defence. As usual Georgio came out on top. He was the kind considerate man. He was always the kind considerate man. She felt the sting of tears again.

'Why are you armed, and why are you hanging about my house?' she shot at him.

Paddy sighed. 'Because Lewis might try and get to Georgio through you, that's why. If anything happened to you, I think Georgio would die, Donna. He told me that himself. I'm here as a little bit of insurance, nothing more. The chances are, Lewis wouldn't dare come near you. But as you must understand, I wouldn't be Georgio's friend if I didn't try and protect you.'

Donna looked at the water in the pool. The small ripples as the heater blew out warm water looked silver in the night-time light.

172

'Is that why the car lot was destroyed – as a warning?'

'Yes.'

'Am I in danger, Paddy?'

He shook his head vigorously. 'No way. Not while I'm here.'

Donna felt a sudden peace envelop her. Paddy Donovon was here, so she was safe. If only she could believe that . . .

She glanced at her watch. It was nearly five-thirty. The dawn was breaking slowly, orange jets of light crowding the dark sky. She was aware of birdsong, as if someone had turned on a radio. The night was ending, and the day was beginning.

'I'm going to bed, Paddy, you can see yourself out.'

He watched her as she walked towards the door that led into the house.

'Donna.' She turned around slowly. 'Are you all right?'

She smiled at him, a lazy smile that enhanced her good looks. 'What do you think?'

As she walked up the large staircase that led to her bedroom she looked around her home as if for the first time. At the ornate coving, the pale grey walls, the pictures so lovingly placed to their best advantage. She felt her feet sinking into the carpet, saw the sunlight beginning to filter through the set of double doors on the landing that led out to a small sun terrace at the back of the house. How many times had she sat out there drinking wine on hot summer evenings with Georgio? How many times had he picked her up and taken her to bed? She walked along to her bedroom, its splendour meaning nothing to her any more, because the man who had fashioned it with her was gone from her.

But, she reminded herself, she could get him back. She could be the means of bringing him, if not home, at least back into her arms.

He had never lied to her, she accepted that. But what he had done seemed worse.

He didn't tell her anything because he didn't trust her . . . and that knowledge hurt her more than a blow could ever have done. He loved her too much was Paddy's argument. Well, he couldn't hope to have loved her even half as much as she loved him; she lived and breathed for Georgio Brunos. He was the reason she got up in the morning and the reason she went to bed at night. She had always told him everything. Had assumed he had afforded her the same courtesy, but obviously not.

She stripped off her clothes and turned on the shower. The walls of her bathroom were all mirrored, so she saw herself wherever she looked. The ensuite bathroom was bigger than most people's bedrooms. It contained a large circular bath, an enclosed shower, toilet,

173

bidet, and twin hand basins. The fittings were all gold. On the floor was a white lambswool carpet. It was pure luxury, and at this moment she felt an urge to smash everything in it. Smash the mirrors that displayed her body from every angle, smash the expensive toiletries that sat on the deep hardwood windowsill. She hated everything about herself, and about this house.

She stood beneath the water, letting it wash over her face, feeling the sting of mascara as it washed from her eyelashes. She felt empty inside, alone and empty. The house seemed far too big for her and Dolly. It was a house made for children, for a large family.

Without Georgio, it was like a tomb, because it had been Georgio who had breathed life into it. As he walked through the door he had made the house happy, had brought it to life. Had brought her to life.

Even knowing what he had done to her, she couldn't feel anger with him for long. Already, she knew, she was making excuses for him. Because one thing kept her tied to him, the thing that Paddy had used when she was at her lowest ebb.

Georgio loved her.

As long as he never stopped she would put up with anything from him. It had always been the same.

By the time she laid herself down on the big king-sized bed and closed her eyes, she had forgiven him.

Georgio heard the cell door open and jam against the wooden wedge. He looked at his watch. It was seven twenty-five. Five minutes before the usual opening-up time.

He sat up on his bunk, listening to the heavy mumbling of Timmy as he rolled over, hoping for a further few minutes' sleep.

Georgio got off the bunk and went to the door. 'Who's there?'

'It's me, McAllister. Open up, Brunos.'

Georgio removed the wooden wedge. All long-timers kept a wedge on their doors. If another prisoner wanted to smash your brains out, the best time was first thing in the morning. They could steam into a cell, club the person with a weapon, having the physical advantage because their victim was still lying down, and be out again in a few seconds. No one would be any the wiser as to who had done it. In an environment where bumping into someone by accident was enough to merit extreme violence, the wooden wedge was known as a lifesaver.

McAllister walked into the cell and slipped Georgio a piece of paper.

'Come on, you two,' he shouted. 'What you think this is – a fucking holiday camp! Up and out, now!'

Timmy sat up in his bunk, his fat belly quivering with indignation.

174

'Up yours, McAllister. Take your fucking bawling somewhere else.'

The man left the cell and Georgio slipped the piece of paper into his underpants.

'Fucking mouthy git, coming in here like he owns the bloody place. Bleeding ponce, that's what he is!'

Timmy broke wind loudly. Disgusted, Georgio picked up his chamber pot and hurried from the cell. He queued on the landing to empty his chamber, chatting amicably with Sadie.

'He stinks! How do you stand it?'

Sadie lifted her shoulders in a Gallic gesture and said, 'Why do you think I don't bother too much about getting celled up with him? But he ain't a bad bloke, Timmy. You've just got to know how to handle him.'

Georgio laughed. 'I can handle him, it's his go-karts I can't stand.'

Timmy ambled out and joined them.

'Something crawl up your arse and die then, Timmy?' This from a young lag called Peter Barnes. He was in on an eighteen and had already earned the respect of the older men.

Timmy laughed good-naturedly. 'Yeah, a nest of cockroaches. You've got the best part of the sentence to come. You wait till the summer, Peter, they crawl all over you in the night. Bastard things they are.'

Peter Barnes looked decidedly shocked at this revelation and all the men laughed at him.

'This place is running alive with them, sonny boy. Big bastards some of them are and all. Remember last year, we had the races?'

Everyone laughed again, remembering.

'I had one, a big bastard and all, called Trigger. It outrun every other roach on the Wing. I coined it in with him. We run them during recreation. I was sorry when he died, to be honest.' Timmy's voice was as sad as if the roach had been a personal friend.

'What did it die of?' Barnes sounded genuinely interested.

Sadie shouted out: 'He farted when it was in his pocket and gassed the poor little bugger in its matchbox.'

Everyone laughed at this, even Timmy.

Georgio walked back to his cell with his chamber pot and shut the door, shoving the wedge back in once more.

Taking the paper out of his pants, he uncurled it.

Get a number 2.

Ripping the paper into tiny fragments, Georgio put them in his

175

mouth and chewed them up, swallowing it all.

He removed the wedge, and taking off his underpants, picked up a towel and went back out on the Wing towards the showers. He was wolf-whistled three times and minced like Sadie to make people laugh.

Once in the showers he thought about the note, then dismissed it. The only person he could trust, really trust, was Donna. Plus, she had the added bonus of being completely above suspicion. By Lewis and the Old Bill.

He began washing himself.

So Donna had been to see Alan, and now the ball was well and truly rolling.

Georgio started to sing to himself.

Alan Cox opened his eyes slowly. The room was in darkness. Getting out of bed, he padded naked to the window and pulled back the curtains. The reason he liked living in Soho was because the place never really shut. Even at seven-fifteen in the morning it was already buzzing. Street cleaners were milling around, early-morning stragglers, toms as well as doormen, were moving through the streets, and the shop-keepers were already cashing up. He stretched and yawned, his long body feeling the ache of his advancing years even as its youthful firmness belied them.

He turned back to the bed and frowned.

Lally was twenty-nine, though she swore she was only twenty-two. She had been his girlfriend on and off for two years. Earlier in their relationship, he had made the mistake of giving her a key. She had been there already, fast asleep, when he had trundled home in the small hours, and he had been too tired to throw her out.

'Come on, Lally, up you get.'

She turned in the bed, displaying a small breast. Her short red hair was spiked and ruffled. She looked very lovely. Sighing, knowing the signs so well, Alan went out to his kitchen and made a pot of coffee. As it perked he savoured the aroma of the Colombian brew and set out two mugs.

Alan enjoyed the early morning, being able to get up without restrictions, no waiting for someone to unlock the door, no sharing with a big hairy-arsed scouser. Since being released from prison he had guarded his freedom with a fervour that Lally and others of her ilk had found hard to understand.

Taking a mug of coffee through to the bedroom, he placed it on the night table and shook Lally gently awake.

176

'Come on, wake up, love. I've got to get moving in a little while. Got a busy day.'

Lally opened one eye carefully, shutting it immediately against the harsh daylight. Alan could see the lines appearing around her mouth and eyes.

'You look rough, girl, you should lay off the gear.'

'Piss off, Alan. It's too early in the morning for lectures, even from you.' She sat up in the bed, making no attempt to hide her nakedness. 'Give me a cigarette, Al.'

He passed her a pack from her handbag, which she had dumped on a chair by the window. She lit up and breathed the smoke deeply into her lungs. As the coughing attack hit her, Alan shook his head.

'You abuse yourself, Lally, but you know that, don't you?'

She nodded her head, coughing with all her might, her face red with the effort. 'Cup of tea and a cough, the great British breakfast!'

Alan picked up the mug and gave it to her. 'This is coffee, Lally. You don't drink tea, remember?'

She took another drag on her cigarette and sipped at the steaming coffee.

'Where were you last night? I thought you'd have closed up by two-thirty.'

Alan walked out of the bedroom without bothering to answer. As he sat at the kitchen table she ambled through with coffee, cigarettes, and his bathrobe draped over her body. She hadn't bothered to tie it up and he knew it was a calculated gesture. He tied it for her.

'Listen, Lally, I don't want you coming and going here as if it's your place. I gave you the key for emergencies only. Now, if you don't mind, I want it back.'

She sat at the table and smiled. 'Why do we always have to go through this, Alan? You'll get in the shower and I'll follow, you'll make love to me, and then I'll watch while you cook us a bit of breakfast. Then we'll be all right until the next time.'

Alan shook his head vigorously. 'There ain't going to be a next time, Lally. I don't like this. I don't like my space being invaded. You know what I'm like, love. I don't want anything permanent.'

Lally sniffed disdainfully. 'Who said that I do then? Don't fancy yourself too much, Alan Cox. I don't want anything permanent either. You're not the only bloke I see.'

Alan looked into the clear blue eyes and said softly, 'But you'd like me to be, wouldn't you?'

Lally had to drop her eyes then, aware of the truthfulness of the statement. She stamped her foot like a child.

'Why do you do this to me, Alan?' Her voice was a low whine.

177

'Why do you shut me out? Can't we just try it together?'

Alan softened but shook his head nonetheless. 'Not in a million years, darlin'. I don't want anything permanent, and if I did it wouldn't be with a tom, no matter how high-class she was.'

He felt bad saying that to her, because in reality he couldn't care what her job was, but he knew it was the only thing he could say that would wound her enough to make her leave him in peace. Over the years he had known toms he would rather have over fifty so-called respectable housewives, and he'd had a few of those as well, which was why he preferred the toms. They didn't pretend, they were real, you knew exactly what you were getting.

He saw the shine of tears and sighed again. 'I'm sorry Lally.'

She stood up, her dignity all she had to shield herself with. 'I didn't deserve that, Alan, and you know it.'

She watched the man before her, his blond hair tousled from sleep, his broad shoulders held back as if warding off a blow, his deep blue eyes with the perfectly placed laughter lines around them, and felt the pull of him. Never before had she wanted anyone so badly.

'We can still be friends, Lally, only I want us to be proper friends who ring each other before they drop in, who don't just land on each other's doorsteps.'

She nodded. He had never rung her, not once. He had never dropped in to see her ever. He was trying to save her dignity and it hurt her more knowing that.

He pulled her into his arms, contrite now because he had wounded her, but sure enough of himself to know she had finally got the message. He could be the big man now, could comfort her.

'I'm sorry, Lally, you're wasting your time on me. No woman will ever share my bed or my life again. If any woman was going to, it would have been you, I swear. I just don't ever want all that again.'

Lally pushed her body into his, feeling the strength of him, smelling his particular odour.

'I understand, Alan, I won't ever do anything like this again. I'll still see you though won't I?'

He smiled down into her eyes. 'Course you will.'

But they both knew he was lying.

An hour later there was no trace of Lally in the flat, and Alan was on the telephone organising his day. He was excited about what Georgio had asked him to do. He had been too long away from the stimulus of the criminal world. Alan was actually enjoying himself.

Donna woke at one o'clock. She lay on the bed, her eyes heavy, her limbs weighted with tiredness. As she sat up she saw herself in a

178

mirror and frowned. Her hair had dried all over the place. Pulling herself from the bed, she went into the shower once more.

She felt lighter as the water hit her in hot jets. The last of the sleep left her body and life tingled back into her muscles.

At two-thirty she was walking downstairs, dressed, made-up and immaculate. As she entered the kitchen Dolly sat at the table shelling peas. She smiled at Donna.

'Have a good sleep?'

Donna smiled back. 'I take it you knew about Paddy keeping guard on the house, Dolly?'

Dolly had the grace to look ashamed.

'It's funny, you know, but you keeping this from me hurts more than anything that Georgio or anyone else could do to me. Because I really thought we had a deep friendship, a mother and daughter relationship even. It seems I was wrong.'

Donna flapped a hand at the older woman. 'No, don't bother getting up. I'm going out now and I don't know when I'll be back.' She smiled maddeningly as she added, 'So don't wait up, will you?'

Picking up her car keys she marched out of the house, leaving Dolly stunned at her words.

Two hours later, Donna was sitting in Amigo's, nursing a white wine and soda and listening to Alan Cox as he explained why he thought someone else should be the go-between.

Alan's eyes were all over the restaurant as he spoke to her. Even deep in conversation he kept his eye on his staff and his customers.

'The thing is, love, I don't think you're cut out for this kind of thing. That's no offence or anything, in a way it's a compliment. But this could get a little bit scary, you know? There's people I need to involve who'd scare Old Nick himself, do you get my drift?'

Donna watched him without saying one word.

His eyes stopped their wandering to look at her properly. 'Are you listening to me?' His voice had risen two octaves and he looked cross. Donna guessed most women hung on to his every word, and he wasn't used to the reaction he was getting from her. Boredom.

'I don't have much choice, do I? You talk enough for a battalion. You're like Georgio in a lot of ways. You expect people to listen, especially people like me: women, menials. Well, Mr Alan Smart Arse Cox, I've been listening to you for ages. If you bothered to make eye-contact now and again instead of looking at every other person in the place, you'd have noticed that much yourself.'

Alan frowned, taken aback at her words. 'Aren't you feeling all the ticket, love?'

179

Donna shook her head slowly in consternation. 'You make me laugh, do you know that? You sit there with your handmade suit and your expensive cigar as if they're props that will make you someone, a somebody. You talk *at* me, not *to* me, and calmly expect me to jump immediately to your way of thinking. Well, Mr Cox, I won't. In fact, I am just about getting sick and tired of being told what I should think, what I should do, and how I should ruddy well do it.

'I have a house that is like Fort Knox, I have a man called Lewis apparently threatening me. Oh no, not me, he's threatening my husband with hurting me – another man who hasn't the decency or brain capacity to mention it to the person concerned! I have a housekeeper who's in on the conspiracy, the great "Let's not let Donna know anything" conspiracy. Even though I am being asked by my errant husband, a man who at this moment in time is hardly in a position to call the shots, if I will kindly break him out of prison. Break the law, put my life, my freedom, and my natural honesty on the line. All for him of course, not for me.

'And you have the gall to sit in front of me and talk at me like I'm a child, and expect me to be grateful and fall in with all your plans without a by your leave. Well, you can go and take a running jump! Is that in language you understand? Only I was never much of a swearer. Unlike you, my husband and others of your ilk.'

Alan Cox sat back in his seat flabbergasted. Then, to make matters worse, he laughed at her: a deep rollicking laugh that caused other diners to turn their heads.

Donna sat, stiff-backed and straight-faced, and stared at him. It suddenly occurred to her that she didn't like the man before her. She didn't like his arrogance, his manner or his clothes. Didn't like his acceptance that anyone and everyone would automatically fall in with his plans. The way his eyes swept over every woman in the room and silently graded them on a scale of one to ten. She didn't like him at all.

She had been going to tell him to find a replacement, but now she couldn't. Because that would make her, in his eyes, what he already thought she was. A bit of skirt, a bit of fluff. Just a woman.

His laughter stopped as abruptly as it had started and Donna saw the Alan Cox that most men saw. His face was now stony, hard-looking. The lines were no longer soft and endearing but now gave his appearance a chiselled quality. He looked for all the world like a man who had indeed kicked another man, another human being, to death and she felt the first prickles of fear.

'You've got a smart mouth, lady.'

Donna smiled, forcing herself to relax. 'It's probably the only thing

180

we have in common, Mr Cox. Let's try and build on that, shall we?'

She picked up her drink and sipped it nonchalantly, aware of his eyes boring into hers.

'Let's get something straight, Mrs Brunos. I don't want you as my number two. I want a geezer, someone in the know. I need someone with experience, acumen and bravado. I want a known face.' All pretence of being a businessman was gone now and Donna noted the fact.

'Well, take a good look at mine, Mr Cox, because this is the only one you're getting.'

Alan Cox looked into the white strained face before him, and his first reaction was to bellow with rage. Alan Cox was used to women like Lally, women who wanted him so badly they automatically fell in with whatever plans he had. In his mind's eye he had envisioned telling her the bad news, giving her a bit of lunch and getting on with what he had to do. Donna Brunos, however, had pissed over his firework, as he put it to himself, and he wasn't happy about it. He wasn't happy about it at all.

Swallowing down his anger, he forced a smile. 'I don't think you understand, love . . .'

Donna pushed her hand through her hair in a gesture of utter weariness.

'I am not your love, Mr Cox. Please don't patronise me with useless terms of endearment which you probably use on the telephone to faceless operators and to your waitresses. I am a grown woman, in case it had escaped your notice. I came to you because my husband looked after your wife and children, probably with far greater respect than you are according his wife. He specifically asked me to be his go-between. I have no criminal record, not even a parking ticket. I have acumen, and I have bravado. I also have a terrible feeling that I don't like you, Mr Cox, I don't like you at all. That feeling is growing stronger by the second.'

Alan was aware that he had been bested. A feeling so alien to him that for a few seconds he wasn't sure what to do.

Realising this, Donna stood up. Holding out her hand, she said, 'I'm so glad we had this little chat. Now, when you are ready to talk business, I'll expect to hear from you. I do hope you don't hold grudges? I find that rather a tiresome trait in older men.' Shaking his hand, she walked stiffly out of the restaurant.

Alan Cox sat back in his seat and watched her leave. Half of him wanted to catapult from the chair and clout a heavy hand across her face. The other half wanted to laugh.

The laughter won. Alan prided himself on the fact he had never,

ever raised his hand to a woman. But Georgio Brunos's little wife had very nearly made him break that vow.

On his dignity now, like Lally before him, he stood up and, as casually as possible, walked up the stairs to his office. In his small bathroom he looked at himself in the mirror. The jibe about the handmade suit and being a somebody had hit home. Basically an honest person, he knew that was why he was so angry. Why he had wanted to slap her.

He was fuming.

Chapter Seventeen

Anthony Calder was a big man. He weight-trained every day of his life, shutting himself in his personal gym and working out all his stresses with the pumping of iron. His head was bullet-shaped, his hair grey and cut into a very short crewcut. His teeth were expensively capped, his complexion ruddy. His nose would have given W.C. Fields a run for his money.

Anthony was fifty-eight years old, with the body of a much younger man, the brain of an ancient, and a wife of twenty-two. He admitted to his ugliness every time he glanced in a mirror, his thick bull neck adding to his overall brutishness. Yet he knew he was attractive to women, always had been, and hopefully always would be. It was the sheer force of his strength and personality that drew them. He looked dangerous and, he admitted to himself occasionally, he *was* dangerous.

Anthony Calder was a fixer; he could fix anything. If a man needed a lighter prison sentence then Anthony Calder was his man. He knew every policeman worth knowing, from the Met to the Merseyside. He knew their prices, knew whom to approach and whom not to approach. He knew whether they wanted cash or holidays, whether they were gamblers or if their tastes ran to women or nice cars. It was his job, his career, and he gave it his all.

Calder was now a millionaire and he didn't have to raise a finger in anger to anyone any more. Gone were the days when he was a paid heavy who would break an arm or a leg for a certain sum of money. His big chance had come when he made the acquaintance of Detective Inspector Billings from the Serious Crime Squad. Billings used Anthony as a go-between in a deal he was setting up with two notorious brothers who wanted suspended sentences instead of life terms. It was at this time he found he had a natural flair for negotiation.

DI Billings had written to the judge saying the brothers were narking for him, and that they were more use on the street than behind bars. The judge had given this careful consideration and, for

183

the princely sum of twenty-five thousand pounds per brother, had allowed them to walk from the court on suspended sentences. Anthony had done his job – and in so doing had found his vocation. Now Calder resided in a large leafy suburb in Chigwell with his little wife, his newborn daughter, and two large Dobermanns. He ran his business from home and socialised with both police and criminals. He was respected by all concerned, especially the police, who saw him as a way of subsidising meagre salaries.

Anthony was pleased with life, and he gave a grin of deep-felt satisfaction as he saw Alan Cox walking across his manicured lawn towards the gym annexe where he spent most of his day.

'Hello, Alan, me old mate, long time no see.' Anthony's voice still had a thick cockney twang.

'All right, Tone? You're looking well.'

Anthony shook his hand. 'What can I do you for then?' The business was starting and Alan was aware of the fact. It was one of the things he liked about Anthony Calder: the preliminaries were few and far between.

'I need a few whispers from you, me old son. I am in the throes of planning a little get-together with an old mate and I need the ear of a few Old Bill.'

Anthony replaced the heavy weight into its carriage and wiped his face and neck with a pristine white towel.

'Where's the setup?'

Alan smiled. 'The Isle of Wight.'

Anthony laughed then. 'I see. Well, that'll cost a few bob, but I expect you know that. Any particular face in mind?'

Alan sat down on a small bench and loosened his coat buttons. 'I need your word on strict security. This could become very nasty.'

Calder shrugged. 'I never open me mouth – you know that, Alan.'

'Not even if it steps on Donald Lewis's toes?'

Alan was aware of the big man's shock.

'What's Lewis got to do with this?'

'Nothing, Tony, and that's how I want it to stay. I don't want him to know anything. He owns most of the Old Bill on the Island, and I want to spring an old mate without Lewis sussing anything about it.'

Tony stared down at him for a moment. 'That's a dangerous proposition, Alan. It'll cost you. Big money.'

'I'm good for it, Tony, you know that. But I have one thing to tell you: if Lewis even gets a faint whiff that something's going down, me and you are going to fall out, do you understand me?'

Tony nodded, serious now. 'I hear what you're saying. But you

184

know that Lewis has his fingers in more fucking pies than little Jack Horner.'

Alan shrugged the statement off. 'That's his prerogative. He's a ponce and I don't like him and he's stepping on a dear friend of mine's toes, which means he's stepping right on one of my corns at the same time. So you tell me who to see and where to see them and I'll do the actual negotiating. That way you're not too involved.'

Anthony sighed deeply. 'I'll have to have a think about all this, mate. It'll take some arranging.'

'I'm well aware of that.'

Anthony was nonplussed for a few seconds.

'I thought you was straight these days', he said eventually. 'I heard you was raking it in with legitimate businesses?'

Alan grinned. 'I am. But like the old saying goes, yours is not to reason why. Especially where I'm concerned.'

He took a thick envelope from his inside pocket and placed it on the bench beside him.

'There's fifteen grand in there in fifty-pound notes. That's just for starters. There's plenty more where that came from. I want this arranged with the best of care and money's no object, OK?'

Anthony picked up the envelope in his meaty fist and weighed it in his hand before he answered.

'Fair enough, but I must warn you, Alan, Lewis's arm is long.'

Alan shook his head slowly.

'And so, my dear Tony, is mine.'

Donna had just emerged from the shower when the telephone rang.

'Hello?'

'Hello, Donna, just a quick call to let you know the books are ready for your perusal.'

'Fine. I'll be over about nine tonight.'

'How's Georgio?'

'Bearing up. Will you try and get in for a visit?'

Stephen's voice was clipped. 'It's difficult, his VOs to me are few and far between. I expect you're the one he wants to see.'

Donna felt the animosity coming in waves down the telephone. 'I am his wife Stephen.'

'Of course you are. It's just I was supposed to be helping you run the businesses and now it seems you don't want to know. I feel very upset at you checking up on me . . .'

Donna's mouth was a perfect O as she listened to her brother-in-law's voice.

'Checking up on you? Now come on, Stephen, I am just exercising

185

a right. I am a partner in your business, naturally I want a working knowledge of it.' Donna's voice was rising and she forced herself to calm down.

It was Stephen's turn to sigh. 'You own a twenty-five percent share, that's all. I have the controlling interest. I think you have a bloody bare-faced cheek, to be honest, and I'm only humouring you because you are my brother's wife. Now let's drop the subject, shall we?'

Donna was amazed to find he had put the phone down on her. Wrapping the thick pink towel tightly around her, she sat on the bed in a daze.

Whatever was wrong with Stephen couldn't simply be the fact that she wanted to see his books. She asked herself now why she was so adamant about seeing them. It didn't really matter either way. But as she sat there, Donna realised exactly what was wrong with her, what had been wrong with her for a good while. *She didn't trust Stephen Brunos.*

It was a startling revelation.

Hattie had listened patiently to Stephen's ranting and now she shook her head sadly.

'She'll find out soon enough, and then it'll be the worse for you and everyone concerned.'

Stephen forced a smile on to his face.

'Nah, she won't. None of them will. I'm too clever by half.' He grinned to lighten the mood, but Hattie just shook her head once more.

'No one's that clever, and you're playing with fire, my lad. You can't run with the fox and hunt with the hounds. No one can.'

He stood up impatiently and kissed Hattie on the top of her head.

'Stop worrying, Hat, I'm as safe as houses.'

Hattie sipped at her vodka and tonic. He was too handsome by half. All her life she had been a sucker for a pretty young man and she realised now that, even going into old age, she wasn't going to change.

'Does she know everything about Talkto Enterprises?'

'No, she doesn't, and there's no reason why she should. Now I've got to go, Hats. I'll pop in later tonight if you're not too busy?'

Hattie couldn't refuse him.

'I'm never too busy for you.'

Smiling widely, he left and Hattie stood where she was in the centre of the room, brooding. He was playing a dangerous game. She only hoped it didn't backfire on him.

186

★ ★ ★

Donna walked into the Talkto offices at nine-thirty as arranged and was surprised to see no sign of Stephen, only a young woman in a tight black cocktail dress waiting for her.

'Mrs Brunos?'

Donna nodded, smiling.

'I'm Cathy Harper. Mr Brunos asked me to let you in. The books are here on this desk. Can I get you a cup of coffee?'

Donna nodded at the earnest young girl in front of her. Cathy was plastered in make-up, taking the edge away from her natural fresh-faced good looks. Her plump young body encased in a black beaded dress gave her an air of tartiness, and Donna wrinkled her nose at the overwhelming smell of Charlie perfume and fresh sweat.

She sat behind Stephen's secretary's desk, noticing that the rest of the offices were locked up and aware that this was a subtle insult to her. The girl plonked herself down on a settee and lit a cigarette.

'Are you going to wait for me?' Donna asked.

She nodded absentmindedly. 'That's what Mr Brunos said. He told me to let you in and to sit and wait until you'd finished. Then I was to let you out and lock the door behind me.'

Donna smiled once more. 'Is he nearby, waiting for the keys to be delivered back?'

'As far as I know, he's still in the club in Wardour Street,' the girl told her, 'but he could have gone by now. I'll just give the keys to Daragh.'

'Daragh?'

Cathy Harper smiled at the question in Donna's voice.

'Daragh O'Flynn. He's an Irish bloke who runs the club for Mr Brunos. Funny name though, ain't it? We all laugh at it – behind his back, of course.'

Donna laughed with the girl and said conspiratorially, 'Of course.'

Cathy beamed, happy to find that the woman was fun. She had been wary of her mission, knowing that some of the people Mr Brunos dealt with were not exactly the answer to a maiden's prayer, being rough, determined, and for the most part vicious. This pretty woman, with the chestnut hair and the subtle make-up, was like a breath of fresh air. Cathy settled herself further into the sofa and picked up a magazine.

Donna took her cigarettes out of her bag and lit one, slowly savouring the smoke as it was drawn into her lungs.

'Where do you work, Cathy?' The question was innocent enough, but hinted that Donna knew more about the operations than she did.

187

'I work in the clubs and I do the peepshow on Mondays and Fridays. It's easier for me like this, gives me a bit of time with the kids, like. I prefer the peeping to be honest. I ain't got to actually do nothing and the money's regular. In the club you can sit all night with some bloke and only come out of it with the hostess fee. Some of the customers are as mean as catshit, know what I mean?'

Donna nodded, looking as if she had been there once or twice herself. Cathy warmed to her even more.

'What peepshow are you working in?'

'La Bohème, just off Dean Street. A right shithole it is and all. The smell! It'd knock you down, but you get used to it, like.'

'You work there for Stephen . . . Mr Brunos?'

Cathy nodded. 'I've worked for Brunos since I was nineteen. He ain't too bad, none of them are. But I expect you know that, being married to one yourself.'

Donna felt that she was only being treated as she was by this girl because her name was Brunos. She spoke the name with respect. Donna smiled again.

'How about that coffee?' She took a ten-pound note from her bag. 'I'd also like a cheeseburger. Would you mind nipping round to McDonald's?'

Cathy took the proffered money and hesitated for only a second. Mr Brunos had told her not to leave the office while this woman was looking over the books.

Donna saw her hesitate, and pulling out another ten-pound note, she gave it to the girl, saying, 'No one need know you left me here, and I'm dying for a cup of coffee and something to eat.'

The girl snatched the other ten-pound note and left the offices. Donna smiled as she saw the keys still on the settee where Cathy had left them. Getting up from her chair, she stubbed out her cigarette, picked up the keys and let herself into Stephen's office. Turning on the lamp on his desk, she began going through his drawers, looking for anything that might catch her eye. She was certain now that Stephen was hiding something from her, and she also had a premonition that whatever it was, he was hiding it from Georgio as well. She couldn't put a finger on why she felt as she did, it was just a gut reaction. Stephen was acting out of character. Maybe it was because she'd found out that his business dealings were not strictly kosher, maybe it embarrassed him, but she didn't think so.

Pulling on the last drawer in the desk, Donna was met with resistance. Taking the keys, she tried two before the drawer lock clicked open. Lying at the bottom of the drawer were two black-bound ledgers. Picking them up, Donna stiffened. Seating herself

188

behind the desk, she began looking through them.

Twenty minutes later when Cathy arrived back breathlessly with a couple of cheeseburgers and a large Polystyrene cup of coffee, Donna was once more in the outer office, looking over the books left out for her by Stephen. Cathy was aware that Mrs Brunos had something on her mind; she wasn't as chatty as she had been.

Locking up after the visitor, Cathy made her way to O'Flynn and after a gram of amphetamine felt much better. By eleven o'clock Donna was gone from her mind.

Alan was not surprised to see Donna standing in his office. He had had a feeling she was going to show up. He poured her a small brandy and as she lit herself a cigarette, he sat back in his chair, enjoying the sight of her. She was really a sweet-looking little thing, even if she did have a tongue like an adder.

'So Mrs B. What can I do for you?'

The sarcasm wasn't lost on Donna. Taking a deep draw on her cigarette, she said gently, 'I need to know what's going on, Mr Cox.'

Alan lifted an eyebrow. 'Sorry?'

Donna could feel herself getting annoyed and forced herself to calm down. She tried another tack.

'Look, Mr Cox, I was hoping we could forget about what happened and start fresh. Georgio is depending on us, and I don't think it's a good idea if he knows that we aren't getting on very well. I think we should at least give it a try, and if it doesn't work out in say a month, we'll both have a rethink. What do you say?'

Alan tut-tutted gently.

'In case it's escaped your notice, I have invited you into my office, I have poured you a brandy, and I have lit your cigarette for you. Now, lady, according to my lights, that is an act of forgiveness. *I* will give *you* two weeks – and if you don't show enough savvy, me and you are parting company whether Georgio likes it or not. Fair enough?'

'Fair enough.'

Donna was shrewd enough to realise that this was as close as Alan Cox would ever come to any kind of apology.

'May I ask you something, Mr Cox?'

She observed the exaggerated shrug and felt once more the prickle of annoyance he always provoked in her. 'Do you know anything about Stephen Brunos at all? Either before Georgio was put away or since?'

She watched his pupils dilate and felt a stab of satisfaction. 'What I'm asking you, Mr Cox, is do you know anything about Talkto Enterprises?'

189

Nonplussed for a second, Alan felt his own temper rising inside him.

'What the fucking hell are you on about now?'

Donna sighed and started to talk calmly and reasonably. 'All I am asking is this. Talkto is supposedly a telephone business – you know the kind of thing: how to cope with arthritis etc. It's got a good turnover and it's making a handsome profit . . . except I found another set of books tonight, and these books have only a list of names and amounts of money written beside them. For example, one entry said, "Gilly, fifty-five minutes, sixty-five pounds". Then beside that in a separate column, "ten pounds". I take it those were Gilly's earnings. Then in another book I find shifts written down, once more with girls' names, times, et cetera. There was a young lady at the offices who worked in a peepshow. I think the second set of books are about that. I wondered if you could shed any light on all this?'

Alan downed his brandy and said testily, 'Are you trying to accuse me of pimping?'

Donna's eyes widened in shock. 'Of course not . . .'

'Well, why would you think I'd know anything about that then?'

Donna was frightened by his reaction.

'I am not accusing you of anything, but as you seem to be a member of the Soho élite I just thought you might know what it was all about, that's all. I am not, I repeat *not*, accusing you of anything untoward.'

'I should fucking hope so and all! Let me give you a bit of advice. Whatever Stephen Brunos is doing is his affair, all right? Not yours, mine or anyone else's. That's one of the first things you need to know. Don't judge anyone, don't question anyone, and never, ever under any circumstances ask anyone what they do for a living. Even a peepshow hostess. It's the unwritten law, love. Keep your beak out of everyone's affairs. It can become very unhealthy if you know too much about anyone, do you get my drift? If Stephen Brunos is running a few toms then that's his affair, not yours, and fucking certainly not mine.'

Donna lit another cigarette and said in a trembling voice, 'Why are you so aggressive towards me? Swearing upsets me.'

Alan really did laugh now.

'Swearing upsets you and you want to be my number two!' His voice was incredulous. 'Darlin', swearing around this gaff is like "God bless you" in a vicarage. Said all the time without a second thought. So get used to it. Now, let's look at all this from Stephen Brunos's point of view, shall we? I reckon he went to Georgio and said, "Right, got a bit of collateral, bruv?" "Yeah," says Georgio,

190

and bungs him a few grand. He's a sleeping partner now, ain't he? In fact, he wasn't just a sleeping partner; if I know Georgio he was in a fucking coma! Which is exactly how I like *my* sleeping partners, how everyone likes their sleeping partners! That, my little love, is why they're called fucking *sleeping partners*!'

Donna sat upright in her chair, her face flaming red with embarrassment.

'I just wanted some advice—'

Alan cut her off. 'And that is exactly what you got. And I'll give you another bit of advice while you're here. When we get going with this little lot, I hope you don't intend to pull any more stunts on me like this. Checking up on me, trying to be Girl Wonder, because if you do, me and you will have a little falling out. If I tell you to jump off a cliff, then you jump. No questions – nothing. Your job is to do what the fuck I tell you and relay the messages back to Happy Harold on the Island. That's it. I am in charge, let's get that straight once and for all.'

Donna was shocked and hurt by his words. She did not know that Alan was worried for her. After requesting another number two, he had been given word that this woman in front of him was what he had, whether he liked it or not. She was attractive, a nice person, but for company, not for working with on a daily basis on something that could get dangerous, nasty, and already had the bad luck to have Lewis hanging over it like the Sword of Damocles.

Donna stood up unsteadily. Picking up her handbag, she turned to leave the room. Alan sighed.

'I'm sorry, Donna.'

She turned at the door and he saw in the harsh light the glimmer of tears in her eyes. Walking over to her, he pulled her into his arms. The action made Donna really start to cry. She cried as she hadn't since the day Georgio was sentenced. She breathed in the smell of Alan Cox, the cigar and brandy odour mixed with a hint of lemon from his aftershave, she felt strong arms around her, pulling her frail body into his, and the longing for her husband overcame everything else, everything that he had said to her, and she found herself holding him, squeezing herself into the confined space of his arms. Frightened in case he let her go too soon and she couldn't assuage the grief that was inside her.

Alan held her while she cried, unable to understand his sudden tenderness towards her, his feeling that holding her was the right thing to do. Seeing her sitting in front of him, with her face drawn, her active mind concentrating on Stephen Brunos instead of on the job she was already up to her neck in, had angered him. Angered him

191

because he felt ineffective. Georgio wanted her, and so she was the number two. He wanted to ask her how she felt about her husband putting her life in danger, because that was exactly what he had done. It wasn't just a jailbreak here, and God Himself knew that was enough. It was a jailbreak under the nose of, and without the knowledge of, Donald Lewis.

He could feel her trembling, and when finally she pulled herself away from him, he was sorry. Desperately sorry. Because he was enjoying the nearness of her, the smell of her hair, her perfume.

'I'm sorry, Alan, you must think me a fool.'

He smiled gently down into her face. Her make-up was smudged, her eyes red and swollen, yet she looked more desirable to him then than any woman had before.

'You're upset, Donna, and I'm not surprised. I was a bully, and I'm sorry. I don't know what came over me.'

She took a deep shuddering breath.

'I think we were both at sixes and sevens today. Both in the wrong place at the wrong time. I'm not usually a crier – Georgio can bear me out on that.'

It was as if his name had opened up a gulf between them, and each subconsciously took a step back from the other, distanced themselves in case the embrace should be repeated.

'Let's both have another brandy,' Alan suggested, taking charge again, 'and then we'll talk properly about what you came here to ask, shall we? I promise not to bite your head off.'

Donna wiped her eyes once more with her fingers and smiled tremulously. Alan handed her a large white handkerchief and she patted her face carefully, dismayed at the black streaks appearing on the snowy linen.

Alan poured them both more drinks. Opening a box on his desk, he took out a cigarette and lit it, handing it to Donna as she once more seated herself in her chair. She took it gratefully, pulling on it hard, drawing the smoke down into her lungs as if it was oxygen and she was dying for lack of it.

'Drink your brandy.' Alan's voice was still low. He could feel the electric charge in the room and knew that Donna Brunos felt it as well.

'I'm afraid I had what is known as a shitty day today, Donna, and you came in on the tail end of it—'

She interrupted him. 'No, Alan, you were right in all you said, really. I should never have come here asking your advice like that. You have known Stephen a long time; this is your patch here, Soho, your way of life. I turn up like a silly schoolgirl asking stupid

192

questions on a whim – and it was a whim, you know. Nothing concrete, just a gut feeling.' She laughed gently as she spoke, feeling foolish once more. 'I'll ring Stephen tomorrow and apologise to him. He must feel like I have taken his kindness and kicked it back into his teeth. He really was a boon when Georgio was sentenced. So please . . . don't apologise. It's me who should be apologising, for bothering you in the first place.'

Alan grunted. If only she wouldn't be so bloody humble!

'Look, Donna, I don't mind you asking me questions, honestly. It's just that today I was a bit overwrought, that's all. Now as to what you said about Stephen, I think it would be best for all concerned if you left him to run Talkto. OK? Just leave him doing what he knows best. Really, Donna, it's the only thing you can do. I have set the ball rolling for the other business and believe me when I say, once we get our tongues around that lot, there won't be time for a shit, a shave or a shampoo.'

Donna laughed at him. She felt as if she had somehow been reborn. He was right, of course, she had no reason to try and tell Stephen how to run his businesses. He had done perfectly adequately without her. Who did she think she was anyway? In her mind's eye she had a vision of what Georgio would have said to her regarding Talkto and was uncomfortably aware it would be along the lines of Alan Cox's advice.

'Drink your brandy, ducks, and let's relax for a moment. Just through that doorway there is a bathroom. When you're ready, go and wash your face, you'll feel much better.'

Five minutes later he was listening to the taps running and cursing himself for what he had done. But he also told himself that as much as he had upset her, and he knew that he had, she would be much more upset by the time she was through with the next step of this operation. She had cried tonight because he had told her off. How would she react to people like Anthony Calder? And poor old Tony was one of the good guys!

Alan hoped deeply and honestly that before too long Donna Brunos would retire from the fray and let him get on with it his own way. As it was she was becoming a liability. Not least because he felt a bit too much for her, and at the end of the day, as he told himself over and over again, she was Georgio Brunos's wife, and Georgio had done him more than a few favours.

As she walked out of the small bathroom he smiled pleasantly at her, all the while planning a visit to Georgio to try and talk some sense into the man. Once he had decided that, he felt better.

Donna, for her part, was still embarrassed and humiliated. Even

193

though she accepted that Alan Cox was right and sensible in what he had said about Stephen she knew deep down that there was more going on with Stephen Brunos than met the eye – and she was determined to find out exactly what it was . . . Alan Cox was right to an extent, as she had just realised. Her name was down on Talkto. If she was a partner, silent or otherwise, and if Stephen was doing something illegal, surely that affected her? So she made up her mind to carry on looking into Talkto's businesses, even if Alan, and Georgio if he could have, advised her to stay away.

The couple sat opposite each other, both scheming, both smiling, and both glad of the other's company. Both hoping to forget what had taken place, because it had affected them more than either would have liked to admit.

Chapter Eighteen

Georgio and Timmy sat at a small table eating cheese omelettes and salad, made for them by Sadie.

Timmy shovelled half the omelette into his mouth on his fork. He chewed noisily, unaware of the faint look of revulsion on the faces of both Sadie and Georgio.

'This is handsome, Sade, do us another one.'

Sadie tutted and left the cell to go into the kitchen once more and resume cooking.

'She ain't a bad old stick, my Sade, is she, Georgio?'

Georgio smiled. 'No. In fact, she's all right really.'

Pleased with Georgio's answer, Timmy shoved the other half of the omelette into his mouth and chewed on it noisily.

'Didn't anyone ever learn you any manners, Timmy?'

The big man shrugged. His mouth full of food, he mumbled: 'Nah, what for? I ain't going to be eating with the Queen, am I?'

Georgio grinned. 'I think we can safely assume you're right there, Timmy. Honestly, you eat like you ain't eaten in months.'

Timmy picked his front teeth with his fork.

'Well, it's good scram, ain't it? I don't know why you're always going on about the way I eat, the way I smell and everything. I'm a man, ain't I? Men are a bit . . . well, manly.'

Georgio pushed the rest of his omelette on to Timmy's plate.

'Just because you're a man don't mean you can't have a wash or eat with your mouth closed, Timmy,' he said good-humouredly. 'Christ Almighty, how far do you think Sylvester Stallone would have got if he ate like a pig and smelled like a poke of devils? It's like torture in this cell some nights with the hum of you. Honestly, Timmy, I'm telling you as a mate.'

Before the big man could answer, Lewis walked into the small cell. 'You should listen to him, Timmy. Our Georgio likes his men to smell nice. He'll have Sadie off you if you're not careful.'

Timmy carried on eating, ignoring the man in front of him.

'I think it's about time you went into the kitchen with Sadie while I

195

have a little chat with my friend here.'

Timmy picked up his plate and walked towards the cell door. Lewis called after him.

'By the way, Timmy, I want you showered night and morning. You stink. You offend me.'

Timmy nodded slowly. 'Yes, Mr Lewis.'

Taking out a clean handkerchief, Lewis dusted off the chair Timmy had used and sat down.

'I don't know how you stand it locked up with him. I'll get him moved in with Sadie for you, OK?'

Georgio sipped his coffee. 'And then who will you put in with me?'

'A little mate of mine called Chopper Harris.' Lewis grinned, a feral, nasty grimace. 'You know my Chopper. He's as sweet as a nut.'

Georgio put down the coffee cup. 'I like sharing with Timmy. The guy's all right.'

Lewis shook his head. 'Sorry, Georgio, I have spoken. Chopper it is. He will be in this afternoon. Timmy will be informed in due course.'

Georgio felt his hand squeezing the thick white mug hard. It was pointless saying anything, as Lewis had just told him. He had spoken. And when Lewis spoke, people in this place jumped, whether they wanted to or not.

'But I'm quite happy with Timmy.' He tried one last time.

Lewis laughed softly. 'Surely you wouldn't stand in the way of love's young dream, would you? It gives the screws a laugh watching them try and get it together. They'll have to look elsewhere for their amusement now. I'm sorry, Georgio, I have already cleared it with everyone; you haven't any say in it.'

Georgio nodded. He was beaten and he knew it.

'You remember Chopper, don't you?' the insinuating voice went on. 'They're shipping him here from Durham for late this afternoon. He will be working for me while he's here. Me and Chopper go way back. I'll enjoy seeing him.'

Georgio stared at the table.

Lewis stood up and glanced at him.

'You'll like my Chopper. He's doing a twenty. Murdered two men, both villains. He cut one bloke's head right off. Nice bloke, old Chopper. You and him should get on like a house on fire. He's a scouser, my Liverpool boy.'

Georgio heard Lewis's laugh as he walked along the wing towards his own cell and gritted his teeth in rage and frustration. He had to get out, and soon. Now that Lewis was banging him up with one of

196

his trained gorillas, the need to escape was becoming more urgent by the second.

Alan and Donna were sitting in Joe Allen's eating Eggs Benedict and sipping ice-cold white wine.

Donna's appetite was fading by the second as she listened to Alan talking.

'The thing is, Donna, we need to get up to Scotland at the weekend. That's where we'll be meeting with Jimmy Mac. He will then take us through his armoury, which will be imperative if we're to spring Georgio.'

He was interrupted by the waiter who replenished their glasses. Donna smiled tightly at the handsome young man, swallowing her food with difficulty.

Alan carried on talking.

'We'll need to know exactly what we're going to use. We'll go to the Island tomorrow and see what we can suss from there. I reckon it'll have to be done by helicopter. Parkhurst is one of the hardest jails to escape from, but like most so-called fortresses it's got its blind spots. It's our job now to look for them.'

Donna placed her knife and fork neatly in the centre of her plate.

Alan chuckled. 'Lost your appetite?'

She could hear the sarcasm in his voice and pursed her lips. 'Not exactly. I'm interested in what you've got to say.' She wondered, not for the first time, why he always managed to put her back up.

'Well, as I was saying, we need an idea of where to take him. Myself, I think we should try and get him when he's off on a laydown, or else get him to play sick and be moved to a civilian hospital. We'll cross that bridge when we come to it. For the moment we'll just go and have a reccy.'

Donna lit a cigarette. 'Have we any way of getting a plan of Parkhurst?'

Alan grinned. 'I've already got one, love, and a plan of Durham, just in case. Normally on a big one you go to either Durham or the Island. So in case they decide to move him before we're ready, I'm not going to take any chances. Durham might be a better bet in a lot of ways, but it's swings and roundabouts. Either place will be hard to get out of.'

'Parkhurst looks pretty formidable to me.'

Alan wiped his mouth with a napkin.

'It is. For a start off, you've got a twenty-five-foot wall around the place. It's rounded and smooth at the top, you'll never be able to get a rope up there no matter what. Then inside that you've got a

197

twenty-five-foot electric fence with tremblers all over it. Anything over seven pounds lands on it, the alarms go off. On top of that is three lots of razor wire – no one is going over that! – then there's the cameras. They are everywhere, plus floodlights, dogs, the whole shebang. The only way out is straight up. That's where a helicopter comes into it. So as you can see, it's a big operation.

'Once he's out, we need to remove him quickly. Now he ain't going on the ferry, is he, so we need a boat of some description, then a secret destination for the boat to take him – a place where he can be picked up and subsequently helped to disappear. I think Southern Ireland's a good idea. Everyone else legs it to Spain. Ireland's a small place, but there's plenty of places to hide away until we can ship him off properly when the heat dies down.'

Donna sat listening to Alan in dismay. Now it was actually happening she felt a cold hand grip her heart. Pulling herself together, she stubbed out her cigarette and said: 'So once he's out of Parkhurst itself, we arrange a boat to Ireland?'

Alan shook his head. 'No. We arrange a boat to take him along the coast. Then we change him to a vehicle of some kind. We make our way to Scotland, and from there he'll go to Ireland. They'll be looking for a boat, won't they? If we sink the boat they'll still be looking for it. No one will guess he's in Jockland for a good while. When someone escapes they keep a look out on a fifty-mile radius. It's very rare for someone to be on the trot for any length of time. It's normally luck that stops them getting caught at once, but the luck usually runs out after a couple of days.

'What we need is to be well-prepared for any emergency. Have a back-up plan in case anything goes wrong, and to keep level heads. Georgio is depending on us now. He knows the ball's been set in motion and is trusting us to deliver the goods for him. What I need to know is, after hearing all this, are you sure you can handle it?'

Donna smiled, a tight, deliberate smile.

'Don't worry, Alan, I can handle anything you throw at me.'

She regretted her words immediately as she heard his answer.

'Well, I'm glad to hear that, love, because you'll have more than a bit of mud thrown at you before this lot's over, starting on Friday in Scotland.'

Picking up his wine glass he toasted her silently and Donna was hard-pressed not to slap his smug smiling face.

'Scotland?' Dolly's voice was high. 'What on earth are you going there for?'

Donna tensed irritably. After listening to Alan Cox telling her in no

198

uncertain terms that he thought she wasn't up to helping him, she now had to get the third degree from Dolly.

'I'm going for a weekend break, what's wrong with that?'

Dolly caught the nervousness in Donna's voice and kept her peace.

'Christ, Dolly, surely I can go away for the weekend if I want, can't I?'

'Of course you can, darlin', it was just unexpected.'

Donna wiped her hand across her face in agitation. 'Has Paddy rung in at all today?'

'No, love. I expect he'll phone about seven-thirty as usual.'

Donna nodded curtly and walked from the kitchen into the small office. Closing the door, she curled up in the deep easy chair in the foetal position.

She was in over her head even before it had all started. Listening to Alan today had been a frightening experience; she had felt the fear seeping out of her pores even as she sat there in Joe Allen's. All her big talk was forgotten. As much as she loved Georgio, and she did love him dearly, the full significance of what he had asked her to do had now come home to her. Donna Brunos was being asked to set up a prison break-out with men she would rather not know even existed, let alone have to meet.

She was expected to keep a level head, help with the arrangements, sort out the businesses as well as get her husband his freedom. Suddenly she realised that what she had taken on was too much for her. She wasn't strong enough to cope. When she was sitting with Georgio she could cope; when she was lying in bed missing him desperately she could cope; now the first steps had been taken, she wasn't sure she could cope with any of it. Alan Cox's smug grin had shown her that he could read her like a book, that he knew the fear his words had evoked. That the real truth of the situation had finally dawned on her.

Dolly knocked on the door and brought her in a cup of coffee and a letter.

'This came from your man by second post.'

Donna took the letter as if it was a live snake. Placing the coffee on the small table by Donna's chair, Dolly left the room to give her some privacy.

Opening the letter, she read the familiar words of love, loneliness and need. She read between the lines his plea for her to help him escape. She felt the waves of frustration coming off the two pieces of ruled prison paper. The well-worn phrases: *I love you, I miss you, and I need you*, were interspersed with, *I am depending on you*. Reading the letter again she knew that there was no going back now. For better or

199

worse, she would have to keep her part of the bargain. Folding up the letter, she let it drop on to the thick carpet. She was to realise later on, during a sleepless night, that much as she loved her husband, a new element had entered her feelings about him. It was resentment.

She resented him for asking so much of her now, after never asking anything of her before.

Slowly she felt panic rising inside her, felt the cold heavy sweat across her back and shoulders that always accompanies acute fear. Lighting a cigarette with hands that trembled, she sat and pondered her situation properly for the first time.

Before today it had been talk, just talk. Now it was fact, she was really into all this, up to her neck. She was now part of it all and it was scaring her. It was all somehow coming true.

One thought was with her constantly. No matter what she felt, how frightened she became, she would go through with it. She owed Georgio that much.

Outside in the kitchen Dolly was on the phone to Big Paddy. He was as surprised as she was to hear that Donna was going off to Scotland for the weekend.

Paddy quickly understood that Donna's seeing so much of Alan Cox and now going away could mean only one thing: they were going to spring Georgio. And he also knew that Donna, whether she let him in on the secret or not, was going to need all the help she could get.

Maeve was listening to Stephen as he talked with his brothers. She could hear the peculiar whine in his voice that he affected whenever he spoke these days about Donna. Maeve knew that somehow the two had fallen out, but about what she couldn't even begin to guess. The worst of it all was, she wasn't in a position to ask. It was a situation where once you found out, you would be dragged into the centre of it and asked to take sides.

That was the last thing she needed at this time. With Georgio's being away, the family was already minus one member. She didn't want to open her mouth and estrange another two.

Nuala's voice was tight as she spoke to her brother. 'What's this with you and Donna all of a sudden? Why the upset?'

Stephen shrugged. 'There's no upset really, I just wish she would stick to her own businesses and leave mine alone.'

Nuala tossed her dark hair impatiently. 'You were on to her about taking on everything, we all were, she's only doing what was expected of her. Myself, I knew she'd be great at it all.'

Stephen carried on drinking his coffee. Then, 'All I'm trying to say

200

is, she should keep her nose out of my affairs. When I asked Georgio to be a silent partner, I didn't think for one moment I'd have his little wife, dear Donna, breathing down my neck.'

Maeve was disturbed and upset at her son's tone.

'What have you to hide then, that all of a sudden your business is so private? What's the rub, Stephen? That child is only doing what her husband wanted, nothing more, and as Nuala says, it's what we all advised at the beginning.'

'That "child" is a grown woman, Mum,' he said viciously, 'and she can take the helm of all Georgio's businesses if she wants, I don't give a damn about that. It's her interference in *my* operations that is annoying me.'

Maeve smiled nastily. 'So, I ask you again, what have you got to hide that's so important Donna can't know about it? Is it something to do with Talkto at all?' Maeve's voice was heavy with innuendo and Nuala listened in dismay to the burgeoning argument between her mother and brother.

'Talkto is a good money-making company—'

Maeve interrupted her son, her voice rising in temper. 'Do you think I'm some kind of fool, me laddo? I knew from day one what the escort agency really was, and it didn't take me long to suss out this Talkto crap. You're me son and I love you, Jaysus Himself knows that, but sometimes I wonder just how eejity you think me and your father are.

'I've seen some of the so-called girls that work for you. Even that secretary, the one with the face like a boiled shite, even she isn't as good as she tries to make out. How she can take your calls and still hold that snooty beak of hers in the air, I don't know. So don't you sit there with your big galoot-looking features and come on at me about Donna Brunos! You should take a leaf out of her book, son, and see how a business should be run. I've a good mind to take me hand across your arse, as big as you are.'

'Mum!' Nuala's voice was scandalised.

'Don't you "Mum" me, Nuala. This one here thinks he's some kind of gift from God. Well, it's about time he was knocked down a few pegs. I've known for years he was whoring. Sure, your father knew straight off. Escort agency, my arse! Now he has the gall to sit and pull my Donna apart like that because she's likely found out what he's up to and, being a decent kind of girl, wants no more to do with it.

'Him and Georgio were both great disappointments to me, Georgio because he could never see what he already had, only what he wanted, and him because he's not man enough to get himself a real job, a real

201

business. When I think of them women it turns me stomach inside out. So now you know, Stephen Brunos, that I know all about ye, and I don't like it.'

He stood up unsteadily. 'I will forget what you just said, Mum. I can see you're overwrought.'

She laughed scornfully. 'You were always the man with the words. Even as a child you could talk the hind leg off the table. Well, let's clear the air here once and for all. Every time I think of what you're doing I feel as sick as a priest at a Jewish wedding. You and Georgio broke me heart between you, and now I've had it up to here.' She poked herself in the forehead to emphasise her point. 'When I think of how you spoke about Donna, you two-faced bastard of hell, I could cut the legs from under ye.'

'I think I'd better go.'

Nuala pulled on her brother's arm, shocked to the core at all her mother had said.

'Oh, let him go, Nuala, I'm sick of the sight of him.'

Nuala watched her brother walk from the room and Maeve ran to the doorway and called down the stairs to where Stephen was opening the front door.

'And tell that fat bitch you're knocking off it's a sin against God. She's old enough to be your mother!'

Nuala stood with her fingers across her lips at her mother's parting words. Maeve pushed past her daughter and stormed back into the tiny front room.

'The cheek of that one! I saw him with me own eyes, kissing and pawing at an old biddy, be Christ. I could have ripped the head off the two of them. What have I bred, Nuala girl? One away till Judgment Day and the other a granny lover. If it wasn't so sad it'd be hilarious.'

'Oh, Mum!'

'Jaysus and Mary, is that all you learnt at that convent? "Oh, Mam!" I only told him the truth, it's about time someone did.'

She lowered herself on to the old settee which groaned under her weight.

'This room used to be full of children. I felt blessed because my seven kids were eating well, were healthy. I used to thank God every night on me knees for it all. Now I ask Him what happened? What went wrong? Mario is as queer as a nine-bob note, Georgio's away for eighteen Christing years, and Stephen . . . clever, handsome Stephen is running women, and living the life of Riley on the proceeds. Only you, Mary and Patrick seem half-normal, and Mary is so boring you'd fall asleep on the phone to her. All her talk about the neighbours, and

202

what will people think, and all the rest of it. Jaysus, she's another one!

Nuala shook her head in wonderment. In all her life she had never heard her mother talk as she was now.

'Oh, Mum.'

Maeve lit herself a Number Six and said through clenched teeth. 'If you "Oh, Mam" me once more, I'll rip every hair out of your fecking head, and trample it into the carpet!'

Nuala stood dumbfounded as her mother smoked her cigarette in short, erratic puffs. After a while she said gently, 'Shall I make you a nice cup of coffee, Mum?'

Maeve shook her head. 'No, lass. Take that look off your face, it's tearing the heart out of me. Me and you will go to the restaurant now, and open a good bottle of brandy. We'll drink till we start laughing. But I warn you, child, that could be some time.'

'Oh Mum, what's happened to this family?'

Maeve stood up painfully. 'Nothing much happened, Nuala love. You all grew up, that's all.'

Her mother's voice had tears in it and Nuala held her in her arms, fighting back tears of her own.

Dolly tapped on the office door and entered quietly.

'Are you all right, darlin'? I was getting worried about you.'

Donna looked into her face and felt a surge of shame at the way she had spoken to her of late.

'I'm all right, Dolly. Come away in and pour yourself a sherry.'

Dolly poured herself a generous measure of sweet sherry and sat in a deep leather chair by the window.

'I always liked this room, Donna. If I close me eyes I can see Georgio sitting where you are and shouting the odds over the telephone, winking at me at the same time. He was a lad!' Her voice was filled with sadness and nostalgia.

Donna sat forward in the chair, listening intently to what Dolly was saying.

'Do you remember the time you were going to Blackpool and at the last minute he made me come with you? Those were the days, I wish to God they were still here. He was a great man, Georgio, a good man.'

'Dolly, he's still with us, woman, he's not dead!'

The housekeeper shrugged and sipped her sherry.

'Well, he might as well be, stuck in bleedin' Parkhurst. I ask you, Donna, what kind of life is it for him? It's bad enough for you and you've got your freedom.'

Donna watched as Dolly's face brightened.

'Here, Donna, do you remember that time my old man came after me and started yelling and carrying on at the front door! His face when Georgio came out to him. It was a picture that I'll never forget. Georgio went ballistic! I can still see him kicking me old man up the khyber as he slung him off the driveway.'

Donna smiled at the woman's glee.

'He was a bastard to me, my old man.' Dolly's voice had lost its jocularity now. 'When I was pregnant with me boy, he knocked me from one end of that house to the other. I remember going up Mile End Road Hospital . . . oh, it must have been 1943. The bombing was well underway then, in the East End anyway. I had a black eye and a fat lip and the baby hadn't moved for three days. I knew it was brown bread, like. He'd kicked me in the stomach. That was always old Joey's finale. The kick in the guts.' She flapped her hand in a gesture of contempt.

'Anyway, in I went, all sorry for meself like, and they deliberately ignored me boatrace. Like I looked normal or something. In them days, see, it wasn't discussed. Not like now, with all these shows on with people telling everyone how they can't stop thieving or can't stop gambling. In them days you kept your own counsel. Once you were married to the fucker, that was it, for better or worse, for richer or poorer. And believe me, girl, for most of us it was worse and poorer, not the other way round!

'I was fifteen when I lost that little boy. Hard to imagine anyone married at fifteen, ain't it? But back then, well . . . I had a belly full of arms and legs. The old man beat him up, we got wed, and that was it, the rest of your life. He was eighteen, with a cock that stood to attention if a breeze went up his trouser leg! Randy bugger he was. Probably still is.'

Donna listened to Dolly's sad voice and felt the usual wave of anger at the treatment she and other women like her received.

'Why did you stay with him, Dolly?'

'That's the hard one, girl. That's the sixty-four-thousand-dollar question.' She put her head to one side and thought for a few minutes. 'One, because I had nowhere else to go. I couldn't go back to me mother's. She still had six left at home younger than me, even if she was married. And two, because in a strange way I loved him. I loved him for a long time, you know. I know it's hard to believe, but you must understand, in the war marriages were quick because you never knew what was around the corner, see? You could be bombed out, blown up, anything. So you did things you wouldn't have ordinarily. Like let an eighteen-year-old bloke give you one in your

204

back garden, up against the coal shed. It was the most exciting night of my life. He could have had the pick of all the girls and he chose me. Everyone was after him!'

Dolly grinned snidely. 'I wish to fuck one of the others *had* got him. Sally Lancaster was so jealous when I married him she never spoke to me again. She married an insurance salesman after the war, and moved to Penge. I used to think that was the epitome of sophistication. Penge! Always looked nice she did, her kids was always immaculate. In those days that was your yardstick.'

Donna refilled Dolly's glass.

'You're happy now though, aren't you?'

Dolly nodded. 'Take no notice of me, love, I'm just missing the big fella. You and him have always treated me decent, like. I've got a little niche here, something I never thought I'd have. There's me little flat, me work, and you two. It's more than I ever thought I'd get and I often think it's more than I deserve.'

Donna looked into Dolly's eyes and felt a great rush of love for her.

'We were the lucky ones, Dolly. We were lucky to get you.'

'Lucky? Well, perhaps you were, girl. If you knew the number of women who have to live lives similar to the one I lived with my old man, you'd be really shocked. At least Georgio loves you – you can see it in him. It shines from him. I envy you that, in a nice way of course, but it's envy all the same.'

Donna looked into her glass and sighed heavily.

'I miss him so much, Dolly. Since he's been gone everything seems to have gone to pot. I miss him so much.'

Dolly heard the loneliness in Donna's voice.

'Once your man's home, we can all get back to normal, eh?' she said gently.

Donna sat back in her chair and pushed her heavy hair off her face.

'Do you think Georgio is guilty? Honestly now. Do you think he deserved what he got?'

Dolly shook her head vigorously.

'What the hell are you asking me that for? Of course he didn't deserve it! He's innocent as a newborn babe. What's come over you, Donna Brunos, to be asking me a thing like that? I can't believe I heard right.'

'Oh Dolly, calm down. I'm asking you this in private. I want to know if you think my Georgio was involved in any of the things he was accused of?'

Dolly shook her head once more vehemently.

'No way. Never. He had his faults, but at the end of the day, he wasn't bad, not at rock bottom. He wouldn't have ordered those men

205

to kill the guards or anything like that. He cried when the dog died. Can you really imagine him planning something like that? He might have supplied the cars, I wouldn't be surprised about that, but the other? Never, not in a million years.'

Donna pulled on her cigarette. 'You sound very sure about that.'

Dolly stood up. Tossing back the last of her sherry she said bitterly, 'Well, it's just as well one of us feels sure, ain't it? Only it doesn't sound as if you know what you think. I'll give you a bit of advice. Don't think too much, Donna Brunos, it's not good for you. Once you start thinking too much, you get to brooding, and brooding leads to trouble. Take my word for it.

'Now, if you'd been married to my old man I could understand it, but not with Georgio. That man worshipped you, and I always thought you worshipped him. I know you did. So don't you start doubting him now. It would kill him. He ain't dead, you're right there, but as I said, stuck in Parkhurst, he might as well be.

'Everything he ever wanted or ever cared about is in this house, remember that. If he loses you, he's lost everything. He's depending on you to see him through this, to have faith and confidence in him. Bear that in mind, young lady.'

Donna watched as Dolly practically bristled from the room. That word always seemed to be in the back of her mind lately. *Depending*. Georgio was depending on her, they were all depending on her to keep everything going for him. It was like a death knell.

She stared down at the now-cold coffee and bit her lip. Life wasn't fair. In all her years with Georgio she had loved him, looked after his home, cared for him and depended on him emotionally. Now it seemed he was depending on her – and she was finding it difficult to accept.

After years of just being there for him, at his whim, the novelty of being the strong one, the organiser, was beginning to wear off. He needed her all right, he was depending on her all right, but only because ultimately there was no one else he could really trust.

It was this that was really galling her.

Dolly was already talking about him in the past tense; most people did. It was all about before he went away, never about the present. Talk of 'when Georgio gets out' was growing less and less, even from his family.

He was depending on her to spring him from one of the most secure jails in the country. He was asking her to take her life, her very own freedom, into her hands – because if they were caught she would be sent to prison too. Yet she knew that as far as he was concerned, and indeed everyone else, she owed it to him. He was depending on

206

her. After listening to Alan Cox today, the enormity of what Georgio was asking her to do had finally hit her.

It went against everything she believed in. She had always been a law-abiding, upright citizen, and had never in her life had any dealings with the police. She was praying now that things would stay that way. The thought of going to prison terrified her, yet what was the alternative?

No one else could be trusted, or so Georgio said. Yet he trusted Alan Cox. In fact, as much as she hated to admit it, Donna also trusted Alan Cox.

Now she was in way over her head and there was nothing more to think or to talk about.

Their course was set. She was going to Scotland on Friday to negotiate with a man called Jimmy Mac, instead of having her hair done and maybe going into the West End to do some shopping. Her world was upside down, and she was too far in to get out without a fight. Georgio would never forgive her if she let him down. *He was depending on her.*

Taking a last puff on her cigarette, she put it out carefully and stood up. She'd take a pill and have an early night. Put it all out of her head until the morning.

But Donna didn't sleep, even with the pill inside her. She would not have been comforted to know that Maeve Brunos was also lying awake in a similar state.

Both women were feeling let down by people they loved and trusted.

But one of the women was willing to put all she possessed, from her freedom to her good name, on the line for one man.

Because Donna Brunos loved her husband, no matter what he had done.

In a funny way she could even sympathise with Dolly.

Georgio also had trouble sleeping.

As he lay on his bunk, Chopper ensconced above him, he heard the pitiful wailing of a young man of twenty-one who was doing a life sentence for robbery and attempted murder. The boy's painfully lonely cries brought tears to Georgio's eyes because he could hear an echo of them in his own heart.

The sound travelled along the landings and into the cells. All over the Wing men were putting themselves in the boy's place. Most were over the most difficult period of adjustment. It took a young lad, after a visit from his mum, to put it all into perspective for them once more.

They were trapped, for good or bad. Trapped.

207

Chopper turned over noisily on the bunk above. 'Ah, the poor little lad. I wonder if the old woman he robbed cried herself to sleep?'

'He ain't in here for robbing an old lady.' Georgio's voice was tight.

Chopper laughed nastily. 'Maybe not, but you can bet your bottom dollar there's an old biddy somewhere with a memory of him. That's how we all started.'

Georgio fluffed up his pillow which felt as if it was stuffed with pieces of flint and said, 'You speak for yourself, mate.'

Chopper sniggered, glad he'd raised Georgio's hackles.

'Oh, but I am, Georgio. I am. I'd murder me own fucking sister if the price was right. Let's get that straight right away.'

Georgio closed his eyes even as he knew it was a futile thing to do. After what Chopper had said, sleep would be the furthest thing from his mind.

The boy's crying was getting on his nerves now. It was almost eerie in the darkness of the cells. Five minutes later, it seemed most of the men felt the same way. A man shrieked: 'Put a fucking sock in it, will ya?'

And the place was quiet once more. Except for the snores, groans and loud bursts of wind that were usual in any prison.

208

Chapter Nineteen

Georgio was awake well before the bell rang. He lay in the silence of the early morning, listening to the heavy sound of his own breathing. In the bunk above him, Chopper's snores were low and regular. He was asleep. Georgio toyed with the idea of getting up quietly and hammering him with the metal slop bucket, but dismissed the notion as soon as it wandered into his mind. Anything he did to Chopper would be repaid tenfold. That much, at least, was a certainty.

He knew the man above him was Lewis's plant – at least Lewis made no bones about that. He also knew that in order to live he had to keep on the right side of Lewis, Chopper, and any other henchmen Lewis employed.

One good thing about Chopper, he showered, washed out his socks, and put his books and shaving stuff away neatly – a result after Timmy. Though Georgio was missing Timmy now, even with his smell and dirty habits.

Chopper moved in the bunk, and the noise was heavy in the confined space. This huge hulk above him would, and could, kill him on a whim. Lewis's whim. It was this that was making Georgio so uneasy.

As he heard the distant clanking of doors, and the early-morning noises of the prison, he relaxed. The days were just about bearable; now the nights would be like torture.

He consoled himself with the thought that Alan and Donna were working for his release and it cheered him. Christ Himself knew, he desperately needed something to latch on to. Even his early-morning erection had died a death at the thought of Chopper, Lewis and the rest of them.

As Georgio slipped a hand into his boxer shorts, Chopper was off his bunk in one swift movement.

'Wanking already, Brunos?'

Georgio snatched his hand out of his boxers as if he'd been burnt. 'No, scratching me nuts.'

Chopper laughed, and stripping off his underwear, stood in all

209

his glory before Georgio, a half-smile on his face. Georgio's eyes were immediately drawn to the biggest penis he had ever seen in his life.

Chopper, obviously used to the reaction, grinned, showing incredibly white teeth.

'You'll get used to seeing it, man, it always takes people like that the first time, especially the women!'

Walking to the cell door, Chopper removed the wedge and started banging on the metal with his fist.

'Open this fucking door up, will you? I want to have a shite!' Turning to Georgio he said nonchalantly, 'People always think my nickname's because I use an axe. But as you now know, that's not true.'

The door was opened by a warder and, picking up a towel, Chopper walked out on to the landing.

Georgio followed him, in spite of himself amazed at the reaction of the men around them. Chopper, stark naked, strolled down to the showers like a prize stallion. Sadie, coming out of his cell, squealed with delight. 'Oi, love, I'll have half!'

Grinning, Chopper walked into the shower room.

Making a face at Georgio, Timmy said in awe, 'Fuck me, he must use a bar of soap just washing his donger!'

Lewis was already in the shower room. He had finished his ablutions and smiled at Georgio as he passed him.

Big Petey Jones called across the shower room: 'All right, Chopper? Long time no see. I heard you'd stuck your cock out the window in Durham and half the nick disappeared over the wall by sliding down it!'

Chopper, still grinning, put down his towel. Taking his bar of Camay, he went over to a bull-necked Irishman called Davey O'Keefe.

Davey was watching him warily, and the men realised that something was going down.

The shower room went silent.

'Hello, Davey, long time no see.'

He nodded. 'All right, Chopper?'

Chopper put his hands on his hips and said loudly, 'Now when was the last time we met? Oh, I remember. It was in Durham top security. You'd just grassed me up on an attack I had made on your mate – what was his name?'

Davey stared at the Colossus in front of him without saying a word. He was resigned; he knew he was for a hiding and he just wanted it over with.

'That's it – Tommy Blackmoore. A slag of the first water. I know you was his mate, Davey, so don't take this too personally.'

As Chopper raised his fist, Davey O'Keefe was underneath his arm and on his way out of the shower room. Suddenly, the thought of the hiding was more than he could bear.

The next thing, the two men were tearing along the landing, both naked, both excited. Mr Ellington, the warder on bathroom duty that morning, was just leaving his little office as he saw them run past. He stepped back inside it and put the kettle on. Picking up his copy of the *Sport*, he decided, wisely, to sit the lot of it out.

Mr Borga and his assistant watched with smiling faces the antics of Davey and Chopper. As Chopper grabbed at Davey's hair, and dragged him backwards, they shook their heads with glee. All the cons were watching now. It was a bit of light relief, a bit of excitement in an otherwise boring day.

After punching Davey a few times, Chopper picked the man up, standing with him above his head for a few seconds, like a champion weightlifter, before he threw him over the landing, to the roar of the men and warders alike.

Davey screamed as he hurtled through the air and landed in one of the nets kept in place for events such as this and for attempted suicides.

The younger men all gathered around and the warders pulled Davey O'Keefe back on to the landing.

'Did you see him belt him! Did you see the size of that bloke's hands? Like bunches of fucking bananas!'

Mr Borga said loudly, and to the amusement of the whole Wing, 'It could have been worse, son. He could have smacked him one with his cock. Now that *would* have hurt!'

Georgio watched as Chopper swaggered back to the shower room, a half-smile on his face.

Chopper had done a great PR job on himself in two minutes. One, he had put himself on the men's side by paying back a debt of honour. To grass was to die, even if it was over a mate. Two, he hadn't really hurt Davey, just terrified him, which was a fair logic because Davey O'Keefe wasn't a hard man. Three, his enormous member, and his good-natured acceptance of the remarks about it, had made him into a decent bloke. His chopper would be the talking point of the day with screws and cons alike. This was the man Georgio was banged up with, a man he knew would hurt him at the drop of a hat.

Thoughtfully, Georgio wandered back to the showers. As he watched Chopper under the water, he wondered just how long it

211

would be before Lewis got fed up with waiting and demanded his money again.

Alan Cox was up early, had breakfasted alone, and was now on his fourth cup of coffee. He lit his first cigar of the day, a small cheroot, and blowing the smoke lazily out of his mouth, grimaced as the first spasm of coughing attacked him. He had a lot to do today, a lot of arranging. He had missed pitting his wits against the police, missed the element of uncertainty that became like a drug to many bank robbers and that always proved their downfall. He'd missed the suppressed excitement of knowing something big was going down and being a major part of it.

Amigo's was doing well, exceptionally well, but the urge to succeed was long gone, as he'd known from the first few nights of its opening that it was already a foregone conclusion. Alan liked setting things up. Once they were up and running and doing well, they bored him. He liked the element of risk. Now he was arranging Georgio's break out, he felt the familiar rush of adrenaline and thanked God for it. It was what he had needed.

The only bugbear was Donna Brunos. He had tried every trick in the book to put her off taking the job of number two. He knew in his heart that she was shit scared, yet still she insisted she was going to do it. He admired and respected her for that, even as she annoyed him, because he had a feeling she would prove to be a liability.

In a way, Alan also admitted to himself, he was a bit jealous of Georgio. His own wife would never have even countenanced doing anything remotely similar for him. She would have been scandalised and disgusted if he had even suggested it. Yet Georgio had, Georgio Brunos, 'the hostesses' friend' as Alan used to call him, who ran around on that lovely wife of his with young tarts – and they were tarts. By Christ, a few were jailbait, barely out of school. One girl Georgio had had couldn't have been more than fifteen for all her big tits and backcombed blonde hair – yet Georgio's woman, Donna Brunos, was willing to risk a prison sentence for him. It was laughable really. But then she didn't know the half of it. Which was probably just as well.

What really troubled him was why Georgio was involving her. There was something fishy about it, nothing that Alan could put his finger on . . . but it just seemed wrong somehow.

Maybe, he conceded, it was his own natural sense of fair play. He would no more have asked this of his wife than he would have asked it of his mother or daughter. It was best to keep family out of the criminal part of your life; it was the code most villains lived by. Even the

212

Krays had kept their mother out of their dealings, and that was more power to them. Womenfolk were to be loved, respected, cared for. You did not bring them on a bank robbery or ask them to get rid of stolen booty. It was an unwritten law. Anyway, most women couldn't keep their traps shut. If they knew their old man was out blagging, by the time they'd told their mates, discussed it with their mum, and chatted to a few acquaintances, the Old Bill would be waiting at the car for him as he raced back from the post office or bank, his shooter at the ready and his balaclava full of nervous sweat and spit.

That was what had been bugging him!

Why was Georgio so adamant that his number two had to be his wife? Why not Stephen, his brother? Why not Big Paddy, his oldest mate? Why a little slim woman with large blue eyes and the most gorgeous hair and legs Alan had ever clapped eyes on? Yet, even as he cursed the fates that had made her go against his unspoken advice yesterday, as he cursed her for being so hard-nosed about helping her husband out, a little part of him was pleased. Because he realised, with a flash of insight that should have knocked him down, how glad he was that he would still be seeing her regularly. It was a long time since a woman had interested him so much.

Later on as he showered, and the London skyline was just beginning to appear with the dawn, he reminded himself of all Georgio had done for him, and reminded himself too that Donna Brunos was his best friend's wife.

Maeve and Mario arrived at Donna's house at eight-fifteen. Maeve parked her Lada in the drive, the old familiar surge of pleasure rushing through her at the sight of the mansion. Donna answered the door to them herself, a large smile plastered on her white face. Maeve took in the black circles under her eyes, the tightness of her skin and the slump to her shoulders, and silently cursed Georgio even as she asked brightly how he was.

Mario, in his usual quiet way, kissed Donna gently and asked her if she was sleeping all right.

Pleased to see them, Donna assured him she was fine and led them through to the large kitchen for coffee.

Dolly beamed at them as they walked in, taking in Maeve's old lilac coat with a wince, remembering the suede and leather coat Georgio had bought for her and which, to Dolly's knowledge, she had never worn.

'Hello, Dolly love. This one is so bloody busy these days, I said to Mario here, "We'll descend on her early in the morning, we're bound to catch her in then!" '

213

Mario grinned. 'You're looking well, Doll, it's nice to see you.'

She nodded and set about making the coffee. She observed Mario surreptitiously, taking in the effeminate features and gestures. He was like a poor man's Georgio, except where his brother's face was chiselled and manly, Mario's was womanish. Indeed, it seemed a shame to Dolly, and Maeve if she could have admitted it out loud, that Nuala hadn't got Mario's features and he Nuala's. Dolly watched the way he picked up his cup and sipped his coffee fastidiously. The way used his fingers as a comb to push his hair out of his eyes. The way he raised his eyebrows as he spoke to emphasise a point. Dolly sighed heavily. He was as bent as a nine-bob note, all right. She would lay money on that.

Maeve watched her son eagerly. He had always had a rapport with Donna and now he was making her smile and Maeve could have kissed him for it.

'Are you still working with John?' Donna asked.

Mario shook his head. 'No, Don, I'm afraid we had a bit of a falling out. I'm seriously thinking of going abroad for a while. My Uncle Costas in Rhodes has offered me an opening out there. I'll see how I feel. I quite fancy a year or two in Falaraki. I know it's a bit of a shithole, but I thought if I moved into a small apartment in Lindos, I could have the best of both worlds. You know, the madness and frenetic pace of Falaraki and the tranquil beauty of Lindos. Also my friend Casper lives there and I can bunk in with him for a while till I get me bearings.'

Donna saw the tightening of Maeve's lips and felt an urge to giggle. She must know Mario was homosexual, he seemed to exude it as other people did sexiness or charm. Unlike Maeve, Donna would have been thrilled to have been given a son like Mario. Homosexual or not, he was a good, kind, respectable person and that was the main thing as far as Donna was concerned. He had never been a day's trouble to Maeve and Pa Brunos. He had worked hard at school, gone on to the Poly in Barking, which was now the East London University, and had done very well for himself.

The only thing he had supposedly done wrong was to fall for a tall blond boy called Casper. And after a few fraught years, Maeve's tantrums, and Georgio's and Stephen's jibes, he had broken up with the boy. Donna knew that Georgio and Maeve, indeed all the family, had felt it was a phase he was going through, and that some red-blooded female would come along and show him the error of his ways. Only Donna had accepted him for what he was, and consequently they had become very close.

'I think a year or two in Greece would do you the world of good,'

214

she said now. 'Does Casper still run the bar in Lindos?'

'He's thinking of buying another one now,' Mario said happily. 'In a little place called Afando, near Falaraki. So I can work for Casper or Uncle Costas really. Work's not the problem.'

Maeve pursed her lips and changed the subject.

'What are you doing on Sunday, Donna? I thought maybe the two of you might like to come over for dinner.'

Donna shook her head sadly. 'Sorry, Maeve, I'm away at the weekend. I'm going to Scotland.'

Maeve's eyebrows were raised practically off her forehead.

'Scotland! What on earth are you going to do up there?'

Donna laughed gently. 'Anyone would think I was going to the Himalayas! I have to sort out a bit of business for Georgio that's all. It's complicated, so I won't bore you with it. But I'm sure Dolly would like to come to you for dinner.'

'Please, Maeve. After a weekend here on me Jack Jones, I'll be ready for a bit of jawing.'

'I'll send this fellow here to pick you up about one then,' Maeve decided. 'OK? We don't eat till late on a Sunday.'

Dolly nodded. 'I'll make a nice dessert then. That can be my contribution.'

'Make that cake I like, Death by Chocolate.' Mario's voice was filled with longing.

Maeve shook her head. 'He eats like a fecking horse and never a spare bit of flesh on him. It'd tear the heart out of you to watch this one eat!'

Mario grinned and in a perfect parody of her voice said: 'And it'd tear the ears off you to listen to this one rawmaishing all day!'

Everyone laughed and Donna realised that Mario had been a blind without her realising it. She knew Maeve and Dolly wanted the lowdown on why she was going to Scotland, and thanks to Mario she didn't have to go through the third degree. It occurred to her that this business with Georgio was going to be even harder than she had anticipated, and God Himself knew, she was already more than aware of how hard it was. On top of everything else she now had to try and get out and about without the two older women growing suspicious about her movements. Once more the sheer enormity of what she was doing almost crushed her under its great weight.

Only Mario noticed how quiet and abstracted she had become, because Dolly and Maeve were now discussing the merits of dishwashers and microwaves. His heart went out to her. She looked so small, so alone, and for some reason, absolutely terrified.

★ ★ ★

215

Donna was in the car lot offices going through the paperwork. Carol was sitting opposite her, her face settled into a tight mask of displeasure.

'The thing is, Carol,' Donna was explaining, 'I did the credit checks on Masters myself. He's blacklisted. I told Davey that. Now I see he has become the proud owner of a Mercedes Sports and is buying it through JCY finance. A finance company I seem to keep coming across, though I can't find it in the Yellow Pages.'

Carol took a deep puff on her Rothman's and grinned.

'You wouldn't find them there, love. JCY is a subsidiary of a company called Talkto. It's a private loan company we use for people who can't get credit because they've been made bankrupt or whatever, but we know on good authority they're OK for the dosh. It's simple.'

Donna had trouble hiding the shock she was feeling at being told Talkto had a subsidiary which was in effect a loan company. Or loan shark would probably be a better term, because you didn't borrow large amounts of money without a guarantee that it would be paid back, even she had learnt that much.

'So what happens if Masters can't pay for some reason?'

Carol licked her lips. 'Don't worry, he'll pay. Masters is an Essex Man, love. He has a big house, a big car, a good lifestyle and no real employment. That's all I can tell you. He's always bought his motors from us, and he always will. It's as simple as that. Every now and again he does us a right favour and we return it. Let's just leave it at that, shall we?'

Donna pushed back her heavy chestnut hair and shook her head. 'I'm sorry, Carol, but I can't leave it. I want to know what Masters's favours are and why we're so grateful.'

Carol's face became hard, and for a few seconds Donna was afraid of her. Carol Jackson was a known hard woman, Donna had always been aware of that. Even the police would think twice before going round to her house. She was like a man in that respect. Had the same attitude. She was a fighter, a physical fist-fighter. Donna, though, stood her ground. The mention of Talkto guaranteed that.

'Listen to me, Donna, and listen fucking good! There's some things that you don't need to know about. And Georgio don't need to know about, neither. Me and Davey ran this place perfectly adequately before Georgio was banged up. Now I will hold me hand up to a bit of skulduggery here and there, but that is down to Davey and me. It has nothing to do with you or your old man. Do I make myself clear?

'Over the years Georgio has picked up his money, and been bloody

216

glad of it at times and all, when it's bailed him out of difficult situations. He never, ever questioned our methods of getting it. In nine years we ain't never been tucked up once by Masters, or any of the others who use our finance company. So please, leave it at that.'

Donna felt the sheer weight of Carol Jackson's anger. Even her body language was aggressive. Her face was a tight mask, her arms and torso stiff with indignation. Suddenly, Donna wished she had never got involved in the car firm. It had spelt trouble from the first.

'Have the insurance company been in touch yet about the payout for the cars?'

Carol relaxed. Donna was having the good sense to change the subject; she could afford to be magnanimous.

'Yes, actually they have. Their assessor is coming again on Tuesday. This kind of thing can take a year or two to sort out. They take your money for the insurance, but they don't like giving it back.'

Donna stood up silently, her face drawn and white.

'Answer me one question, Carol, and I promise I'll never ask you anything about JCY again. How long have you been using it as a finance company?'

Carol wiped her heavily jewelled hand across her forehead. 'Six and a half years to be exact. Georgio introduced us to it, as it goes. All dealers use different finance companies. You know your trouble, Donna? You're too naive for this kind of caper. Well, let me tell you one last thing. To survive as long as we have in this business, you need an edge. JCY is that edge for us. You only have to drive through Leigh-on-Sea, Romford, Manor Park, Ilford, Dagenham, Chelmsford, fucking Barking, in fact anywhere in the south-east, and you will see car lot after car lot. Well, in competition that tough, you need to be able to offer that bit more. JCY is our little bit more. Be grateful to it. It bailed your old man out of the shit more than once.'

Donna sat down again heavily and Carol took pity on the woman in front of her because she knew Donna was not really ready for the big bad world as everyone else knew it. Georgio had cushioned her from so much. Now she was finding it all out, the hard way. Carol's voice was softer as she said: 'Listen, Donna love. You've done a great job with everything, the sites, here. You know, you've been a brick. But you must learn to accept a bit of ducking and diving as the norm. We all do. Even the Old Bill have their perks, love. If we couldn't offer JCY we'd be like every other little tinpot car dealer. There's a whacking great recession out in the real world, Donna, and everyone has to do their little bit to ensure they don't go under. Whether you're a bigwig or a small concern.

'How many little builders are doing work cash in hand, no VAT, to

217

keep a roof over their kids' heads? How many people are torching their motors to get a few grand cash back? I'll tell you how many Donna – hundreds. Thousands even. It's part and parcel of the world we live in. It's called survival. What we're doing ain't even illegal really. They sign a contract, they honour it. That's the long and the short of it all. They've been bankrupted in the courts yet they'd put a bit away for a rainy day. In their wife's name, their kids' names, or their mother's.

'It's why you found out you owned your house. It's called covering your own arse. If we put the paperwork through the correct channels, the bailiffs would be battering their doors down. We just do them a favour, that's all.'

Donna stood up and picked up her handbag.

'Fair enough, Carol, I understand what you're telling me. OK, I'll never mention it again. I'm away for the weekend, so I won't see you till next week sometime.'

'That suits me fine. Do you good to get away, have a break. It's what you need.'

Donna gave her a tight strained smile, and left the offices.

On her way to the car she felt crushed by worry. Since Georgio had been sentenced, life had become one big chore. Her euphoria at the thought of him coming home, no matter what, had evaporated drastically in the full knowledge of what she was supposed to do to achieve that end. She now knew that Talkto was something Georgio had set up with Stephen as a blind. Talkto was probably the main company now that telephone sales and sex had become a part of everyday life. JCY was probably the beginning of Stephen's little empire in Soho.

She sat in her car wondering what she should do. Should she ignore what she had found out? That seemed the most viable solution. She had lived twenty years without knowing anything and at this moment she yearned once more for her days of ignorance. The worst thought of all was that Georgio was really bent, really had been involved in a lot of things she could not even have guessed at.

She saw Carol watching her through the office window and turned the key in the ignition. Carol could cope with everything; in fact, knowing Carol, she was probably the real brains in her marriage. Donna knew instinctively that Davey Jackson would think long and hard before doing anything without her knowledge, and Donna envied Carol for that. Davey afforded her the respect she deserved.

Had Georgio ever done that for her? The question once asked frightened her, because she already knew the answer, had always known the answer, deep inside.

218

Well, she would show him. She would do what he asked. It could only make them closer in the long run. It saddened her that she had to break the law to prove to herself and her husband that she was worthy of him, that she would do anything for him, no matter what. Yet she was aware that it was making her more determined to do what he asked. For the first time, she really was on top where Georgio Brunos was concerned. This fact staggered her even as it frightened the life's blood in her veins and turned it to ice water. Finally she pulled out on to the road, Carol Jackson's angry countenance fresh in her mind. She would have to toughen herself up, and do it soon. Before the real work started. As she drove home she decided to take a leaf out of Carol's book.

Whatever Davey was up to she made a point of being there with him, organising and taking an active part. Well, Donna decided, she would do the same.

Happier in herself, she drove home with a lighter heart.

The course was set, she was into this already, up to her neck in fact. A police car drove past her on the A13 and she smiled sadly. Would the time ever come again when a police car would be seen by her as a blessing? Would she once again feel safer because it was on the road with her? Or would she become like Georgio, and see the police as the enemy? Would she live her future life looking over her shoulder?

Once Georgio was out, they would in effect become outlaws. Her little world would be blown open; they would never return to England again. Suddenly the Essex countryside looked very beautiful, the fields laid out in neat squares, the farmhouses of red brick picturesque and homely. They would be forced to live abroad, and it would be in extreme heat if she knew Georgio. He loved the sun, always had. It occurred to her that she was giving up an awful lot to have her husband back with her once again, but it was worth it. Even leaving her life here was worth it; anything was worth Georgio's being beside her once more. All she had found out about him was as nothing compared with her love for him. Her need of him. Donna pushed Dolly and Maeve and Pa Brunos from her mind, because once they left England, she and Georgio would be leaving them also.

As she approached her house, she stopped in the village and went into Carpenter's, the estate agents. Georgio had asked her to put the house up for sale, as they would need as much money as possible. Once they were out of the country, their assets would be frozen. It would become difficult to gather funds together. She was preparing to lose her adopted family, Dolly and her lovely home, yet Donna

219

didn't falter as she stepped into the estate agents.

This was for Georgio and for herself.

They would be together for ever. That was what she had to keep telling herself, no matter how hard any of it became. She shook herself mentally, reminding herself that her husband was sitting in a maximum security prison being tormented by a man who would terrify Jack the Ripper.

Donna allowed herself a small feeling of satisfaction as she spoke to the estate agent; she was getting good at lying. Georgio would be proud of her.

'What is the joke, madam?' The handsome young man before her was looking at her quizzically.

'Oh, nothing you would understand.'

She made her goodbyes and left, wondering what Dolly's reaction to the sale of the house would be. After all, it was her home as well.

Sidney Carpenter grinned in satisfaction at his boss.

'You know who that was, don't you?'

'Yeah, Georgio Brunos's little wife. So the house is going on the market now, eh? She must be feeling the pinch with her lord and master banged up in Parkhurst. Never liked him myself, he was an arsehole. All the money he earned and still he argued the toss over getting the commission down on any of his properties.'

Peter Downs walked into his small office and picked up the telephone. He dialled the local Town Hall and asked for Councillor Robertson.

Harry Robertson had just left a planning meeting and was feeling great. He had voted against another large superstore car park, knowing the paving specialist would up the ante on his next approach to him. He picked up the telephone with the air of a man who was happy with himself, happy with life.

'Hello, Harry Robertson here.'

He never called himself 'Councillor', preferring to be known as the plain man's friend. No titles for Harry, not from the electorate anyway.

'Councillor Robertson, how are you?'

Harry frowned. 'Hello, Peter. Long time no see, old chum.' Harry could sense the other man smiling down the phone. Downs always smiled, even when he was imparting bad news.

'I had a visitor today, Georgio Brunos's wife actually,' the voice said excitedly. 'She's put her house on the market. Quick sale by all accounts.'

220

Harry knew he had to answer, but he was having trouble breathing.

'Really, Peter? Now what made you think that would be of any interest to me?'

Peter laughed gently. 'Well, knowing how close you all were, I thought you might like to be told about it. I organised the sale of all the properties Georgio built, if you remember rightly. I know you always had a penchant for Georgio's place, thought you might have been interested, that's all. It's a lovely property – swimming pool, tennis court, and it's going for a song really – three-quarters of a million in fact. She seems in a hurry to get out. Maybe the upkeep is getting too much, eh?'

Harry decided he had humoured Peter long enough and now was the time for him to act the councillor. Peter was a tad too disrespectful for Harry's liking.

'Look, Downs, fascinating as all this is, I really have to go now. I have a planning meeting scheduled for two-fifteen and I want to grab a bite of lunch.'

'Don't worry, old boy, I know what you're like when you want to grab something. Give my regards to Bunty, won't you?'

Harry found himself holding a dead telephone and cursed under his breath. Downs was getting too big for his boots, but this phone call had proved something to him. Georgio Brunos and all his dealings with him were not going to go away.

Harry had made a point of distancing himself from Georgio on the night he was arrested, feigning shock and horror and any other emotion that would put him in a good light with councillors and contractors. But he was in over his head with Georgio and he knew it, and now the phone call from Peter Downs was confirming his worst suspicions. Georgio was selling up. Donna wouldn't shit unless Georgio gave her permission. It was Georgio who wanted shot of the property. Maybe money was tight. That was one reason for a quick sale.

But the house aside, Georgio knew an awful lot about Harry's business dealings and other activities . . . The man began to feel extremely worried. He regretted dumping Georgio and Donna so quickly. He should have made a point of standing by her – in private, of course. It wouldn't do to be seen openly consorting with the wife of a local villain, and that's how Georgio had come over in the trial. If he hadn't been so greedy they would have been raking it in by now.

Harry groaned. Raking it in was an understatement. They would have been worth small fortunes, and neither he nor Georgio was exactly short of a few bob.

Harry's secretary Sally walked into the room at that moment, swinging her hips and smirking delightedly, and for the first time ever, Harry didn't register a pretty, eager face.

He was too absorbed in what was going on in his mind.

Once Donna moved, she was out of his orbit and he couldn't afford that at this time. While he knew where she was he could keep an eye on her. Did Georgio have any idea of doing a deal to get out earlier? Was he going to sell Harry down the river? It was all very worrying. He had a few big deals coming off and a scandal could ruin him. But more than that, if Georgio opened his mouth about the software industry they were going to create, he would be behind bars, disgraced and doing a long prison sentence into the bargain. His bowels were growing looser by the second.

'Harry? Do you need me any more or can I go for lunch?'

Sally's sweet features were a blur to Harry who felt as if he had been punched none too gently in his nether regions.

'Oh, it's you. Look – piss off girl and get your lunch, for Christ's sake.'

Sally's eyes widened, and her face took on the hurt expression of a dog that's just been beaten. Pink and tearful, she raced from the room.

Harry put his head into his hands. He'd have to apologise to her now, before she mouthed his words all over the Town Hall. Sod Peter Downs, and sod Georgio bloody Brunos!

Just when everything was going so well, this had to happen. Well, he hoped Donna was moving to be nearer the prison, that wouldn't be such a bad thing. It was if she was moving away before the bomb was dropped that was worrying him.

He made a mental note to get Bunty to go round there, all sweetness and light, and try to patch up their rather curtailed friendship. He heard his outer door slam and bit on his thumbnail. Sally was more upset than he'd realised.

Picking up the phone, he prepared himself for Bunty's strident voice and guaranteed rage when he told her what he wanted her to do. In a lot of respects he had envied Georgio his meek little wife; now he was positively green.

Bunty was not a woman you told to do things, not if you knew what was good for you.

Taking a deep breath, he dialled his home number.

222

Chapter Twenty

Bunty Robertson was fit to be tied. She stood in the centre of her dining room and scowled at her husband as he tried to pacify her.

'Bunty, darling.' His eyes were beseeching her.

'Shut your stupid fat mouth, Harry. I will not, I repeat, will *not* go round to that bitch's house for love nor money. Get it? Or do you want me to tattoo it on your forehead?'

Harry felt his heart sinking below his navel.

'Bunty, listen to me, for God's sake. You have to do this. If Georgio opened his mouth we would all be in it up to our necks. You and your father included.'

Bunty's long horsy face was fixed in a sneer. She made an unladylike snorting noise through large nostrils.

'Forgive me if I seem a bit dense, Harry darling, but if Georgio was going to open his mouth I would have thought he'd have done so by now. What on earth would it gain him to tell all now? He's already doing eighteen years. I would have thought even you could have grasped something that simple.'

His wife's high-pitched voice finally broke through his fear of her and Harry Robertson shouted for the first time ever at his long skinny wife.

'He's trying to get a fucking appeal going, you stupid cunt. If he doesn't, he could do a deal. Did that ever occur to you, or your father for that matter? Did it not come into your father's reasoning about all this then? That Georgio might ask for leniency for opening his trap about a scandal that would leave us both waist-high in shit, and about a business that would be the talk of everyone in the country – a disgusting industry that you were all for. Even I baulked at it at first. Now I wish I had listened to myself for once instead of you and that ponce of a father of yours. Major Browning, my arse! The nearest he ever got to the Army was the fucking glasshouse for desertion. Now stop whining and get round there and pacify that bitch of a wife of Georgio's.'

Bunty's eyes were wide and staring. Their icy blue held a glint of

223

steel as she tried to cut her husband in half with their glare.

'How *dare* you! How dare you talk about my father like that? The major is a respected man . . .'

Harry groaned out loud and cut his wife off. His voice low now, he said sadly, 'Why do you insist on this charade, Bunty? I am Harry – your husband, remember? I met you years ago when you were living in Huddersfield and Daddy was banged up in Strangeways for fraudulent deception. Your father is a conman, love – a good one I admit, but a conman all the same. You never went to private school, you never owned a pony, and you never lived in Singapore. So please stop pretending with me, eh? Just listen for once. Get in your car, drive over to Donna Brunos's house and give her a load of old fanny. Make sure she knows we're on her husband's side. Tell her we waited until it had all died down before we made our move. She'll understand that much, she's more intelligent than you ever gave her credit for. Find out what the score is, and what's happening with Georgio. Do this, Bunty, because all our futures are in Georgio's hands at the moment. Mine, yours and the Major's.'

Bunty listened to the tone of her husband's voice, saw the desperation in his eyes, and sensed his animosity towards her father. She decided it was better to retreat on this occasion. Harry could be henpecked, he could be manipulated, he could be utterly stupid. But once he laid down the law, Bunty was inclined to listen, mainly because if he pushed the issue, he was generally in the right. Harry had one thing in common with his wife: both were marvellous at saving their own arses.

Smiling evilly Bunty spat out: 'All right, Harry, if you insist. But I warn you now – one snide remark from her and that's that. Let them do their worst. I'll not be held over a barrel by that skinny bitch or her thug of a husband.'

Harry gave a great sigh of relief.

Leave it to the women. He was a great believer in passing the buck. Whatever happened now was down to Bunty, and for all her hard talk and crassness, she knew better than to push Donna Brunos too far. Bunty could grovel for England when the fancy took her. He smiled to himself. He was half-sorry he would miss the performance.

Harry had panicked the night of Georgio's arrest and had completely blanked out the couple from his life. Feigning surprise, then pretending he had had his suspicions all along about Georgio, he had agreed with the opinion of whoever he was talking to. Deep inside, he had had to convince himself that Georgio opening his mouth about the deals in Sri Lanka and Bangkok would only land

224

him in more trouble. The idea that he might eventually use them as a way to gain a lighter sentence had occasionally filtered into his mind in the dead of night, just after Georgio had been given eighteen years. Knowing that he himself would have sold anyone down the river in those circumstances had made him aware of the precarious position he was in.

However, knowing that Donna was nearby had given Harry a false sense of security. While he could still pass Georgio's house, see the familiar car in the drive, he had convinced himself that Georgio was still holding out for them all. Now Donna was leaving, Harry was worried. Once she was gone, he had no way of finding out anything, until the knock came on his front door as it had on Georgio's. He felt himself break out in a sweat just thinking about it. Harry Robertson, planning officer, pillar of the community, actually being arrested. It didn't bear thinking about.

Especially when the reason for the arrest would be enough not only to shock his contemporaries, but also disgust them.

Dolly was out shopping, and Donna was enjoying a coffee and a cigarette in her conservatory. She looked out over the swimming pool and across the perfect lawns to the tennis court. She had planted the lavender bushes herself, also the honeysuckle; on a summer evening the scent was overwhelming. When they had moved into the house the grounds had been a great muddy wilderness. Donna had planned her garden with care, expecting to stay there until she died. She had decided on every plant, every ornament, every blade of grass. She had watched over it, nurtured it, and engaged a gardener who loved the grounds almost as much as she did. The apple trees, pears and the fig tree, had all been lovingly tended. The rose bower was her idea, as was the winding pathway that led around the side of the house to the herb garden. The large conifers provided a natural screen, and the huge weeping willow had been left. She had worked around them, believing that a tree should never be cut down.

She knew she would miss it all terribly. Knew that it would be a wrench. But she also knew she would do it because of Georgio. Anything was worth losing if it brought Georgio back to her. The estate agent was coming at around four-thirty in the afternoon, and Donna still hadn't plucked up the courage to tell Dolly she was selling up. She was wondering if she should actually tell her everything, felt she should because Dolly was so loyal, but didn't know whether she could involve the older woman in something that was not only illegal but also dangerous.

Her eyes strayed to the photograph on her lap. It was of Georgio. It

225

had been taken a few weeks before his arrest and it showed him smiling heartily, his perfect white teeth and dark good looks set off to their best advantage. Just looking at it gave Donna a thrill. He was gut-wrenchingly handsome. Always had been. Then the deep depression that accompanied the sexual urge overwhelmed her once more. To have him back, sitting opposite her or slipping into bed beside her, was not just a want, it was a pure physical need.

She stared over the garden once more, her earlier feelings of sorrow at having to leave it gone now. She was left only with her need for the man she had married. She would have him on his terms, anywhere he wanted to be. Without Georgio this place was just a house. With him she would once more have a home.

The loud ring of the doorbell broke her reverie and she strolled through the house, expecting to see Dolly on the doorstep. She was shocked to see instead the familiar outline of Bunty Robertson. Opening the door, she stared into the woman's face.

'What can I do for you?'

Bunty smiled brightly. 'How are you, Donna dear? I thought I'd pop in and say hello.' She clearly expected to be invited into the house.

For the first time ever, Donna Brunos looked at Bunty Robertson and didn't feel small, didn't feel intimidated by her nasal tones, upper-class accent and designer clothes. Instead she felt as if she was the one in control.

'Hello then. Now, if you don't mind, Bunty, I'm quite busy.' She watched with satisfaction as Bunty's face dropped into its usual sour lines.

'I say, Donna, that's no way to treat a friend.'

Donna grinned. 'Isn't it? Maybe you would prefer it if I cut you dead in the village? Or didn't return your calls? That's what you do, isn't it? To your *friends*.' Donna frowned as if in earnest consideration and she was delighted to see Bunty's face redden.

'Come on, Donna, surely you must have expected that at first? Harry, after all . . .'

Donna finished her sentence for her. 'A councillor and local dignitary. I know, Bunty. My husband helped him get there, remember? Now I think about it, my husband did a lot for both of you at one time, and not even a phone call or a note from you to tell him you believed in him. In his innocence. Go away, Bunty. We have nothing to say to one another.'

Donna went to shut the door, but Bunty thrust her foot into the doorway.

'Please, Donna, let's not part like this!'

'Take your foot out, Bunty, or I'll slam the door on it. Shall I tell you something? I never liked you, ever. I put up with you and your drunken overbearing husband because of Georgio. Now he's away I don't have to listen to your phoney accent, or endure your husband's groping hands. In fact, that was the only good thing that came out of all my troubles. So remove your foot now, get in your car, and as my housekeeper would say, *piss off!*'

Bunty removed her foot slowly.

'I understand the house is up for sale. I came here to offer the hand of friendship, to see if we could help in case you were having financial problems. I never expected to be insulted for my trouble.'

Donna laughed now, a low, bitchy laugh.

'Well, news certainly travels fast around here, doesn't it? As for offering the hand of friendship . . . if I was stuck on a sinking ship I wouldn't share a lifeboat with you, Bunty. If I needed a pound to keep from starving, I would rather starve than take anything from you. But all that aside, I have taken over all Georgio's businesses and am doing very well with them, thank you very much. Tell your husband that from me. I'm doing *very well*, and have no need of freeloaders, OK? Now, for the last time, get off my property.'

Bunty's face was a picture of amazement and stunned disbelief. 'You've taken over all his businesses? All of them?'

Donna smiled. 'That's right. When and if I ever need you, I'll let you know. Now, I'll say goodbye for the last time.'

Shutting the door, Donna walked back to the conservatory with a soaring heart. It had done her the world of good seeing Bunty Robertson on her doorstep. Telling her what she thought of her, and finally getting the upper hand.

Looking once more at the photo of her husband, she whispered, 'You'd have been proud of me, Georgio. I'm finally growing up.'

'I hate Thursdays. I hate every day.' For once Sadie's voice was depressed.

Georgio smiled at her. 'Cheer up, Sade, it could be worse.'

Sadie smiled back infectiously. 'Could it? Oh yes, I know. The four-minute warning could go. Fat chance we'd have in here, all the screws running to get out and locking us all in on their way!'

'That's better. You always have a crack, no matter what's wrong in here.'

'That's my trouble,' Sadie told him. 'I always look for the good things in life, and believe me when I say there ain't been that many to really get excited about.' Sadie's deep brown eyes were sad once more. 'I mean, look at me. I'm not even thirty yet, but here I am

227

doing time for murder. I'm as queer as a two-bob clock, I prefer dressing as a woman – I *feel* like a woman, that's been my trouble all my bleeding life – but all that aside, I now have one really big problem.'

Georgio stared at the character in front of him, sorry for the sad eyes and drooping shoulders.

'Lewis came on to me in the showers, Georgio. What the hell do I do?'

Georgio's eyes widened. Lewis coming on to Sadie? Lewis who kept as far away from the TVs as possible? Lewis who saw his homosexuality as a macho thing, an image, the hard man, the hard queer. You could almost hear Lewis's voice saying: 'Come on then, I dare you to make a joke about queers,' as he walked into a room. Lewis coming on to Sadie? It was unbelievable.

'Christ, Sade. Are you sure?'

Sadie's eyes flashed in temper. 'I'm a lot of things, Georgio, but stupid isn't one of them. He felt me up all right and asked me if I would be so kind as to have lunch with him. Poor Timmy. He'll be gutted. He really cares about me, you know.'

'So you're going to do it?'

Sadie nodded almost imperceptibly. 'I don't have much choice really, do I?'

Before Georgio could answer a screw walked into the recreation room.

'Visitor! Brunos, get your arse in gear.'

'I'll speak to you later, Sadie.'

She smiled up at him. 'Hope it's your wife.'

'Not today. I've other fish to fry today.' Giving Sadie a quick wink, he walked from the room.

Donna strode through the electric doors into Parkhurst prison. As she waited for the inner doors to open she fished out her Visiting Order from her handbag. Sensing eyes on her, she turned around to see a tall blonde girl staring intently at her. Donna smiled, but the girl turned away abruptly. Just then, a small dark-haired boy of about eighteen months toppled over, and forgetting the girl's strange look, Donna rushed to help him up. He was bawling his head off. As Donna reached him, the tall blonde picked him up.

'He fell really hard. I hope he's OK?'

The girl's delicate features and long highlighted hair belied her rough voice.

'He's always falling over. He'll survive.'

Donna looked at her closely.

228

'Do I know you? Only I saw you staring at me earlier.'

The girl smiled naturally. 'I was staring at your suit, as it goes. It's very nice.'

Donna relaxed. 'I've had it for ages to be honest, but it wears well on long journeys. Is this your son? He's really handsome.'

'No. I'm here with me sister, looking after him while she goes in for a visit. The doors are opening. You'd better get a move on or you'll be ages getting in line.'

Donna ruffled the child's hair gently. 'Thanks. He's a darling – your sister is very lucky,' she said.

The child was snuggling into his auntie's arms and crying softly.

Donna watched her walk out of the prison, and shoved her way through with the rest of the visitors to be searched, identified, and taken through to the visiting room. The usual overpowering smell of cheap perfume and children's sweets accompanied her. Nodding here and there at familiar faces she went through all the procedures, and finally, after depositing her handbag in the locker, she walked into the visiting room, the constant closing of doors behind her giving her a small insight into how Georgio must feel living with it constantly.

As she entered the visiting room, she was astounded to see Georgio already there, apparently waiting for her. His face was a mask of surprise and pleasant shock.

She rushed towards him, feeling the familiar rush of longing as she looked into his face.

'I bet you weren't expecting me, were you? I talked Paddy out of his VO. It was a good idea to put my name on everyone's. I told you it would be, didn't I? Then if they can't make it, or I can con it from them, we can see more of one another.'

Georgio was staring at her as if he had never seen her before.

'Well, aren't you going to kiss me?'

He pulled her into his arms and kissed her hard on the mouth.

'I couldn't be more surprised or pleased,' he said. 'I was expecting either Paddy or Stephen. Now I've seen you I'm over the moon. How are you, darling?'

Pleased with herself for surprising him, Donna said: 'I'm fine, Mr Brunos. Now sit yourself down and today I'll go and get the teas, and the KitKats, and the Mars bars. I broke into my piggy bank on purpose!'

Ten minutes later they were sitting hand in hand.

'I must be honest, Georgio, I pinched Paddy's VO for a reason. Tomorrow I'm off to Scotland with Alan Cox. We're seeing a man about a break-out!'

Donna saw his expression change and looked enquiringly at him.

229

'What's wrong, Georgio? I thought you'd be over the moon.'

He squeezed her hand painfully. 'What do you mean, you're off to Scotland with Alan Cox?'

Georgio's face was dark and he was more than surprised when Donna began to laugh deliriously. She put back her head and literally roared with laughter.

'Give over, Donna, everyone's staring at us.'

She clapped a hand over her mouth, stifling the loud guffaws, shoulders heaving with suppressed mirth.

'Oh Georgio, you're priceless, do you know that? I can't believe it – you're jealous! You are actually jealous. You talk me into doing all this and then when it gets under way, the first thing you do is get all jealous. If it wasn't so funny I would be really annoyed.'

Georgio heard the underlying anger in her words and admitted to himself for the first time just how much his little wife had changed. She questioned him, challenged him, stood up to him – something she would never have done before his sojourn in Parkhurst. Yet he knew that she was absolutely right. The thought of her and Alan Cox going away for a weekend was like gall in his mouth. He had expected Alan to do all the collar and Donna to relay the messages; he had never expected Cox actively to involve her.

'Donna, I think we should get something straight here, love. I want you as nothing more than a go-between. You can give up any ideas of jaunting off to Scotland this minute. It's a dangerous thing you're taking on and the less you have to do with that side of it, the better. Tell Alan I trust him to keep you out of it. What the fucking hell's he playing at, eh? What's the next step? You going to turn up here riding shotgun on a fucking helicopter or what?'

Donna's voice dripped ice as she answered her husband.

'Don't swear at me, Georgio Brunos. Sometimes I wonder where the hell you get off. You talk me into putting my liberty on the line, my life in Alan Cox's hands, and then you have the audacity to sit there and out of petty jealousy tell me that I can't go and do the job you specifically asked of me.

'Did it ever occur to you,' she went on hotly, 'that I can walk into a lot more places than you or Alan Cox? That I have a better cover for what we're doing than anyone? That I have a bit more brain in my head than you obviously give me credit for? And, finally, that I might *want* to help out properly? It's bad enough that Alan Cox thinks I'm about as much use as a chocolate fireguard, without my husband agreeing with him – and to my face as well. Thank you very much! Shall I take up knitting then? Or shall I get myself a lover? A lot of the women do, you know. Oh, I'm not as sheltered as you think. I

230

keep my eyes and my ears open. Some of the talk on the ferry coming over here would make even you blush. So you tell me, big man, what am I to do?'

Georgio listened with increasing annoyance, yet he knew that he needed this woman in front of him, and more than she needed him at this time. This wasn't his little Don Don, who jumped at his whim, this was a grown woman, and in all his years with her she had never looked as desirable as she did now. Her hair was awry, her eyes were glinting with temper, and her face was flushed. She had what he called 'the just-rogered look', and what he wouldn't give to have been able to put that look on her face properly!

'I'm sorry, Donna. I worry about you, darlin'.'

She relaxed slightly and said softly, 'It's a pity you didn't worry so much before all this, then neither of us would have to be here today.'

The look of hopelessness on Georgio's face as she uttered the words made her feel a prize bitch. Gently caressing his face she said: 'I love you, Georgio. Christ knows, I love you with every ounce of my being. For the first time ever I am really of use to you, I can be equal with you. Don't you understand how that makes me feel? We haven't talked so deeply in over ten years, not since we lost the boy. It gives me a reason for going on. I want you back, I want you beside me, can't you at least understand that? After my initial fear, my worry about what I was doing, I am finally resigned to it all. How can you deny me this now?

'I want to help you in any way I can,' she said softly. 'While you're locked in here, I'm only half-alive, I might as well have been locked up with you. Leave me be now, darling. Let me work for you, beside you and with you on this. Just this once, Georgio, don't throw it all back in my face. Not after all the trouble I've taken.'

Georgio took a deep breath. He needed this woman more than anything. Instinctively, he knew that while Donna was rooting for him, he had no worries. His moment of petty jealousy was over as quickly as it had come. As he had said to Sadie, he had other fish to fry.

'I'm sorry, Donna, but you're a very attractive woman.'

She smiled now, gently and heartwarmingly.

'I'm glad you finally noticed, Georgio.'

He wiped a hand over his face. He had expected a lot of things today, but Donna and her newfound independence wasn't one of them.

'I put the house up for sale by the way,' Donna suddenly announced, 'and guess what! I had a visit from Bunty Robertson into the bargain.'

231

Georgio's face darkened. 'What did that parasite want?'

'Well, that's the funny thing, Georgio. I was amazed to see her on the doorstep after the way she treated me when you first got put away. I was annoyed she had already heard the house was going up actually, because it's not as if there will be a For Sale notice or anything. I want it all low-key, like you asked me. Anyone looking in our price range will be given a colour brochure. I have no intention of letting people knock the door just for a glimpse around our home, and that's what most of them would be after. I phoned the estate agent and gave him a piece of my mind.'

'I can believe that.' Georgio's voice had regained its equilibrium.

Donna sighed. 'I seem to be giving a little more out each day. If I'm not careful I won't have any left!'

'You seem to be doing all right. If you get a bite on the house, I'll give you an account number to place the money in offshore. The last thing we want is our cash going into Nat West, ain't it? We need it transferred out of the country. So whatever happens, you tell anyone interested that you can't move until whatever date we have for me going on the trot.'

Donna nodded. 'OK. I don't think it'll take long, to be honest. I put it up for three-quarters of a million. That's a saving of at least two hundred and fifty thousand, so anyone with half a brain will jump at it.'

Georgio grinned. 'Good girl. A bargain is a bargain. Shame really, when you think of all the work that went into the place.'

Donna grasped his hand and sighed again.

'I thought of that actually, and it really made me sad. But wherever we can be together will be home to me. It's taken me an awfully long time to come to terms with everything, you know, Georgio. I realise now how naive I was. I didn't think for one second you were into any kind of dodgy deals. The mere thought would have shocked and horrified me, to be honest. Now all this had happened, I realise I couldn't give a monkeys' what you've done as long as I can still have you. As long as we can be together.'

Georgio stared down at their joined hands, his breath suddenly coming in short gasps. Donna's open adoration of him, her naked longing, hurt him to watch.

'Thanks for everything, Donna. I'm just sorry it had to come to this. I love you, girl. I'll always love you.'

Donna basked in the glory of his words.

'I still haven't broken the news to Dolly that we're moving,' she said after a minute. 'What do you think I should tell her?'

Georgio shrugged. He picked up a Mars bar and opened it nonchalantly.

232

'Don't tell her nothing. Just say we're looking for a smaller place now. You can give her the bad news nearer the time.'

Donna frowned slightly. 'That seems a bit callous after all the years she's been with us.'

'Listen, Donna, we've done her proud over the years, right? This is no time for sentiment. I will be leaving my parents, my brothers and sisters, everyone I care about. So Dolly for me is quite low on the list. I need to get out of here, and soon. I can't fucking hack it here much longer. So don't give me grief over bloody Dolly. She'll survive.'

Donna bit her lip at his harsh words, realising the position he was in. Desperate times meant desperate measures. But his cavalier attitude over Dolly stung her to the quick.

Georgio read this in her face and his features softened. 'Listen, Don Don, Dolly will be given a lump sum, a golden handshake. She ain't going to be badly off, I promise you that. All I'm interested in at the moment is getting out of here. I have Lewis and his henchmen breathing down my neck. Let me get out and I'll sort out Dolly and everyone else, OK?'

'Okey doke. Back to Scotland. We're going to arrange your route once you're off the Island. Probably most of it will be overland. I'll have more to tell you next time I visit, OK?'

Georgio found himself smiling. 'You sound like a bleedin' gangster's moll!'

'I feel like one!' Donna giggled. 'Whoever thought I'd be laughing about something like this, eh? Me, timid little Donna, afraid for years to open my mouth unless you'd already briefed me on what to say! Wheeling and dealing in the London underworld no less! But in fairness to Alan Cox, he tried to frighten me out of it all. Once he knows I'm capable of looking after myself, he'll change his tune. To be honest I get the impression he isn't too chuffed with you for having me as the number two. But then, he doesn't know me like you do, does he?'

'Be careful this weekend, won't you, love? This ain't a game, you know. You're going to meet some dangerous men and some violent people. Watch your step, and for Christ's sake dress down. You're too good looking for the cretins you'll be meeting up with. Their idea of foreplay is not to smash the old woman around the head before sex!'

Donna smiled at his words but picked up the meaning behind them.

'Stop worrying, Georgio. I intend to work at anything and with anyone to get you home. After my initial upset, I realised I would

233

have you on any terms. Nothing you could do, could ever stop me loving you or wanting you.'

Her eyes were wet with tears and Georgio put an arm around her shoulders.

'I never deserved you, Donna. In fact, if the truth's only known, I still don't deserve you.' He smiled proudly. 'Who would have thought that my Donna could have come up trumps like this?'

Before she could answer her husband she heard a cultured voice call his name.

'Georgio! Introduce me to your lovely companion.' The words were clipped, and without real emotion.

Donna glanced up at the man before her. He wasn't very tall, or very well-built, but his whole demeanour spoke of a violent nature.

'Donna, this is Donald Lewis.' Georgio's voice was flat. She could feel his embarrassment at having to kowtow to the little man before him.

'How do you do, Mr Lewis?'

Donald looked down at the strained white face and despite himself he was impressed. He could almost taste her fear as she looked at him, and he decided there and then to be charming. It would have been fun to intimidate her, get Georgio's goat well and truly up. But something inside decided him against it. He was amazed to find that he rather liked the look of her. She had the same bearing as his mother, was similar in looks. Also, she was a smart dresser and her voice spoke of a good education and upbringing, things he had always admired. No, he would leave the frightening of her to another day; today he would be nice. He sat beside her, aware that his intrusion was being witnessed by more than a few people.

'Georgio has told me a lot about you, my dear – may I call you Donna?' Before she could answer he pressed on, 'But he never told me just how beautiful you are. Why, I'm amazed a woman with your assets is still bothering with a man like Georgio. He is indeed a very lucky fellow. I was rather under the impression his taste in women was not so refined. It just shows you how wrong you can be, doesn't it?'

Lewis was enjoy Georgio's discomfort. He ignored him, secure in the knowledge his taunts had found their mark.

'I hear you have taken over the businesses, too. My mother is a strong woman, Donna. I have always respected women, though I'm not a great lover of them in general. My tastes run more to masculine friendships, you understand. But now and again a woman comes along whom I like, and I have a feeling you're going to be one of them.'

234

Donna nodded graciously. 'Thank you, Mr Lewis, I shall take that as a compliment. Is your mother visiting you today?'

He shook his head. 'Not today. Maybe on Monday. It's a very tiring journey for her. She's well into her seventies, but marvellous for her age. I have her chauffeured down every two weeks by a friend on the outside. It's wonderful to have friends on the outside, isn't it, Georgio? Especially attractive ones. They brighten up the dreary days in here.'

'I'll look forward to meeting your mother, Mr Lewis, she sounds an amazing woman. I lost my parents when I was very young. I always feel that mothers are very special, particularly to their sons.'

For the first time ever Georgio saw Donald Lewis actually smile genuinely at someone, and he was even more amazed to find the smile bestowed on his wife.

'You're a very astute girl and I see I was right in my first impressions. I think you and I will be great friends, Donna Brunos.' He looked at Georgio. 'I hope you appreciate this girl, Georgio?'

He relaxed visibly. 'Don't worry, Donald. I not only appreciate her, I depend on her in a lot of ways.'

Donna smiled sadly. Georgio depended on her. There it was, that word again. But this time at least, it didn't frighten her so much.

Donald Lewis not only frightened her, he positively terrified her, but she kept on smiling and chatting to him, knowing that her husband's stay in prison depended on this man's goodwill.

As small and amiable as Lewis seemed at this moment, she could see the latent violence of his nature in the pointed way he talked to Georgio.

She was shocked at her husband's obvious subservience in the presence of this man, and it made her all the more determined to get him out – and fast. Five minutes of Donald Lewis was wearing enough. What must it be like to have him watching over you day in and day out? Lewis was capable of murder, and she recognised that he was also capable of great charm.

The combination of the two was more frightening than anything.

235

Chapter Twenty-One

'Lewis is a terrifying guy, love. Believe me, I've had a few run ins with him myself over the years.'

Donna looked out of the car window, half-enjoying the changing scenery.

'Well, he frightened me, I know that much. There's a sort of pent-up menace about him, as if at any moment he could attack.'

Alan laughed loudly. 'That's the understatement of the year, Donna. I could introduce you to a bloke in Soho who had what's called in the trade "facial scalping". No ears, no nose, the bare minimum of eyelids. That's what happens when you upset Donald Lewis.'

Donna blanched. 'You're joking!' Her voice was small, breathless.

Alan realised that what he had said would only make her more concerned for her husband. He flicked a glance at her, and seeing the strained white of her face, felt like kicking himself.

'No, I'm not joking. But don't worry, Georgio won't get anything like that from Lewis. I can guarantee it.'

'And how can you guarantee it?'

Alan lightened his voice. 'Because the bloke it happened to was one of Lewis's amours, that's why. And he made the mistake of taking on a little friend. Lewis didn't like that. He owns his boyfriends, you see; they're his property. Especially when he's laid out a small fortune on setting them up in a flat and playing at mums and dads, know what I mean? If he was going to hurt Georgio it would be done in a much more civilised way. He'd just have him killed.'

'Well, that's made me feel a whole lot better, I must say! Thank you very much, Alan, I really needed that today.'

He pulled on to the hard shoulder of the motorway. Cars and lorries whizzed past his Mercedes. Grabbing Donna's arm, he pulled her round to face him. Sorry for the fear in her face, but also annoyed at her childishness.

'Listen, Donna, I know you're a nicely brought up girl and all that, but at this moment you are on your way to meet some people even

236

Lewis would balk at upsetting. Now we both know Georgio is skating on thin ice, and knowing him as I do, he probably brought it on himself. Well, that aside, me and you are in the throes of springing him from one of the most secure nicks in Britain. Now if you want to act like we're going on a picnic, that's your prerogative. Meself, I intend to watch my arse, my back, and anything else that I can watch without breaking me neck. I suggest you do the same. All this being frightened and shocked and ladylike ain't worth a piss. The sooner you realise that, the better off we'll be. I can't look after you all the time, and I don't see why I should. Now I can drop you off at the nearest train station or I can carry on up this bleeding motorway towards Jockland. It's up to you.'

Donna pulled herself free. Her face was pale, but this time with anger.

'You bastard, Cox! You love all this, don't you? You set out to scare me, and when you know you have succeeded, you always turn on me after. Well, I might be a little ladylike woman in your eyes, I am in my own. But if I wasn't intent on what I'm doing, I wouldn't be here. All the same, that's no reason to keep pushing down my throat the danger we're in. I know that, for Christ's sake. I can't sleep properly for thinking about it. But I'm here, and surely that must tell you something? I came with you, I'm trying to do my bit, and believe me when I say you are not making it any easier. You're an arsehole, mate. A twenty-four-carat arsehole, and I wish at this moment I had never clapped eyes on you. You have no respect for anyone or anything, and worst of all I think you enjoy frightening me. Facial scalping! Are we talking about Lewis or bloody Haiti? Do you know what I think? I think all this violent talk is just to scare me off. I think you're frightened – frightened I might just do it all right.'

Alan shook his head as if in sympathy.

'Shall I tell you something, Donna? If I told you the half of it you'd wet your tiny scrap of knickers, and probably follow through as well. I ain't told you nothing yet. *Nothing!* And, yes, I do wish you'd fuck off out of all this. Georgio must be going into fucking premature senility to want you on this team. But I promise you this much now: I won't open me trap again. Let's see how you get on with the Jocks. Then afterwards me and you can sort out once and for all whether you can kick all this or whether you want to sit out the last dance. How's that?'

Alan stared into the miserable face before him, hating what he was doing yet unable to stop himself. The thought of this naive girl-woman coming up against Lewis and others like him was anathema to Alan. He knew what they were really capable of. He knew exactly what was on the line here – not only the violence but the prison sentence they could end up with, and he knew she wouldn't last five minutes in a police station cell, let alone Holloway or even Cookham Wood. It was laughable, excruciatingly laughable, that Georgio could put this woman's life and liberty on the line and still sleep at night. But then, he had always been a selfish bastard, only this Donna didn't seem aware of that fact. Alan felt a strong urge to tell her all he knew, but buttoned his lip.

Mainly because she wouldn't believe him, but also, he admitted to himself, because he admired her spunk. Well, he had done his bit, he reasoned, tried to stop her from becoming involved in every way he could. The ball was well and truly in her court now. He sighed deeply, restraining an urge to apologise as he saw the fine lines around her mouth, the deep smudges under her eyes. But he consoled himself with the fact that it was Georgio who had put them there, not him. He would look out for her, it was all he could do. But at this moment in time, if Georgio was in front of him, he'd hammer him to within an inch of his life.

He put the car into gear and pulled back on to the motorway. As he turned on his CD player, the car was immediately filled with the sounds of Freddie Jackson singing 'You Are My Lady'. Donna stared once more at the shimmering landscape. The day was suddenly overcast, the sun hiding behind thick cloud. She swallowed back frustration and tears and made a resolution.

She would show Alan Cox, and Georgio.

She would show them all.

Exactly what she was going to show them, she wasn't sure.

They drove towards the Scottish hills in silence, Freddie Jackson's haunting voice drowning out the purr of the car's engine.

'I would appreciate it, Mr Cox, if you would refrain from swearing at me.'

Alan nearly smiled as he marvelled at a woman's knack of having not only the last word, but putting you well and truly in your place while having it.

Sadie sat with Donald Lewis in the recreation room. The TV was blaring. *Neighbours'* Australian slang was reverberating around the room.

'I'd give her one.'

Someone called out from the card table. 'You'd give my fucking granny one!'

Timmy glowered at Lewis and Sadie as he watched them playing dominoes. Sadie caught his eye and Timmy read the hopelessness there. Sadie's hair was back in a neat pony tail, and her face was

238

devoid of make-up. She was wearing a regulation denim shirt and tight-fit jeans, nick fashion for a gay's straight clothes. Gone was the shirt tied under the breastbone, the swaggering walk, the thick eyeliner. She was conforming to what Lewis wanted in a partner.

Everyone was amazed at Lewis's decision to take Sadie on board. He liked young fresh-faced boys with muscular bodies and clean-cut good looks. There was method in Lewis's madness, but as yet no one had sussed out what it was.

'Get me a cup of tea, Timmy, there's a good lad.'

The room was static with tension as Timmy hoisted his huge bulk out of his chair and stood up. Every man in the room, screws included, knew that old Timmy loved Sadie in his own way. Outside the confines of prison Timmy wouldn't have given her the time of day. But as a man who had spent over half his life locked up in top security, he had two sets of principles, one for the inside and one for the outside.

Outside, Timmy had his wife and children, whom he adored in his own rough fashion. Inside, he always picked himself up a galboy. He liked the sex, the friendship, and the fact that the boy needed him.

Timmy didn't know the exact meaning of love, could not have explained it to himself or anyone else. What he did know was he liked being with someone, liked looking after someone, and they took the place of his wife, Vi. He could share confidences with them, and they made the time pass that bit quicker. Sadie had been his wife, lover and child all rolled into one.

Now she was with Lewis, and it was small consolation that he knew Sadie wasn't pleased about it. Another galboy might have enjoyed the notoriety Lewis could afford them, but Timmy knew that Sadie had a lot of affection for him. She was genuine, in a world where that was a hard-won commodity. Sadie was a diamond.

Lewis watched Timmy amble from the room, his hugeness a balm to Lewis's ego.

'What's the matter, Sadie, missing your old beau?'

She concentrated on the dominoes. 'You know me better than that, Mr Lewis. But Timmy and I were good friends.'

Lewis outlined the delicate features of her face. 'Do you know why I picked you, Sadie?'

He watched her shake her head.

'I picked you because for all you look like a little tart, and I know that you are one, you have a certain vulnerability I like. I can be a bastard to you, and as much as I'll enjoy it, I'll also feel a tinge of guilt. Which makes it all the better. I don't expect you to understand that, but I decided to tell you anyway.'

239

Sadie looked full into his eyes, and Lewis was surprised at the understanding in them.

'Mr Lewis, people have been doing that to me since I was a child. I know more than people think. Whether it was the businessman I picked up for a quick blow job, or a big hairy-arsed plasterer, ashamed at what he wanted to do. I cashed in on it in the end because it became all I knew how to do. You scare me, Mr Lewis, but for all the wrong reasons.'

Sadie wondered if she had gone too far. Lewis's face was tight now, the skin shiny over the cheekbones. She knew Lewis was gritting his teeth.

He smiled then.

'As long as you're scared, Sadie, that's all that matters. Why you're scared is your own affair.' His voice rose. 'Now where's that cup of tea?'

Timmy walked in slowly, holding the thin cup and saucer, careful not to let any tea slop over. He placed it beside Lewis with exaggerated care.

Lewis looked into the cup as if worried what he might find in there.

'Where's Sadie's cup of tea then, Timmy?'

Sadie barked out. 'I don't want a cup of tea, Mr Lewis, thanks all the same.'

There was an argument going on in *Neighbours*, the voices loud and strident in the already tense atmosphere of the recreation room.

'Turn that crap off!' Lewis's voice was harsh. The TV was turned off immediately. In the silence of the room, his words were menacing.

'If I say you want a cup of tea, Sadie, then that is exactly what you want. Get her the tea, Timmy.'

Georgio watched the changing emotions on Timmy's face, before he saw him turn and walk from the room. Twenty pairs of eyes watched him leave, amazed at his calm acceptance of what had taken place. Yet not one man felt any less respect for him; they all knew they would do the same. Would have to do the same to survive.

Lewis, enjoying himself now, picked up a domino. 'Double six. Looks like I won, Sadie.'

Sadie gazed once more into his eyes. Voice soft and feminine, she said slowly, 'You always win, Mr Lewis.'

Georgio heard the conversation around them gradually starting up once more; heard the clatter of ashtrays and the striking of matches. He saw the men in the room turn back to what they were doing, trying to put Timmy's plight out of their minds. Lewis was once more engrossed in setting up his game of dominoes. Georgio observed him intently. With Timmy now upset over the loss of Sadie, he realised he had an ally.

As he looked at the hardest of Britain's criminals it amazed him that one man could cow them all so quickly and so utterly. When he was sprung, he would make a point of letting everyone know he had got one over on that sick-minded individual Donald Lewis. The thought was a balm to him, because until he was well and truly away, he had to toe the line like everyone else.

He watched Sadie rolling a cigarette and felt respect and also affection for the boy.

Sadie was on his side. Timmy was on his side. He wasn't so alone.

Georgio went back to his letter, only looking up when he saw Timmy come into the room with Sadie's tea. The expression on Timmy's face was one of suppressed hatred, and for a second Georgio hoped that he was going to do something to Lewis. Blades were plentiful in here, as were home-made one-shot guns.

If Timmy was upset enough, he might just take Lewis out of the ballgame.

It was a thought that stayed with Georgio through the evening.

'Hello, Paddy.'

Paddy turned in shock on hearing the voice.

'Hello, Maeve. What brings you to this neck of the woods?'

Maeve smiled slowly. 'What do you think brought me here?' She picked up a dirty donkey jacket and dropped it on to the floor before sitting on the chair. 'How the hell you ever make rhyme or reason of these sites I don't know. Me poor boots are ruined.'

Paddy sat behind the small desk in the Portakabin. Wiping a hand across his face, he waited for Maeve to speak again.

'What's the matter, Paddy – cat got your tongue? I asked you a question.'

He felt uncomfortable. Maeve Brunos was well-known to him. He had eaten in her kitchen, and in her restaurant. He had known her and Pa for a good deal of his life. He respected them, cared for them, and, most importantly, he worked for their son.

'I don't know what brought you here, Maeve. Thinking of branching out into the building trade, are you?'

She pushed up her bosom, an unconscious gesture reminiscent of Old Mother Riley.

'What's going on with Donna, with Georgio, and with all the businesses?' She stressed the 'all'.

Paddy's face was blank. 'In what way? Donna was overseeing everything as you know . . .'

241

Maeve butted in, her voice impatient, 'You're not a stupid person, Paddy, and neither am I. Nuala told me that you are now the main runner for the businesses. Fair enough. Now I also find out that Davey and that eejit of a wife of his are running the car lot. Dolly informs me that Donna is out morning, noon and night, here, there and everywhere. So I ask you again – and I'm rapidly losing the little patience I've got, mind – what is going on?'

'That's another question, Maeve . . .'

'Oh, for God's sakes, stop playing around, Paddy! I'm not in the mood. There's my Stephen walking round with a face like a madman's arse. Donna is out annoying the life out of him. Dolly is telling me things, but not all she knows. You're looking at me as if I've just grown another head, and to top it all Donna's on her way up to Scotland for the weekend. Now I ask you one last time before I rip out the few remaining hairs on your head: *what is going on?*'

Paddy picked up his hip flask and took a deep swig.

'Nothing's going on, Maeve.'

She shook her head sadly. 'I always liked you, Paddy, you are a good Corkman. I remember you when you came over and started work with my Georgio. I visited your wife in hospital, I attended her death and her burial. I babysat your children. I reminisced about the old country with you. And now you have the gall to sit there and try to pull the wool over my eyes!

'Pa is convinced something's afoot, and so am I. Stephen is like a loony, he's convinced that something's going down that he doesn't know about, and for once I think he's right. If you don't stop rawmaishing now, Paddy, and tell me what's up, I'll go and ask Georgio myself.'

Paddy took another long swig from the hip flask, the Jameson's burning into his stomach.

'I can't tell you, Maeve. The fewer people in the know the better. I'm not going to insult you by pretending there's nothing going on. Just be content when I tell you I can't discuss it.'

Paddy's heart sank as he saw Maeve's mouth settle into a hard thin line.

'Right then. If that's what you say, I'll go to Georgio himself. Stephen can come with me. In fact, I think I'll get Stephen to make some enquiries . . .'

Paddy interrupted her.

'The further Stephen is from all this, the better, Maeve. Don't let on to him about anything. That is one thing Georgio is adamant about. He doesn't want him involved at all.'

Maeve's eyes narrowed to slits. 'Why? His own flesh and flood. Is it dangerous?'

'Could be.' Paddy's voice was clipped, low.

'But not too dangerous for Donna, I take it. Where is she going this weekend?'

'To Scotland.'

Maeve shifted in her seat in agitation. 'Don't get flippant with me, Paddy Donovon. I mean, where in Scotland and to see whom?'

Paddy held out his hands in a gesture of helplessness. 'You know as much about that as I do. Even I'm not privileged to share that information. All I do know is, she's going up there for Georgio. I think it's probably something to do with one of the businesses.'

Maeve nodded her head slowly. 'And which sort of business would that be? Legal or illegal?'

Paddy shifted uncomfortably in his chair. 'Come on, Maeve, would you give a man a break?'

'No, Paddy, I won't. Is something happening that could put Donna in any kind of danger?'

'I don't know, Maeve. I know nothing.'

Maeve stood up abruptly. 'Well, thanks for nothing. I think I will have to ask me son, won't I?'

'You do that, Maeve.' Paddy exhaled loudly.

She stared into Paddy's face, her intense gaze unnerving him.

'Pa will be told about this conversation, Paddy. I can promise you that much. I think me and him have a right to know what's going on around us. Georgio is my son. He may be your friend, but he's my son. I birthed him, fed him and nurtured him. I have a right to know what he's up to.'

Paddy watched her walk from the small office, her back ramrod straight and practically bristling with indignation.

He finished the whisky in the flask and sighed. Sod Maeve. He had better get in contact with Georgio. Once Pa was involved there would be murders. As amiable as Pa Brunos could be, you had to get up very early in the morning to get one over on him.

Very early indeed.

Maeve slipped into the car beside Mario.

'Nothing. He told me nothing, but there's something going on all right.'

'So what are you going to do?'

Maeve shrugged and started up her Lada, enjoying as always the scrunch of the gears.

'What do you think, child? I'm going to talk it over with your father.'

She pulled out on to the road, her erratic driving causing panic amongst oncoming vehicles. Maeve ignored them and spoke again.

243

'It's funny you know, Mario, but Paddy told me that Stephen should not be told anything.'

Mario nodded. 'I think Paddy is right. I don't trust Stephen as far as I can throw him. Never did. Neither did Georgio, not with important things. Remember that, Mum.'

Maeve skirted a corner, scraping the kerb with her wheel. 'What a life! My son's locked up till time immemorial, and now I find out that my children don't trust one another. Well, you know what they say, don't you? You live and learn.'

Mario grinned. 'We trust one another, Mum; it's just that none of us really trusts Stephen.'

Maeve shook her head. 'It's a terrible thing to say, I know, but I don't entirely trust him myself. Even as a child, he had a way with him. Oh, you wouldn't understand.'

Mario put his hand gently on to his mother's arm. 'I understand more than you think, Mum.'

Maeve sighed. Smiling gently to herself, she said, 'I suppose you do, Mario, I suppose you do.'

They drove home to Canning Town in silence.

It was late evening when Alan and Donna pulled into a Bed & Breakfast outside Edinburgh. Taking their bags from the boot, Alan rang the doorbell of the tall four-storey house. It was answered by a small dark-haired woman in her thirties.

'Can I help you?'

'We need two rooms for the night, please. Breakfast in the morning and maybe a sandwich now to be going on with.'

Alan's voice was different, more cultured, and Donna stood in the shadows of the long drive, watching him in surprise.

'I can manage that much, laddie. Away in.'

The woman opened the door wider and Alan entered. Donna followed him slowly. They had hardly spoken for nearly six hours, stopping once at motorway services to eat what passed for shepherd's pie and tasted like shepherd's socks.

The woman showed them into a sitting room containing a small sofa, two occasional tables, and a portable TV. The walls were painted oatmeal colour, and along one of them stood a metal holder, full of different pamphlets about Scotland and the highlands. It smelt of Mr Sheen and stale food.

'Sit down and I'll bring you in a pot of tea and something to eat. I have a wee bit of bannock outside, could you fit that in, maybe?'

Alan smiled. 'Anything. We're starving. What a lovely place you have here.'

The small woman glowed with happiness at the compliment and bustled out of the room.

'This is hardly what I expected, I must say.'

Donna's voice felt rusty through lack of use and nervousness. Since the argument earlier on there had been a tension between them that she knew would now be hard to break down.

Alan shrugged. 'We don't want to attract any kind of attention. This will do for what we want. It's clean and out of the way. I hope the tea's all right, I could murder a cup right now.'

Donna opened her bag and took out her cigarettes. Alan watched her light one, amazed that she could perform the act with such natural grace.

'You'll be glad of a bath, girl. We both will.'

Donna nodded.

'What do you think of Scotland then?'

Donna enjoyed Alan's discomfort. He wanted to talk now, did he? She shrugged nonchalantly.

'It's all right from what I've seen of it.'

The woman bustled in with a small trolley laden down with sandwiches, cakes, buns, tea and a large bottle of Grant's whisky.

'What a sight for sore eyes, Mrs . . .'

'Mrs MacIntyre. But you can call me Emma. When you've had your fill I'll show you to your rooms. It's twenty-two pounds a head, payable in advance, and that includes a full Scottish breakfast.'

She laughed as she spoke. 'That's eggs and bacon, by the way – with porridge to start.'

Donna looked at the tantalising array of food and smiled wanly. 'This looks absolutely lovely.'

Emma nodded as if acknowledging a great truth.

'I do all my own baking. That fruit cake was fresh made this morning, as was the bread and bannock. The sandwiches are beef – Aberdeen Angus of course! I also made you a few ham and tomato. I like to see my guests eat well. Now if you need anything else, I'll be through in the bar. It's open till two-thirty in the morning if you fancy a bit of company. My husband will be glad to meet you both.'

Donna smiled at the woman. 'Thanks, we might take you up on that. What do we owe you for all this?'

'We'll sort that out later. Eat up now.'

When Emma had left the room, Alan grinned.

'Bit of all right this, ain't it?' He picked up a thick boiled ham sandwich. 'Me mum used to boil her own bacon. Beats that shop-bought crap into a cocked hat.'

245

He poured out two large measures of whisky.

'Get your laughing gear around that, Donna. It'll help you sleep.'

She took the whisky and sipped it, while Alan, a sandwich stuck in his mouth, poured them both hot tea.

'I feel so tired, I don't think I'll need anything to help me sleep.'

'You're not nervous then?' His voice was low.

'No, I'm not, actually, and I don't want to go into all that again, if you don't mind. I think you made yourself clear earlier on today.'

Alan swallowed the last of the sandwich.

'You didn't do too bad yourself. You certainly put me in me place.'

Donna picked up a beef sandwich. 'Well, at least some good came out of it then.' She bit into the smooth creaminess of real butter and thick beef. 'This is lovely!'

They ate in greedy silence for a while.

'I never meant to hurt you today, Donna. It's just, I'm worried about you, that's all.'

She sipped her tea. 'Well, don't be. I can take care of myself.'

'If you insist then. But I wonder what your old man's playing at? I wouldn't ask of my wife what he's asking of you.' His voice was low, serious.

'Maybe you and your wife didn't have the same kind of relationship. Georgio and I are very close. Even with all that's happened to him, and all I've found out, I still love him. In fact, I think I love him more if that's possible.'

Alan tossed back his whisky. 'That's what surprises me. Doesn't it bother you – all you've found out?'

She shook her head firmly. 'Nothing I could find out about Georgio after this could really bother me.'

Alan picked up another sandwich. 'Are you sure about that?'

Donna slammed the cup back into its saucer. 'Yes, I *am* sure of that. Are you going to start all this again? I mean, what is it with you? You tear into me today because of what I'm doing. Now you try and make snide remarks about my husband – your so-called friend. If you have anything to say, Alan Cox, I wish you'd just open your big mouth and get it over with. I'm fed up with playing games! Christ knows I played enough of them with my husband to last me a lifetime.' She was near to tears and she knew it.

Standing up, she walked across the room and stood at the window staring out into the darkness of the night. She heard Alan moving and sighed. When his arms came around her she pulled herself away from him.

'Oh, please. Give me a break, would you?'

'Look, I'm sorry if I upset you.' Alan looked contrite. 'I don't know what's got into me.'

Donna licked her lips slowly. 'Can't you just try to get on with me? I know you think I'm a liability, but believe me when I say I will be all right. Georgio trusts me implicitly, so can't you just try and have some of his faith in me? This is difficult enough as it is, without you making it harder for me. I am trying, really trying, to help my husband, to get him home. I tried to do it legally, now I am willing to do it illegally. Whatever you say or do, you can't change that. Georgio is all I ever had, all I ever wanted. He gave to me for more years than I care to remember, now I want to give something back to him. I want to help him, I need to help him. He's all I've got.'

Alan stared down into her beautiful, unhappy face. Took in the highlights of her hair, the lines around her mouth, and the pallor of her skin. He could smell her odour of cigarette smoke and Chanel Number Five.

'If he's all you've got, love, then I pity you.'

Donna closed her eyes and turned back towards the window.

'I wish you'd stop all this.' His voice was low.

She laughed without humour. 'I can't. Now let's get on with what we've got to do.'

She could feel his breath on the back of her neck.

'All right then, Donna, you win. We'll do what we have to do – on one condition.'

'What's that?'

Alan turned her around gently and stared into her eyes. 'Promise me that when it does get too much for you, you'll tell me? Until that time I'll give you every bit of the respect I would give to Georgio, OK?'

Donna nodded. 'I promise that if it all gets too much, you'll be the first to know.'

'I didn't say *if*, Donna, I said *when*.'

'The most irritating thing about you, Alan Cox, is that you're so sure you know everything.'

He laughed. 'My wife used to say that.'

Donna pushed past him and went back to the sofa. 'Your wife also divorced you. I can see why.'

'All right then, this round goes to you, but what I said still stands. When you want out, just let me know. Now let's finish these sandwiches and get some shut eye.'

Donna poured herself another cup of tea. 'My sentiments entirely, Mr Cox.'

247

Alan closed his eyes to hold on to his temper. 'You've always got to have the last word, haven't you?'

Donna bit into another sandwich and said through a mouthful of ham, 'Yes, actually, I have. Especially where you're concerned.'

Chapter Twenty-Two

Mr Ellington and Mr Borga were amazed to be invited into the cell of Eric Mates, normally a quiet man who kept himself to himself. The offer of a cup of tea and a look at his new paintings was too good to miss. Eric Mates was in on what was commonly termed a 'lump' – a really big sentence. Convicted of murdering his wife, his children and his wife's alleged lover, he was not getting out at any time. He had spent fourteen years on the 'Nutcracker Suite' – C wing, where the psychiatric cases were – and was noted for the number of 'tear ups' he'd had with cons and screws alike. Then he had discovered painting, and that was his salvation.

He painted stark pictures of the world as he saw it. He painted the children of Bosnia, dying, bedecked in flowers. 'The beauty among the evil' was what he called it.

His paintings were raffled for charity and he was now getting himself a name in the art world. He was respected by all, an unassuming man who made people forget within five minutes of talking to him exactly what he was banged up for. His days of tearing people to pieces, either physically or verbally, were long gone.

So the offer of a cup of tea and a look at his latest masterpieces was too good to miss. Mr Borga was contemplating the amount he would get from the *Sun* or the *Mirror* for this information. Mr Borga always had his eye on the main chance, which was why he got on well with the prisoners.

They could respect that.

As Eric slowly made the tea, the two men enjoyed looking at the paintings, unaware of what was going on outside the cell door, on the landing.

Benjamin Dawes wanted something, and he had wanted it for years. He had finally seen a way to get it and that was why Eric Mates was keeping the two screws company.

There was an unwritten law in Parkhurst SSB Unit. If you could get something back to your cell without the screws seeing it, it was yours to keep.

249

What Benjamin wanted was beyond the imagination of any of the screws and a good number of the cons themselves. However, when word went round the Wing what was going down, laughter was heard everywhere.

Twenty minutes later, when Mr Borga and Mr Ellington emerged from Eric Mates's cell, the laughter had died down, joints had been lit, the air was heavy with the scent of cannabis and everything seemed normal.

Except there was a bed out on the landing.

'Whose bed's this, then?'

Benjamin Dawes strolled out of his cell.

'Mine. I don't want it any more.'

Mr Borga laughed. 'The old back giving you one up?'

Many of the cons slept on the floor of their cells on a mattress. A bed abandoned on a landing wasn't really a big deal.

'Okey doke, I'll get the cleaning crew to dismantle it. Don't you want the mattress then?'

Benjamin Dawes laughed. 'Nah, that's all right. It won't fit in here now I've got a three-piece suite!'

Everyone laughed and Benjamin walked back into his cell and shut his door.

'Three-piece fucking suite! He wishes, eh, lads?' And Mr Borga creased up laughing and carried on with his work. The bed was gone within fifteen minutes and the Wing went quiet, everyone waiting eagerly for the count-up after lunch. The air was alive with excitement, the men's spirits were buoyant. The screws put it down to the large amount of skunk on the Wing. No one was that bothered, if as a result the prisoners were relaxed, happy and cheerful.

It made their job that much easier.

'I want to know where you were, Davey, and I want to know now!'

Davey wiped a hand across his face in agitation.

'Look, Carol, we're married, not joined at the fucking hip. I went for a drink with a bloke, and that's it.'

Carol snorted in a very unladylike fashion.

'My name's Gilly Hunt, not silly cunt, and I ain't changing it for you or anyone else, mate. Now tell me the truth or I swear before God I'll stick a fucking knife through your guts!'

'Mum, can I have packed lunch tomorrow?'

Jennie Jackson, used to the violent arguing of her parents, walked casually into the room.

Turning on her daughter like a maniac, Carol bellowed, 'Ask your father, because if I don't get any answers here today, I'm fucking off

250

out of this house and he can have the lot of you!'

Jennie, raising her eyes to the ceiling, said in a resigned voice, 'I'll take that as a no then, shall I?' She wandered out again.

Carol stared into her husband's face. Her voice lower now, and with a hint of tears running through it, she said, 'I mean it, Davey. If you're out shagging again, that's it this time. I've taken just about all I can. There's a bill for a restaurant in your trouser pocket, it's for over a hundred nicker, and you sure as Christ never took me there!'

Davey stared into his wife's miserable face. He could see the tiny thread veins that ran through her cheeks, from too many nights spent drinking Bacardi while waiting up for him. He saw the deep circles under her eyes and the faded blue of their irises. Her heavy figure, encased as usual in a dress two sizes too small, was a legacy of the kids and takeaway dinners. He felt a moment's affection for her. Deciding that with Carol in this mood, and the odds on getting knifed growing shorter by the second, he would tell her the truth. One thing with Carol, if you held your hand up, she was quite fair.

'You know me, Carol, a pair of bristols and I'm away. She was only a slag.'

'Who was it, Davey? Do I know her?'

He sighed heavily. 'Of course you don't know her, what do you take me for? When have I ever made a grab for one of your mates? Give me a bit of savvy, would you? I might bat away from home now and again, but I have got some fucking morals, you know!'

Carol grinned now, and Davey knew he was halfway home. He might get a plant around the head, but the knife was no more a threat.

'I still want to know who it was.'

'Just some little bird,' he said wearily. 'I can't even remember her name. She had a micro skirt on, plenty of perfume – Opium, I think – and loads of make-up. Her boatrace left a lot to be desired, but I'd had a drink.' His voice was whining now.

'Fucking hell, Cal, it's not like it's the first time, girl, is it? Why do we have to go through all this every time? I come home, don't I? They're just dogs. You're me wife.'

Carol swallowed deeply. 'You're a piece of shite, Davey, do you know that?'

Smiling devilishly, he said, 'So you keep telling me.'

As he walked out of the lounge doorway, a large terracotta plant pot hit him on the back of the head. It only grazed him, but he decided to play up to her.

Holding his head with both hands, he bent over, groaning.

'Fuck you, Carol, that hurt!'

Jennie, pushing past her father, picked up her jacket from where it

251

was hanging on the banisters and said gaily, 'See you all later.'

As she opened the front door she stood stock still. 'There's a bird out here, Mum.'

Grinning at her father's white face she tripped down the pathway back to school.

Pulling the door open properly with a meaty arm, Carol glared at the tall thin woman before her and snapped: 'Yeah? What do you want? A bit off the beaten track here love, ain't you?'

Bunty licked dry lips and said in her nasal tones, 'May I speak to Mr Jackson, please?'

Davey, his face devoid of colour, stood behind his wife, slowly shaking his head as if to warn off the woman before him.

'You'd better come in before the neighbours see you.'

'Well, they must certainly have heard you, Carol. I heard you from the bottom of the road.'

She frowned. 'What do you want, Bunty?'

'I need to see Davey.'

His face was a picture and Carol, noticing this, said: 'He looks a bit green round the gills because he's just had a plant pot in the back of the head.'

Glancing at the dirt-covered carpet and broken plant pot, Bunty said sarcastically, 'I never would have guessed.'

Underestimating Carol Jackson was her first big mistake of the day. Pointing a finger into the older woman's face, Carol said nastily, 'You know something, lady? You want to watch that big trap of yours before someone decides to fucking shut it for you – permanently!'

Davey pushed between the two women.

'All right, Carol, go and make a cup of Rosie Lee.' Steering Bunty into the lounge, he said, 'Did your old man send you round here?'

Shutting the lounge door in Carol's face he lowered his voice, praying in his heart of hearts that his wife wouldn't insist on knowing what exactly was going on.

She knew too much already.

Stephen was in The Bordello, one of his peepshows in Soho. As he lifted the takings from the manager, they chatted about the general state of the economy. The manager was saying what everyone in the know in London believed, from black cab drivers to porn merchants and politicians.

'Listen, boy, if the toms ain't making it, then there's no money about. Even the fucking tourists are few and far between, thanks to the IRA. All that lovely American money going to waste, eh? I wish they'd sort something out over there, I really do. I mean, we're doing

252

all right, but fuck me, not like last year, eh? Money was creaming in last year and the birds were right fucking ropey, some of 'em.'

Stephen nodded in full agreement.

'It's been a lousy summer, I grant you that. How much you salting away this year then?'

The two men smiled at one another.

'Not as much as I could, Brunos, you know that. It's why you employ me. I never did take the piss.'

Stephen grinned now.

'Fair comment. How is the place?'

A record came on, a strident rock number, and the small office space was literally shaking with the bass line.

'How the fuck that bird can even pretend to dance to that crap, I don't know!'

Before Stephen could answer they heard a loud shriek.

Rolling his eyes at the ceiling, the manager pulled himself from his seat and barrelled along the corridor to the work area.

'Oh, bollocks! Micky, get off that door and get down here!'

Stephen watched in amazement as the manager, Terry Rawlings, stepped through a hole in the wall. One of the peep cubicles was completely gone and a heavyset man was laying into a half-naked girl lying on a double bed.

The sheets were already staining with blood.

Black Micky, the bouncer doorman, and Terry pulled the man off her. Holding his arms behind his back, they forced him to a kneeling position.

'What's your problem, mate! Fucking calm yourself down, will you?' Terry's voice was exasperated.

The man was obviously as high as a kite and his voice, when he answered, had a slight German accent.

'She was laughing at me. I could see her laughing at me.'

Micky shook his head and smiled.

'Course she was laughing, mate, that's her job. You wouldn't want her crying, would ya?'

Terry tutted. Turning to Micky, he said. 'Clear this cunt's pockets. Take his traveller's cheques and cash the lot. He can pay for this damage. Looks like he could stand a few quid. Then give him a slap.'

Micky dragged the man along the corridor towards the back of the building. He was shouting now in German and English but no one was taking any notice.

Terry tidied his hair with a large bony hand. 'What a fucking nonsense he was! I tell you, Stephen, we get them all in here.'

The girl was sitting on the bed, her right eye swollen to three times

253

its normal size, blood seeping from wounds to her eyebrow and lip.

'What about me!' Her voice was very young-sounding and trembling with shock and fear.

Terry looked at her as if he had forgotten about her, which he had. 'What do you mean?'

'Well, what do I do?'

He checked her face over with a practised eye, careful not to touch the blood.

'You'll survive. Get yourself to the hospital. A couple of stitches will sort you out.'

Walking with Stephen back to the office, he said, 'I'll get a chippy in. We'll be back in business in two hours. What a fucking nutter, eh?'

Ten minutes later Stephen pulled away from outside the club in his Mercedes.

The girl was trying frantically to get a black cab, but her attire, the location and the copious amounts of blood guaranteed no one would stop for her.

She was crying.

The men on the Wing were all still high with excitement. Celled up after their lunch, some took a nap while others read; most just got stoned. When Mr Borga began to count, every cell went quiet, waiting for the balloon to go up.

Mr Borga opened the small spyhole with his finger, looked inside and called out the cell number, then 'present'. But only after he had seen for himself that the people in there were who they should be and were also definitely present.

As he came to Benjamin Dawes's cell the men heard him shout: 'Cell nineteen, present.'

Then his footsteps as he moved to cell twenty.

Then they listened to the blakeys on the bottom of his shoes tapping once more across the floor as he retraced his steps and lifted Benjamin Dawes's spyhole again.

The balloon finally went up ten seconds later when Mr Borga said in a high, shocked, and disbelieving voice: 'This cunt's got a fucking three-piece suite in here!'

The whole Wing erupted into laughter.

They heard the door being opened and Benjamin's voice bellowing, 'I told you I had one earlier, that's why I dinged out me bed.'

Georgio and Chopper were crying with laughter as they heard the exchange, as were all the men on the Wing, screws included.

Mr Borga's voice, still full of disbelief, was heard shouting, 'Don't

254

you dare try and tell me this was handed in on a visit, Dawes, or I'll have you on a fucking charge! Where did you get it? Come on, I want to know.'

Benjamin, walking out of his cell so all the men would be able to hear his words, said in a contrite voice: 'Remember when we used to have the drama classes?'

Mr Borga answered warily, 'Yeah?'

'And remember they were stopped because they found out that a lifer was trumping the drama teacher?'

Even Mr Borga laughed now. 'Yeah, I remember that, Benjamin.'

'Well, all the props were locked in the stage room, weren't they? This beautiful pink Dralon three-piece was just sitting there, doing nothing, and I thought to meself: I can't have that! Not when it would fit in my cell, like.'

Mr Borga roared with laughter. 'I don't fucking believe you lot! I've been in this nick for twenty years and you can still amaze me! That's why Eric invited us in for tea and fucking artworks, ain't it?'

Benjamin nodded his head vigorously.

'You should have seen us, Mr Borga, trying to get this lot onto the Wing without you hearing or seeing us. It was a right laugh! We had to get it past Eric's peter and all! Carrying the settee on tiptoes, we were.'

Mr Borga's laugh was nearly hysterical now.

'Can I keep it then?'

Pulling out a great white handkerchief, Borga wiped his eyes and said loudly, ''Course you can, Dawes. Anyone who can pull a stunt like that, right under my nose, deserves to keep whatever he got. Jesus H. Christ, this one will go down in the folklore. A fucking three-piece suite! This even beats the seven sacks of potatoes, this does!'

All over the unit, joints were being rolled, beers were being cracked open, and laughter was the order of the day.

The wardens knew that Benjamin and his three-piece were here to stay, and all were glad of the laughter it had provoked. On a Wing like this, you could be laughing one day, and stabbed the next. But it also reminded them of how devious the men could be. No one asked who had actually opened the door to the stage room.

Harry was in a spin, and Bunty watched him with no small measure of satisfaction.

'Are you sure about this?'

She nodded. 'As sure as I'll ever be. She knows about the hotels all right. But Davey isn't too trashed about it, so why should we be? In a

255

way, her working in Georgio's businesses can only be a good thing. Everyone can keep an eye on her then.'

'What about Carol Jackson?'

Bunty laughed now, a thin malicious sound. 'She knows less than she thinks, and that's a good thing. Got a touch of the puritan inside that foul-mouthed head of hers. Jesus, you should have seen the antics there today. She'd just crowned him with a bloody plant pot!'

Harry didn't bother to answer. Bunty in a bad mood was worse than any screaming harridan, but he wisely kept that opinion to himself.

She studied her husband's weak face and sighed. 'You're really worried, aren't you?'

It was a soft voice, unlike her usual tones, and Harry looked into his wife's face and nodded.

'I'm terrified. If any of this came out, *any* of it, I'd be finished. The land scandal alone would be enough to do it, without the rest.'

Bunty, bent on self-preservation, went to her husband and kissed him gently on the lips.

Looking into her hard face, Harry saw briefly the girl he had met all those years ago, with her phony accent that had taken him in, and her rogue of a father who had not.

He had lifted himself from a council house, had worked to achieve a good life, a decent standard of living. And he had never done any of it legitimately, always sailing too close to the wind. For a few seconds he wondered why he'd bothered. They didn't even have a child to leave it all to.

Then Bunty smiled, and he knew why.

Because this thin, vicious bitch of a woman had got under his skin when she was seventeen, and had been there ever since.

Lewis admired Benjamin's cell, and nodded with approval.

'What you need now are some curtains. A nice biscuit colour would look good.'

Donald Lewis was in his element; he was the acknowledged master of the colour scheme, followed a close second by Sadie. No one asked Eric, who though classed as artistic was considered a bit too macho for that kind of thing.

Benjamin said sagely: 'I'm going to sort something out, Mr Lewis. I want a nice rug now for the floor.'

Georgio listened to the discussion with a growing sense of unreality. Pushing himself away from the wall, he walked down to the kitchen and watched Sadie preparing goulash.

'How's it going, Sade?'

256

Face pale and devoid of the usual make-up, she shrugged. 'How do you think? Would you like Donald Lewis stuck up your arse?'

Georgio closed his eyes in disgust. 'What are you going to do?'

Sadie shrugged again, and the sad inevitability of this young man's fate angered Georgio.

'What can I do? It's Timmy I feel sorry for. He's like a little lost kid. I know people took the piss out of us, but I care about Timmy. In my world, people like him are few and far between. He would listen to my dreams and my wants. Oh! I know he's a big fat ignorant git, but he cared for me, Georgio, and to someone like me, that means a hell of a lot. He made me think that I could do the things I want to do. He was genuinely interested in *me*, Albert, known as Sadie. The man who ain't a woman. The person underneath all that.'

Georgio nodded.

They were silent for a few seconds, while Sadie chopped onions and crushed garlic.

'Timmy and me were an item. I knew that once he walked out of this nick I'd be gone from his mind, and I accepted that. But while we was together I had a bit of protection. You'd be surprised at the blokes who come on to me, you really would, Georgio. Some of the biggest queer-baiters in here have tried to get it on with me. Last year a known face raped me with two of his mates when I was on a work detail. A bastard screw set it up and watched the whole time. I never told Timmy but he guessed, bless him. The three ponces who done it wore condoms, can you believe that?'

Sadie shook his head in bewilderment.

'They hate queers, blame us for the spread of AIDs, but after a few years banged up they're not averse to holding you down and raiding your arse. But they're not arsehole bandits, oh, no!' His voice was bitter.

'No, they're just having a laugh. Now it's a strange thing, Georgio, but the Greeks revered pooftas. Did you know that? I think that most men, no matter how homophobic, will eventually turn to another geezer if women aren't available to them. Any port in a storm, if you'll excuse the pun. Those blokes who raped me did it because they thought it would be the macho way to get my arse. They couldn't approach me nicely, like, and negotiate because that would have made them shirtlifters, see? And they're not, are they? What they are, are macho men who raped a queerboy. It was just a laugh, see.'

He paused, and wiped a finger across his eyes to stem his tears.

'And they say *I'm* mixed up. One of the best arguments for

257

conjugal visits is the amount of male rape that goes on in nicks.'

Georgio was moved by the boy's words. Before he could answer, Timmy slipped into the kitchen.

'All right, Sade?'

Sadie smiled at him. 'Hello, Timmy love. I've done a bit extra for you. After I've served me and Lewis, you come in and get yours out of the oven, all right?'

Timmy beamed with pleasure at the thought of his dinner.

Watching them, Georgio sighed.

'All right, Georgio? How you getting on with Chopper?'

He held out his arms. 'How do you think?'

Timmy nodded. 'That Lewis wants to watch himself. They all want to watch themselves.'

Sadie stopped cutting carrots and said to Timmy in exasperation, 'Please, Timmy. He'll get fed up with me soon enough and then we can all get back to normal. Be patient.'

Timmy shook his head, his heavy-jowled face shaking with the force of his emotions.

'I mean it, Sade. I ain't swallowing this, girl. He's made me look a right fucking Herbert.'

Sadie leant on the table and said gently, 'You *are* a right fucking Herbert. But all that aside, just forget about it. No one thinks any the less of you. There's not many men would fight over the likes of me in the first place, and none of the people in here would fight Lewis over me, you, or anything. Just let it go, Timmy.'

Georgio picked up a piece of carrot and popped it into his mouth.

'Sadie's right, Timmy. No one thinks any the less of you. Look at me, Lewis has got me by the bollocks. Just go with the flow, mate, and wait till he gets fed up.'

Timmy shook his head. 'I know you mean well, but I have to sort this lot out for meself . . .' Changing the subject abruptly, he said to Sadie, 'What did you think of the three-piece suite scam! Cor, it didn't half make me laugh!'

Timmy's face was open and smiling, and Sadie felt a rush of affection for the large-bellied man before him.

'It was so funny. Especially when old Borga was doing the count. I nearly pissed meself.'

Georgio grinned. 'He's a headbanger, that Dawsie. Me and Chopper were in hysterics.'

The three men laughed but the atmosphere in the kitchen dropped to zero as they saw Donald Lewis standing in the doorway.

'How's my dinner coming on, Sadie?'

She smiled pleasantly. 'I'm well ahead of me schedule, Mr Lewis,

258

and I'm cooking it in the pressure cooker, so it'll be done in the next forty minutes.'

Lewis looked at Timmy and Georgio and after a few seconds he said loudly, 'Lovely little cook, my Sadie. Good with her hands – but then you already know that, Timmy, don't you?'

Timmy stood stock still, his face devoid of colour. When he didn't answer, Lewis walked a few steps closer to him and said huskily, 'Good with her mouth and all. Lovely tongue, eh, Timmy? I bet you miss that, don't you?'

Then, laughing gaily at Timmy's dark countenance, he said to Georgio, 'You should have a try out of Sadie, Brunos. I hear the Greeks like a bit of shirtlifting.'

Georgio shook his head. 'Not this Greek. And anyway, I'm English.'

Lewis smiled, his flat grey eyes like pieces of concrete. 'You're not English. You're second-generation Bubble and Irish. Two nations of scum. You're not English, not by a long chalk.'

Turning to Timmy he said, 'Out! Now! And if I see you near Sadie again, I'll make you wish you were dying of cancer.'

Timmy hesitated for a fraction of a second and Lewis bellowed into his face: 'You heard me. Get out!'

Timmy rushed from the room.

'Now then, Sadie, make me a nice cup of coffee and Georgio can bring it to my cell. They're airing *Carmen* on the radio today. I do enjoy a tragic romance, don't you?'

Georgio watched Lewis's calculated gestures of intimidation and marvelled once more at the power of the little man. Because even though Georgio had three stone on Lewis, he knew he would have to think twice about fronting him up.

Lewis had mental strength on his side.

He was mental enough to do anything.

259

Chapter Twenty-Three

Chopper watched Lewis and Sadie with a snort of distaste. Homosexuals didn't bother him as such, it was the queens like Sadie he couldn't stand. The thought of men walking round acting like tarts went against his rather macho grain.

'What's the matter, Chopper? Don't you like my little friend?'

Chopper amazed everyone in the shower room with his answer. 'Not really. He's a prick.'

Steam from the water was thinning in the cold air. Men of all shapes and sizes soaped themselves, washing off the stink of the prison.

Lewis laughed, tweaking at Sadie's long hair. 'I don't think he likes you, my little love. Maybe you ought to try and be a bit nicer to him.'

Chopper moved under the jet, his face immersed in the water.

Georgio stood with a towel over his shoulder, waiting to get under an empty shower, when he noticed Timmy walk in with a towel over his arm. He smiled a greeting, then saw what Timmy was holding, and leant back against the wall watching in anticipation. Lewis was under the shower, two of his minders beside him, Sadie standing dripping wet by his side.

Chopper watched along with Georgio, aware that Lewis had not given Timmy or his feelings enough consideration. Timmy was of the old school of villain. Whatever he thought of Sadie, the fact that Lewis had taken her from under his nose, and in full view of the whole Wing, was eating at him like a cancer. Sadie was also displaying bruising around her buttocks and on the back of her legs. Lewis's nastiness was well-known. Sadie for her part stood quietly, as she knew she was expected to.

Lewis had just put shampoo on to his hair and was lathering it up, his hard, contained body, without an ounce of fat, glistening with the running lather, when Timmy slammed the hand covered by a towel into his back.

Lewis's eyes opened wide, his expression one of amazement. He put a hand on to his kidneys and brought it back covered in thick red

260

blood. Before Timmy could repeat the action, Chopper was on him.

Lewis stared at Timmy, dumbstruck.

'You stupid, stupid cunt! I'll kill you for this, you fat ponce.'

His words were lost as he sank on to his knees, lather from his hair rushing into his eyes, the blood seeping from his torn back running into the drains along with the water, turning it pink.

Maddened with anger, Timmy pushed Chopper off easily.

'You won't do nothing to me, Lewis, hear me? Nothing, mate. I've taken all I fucking well can from the lot of you.' He held the home-made knife out menacingly. 'Anyone else fancy their chances, eh? Come on then! Come on take me.'

Two screws stood silently at the door of the shower room. Neither attempted to get help or raise the alarm. This was between Lewis, Timmy and Lewis's henchmen. If Timmy was going to get his lights put out, then they had best let it happen at the same time as Lewis's accident. Both men's faces were straight, no trace of fear or favour. Let the best man win.

Chopper stood back, watching the two men Lewis had assigned to look after him. Neither seemed as if they wanted any truck with Timmy, who looked demented.

'Here, Sade. Get back to me cell and wait there for me.'

Sadie shook her head in distress.

'Oh Timmy, you bloody fool.'

'Move it!' His voice was loud and easily drowned out the hissing of the water from the shower heads.

Sadie practically ran from the room.

Lewis was kneeling down. Groaning now, he tried to rise. Georgio saw Timmy go in to finish him off, and he stood in front of the bigger man.

'Give me the knife, Timmy. You don't want to add another five years to your sentence, do you? He ain't worth it.'

'Out of me way, Georgio. I've took all I fucking can in this shithole, I'm telling you. I'm sick of this perverted little ponce telling me what I can and can't do. Who I can have. He took my Sadie away from me. You know that.'

Georgio saw that Timmy was near to tears. He also saw the unnatural light in his eyes. He was high as a kite. Lewis's drug-running had finally backfired on him. Whatever Timmy had dropped, it had given him the courage to go after the top man.

'Give me the knife, Timmy.'

He watched as Lewis slumped on to the floor of the shower room. Chopper made a move towards Timmy, who jabbed the knife to within an inch of his face.

261

'You want some, you scouse bastard, do you? Come on then.'

'Give Georgio the knife, man. You're in enough stook as it is.' Chopper's voice was low. 'Do yourself a favour, eh? You've done what you set out to do. He looks dead enough to me.'

Timmy looked down on Lewis and smiled gently. 'He fucking better be, because if he ain't I'm a dead man myself.'

Georgio removed the knife from Timmy's hand, passing it to Chopper as he took Timmy by the arm.

'Let's go and get a cup of Rosie Lee and a bit of Holy Ghost, eh?' Timmy smiled vacantly.

'Tea and toast. We'll celebrate that wanker's demise, shall we?'

Georgio nodded sagely, then led Timmy past the two screws at the door and shook his head at them in a gesture of warning. The two men stepped back, allowing Georgio to pass them by.

The shower room was still silent with shock. One of Lewis's minders, Michael Clarkson, spat on to the inert form. Then, picking up his towel, he walked from the room, whistling lightly under his breath.

The elder of the prison wardens knelt down beside Lewis and took his pulse.

'You'd better get the quack, Daniels. He's still alive.' Standing up he looked at the men in the shower room. 'This puts a different complexion on things, don't it? Did anyone see anything?'

Slowly each man in the room shook his head; some even carried on with their showers. Shrugging the warder sounded the alarm and oversaw Lewis's removal to the hospital wing.

Ten minutes later it was just a normal morning in any maximum security prison.

Benjamin Dawes was washing himself once more when he shouted out: 'If Lewis croaks, I bagsy his rug and his curtains. They'll go lovely with me three-piece suite.'

Everyone cracked up with laughter.

Donna's introduction to the underworld of Scotland was a shock, the more so because the first taste she had of it was being driven by Alan to a large house on the outskirts of Edinburgh.

The house had a long winding drive, a gabled roof, and enough ivy along its Georgian exterior to cover her own home five times over.

'Nice drum, ain't it? Everyone always pictures the slums when they think of villains. Well, that might be where we all started out, and some never leave them, but a few of us, Georgio included, go for the high life.'

Donna didn't bother answering him.

262

Three large German Shepherds were barking at the car as they drove through the electric gates.

'Don't attempt even to open a window till Jamesie gets here. They'd rip you to pieces.'

Donna looked out in dismay at three identical sets of teeth as the dogs jumped on the car.

'They fuck up me paintwork every time.' Alan's voice was resigned.

'Listen, Donna, don't say nothing unless you know what you're talking about, right? Jamesie is a bit of a lad, a laugh, but at the same time he don't suffer fools gladly, know what I mean?'

Donna carried on staring at the three large dogs, whose barking was beginning to give her a headache.

A small man of indeterminate age walked down the steps from the house. He whistled and the dogs immediately became like pets, wagging their tails and jumping up at him. He patted them roughly. Smiling pleasantly, he nodded at Alan.

'That means we can get out of the car.'

'But the dogs?' Donna's voice was frightened.

'They won't come near you once Jamesie's there, don't worry.'

Alan slipped from the car and walked cautiously towards the smaller man. The dogs began scampering around him, sniffing him and waiting to be petted.

Alan stroked them all in turn, murmuring endearments.

'What's the matter with your companion? Is she frightened of my wee boys?' Laughing, Jamesie went to the car and opened the door. 'Come on, dearie, they won't hurt you. Give them a stroke and you'll have friends for life.'

Donna, an animal lover, stroked the thick warm fur and gingerly slipped out of the car.

'Sit down, you buggers, before you ruin her good suit!'

The three dogs sat obediently and Donna smiled widely.

'They're gorgeous. They certainly know their jobs, don't they?' She knelt down and put her arms around the largest of the dogs, kissing its furry muzzle.

Jamesie grinned. 'See? There's nothing to be afraid of. The only people I canna keep them from attacking is folk in uniform, but I don't worry too much about that. I was never a lover of the polis myself!'

Alan laughed and took Donna's arm as they followed Jamesie into the house. The three dogs sat once more by the front door, as it was shut in their faces.

'As much as I love them, their place is outside. In Germany they

263

sleep in six foot of snow. If you bring them into the house they moult all bloody year. It's the central heating, you see. Come away in and I'll make us all a drink.'

As they followed him through the impressive entrance hall into a large drawing room, four small Jack Russells set up a cry.

Donna knelt down to stroke them all, impressed despite herself by the house and the animals.

'How many dogs have you got?'

Jamesie shook his head. 'Too many to count. I'm a breeder, you see – I have kennels in the grounds. My dogs are very sought-after. You like dogs, I take it?'

Donna nodded. 'I love them. My old dog died about two years ago, and I still miss him.'

'You do get attached.' Jamesie began making them all hot toddies. Donna was absolutely fascinated by the small kettle hanging over the wood fire. Picking up a tea towel he took the kettle from its hook and poured steaming water into three thick glasses.

'About a year ago, I sold two beauties to a dealer from Wales, a woman and a man. Funny pair. The dogs were over a grand each, so they had a few bob. Well, I like to keep an eye on my animals even after they've been sold so I took a dander down to their place one day.

'Ach, those poor dogs! The bitch was tied in a small pen, her puppies around her, her own shite stuck to her fur. Two of the most beautiful Rottweilers you've ever seen, and great little personalities they had. To see them in that squalor broke my heart. I razed the place to the ground before I left – the outbuildings, that is. I didn't touch the house because they had children. But my temper was up, I can tell you. The kids were no better treated than the animals. I brought them home. Puppies, the lot.'

'That's terrible, how are they now?'

'I'll take you out to them later. I must say Georgio did himself proud with you. I never gave him the nous to have a brain where women were concerned . . .'

Alan hastily interrupted him. 'Devoted he is to her, Jamesie, absolutely devoted.'

Jamesie carried on making the hot toddies, his face closed now. Donna sat on the edge of a chintz sofa watching the four Jack Russells settling at her feet.

Jamesie gave them both a glass and held his up in a toast. 'To Georgio, the fucker!'

Alan and he laughed and took long draughts of their drinks. Donna sipped hers and placed it on a small onyx-topped table. Jamesie sat down and looked at Alan.

264

'So what exactly do you want from me?'

Alan sipped his drink before answering. 'We want to spring Georgio, Jamesie, and we want to do it soon.'

Jamesie nodded his head sagely. 'I had a feeling it was going to be something like that.'

Sadie sat in the cell with Timmy, her heart racing. Since the attack earlier in the day the whole Wing had been on tenterhooks. No one had admitted to seeing anything. All had been washing their hair and had had shampoo in their eyes. The two wardens had been looking the other way. To all intents and purposes, Lewis had stabbed himself in the kidney.

Georgio came in with three teas.

'It's like a nightmare out there, Timmy. Rumours are flying round. One is that he's dead, another is that he's being operated on, another – and this is from Benjamin – that he's been taken away by a load of birds from the *Sunday Sport* to do his time in the punishment block.'

Even Sadie smiled at that. 'I hope he is dead, Georgio, for Timmy's sake.'

Timmy shrugged and sipped at the strong liquid laced with prison hooch. 'I hope he's dead and all. I hate that bastard. It's funny, you know, but as frightened as I was of him, I felt as if I'd just about taken all I could. Then seeing my old Sadie here . . .'

'Not so much of the old, Timmy, if you don't mind.'

Georgio shook his head in wonderment. 'Chopper's been keeping a wary eye out. We'd all better watch our backs anyway. Lewis looked dead to me, but I've a feeling he's a hard bloke to get rid of, know what I mean?'

The cell was quiet once more, each deep in their own thoughts when Mr Marvello, a neutral screw, came into the tiny room.

'There's murders going on, if you'll excuse the pun. The Governor's like a teenage virgin on a date with Casanova. He wants to know why no one saw nothing. I have to laugh, you know, chaps. I often wonder where they gets these pricks from. Never been in a fucking nick in his life, then comes in here on a large wage and starts telling us what to do. It's laughable. Anyway, all that aside, lads, Lewis has had his kidney removed. He's in intensive care at the civvy hospital. Hopefully, he'll kick the bucket then we can all get back to normal.'

Sadie looked into the screw's face. 'What's normal, Mr Marvello? I've forgot.'

Marvello grinned. 'With respect, Sadie, it ain't something I'd have thought you was familiar with. Keep your fingers crossed anyway.' He slipped from the cell.

265

Timmy drank his tea in three large gulps. 'I'm a fucking dead man, I know it.'

Georgio shook his head. 'Wait and see what happens, Timmy. If Lewis snuffs it, you saw the reaction from the other cons. Most of them are hoping he's out of the ballgame. Either way, Lewis is out of our road for a while. We can all breathe easier now.'

Sadie stood up. 'I'm going down the reccy room, see what the buzz is in there. Coming?'

Timmy shook his head. 'I can't believe I done that. Not to Lewis anyway. Oh Sadie, I'm shitting meself.'

Sadie stroked Timmy's head. 'Well, it's done now, as my old mum used to say. I'll nip down and see what the general consensus is. I won't be long.'

As usual the recreation room was loud, with a TV blaring and a cassette recorder playing. Men shouted to be heard above the din. Sadie went inside hesitantly.

'All right, Sade? How's your old man?'

Benjamin's mouth was wide with laughter. 'That right they removed his kidney? Keep away from the meat pie, lads!'

Big Ricky the Rastafarian was rolling himself a joint. Sadie knew that if Lewis was out of it, Ricky would be the next contender for the crown. He was big enough and violent enough to take over. Already Lewis's henchmen were ingratiating themselves with him. Sadie was pleased. Ricky was all right. He was prison-minded, he left the gays alone and only really hated nonces. There was a big difference in the men's attitude towards consenting males and men who touched little boys or girls.

Chopper was sitting alone in front of the television watching an old black and white movie on Channel Four. Sadie watched as Lana Turner sat on the bedside of her maid and cried bitter tears.

'*Imitation of Life!* I love this film.' She sat by Chopper and three other men who were also engrossed in the film. 'I love the bit where she goes to the night club to get her daughter and pretends she's her maid.'

Chopper nodded. 'I know, it guts you watching it.' He leant out of his chair. 'Turn that fucking wogbox off, will you? I'm trying to watch me film!'

The music was hastily turned off. Ricky stood up and switched it back on, turning the volume up full. Steel Pulse blared out into the room. The strains of their song 'Ku Klux Klan' were audible to everyone in the Wing.

Chopper stood up menacingly and Ricky flexed his muscles. Everyone had been waiting for this all day. Someone had to take over

266

the Wing, and the main betting was on Ricky, a known lunatic.

'Calm down, lads. Let's see what the score is first.' Georgio's voice was loud. 'Lewis has had a kidney removed. Let's see whether or not he gets back home safe and sound, shall we, before the Third World War erupts?'

Lewis's henchmen stood back from Ricky, unsure what to do.

'Fuck Lewis, Brunos, and fuck you and all, you Greek ponce!' Ricky's voice was loud. 'This is between me and him.'

Chopper slipped off his denim shirt. Excitement was mounting in the room. Six wardens arrived and as they had all had a good shaking down from the Governor, they did what they were paid for.

Broke up the fight before it started.

The last thing they needed today was another incident, another killing. It was much better in their eyes when the criminals hanged one another. That you could smooth over with the Home Office.

'Come on, lads, this ain't the time or the place. Lewis ain't dead yet. The Governor's like a cat with a sore arse as it is, don't give him more reasons to take away your privileges.'

The tension in the room was tangible. At some point someone had turned off both the TV and the cassette player.

Ricky and Chopper stared into each other's eyes.

'You'll keep, boy.' Ricky's voice was deep and low. But everyone noticed that for all his talk, Ricky was the first to look away.

Sadie and Georgio made their way back to Timmy.

'What's the rowing about?' he asked.

Georgio sighed deeply, running his hands through his thick dark hair. 'Let's just say, the king's not dead yet, but it ain't stopping him being overthrown.'

Timmy looked puzzled. 'What's he on about, Sade?'

She shook her head. 'Let's just wait and see what happens, shall we? I thought that Lewis's going could only be for the good, now I'm not so sure.'

Georgio grinned rakishly. 'Well, I ain't complaining.'

Sadie giggled. 'Now I come to think of it, neither am I!'

Timmy stopped the two men's laughter by saying, 'But that's just it, ain't it? He ain't dead yet.'

Silence descended on the three once more, all taken up with their own thoughts. But all thinking about the same thing.

Lewis.

Jamesie whistled through his teeth in wonderment.

'We're talking Armalites, helicopters, the works. Parkhurst is hardly the easiest place to escape from. It'll mean big money.'

267

Alan wiped his mouth with his napkin. The poached salmon was perfect, as was all the food before him.

'I'm well aware of that fact. You're the only person I trust to supply us with what we want. You're the man, Jamesie, everyone knows that.'

Donna watched the little man preen himself in satisfaction.

'I get a lot of my stuff from the Army, as you know. I could easily arm my own little corps if I wanted. Christ knows I've done it for enough African countries. I draw the line at the Arabs though, never had a lot of truck with them.'

Donna smiled, acting the part of willing negotiator with everything she had. 'I thought the Arabs had it sewn up?'

Alan nearly choked on his salmon at her words.

'That's only rumours, my dear,' Jamesie said brightly. 'I could name a few other biggies for you. I deal mainly with people from the continent these days. What with Glasnost and everything else out there, I could get you some plutonium if you really wanted it. The things I've been offered, you wouldn't believe!'

'I would,' Alan interrupted. 'I was talking to Peter the Pole the other week. He's doing a lovely sideline these days – ex-Army flame-throwers. They're going like hot cakes, by all accounts.'

Jamesie wiped his chin with thick stubby fingers. 'It's surface-to-air missiles that are the real moneyspinners. Believe me, I know. Everyone's arming themselves, whatever governments might say. I was in Cuba a while back, on holiday. Now there's a country ripe for a takeover, you mark my words. As for Haiti . . . that Aristides couldn't look after a fucking terrier, let alone a whole country. It's a joke, I tell you. I don't even watch the news any more. I could get myself a new sideline telling the papers what's really going on.'

Donna listened intently, shocked at the revelations. Of all the conversations she had expected, this was not one of them.

'Do you travel a lot?'

Jamesie looked into her face, enchanted with her good looks and bright brain.

'All the time – South America, Africa, the Soviet Republic . . . now Moscow is the place to visit before it becomes Eastern Europe's Benidorm. You want to see it out there. Man, I tell you, it'd knock your socks off. I deal with a lot of the new rich from there. Villains, like meself. I have a friend in London, a banker, he's their contact. They pay out about three-quarters of a million cash for a house in, say, Knightsbridge or wherever. Then they borrow money against the property. That way the money's clean, you see?'

He smiled at Donna. 'From there it's just a small step to offshore. I

268

tell you, love, it's becoming the laundry capital of the world. And anyone with half a brain will cash in on it. I know Georgio was going to. Last time I spoke to him he was expanding his money business, the borrowing games, pennies and halfpennies. It's the laundering that is the main winner now.'

Donna nodded as if she knew what he was talking about. The perfectly cooked salmon was beginning to curdle in her stomach.

'Sometimes I wonder if there are any pies left for Georgio to push his greedy little fingers into.' Her words came out calmer than she expected.

Jamesie carried on eating, unaware of Donna's pallor. Alan hastily took over the conversation.

'So what do you think we're looking at then, Jamesie? I'm rounding up the men – all handpicked, of course. But I need a good armoury. I was wondering if I could rent the guns, like – on a sale or return basis. I won't have much need of Armalites, you know that, and I don't much fancy selling them on. Can you imagine a blagger with an Armalite or a hand-grenade? It just don't bear thinking about!'

Jamesie chuckled. 'I'd already thought of that,' he said. 'I have a cachement coming in on the fifteenth of October. That's four weeks away. I could sort you a few little bits from there.'

'That's a result anyway.' Alan looked pleased. 'How's the dog-breeding going these days?'

Donna was more than aware that Alan was changing the subject.

'Oh, the dogs are doing fine,' Jamesie said, satisfaction in his voice. 'I had another one of my boys won Crufts last year. I can't lose with them. I must show you around the kennels, Donna, I know you'll be impressed. My dogs get the works – central heating, the best food – nothing is too good for them.'

She smiled, glad to be back on a subject she understood. 'I'd love to see the kennels, thank you.'

She sipped her wine, wondering what the hell she was doing chatting about dogs, Crufts and Armalite rifles!

The prison was in darkness. Georgio rolled over on his bunk, unable to sleep. He could hear Chopper whistling through his teeth, a sound that drove him to distraction.

'You awake, Georgio?'

'What do you think?'

Chopper laughed softly in the darkness.

'I had a feeling you might be having a bit of trouble with your zeds. Listen to me. I think Lewis has had it, don't you?'

269

Georgio shook his head wearily. 'Oh Chopper, just how well do you know old Donald? Only, I remember when he got shot in the early seventies. He took six bullets, was left for dead, and three weeks later the man who tried to finish him was found tied up, gagged and tortured to death. Until you see Lewis go in the ground, mate, with your own eyes, don't bank on nothing.'

Chopper absorbed Georgio's words. Then 'I know he's a hard old bugger, but every dog has its day.'

Georgio sat up. Swinging his legs over the side of the bunk, he scratched his stomach aimlessly.

'Well, I have a feeling that Lewis's days are still here, know what I mean? You forget he still owns a good portion of this nick. Now his nancy boys might have taken the coon's side today, but once Lewis hobbles back on this wing, he'll take over the reins again. Believe me, because I know him. I know him bloody well. He would buy all he needed. He's mega rich, and mega bad. He is, in fact, your worst nightmare, because once he finds out what's been going down, he'll pay everyone back. And pay them back as viciously as possible.'

'You seem to know a lot about him?'

Georgio answered with a toughness in his voice he didn't really feel: 'Listen, Chopper, I knew Lewis from a kid. My old man knew him. Unlike most hard men, the stories you hear about him are true. You wouldn't *need* to exaggerate them. I know for a fact that he's been responsible for the murders of a good many blokes, and a few women too. He is bad, exceptionally bad. Go careful.'

Chopper got off his bunk and lit himself a roll-up, his face eerie in the light of the match.

'You seem to be doing all right. I hear you owe him a lot of money – money he wants back. And you're not telling him anything, I notice.'

'That's for the simple reason that once I tell him, I'm finished. There ain't a lot of people that can frighten me, but Lewis is one of them. I mean it: go careful, Chopper. I'm telling you that not because I like you, but because I have a feeling you could end up causing us all trouble. Let it all lie. Once we know what's going down, we can all make our plans.'

Chopper took a deep drag on his cigarette.

'And what are your plans? I get the impression you're waiting to go somewhere. You don't get involved in anything, you're distant to most of the men. You seem to me like you're only here on loan.'

Georgio laughed. 'I'm waiting for my appeal, Chopper. I thought that was common knowledge.'

'Yeah, and the Queen Mother is coming in tomorrow for soliciting!

270

What do you take me for? I've spent the best part of my adult life in places like this. I can read people. I see more than you'd think.'

'Then this is one time you're wrong. I want to do me time with as little fuss as possible, that's it. End of story.'

Chopper sat on the bunk next to him.

'You intrigue me, Brunos. What are you bothering with Sadie and Timmy for, eh? Why don't you use your reputation to make life easier for yourself in here? I know all about you, what kind of stuff you're involved in. You're doing eighteen years, boy. That's not a nonce's sentence. Why are you toeing the line with Lewis?'

Georgio sighed. 'As I already told you, I know him better than anyone. Lewis isn't dead until he's buried, take my word for it. Even then I wouldn't put it past him to carry on from the grave. You know so much about me? Well, my advice is to find out about Lewis – *really* find out about him. You might just get a shock. Ask around about Jimmy Lansdown. I take it you've heard of Jimmy?'

Chopper nodded.

'Then you know how he died. Lewis was behind that or I'm a fucking Dutchman. Don't let his homosexuality make you think he's no threat, because one thing I've learnt over the years is this: the queers are always underestimated, especially by the macho men like you. Lewis is a dangerous man, remember that at all times. He'd slip a knife into you while he was smiling.'

Chopper listened carefully. 'Do you think he'll come through this, really?'

Georgio laughed again, harder this time.

'If he can come through six bullet wounds, having his kidney removed ain't gonna trash him. In fact it wouldn't surprise me if he has it grilled with a bit of liver and eats it with a nice Chianti. He's capable of it.'

Chopper got up and climbed back on to his bunk.

'We'll see.'

'See what?'

Chopper settled his bulk and answered nonchalantly, 'We'll see how it goes. But I warn you now, if he's out of the ballgame I am in, and I'm expecting you to back me up, Brunos. It's about time you pulled your weight in this nick. It's getting boring watching you sit on the fence. Before you know it you'll fall off, and then where will you be?'

Georgio didn't bother answering.

He lay awake wondering how Alan and Donna were getting on in Scotland. If Lewis came back he could handle it; he hadn't done anything detrimental. All he wanted was to keep his head down and

271

sit it out until such time as he could make his move. And the sooner that was the better.

The Wing was deathly quiet, the usual night sounds muted. Georgio knew that all minds were on Lewis, and what was happening to him.

Please God let him die, he prayed.

He wondered for the umpteenth time why he had not let Timmy finish what he'd started. He should have left Timmy to cut the bastard's throat. It was the chat with Sadie that had done it. They were friends now, and in a place like this, friends were your all.

He had just found that out.

Chapter Twenty-Four

The day dawned wet and Donna shivered in the car as they drove towards Glasgow. Yawning widely, she settled back in her seat.

'I know this is an early shoot, Donna, especially after last night, but we have so much to do this weekend. Important things.'

She watched the scenery gradually change from green fields to grey concrete and nodded.

'Jamesie seemed such a nice person, not the type to be involved in arms deals or robberies . . . Oh, you know what I mean.'

Alan slowed the car to allow some children to cross the road. 'I understand what you're saying but you must remember, hardly anyone is what you think they are. Even the average housewife has something she wants to hide.'

Donna laughed nastily. 'The average housewife? Now I've heard everything. God, you're a bloody chauvinist! What, may I ask, is an *average* housewife? You sound as though you're an expert on the subject.'

Alan felt his temper rising. Donna was getting more and more touchy by the hour. Swinging the car round a bend, he answered her in a loud voice.

'Well, my mother was an average housewife – not that you'd know one if she fell out of a tree and hit you on the head. The average housewife lives in a council place, with three or four kids, no holidays, very rarely enough money, and an old man who spends his time between the dole and the pub. She reaches thirty and looks forty-five, her figure goes after the second child, she becomes loud-mouthed to compete with the neighbours who are all streetwise, and she fights to give her kids that little bit more. She dresses them from catalogues, does a bit of ducking and diving for extra cash, and finally expires at about sixty-odd after living for years in damp accommodation and taking the back of the old man's hand.

'She gets the doctor for her kids but never for herself. She dotes on her grandchildren, visits sons in nick or boasts because they've got a job. She makes sure her daughters try for better and is deeply

273

saddened when they plump for what she had. Her telly and her drop of sherry are her lifeline. And of course Bingo where she can meet her cronies, have a laugh and slag off the neighbours. That, Donna Brunos, is the average housewife.'

She listened to him in silence.

'All right then, Alan, so what would her big secret be then?'

He grinned. 'Her big secret would be the bloke who got away, the one she was young with, the one she should have married instead of the ponce she ended up with. She daydreams over shitty nappies and greasy dinners about the fella who fancied her when she was young, the fella who was well-spoken, quiet, classed by her peers as a bit of a snob. Then she remembers her old man in his Teddy boy suit, his slicked-back hair, and his devil-may-care attitude. She took second-best and she knows it. That, Donna, is her secret.'

She tossed her hair in consternation.

'Well, forgive me, Alan, but that's not exactly on a par with Jamesie, is it? We were talking about living a lie, not living with regrets.'

Alan flicked a glance at her.

'You know something, Donna? That's your problem. You don't really know the difference. The lie she's living is that she is there. All her married years she's looking for that extra few quid to come in so she can dump the old man, get the kids out of their environment, help them better themselves. She daydreams of that, of the man coming back for her and finding her and taking her away from it all. Yet she sleeps in the same bed as the man she has come to despise. She allows him access to her body, but never to her mind. He isn't even aware she's got one. She puts up with all sorts of trouble and humiliations for him, and through him. Yet the lie, Donna, is always there.

'She has his children, she's the mother of his children, and that is all she is and she knows it. There's no real respect, no real love, and she knows that as well. Her old man watches Benny Hill, reads the *Sun* and the *Sport*, and treats her once a year to a birthday present, usually something for the home – an iron or a kitchen set. She is a non-person, and the more time goes by, the more obvious it is to her. So she retreats more and more into what could have been, and what she should have been.

'She is living more of a lie in fact than Jamesie, because he's a man and can do what the fuck he likes. That privilege is rarely afforded to women, especially working-class women. You think you've got problems? Your old man's banged up, big deal. You should try looking after three kids on the fucking Social. That would soon put

274

paid to your smart mouth, I can tell you.'

There was silence in the car. Both were aware that Alan had gone too far and neither really knew what had brought on this tirade. All he knew for sure was that her long face was getting him down. He didn't want her there, didn't want her meeting people like Jamesie and others of his ilk. He wanted to protect her from it all, yet at the same time her complete disdain for his way of life, Jamesie's way of life, and the mess they were all in, annoyed him. He was doing her old man a bloody big favour, and consequently he had to put up with her. It was all a mess.

Donna's voice was quiet as she answered him.

'For your information, Alan Cox, I would gladly have lived in a council flat if I could have had even one child.'

Alan heard the yearning in her voice, and realised what he had said. He should have remembered all Georgio had told him over the years about their quest for a child. Even adoption was out because of his nefarious activities. He could have taken his foot and slammed it painfully into his own mouth. Stopping the car, he turned to face her.

'I'm sorry, Donna. That was uncalled-for. I just wasn't thinking. Forgive me.'

She stared out at the blurred landscape and forced back the tears. If Alan Cox knew how she still yearned to hold a baby, to snuggle it into her arms and know it was hers! She would gladly give up everything she possessed for that.

He placed his hand on her arm and she shrugged it off.

'I'm fine, Alan. Let's get going, shall we? Now I have been put well and truly in my place I will remember to act the subservient little woman in future.'

Alan felt an urge to turn her around and pull her into his arms but he knew it would be fatal.

'Shall I tell you something, Donna?'

'Would it stop you if I said no?'

'I'm being serious, darlin'. You bring out the worst in me, I don't know why but you do. There's something about your whole demeanour that irritates me in the extreme. You're so sure of yourself, you look down on everyone, yet you need these people to get your husband – who incidentally is doing eighteen years – out of nick. You are mixing with the scum of the earth for that one reason. You look down your pretty little nose at them, yet you are no better, not now. You were before you became embroiled in all this, but not any more. You're as crooked as them now and the sooner you realise that and stop trying to fucking be Mother Theresa of Alcatraz, the sooner me and you will get on.

275

'Like I was saying before, the average housewife has the housewife mentality: the man in her life is what brought her low. Remember that, love, because it applies to you as well. You don't go to Bingo, you go to fancy restaurants and clubs. You don't have a beano to Southend now and again, you go to the Caribbean. Same meat, Donna, different fucking gravy. Now you're making me all annoyed again. Why the hell is that!'

Donna turned on him, her eyes blazing.

'I don't know why I irritate you, Mr Cox, but I can honestly say that the feeling is mutual. As for all this old rubbish about housewives, what are you, some kind of sociologist? I have a degree in Sociology, you may be interested to know, and I never read anything remotely like the crap I've heard today.'

Alan shook his head. 'What I know you can't learn from books, love, you learn it from experience. Remember that.'

He stared into her face, feeling the familiar pull of her, the pull he'd noticed the first time he'd clapped eyes on her. He sighed. Her blue eyes were glittering, emphasising her anger; her hair was like a thick mane. Her stubborn little chin was set; her mouth quivering with indignation. Alan groaned inwardly. What he'd really like to do was strip her off in the car and fuck the arse off her. That was what was wrong with him and he knew it. He was picking on her, and had homed in on the thing that would hurt her most, her inability to have children. He was a nasty, evil-minded man, and he was ashamed because he still didn't feel sorry. Inside himself he knew she needed knocking down a peg, and he wanted to do it before they got to Glasgow and she met the people he had been talking about. Her idea of a slum was living in Canning Town, like Ma and Pa Brunos did. She had never in her life been subjected to a real dump, with hard people. Glasgow would be an education, as would Liverpool or the seamier parts of London.

He stared into her face, willing himself to calm down. She couldn't help being what she was; she was lucky she had never had to live as he had. Was lucky never to have had to scrimp or save or wonder where the next meal was coming from. She had been lucky all her life.

Mrs Good Woman soon lost all her fancy values when Mr Good Man got banged up though, even though Mr Good Man was as bent as a nine-bob clock. Yet still she looked down on Alan, and the people they were dealing with. It was a pity she didn't look down her nose at that husband of hers. She didn't know the half of it where Georgio was concerned . . .

His bad temper was over now.

'I'm sorry, Donna.'

276

She licked her lips slowly, an unconsciously erotic act. 'No you're not, Alan. To you I'm a stuck-up cow and I know it. Well, let me tell you something – I'm glad I am. I'm over the moon, because I know deep inside that whatever I may be involved in now, it's for one reason and one reason only. My Georgio. I didn't choose any of this, it was thrust on to me. What's your excuse for the way you've lived your life? A murderer, a self-confessed murderer. My God, you people are laughable. Don't tell me about poverty, I know all about it! People like you shove it down my throat all the time. Well, here's another little gem for you to put in your pipe, Mr Cox. *People* make slums, not houses. Remember that when next you step up a flight of stairs on one of your council estates and encounter filth, condoms and urine. You didn't have to be a villain, you *chose* to be one. Not every poor boy becomes a gangster or a robber. It's a choice you make. So keep all your bleeding heart stuff to yourself in future. It don't wash with me.'

Alan felt a rush of rage again and swallowed it down like bile.

'Your old man is no different to me, love, and don't you forget it.'

Donna smiled, her face rosy once more, complexion bright. She looked stunning in the morning light.

'But I don't love you, Mr Cox, and I happen to love my husband very much. No matter what he's done. Now, are we going to Glasgow or are we staying here all day?'

Alan put the car in gear, aware that his hands were shaking. He felt an urge to put them round Donna Brunos's throat and choke the living daylights out of her.

That was how she affected him. When he wasn't yearning to kiss her, he wanted to kill her.

As they pulled away he sighed heavily. What a situation, and he was lumbered with her for a long time to come. He didn't know if the prospect pleased or appalled him.

All he knew for sure was that her legs, sheathed in black stockings, were drawing him like a magnet; and her face, with its expertly applied make-up, was also drawing him to her; and her feisty personality was the icing on the cake. The more she fought back, the more he wanted her. The more she annoyed him, the more he wanted her.

That was the trouble: he wanted her so badly he could almost taste her. Could smell her scent close to him, and couldn't stand it for much longer.

She was Georgio's wife, a bit of class.

And he wanted her.

★　★　★

277

Lewis came around in the Intensive Care Unit. He opened his eyes to the bright lights and squinted, listening for any sounds he recognised. All he could hear was the bleep-bleep of the monitor by his bed. Opening his eyes fully, he observed a policeman sitting by the bed reading the *Daily Mirror*. His throat was dry, his eyes gritty with sleep. He could smell the peculiar odour of anaesthetic.

Then it all came back to him. He felt the searing pain as the blade entered his back. He tried to move in the bed, feeling renewed pain as he did so.

He smiled.

He was alive then.

The policeman glanced at him and saw he was awake.

'Mr Lewis, are you feeling all right? I'll get you a nurse.'

The man had a gentle Yorkshire accent. As Lewis opened his mouth to answer him, nothing came out except a small croak. He needed a drink of water, his teeth cleaned, and to know what was going on, in that order. The policeman walked up the ward while Lewis moved first his hands and then his feet.

He wasn't crippled.

The thought was like a balm to him. He knew his back had taken a good slice; if the knife had been slipped into his spine he would have been well and truly finished.

In his mind's eye he saw Timmy, his face turned into a mask of grief, and Lewis smiled again.

Timmy would pay, and pay dearly, for his little temper tantrum. It would keep Lewis going. While he recovered he would set his mind to thinking up something elaborate for Timmy.

Lewis was renowned for paying his debts.

This one would be repaid one hundredfold.

Glasgow was a shock to Donna. The beautiful buildings were not at all as she had pictured them. When they came towards Govan Southside, though, her preconceptions were confirmed. The shops had thick, security wiring over the glass and the streets seemed to be full of women with pushchairs, men wandering aimlessly, and stray dogs. Alan had only spoken to her perfunctorily since their argument. It was now early afternoon and she wanted a drink, something to eat and a pee in that order.

They drove into a maze of low-rise flats, some with boarded-up windows, others with bright net curtains. Children played everywhere, their aggressive mien noticeable even from a passing car. Donna felt tension in the air.

'Where are we?'

Alan smiled grimly. 'This is a place called Govan.'

Donna faced him. 'What does that word mean?'

Alan parked in front of a squalid block of flats and shrugged his shoulders.

'I don't know. It's probably a Gaelic word for "arsehole of the world". Come on, get everything out of the car. We ain't leaving nothing. They'd smash your windscreen here for a packet of fags left on the dashboard.'

Donna emerged from the car, looking around her helplessly. This wasn't what she had expected. After Jamesie's grand house she thought everywhere else would be the same. What on earth could they be doing here?

As they walked into the small block of flats they were nearly knocked flying by three teenage girls who ran through the lobby doors, laughing wildly.

The tallest of the girls said something unintelligible to Donna and the other two sniggered. Donna felt her face burning. Whatever the girl had said had been accompanied by a sneer as she looked Donna up and down like so much dirt.

Alan held the door open for her and she walked into the foetid warmth of the block. There were two doors on the first floor. Each had a black binbag outside, overflowing with rubbish. The tiled flooring was filthy; the stench of decay filled their nostrils. Propped against a wall was a child's cycle and a large bag of cement. The bag was broken open and cement was strewn all around the floor. It had obviously been there for months. Alan knocked on a battered green-painted door and waited patiently. No one answered. He banged on the door again, harder this time. Donna could hear voices coming from the flat. Loud raised voices, one of them a woman's.

The door was thrown open by a child of about nine. The boy had short cropped hair, a striped jersey, dirty jeans and a pair of Fila bumpers.

'What?' The child's voice was harsh.

'Is your dad in?'

He wiped his hand across his nose and looked Donna up and down before answering.

'Who wants to know?'

Alan knelt down until he was the same height as the boy.

'Listen, little hard man, is your fucking dad in or not? If he is, tell him Alan Cox is here. If he ain't, give me the name of the pub he's in and I might, just might, give you a couple of quid.'

The child stared into Alan's face, debating whether to tell him anything or to keep his peace. He was saved from answering by the

279

appearance of a small bull-necked man with the biggest beer belly Donna had ever seen in her life.

'Hello, Alan, me old mate. Long time no see.'

His Cockney accent was like balm to Donna after listening to he thick Glaswegian tones of everyone else. The child moved silently aside to let them pass.

'Annie! Get the kettle on, girl, we've got visitors.' He turned to Alan, grinning cheerfully. 'You'll have to take us as you find us. You know my Annie. She never was a one for clearing up.'

Alan laughed. Then a good-looking blonde woman of about thirty-five walked into the hallway. Her hair was immaculately brushed, her clothes cheap but well-pressed. She had on impossibly high heels, and Donna was amazed to see that under her leggings and the big shirt, the woman was heavily pregnant.

'Hello, Alan.' Her voice was pure Scots. She smiled at him seductively, even in her advanced state of pregnancy.

Donna was ignored, and knew instinctively that she would always be ignored by this woman while there were men about. All Annie offered her was a perfunctory glance.

'I'll make the tea.'

Her voice didn't have the harsh tones of most of the Scottish people Donna had encountered, but was soft and musical.

Donna walked after the men into the small front room and was shown to a seat on a surprisingly good leather sofa.

The front room was Annie's pride and joy. It was filled to capacity with what she termed 'good stuff'. There was a thirty-two-inch TV and state-of-the-art video, the leather suite was black, the walls painted white and hung with pen and ink drawings depicting different scenes from the Clyde. A thick Axminster carpet covered the floor, and the fireplace was Adam style with a black marble hearth. Tables abounded, and a large black ash wall unit dominated the back of the room, covered in all sorts of blue-painted plates, jugs and glassware. Donna secretly abhorred the style but was admiring of the fact that it had been done at all. After seeing the outside of the flats and the hallway, she was pleasantly surprised to find herself in relative comfort.

Alan and the man settled themselves. A small child crawled into the room and Donna was amazed to see Alan pick it up expertly and cuddle it.

'She's got big, Jonnie. How old is she now?'

He shrugged. 'Nearly a year. She still ain't attempted to walk. Justin and Wayne were both early walkers but she's a lazy cow.' He pushed his face close to his daughter's and the child grabbed at his

280

nose, laughing. 'Aren't you, my little darling? Who's Daddy's best girl then, eh?'

The child crowed with joy and Donna felt herself relax. If children were in the house then at least this wasn't going to be dangerous. She felt hypocritical to have judged this man by his home after spending the previous night in the palatial residence of an arms dealer.

'This is Jonnie H. Jonnie, this is Donna Brunos, Georgio's wife.'

As he spoke Annie walked into the room with a tray of tea. She looked at Donna with new respect.

'You're Georgio's wife? Well, well, well. I always thought him having a wife was just a vicious rumour. So you actually exist? Wonders will never cease.'

She scrutinised Donna then, as if seeing her for the first time, taking in the black suede shoes, matching handbag and expensive silk suit. She registered the sheer black stockings, the thick chestnut hair and dark blue eyes – and decided she didn't like Donna Brunos one bit.

She passed her a chipped mug full of weak tea, the mug she had been going to have herself. Donna nodded her thanks and Annie ignored her once more.

'So what brings you to this neck of the woods?' The musical voice was turned on Alan.

'I came to see your old man, Annie. I have a bit of a tickle for him.'

She smiled, showing even white teeth. 'As long as it's not a robbery, Alan. I'm nearly due and all I want is to get this bairn born with Jonnie beside me as usual.'

Alan smiled widely, his teeth sparkling in his tanned face.

'This is as sweet as a nut, Annie. A good bit of wedge for one day's work.'

'How much is a good bit of wedge?'

Annie's voice was brisk, businesslike, and Donna watched amazed as Jonnie H. waited for his wife to have her say.

'A good few grand.'

'And what will my Jonnie be doing for his good few grand?'

Alan grinned again. 'He'll be helping me to spring a mate from Parkhurst, that's what he'll be doing.'

Annie stared at her hands for a few seconds, digesting what he had said. Then she looked up into Alan's eyes and said seriously, her musical voice taking on a hard edge, 'Fifteen grand, eight up front, and my Jonnie is yours, Alan.'

He laughed out loud. 'Your wife's a fucking con artist!'

Jonnie H. grinned mischievously. 'My wife knows my worth, and don't you ever forget it, Cox!'

Alan held the small child up in the air and cooed at her. 'Your mum's the best negotiator in the business, sweetheart.'

The baby chortled, her chubby legs moving in a cycling motion.

Alan placed the child back on the floor. Looking at Annie he said: 'Fair enough. It's a deal. Now, I want you to find me some other men I can trust. No one will know what's going down until the day before the jump, right? I want men unknown around the south-east, men who are hard, who can take a few knocks and who can keep their traps shut.'

Donna watched Annie carefully assessing what Alan said. Despite herself she was impressed with the woman.

'I'll tell you what, Alan. I've a proposition. We give you the names and for every one you decide to take on, we get a ten percent cut for commission. How's that? We'll recruit them for you if you want. Jonnie's got a few good mates up here in Govan. Christ knows, they could do with the money.'

Alan nodded. 'That's the ticket, girl. You do the recruiting. The only stipulation is, they must be able to keep their traps shut, before the jump *and* after. Especially after.'

'Understood. Now, who wants more tea? I have a nice bit of ham in. I'll make a few sandwiches then you and Jonnie can go through the names and their specialities and we can work from there. Would you like to give me a hand?' She smiled at Donna for the first time.

Donna stood up uncertainly and followed her out into the small kitchen.

'The bread's in there and the butter's in the fridge. Get buttering.'

Donna did as she was told, swallowing down her annoyance at the woman's attitude.

'So how's Georgio these days? We haven't seen him for a while. Jonnie H. was a good friend of his years back.'

Donna licked some butter off her thumb. 'Georgio's fine, thank you, Annie. I'll give him your best, shall I?' Her tone was hard.

Annie laughed. 'You do that. Tell him Annie asked after him. Just that.'

Donna smiled tightly. 'He'll know who you are, then?'

Annie rested her arms on her huge stomach. 'Oh, he'll know who I am, all right, don't you worry about that.'

They worked in silence for a while, the atmosphere thick in the small confined space of the kitchen.

Annie spoke again. 'How come you're with Alan? Georgio wouldn't like to know you were out and about together, would he? Especially while he's away. I remember when my Jonnie was banged

282

up in Barlinnie, I nearly went out of my mind. Have you any wee ones?'

Donna shook her head. 'Georgio knows I'm here, Annie. As for children, we don't have any.'

Annie sneered at her. 'You don't look the type to get pregnant, not the way you dress.'

Donna slammed down the knife she was cutting the sandwiches with.

'And what would you know about that, eh? What are you, some kind of bloody oracle, you know everything suddenly?'

Annie grinned annoyingly. 'Calm down, Donna. I was only making a statement of fact. I bet you wouldn't be seen dead looking like I do.'

Donna felt the fight leave her body. What with Alan and now this Madonna of the Scottish Slums, she was finding it hard to cope.

'Then that just shows you how much you know, doesn't it? I had two miscarriages and a dead boy, if you must know. I wasn't very lucky where children were concerned. Satisfied?'

Annie was about to answer when Alan walked into the room.

'Everything all right, girls?' His voice was artificially bright. 'Jonnie H. has gone down the offie for a bottle of scotch. Can I give you two a hand?'

Annie shook her head. 'No thanks, Alan, me and Donna are fine.' She smiled at him reassuringly and he had no choice but to leave the room.

Annie went to Donna's side and touched her arm gently.

'I'm a bitch, take no notice of me. It was your lovely clothes and your slim figure that annoyed me. I'm sorry for what I said, heart sorry.'

Donna finished cutting the sandwiches.

'I don't want your sympathy, Annie. I just wish everyone would stop treating me like I was something they dragged in off the street on their shoes. I know the impression I create and I'm sorry, but that's me. I never had to fight for anything in my life until now. But believe me when I say, for Georgio I'd fight anyone.'

Annie smiled again, wider this time, a genuine smile.

'Och, you'll do, lassie. And let's face it, Georgio is worth fighting for, eh? You're a lucky girl, keeping him all these years. That's no mean feat. Georgio is too good-looking for his own good. Or anyone else's for that matter!'

Donna laughed at the underlying message in what Annie said and the two of them bonded then as only women can.

In the lounge Alan sat with the baby and thought of what he had heard Donna snap at Annie.

283

A dead boy. His heart went out to her. Especially after all he had said to her in the car earlier. How could he have been so dumb, so stupid? Donna Brunos was no ordinary housewife, he had deliberately set out to upset her. Now he realised just how he had achieved that end.

A dead boy. The words ran around his head and every nuance of her heartbreak was in those three little words.

A dead boy.

No wonder Georgio was her all. At her age she didn't have anything else to look out for, to look forward to.

He decided then and there that if it was the last thing he did, he would see that she got what she wanted: Georgio.

He would move heaven and earth to achieve that for her.

Jonnie H. came back with the scotch and the girls brought in the sandwiches, smiling at one another like conspirators now. Alan shook his head at the ways of women.

'I was going through names while I walked down the offie and I think I might have just the people you're looking for. Three brothers. They stick to each other like shit on a blanket and they're all kosher. One went down for five years for a mate, because he wouldn't grass him. They're called the McAnultys and they're bastards, but trustworthy bastards. Know what I mean.'

Alan nodded.

As he listened to Jonnie H. he watched Annie and Donna looking after the baby, saw how Donna put the child on her lap and kissed its downy head. He could see the naked hunger in her eyes and it was like a knife going through his very soul.

He would give her what she wanted; he would hand her Georgio on a plate if that's what it took to keep her happy.

He only wished he could give her what she really deserved.

284

Chapter Twenty-Five

Alan and Donna walked out of the flats and he checked the car over before they got into it. They were both amazed to find it intact. As they drove out of the inaptly named Harmony Row towards Argyle Street, Donna settled back into the comfort of the seat.

'What did you think of Annie?' Alan asked her.

She shrugged. 'I liked her, but not at first! Once we had had a little chat we were fine, though. I was surprised to find that Jonnie H. was a Cockney. It seemed strange hearing his voice after all the Scottish accents.'

Alan laughed with her.

'There's a story there with Jonnie H. and Annie. When he was in the Smoke, he was a sod for whoring. He patronised Shepherd's Market and Kings Cross. It was a standing joke with everyone. He always went for the rough trade. Then, all of a sudden, Jonnie H. was getting married. We were all amazed. I done the food for his wedding, Georgio will tell you . . .'

Donna turned in the seat. 'You mean, he was there? At their wedding?'

Alan swallowed heavily. Taking a deep breath, he said, 'Nah, of course not. I mean it was the talk of the town, like. Nothing more.' He saw Donna visibly relax.

'Anyway to get back to me story. It turned out that Annie, she was only about seventeen then, was a tom from the Market itself. He picked her up one night in his motor and that was that. He took her away from it all. She was a right looker and all. I mean, she looks all right now and she's ready to drop her chavvy any day. It caused a sensation at the time, but as Georgio said to me once – in reality, Jonnie done himself a favour. He got what he wanted and he's happy. He paid the toms to do what he wanted. Now he has one on tap, if you like.'

Alan roared at his own humour.

Donna stared at him stonily. 'They seem very happy to me.'

Alan waved a hand at her. 'They *are* happy – happiest couple I've

285

ever seen. He worships her. But myself, I couldn't marry a tom. I know it sounds nasty, like, but I just couldn't do it.'

He hung a left off Argyle Street and made his way to The Waterloo public house. Pulling up outside, he turned the engine off and faced her.

'Have I said something wrong?'

Donna shook her head. 'Annie seems to me to be very much the stronger of the partnership.'

'Oh, she is,' he agreed. 'Before they married he'd do a blag, piss all his money up the wall and be looking round for work again. He also sold himself short. It's Annie what got him into this business. She's his negotiator, and she looks after the dosh. That flat in Harmony Row is just a front. Eventually him and her are going to get right out of it, buy a place for cash then carry on from there. She's shrewd, old Annie. She knew what Jonnie H. could offer her and she took it. Like most brasses she's loyal to him. They're always loyal, brasses. Funny that. They're loyal to their pimps, their boyfriends and their husbands. Never ceases to amaze me.'

He jumped from the car and held Donna's door open for her.

'What are we doing here?'

'This, Donna, is where we pick up the front men. I know a few faces here who can help us.'

She followed him into the stagnant warmth of The Waterloo. It was a known haunt of homosexuals and Donna breathed in perfume, aftershave and sweat as they pushed their way to the bar. The music was loud and heavy. Leather and earrings abounded.

'Two large scotches, please. Is Nick Carvello in at all?'

The barman nodded and jerked his head at the corner of the room. Alan paid for the drinks and they squeezed through towards Nick Carvello and his friend Albie Doyle.

Nick was tall, slender and very good-looking, with thick red hair tied back in a ponytail and green eyes like a cat's. Albie was short, dumpy and dressed in overalls. Donna felt as if she had gatecrashed a Village People concert.

Nick squealed loudly. 'Alan! Oh, what a pleasant surprise. Look what the cat's dragged in, Albie.' He was looking Donna over as he spoke. 'Love the suit, dear, very Sharon Stone. Now let's sit down and get settled.'

He walked to a table where four men were sitting chatting. He made a waving gesture with his hands and the four beat a hasty retreat.

'Come and sit down, and let's catch up. Sit beside me, Albie dear, but first go and get another round of drinks. And ask Phillip if he can

286

put on some Stylistics. This shit is giving me a headache.'

He turned to Donna and said conspiratorially, 'Ever since that shit "Relax" came out, they think we all gyrate to rubbish like that. Sickening, isn't it?'

Donna smiled, feeling very out of place. 'You're not Scottish?' she said tentatively.

Nick screamed with laughter. 'Essex born and bred, dear, that's me. Typical Essex Man if people only knew it. The things I could tell you about that county would make your hair curl up and fall out! Mind you, I was a Londoner for a long time. Ever heard of the London Boys? Bowie wrote a song about us once. I live up here now, doing me bit, like we all do. What's your name, dear? I hope it's as glamorous as you are.'

Donna looked into his perfectly made-up face and said: 'It's Donna, Donna Brunos.'

She saw Nick's eyes widen. Then he looked at Alan quickly before saying *sotto voce*. 'We *are* a lucky girl, aren't we?'

Donna was saved from answering by Albie coming back with the round of drinks.

'Oh Albie, you are a darling. Albie, meet Donna Brunos. Georgio was hiding her from us all for years. Pretty as a picture, isn't she? Love the hair. Is it natural?'

Donna found his high breathless way of talking amusing, especially as he jumped from one subject to another so hastily. She realised that most of his questions weren't to be answered but were delivered as compliments.

'So, Alan. What's to do, dearie?'

Alan grinned and knocked back his scotch. 'Stop fucking camping it up. You know I hate it.'

Nick's face was serious as he answered in a deep voice, 'That's why I do it, love. Got to give the punters a show, eh?'

Alan sighed. 'I've got a bit of business for you and Albie. I need a boat, a straight house – and I mean *straight* – and some supplies.'

Nick sipped his rum and Coke and licked his lips before answering.

'What kind of boat do you want, and where do you want it docked? If you're travelling over the water, I'll get you a nice fishing vessel. If you need a speedboat, I've got a choice of three. You tell me what you want to do and I'll tell you if I can do it, how much it'll rush you and whether or not I think the risk is worth it. I don't do drug running any more. My Petey got a life for it and I don't need the hassle, OK? Now it's your turn, Alan, and keep it short and sweet.'

Donna was amazed at the turnaround in Nick Carvello. Now he was like any other businessman, except instead of a suit he wore a

287

bright green Lycra bodystocking, and green eyeshadow to match. The Stylistics came on singing 'Betcha, By Golly, Wow' and Nick listened to Alan while swaying in time to the music.

He looked at Donna and winked in a friendly fashion.

Alan began talking. Donna was amazed at the way he didn't take any notice of the people around him. He seemed at home with them.

'I need a fishing boat, but one that can shift, know what I mean? I need a house to hole up in just in case we don't make it to the boat in time. I need a good crew, trustworthy, who can keep stumm. I also want a chart for getting over to Ireland. That's where the parcel is gonna be landing first off.'

Nick nodded. 'This ain't nothing to do with the Irish, is it?' His voice was hesitant.

'In a way. He's half-Irish and we're gonna spring him.' He nodded towards Donna as he spoke.

Nick grinned. 'I get it – old Georgio is for the off! In that case I'll work you out a good deal, Alan. A mate's a mate after all, and in my game you can do with as many of them as possible.'

He held up his glass in a toast and swallowed down the rest of his rum and Coke. 'Another round, Albie dear, if you don't mind.'

Albie smiled and went to the bar once more.

'He's very quiet, isn't he?'

Nick laughed gently. 'So would you be, love, if someone cut your tongue out.'

Donna wasn't sure whether it was a sick joke. She looked askance at Alan who nodded his head slowly.

Nick carried on talking. 'He was a rent boy with me years ago, before I came into my present occupation. A punter done it because he didn't like the blow job. I've looked after him ever since. I found him and I kept him. I've got a thing about strays.' His voice was once more pure camp and Donna knew it was to hide the sadness behind his words.

Inexplicably she felt tears come into her eyes and Nick, seeing this, held her small hand in his large scarlet-nailed one. 'Sad, love, I know. But he's all right now. I give him a good life, dear. You're too chicken-hearted. I'm the same. I cry at *Lassie* films.'

Alan watched the incongruous twosome and shook his head in defeat.

Donna was holding her own and making friends wherever they went. It could only augur well for the future and Georgio's jump. He smiled at her, watching her beautiful face as she stared into Nick's heavily made-up eyes.

She had passed the test, she had held her own, and Alan realised

288

that in a lot of ways she was an asset to the operation. Everyone had always wondered about Georgio's wife; Brunos was into so much more than Donna would ever be able to comprehend. She was an enigma to people, for she was interesting, and she looked and acted shrewd.

In fact, he told himself, if she'd been anyone else's wife . . .

Georgio and Chopper sat in their cell and played poker. Chopper was holding all the winning cards. He took a deep swig of the prison hooch – a dangerous whisky made from potatoes and smelling suspiciously of paint-stripper – and breathed out harshly as the alcohol burned his mouth.

Georgio laughed. 'I don't know how you can drink that shit.'

'Needs must when the devil drives,' Chopper grinned.

The cell door was opened by one of the night screws, a tall heavyset man with a large handlebar moustache.

'Lewis is out of danger and should be back on the Wing within ten days,' he announced. 'I've got a message for you, Brunos. Mr Lewis says you're to be his eyes and ears till then.'

The door clanged shut.

'I don't know what Lewis is playing at,' Georgio said.

Chopper shuffled the cards expertly. 'Don't you? I do. He knows your head's in the noose so he wants a grass. He figures you already owe him and you'll want to even the score a bit. It's common knowledge he wants a hefty wedge from you and you ain't saying where it is. He thinks you'll spy for him to get in his good books – it's as simple as that.'

Georgio stood up and stared at himself in the small mirror leaning on the windowsill. His thick black curly hair was showing grey around the sides; his deepset eyes had bags beneath them. He noticed the prison pallor was already evident.

'Don't worry, Brunos, you're still good-looking.'

He ran his hands through his hair. 'I don't understand you, Chopper. According to Lewis we was deliberately banged up together. You were his eyes and ears in here, so to speak. He gets a caning, and you want to be number one. What's your scam? Come out into the open and let's clear the fucking air.'

Chopper laughed. 'You make me die, Brunos. You was a big fish in a little pond—'

Georgio cut him off. 'Then that just shows how much you know, don't it? If I wasn't banged up in here with Lewis and his silly henchmen, I'd have wasted that ponce ages ago. I'm getting sick of this place, I'm warning you. I'm sick of the smell, the setup, and the

289

people. Don't push me too far, Chopper. You don't scare me and your juvenile name don't scare me.'

'But Lewis does, I take it?'

Georgio nodded, his face set. 'In here he does, yes, and if you're sensible you'll bear that in mind. Lewis owns this nick, he has the dosh that's needed to do it. He owns about two-thirds of the prison service in one way or another. Believe me when I tell you he could walk out of here in the morning if he really put his mind to it, but he's shrewd enough to realise he's too well-known to go on the trot. And he's British through and through, like a fucking stick of Blackpool rock. He couldn't hack living in Spain or South America. Anyway, his mother wouldn't go and you know what he's like about her. He'll do his time here, with a holiday now and again in Durham or somewhere else to break the monotony, and he'll own them nicks.

'He went out a while ago on a fucking day trip to see his Harley Street surgeon. On the way back him and the two screws had dinner with one of the biggest blaggers this country's ever known. Lewis is no silly old bastard. He's a dangerous, vindictive and shrewd customer. It would do you good to bear that in mind, if you're thinking of stepping into his shoes.'

Chopper lit a paper-thin roll-up and grinned. 'Anyone would think you were worried about me.'

Georgio shook his head. 'That's just it, Chopper – I am. I don't want to see you sliced up in the john one morning, because that's what's going to happen to Timmy, and he knows it. Lewis will be off on one of his jaunts soon, Durham probably, then we can all breathe more easily for a while. But take the advice of someone who knows. Lewis isn't worth the hag he's gonna be causing you if you carry on this vendetta with Big Ricky. Even that black ponce will draw in his horns once he knows Lewis is on his way home.'

Chopper listened to Georgio in silence, taking in the words and also the inflection in his voice.

'So I take it you'll grass for him then?' he said.

Georgio shook his head and smiled. 'Of course not – what do you take me for, eh? I'll give him a load of old fanny. I don't want a knife in me ribs off someone else, thank you very much. I have enough trouble getting through the days with Lewis on me back. Enemies I got plenty of, I don't need to make any more.'

'Why are you telling me all this?' Chopper's voice was low, genuinely interested.

'I'm telling you this, Chopper, because we are banged up together, and as Timmy once pointed out to me, if you get torched one night, so do I. Just before I came in here Lewis had a bloke burnt alive on

290

another wing, and do you know why? Lewis thought he had given him a dirty look in the chapel. Now if that don't tell you what you need to know, nothing will. He's a bona fide headcase, you mark my words. Timmy will be skinned alive one night, and that's if Lewis arrives back in a good mood. He has the backing of a lot of major criminals, mate, he's hand in glove with them all – the real big ones. He made a point of cultivating them over the years, now he can call on literally anyone to help his end. If you've got a fucking death wish, then put in for a cell transfer before you make any moves, OK?'

Chopper took a deep drag on his roll-up, then blew out the smoke slowly, digesting what Georgio had said.

'Lewis warned me to put the frighteners on you, but you know that – I told you before. You have the look of a man who's going places, Brunos, and maybe, just maybe . . . I might want to go with you.'

Georgio sat on his bunk and pushed his hands through his hair. 'I dunno what the fuck you're talking about. All I do know is, if Lewis can move around, then he'll be back here in the prison hospital. And when he is, he might just as well be in your jockey shorts with you, that's how close to us all he'll be. If, and I mean if, I go on the trot, you will be the first to know. But at the moment I just want to get through me time in peace.'

Chopper nodded nonchalantly. He had made his point and he knew it.

'You're a funny bloke, Brunos. I heard you was a hard card of a man.'

Georgio nodded. 'I am. But I am also a shrewd man. I know when to keep me trap shut and listen, and when to open it and get things done.'

'That's the kind of man you are, is it?'

Georgio looked at him. 'I'm also a frightened man. Lewis frightens me and I ain't ashamed to admit he. He makes Saddam Hussein seem like one of the Three Bears. I'm frightened all right, and if you had an ounce of brains in your head, you'd be shitting about it now.'

Chopper answered slowly this time. 'I think you're talking sense, Brunos. I might heed your warning.'

Georgio slammed himself back on his bunk. Lying flat, he put his hands behind his head.

'Do what you fucking like, but remember what I told you. If you persist with your plan of action, get a cell change first.'

Chopper leant towards him as he opened his mouth to speak. Georgio pulled a long thin blade from out of the mattress.

'Shut it, Chopper. You're beginning to get on my fucking nerves now, all right? I might just flex my muscles on you, boyo, and

291

wouldn't that please your Mr Lewis, eh?'

Chopper was amazed at the change in Georgio's face. He eyes were burning with hatred and his teeth were bared; an almost feral look was on his face. Chopper realised that he had underestimated Georgio because of his outward demeanour. Moving cautiously away from the blade, he slowly held up his hands.

'You'll keep, Georgio.'

The other man laughed harshly. 'Don't push me, you scouse cunt. You've trodden on my toes once too often for my liking. I've given you good advice, now take it or shut the fuck up. Do what you've gotta do but leave me out of it – OK? I have enough on my plate with Lewis, without you putting your two bob's worth in.'

Chopper picked up some cards from the desk and began shuffling them, his face closed.

He knew what he wanted, and Georgio would keep for a while. But he would lay money on the fact that his cellmate was for the out, for the jump, and when he finally jumped, Chopper wanted to be right behind him.

Donna walked out of The Waterloo into the cold night air. She shivered slightly as they made for the car.

'What did you think of Nick?' Alan's voice was curious.

'I liked him, actually. Once you get past his funny clothes and camp way of talking, you discover a very intelligent man.'

Alan opened the door for her and as she sat down, he said, 'Shall I let you into a secret? Nick ain't gay. He's a cross-dresser who got caught up in the gay scene years ago. He takes a woman now and then.'

Donna's eyes widened at the thought.

Alan climbed into the driving seat and grinned.

'Honestly, it's as true as I'm sitting here. Some old lag told me that. He plays on the camp angle. And let me tell you, it's the perfect cover for him and all.'

Donna nodded. She opened her bag and checked over her make-up, talking all the while.

'Where are we off to now?'

They were once more cruising along Argyle Street.

'Me and you are going to have a nice meal in a Chinky I know. It's the Amber House Restaurant – you'll love it. The best Malaysian food this side of the Clyde.'

Donna was delighted. 'I'm starving. We haven't eaten since that ham sandwich this afternoon, and the amount we've drunk!' Her voice was slightly louder than usual and Alan laughed gently.

292

'One thing in my favour, Donna, I could always handle me drink. I take after me old man in that way.'

Donna moved sideways in her seat so she could look at him as he drove.

'Do you come up this way a lot? Only everyone seems to know you and Georgio.'

Alan carried on talking as if he hadn't heard her. 'My old man could drink anyone under the table. In fact, it was a scam he used. In a pub, right, my old man would bet the biggest navvy in the place that he could drink him under the table. He'd put a ton on the bar and ask him to match it. Then he'd drink the fucker under the table!'

He snorted at the skulduggery of his father. 'Old ponce he was, I hated him.'

He pulled into a parking space and said gaily, 'Here we are then, girl. The Amber House.'

A few minutes later they were sitting inside the restaurant. The proprietor knew Alan and he showed them to a quiet table. Donna lit a cigarette. Leaning on the table she said, 'You didn't answer my question, Alan. Do you come up this way very often, and how come everyone knows Georgio? If you don't answer me I might start doing a little bit of investigating myself.'

Her voice was jocular, but he heard the steely undertone.

'You smoke too much, lady.'

Donna gave a nasty little laugh that jolted him.

'You must think I'm stupid, Alan Cox. I'm a grown woman, and I want an answer to my bloody question! I'm not a child to be put off with anecdotes and smarmy references to my general health and well-being! Now, are you going to answer me?'

He sipped his scotch and grinned annoyingly. 'Why do you always want to know everything? Why can't you just get this little lot sorted out and be done with it? Jesus, I don't envy Georgio being married to you, love. It must feel like being shacked up with someone in the CPS. Always asking questions – questions, I might add, you probably wouldn't like the answers to.'

The moment he said the words he regretted them. It was the drink speaking and he knew it.

But he did honestly wish she wouldn't keep asking questions he couldn't answer. In fact, the only person who should answer them was Georgio, and he wasn't saying anything!

'Thanks a lot, Alan, it's really nice to know I can trust you so much and that the feeling is mutual. Everywhere we go, people look at me as if I am an interesting specimen. Annie, Jonnie H. Nick, even poor dumb Albie. They all know you and Georgio. Yet I ask you one civil

293

question and you talk down to me like I'm dirt. You afford a greater measure of respect to rent boys and ex-prostitutes from Shepherd's Market. Now, if you don't give me a straight answer, I am getting up and going home. I am going to tell my Georgio to leave the whole lot in your capable hands, as well as ask what is going on with him, Scotland, and all the people we've met since we've been here.'

Alan shrugged helplessly. 'You do what you've got to do, love. All I can say is, as far as my interests are concerned, they're fuck all to do with you. I ain't got to tell you nothing about my dealings, or anything else come to that. As for your old man's business, that's down to him to tell you, not me. Be fair, love. I ain't got to tell you nothing. You ask him, all right? About the respect, well, I'm sorry if I've offended you, but there you go. These people, Annie included, are a big part of my life, love. How and why I know and respect them is my business again, OK?'

Picking up a menu he glanced at it as if engrossed. Donna fought down an urge to get up and walk from the restaurant, knowing in her heart that it was exactly what Alan Cox wanted. She was shrewd enough to realise that he hated her tagging alone.

Looking into her face, he smiled gently.

'Look, Donna, is it my fault you don't trust your old man?'

She lit herself another cigarette and sipped at her glass of Perrier. Alan Cox had just hit the nail on the proverbial head.

She didn't trust Georgio. Which was why she was in Scotland.

The revelation shocked her.

'I don't like you, Alan Cox. I tolerate you for my husband's sake. Don't worry, I'll never question you again.'

Alan raised his eyebrows whimsically. 'I take it you're leaving then, so I'll just order for myself, shall I?'

As he scanned the menu he realised he had hit a raw nerve, and the knowledge saddened him. He looked over at her, and was astonished to see the glassful of water coming straight towards his face. It was too late to duck.

Soaked to the skin, he sat back in his seat and shook his head slowly before saying through gritted teeth: 'If you was anyone else, Donna, I'd smash that glass into your boat without a second's thought. Now I'm going to the toilet to sort myself out and calm down, because I'm fucking annoyed, woman. If you're still here when I come back, I want an apology, and then we'll see if we can go on from there. But if you ever pull a stunt like this again, I'll give you the hiding of your fucking life!'

Stunned at what she had done, her face devoid of colour, Donna watched him as he pulled out his handkerchief and wiped at his face. As he stormed across the restaurant towards the toilets she realised

294

exactly what she had let herself in for.

Alan Cox was dangerous, and so was her husband.

The drink she had consumed was weighing heavily on her stomach and she looked at the empty glass with a feeling of shocked triumph.

She didn't trust her husband. That new insight continued to shock and sadden her. Her involvement in all this was a blind. What she had really wanted to know all along was how far up the scale of villainy her husband really stood.

She refilled her glass from the large bottle on the table and sipped the water slowly. The knowledge that Georgio was involved with the likes of Annie, Jonnie H. and Nick Carvello had shocked her. But even with Alan Cox threatening her, she realised she still didn't want out from it all. *All she wanted was the truth.*

She reasoned that eventually she would get it – and that she would probably find it a bitter pill.

As Alan Cox walked back towards her she rehearsed her apology in her mind.

She hadn't wanted to throw the water at him; she had wanted to throw it in her husband's face.

She had a strange feeling that Alan Cox had realised that before she did.

BOOK TWO

Odi et amo; quare id faciam,
fortasse requiris.
Nescio, sed fieri sentio et excrucior
I hate and I love; why do I so you may well ask.
I do not know, but I feel it happen and am in agony—

Carmina No. 85, Catullus, c.84–54 BC

At twenty years of age, the will reigns;
at thirty, the wit;
and at forty, the judgement—

Poor Richard's Almanac (1741 June), Benjamin Franklin, 1706–90

Chapter Twenty-Six

Jack Coyne was a thick-necked Liverpudlian of almost pure Irish ancestry. The name was Irish, the deep blue eyes were Irish . . . but Jack's mother had been a Vietnamese women of uncertain age and even more uncertain virtue. He grew up in an atmosphere of suppressed violence, strong maternal love, and hardship.

Kek To, his mother, had lived in a small tenement building in the heart of Handsworth, supplementing her meagre Social Security with turning tricks along Lime Street and the Dock areas. She was small, quietly spoken and amicable, which meant she attracted large brash individuals who wanted a weekend's leave in a warm house with a warm woman – and the advent of a large half-caste son was often a bugbear. Especially as Jack hated more than anything his mother's 'friends'.

Kek To had died when he was thirteen years old. Already five foot ten, and looking much older, he got himself work in the Docks, loading the tall ships that came in, and keeping himself to himself. At seventeen he was already a world-weary man and that was when he met JoJo O'Neil. JoJo was thirty-five, already a big name in Liverpool Dock circles as a pimp and procurer, and he saw the potential for violence in hulking young Jack Coyne.

Taking Jack as his minder, JoJo had taught him the finer points of pimping, fencing, and countless other ways of making a dishonest few pounds. Together they became a mighty force, and twenty years on Jack and JoJo were still together, only now they were partners and ran a good many of the Liverpool rackets. Neither had ever darkened the doors of a prison and neither wanted to.

To look at, the pair were semi-respectable – both drove nice cars, wore decent clothes, and owned among other things two night clubs and a brothel. JoJo had only one interest – young women – which he pursued with a fervour belying his age. Jack Coyne on the other hand had an Achilles heel – his wife Bethany, a small dark-eyed West Indian woman, five years older than him and the mother of his six children.

299

Jack adored her, even though she was showing the wear these days and he was in a position to buy any kind of company he liked. Bethany was his mother, sister and lover rolled into one; the product of a white woman and a black man after a one-night stand. They had an awful lot in common; they both adored each other and their children in that order, and Bethany turned a blind eye to her husband's businesses, enjoying the feeling of security the money and the respect brought them. Their children were beautiful, taking only the best from their ancestors; they were clever, industrious and loving.

The Coyne family lived behind the walls of a large house in Cheshire, in the upmarket hinterland of Liverpool, and the neighbours, who included a top female TV star and three producers, were always polite to the Coynes even though their overtures of friendship were never reciprocated. The Coynes never accepted invitations to dine or attend parties. They were an anomaly, and eventually the neighbours left them in their large property and just waved now and again if they saw them on the drive. Bethany's mother visited on a daily basis and Bethany needed no one else. Just Jack, her mother Violet, and her children, four sons and two daughters.

The house had twenty rooms, an outdoor heated pool and a large thirty-by-thirty-foot pond in which Jack kept his Koi carp. The grounds, which sprawled for nearly an acre, held numerous animals belonging to the children, including a pot-bellied pig and three Shetland ponies.

Bethany cooked and cleaned the house by herself, grew her own herbs outside the back door, and had never learnt to drive or use a video. She dressed well, kept herself neat, and never wore make-up. Jack looked on her as his dark Madonna. Now she was pregnant once more and enjoying the condition as always.

It was to this strange household that Alan and Donna came on the Sunday afternoon, on their way back to London from Glasgow. The atmosphere in the car was uncomfortable.

After Donna had apologised, they had left the Amber House Restaurant without ordering; Alan had driven them straight back to their hotel, leaving her at her door. Donna had gone into her room, and cracking open a bottle of Jameson's, had sat on her bed and thought long and hard about the events of the last few days. It was a different woman who came down to breakfast the next day, and they both knew that.

Alan pressed the intercom on the wall by the double gates. As they opened electronically, Donna drew in a deep breath on seeing the house that was hidden behind them gradually revealed. It was a long,

300

low Scandinavian-style building, with floor-to-ceiling windows and flat roofs. It seemed out of place in Liverpool, and in the weak sunshine looked as though it should have been covered in snow on some mountainside in Europe.

'What a house!'

Alan gave a weak smile at the awe in his passenger's voice. In the South of England, the house and its grounds would easily have been worth in excess of two million. It was one of the most beautiful properties he himself had ever seen. Its windows gleamed like diamonds in the sunshine and the house looked as if it was actually watching you. It was constructed on three levels, but from the front looked as if it was a bungalow type. It wasn't until you went inside that you realised it had been literally built into the ground. The entrance hall was on the top floor, and the rest of the considerable area in the lower levels. Donna was enchanted as Alan had known she would be. They were once more greeted by dogs, but this time by two mongrels with shaggy black hair and friendly yaps. Alan got out of the car on the circular driveway and scratched both animals behind the ears.

'Hello, old boys. Donna, meet Happy and Grumpy. They're Jack's kids' dogs. Friendly pair of buggers they are and all. He saw someone throw a sack into the Docks and jumped in when he realised it was moving. These were the culprits.'

Donna knelt down and allowed the dogs to nuzzle her face, letting them lick her neck, enjoying the sensation. Then, laughing, she turned to look at Alan and froze. In the doorway of the house stood possibly the biggest man she had ever encountered in her life. He made Geoff Capes look like Finn McCool's little baby. Behind him was a small, painfully thin black woman.

The big man lumbered down to greet them, his face twisted into a smile. Donna saw the oriental look about him and found herself holding a hand so big it could easily have swallowed her arm to the elbow. He was surprisingly gentle.

'How do you do? You must be Georgio's wife.'

He inclined his head as he spoke, as if she was a queen or at least a princess, and Donna knew instinctively that this was a man who liked and respected women.

'This is Jack Coyne, Donna, and his wife Bethany.'

Bethany had held back. Now she was properly introduced she came forward timidly and shook Donna's hand also. Her grip was firm, her skin cool. Donna said a shy hello and the two women were about to talk more when all hell broke loose. Six children of different shades and appearance broke out of the house, shouting and laughing at the tops of their voices.

301

Jack waved a hand at them and they all stood silent as they were introduced to Donna with proper ceremony.

Jack smiled at the children and said with pride, 'My daughters Jade and Ruby.' Two tall girls with budding breasts and long legs smiled a hello. Both had inherited the slanted eyes of their grandmother except theirs were a startling shade of blue.

'My sons, Jack Junior, Petey, Davie, and the youngest, Harold.'

Jack Junior, Petey and Davie were coffee-coloured, handsome boys with thick lustrous hair like their father's. The youngest boy, Harold, had the tight curls and deep black skin of an African. He also had blue eyes like his brothers and sisters. Each child was exotic and stunningly beautiful, taking Donna's breath away with their sheer perfection.

'They are very beautiful children, Mr Coyne. You must be very proud.' She smiled at him as she spoke and watched his chest swell with pride. Donna was secretly pleased that these children would have the buffer of money, knowing immediately the trouble their appearance would have caused them in a less privileged environment or even a middle-class area. With money their appearance was another asset, to set them apart, and these children would always be set apart from everyone else. They were a tangled mixture of colours and cultures and they looked happy and healthy.

Inside the house, Donna's eyes were drawn to many lovely different features as they made their way down to the bottom floor and the living rooms. Everywhere was light, space and glass. The house was absolutely individual.

Inside the forty by twenty foot lounge Donna was seated on a white leather sofa and given coffee. The outer wall consisted of glass doors overlooking the landscaped grounds. It was a house made especially for these strange people.

'I designed the house myself,' Bethany said, almost reading Donna's mind, her thick Liverpool twang at odds with her frail appearance.

Donna took a deep breath. 'It's fantastic. Are you an architect?'

Bethany laughed, a breathy sound reminiscent of fluttering wings.

'I can't barely write my name, Mrs Brunos. I drew a picture and the man worked out the plans for me. We were very satisfied with it. Jack had it built to please me.'

He nodded and Bethany stood up.

'If you don't mind, I have to get the children ready. The girls have got dancing tonight and the boys go to karate. I won't be long.'

Such normal behaviour and homely talk seemed out of place with the mission that was on their minds. Donna looked at Alan and knew he was experiencing the same feeling.

302

'So, Alan, what can I do for you? JoJo won't be here for a while yet, so drink your coffee and relax. I know you've had a long journey. Bethany's made up a couple of rooms in case we run late and you want to stay the night. Before I forget, what's the scam with Dirty Freddie? I heard he was out of the game now?'

Alan relaxed back in his chair and began to talk about a violent London pimp. Donna knew then that the first magic of the house and its occupants would never come back to her again. Sighing she sipped her coffee, staring out over the beautiful grounds.

303

Chapter Twenty-Seven

Timmy was lying on his bunk, his fat moon face sad. Georgio could practically smell the fear emanating from him.

'Are you sure you don't want to come down to the rec room, Tim? Have a game of cards or something?'

Timmy shook his head. 'Nah. You go, Georgio. I'll be all right. I just want to lay down and think.'

Georgio left the cell and the foetid pong of Timmy's feet. He passed the kitchen just as Sadie walked out of it.

'I put the pie in,' she said fussing. 'Timmy loves a rhubarb pie. Where you off to?'

Georgio pointed down the corridor. 'Where do you think? The rec room. I can't sit in that cell any more. Why don't you come down for a while? The film should be starting in a minute on Channel Four. It's *The Winslow Boy*. You need a break and all, Sadie.'

She looked towards Timmy's cell for a second then followed Georgio down to the recreation room. Old black and white movies were her favourites.

Inside, the noise was deafening. Chopper and Ricky were playing the game, the game being fronting each other up. All the other cons watched them surreptitiously while playing pool, cards, or Scrabble. Benjamin Dawes was regaling everyone with jokes as usual. Georgio sat down at an empty table and began to watch Leroy, Ricky's number two, cutting out pictures of naked women from a copy of *Parade*.

'I never noticed before how many women in magazines are blonde. Strange that, ain't it?' Leroy's voice was amazed. 'I never had much need for this type of thing on the outside, always had a bird in tow. Now I get me jollies by looking at pictures. Fucking pathetic really, ain't it?' He threw the magazines on to the table and sighed. 'Want a game of chess, Georgio?'

Georgio was surprised. 'Do you play?'

Leroy laughed out loud. 'Do I play? You're looking at the Hollandsy Bay Borstal chess champion, mate. Mind you, it was easy

304

because most of them played it like drafts! I'll get the board.'

Benjamin's voice sang out loud. 'That pie smells the dog's bollocks, Sadie. Can I have a lump when it's cooked?'

She grinned girlishly. 'You're such a bleeding greedy guts, how did your mother stand it?'

Benjamin sucked his teeth. 'My mother never cooked, Sade. All she ever did was go out with blokes. Said cooking was for mugs, which didn't do a lot for me, I can tell you. I spent the first five years of my life living on tinned stews. Hate the fucking things now, I do. Go on, Sade let me have a lump. I like your cooking.'

She rolled her eyes. 'Oh, all right then. I wish that Harrison hadn't broken the video. I'd like to have taped this film.'

The Winslow Boy had come on and Sadie was sitting with about six other men looking up at the TV, which was ten feet up the wall on a small shelf.

Benjamin called out to Georgio: 'Did you hear the one about the little boy who went into school and said, "Sorry I'm late, Miss, me dad got burned this morning." And the teacher said, "How terrible, was he burned bad?" And the kid said, "They don't fuck about down the Crematorium, Miss".'

The whole place erupted into laughter again.

'You're mad, Dawes.' Ricky's voice was full of mirth.

Benjamin shrugged, grinning childishly. 'If you didn't laugh you'd go mad, wouldn't you? How about this one then . . .' And he launched into another joke and once more everyone was laughing.

Sadie's voice was loud and bossy at the end of it.

'If you don't stop that noise, Benjamin Dawes, you won't get no pie. I want to watch this film!'

He hunched his shoulders and rolled his eyes, in a mock fearful expression. Everyone chuckled again.

'I mean it, Dawes.'

The smell of the baking pie was now very sweet in the rec room and Sadie was aware that before the pie was cooked she would be offered cigarettes, tea and coffee by men hoping for a slice.

Chopper and Ricky still eyeballed one another, and the men still observed them. The conversation died down to a muted hum, and Georgio began his game of chess with Leroy.

'There's going to be trouble between them two and Lewis is not going to like it.' Georgio's voice was low.

Leroy shrugged and took Georgio's black pawn.

'Let 'em get on with it. If Ricky needs an hand I'm here, like all the black contingent. Don't lose any sleep over it, Georgio. Lewis may not come back. We don't know what's going on yet.'

305

Georgio fretted. 'And what if he *does* come back?'

'Then we play it by ear. Now, will you concentrate on the game, please? I take my chess seriously. And don't leave your queen wide open like you did when you was playing Lewis. I don't mind losing.'

Georgio gritted his teeth at the inference and made his move. Suddenly the air was split by the sound of a fire alarm going off. Looking up, Georgio smelt a faint whiff of burning. Sadie jumped from her seat.

'Oh fuck it, me pie's on its way out!'

She rushed from the room, and everyone settled down once more as the noise of the alarm clanged through the Wing.

'Turn that fucking thing off, we're trying to concentrate!'

Leroy bellowed, his voice loud and harsh, but the alarm bell kept ringing. Then a denser smell permeated the room just as Sadie started screaming. Everyone was catapulted from their chairs in record time and the corridor was suddenly filled with men.

Georgio realised for the first time that no screws were to be seen anywhere. Black billowing smoke was coming from the cell block. Before they got down there all the men knew what had happened.

Timmy was burning like a Guy Fawkes dummy, lying on his bunk, not a movement from him. The stench of rubber was strong and another smell was evident. Georgio's nose twitched as he tried to remember where he had smelt it before. Then his mind was taken over by what was on Timmy's face. Someone had shoved a rubber mask over it, and the rubber was burning into the skin. Sadie was still screaming, out of control; Ricky slapped her face sharply to stop the noise.

The corridor was quiet now, apart from the crackling sounds from Timmy's body as it was engulfed in flames. Even the fire bell had stopped. His hands were on fire and twitching. Georgio realised that he was still alive but paralysed somehow.

Running to the doors, he banged on them hard, shouting: 'Get in here and bring the fucking fire extinguishers! He's still alive! He's still alive!'

After what seemed an age, four screws came through the doors in riot gear, looking weirdly out of place. All the men stared at them in wonderment. They were armed.

'Move back to your cells now! Come on, we don't want no trouble from you.'

The men looked at the screws then at each other.

'Timmy's burning, for fuck's sake, you've got to get the medics.'

'The sooner you get back in your cells, the sooner we'll fetch the medics. Now MOVE!' The last word was practically screamed at them and the men obeyed without thinking.

The last Georgio saw before he returned to his cell was Timmy's hands and feet, burning. Sadie was bundled into the cell behind him.

Benjamin Dawes was calling out: 'Oi, turn off Sadie's rhubarb pie, won't you, Mr Jackson? Don't let that get burnt and all.'

Georgio slumped down on the bottom bunk and put his head in his hands. He had to get out of this place.

He had to get out.

JoJo O'Neil was someone Donna knew she wouldn't like the moment she clapped eyes on him.

He was dressed in a blue silk Armani suit, with a white poloneck and Timberland boots. His hair was greased and slicked back, his teeth were bad and his skin sallow. His eyes looked as if they had seen too much and too soon for the rest of his body. He was loud-voiced with a thick Liverpool accent and he looked at Donna as if she was a piece of meat.

'So, Alan, you arrived then – and this is Georgio's old woman, is it?' He poured himself a drink and stood before the fireplace as if the house was his and not Jack's.

Donna saw Alan look at the man with loathing, and she felt a prickle of fear.

'Still nattily dressed, I see, JoJo. Where do you shop these days – the Oxfam shop or the Sally Army?'

JoJo laughed mirthlessly and shook his head.

'You've got a fucking nerve, Cox, coming here and asking the earth. When Jack told me what you wanted I nearly wet meself with laughter. You and Brunos are a pair of fucking scallys and the sooner you realise that the better.'

Alan got up and Donna felt the tension thicken in the room. Jack went to rise from his seat and Alan pushed him back down as if he was nothing, no weight at all.

'Don't even think about it, Jack. I always carry insurance and you know that. Anything happens to me and about fifty blokes will be haring up the M1 like raving lunatics. Remember the north-south divide, son, and keep yourself out of this.'

He walked towards JoJo who was about the same height and build, but softer bodied, not hard-looking or trim.

'I don't like you, you're a cunt, O'Neil, but you owe me and you owe Georgio. Now I've come to collect for the both of us.' He looked at Jack. 'I'm surprised you got into this business with him, mate, you being a family man and all. I'd have thought even you'd have balked at it. Now, as you both know, I killed a man for less than this ponce is

307

doing at this very moment, and I swear an oath I'll rip you limb from fucking limb if I get any more of your cheek, OK?'

JoJo stood straight, his face a mask. Donna couldn't even begin to guess what he was thinking. Then, without warning, the man smiled, a wide, cheerful, good-natured smile that didn't quite reach his eyes.

'I looked after you when you got banged up, Alan. I don't owe you fucking fuck all, mate. I made sure you was all right in nick, I saw to everything for you, but you had to do it in public, didn't you? You couldn't have waited for the Chinky ponce in a dark alley, oh no, not Alan Big Man Cox. You had to do it in front of everyone, even fucking tourists! I don't owe you – you owe *me* mate. I kept my end of the bargain. I never tucked you up. We all lost a lot of sobs over you, mate, we lost a fortune.'

Donna had no idea what they were talking about and her face showed her bewilderment.

'You never sent me a fucking brass razoo in stir, boy, it was Georgio who watched out for me and my family. *Georgio*. He came up trumps for me while you done a fucking runner. You legged it so fast it's a wonder they never asked you to run in the Commonwealth Games!' Alan's voice was now a fierce roar.

'You owe me, you little turd. You'll always owe me, because I killed a man you wanted out of the way. I was a convenient fall guy for you, and then I find out off of Georgio that you was hand in glove with the Chinese ponce. So don't wind me up today, boy. I ain't in the fucking mood! I never liked pimps or ponces, you should know that better than anyone!'

Donna watched JoJo's face as he visibly gritted his teeth, then spoke. 'What do you want us to do though? If you've got the Jocks sorting it all out—'

Alan interrupted him impatiently. 'Don't talk like a prat. You know I can't be running up here morning, noon and night. I want you two to watch over everything from here. I also want you to sort out another safe house that doesn't have my name or Georgio's involved in its creation. You know what I need, O'Neil, you've done it enough times for others. Now you can use your expertise for me and Georgio – and let me give you one more warning. Brunos is into heavy stuff, heavier than you'd ever guess mate, so be careful. He has friends in strange places, old Georgio, and so do I. Be careful who you talk to, boys, because I'm like a fucking grasses' heaven – they tell me everything. That's why I'm here demanding and you've got to do what I ask.'

JoJo tried to salvage some dignity.

'OK, we're in,' he said. As if he had a choice in the matter.

308

Alan shook his head. Looking at Jack he said, 'How do you stand this prat, eh? Come on, Donna, we've done our bit. Let's make a move.'

She hastily picked up her bag and followed him to the door. Outside in the hallway Bethany stood clenching her fists. Donna could see the same fear mirrored in Bethany's face as was on her own.

Georgio lay on the floor of his cell listening to the soft snores of Sadie who had been given an injection by the medic. Chopper sat on the edge of his top bunk, a roll-up in his mouth.

'I know what that smell was, Chopper,' Georgio said suddenly. 'It was tetrachloride! I remember it from when I was first in the building game. It was the only thing we could use to thin out rubber paint. Jesus, how the fuck did they get it in here?'

Chopper shrugged. 'In a flask – a soup Thermos or a hip-flask, of course. It's a similar burning to one I witnessed in Durham. That was a child molester though. No one gave a fuck.'

Georgio's head was reeling with the sights he had witnessed. 'How was he paralysed though? He was still alive – I saw him moving.'

Chopper smiled slightly. 'Nah, man, he wasn't paralysed in that way. He had something pushed down his throat, probably a ping pong ball or an old sock. Then he was trussed up with chicken wire – you just couldn't see it because of the burning, the smoke and that. Then the rubber mask was pulled over his face and the tolly was poured all over him. After a while they dropped a match on him and that's when the smoke started. It's a well-known trick in northern nicks.'

Georgio felt the vomit rising in his stomach and took a deep breath. Chopper laughed louder this time.

'You make me laugh, Brunos. Anyone can see you've never been in a nick before. You think this is bad, you should try some of the others, mate. You have to harden yourself up, get used to it all if you want to survive. That wasn't as bad as some of the things I've witnessed. I've seen men have their wedding tackle removed and shoved in their mouth, then their lips sewn together with the thick needles and twine used in the workroom. You have to sort yourself out. I thought you was a hard man?'

Georgio shook his head. 'I am hard when I need to be, don't you worry. But only an animal would countenance this. No human could order it.'

'Well, at least we're agreed on that one,' Chopper sniggered. 'Lewis is behind it as we both know and he *is* an animal, a subhuman arsehole, and he'll be back before we know it. That little display

309

today was for the benefit of you, me, everyone. Another way for Lewis to let us know he has a long arm.'

'I could kill him myself.'

'Now that's the most sensible thing I've heard all night! Between us, me and you, we could kick that arsewipe off the face of the earth. Think about that, Brunos, instead of your Kentucky Fried friend. I'm going to sleep. There'll be hell to pay in the morning while the guards question us and pretend they knew nothing at all about the events of today.'

He lay back in his bunk and Georgio settled himself on the floor of the cell on the thin blanket.

The smell of burning was still acrid and the faint stench of the tetrachloride pricked his nostrils. The thought of Timmy's pain as the tolly burnt into him, and the rubber melted into his face, into his eyes and mouth, made Georgio feel sick to his stomach. Timmy didn't deserve that.

He hadn't done anything worth that.

As Chopper said, it was Lewis showing his strength once more, and the thought made Georgio see a dull red behind his lids.

That bastard Lewis needed taking down a peg, and after Timmy's maiming and Chopper's words, Georgio thought he just might be the person to do it.

He finally slept . . . and he dreamt about Timmy, Timmy's wife, Timmy's kids . . . and Sadie.

He felt no better for the sleep, his dreams so vivid and disturbing. He finally vomited into the toilet bowl at four-thirty in the morning.

He wasn't sure but he could have sworn he heard a dull chuckle come from Chopper's bunk.

310

Chapter Twenty-Eight

At four-fifteen in the morning, Alan pulled up outside his flat in Soho. He turned off the car engine and stared at Donna who was sleeping gently beside him. He watched her for a few moments in the muted light of a street lamp, her face sweet in repose, dark eyelashes casting long shadows across her cheeks. He put out a hand tentatively and placed it on her shoulder. Donna opened her eyes and smiled trustingly at him, then, memory returning, she sat up abruptly.

'Where are we?' Her voice was still full of sleep and Alan grinned in the half-light.

'Outside my drum. We're back in the Smoke. Come on, I'll make you a coffee, then you can freshen up and drive yourself home.'

Donna grabbed her bag and followed him into the tall building. Inside the flat, she was surprised to see it was almost too tidy. Even the telephone pad on the hall table was neatly placed alongside the phone with a pen and a pencil either side of it like a dinner setting. In the comfortable lounge she sank gratefully on to a well-upholstered blue silk sofa and closed her eyes. Sleep was still threatening to envelop her. She was both physically and emotionally exhausted. Alan looked at her with pity and put on the electric kettle for some coffee.

'Why don't you go and have a shower?' he suggested. 'Freshen up. I'll bring in your case and you can get changed, eh?'

Donna nodded gratefully. The journey from Liverpool had left her feeling a wreck.

Five minutes later she was standing under a hot shower, letting the water cleanse her inside and out. As she picked up the bar of Lux and began to soap herself all over, it occurred to her that Alan had probably used it to do the same thing. The actions became almost lazy then. She breathed in deeply. The scent of him was everywhere, even the tang of his cigars was all around her. She closed her eyes and let the water run over her face, allowing it to wake her up, to give her back some of her energy.

Finally, she soaped herself between her legs, luxuriating in the

311

feeling. It had been too long since a man had touched her there . . . Drawing her fingers back as if they were burnt she hurriedly finished her shower and wrapped herself in a large white towel. Then, picking up a hand towel, she folded it like a turban around her head.

Donna stared at her reflection in the mirror over the hand basin. She looked good, she knew that. Her skin was glowing from the hot water and her eyes were glittering like black diamonds. It was at times like this she missed Georgio more than ever. She had always been a healthy woman, and craved sex at times like other people craved chocolate. It was the only time she was truly connected to her husband. Breathing deeply, she turned from the mirror, pushing both Georgio's face and Alan Cox's out of her mind.

Spotting a large black bathrobe hanging on the back of the door, she slipped it on, folding up the bath towel and replacing it over the heated towel rail. Her eyes scanned the bathroom to make sure everything was neat again and then she slipped out of the door. As she saw Alan standing in his bedroom she felt a flush creep up her neck and face, the heat making her feel faint with embarrassment.

'I brought you in a cup of coffee; your case is on the bed.'

They stared at each other for a long moment, Donna realising that there was something in Alan Cox that called out to her. Suddenly she knew why they argued so much, why they couldn't get along.

The insight was a revelation to her. No longer meeting his gaze, she smiled tightly.

'Thanks. I won't be long now then I'll get myself off home.'

Alan took his cue and walked from the room.

Donna dried herself off and dressed hastily, chiding herself the whole while. She had to get out of Alan's flat and back on to her own territory as soon as possible. She'd been too long on her own, that's what was wrong.

Once Georgio was home everything would go back to normal.

She was so busy with these thoughts, she didn't notice Big Paddy parked outside.

Alan was listening to the early-morning news on Radio 4 when his buzzer sounded. Frowning, he pressed the intercom switch. 'Who is it?'

He was relieved to hear Big Paddy's voice.

'It's me, Alan, open he door.'

Two minutes later, Paddy was standing in Alan's hallway, an anxious smile on his face. He took in the dressing gown and recently washed hair.

'I was hoping to hear from you, Paddy,' Alan said. 'I just assumed it would be at a normal time of the day or night.'

312

Paddy followed Alan through to the kitchen.

'Coffee or tea?'

Paddy shrugged. 'Whatever you're having.' He sat at the kitchen table and glanced over the newspaper headlines.

Alan placed a cup of coffee in front of him and said tersely, 'So? What do you want?'

Paddy eyed him for a moment. 'I just saw Donna leaving, I was under the impression that Donna's only to be the messenger, nothing else. Wonder what Georgio will have to say about her leaving with wet hair? I know he wasn't that impressed with her going off for the weekend with you in the first place.'

Taking his time, Alan lit himself a large cigar. Blowing the smoke across the table into Paddy's face, he said viciously, 'You tell fucking Georgio that his wife is in this up to her neck. She took him at face value and now she wants to organise everything with me. If he don't like it, then that's tough shit. I am doing him a right favour and he'd do well to remember that. And before you open your trap, Paddy, remember just who you're talking to.'

Alan sipped his coffee, a vision of Donna still before his eyes, and then he said in a low voice: 'I don't believe what I'm hearing. You have the fucking gall to sit there and tell me that Georgio is still calling the shots from Parkhurst? He involved her in all this himself – I never wanted it from the off. I even sent a message in telling him I wanted another number two. But no, I got sex on legs, whether I wanted her or not.

'Well, Paddy me old mate, she knows too much now, and believe me when I say she's quick on the uptake. She has been an asset on this trip, a bona fide asset. Tell Georgio we left school over thirty years ago. If he wants to go into his dotage, that's his lookout – but he can get off my fucking back. You can also tell him that if he has any sense he'll gets off hers as well. *I'm* doing *him* the favour, remember?'

Paddy sighed gently. 'What's the score with Jockland?'

Alan grinned. 'How much do you know, Paddy, and how much are you guessing, eh? I know for a fact you ain't had a visit in a month. Only Donna's been up and she nearly frightened the life out of Georgio by turning up on the same day as one of his other friends. So where's your information coming from, eh? Is it from Dolly, or is that you're putting two and two together from his messages?

'Whatever it is, you can get this straight: Donna's attractive enough, I will concede that but me and her have nothing in common but Georgio Brunos – who, as I said earlier, I am doing a right favour for. Now if you don't mind, Paddy, until Georgio instructs me otherwise, I can't tell you fuck all else. And one last thing, if you ever

313

insinuate anything about me and Donna again, you'll regret it. Believe me you'll regret it.'

Paddy dropped his eyes and then sipped at the hot coffee. 'Did you know Lewis was cut up, lost a kidney?' He had the satisfaction of seeing Alan's eyes widen.

'Not by Georgio, surely?'

Paddy shook his head. 'Nah, he was cut up by a small-time blagger. No one we would be interested in. Lewis is all right, though, more's the pity. Seems he poached the bloke's bird, a little queen called Sadie.'

'But Georgio is all right?'

Paddy nodded again. 'Oh yeah, he's champion. It got Lewis off his back for a while. He's due back in the poke in ten days.'

'This Sadie is on the same wing as Georgio?'

'So is this Timmy, the boyfriend – though he was roasted alive on Saturday night. You know the old scam, chicken wire and tolly. Always a northern scam that. But Lewis's arm is long. He's dying, I heard, this Timmy.'

Alan frowned. 'I hope he is, poor bastard. I remember a bloke having that done to him when I was in Durham. He survived it, and I think he was sorry he did. He topped himself the day they put him back on the wing. He looked fucking rough, Paddy. No eyelids, nothing. The tolly burns through everything – skin, bone, the lot. He'll be lucky to keep his sight.'

Paddy shrugged. 'That's his problem. At the moment I think Georgio just wants you to get things moving as quickly as possible.'

'I'll do that. Lewis is a game old fucker though, isn't he? I was there when he got shot in 1974. I thought he was a gonner, we all did, and yet the old sod walked out of hospital six weeks later, harder than ever. You have to admire him, even if you can't stand him.'

'That's a fact. You'll be in touch with Georgio, then?'

Alan nodded. 'You give him a message. Tell him I'll swallow this morning because I know what it's like to be banged up, but if he ever casts aspersions on me or Donna again, I'll leave him high and fucking dry, all right? I don't need this shit.'

Paddy got up and nodded again, his great red beard hiding his real thoughts on the matter.

After Paddy lad left, Alan sat smoking, waiting for the anger to seep from his bones.

So Georgio thought he might make a play for his wife? Well, as Alan now admitted to himself, that's exactly what he would like to do. And knowing all he knew about Georgio Brunos, he could probably get her.

314

★ ★ ★

Sadie was terrified and Georgio knew it. There were three new prisoners on the Wing. One was a black man called Eros, a heavyset geezer, typical pimp turned gangster. The Yardies were everywhere now. He was a schizophrenic as well. The other two were a different kettle of fish. Both were in their fifties, fairly big and obviously friends. They didn't talk to anyone and any overtures were rebuffed, albeit in a friendly fashion. The shorter of the two spoke a lot but said nothing.

Georgio watched the men and smiled to himself. He knew exactly who they were and so would Lewis. He also knew what they were in for and he toyed with the idea of blowing their world wide open. He decided against it for the time being; they would keep until they came in handy. He ignored them and they ignored him, though they knew who he was as he knew who they were. One hard look from Georgio was enough to make them keep their traps shut and he made a point of pushing them both aside roughly as they went out on exercise.

Sadie also knew the men, which is why she was frightened. She had first encountered them years earlier as a fifteen year old in Soho. Sticking to Georgio's side, she watched the two men warily. Out in the exercise yard she said to him, 'I know them two. They're bad news, Georgio. Jesus, they're the biggest nonces this side of the water, and sadistic with it. They were pulled in for that paedophile ring murder last year. How they're still walking around here, I don't know. If anyone knew who they were . . .' She rolled her eyes.

Georgio looked at the two men.

'I know who they are all right, and I'm sitting on the information until such time as I can do something about it – so keep stumm, all right? I think they'll take Lewis's mind off everything else when he gets back, don't you?'

Sadie saw the logic in this and nodded.

Georgio walked casually over to a guard and asked for a light. As the man struck the match Georgio whispered, 'Keep a lid on them two until Lewis gets here. He asked me to be his eyes and ears while he's away, OK? Let him deal with them when he comes back. He's got a score to settle with the bald one.'

The screw nodded almost imperceptibly and said, 'Timmy died an hour ago.'

Georgio walked back to Sadie. Despite her strange appearance and ways, Georgio liked her and was sorry for the news he had to impart.

Sadie cried like a baby, as everyone knew she would.

Anthony Calder was talking to Jonnie H. on the phone while

315

watching his baby daughter crawl around the floor.

'I can see what you're getting at, Jonnie, me old mate. But are you sure it's for the best? This way we only have one stab at the jump. Tell you what, you let me talk to Alan and I'll get back to you, OK?'

He put the phone down and picked up his daughter, kissing her soft downy head.

'Hello, beautiful girl.' The child crowed with delight. Settling her on his lap, he punched out Alan's number. Alan was there within the hour.

Anthony Calder was changing his daughter's nappy and still talking on the phone when Alan arrived. He rolled his eyes at the ceiling as Alan smiled to himself.

'Just get yourself home, will you? I have work to do. No, I don't mind if you buy the blue suit – buy the whole fucking shop, Sharon, if you like, but get home, will you? The baby is driving me up the wall.'

He put the phone down and laughed ruefully at his visitor. 'So much for the New fucking Man, eh? I get left holding the baby while she swans round Oxford Street, her mobile phone in one hand and a bunch o' credit cards in the other. They'll both need the kiss of life about four o'clock!'

Alan roared with laughter. 'You love it, mate, and you know you do.'

Anthony finished putting on the baby's Pampers and grinned. 'She's a little doll. Ain't you, my darlin'?'

He placed his huge face on the baby's belly and blew out his lips. Then, picking up the child, he settled her once more on his lap and said seriously, 'Jonnie H. rang. He thinks we'd be much better getting Georgio out on a laydown. Seems Parkhurst is too extreme a nick to actually walk out of, know what I mean?'

Alan nodded. 'But how will we know if there's a laydown? No one knows that, not even the guards. Only the Governor knows and that's the day it's happening. I imagined us getting out with a helicopter and a few blokes riding shotgun. Like they did in Durham.'

'That's just it. From what I've heard, there's no blind spots on the Island any more. They've got the wires everywhere. No chopper is landing anywhere near that nick. I think the laydown is a good idea myself, except we'll only get one shot at it, see. The laydown from Parkhurst is always Wandsworth, ain't it? So we can sort the route from there. It'll be a case of backing and fronting the sweatbox, and getting the driver out. We have to get him out because without him we can't get to Georgio in the back.'

Alan nodded.

'Georgio's A grade, you know that,' Anthony went on. 'There'll be the sweatbox, a Rover, two motorcycles, and a Range-Rover on his arse. It's too big a deal to go through with all that. That's not

316

forgetting the local police who'll have to open the roads for us. You know there's no way the entourage will stop for anything.'

Anthony thought about Alan's words as his daughter chewed on his fingers, her face covered in spittle. She grinned toothlessly at Alan and he grinned back.

'She's a real darling, ain't she,' he said dotingly. 'Good job she don't look like you. Except for the bald head, of course.'

'Up yours, Coxy Apples. Remember that from school?'

'How could I ever forget it, eh? I lived with that every summer of my life.'

The two men laughed, then Anthony said seriously, 'What we have to do is arrange the route. Once we fix that, we can concentrate on getting him out on some pretext.'

'I've got JoJo O'Neil and his lumbering sidekick sorting out safe houses up north, just in case, and the queer feller in Glasgow is sorting out the boat. We should be all right in that way at least. Jimmy Mac is sorting the rifles. Do you think we'll still need a helicopter?'

Anthony shook his head. 'Not now. We don't need a helicopter but we'll need scrambling bikes for the chop. We need to check the route from Portsmouth to Wandsworth and find the right spot for the jump. It will need to be near a footbridge of some kind for the chop itself, the changeover from bikes to cars. If the Old Bill's following they can only go by foot then, see. By the time they drive round we'll all be long gone.'

Alan nodded, feeling the sense of excitement filling him once more. 'Let's all have a good think, get the route sorted and the safe houses. The boats are ours from next weekend. We could spring Georgio in a month to five weeks, top whack.'

Anthony grinned. 'I'll drink to that. There's a bottle of scotch behind you. Bring it over with the glasses, would you?'

Alan poured out generous measures for them both. Anthony put a meaty finger in his glass and rubbed it on his daughter's gums. 'Sharon would have a fit if she saw me doing this, but my old mum swears by it. Cheers!'

Alan smiled as the baby's face screwed up and she spat out the scotch as if it was hemlock.

'Like I said, good job she don't take after you apart from the hair. She don't like whisky either!'

Anthony grinned and sipped the burning liquid. 'If we get our thinking caps on we should be all set before we know it, then it's just biding out the day. That will be the hard part. We'll definitely need the Armalites now – the sweatbox windscreen is bulletproof. The

317

screw will laugh in our faces until he sees the Armalite, then he'll shit himself.'

'I'll get the Ordnance Survey maps later on and I'll drive the route some time this week. I'll keep you informed.'

Anthony smiled. 'You're enjoying this, aren't you?'

Alan grinned back at his friend. 'You could say that, Anthony. Yes, you could say that!'

Donna had been listening to Dolly's chatter for twenty minutes and it was beginning to wear on her nerves. Since she had walked into the house Dolly's mouth had not stopped except for the odd breath.

'Paddy's going up to see your man today. I expect he has a lot to sort out with him.' Dolly glanced at Donna as she spoke.

Donna nodded and sipped her coffee.

'How did the weekend go then?'

This question was what Donna had been waiting for.

'OK, thanks. How did your dinner go at Maeve's?'

Dolly smiled, a steely glint in her grey eyes. 'OK. Your mother-in-law is a demon of a cook, the Yorkshire were like diddy men, the size of them! But I'm more interested in Scotland. Where did you go? Did you visit anywhere nice? I hear the food is great and the people aren't as bad as the comedians make out.'

'It was lovely, and the people were lovely too.'

Dolly wasn't to be put off. 'Did Georgio know you weren't going alone, like?' Immediately the words were out of her mouth she regretted them.

'I beg your pardon, Dolly! Exactly what are you getting at?' Donna fixed dark brooding eyes on the small woman in front of her and saw her visibly pale. 'Are you trying to insinuate something here? Have I missed something? I was away on business, nothing more. Remember when Georgio used to swan around on business – all over the world, in fact? Bangkok, Sri Lanka, Italy, Germany . . . to name but a few of his trips. Trips he made alone, Dolly. Trips where he was sometimes gone for six weeks at a time, while I was banged up in here with just you and an old black dog for company. So let's get something straight here. If I want to leave the house I don't have to answer to you, Georgio, or bloody King Street Charlie about where I am or who I'm with. You would do well to remember that. This is my house, the money in the accounts is mine, the businesses are mine, and I will look after them as I see fit.'

She only just stopped herself from telling the older woman that the marvellous Georgio would be quite happy to dump his longtime housekeeper out on the street without a by your leave.

318

'The estate agent rang, by the way,' Dolly told her in a choked voice. 'He has a couple who want to view the house. I told him to wait until you came home, as I knew nothing about it at all.'

Donna dropped her eyes. Dolly had hit her where it hurt and knew it.

'I was going to tell you about it,' she began awkwardly. 'Georgio wants the place sold up. It's too big for just the two of us—'

Dolly interrupted her. 'It was much too big for the three of us but he never wanted to sell it before.'

Donna slammed her fist on to the table. 'Well, he does now! We need the money, Dolly. The bottomless pit has dried up and the goose that laid the golden eggs is vegetating in Parkhurst. Think about it, will you? The gas bill in this house is over seven hundred pounds a quarter in the winter, the electric is the same. That's without everything else. The pool alone costs over two hundred a month, what with the Voxanne and algae killer and the rest. It's just too much at the moment. I need something smaller.'

She saw the haunted look on Dolly's face and the woman's next words shattered her.

'What about me, then? Am I part of all this cutting back?'

Donna rushed from her chair. 'Of course not Dolly. Don't be silly.' She held the woman to her and hugged her. 'How could I ever get along without you, eh? Even if you do drive me to distraction sometimes.'

Dolly grasped Donna's hand, lying across her shoulder. 'You're like me own child, Donna. More to me, in fact.' Her voice broke. 'Since Georgio got caught, everything's been so different. I'd give ten years off me life to have him walk in that front door now and kid around as usual. It's all gone wrong, everything has changed, and I'm too old for change now. I'm too set in my ways.

'I loved Georgio Brunos like me own, too,' she said tearfully. 'I love both of you, and I can see the rift coming now even if you can't. Why would you go away to Scotland with Alan Cox, eh? Why him? Georgio had no business dealings with him, did he? Alan's as straight as a die now.'

Donna stared down on to Dolly's grey head and the words 'Georgio got caught' and 'Alan's as straight as a die now' whirled around inside her head. With stunning clarity she realised that Dolly, Paddy – all of them, even his mother – knew Georgio was guiltier than he had made out. From day one they were all aware of what he was up to. Everyone was, except her – his wife.

She knelt down on the Italian tiles and made Dolly look into her face. 'You knew he was guilty, didn't you? You always knew.'

Dolly gently stroked Donna's cheek. 'I never knew for certain, but I'll tell you this much. Coming from where I do, and knowing what I

319

know, Cockney boys don't get all this through collar and sweat. Georgio was a wise man, and he used what he had to better himself, and while he was at it, he gave you the earth, girl. Remember that. Alan Cox is a cold-blooded murderer, you'd do well to keep that in mind when you're dealing with him. He kicked and punched a man to death on a crowded street. It was a vicious, senseless killing. Don't be too hard on Georgio when you can spend a weekend with the likes of Cox.'

'I did not spend the weekend with him, Dolly! I went away on a business trip with him. Christ Almighty, Georgio had more women over the years than bloody Warren Beatty! If I had had an affair, which I didn't, it would be nothing to what he's done to me over the years.'

Dolly smiled gently. 'Oh it would, Donna. It would be much worse.'

Donna sighed. 'How do you make that out?'

'Because you would be emotionally involved. Georgio was out shagging – there's a difference. He only ever loved you, girl.'

Donna shook her head in exasperation. 'Oh Dolly, I suffer from the same blindness as you do. I only ever wanted Georgio, whatever he's supposed to have done, real or imagined. In my heart I don't really care. Stop worrying about Wonder Boy, he'll be all right. He'll always be all right. Especially while there's women like us around to support him.'

'And Alan Cox, what about him?'

Donna shrugged. 'What about him? He's a man, a good-looking man, who committed, in your words, a cold-blooded, vicious murder. He is helping Georgio out now, and that's all. Georgio knew I was going up to Scotland. Georgio knows everything.' She nearly added: *Thanks to you and Paddy*, but stopped herself. If only Dolly knew how ruthless Georgio really was! Then it occurred to her that when she had finally realised how ruthless, selfish and self-involved he was, she herself had still loved him. Dolly would probably be the same.

Dolly lit a cigarette, drawing the smoke deep into her lungs. 'You've come so far, stood by him through so much, don't let him down now, girl. He's depending on you. I don't know for certain what's going on but I keep my eyes and ears open. If Georgio's for the jump, then you make sure the jump is high enough and long enough to get him out of England. Now, shall I make us some fresh coffee?'

Donna was not surprised to hear that Dolly had sussed out what was going down. Nothing surprised her any more.

'You sit there, Doll, I'll make it.'

320

She went to the sink to fill the kettle and Dolly said quietly, 'If I can help, you only have to ask, love. I'd do anything for that man. Anything.'

Nick Carvello was fast asleep. Devoid of his outrageous make-up and outlandish clothes, he looked an altogether different person. He turned in the bed and cuddled up to the woman lying beside him. She stirred, snorting slightly, and settled into his arms. Opening one eye she said lazily, 'It's late afternoon, I have to be going soon.'

Nick kissed her earlobe gently. 'Make a cup of tea, Sandy, and I'll drop you off at your mum's.'

The woman grinned, showing small white even teeth. She pushed a hand through her short black hair, fingernails bitten to the quick.

'You're a lazy sod, Nick.'

He laughed, his eyes still closed. 'I'm getting another hard-on, actually.'

Sandy slipped from the bed. Her body was lean, small-breasted and compact. Not an ounce of spare fat anywhere. Nick watched her lazily. A few white lines above her pubic hair showed that she was a mother.

'How's the little fella?'

Sandy stretched. 'Growing like mad. I'll bring him Friday if you like?' Her voice was hopeful.

Nick shook his head. 'Bring some more photos, love. They'll do.'

Sandy pulled on a pair of jeans and a small crop top. 'I'll make the tea.'

As she walked from the bedroom, Nick relaxed in the bed. His son was an anomaly to him. He loved the thought of his flesh and blood growing steadily somewhere, but he was afraid of seeing him in person. Frightened of getting too involved. He sat up in the bed and reached for his cigarettes.

Then all hell broke loose.

His front door was unceremoniously battered into the hallway by two men with sledgehammers. Before Nick could utter one word his bed was surrounded by men.

He lit himself a cigarette and smiled sleepily. 'Hello, JoJo, still like to make the odd entrance I see?' His voice was once more pure camp, his body language effeminate.

It didn't fool any of the men around his bed. If you wanted to scare Nick Carvello, you came mob-handed.

Nick looked the men over slowly, savouring their discomfort as he eyed their trousers longer than their faces.

321

'What's the matter then, boys? Liverpool been bombed, has it? Not before fucking time anyway. Don't stand there like a cunt, JoJo, sit down and tell me what all this little show is all about. I'm beginning to get bored.'

JoJo O'Neil, to the amazement of his paid muscle, sat on the bed and started laughing.

Nick looked towards the bedroom door and grinned. 'Hello, Albie love, come in and say hello.'

The men looked towards the door and their faces paled. Albie, his tongueless mouth grinning, had a compact Uzi in his hands.

Nick tapped JoJo's face gently with his fingers. 'Never underestimate a queer, JoJo. You of all people should know that. Now what do you want?'

'I want to know everything you have on Georgio Brunos and Alan Cox. Your little mute friend don't scare me, Nick.'

He smiled lazily then nodded at Albie, who walked a few feet into the room and opened up two shots into the carpet by JoJo's feet.

'You should be scared, JoJo, you should be very scared, because I know everything that's going down with you and Coyne and I think it stinks, personally. Albie, let him have one in the hand to teach him a lesson.'

Albie shot JoJo's hand. Three fingers were severed with the first shot. Two more shots hit him in the thighs.

JoJo's henchmen were silent and wary. All were armed and all were too intelligent to go for their equipment. Albie looked the nutter he was and they automatically respected that.

Nick tutted loudly. 'Listen to me carefully, boys. I want you to take this piece of shite out of my home, then I want you all back in Liverpool as soon as possible. If ever I get wind that any of you is within shitting distance of me again, there'll be big trouble. Now take JoJo home. He's bleeding all over me carpet and bedspread.'

Five minutes later the flat was clear and Nick was sipping his tea in silence while Albie started to clear away the remains of the front door.

Sandy shook her head sadly. 'He'll be back, Nick, with Jack Coyne in tow.'

'No he won't, love,' Nick grinned. 'He's found out what he wanted to know, so don't worry your pretty little head about it. Now I'd better get me make-up on, I have people to see today.'

The conversation was closed.

As she watched Nick fluttering around the flat she reasoned with herself about her feelings for him. No one, her mother especially, could understand her fascination with him. But they didn't know the Nick she knew, the man in the dark of the night when he was himself.

322

When he loved her body and her mind. He was more of a man than most of the so-called macho types.

But only she knew that, and if she wanted to keep him, she had to keep the information to herself.

And Sandy wanted to keep him.

'Why did you let Albie shoot him?' she asked.

Nick smiled. 'Because he's a nonce, love, the same kind of nonce who cut out Albie's tongue. Don't feel any pity for JoJo O'Neil. I only wish Albie had shot his fucking balls off!'

Sandy stilled the beating of her heart. 'Shall I make you more tea?'

Nick smiled at her lovingly. 'Okey doke, love. I'll have to get Skinny Bill round to clear this lot out. There's more claret on my floor than at a Millwall at home game.'

Sandy made the tea.

Alan was surprised to see Anthony Calder sitting in Amigo's at six-thirty. He had the delectable Sharon in tow and she'd settled herself at a table where she could get a good look at the waiters. Sharon was twenty-two, short, with big breasts and streaked blonde hair. Alan could see nothing about her good enough to marry, but Anthony was besotted with her. Alan put it down to the child. He worshipped the child, and therefore he worshipped the mother. It was his only blind spot. Sharon had a voice that could break glass and a laugh you would only expect on a Jimmy Jones video. She was ordering a double vodka for herself when Alan and Anthony went upstairs to the office. Once inside the office Anthony burst out laughing.

Alan grinned. 'What's the joke?'

'You know Nick's Albie? He shot fucking JoJo O'Neil this afternoon. Straight up. Shot him in the hands and thighs. He's lost three fingers and a lot of blood. Jack Coyne told me.'

Alan's eyes widened in wonderment. 'You're having me on?'

Anthony laughed again. 'Straight up. With a fucking Uzi and all, if you don't mind. I knew there'd be conflict there, but fuck me, I never expected anything like this, did you?'

Alan shook his head. 'No, I didn't, but like the advert says, I know a man who does.'

'You don't think Georgio . . .' Anthony's face clouded. 'Why would he want to do that?'

Alan poured out two small brandies and said quietly, 'I know why, and believe me when I say I'd love to tell you, Ant, but I can't. He's used us to settle a score, but then that's Georgio all over, ain't it? I'll fucking slaughter him for this. I should have sussed it from the first.'

323

Anthony sipped his brandy. 'What's going down, Al? I have a right to know if I'm in on it and all.'

Alan sighed. 'It's a long story. I only know the half of it myself, but I know enough to suss out the rest. If I could tell you, I would, but I can't. I owe Georgio one, a big one, and he knows it. All I can assure you of is this: that will be the end of it. JoJo has had his warning, and he'll heed it.'

Anthony shook his head in bewilderment. 'Do you honestly think Jack Coyne will swallow his best mucker being shot at? Are you off your fucking rocker? There'll be murders up north. We won't be able to set up a friendly game of football after this lot!'

Alan held up his hand.

'All I can say is, Nick knew the score. He owes Georgio one and all. He knew what was going down and he played the game. Jack Coyne will not be retaliating, because Jack knows the score, too. It will all settle down in a few days, I take oath on that.'

'So what you're saying is, Georgio used me and all?'

'In a way, I suppose he did.' Alan sighed heavily. 'Look, Ant, if anyone should have the fucking tit and bump about it, it's me. I should have seen it coming. So don't you get the hump and all. That's all we fucking need now! It's over and done with, leave it at that.'

Anthony Calder leant across Alan's desk and said through his teeth: 'You tell Georgio fucking Brunos that if he *ever* pulls a stunt like that again, Lewis won't be in it when I fucking get going! I don't like people using me for anything, especially not jumped-up bubbles from Canning Town who need me a damn sight more than I need them. I'm a fixer by trade, and if he wanted JoJo fixed I'd have sorted it for him. Properly, mind you. I don't get personally involved in any of my deals. And you tell Georgio that if he ever steps on my toes again, I'll rip his fucking head off and shove it where the sun don't shine!'

Alan grinned. 'In those exact words, Ant? Only it'll cost me a fortune to get a message like that inside. It'll be bigger than his fucking court transcript!'

Anthony laughed, but his heart wasn't in it, they both knew why.

'You know what I'm saying, Alan. Get it sorted. That could have caused hag for us all. I use Jack and JoJo a lot in my dealings, as I do Nick Carvello. I can't afford them all to take umbrage with one another at this moment in time. Let's face it, even I'm wary of Jack Coyne, and so are you if you're truthful about it. He's a bona fide nutcase.'

Alan shrugged. 'Jack Coyne and JoJo have had their day, believe me. Georgio was just warning them – through Nick. It's a personal score he wanted settled.'

Calder finished his brandy in thoughtful silence.

'Listen, Alan, I'm a man of the world, you're a man of the world . . . has this got anything to do with Georgio's dealings abroad at all? I heard a whisper about them. Can I second guess from what I heard?'

Alan shook his head. 'I can only promise you this: when I can, I'll tell you the lot.'

He stared into Anthony's eyes and the two men looked away simultaneously. Alan knew Calder had put two and two together and would no doubt soon be making the miraculous four.

'I'd better get down to Sharon, she'll be pissed otherwise.' Anthony stood up. 'One last thing, Al. Why are you helping Georgio so much?'

'For old time's sake,' Alan told him. 'He done me a right favour when I was banged up inside, a favour you have to repay. Without him, I wouldn't have had a lot to come out for, you know.'

Anthony nodded. 'I never really liked Georgio,' he confessed. 'I never trusted him. I don't know why, he never did anything to me personally, like – it was just a gut feeling. I've got that feeling now.'

Alan stood up and looked into his friend's face.

'Remember this, Ant. It's me who's paying for everything, so keep that in mind. The favours are for me: not Georgio Brunos. Remember that won't you?'

Anthony nodded. At the door he turned and said gently, 'Make sure Georgio knows how I feel about what went down. Make sure he knows that whoever's paying don't mean a flying fuck when he puts my contacts on the line like that, OK?'

'I'll tell him, Anthony. Don't worry. By the way, the meal's on me. Enjoy yourself.'

Anthony shook his head. 'Thanks all the same, Al, but unlike Georgio Brunos, I pay me own way. See you soon.'

Alan watched him leave the room, and inside felt the balloon of anger welling up.

Georgio had managed to poison a friendship Alan had nurtured for years. Anthony Calder would not trust him for a long time to come and it galled him.

Because of the two of them, Anthony and Georgio, he preferred Calder any day of the week.

325

Chapter Twenty-Nine

Donna drove past the car lot on her way to Maeve's. As she glanced towards the forecourt she was amazed to see Stephen Brunos and Davey Jackson loading boxes into the back of a white Ford transit van. Parking her car, she walked back towards the forecourt and quietly went over to the two men.

'Hello, Stephen, Davey. Thought I'd pop in and see if the insurance has been paid out yet.'

Davey dropped the box he was lifting on to the concrete and turned to face her.

'Hello, Donna love, all right? Come inside and I'll make us a cup of coffee. Fill you in on everything.' He glanced over his shoulder at Stephen. 'You'll be all right here, won't you?'

'Course I will. You two get inside. I'll ring you later, Davey.' He carried on loading the boxes.

'What are they?' Donna's voice was high. 'I mean, what's in the boxes?'

Davey shook his head ruefully. 'Believe me when I say you don't want to know, love. Just a bit of hookey gear we're shifting for a friend.'

She frowned, and as Davey went to take her arm, she shrugged him off. Even Davey was surprised at the action.

'Hookey gear – hidden on my car lot, with insurance people crawling all over the place? Hardly an intelligent act, is it? What kind of stuff is it anyway?'

Stephen placed another box in the van and turned towards Donna, his face dark with anger.

'Listen, Donna, this is fuck all to do with you, love. Now go inside and have a cup of coffee, and keep your big nose out of this, all right?'

She felt the heat burning in her cheeks as she flushed with embarrassment.

'Don't you speak to me like that, Stephen Brunos. I've taken just about all I can from you over the last few months . . .'

Stephen sighed dramatically. He looked at Davey.

326

'How my brother swallowed this nosy bitch breathing down his neck I don't know. Well, listen to me, Donna, you have no right to know anything, get that? Anything. So get back in your car, and get back to your own businesses. Go and play at grown ups if you want, but not with me, all right? Can you get a simple message like that or shall I put it in simpler words still? Piss off!'

As he turned back towards the van, Davey Jackson grabbed him by the arm and spun him round.

'Don't you talk to her like that, Stephen. I won't have it, and your brother wouldn't either if he was here.'

Stephen laughed nastily. 'Oh, my Gawd, don't tell me you want to get your hands up her skirts and all. By Christ, Donna, you've never had it so good, have you? Wait until I tell Georgio this one. Not content with swanning off to Scotland with Cilla Black's answer to a good blind date, you're sweet-talking fucking Davey Jackson. Well, look out for Carol, love. She'll eat you for breakfast and spit out the bones.'

Davey stepped towards Stephen but Donna pulled him away roughly.

'You're dirty-minded, do you know that, Stephen? Well, wait until I tell Georgio that you're hiding knocked-off stuff on the premises. Let's see what he has to say about that!'

Stephen laughed contemptuously. 'Oh piss off, for Christ's sake, you stupid tart. You're getting on my nerves.'

Davey's voice was low as he spoke again.

'I told you not to talk to her like that, Stephen. Now take note of what I'm saying because I'm beginning to lose my temper.'

Donna saw the subtle shifting in Stephen's face and realised that he was frightened of Davey, of what Davey might do.

'Leave it, Davey,' she told him. 'I can look after myself.'

Stephen stared into her face. It was white now, her eyes glittering with temper and also, he realised with a lift of his spirits, with fear, a veiled fear. This excited him. He liked frightening her.

'You make me laugh, Donna, do you know that?' he said spite-fully. 'You swan around in your expensive suits and your handmade shoes, and you drive around in your flash car, and it was my brother who gave it all to you – the house, the lot. Without him you'd have been stuck in a fucking semi, rattling around in it on your own because any other man would have dumped you quick smart when you couldn't produce a child. My brother raised you when he married you and you could never see it. You looked down your nose at my mum, at my dad, at all of us – you stuck up fucking bitch!'

Donna's eyes stared in shock as she listened to what he was saying.

327

She watched him push Davey aside and storm round to get into the van. Wheelspinning the Transit, he screeched out on to the road and disappeared.

Donna put her fingers to her mouth as if warding off the sickness inside her stomach.

Davey looked at her haunted face and felt the familiar protectiveness well up inside him. She didn't deserve that, she didn't deserve any of what Georgio and his family were laying at her door. Donna was a woman to aspire to, if only that prat Georgio had realised it.

'Come inside, love,' he said into the stillness. 'He's a ponce, Stephen, always was. Don't listen to him, he's a fucking hypocrite.'

Donna looked at Davey and wiped a dry tongue across even dryer lips.

'He hates me and yet I never knew it before.

In a rare flash of insight Davey shook his head gently.

'He don't hate you, Donna, he wants you. He always did. That's the crux of the problem.'

Picking up the last two boxes from the ground, he carried them back into the office. Donna followed him, crushed under the weight of everything that had happened in the last few minutes.

'I'll put the kettle on, shall I?'

Placing the boxes by the door, he went into the little kitchenette. Donna heard the water being turned on and the clatter of crockery. Pulling up the flap of the box nearest her, she looked inside. Her heart sank. It was fully of three-inch floppy discs. She had taken all that flak over a few floppy discs.

Picking one up, she stared at it in wonderment. As Davey popped his head round the door she slipped the offending article into her pocket.

'Don't worry, Donna, he don't mean the half of it.'

She took a deep breath and said in her strongest voice, 'I don't want this place used for stolen property ever again, and I mean that, Davey. We've too much to lose if we get caught out, especially with the insurance people crawling all over us. They're already suspicious because I insured this place up to the hilt just before the ram raid. So think about it in the future. Your livelihood and Carol's and the kids' depends on this place.'

Davey nodded, then went back to finish making the coffee.

The prison wing was quiet. Timmy's death had affected them all in one way or another.

As they trooped from their cells for their morning shower, the general mood in A Wing was subdued. Even the Wing's joker

328

Benjamin Dawes was quiet. The two new inmates showered side by side. Georgio watched them as they chatted quietly to each other, relishing the knowledge that he would soon smash their world wide open.

The prospect eased his grief over Timmy. Sadie was still being supplied with Valium to calm her nerves. Even the screws were saddened by her abject misery over Timmy, bringing her cups of tea and cigarettes, never forgetting for one moment that she was the property of Donald Lewis and until he dumped her she was to be afforded a measure of respect.

Georgio washed himself absentmindedly. Timmy's large lumbering presence was more of a loss than he'd ever have suspected. His death had brought home to Georgio just what a precarious position he himself was in. He knew in his heart that at a whim of Lewis's he could die in the same way, and Lewis would never be brought to book over it. Nor would he lose any sleep either. To Donald Lewis, people were as expendable as elastic bands or condoms. You used them, then threw them away. It was a frightening thought.

Tying his towel around his waist, Georgio walked from the showers. As he reached his cell a new screw was standing by his window. Sadie was nowhere to be seen.

'Where's Sadie?'

The man smiled pleasantly. 'The quack wanted to see her. Shut the door, Brunos, and shove in the wedge, we need to talk.'

Georgio stared at him for a few long moments, sizing up whether he should listen to him or throw him out. Lewis wasn't above setting him up and Georgio was aware of it.

The screw seemed to read his mind. He shut the door himself, forcing the wedge into place with his booted foot.

'My name's McNamara and I'm assigned to you from today. I work for Alan Cox. You're in deep shit, mate, and my advice is to listen to me carefully. I am going to be bringing you in messages, regular messages. The first one is this: Cox and Anthony Calder want you to know they are both extremely annoyed at the setup with O'Neil and Carvello. If anything like that happens again, they'll pull and leave you to it.

'Cox also says that if you so much as hint at anything untoward between him and D, he'll leave you high and dry. I'll be back with more news soon.'

As he walked towards the door, McNamara looked over his shoulder and said, 'Oh by the way, Lewis is back in four days. Made a miraculous recovery by all accounts, but his stitches will hinder him for a while. Losing a kidney takes it out of you, like. But his brain's

329

back on track – as I expect you've already guessed. Be seeing you.'

Alone once again, Georgio sat on his bunk and felt the anger welling up inside him. He needed Calder and he needed Cox, but once he was out he could do what he liked. He hung on to that thought to stop himself from screaming out loud. Four days and Lewis was back . . . it was like a death knell in his mind. Four days until everything was back to square one: watching his back, watching his words, and watching Lewis and his henchmen. He had to see Davey Jackson and soon. Whether his dear little wife liked it or not, she'd have to forego a visit, and Georgio admitted to himself that after her little performance in Scotland, he wasn't sorry about it.

At that moment, Sadie walked into the cell and lay down on the bottom bunk. 'Fucking doctors, what do they know? Gave me another AIDs test. I'd already told them I was clean. I've had regular checks since the late eighties. I mean, in my game you have to, don't you?'

Georgio nodded.

'Cheer up, Georgio, it could be worse. You could be dead. Especially with Lewis around.'

'Bollocks to Lewis, Sadie. He's the least of my problems at the moment. In fact, if he opens his big mouth I'll rip his stitches out, see how he likes that one.'

Sadie closed her eyes and said quietly, 'Alan Cox is a lot of things, Georgio, but he ain't a philanderer. Your wife's safer with him than anyone else. Paddy needs a kick up the arse for telling you different.'

'Nah.' Georgio shook his head. 'She came out of his flat, Sadie, with her overnight bag and wet hair. Don't tell me she was in there having a shower for fun, love. Even I ain't that fucking stupid!'

Sadie sat up and grinned. 'Really? Then why all this performance? Speaking as a woman, which I am you know, in me own way, I think she's as sweet as a nut. I mean, let's face it. If she was shunting Alan Cox, why would she be fighting hammer and tongs to get you out? Maybe she needed a shower to liven her up after a night on the road from Liverpool. Don't fall into the trap of a lot of lifers: your old woman's on the outside and there's nothing you can do to her there except have her harmed. Is that what you want to do, then? Send someone round to smash her face in? I've known plenty of blokes who have done that and regretted it, mate. Deeply regretted it. She's all you've got going for you at the moment if you could only see it. Men always think they own their wives, and that's their fatal mistake.

'She could have had a shower for a whole host of reasons, but no, you have to think of the most obvious one of all – she was in there shagging with him. According to Paddy they were in and out in an

330

hour, then she picked up her car and drove home. She was probably asleep for a good part of the journey back, for crying out loud. So she had a shower, changed her clothes and shot off. Don't tell me you wouldn't have done the same thing yourself because I know you would.'

Georgio shook his head. 'She's my fucking wife. I wanted her to help me out of here; I thought I could trust her. But like most women, once I was off the scene she was out and about. It's as simple as that, Sadie, and nothing you or anyone else says can make me think any different. Alan Cox knows the rules. You don't invite your mate's wife into your home, you just don't do it. He thinks he has me where he wants me. Well, he don't, and neither does she.'

Sadie closed her eyes and lay back down.

'You've got what's known as prison paranoia. A lot of blokes get it. It's caused by being banged up and thinking too much. You'll start distrusting your own brothers soon, when they give her a lift down here. You'll be convinced she'd changed towards you, that she's distant, and you'll automatically assume it's because she's being serviced by someone else.

'But it's not because of that, Georgio. It's because every time she visits it'll become harder and harder to talk to you. You'll always be listening for her to say something incriminating, something you can pounce on, and eventually she'll lose patience and you'll be convinced you've been proved right. When in effect she'll dump you because it's all too much like hard work. *That's* when she'll meet someone else, mate, someone who tells her all the things you should be telling her only you're too stubborn and too ignorant to bother. Because you sit here day in and day out imagining her on the job with every Tom, Dick and Harry. You're a fool, Georgio. A twenty-two-carat fool.'

Georgio listened to his little friend with shock. Never had Sadie spoken to him like this.

'What makes you such an authority then?'

He smiled. 'I'll tell you what makes me such an authority. I've spent the best part of my life banged up, mate, and I've seen many men like you. Straight men, gay men, you name it. Murderers, arsonists, blaggers. Even fucking rapists. Once you're banged up, you're out of life. Life for you is four walls and the brutality of whoever is bigger and harder than you. The wife or girlfriend, on the other hand, who has committed no other crime than that of loving or marrying you, gets the brunt of your feelings. You channel all your energies into trying to make out they're also betraying you . . . when the only person who betrayed you was yourself! By getting banged up, you fucked up. It's as simple as that.'

331

Georgio listened to Sadie and although a small part of his mind acknowledged the truth of what she was saying, another part dismissed it all.

Wet hair and an overnight bag was heady stuff to a man in prison. Especially when the news was delivered with the maximum of innuendo.

Paddy had given Georgio the bullets, and he was about to fire them.

Nick Carvello looked over the boat and nodded. It was a small motorised fishing vessel that looked well-used and serviceable. In fact it had a powerful engine on board and also a well-stocked bar, a comfortable bed, and a high-frequency radio. It could gather dangerous speeds, but was small enough to lose quickly if necessary. He nodded again to the man cleaning out the interior.

'I want this fully operational by Sunday latest and then I want it moved away from here and put in the safest boathouse we have. I don't want anyone remembering it was ever here, OK?'

The young man nodded, his face obscured by the thick knitted hat he was wearing.

Nick looked the boat over again, then, pleased with himself, he dialled Anthony Calder's number on his mobile phone.

'Hello. We're all operational here and ready to go whenever you want the jump. I'm ready as well, OK?'

He placed the mobile in the pocket. Turning once more to the younger man he said conversationally, 'Could you stock up with some decent food, tinned stuff of course, and also a good bottle of claret. Oh, and a litre bottle of Glenmorangie; my client favours that whisky. Then I want you to do another favour. I want you to find Little Dicky for me, and tell him I need to have a word – it's urgent. Do you think you could remember all that?'

The youth faced him and smiled. 'I can.'

Nick squirmed in imitation of a bimbo. 'So manly, so strong. Give us a kiss!'

The youth stood up straight and grinned. 'You'd get a big shock if I said yes, Nick.'

Nick's face dropped for a second in mock sadness. Then in his own voice he said, 'You bet your life I would. But not half as big a shock as your old woman when I told her.'

They both laughed in easy camaraderie.

Jonnie H. listened intently to what was being said to him. He deliberately didn't look towards his wife; he would soon garner her thoughts. Annie was never backward in coming forward. Once

332

people realised that she was the real negotiator they were first shocked and then pleasantly surprised at her acumen.

Danny McAnulty was a small stocky man with a thick Glaswegian accent. His brother Cyril, a name that had made his mother proud and himself violent, sat quietly as he negotiated on their behalf. A third brother, Iain, would abide by whatever they decided for him. Danny knew that this jump would be lucrative and also quick – the kind of work he enjoyed. They would be down south overnight and back in bed before the Old Bill started pulling files. It was perfect work. But he knew that Jonnie H., although a fair man and well-respected all over the UK, was also a shrewdie – or, more to the point, his old woman was.

'We think we need at least seven grand each for the day's work. We're putting ourselves on the line—'

Annie interrupted. 'It'll be two hours' work. All you have to do is to be waiting at the chop. Nothing else. You will not be involved in the jump itself. I'm offering you five grand each and that's that.'

Danny shook his head and Cyril followed suit as they all knew he would.

'With respect, Mrs H., we will be the most important people there. It will be us who takes the jumper to his final destination . . .'

Annie interrupted again. 'No, you won't. You will drive him only a few miles, then you will be out of the ballgame. Five grand each and that's it.'

Danny looked at the heavily pregnant woman and sighed. 'Eight.'

Annie grinned. 'Seven.'

'Done.'

Jonnie H. grinned too as Danny shook hands with Annie. 'I'll let you know the dates nearer at hand. It'll be within the next few weeks. The car will be supplied as will your clothes for the actual going to work. All you have to do is keep out of fights and we'll all be on the go before you know it.'

'Nice doing business with you both.'

Annie smiled and showed them to the door. As she walked back into the front room, Jonnie laughed at her.

'You're a girl! You know we'd earmarked ten grand apiece.'

'And that's exactly what Calder will think they're getting. We deserve to make a few quid on this one. Actually I was out to offer eight. Men, eh? You never value yourselves highly enough. Leave it to a mere woman to rip you off!'

She placed a hand across her swollen belly. 'This baby had better get a move on, Jonnie. Once this blag's over we'll be at the hundred grand mark.'

333

He grinned. 'I've already seen a smallholding in Wales. Thirty-seven grand. That'll leave us plenty to live on, with just the occasional bit of work. I want to get the kids out of this slum.'

Annie raised her eyebrows and said seriously, 'But will we ever get the slums out of the kids, eh?'

Jonnie shook his head. 'That, my love, remains to be seen.'

Annie settled herself on the leather settee and picked up her knitting. 'You'd better let Calder and Alan know the score. We're ready for the off. At least, as ready as we'll ever be.'

Jonnie nodded. 'I'll ring them now.'

Annie began to knit the small bootees, she said over her shoulder, 'By the way, stick the kettle on while you're out there. I could murder a cup of tea.'

Jonnie H. chuckled as he dialled Alan's number. Only his Annie could have ever made him so happy. She was phenomenal. His father had said to him years before in a joking way: 'Marry a whore, son, she can't sink no lower.'

Well, his father had been right in a lot of respects. When you were a whore at Kings Cross, the only place for you was up, or into the ground itself. Annie wanted to go up and she had taken him with her.

For that he would always be grateful.

Jamesie stroked the Rottweiler bitch's head and spoke to her soothingly.

'There, my little darling, out it comes. There's a good girl. There's a beauty if ever I saw one.'

He lifted the new puppy and placed it gently at the bitch's head. She began to lick it, pulling it out of the birth sac with the help of Jamesie and her own teeth.

Jamesie's kennel maid stepped nearer and the bitch snapped at her, showing dangerous teeth, growing, making to lift herself up.

'Keep back, Janet, the dog's not herself! Go and make me a hot toddy, and one for the dog here. Put her a large drop of Glenfiddich in warm milk, it'll settle her down. The birthing's nearly over.'

Janet left the warmth of the kennel gratefully. She didn't trust that bitch, never had. But Jamesie could always do what he wanted with the dogs. It was as if they felt he was one of them, as if he had the same smell.

Jamesie saw the last head appearing and grinned. Six little beauties. He was over the moon.

Ten minutes later the bitch was being fed the hot milk and whisky and he was sipping on his toddy, admiring the newborn babies, when his mobile phone rang.

334

He turned it on and beamed as he spoke.

'Hello there, Alan. I've got six beauties here, newborn and as handsome as anything. Yes, don't worry, everything is ready and waiting for you. I've got a paraffin budgie on standby just in case you change your mind. I've got to go, man. Speak to you tomorrow.'

He turned off the phone and stroked the bitch's head again, settling her down.

'There, my beauty. You just relax and I'll be back in a short while.'

Ten minutes later, he was in the cellar of his house; it was like a military arsenal down there. He picked up an Armalite and checked it over, then he began preparing the other weapons that would be needed for the jump.

He was humming with happiness while he worked.

Jack Coyne was visiting JoJo. He listened in silence while JoJo described in graphic detail exactly what he was going to do to Nick Carvello once he was on the mend properly. Jack sighed heavily.

'What you sighing about, Jack?' JoJo's voice was harsh.

He slumped even further down in the uncomfortable hospital chair. 'Did they find your fingers?'

JoJo snorted. 'Did they fuck! That ponce is probably having them dipped in gold and made into a necklace. But I promise you this much: once Georgio is out, I'll pay back the lot of them, him included. He was behind all this from the off. He's letting us know that he don't trust us. Well, if he wants his money from the deal, he'd better start showing me a bit of respect. I never wanted to get involved, it was his idea and now he's trying to keep my trap shut, and yours as well, in case we blow the lid while he's banged up – and banged up with Lewis of all people. Lewis wouldn't touch a deal like this one – he thought he was going into property, the stupid fucker! Well, I've lost more than my fingers now. I've lost face and respect and Georgio has to be made to realise he can't do that to me.'

Jack shifted once more in the chair.

'Will you keep fucking still?' The patient complained irritably. 'You're giving me the heebie-jeebies.'

Jack rolled his eyes at the ceiling. 'I don't want any part of this any more. It's all blown up in our faces. We should never have got involved in it. Whatever way you look at it, it's all wrong, JoJo.'

JoJo couldn't meet the other man's eyes, but he said quietly, 'Wrong it may be, mate, but at the end of the day it's the biggest moneyspinner in the world at the moment and we are in at ground level. Once we make a killing we can walk away from it all richer than we ever believed. And it's very nearly legal.'

335

Jack shook his head miserably. 'I still don't like it, JoJo, I never did. I should never have listened to you about it all.'

JoJo started to get worried. In all their dealings, Jack had calmly done whatever he asked. It wasn't Jack talking now, it was that skinny wife of his.

'Listen,' he told him now, 'all we ever did was put up the money. The distribution was down to Georgio. He'll take the flak from it all once it hits the streets. No one is to know that we put up money unless Georgio tells them, and he wouldn't do that. He second guessed us on this, knew that once he was banged up we would get worried. That's what my hand's all about. Nick Carvello must know something because he was quick enough to blast me. So don't worry on that score. Once Georgio's out he can pick up the reins from wherever he is. This stuff travels through the air, boy, you can distribute it from anywhere in the world.'

Jack realised that JoJo was trying to calm him down. It seemed he didn't entirely trust his partner to keep a level head. That knowledge should have upset Jack.

It didn't.

Jack Coyne knew his own capabilities, none better. Sometimes it was the only thing that gave him the edge in the world he lived in. Jack knew he was a heavy, a bully boy, a pimp. He was good at it and it was a lucrative business. It had kept his head above water for years and eventually it had given him a lot of money and a lot of happiness. He didn't want to endanger this life he had created because of JoJo or that bastard Georgio.

'Listen, Jack, how about I ring up Alan and tell him he'll have to find two other mugs to oversee things this end? We can't be expected to watch over Calder now, not without trouble. Alan will see the sense in that. This way, we're out of the jump and Georgio can think what the fuck he likes. Shall I do that, eh?'

Jack digested what JoJo said and finally, after what seemed an age, he smiled agreement.

JoJo relaxed. He wanted an out and now he had one. For all his big talk about Nick, he didn't particularly want another run-in with him. What he did want was the money from the scam and to disappear off the face of the earth.

It was untold riches, and unlike Jack, JoJo had no qualms about what he was doing. He would get himself overseas, give himself a new identity, and set up the business in a big way. It was the money-making scam of the future, and whatever legislation they brought in, it was here to stay.

'Do you think Alan will go for this then?'

336

Jack's voice brought him back to reality.

'Of course he will.' The irritability had reappeared in JoJo's voice. 'How can he expect me to oversee a man who's shot me fucking fingers off? Use your loaf, Jack, for fuck's sake.'

Jack nodded. 'Can I get you a bottle of Lucozade or anything?'

JoJo rolled his eyes. 'It's costing me over a grand a day in here. Ring the bell and they'll deliver you a large scotch if you want one. But for fuck's sake, Jack, never, and I mean *never*, order a Lucozade while you're here. I couldn't live it down.'

Jack sighed and lapsed once more into silence while JoJo talked on, as if the sound of his voice would grow his missing fingers back.

Alan Cox got the message from Anthony Calder and smiled into the mouthpiece of the phone.

They were ready for the off, they were ready to go. All that was left was the actual jump.

Anthony was arranging a meet with a man who could get you out of a Turkish prison, a Thai prison, or who could snatch your child off the street anywhere in the world. He was an ex-paratrooper, an ex-mercenary . . . and he knew the prison system backwards and forwards.

Alan felt the adrenaline rushing through his veins. He had been too long out of the ballgame. Now he was back and loving every second of it.

Once the jump was actually up and running, he could relax and enjoy the spectacle.

All he had to do now was phone Donna Brunos and arrange to meet her for dinner to explain everything to her. He could have done it over the phone but he didn't want to. He kidded himself he didn't trust the phones. Privately, he knew he just wanted to see her. She was part of the excitement.

As he dialled her number he pictured her in his bedroom, without the towel and without her inhibitions . . .

He wished he could envisage her without Georgio.

337

Chapter Thirty

Little Dicky was a seventy-year-old gay man. He was only five foot one, hence the name. He was thin to the point of emaciation, and his hair was long gone. His finely chiselled features had aged well, though, and coupled with very expressive brown eyes made him look like anyone's idea of a dear old man. In reality, Little Dicky was a listener.

Instead of being paid by the police for information, Little Dicky traded with the bad boys. If you wanted to know where a scam was going down, Little Dicky was the man to ask – especially if you were the person organising it. Dicky found out all he could and reported back. That way you had an idea of who was blabbing in your organisation, and whom you could trust. Through a network of whores, pimps, gays, robbers, burglars and publicans, Little Dicky heard everything, and anything he didn't hear about, wasn't worth knowing. It was a lucrative business. Word on the street was that Little Dicky never talked to the filth, and that made everyone, including Little Dicky, feel safe. Dicky knew his very life depended on discretion.

He turned up at Nick's place at five-fifteen, smiling and friendly, like a little brown teddy bear. Nick, however, knew different. Little Dicky had used a knife since childhood. It was rumoured he could cut anyone, anywhere, without even taking his eyes off the pavement. He was a bundle of hatred behind his big cheesy smile and amiable countenance. You didn't grass on your own for fifty years without being able to take care of yourself.

'Hello, Dicky boy. How's things?' Nick's voice was normal. He knew Dicky too well to play the game with him.

Little Dicky shrugged, a charming, graceful gesture. 'OK, man. Yourself?'

Preliminaries over, the two of them sat in Nick's kitchen and shared a bottle of white rum.

'What do you want to know, Nick? Is it about JoJo or Jack Coyne?

338

Nick Carvello chalked one up mentally to Dicky. 'News travels fast.'

Dicky laughed. 'Tell me, man, what the fuck did you do with his fingers?'

Nick chuckled with him, softly, as if they were sharing a huge joke. 'I flushed them down the crapper.'

Dick grinned, showing surprisingly white teeth capped with gold. 'Best place for them if you ask me.'

Nick stopped smiling. 'But I'm not asking you, am I? What you're here for is to tell me what you've heard about me, JoJo, Jack, or King Street fucking Charlie. Spill it, Dicky, I ain't got all day.'

Little Dicky sipped at his white rum and shrugged.

'Well, everyone knows about the shooting, except the police of course. But that's how it should be. And what I hear besides is this: you're planning a jump for someone and that someone is assed off with JoJo. So you sort of done him a favour, without realising it. I also hear that there's a few people down south who want to know what's going on and they're willing to pay a lot of money to find out. That's what I hear, Nick. Care to enlighten me further?'

Nick ran his tongue slowly across his teeth. 'Who told you this?'

Little Dicky smiled again, his biggest, whitest smile.

'Now you know I can't divulge that kind of information, Nick. That's what's kept me alive for so long. Little Dicky never opens his mouth about anyone. You of all people should realise the sense in that.'

Nick nodded. 'Listen to me, Dicky, this is a big one, but you already know that. Now listen to me good. I'll put you on a retainer, working exclusively for me, just until all this is over. If anyone offers you a cent you refer them to me, through the grapevine of course. I'll pay them a visit personally, you don't have to soil your hands. I'll watch your back, and I'll set you up, but I need your word you'll only work for this baby. Any double crossing and you'll be found minus your head, tongue and cock. Do you get my drift?'

Little Dicky sat for a few seconds as if thinking over the proposition. Both Dicky and Nick knew he had to accept it. Nick was the undisputed King of the Gays and owned too many people. Little Dicky respected the fact he was pretending to ask him. It cut ice with the older man, afforded him a measure of respect. He knew how to play the game and he played it.

'OK, but I want five grand up front and I want your assurance I ain't got to deal with Albie. That boy gives me the creeps.'

Nick grinned now, a friendly grin.

'You'll get three grand up front and you'll suck Albie's cock if I tell you to. Now first things first. Anything you hear on the street comes straight to me. I'll give you my mobile and car numbers – I want everything hot off the press. Anything else you find out, no matter how irrelevant, I want to know about. Any big scams going down, anything where guns or a crew are involved, especially if it's down south. I want to know when JoJo O'Neil shits and eats, I want to know all about his businesses, I want to know what size bra Jack Coyne's old woman wears, where he's been seen, who he's talked to. In short, I want to know everything.'

Dicky nodded. 'Does that include Alan Cox?'

Nick laughed at the older man's innocent expression. 'I also want to know why you know all this already! Who's the weak link, Dicky? Tell me that now and I'll give you the other two grand up front.'

'It was Jonnie H.'

Little Dicky watched Nick's face fall and then grinned. 'But don't worry, Jonnie hasn't said a word. It was just something I overheard in a club. Jonnie H. had a visit from a big man and a good-looking woman in a flash car. It didn't take me long to suss out who it was, with all the other talk going round. When you been listening as long as I have, you don't need much to make up two and two. Cox was a fool. He should have known better than to visit on the Clyde. Christ, someone paying their milkman two weeks on the trot is talk over there! I ain't heard Cox's name mentioned anyhow, so stop worrying. Your secret's safe with me. I also heard that Jonnie H. was looking for the McAnultys. Knowing Jonnie, he found them. I hear everything, man, everything, and if I don't hear about it, then it ain't worth knowing.'

'But you can also keep a secret, can't you?'

Little Dicky finished off his rum and poured himself another.

'Like the grave, man, like the fucking grave. Especially when I'm getting paid up front. A lump of money is a good hearing aid, know what I'm saying. It also helps me to remember what I heard and who I should be telling it to.'

Nick wasn't offended by the older man's speech. He had always respected the power of money. Without money you were powerless; with it, you could at least have an inkling of what was going to befall you.

'I'll bring the money to your place tonight,' he promised Little Dicky. 'Keep your ear to the ground, boy, and remember – you're listening just for me.'

Maeve arrived at Donna's beaming and carrying a chocolate cake. Dolly let her in and their loud voices penetrated into Georgio's office where Donna was going once more though all his papers. Sighing, she walked from the room, plastering a large smile on her face as she entered the warmth of the kitchen.

'Hello, darlin'. I was just passing and thought I'd pop in.'

Donna smiled. There was no way anyone just passed her home. The three women knew this and all played the game.

'I'll make a pot of tea.' Dolly began preparing it and Maeve stared into Donna's face and inclined her head towards the back door. Donna frowned.

'I heard the house was up for sale. Any takers yet?'

Donna shook her head. 'No, but there's a couple coming to look later on today.'

Maeve nodded. 'How's the garden looking?'

Dolly turned to answer this one. 'It looks good as always, the gardener sees to that. Donna hasn't the time these days, what with everything else.'

Maeve walked through the utility room and opened the back door. She stepped out into the garden and Donna followed her cue.

'Give us a shout when the tea's ready, Dolly.'

The two women disappeared and Dolly watched them follow the small pathway to the tennis court.

'What on earth is all this cloak and dagger stuff about, Maeve?' Donna asked.

The older woman sighed. She sounded depressed. 'I heard about you and Stephen. I didn't want to mention it in front of Dolly. She hears too much as it is.'

Donna frowned as she listened to Maeve's sullen voice.

'I think Stephen's in trouble. We had a visit last night, to the restaurant. Three men. And let's just say they weren't respectable businessmen. They said to tell Stephen that Donald Lewis sent them.'

Donna felt her face drain of blood. '*Lewis*? But what would he want Stephen for?'

'You tell me, love. There's something happening, something going on, and I can't seem to get to the bottom of it. I mentioned it to Mario and he just shrugged, told me that Stephen could take good care of himself, but I'm not so sure. I had a feeling it was to do with Georgio. He is my son, but God forgive me, Donna, sometimes lately I find it hard to carry on loving him. Whatever he's involved in, Stephen's in it too, up to his neck. Why didn't they look for Stephen at his offices or his flat? Why did they come to the restaurant? That's what worries me. It's as if they came to our home knowing it would worry Stephen more.'

341

Donna thought for a moment. 'What did they look like?'

Maeve made a face. 'Big galoots with expensive suits and faces like a madman's arse! Typical of Georgio's friends if you like.'

Donna grasped Maeve's hand. 'Did they threaten you, actually threaten you?'

Maeve heard a steely note in Donna's voice and she sighed. 'You're getting just like Georgio and Stephen, do you know that? A year ago you'd have stood and worried with me. Now you feel you want to make them pay. I can hear it in your voice, see it in your demeanour. Listen, Donna, get out of all this while you still have the chance. Let Georgio run everything from his prison cell. I've even lost the yearning to have him home. Don't let him make you like he is, like Stephen is, like Donald Lewis is. That's why they're inside and we're out here.'

'Stephen's not inside.'

Maeve shook her head. 'Not yet maybe, but I know it'll come. If not this year, then next. Stephen is like Georgio, an accident waiting to happen. Make sure it doesn't happen to you.'

Donna was shocked at Maeve's words and the truth of them. The thought of Ma and Pa Brunos getting a visit from Lewis's heavies made her feel a redhot wave of pure rage; for a split second, she wanted to crush them, smash them. Never in her life had she felt like that before. Always the pacifist, always the voice of reason . . . Maeve was right. She *was* changing, and she wasn't sure whether it was for the better or worse.

'I'll tell Georgio,' she said now. 'He'll sort it out.'

Maeve smiled sadly. 'Do you realise we're not even pretending he's innocent any more? And do you know what hurts me more than anything? Your acceptance of that fact. Knowing what he is now, instead of turning your back on him, you're joining in with his wild schemes and his wants, Donna. You're even selling this lovely house.'

She wiped a wrinkled hand across her brow. 'Leave him, Donna, while you're still young enough to get away. In another few years, time will have raced on. Believe me, I know what I'm talking about. Then it'll be too late to follow your own road, because you'll have followed his for so long the habit will be hard to break.'

'Whatever he is, whatever he's done,' Donna said vehemently, 'he is still my husband. He stood by me through miscarriages, upsets, and all sorts of traumas. I have to do the same for him now.'

Maeve shook her head once more. The sadness in her face was such that Donna too, felt an urge to cry.

'He didn't stand by you, Donna. You're remembering with the rosy glow of a woman. He left you in on your own, he travelled the

342

world, he carried on with his life. Every now and again he threw you a mercy fuck, and you were grateful for it. Do you know something? I was so pleased to see how devoted you were to him, I knew he had found a true love. It wasn't until you'd been married a few years that I realised it was all one-sided. Oh, I'm not disputing he loved you, so you can take that look off your face. But he wasn't *in love* with you any more. He loved you like he loved his car or his businesses. He owned you. Why can't you see that, Donna, and get out now?'

Donna stared into her mother-in-law's face.

'If this wasn't so sad, I'd laugh. All those mother-in-law jokes about how the girl isn't a patch on the mother. How the clichés always have the mother resenting the girl who took her beloved son away – and I get you, Maeve. I worship your son and you expect me to leave him high and dry now? After twenty years of devotion you expect me to turn my back on him? If it wasn't so terrible, it really would be a joke.'

'He's using you, Donna, and he's using Stephen. God forgive me, I love the bones of him but I can see him for what he is. God only knows what else he's involved in. Robbery and murder aren't enough for him. He's my son, I bore him and I know him better than anyone. He always had a sneaky way with him even as a child. Georgio goes out for what he wants and nine times out of ten he gets it. Remember that. And he doesn't care who gets hurt in the process.'

Donna lost her temper.

'I'm not listening to any more of this, Maeve. You're obviously overwrought. Whoever visited you probably had a good reason. I'll find out what it is and I'll deal with it. Now will you come inside and have a cup of tea, and let's never refer to this conversation again, OK?'

Maeve sighed heavily. 'So, you'll find out who visited me and you'll deal with it, will you? You sound just like Georgio or Stephen or Davey Jackson. Even Paddy. You're getting hard, Donna, and you're getting in over your pretty little head. I'll take a rain check on the tea if you don't mind.'

And Maeve Brunos walked back to the house alone, her small body bristling with indignation and upset.

Donna watched her till she rounded the bend by the kitchen garden and then she felt the tears come into her own eyes. They weren't tears of sadness though, she admitted to herself. They were tears of anger.

Ten minutes later, she went back inside, walked past a silent Dolly and locked herself in Georgio's office. Here she read and re-read his

343

letters of love and need, drank in every word on the pages and told herself that this was she wanted. Her husband adored her and she adored him, and she would do anything to get him back with her.

Anything.

And if she was getting tougher, then that was all to the good. Softness had never got her anything. For the first time in her life she was her own woman and she was learning to fight for what she wanted.

And if fighting made men like her husband and Alan Cox sit up and take notice, then she would fight to the death.

Paddy sat opposite Georgio in the visiting room of Parkhurst and grinned.

'You're looking well.'

Georgio shrugged. 'What exactly happened with Donna and Alan, Paddy I want to know everything.'

'What I told you,' the Irishman said. 'She went into his flat and came out fifty-six minutes later. She had obviously showered and changed. She picked up her car and went home.'

Georgio looked into his friend's face. 'Do you think there's anything funny going on there, Paddy? I want the truth as a mate. You've hinted as much.'

Paddy looked into Georgio's face and sighed inwardly. 'I really don't know. Knowing Donna like I do, I would say no way. That's not her scene.'

Georgio leant across the table. 'And you know what her scene is then, do you?'

Paddy moved away from Georgio and surveyed him steadily. 'What's that supposed to mean? Only if you wasn't so fucking close-mouthed over everything that's going on, maybe you wouldn't have had to rely on Donna to do all the donkey work. I know what's going down and let me tell you something – I realised from the off what you were planning the moment I knew she was dealing with Cox. And if I sussed it, you can bet your arse someone else has as well.'

Georgio closed his eyes. 'I have got to get out of here, Paddy, and soon.'

'If you'd have brought me into everything, you wouldn't be having the hag you've got now. I run your fucking sites, and believe me when I say your old woman done a brilliant job on them. She is a natural worker. I mean that and all. As for you getting out, it seems you've got that all sewn up as well. I watch Donna and Alan, and you watch them, and we all watch Lewis. Nothing like complicating

344

everything, is there? You should have come to me straight off and we'd have sorted it between us.'

Georgio shook his head. 'No way. Lewis knows we're close. He'd have sussed immediately. The only reason you're here now is because he's off the Wing for a while.'

Paddy grinned. 'But his henchmen ain't. My visit will be all over this nick by teatime. You're involving me now because of Donna. No other reason. You want me to watch her and Cox. Well, I have been, or at least I've had others watching her, put it like that. I'm still watching the house, and I have something to tell you that you're not going to like. Three of Lewis's baboons visited your da's restaurant last night looking for Stephen. He's closing the net, Georgio. If I was you I'd put your hand up and get out of the game. It's getting too dangerous for everyone concerned.'

Paddy was pleased to see Georgio's worried look. He was too sure of himself at times. Even banged up, in the worst trouble of his life, he still had that devil-may-care attitude and sometimes, like now, it really irked Paddy.

'Fuck Lewis! I want to know what's happening with Donna and Alan.'

Paddy lit a cigarette. 'Nothing, I'd lay money on that. Think about it, Georgio. Donna is busting her arse to get you out. Don't put everything in jeopardy because you think Alan is tumbling your old woman. It's senseless, especially knowing what we both know. You'd leave her high and dry in the morning if you thought it would benefit you in any way, and don't try to tell me different, Georgio. I've known you too long to be bullshitted.'

Georgio sighed heavily. 'It's the thought of it, you know. Stuck in a fucking cell, and all you can see after lock-up and lights out is your old woman humping while you're banged up with only a right hand and distant memories.'

Paddy nodded. 'I know, but it's something all long-timers have to get used to. She's on the outside and you're banged up. She can get up, do what she likes. It's the freedom element. You assume her freedom allows her to do things she wouldn't normally do. Like shunt Alan Cox. Stop winding yourself up, Georgio, get back in the real world and get yourself out. Then if you find out you're right about her and Coxy, you can do something about it.'

Georgio swallowed the logic of what Paddy said, and smiled.

'You're a mate, Paddy. You're right. I can't do anything while I'm stuck in here, and if there is anything funny going on then I'd like to deal with it personally.'

Paddy nodded and stubbed out his cigarette.

345

'So what's the score then?'

Georgio looked at him intently for a few moments before making up his mind exactly how much to tell him.

Alan Cox and Anthony Calder waited patiently for Donna's arrival at The Barking Dog public house in Barking High Street. They sipped Guinness and chatted amiably, smiling now and then at the women with their parcels and children enjoying a quick sandwich or a burger after a hard Saturday's shopping. Donna walked in at just after five past two. As usual she looked immaculate and Alan watched as Anthony and three men at the bar openly admired her as she walked towards them.

'Sorry I'm a bit late.'

The two men stood up.

'We haven't time for a drink, love, we'll have one when we reach our destination.'

Two minutes later Donna was in the back of Anthony Calder's black Cosworth and they were on their way to Ilford. The men were silent until they pulled up outside a house in Mortlake Road.

'This is a safe house, Donna. We're meeting the man who's going to be the brains behind the jump. Keep your mouth shut and your head down and listen carefully to everything he says. He will not repeat himself.'

She got out of the car, her stomach quivering with what she wished was excitement but acknowledged to be deep fear. Even Alan and Anthony were subdued. Whoever this man was, he was obviously someone to be respected.

Alan opened the door with a key and the three trooped into the dim hallway. To the right of them was a doorway and Alan tapped gently on the door before opening it.

'Eric? Hello, mate. Long time no see.'

Donna followed Anthony into the front room of the house. The room was comfortable if not luxurious. It was obviously used by people in transit; it had the look of a furnished flat or rented room. A smell of cooking fat underlay the hint of furniture polish, giving the room a stuffy feel. In a chair by the window sat a man of indeterminate age with short grey hair, massive shoulders and an easy if unwelcoming smile. He had steely grey eyes and he wore a cheap Tesco tracksuit.

'Alan, it has indeed been a long time.'

Donna was taken aback by his cultured tones.

'This is Eric. Eric, Donna Brunos. Anthony you already know.'

Anthony shook hands and they all sat down. Donna noticed that

346

Eric, whoever he was, didn't afford her so much as a glance. Instinctively she took the seat nearest the door and let Alan and Anthony sit nearer to him.

He poured out three vodkas and handed them round without asking if anyone wanted a mixer. Donna placed hers on a small table by her chair and licked her dry lips. Never before had she felt such strength in a person, such a sense of danger.

'So, now you've got me, what exactly do you want?'

Anthony sat forward in his chair. 'We are organising a jump. So far we have the facilities, the armoury and the manpower. What we need is your expertise in the planning and execution.'

Eric linked his fingers together and placed them across his chest.

'It'll cost you.'

Alan smiled; this was talk he understood.

'We've got the dosh, Eric, don't worry about that.'

Eric smiled faintly. 'I'm glad to hear that. I'm not a charity.'

The room was quiet as if everyone was letting this little gem sink in.

'Where's the jump from? As if I need to ask with dear Georgio's wife here.' For the first time he smiled at Donna and she smiled hesitantly back.

'How is your husband?' he went on smoothly. 'It's a long time since I had any dealings with him. I'd offer you my deepest regrets, but Georgio was always a man who would one day be locked up. It stood to reason.'

Donna didn't like the way the conversation was going. She looked towards Alan for support, but he was listening intently to what Eric had to say.

'So the jump's from the Island. Is it only Georgio we'll be taking or is there more on the agenda? I had that happen to me a few years back in Turkey. I sprung a young drug-dealer, you might remember him from the papers – Kirkson. He was found with his throat cut outside the prison gates. Foolish boy. I could have had him home and dry within twenty-four hours. He tried to tick me up, as you Cockneys say. Biggest mistake he ever made. If I had been informed he wanted his girlfriend sprung with him, of course I would have obliged. But for a fee, of course.'

'Of course.' Alan's voice was nearly jovial.

Eric knocked back his vodka and immediately poured another large measure for himself.

'So, have you any thoughts on how you want him outed?'

Anthony shrugged. 'We thought of helicopters—'

Eric interrupted him. 'No chance, not on the Island. Since the

347

jump from Durham there's not an ounce of spare space in any of the four maxis. All wired. No chance for chock's away. Choppers no good, chaps.'

He looked at Alan and Anthony as if waiting for more bright ideas.

Alan grinned. 'We thought of getting him on a laydown.'

Eric grinned back. 'That's more like it – except you can't guarantee when the laydown is going to be. No, we need to know exactly when Georgio is going to be on the road itself. That's the only way. Unless you can get news from inside as to when Section 43 is being put into operation, of course.' He looked at the three blank faces. 'Even the prison Governor doesn't know until twenty-four hours beforehand, the Home Office are fuckers for that. It's all the terrorists, you see, not the blaggers, that's who it was brought in for. Barbaric rule if you ask me, but there you go. Pity Amnesty doesn't shout a bit more about what goes on here instead of whining about south America all the time.'

Alan sipped his vodka. 'Can you find out when a laydown is to be brought forward?'

Eric shook his head. 'Not a hope in hell, Alan, old man. They're very secretive about all that, I'm afraid. I have a contact in the Home Office, but he wouldn't know himself until the day before. No one knows except the Chief and his close staff.'

Alan looked resigned.

Anthony finished his vodka and held out his glass for more. Eric filled it nearly to the brim.

'The thing is, even if we knew, could you get the men in place in time? I don't think so. That much activity would be noticed, and also we couldn't guarantee what the posse with the sweatbox would be like. It could be one or two outriders and a Rover, or it could mean helicopters, the works. What we need is a day, an exact day, and then we'll plan accordingly.'

Donna could contain herself no longer. She said loudly, 'But how could we know that, unless we could make it happen?'

Eric began to laugh. 'Astute girl here, chaps. That's exactly what we would have to do. Make it happen.'

Alan frowned. 'But how?'

Eric stood up. 'Can I get you a cup of tea, my dear? I can see my vodka isn't to your liking.'

Donna shook her head. 'No, really, I'm fine.'

Eric picked up a large canvas bag and took out an Ordnance Survey map.

'I've already planned the route. All we need is him outside on the road. On a laydown, they always take them to Wandsworth from

348

Parkhurst. The roads are left open, the local police are brought in. Oh, you all know the scenario. But every now and again, there's a quick move. A laydown that is at the prison governor's discretion. That's how we are going to spring Georgio. We'll never get him out of Parkhurst, never. It's far too tough a nut and we'd be fools to attempt it. While he's inside he can do nothing but stay there. Outside, however, is a different matter. Outside, we can pick him off like a cherry from a tree.'

Donna was listening raptly, fascinated by the man's knowledge and the way he imparted it.

'What do you mean, the Governor's discretion?' she asked.

Tapping each end of the rolled-up map with his short stubby fingers, Eric looked at the three faces around him. Grinning widely he said, 'We'll get him out of there on a GOAD.'

Anthony and Alan laughed with delight.

Donna, not sure what they were laughing at, said, 'What's a GOAD?'

'Good order and discipline is what it is, young lady. And we're going to use it to get your husband home to you.'

'But how? How will that bring Georgio home?'

Eric grinned at the three expectant faces. Picking up his glass of vodka, he held it high in a toast.

'Because, my dear,' he announced in ringing tones, 'your husband is going to shit up the Governor of Parkhurst!'

349

Chapter Thirty-One

Donna listened to the almost manic laughter of the three men and swallowed down her annoyance.

'I wish someone would explain to me what you're all laughing at.'

Eric wiped his eyes. Sitting once more in his chair, he looked at Donna fully.

'If you're in prison for a long term, or you're A grade, you are treated like a subversive – and of course eventually that is what you become. You live your whole life trying to get the better of the system. It's an Us and Them situation. So naturally we have to use this to our advantage. If, for example, a man on the SSB wing decided to organise a work strike, or better still a riot, then the prison Governor could have him removed from the premises at his discretion. That means your husband, dear lady, would be moved with only a sweatbox and probably one Rover car to supervise it. Exactly what we need. The best way to guarantee the out is to accost the Governor. That's where "shitting up the governor" comes in.'

Alan nodded. 'I've done it myself, Donna. You save your big jobs up for a week, until it's nice and watery, and then you offload the bucketful over the Governor when he comes to visit the Wing. If we can get Georgio to cause a disturbance, he can be the main culprit and can do the business on the old man, and they'll have him out as soon as possible.'

'If he does the dirty before lunchtime,' Eric went on, 'then they'll move him in the afternoon. All we'll need is a joey on a mobile at the ferry terminal to say whether or not the sweatbox goes on it. If it does, we're off.'

Donna frowned. 'What if they don't move him until the night, though?'

Eric shrugged. 'Same thing. I'd prefer the daylight obviously, but it don't really make that much difference. As long as he hasn't got the big entourage. Also the local police will not be able to get too organised.'

Donna was confused. 'But why would they move Georgio out so quick if he's A Grade?'

'Think about it, love,' Anthony told her. 'They want the ringleader out to defuse the situation. While he's there the men he's got behind him will want to carry on, won't they? He's got to wind them up, ain't he? Be the big man. The prison authorities won't want him there, and if he wasn't going on the trot they'd take him from the laydown to another nick and segregate him for a few months. There's nothing like three or four months on the block – solitary to you, love – to get people to crack up.'

Eric poured out more vodka for everyone except Donna.

'Are there any nonces on his Wing, do you know? Only that's a good scam. Everyone wants to do the nonces; it's part and parcel of prison life. If Georgio can get a weapon, he can quite happily do all the nonces over. Beat the fuck out of them and then cause uproar. They'll want him out all right, they always do. They don't give a fuck how they're tortured on a daily basis, but a big one with three or four mashed up at once scares them. The *Sun* would be climbing all over their backs for a start. Especially if we make sure they know all about it. Then we nab your man as they trundle him off the laydown.

'That's where the GOAD comes in,' he finished off. 'Good order and discipline. It's an old antiquated rule but it can work for us in this. The GOAD is brought in when you're classed as a disruptive influence, or in the case of nonces, for your own protection.'

'So they could take the nonces with him then?'

Alan shook his head. 'Not until they're out of the hospital, love. Georgio's got to hammer the fuck out of them, and knowing Georgio he'll enjoy doing that. No one likes the nonces. No one. Not even the screws. That's why he has to shit up the Governor as well. It'll be the icing on the cake, see. Once he's been humiliated in front of the Wing, the Governor will want Georgio out of his sight.'

Anthony nodded slowly. 'He'll probably get a hammering himself before he goes but it'll be worth it. This plan's brilliant. We knew we'd have to get him from the outside, but finding out the laydowns is nigh on impossible and the information is not always reliable, see. But this way, we have a ninety percent chance of being on schedule. I've never known a Governor yet swallow a shitting, have you?' He looked around him for confirmation, and both Alan and Eric shook their heads.

Anthony grinned. 'I done it myself at Durham, years ago though. It was such a fucking laugh! If you'd seen his face! I'm going back years now. There was a right loon on our Wing, a black bloke. Nice enough, a laugh, you know. But he was really erratic. Anyway, the

351

screws used to bait him something chronic, and he'd throw a right paddy. Knocked the fuck out of them a few times. Well, at times like that they used to inject him with Valium or something, it was in the seventies and that was the scam then. Drug you up and knock you out, like. Well, whatever they gave him killed him. He was found in his cell . . .'

'It was Librium.' Alan's voice was low. 'The man was Karol Denoy. He had more drugs in his system than fucking Jimmy Hendrix and they forced more inside him. He was a mate.'

Anthony paused. 'Well, after a week, the Governor came down on the Wing to have his usual constitutional around the nick and I caught him lovely. I went, "Sir?" And as he turned around I let him have a bucketful right in his mush. He went fucking mental! The screws was running round like scalded whores and I laughed my fucking head off.'

'What happened then?' Donna's voice was frightened and all three men picked up on that.

Anthony smiled at her amiably. 'They put me in a straitjacket and kicked the shit out of me on the block. But it was worth it. I spent eight months in solitary. They spat in my food, pissed in me tea. You name it, they did it, and I didn't give a flying fuck. It was worth it.'

Donna's face was devoid of colour but she nodded at him in acceptance of what he said.

'Surely they can't get away with all that now?' Alan laughed out loud. 'Don't you read the papers, Donna? The Guildford Four, the Birmingham Six? I've had more than my fair share of hidings over the years. Now when I killed Won Tang it was a different ballgame. The Old Bill treated me like visiting royalty. Getting me tea, fags, magazines. They knew the score with him and I'd done them a right favour. With him off the street they knew their job was a lot easier.'

Eric smiled at Donna, sorry for her but also slightly annoyed with her at the same time.

'You'll learn the rules to live by when you're on the trot with your old man, love. It really *is* a different ballgame. You'll spend your whole life looking over your shoulder, wondering what the next day will bring. Whether you'll be caught, and charged as an accessory. Whether the filth will be waiting when you get home, whether you'll be banged up or allowed bail. You've got it all to come. Do you think you can handle it? Only this could get a bit rough, you know. This isn't TV, my dear, this is real life.'

Donna realised that all three men were watching her intently. The

352

easy camaraderie was gone. Alan and Anthony really wanted to know the answer to their question. Taking a deep breath, she finally and irrevocably put herself on the line.

'I can handle it, Eric. The point is, can you?'

The three laughed, and Donna felt the tension leave the room. She laughed with them, while inside her bowels felt as if they were turning to iced water and her heart beat so loud she wondered how the three of them didn't remark on the sound.

'Oh, I can handle it, my dear. That is my job.'

Donna looked around the dingy room, at the well-used furniture with cigarette burns and greasy marks, at the cold fireplace with the cracked tiles on the hearth, and the faded flock wallpaper.

All she could think as she sat there, cold, friendless and frightened, was that it would all be worth it once Georgio was back with her.

Everything would be worth it.

She needed to believe that more than anything else in the world.

Georgio lay in his bunk thinking about the off. He had to find out something concrete soon or he would go mad. Lewis would be back on the Wing within the next forty-eight hours. That meant going back to living on a daily basis, minding his back and listening out for footsteps, watching for hidden weapons.

Lewis never let anyone feel they were entirely safe from him. It was the edge he had over people. He could smile at you, and joke, and put his arm around your shoulders, oblivious of the fact he had ordered your beating, or worse. It was the 'worse' that bothered Georgio. Lewis's forte was scarring people. Cutting them up and watching them weep. Georgio knew that he had his creds, he was a known villain, respected because he didn't get caught – not until now anyway. But no one was a match for a psychopath like Lewis.

He turned on his bunk, willing the night away and also willing it to stay. He concentrated on his wife. A small smile was playing around his lips. In the dimness he could make out Donna's photograph alongside the others on the cell wall by his bunk. He frowned as he saw the line of her cheekbones emphasised by the half-light.

Donna wouldn't do the dirty on him, Sadie was right in that respect. After all those years of being his wife she wouldn't turn on him now. He had prison paranoia, that's all. All the men went through it at some time. It was the pressure getting to him. If he could have done his time without Lewis hanging around his neck, he would have been all right. But all the stress had got to him.

353

Anyway, he concluded, she wouldn't dare do it to him. Not Donna. She wouldn't have the guts. He'd run around on her all through their married life and she hadn't even had the guts to question it. Knowing in her heart of hearts he would have given her the answer she didn't want to hear. In reality, he mused, he should have unloaded her years before for someone more like himself. But he didn't want to be lumbered with a Carol Jackson, and the life he had lived would have guaranteed someone like her. A decent woman wouldn't have anything to do with him, not unless she was ruthless, and decency and ruthlessness did not go hand in hand.

He liked the way Donna lived her life. She was quiet, contained, and loyal. Too loyal really. Over the years he had despised her in some ways for her easy acceptance of what he could do to her. She allowed him anything to keep him, and Georgio knew that being the kind of person he was, he couldn't, wouldn't plump for a life like that any longer. Maybe if they'd had children he might have felt different. But he could have children, he knew that for a fact. He smiled into the darkness.

If only Donna knew what had really transpired over the years, she would faint. She was a brick though. What she was doing went against the grain with her, and he knew that. In effect he was using her, but he preferred to look on it as payment for all the easy years she'd had, spending his money and living her luxurious lifestyle. He knew she loved him, and the knowledge pleased him. He loved Donna, but he had not been in love with her for years. Not since the boy died. Something had died inside him, too, that night. She had failed him, as she had since the day he married her. She had refused him sex beforehand, and eventually he had married her for it. And the sex wasn't worth it, not really.

Yet he had cherished her, outwardly anyway. Donna never really knew the extent of his feelings for her but he had known hers. They enveloped him as he walked into a room with her. Sometimes the feeling had been like a balm to his spirit; at other times like a suffocating blanket. But she had class, he couldn't take that away from her. He knew men looked at her, wanted her, and he enjoyed the knowledge.

Not like Vida. She was a different proposition altogether. Vida was young, vibrant and beautiful. Tall, willowy and blonde, she had a mouth like a sewer and a mind to match. But she was exciting. She knew what he wanted and she supplied it. She was aware of his weaknesses and his strengths. She gave her body as Donna gave her love, without thought or care or even the smallest amount of embarrassment. She opened to him at any time, gave him thrills of

354

pleasure and also peace of mind. He could mould her into what he wanted before she became like Carol Jackson, the clichéd villain's bird, with heavy make-up, the regulation sexy clothes and the too-knowing mouth. He could turn Vida into a young Donna, into a woman. His woman. And Vida could have a child, she had already proved that. He saw himself living in a palatial villa in the sun with Vida beside him, strong and bronzed. Her willowy figure without clothes or inhibitions. That was the woman he wanted, deep in his guts.

But Donna pushed into his thoughts again. Donna and Alan Cox. He smiled. Alan's idea of a woman was a prostitute like his Lally. Alan didn't want commitment. He didn't want to be tied. Georgio should have had more sense than to think Donna and Alan were getting it on together. In a rare moment of honesty, Georgio realised he was more upset at the thought of Alan fanning the flames in Donna. The flames he had never managed to light properly . . . not since the night the boy died. It was as if after that trauma, sex to Donna became only an act of love. He didn't want sex with love, not all the time, he wanted to fuck her sometimes. All the time. He wanted her on her knees in front of him, abandoned, taking him into her for the pure joy of fucking. He was sickened by her constant declarations of love. Sex was ninety-nine percent in the head, not the body.

Sex to Georgio over the years had become visual; he liked to enact blue movie sequences with women, liked to see them enjoy themselves as much as he was. Not make love like Donna wanted, with the mattress under her back and words of love whispered constantly. Sex to Donna was a reassurance of his love for her. He had known that for a long time. He had climbed from his bed some mornings with a raging hard-on and had left her there, wanting him, because he enjoyed the power he had over her. Now, though, Donna had the power. The power to get him out, the power to get his money and the power to call the shots. Until he was out of here, that was. Once he was free he could do what he wanted, and he would. He needed Donna to get his money because she was the only person in the world he could really trust.

His Donna, the most trustworthy of wives.

But Georgio, being a realist, knew he could never, ever trust himself. And Donna wanted him to want only her, and after all this was over she would demand his allegiance, feel she had earned it even, and Georgio knew he could never promise that to anyone. Not even Vida.

Not even to himself.

355

★ ★ ★

Donna couldn't sleep; the day's events had thrown her off balance. She sat in Georgio's office, a cigarette and a glass of whisky her only companions. She sipped the burning liquid, enjoying the bite as it hit her throat and belly.

Meeting Eric had really shown her what she had let herself in for. She had looked at Alan and Anthony, listened to their easy talk, their easy acceptance of what was to happen, and real fear had enveloped her. Eric was right. Could she live with the constant thought of a knock on the door? Of a police raid? Could she live as a fugitive? She knew instinctively that Georgio could, she had few illusions left about her husband. All that was left, all that was certain, was her deep-seated love for him, a love he had ensnared long ago and which had grown over the years.

She stood up and walked to the window. Glimpsing the car parked to the left of the driveway, she knew that she was still being watched and the knowledge depressed her even more. Once the house was sold and they were off, would this become a way of life? Would they be watched constantly, would they ever know peace? Would Georgio be able to sleep easy in bed only because he knew hired help was watching his house for him? Would she be able to sleep knowing that? Would Donald Lewis find them or the police? Had Georgio told her everything or were there other people he had to watch out for, as if Donald Lewis and the police weren't enough?

Donna knew she shouldn't question herself too much; brooding like this was a bad thing, especially in the night, and with only a cigarette, a glass of scotch and her own active imagination for company. But it all seemed so real now; Eric had made it real. Once she had left Scotland and Liverpool it had ceased to seem real to her, but Eric was real. Too real. He spoke about the jump as if it was a game and she was sure that to him it was, a lucrative game that earned him a considerable amount of money and gave him the opportunity to get one in the eye of the establishment.

Donna stared out of the window and sighed gently. It was all set now. Even if she wanted to pull out, she couldn't, she was in over her head. Georgio knew it, and she knew it. The knowledge upset her. She had envisioned herself keeping apart from it all somehow, being part of it but not actually taking a part. She now knew that she was wrong. She could be arrested at any time; if anyone got the slightest inkling of what was about to go down, she could be hauled into a police station and questioned. She could be charged with conspiracy, and God knew what else. Once Georgio was out she could be put behind bars for a long time if they were caught.

356

Although these thoughts had floated in and out of her consciousness at different times over the last few months, she hadn't really let them take substance, because she knew if she thought about them too much she would have backed out, proved a coward. Now, after meeting Eric, she knew exactly what she had done and she also had an inkling of what she could end up having thrown at her.

When Maeve had accused her of becoming like Georgio she had realised just how astute her mother-in-law was. Donna had felt a rage inside her at the thought of Lewis's henchmen coming to the restaurant. Had the rage always been there or had it developed over the past months? The question frightened her. All she had wanted was her husband. Home. Her husband whom she had been convinced was as pure as the driven snow. She smiled as she thought of her naivety. Had she really thought that over the years – really, deep down? Had she honestly thought Georgio was such a perfect man?

She couldn't answer that. Georgio was Georgio, and whatever he was, she had wanted him . . . still wanted him. And the only way to get him was to fight for him.

She knocked back the scotch and poured herself another. Sleep was beyond her, getting drunk was beyond her. She was at a pitch of nerves that would let her neither rest nor sleep. She had become good at fighting, and Georgio had sat up and taken notice, that was the main thing.

The sharp ringing of a phone broke into her thoughts and she automatically picked up the receiver by her side. Nothing, just a dialling tone. It took her a moment to realise it was the fax on the desk. She went to it and listened in the eerie light as the strange sound emanated from it, stretching her overwrought nerves. As the paper began to spew on to the desk she laughed with relief. She had given herself the heebie-jeebies over nothing. Quickly, she swallowed down more scotch.

Picking up the piece of paper she scanned the page, turning on the desk lamp to see it more clearly. It was written by hand, a scrawling hand. She screwed her eyes up to read it better.

FOR DAVEY AND GEORGIO
TROUBLE AT THE HOTELS. GOVERNMENT TROUBLE.
NEED HELP.
STOPPED SHIPPING UNTIL FURTHER NOTICE.

CANDY

Donna looked at the fax as if she had never seen one before. Who the hell was Candy? The headed notepaper was from the Bay View Hotel

357

in Sri Lanka. She read and reread the fax, but still she couldn't make head nor tail of it. Shipping what? Georgio had already told her that the government had stopped the building, so what could be the new trouble? Her husband vanished from her mind as she studied the message.

She needed to get to the bottom of this – and Davey would have to start answering some questions soon. She saw the fax number on top of the piece of paper and, without knowing why, locked the fax into the desk drawer. Dolly was always around and about and something told her to keep this to herself for a while.

Here was another of the great Brunos mysteries; and knowing Georgio like she did she knew she wouldn't get a straight answer from him about it.

Carol was in the office when Donna arrived and the two women chatted and shared a cup of coffee. Small talk was easy with Carol Jackson; she thrived on it.

'My Chrissy's in all sorts of trouble up the school. I told Davey to give him a right-hander but he won't. I'll have to do it as usual.'

'What's he done?'

Carol shook her head. 'If I told you, Donna, you wouldn't believe me. That boy is just like his father, feet first into everything. He's fifteen going on thirty, that's his trouble.'

Donna smiled sympathetically. 'Where is Davey, by the way? I want to have a word with him.'

Carol shrugged. 'Out. I dunno when he'll be back. He had a bit of business.'

Donna rolled her eyes to the ceiling. 'If we had a penny for every time they said that!'

Carol laughed with shock. Donna was talking like any villain's wife. Carol wasn't sure if she liked the change.

'Can I help you at all?' she asked tentatively.

Donna surveyed Carol carefully before answering. Her make-up was as bright as usual, her hair backcombed to its limit and gold jewellery very much in evidence . . . but Donna saw the softer side of Carol looking at her through all that and so she took her courage into her hands.

'What's going on in Sri Lanka, Carol?'

She saw Carol lick her lips nervously and drop her eyes. 'I dunno. You tell me, Donna.'

Donna took a deep breath, feeling a chill come over the room at her next words.

'Come on, Carol, I'm not a fool. What's going on in Sri Lanka?

358

You know more than Davey, probably. I'm well aware you make a point of knowing everything – so why don't you share that knowledge with me? I am supposed to own the land out there, after all, ditto the land in Thailand. I think I have a right to be told what's going on.'

Carol lit a Rothman's and stared into Donna's face.

'You want the truth, Donna? The truth is that I don't exactly know what's going on out there. Stephen looks after that end, and Davey. It's one of the few things he has never discussed with me.'

Donna heard the underlying worry in Carol's voice and probed deeper.

'Do you think it's illegal then, whatever all this is about?'

Carol laughed wryly. 'Everything they touch is a bit dodgy. It's Stephen being involved that really bothers me. Once he gets into things, they tend to get dirty.'

Donna looked her in the eye. 'Dirty? In what way?'

Carol smashed her cigarette into the ashtray and said through her teeth, 'Just dirty. Filthy rotten dirty. What made you ask about Sri Lanka, Donna? What have you heard?'

Donna swallowed deeply. 'I just found some papers in Georgio's safe and wondered what they were about, that's all. I haven't "heard anything", as you put it.'

Carol lit another cigarette. 'You look rough, girl, really rough. Like a woman with a lot on her mind.'

Donna smiled. 'I didn't sleep much last night, Carol. And I have got a lot on my mind.'

'Missing Georgio?'

Donna nodded faintly. 'Sometimes I hate him, Carol, for what he's done, for what he wants me to do. But even knowing that, under-neath it all, I know I'll do what he wants.'

'I feel the same about Davey,' Carol admitted. 'Oh, I know to you he ain't no prize. But to me he's like my life's blood. I couldn't exist without him, you know?' Her hard features softened as she spoke and Donna saw the girl she had been, many years before.

'Sometimes it wouldn't take nothing for me to batter him to death with a baseball bat, especially when I know he's been out tomming. But the underlying fact of it all is, I couldn't even begin to think of living without him.

'We get older, girl,' Carol went on sadly, 'but men don't. Oh, they do in years but not in the brain. Most men's cocks rule their heads till they're in their dotage. You only have to look at the politicians who get tumbled because of a bit of skirt. What we have to do is swallow it, no matter how much it hurts.'

Donna nodded, understanding flooding through her.

'I could never believe the way those women stood by their husbands after they'd been publicly ridiculed . . .'

Carol laughed. 'I can, because without them they're nothing. They don't want to try and find a new life at forty or fifty odd. They want the bills paid, a good car, a nice drum. They want to be paid out for bringing up the kids and taking the flak all those years. They want what the younger bird wants. They want his protection. Even in the enlightened nineties there ain't many women who can survive without a man as well as they do with one.'

Donna sighed. 'I never thought I would talk like this, Carol. I thought I had it all, and I did. But only because I was ignorant about most of it. No, not ignorant exactly. I was deliberately blind, deaf and dumb. The three wise monkeys had nothing on me. I'm only sorry we didn't get more friendly over the years.'

The two women looked at each other, gazed deep into each other's eyes.

'I hated you for years,' Carol admitted in a rush. 'I hated your self-contained ways, your snooty hooter always stuck in the air. I hated the way you talked, acted. I hated you because I couldn't be like you, no matter how I tried. I could only be me.'

Donna grasped the other woman's hand and squeezed it. 'I wish I was like *you*, Carol. I mean that from the heart. At least you take what life gives you and you throw it back into its own jaws. You're strong. A strong woman.'

Carol smiled. She saw Donna's thick glossy hair and understated clothes. The curve of her small breasts covered by silk. She saw the slim legs, knew Donna wouldn't have a real flaw on her body. No stretch marks, no varicose veins, no black roots.

'You're the strong one, Donna, if you only knew it. You had to be stronger than bleeding Arnold Schwarzenegger to keep a man like Georgio for twenty years. Don't put yourself down, love. You've done a great job. Your strength is greater because you never knew you were fighting for Georgio. You never knew the competition.

'I've watched out for it all my married life. Davey never even tried to hide it from me. I've found letters, phone numbers, smelt other women's perfume, and washed off lipstick that ain't mine. That's why I watch him like a hawk nowadays. You'd be surprised at the silly little bitches who want a bit of excitement with a local villain, and that's all Davey is to them. To me he's Davey from Plaistow, Davey I went to school with, Davey I married, and Davey the father of my four kids. I was seven months pregnant when that bastard finally married me and I even had to fight for that. I've been fighting for him ever since.'

Donna asked softly, 'Was he worth it? All that fighting?'

Carol sat up straight and grinned, her hard countenance back in place once more. Carol the hard nut. Carol the villain's wife. 'Some nights when I laid in bed waiting for the bastard to come home, I wondered.'

'And now?' Donna's voice was even softer.

Carol laughed ironically. 'Now? Now it had better have been, darling, or I've wasted the best part of my bloody life.'

Donna didn't laugh. She lit a cigarette and pulled deeply on it before saying, 'He's wasted his too then, if that's the case, because if he didn't want you, why is he still here?'

Carol bit on her lip and thought before she said seriously, 'Because I'm the mother of his children, love. No long-legged bimbo can compete with that. I had my Jamie at forty-one to keep that fucker in his place. He idolises her, she's his baby. That's all I have going for me these days and I'm honest enough to admit it.'

'Then you've got more going for you than I have, Carol.'

Carol could have bitten her tongue for what she had just said. Instead she shook her head sadly.

'That's what I was trying to tell you – you've kept Georgio without any shackles whatsoever. With a man like him, that's no mean feat.'

Donna stood up. 'Oh, there were shackles, Carol. The only thing was, they were all on me.' She walked unsteadily to the door and opened it. 'If you get any more thoughts on Sri Lanka, let me know, won't you?'

Then she was gone, leaving Carol Jackson wishing she could sew up her big fat mouth. Running to the door, she opened it and called out to Donna, who was walking across the forecourt to her car.

'Donna! If you need me, call. All right?'

Donna nodded. Waving in farewell, she carried on walking, unable to see the tarmac through the tears in her eyes.

361

Chapter Thirty-Two

Donald Lewis walked back on to the Wing full of smiles. He looked grey, older and ill. But he also looked more vicious than before. The steely glint was there to stay now, and the sunken cheeks and black-rimmed eyes only added to the overall look of menace. He walked with a slight stoop, his two sidekicks beside him like warriors. No one in the room would have guessed the pain and torture it was for Lewis to get himself in there. He looked around him, nodding here and there at different men. His only real smile was for Sadie. All he wanted was to get back to his cell and lie down, but he knew any show of weakness would be noticed and filed away for future reference. He sat gingerly in a chair and grinned at Georgio.

'Hello.'

Georgio nodded. 'How are you feeling?'

Lewis carried on smiling and said through his teeth, 'How do you fucking think? My back feels like someone just ripped it open with a red-hot knife, but other than that I'm tickety boo as the big nobs say.'

Georgio looked at him in genuine concern. Up close he could see just how weak the man was, and against his better judgement said quietly, 'Why don't you go and have a lie down, Donald? You look fucking rough, mate. Seriously rough. There's no one here who wants to match you in any way. Go and rest, man, before you do yourself a damage.'

Lewis grinned. 'You make me die, Brunos. You nearly had me believing you there. I'll survive. I lived through six bullets, mate. It'll take more than the loss of a kidney to frighten me.'

Georgio shook his head sadly. 'You survived the loss of a kidney, Donald, because of the medical help. Now you're back on this Wing and you're putting yourself under too much stress. Christ, you've just had a major operation, for fuck's sake. Even you're not God, you know. Even you must be aware of your own mortality. You wiped out Timmy, everyone's over the shock. You're still the king pin, so what the fuck are you trying to prove?'

362

Lewis laughed again, only this time it was harsher, bringing all eyes to their table.

'I'm proving once and for all that nothing can keep me down. Now let's walk back to my cell together and you can fill me in on what's been happening. I hear we have two interesting new occupants and I want you to tell me all you know about them, OK?'

Georgio nodded. Rising, he made the mistake of offering Lewis his help. His hand was knocked away with a ferocity that belied the man's sorry condition.

The rec room watched them disappear through the door with the two minders in tow. Sadie laid her head on her arms and thought about Timmy and Lewis. Suddenly she felt a hand grasp hers and sat up in wonder. It was young Benjamin Dawes, the Wing joker.

'Any chance of a bit of a laugh, Sade?'

Sadie looked into the young man's eyes and felt a deep bitterness inside herself.

'How long have you been away, Benjamin?' she hissed. 'A year on remand, and now what, three months in here, and already you're an arsehole bandit? Let me give you a bit of advice, love. You're in on a good one, I admit, but if you can't control your urges you'll end up with the real big one – HIV. There's already three in here carrying the virus that I know of. Now you do yourself a favour, Sonny Jim. You make your right hand your best friend, and if you ever come on to me again I'll shake your dick till it drops off and then I'll wear it as a keepsake! Do you understand what I'm saying?'

Benjamin stood up, all youth and battered dignity. 'I only fucking asked.'

Sadie, recovering her usual bravado, said in a camp voice: 'I hope you treat the real girls better than you do me, sonny!'

The whole rec room cracked up with laughter. Benjamin stormed off, shouting: 'Fucking queens, you're all the same.'

Sadie rolled her eyes and sighed. 'Now there,' she cried, 'speaks the voice of experience.'

All the men laughed again, respecting Sadie for putting the young man in his place, all knowing that if the boy got caught up with Sadie this early in his sentence he'd be used and abused by the bigger men before he was paroled. In nick you had to be able to look after yourself to stop the raping and the abuse that went on behind cell doors. Especially when you were a youngster like Benjamin, who thought he knew it all and knew nothing really.

Sadie sat back in her chair once more, mind awhirl again with one thought.

Lewis was back.

363

Lewis was back and acting as if nothing had happened.

Lewis had smiled, which meant they were still on, and Sadie could do nothing about it.

If young Benjamin were her only problem, how much easier life would be . . .

Lewis sat down on his bunk and Georgio perched himself at the small table.

'So, Georgio, what's been happening?'

He shrugged casually. 'This and that. There are a couple of nonces on the Wing here, as you no doubt know. I didn't deal with them, I thought I'd let you have the pleasure of that. They're paedophiles, little boys mostly but little girls as well. There's a circle of them, been operating for years. They copped the big one, fifteen and eighteen respectively. They're shite.'

Lewis closed his eyes and nodded slowly.

'I know of them. The people we get in here, eh? What would we do with them if we administered justice ourselves? I don't know, Georgio. The Governor must have been off his fucking trolley to stick them in here with us. Who else knows about them?'

Georgio shook his head. 'Sadie knows, but no one else has said a dicky bird. I've seen big Ricky eyeing them up, but nothing definite's come from him. I thought he might just be trying to scare them, you know. The men are getting suspicious because the two of 'em keep together and don't discuss their cases, which in here is like a page three girl in a vest, ain't it? No way would it happen. Everyone talks their cases through, it's the only way to cope in the first few months.'

Lewis raised his hand for silence. 'What's been said about Timmy?'

Georgio dropped his eyes. 'You was out of order there and you know it. He didn't deserve that, and that's the general consensus from everyone. But knowing you like I do, I don't suppose that'll bother you too much. Let's face it, Donald, you enjoy the notoriety, don't you?'

Lewis grinned, showing small white teeth.

'I had a fucking kidney cut out and you have the gall to sit there and tell me *I* was out of order! How long have I been away? Not three weeks, and you're telling me what you think as if I'm some kind of cunt! I lost a kidney. That prick was lucky I was in the hospital when he got topped. I'd have tortured the ponce with my bare hands if I'd had my way.'

Georgio ran his hands through his thick dark hair and realised that for the first time since walking into Parkhurst, he wasn't scared of

364

Lewis. The guy was weak now. Like a dog sniffing at the leader of his pack, Georgio had discovered that Lewis was weaker than he'd thought . . . and that could only be to Georgio's good.

'Let's be honest about this, Donald,' he said firmly. 'You topped Timmy because you needed to make sure the men didn't forget you or what you're capable of. I'm not disputing you took a blow, I know you did, but at the end of the day you wound Timmy up. You *made* him go for you. For the first time ever, someone tried to get back at you – and so you lost a kidney over a transvestite whore who couldn't even pass these days for a rent boy. Why did you want him, Lewis? Why *did* you take Sadie away from Timmy? What was in it for you?'

Lewis grinned again, wider this time.

'I took Sadie because I felt like it. Who was that bloke who said he climbed Everest because it was there? Well, that's why I took Sadie from Timmy.'

Georgio sighed heavily. 'You're not all the ticket, do you know that?'

Lewis laughed again. 'I am well aware of that fact, Georgio. It's what gives me the edge. Another man who'd been through what I've just been through would still be being spoonfed slops in a hospital bed. Life is all about living, and living is all about being the best, being on top, and in this place that means being the hardest bastard around.

'Now, back to the two nonces. What have they had to say for themselves?'

Georgio shrugged again.

'Like I said before, not a lot. But if they're going to be slaughtered, can I have the job?'

Eric drove the route for the jump with Alan. From Portsmouth they followed the M275 to Cobham and from there the A27 towards Drayton. At Drayton they picked up the A3 until they came to Horndean and drove for nearly an hour, chatting companionably until they arrived at the place Eric had picked out for the jump. It was a quiet patch of road bordered by countryside and parallel to a dirt road. It was also spectacularly beautiful. It was known as the Devil's Punch Bowl.

Eric pulled over into a layby and smiled at Alan.

'What do you think?' he asked in his well-modulated tones.

Alan stepped out of the car and stood looking around him at the cars speeding past and the countryside.

'It's perfect.'

'Better still, Al,' Eric grinned as he joined him, 'there's a farm road

365

a little way down, that takes us on to a quiet country lane. It couldn't be better, could it?'

Alan shook his head slowly. 'It's ideal. Fuck me, it's brilliant! And you're sure this is the route that the sweatbox will take?'

'It's the route, all right, they always take the same one. The local police know the score, see, they know the procedure for the laydowns. It's easier than to keep replanning new routes. They're convinced they have it off pat, and they have. But not for the GOAD, see? If Georgio can get himself removed from the nick then we're all laughing. Because then there's only the sweatbox to take care of. We can back and front it, take out the outriders and the police car if necessary. Then it's just a case of getting the driver out of the vehicle because he'll have the key to the back doors. Georgio will be cuffed in a cubicle in the sweatbox. We need the door open and the police out as quick as possible. Then we can take your man out of it.'

Alan nodded, thinking deeply.

'What about the other cars, though?' he said. 'There'll be motors queuing up once we block the road off.'

'That's exactly what we want, Alan. One man will take the car keys off the first three or four cars and dump them. That means once it's all over the Old Bill will have trouble even getting to the scene of the crime, see? We'll have scrambling bikes and be off over the road to the country lane by then. They'll have so much to sort out it'll be pandemonium, and that'll give us precious minutes.'

Alan looked at the road as if visualising it all.

Eric lit a cigar and pointed in the direction of their car.

'I'll explain it all now, briefly. We'll be over there waiting in the farm roadway with a skip lorry, right? No one will know we're there from the road.' He pointed to the left of him. 'The Mercedes van will be parked up over there, as if it's broken down. We'll have a Police Aware notice on it and everything. In the back of the Merc will be three scrambling bikes.

'As the sweatbox arrives, the skip lorry will pull out and we'll pull out at the same time. That's how we'll back and front it. There will be two minutes before the Old Bill collect themselves, maybe more, but we're working on two minutes to be on the safe side. We all pile out with the guns. I'll take the Armalite and go to the front of the sweatbox. The driver will shit himself once he sees it. I'll blow two or three holes in the windscreen, then pour in some petrol. I'll threaten to burn him alive if he doesn't get out of the van.

'Meanwhile,' Eric went on, taking another pull on his cigar, 'you, Jonnie H. and his boys will be all over the place. One of the men takes the car keys, the others are sorting out the outriders and/or the police

366

car. We'll need to shoot out the tyres immediately they stop, the outriders and the main ones. They're on bikes and they can cause us hag, be off and out of it within seconds – so they're the important ones. I'll say shoot to wound not kill, but it'll be so mad here, Christ knows what'll happen.

'Once the shooters go off, especially the Armalite, we should get some good cooperation. I can't guarantee it, though. You know what people are like when they're shit-scared. They could go one way or the other. However, once they're all taken care of, we're laughing.

'Meanwhile, I'm dealing with the bloke out of the sweatbox. Remember – only the driver will have the key to the doors. It always works like that. He alone knows the procedure for opening them. You see, the lock is like a safe – You turn the keys in special positions. The driver will know them off pat. So, I get him to open the doors, we chin the guards inside, lock them in – and we're off! I'll take Georgio on the bike with me.

'We all shoot across the field and over to the country lane, going in the opposite direction from the one they're expecting us to take, because there's a crossroads there. They'll expect us to be moving *away* from the way they came, but in fact we'll be going in the opposite direction until we come to Gibbet Hill about a quarter of a mile away. We'll dump the bikes there, run over the railway bridge on foot, and that's where the safe cars are. We strip off the boiler suits and balaclavas, dump the guns. Georgio slips into the foot rest at the front of the first car, we let him go with you or me, whatever. The rest go in the second car and then it's up to you for the actual safe houses and all the rest.

'The railway bridge is an excellent scam,' he told Alan enthusiastically. 'It's got high brick walls everywhere in case the Old Bill decide to follow with shooters. We can be over it and off in no time. I'll let off a few rounds of the Armalite as we begin to run. That way they'll know we're well-armed. But myself I don't think we'll be followed by them. If we are, they got a lucky strike, and they'll be woodentops anyway out here. Not worth a wank. So what do you think, Alan?'

Alan had listened with interest and growing excitement. Now he grinned widely at Eric.

'I think it's fucking excellent, mate. Excellent. It's as sweet as a nut.'

Eric was pleased. Throwing his cigar on to the roadway, he stamped it out.

'I've already got the ballies and the boiler suits. I've also purchased five red polo-neck sweaters. We'll cut the tops out and just wear them – that way, any witnesses will describe us all the same: red sweaters,

367

black boiler suits and black balaclavas. At least two witnesses will say we were black, they always do when guns are involved. We'll wear black knitted gloves and boots too. They won't see fuck all. When everyone is dressed alike it just confuses the witnesses more. There's no eye colour, hair colour, nothing to be seen. Only Georgio, and the Old Bill already know what he looks like.

'It's the witnesses we want to confuse,' he went on, 'so we shout all the time, except for me when I'm reassuring the driver to get him to open the door. Shouting is the best form of communication on a jump because your voice is completely different from normal. It also intimidates people, and that's what we have to do, ain't it? Scare them shitless, the Old Bill included. I'll put on an accent for the driver, he won't know me from Adam. I'll have the door open and promise him he'll be home in time for tea if he just cooperates. The driver is the worst to look after, see? He is sure that no one can get to him through the bulletproof screen. Once he sees the Armalite he'll be terrified, he'll drop down under the dash. And when the smell of petrol hits him, he'll just disintegrate before our eyes. No one wants to be burned alive, do they?' Eric laughed at his own cunning. 'He'll be as meek as Mary's little lamb!'

Alan laughed with him, excitement giving way to euphoria. 'I can't wait to see the fucking Old Bill's faces, can you?'

'As long as they don't see ours,' Eric joked. 'That's the main thing! Come on, let's get going. There's a Happy Eater along from here and I could murder a cup of tea.'

They went back to the car. Alan stood for a few seconds enjoying the view of the golf course and the surrounding countryside. He smiled and said to the breeze: 'The Devil's Punchbowl, eh?' And, chuckling, he got into the car beside Eric. 'What a name for the Old Bill to write in their statements. Not a bad name, in the circumstances.'

Eric nosed the Volvo back into the speeding traffic. 'On the maps it's classed as an area of outstanding natural beauty. After the jump the Old Bill will never be able to pass it by without a shiver of apprehension – and that, to me, will be the best part of all.'

Alan nodded his agreement and watched out of the window as the countryside passed by.

Georgio watched Donna as she walked jauntily towards him with the teas and KitKats. He saw her slim legs encased in sheer black tights move beneath the short skirt of her emerald green fitted suit. She looked stunning. The suit had large gold buttons on the jacket and she wore gold earrings and bracelets to complement it. Her shoes

368

were four-inch-heeled black suede, plain-looking but obviously expensive. He noticed the looks she gathered from both the men and the women in the visiting room. He saw a young pretty blonde girl give her a wave, and frowned.

As Donna reached the table he said. 'Who's the little blonde?'

Donna shrugged. 'Oh, just a young girl. I give her a lift sometimes, help her with the kids. Why?'

For some reason he didn't understand, Georgio felt a deep resentment. More curtly than he meant to, he snapped, 'She's a blagger's slag, don't give her a lift any more. Her old man's an ice cream. Stupid little fucker. Keep away from her.'

Donna sat down and looked at her husband in undisguised surprise. 'I beg your pardon?'

Either not noticing the tone of her voice or unwilling to heed it, Georgio said nastily, 'I said, keep away from her. What the fucking hell would you have in common with the likes of that, eh? I don't want you giving her or any of these slags in here, a lift – all right?'

Donna slammed a KitKat in front of him. 'Listen, Georgio, I don't know who's rattled your bloody cage today, but don't you ever think you can tell me what I can or can't do. I have a *lot* in common with that little girl, as it goes, mainly the fact that both our husbands are banged up for a very long time. She misses him like I miss you, and unlike me she has to keep two children on a bloody pittance. If I want her living in my house I'll have her there, Georgio. The days of you telling me anything are long gone.'

Georgio and Donna stared at one another in shock, both aware that something had changed between them and neither willing to take responsibility for it. Donna was frightened and exhilarated all at the same time. Georgio's face hardened and for the first time Donna saw him as others saw him.

'That was a big speech, Donna. Who put them words into your trap then? Alan Cox, I suppose.'

Donna's mouth dropped open in shock. 'What? What do you mean?'

Georgio could hear the strain in her voice, see it in her face, and still he carried on speaking even though he knew he was being unfair. Seeing her with the blonde girl had frightened him. He was shit-scared in case the girl ever saw any of his other visitors and mentioned them to Donna. It was this fear that kept him speaking against his better judgement.

'You heard. I know you had a great time in Scotland. Have a nice shower in his flat, did you? Get in with you, did he? You always liked me slipping in a length in the shower, didn't you, darlin'?'

369

She heard the words and registered them, but her own brain would not allow her to answer. She watched Georgio's mouth moving and felt as if she had been punched heavily in the solar plexus.

'I mean, let's face it, girl. You had a weekend to get to know him, didn't you? Was it any good, eh? Got a nice big one, has he?'

Donna began to stand up, her legs jittery and unstable. She couldn't believe what her husband was saying to her, what filth he was spewing out at her as if she was a nothing, a nobody. Seeing her rise, Georgio grabbed her hand, squeezing the skin between his thick fingers until it hurt her.

'Let me go, Georgio. I want to leave, let go of my hand.' Her face was closed, her voice low, the words spoken through gritted teeth.

Georgio felt a wave of panic wash over him and opened his mouth in distress.

'Sit down, Donna. Please, sit back down. I don't know what the hell is wrong with me. Please, Donna, I'm begging you to sit back down.'

He stared into her white face, his own pleading with her to sit once more, to listen to what he had to say. Donna sat down, her heart hammering inside the emerald green suit, the first beads of nervous sweat appearing under her arms and across her chest.

Georgio's voice was lower now, gentler.

'I'm sorry, Don Don. Christ Almighty! I don't know what's wrong with me lately. I'm so jealous of you, darlin'. I looked at you just now and I felt the most awful feeling of loss inside me, it was horrible. I suddenly visualised life without you. If you left me I'd die inside, Don Don. I would, I swear before God. I couldn't go on. Thinking of you, looking like you do, with Alan Cox. I know him, Donna, he's a slag. I know he's me mate but women don't stand a chance with him once he starts his antics—'

Donna interrupted him. 'You're two of a kind, you mean, Georgio?' she said in a low voice. 'You always liked the ladies, or should I say girls? So I showered in Alan Cox's flat. Big deal. We'd been driving all night. But all that aside, it hurts me to think you can't trust me, that you take me for such a tart. After all these years, you could accuse me of that! Me, Donna, the only faithful half of our marriage.'

She leant forward in the chair and said with heavy emphasis, 'Do you know something? It might do you good if I did have an affair, Georgio. It might just make you realise what you've got. I am putting my arse on the line for you, mate. I am trying to keep everything going and all you can do is talk to me like I'm one of bloody Talkto's so-called escorts.

370

'Well, listen to me, Georgio Brunos, and listen bloody good. You ever pull a stunt like this again and me and you are finished. Get that? Finitosberg, goodbyesville as you used to say years ago. "Slipping in a length . . ." you have the gall to say that to me when you spent the best part of our married life fucking anything under the age of twenty-one that showed a bit of leg and looked available. You've got a nerve, Georgio. You've got some bloody neck!'

Georgio listened to Donna in a stupor of shock so intense he felt an actual wave of heat wash over him, followed by nausea. That Donna could talk to him like this spoke volumes. It showed him just how far his wife had broken free, how the hold he had over her had been destroyed. Half of him was excited by this new, strong-minded Donna and the other half was wary, frightened of her. She had bowed to his will for over twenty years; to realise now that she was a strong person, one to take account of, was a dismaying, even alarming thought. She could make or break him now. She could blow him wide open or she could take him through everything he needed to do. Donna, his little Donna, was in charge. Finally and irrevocably she had thrown off the mantel of underdog, and was meeting him as an equal, as a grown-up woman. He also knew that the Donna he had married, the girl who had catered to his every whim and want, was gone. She would never, ever come back.

Donna had emerged as a mature woman, and the knowledge terrified Georgio because he knew he couldn't handle her as an equal. He could never accept any woman in that way. The worst part of it all was that he knew he had to grovel to her for now, had to tell her exactly what she wanted to hear in order to placate her. It was what Donna had had to do to keep him throughout her married life . . . but Georgio decided not to think about that. Instead he put a smile on his face, but as he spoke to her, a seed of discontent grew inside him as he saw himself, in his mind, debased by and before her.

'I said I'm sorry, Donna, what more can I do? I was a fool, I know. I'm jealous, that's all. You don't know what it's like banged up in here night after night, knowing you're outside, able to do what you want. I love you more than life itself. I can't help feeling insecure in the knowledge that you're a beautiful woman who men want and desire. I know blokes who'd give ten years of their lives for a woman as good as you, only half as good as you. Please tell me you forgive me. I couldn't stand it if we parted company today with this between us. Honestly, Don Don, it would kill me.'

Donna looked at Georgio through new eyes and was surprised to note that his impassioned plea had not reduced her to a quivering wreck as it would have done at any time before he went away. The

371

knowledge hurt her, even while she felt exhilarated by the fact she was strong now. Stronger than she had ever been at any time in her life. As she looked into his eyes she thought: Is this all I had to do to get him to notice me? Should I have made him jealous over the years? Should I have fought back when he was unfaithful? Was it all really this easy? Just let him think I was being approached by another good-looking man?

Suddenly, she felt the futility of what her life had been with this man. She had loved him with every ounce of her being and he had haphazardly loved her back. She had been grateful to him for every scrap of affection he had shown her over the years, believing that he was in charge. He was the leader in their marriage, in their relationship. The knowledge stunned her in its simplicity. It was so easy and she had never before realised it. Now he was looking at her as if she was indeed his wife. He was looking at her as a woman and it felt so good. It felt so very, very good.

She smiled at him, a wide smile that didn't reach her perfectly made-up eyes.

'I'll forgive you, Georgio, on one condition. You never, ever speak to me like that again. I am your wife, man, your wife! Not your mistress or one of your little one-night stands. I am Mrs Donna Brunos and you had better remember that in future.'

Georgio nodded even as he fought the urge to slap the smile off her face. Donna stared into his eyes for another few moments before she looked down at her cup and said, 'The jump is in one week. It's to be the twenty-ninth of November and you need to cause uproar here to get the Governor to put you on a laydown. The GOAD rule must be enforced, but you must make them want to remove you from the actual prison, not just off the Wing. Eric thinks you should attack all the sex-offenders, cause a riot on the Wing, and then you must shit up the Governor to put the icing on the cake.'

Georgio listened to his wife in amazement. Today really was a revelation to him.

'I'll shit up the Governor all right, Donna. I'll enjoy that.'

She nodded. Looking into his eyes again, she said steadily, 'You must cause enough of a disturbance here for them to want you out. Myself, I'd say cause a work strike or something not so violent—'

Georgio broke in. 'Nah, stomping the nonces is the best bet, I can get all the blokes wild with that. I just make sure the screws know I caused it all, that I'm the main culprit. I suppose they'll want me to cause it first thing in the morning?'

Donna nodded.

'Then I'll have to plan this myself. The twenty-ninth, you say?' He

372

grinned. 'I'll have it off pat by then, my love, and then me and you will be home and dry. What's happening with the house?'

Donna licked her lips. 'Nothing. I've taken it off the market actually.' She saw his mouth open and held up her hand.

'I think I'd better sit it out with the house for a while, until after the jump. We can easily get it sold by auction afterwards. The whole thing's caused too much talk already. Harry even sent that prat of a wife of his round. No, Georgio, I think it's better for all concerned if we get you out first and then go on from there.'

He nodded agreement even as he felt a blinding rage at her taking the decision away from him.

'If that's what you want, Donna . . .'

She smiled gently. 'It is. I've thought long and hard about it. Georgio.'

She was lying and enjoying lying to him. She had only just thought of it, and somehow she knew she was doing the right thing. The thought of him out, with all the money from the house and everything they possessed, frightened her even as she told herself that this was her husband, her soulmate. But nevertheless she was glad she had made the decision.

Georgio forced a smile on to his face.

'Whatever you want, my darlin'. You do what you've got to do, my love.'

Donna smiled once more and lit a cigarette for herself. 'Oh, I will, Georgio, don't worry about that.'

She pulled on her cigarette hard and, blowing out the smoke, dropped her biggest bombshell of the afternoon, although she didn't realise that until the words were out of her mouth and she saw her husband's stunned reaction to them.

'Now, Georgio, what's happening in Sri Lanka?'

373

Chapter Thirty-Three

Donna watched in shocked silence as her husband's face drained of colour and his thick fingers flew to his chest like an old fishwife who'd had her worst suspicion confirmed.

'What do you mean exactly?'

Georgio's voice was strained, heavy with emphasis. Donna realised that she needed to know not only what was going on in Sri Lanka, but also what was going on inside her husband's head.

There had been too many things left unsaid over the years, too many questions unasked. Before, maybe, she wouldn't have wanted to know the answers; now, however, she knew enough to want to fill in the gaps.

Donna smiled at him nonchalantly. 'What I say. Exactly what is going on in Sri Lanka? Namely, the Bay View Hotel.'

'Nothing that I know of.'

Donna pushed the point. 'But there *is* a Bay View Hotel? It has been built? Only we had a fax about it a few days ago and I'd like to know when it got built, who owns it, and whether or not we can get Lewis off our back with it. After all, it's through the hotels that you fell out with him, isn't it?'

Georgio nodded, scraping about to find a viable excuse to give to his wife.

'It should be built by now, anyway,' he said hastily. 'It's a beautiful place, Don Don. Really upmarket. We'll make a small fortune out of it.'

Donna lit a cigarette and said calmly. 'How can we manage that? Once you're out of here, how are we supposed to run the businesses?'

Georgio was happier now, they were on ground he knew he could cover.

'That's easy, darlin'. What I'll do is put the lot into Stephen's name. He'll sort it out from there, don't worry.'

She stared into his eyes, all the while smoking, and Georgio carried on talking.

'It was going to be a surprise for you, like. That is where I wanted

374

us to go, for a while anyway. Imagine it, Donna, owning your own hotel. It's a real luxury place, all marble floors and colonial décor. That was where I eventually wanted us to end up, see? I wanted to surprise you with it.'

His voice was soft, and as Donna listened to him, the words he spoke were like music to her ears.

'But what about Lewis, Georgio?' she persevered.

He grinned. 'If it's all up and running, then we can sort him out, can't we? All right he might have lost out in Bangkok, but at least the Sri Lankan deal is still sound.'

Donna sighed heavily.

'That fax, Georgio, the one that came a few nights ago. It said there was trouble, government trouble, and that they need help. It was signed "Candy".'

Georgio refused to let her down him. He needed her to think there were great things happening, and he would make sure she thought it if it was the last thing he ever did.

'Look, the only trouble they can have with the government now the hotel is built is trouble with backhanders.' He smiled. 'Oh, don't go all moral on me again, that's the way of the world out there, love. Everything comes down to who knows who and who can pay the most. Come to think of it, it's pretty much the same as here, eh?'

Donna smiled with her husband. 'But I thought it had all fallen out of bed . . .'

Georgio sat up straight in his chair and said seriously, 'Fallen out of bed? That's a Coxism if I ever heard one.' He laughed then, a harsh sound. 'You're turning into a Cockney, girl. I'll have to knock that out of you once we're on the outside.'

Donna didn't laugh at Georgio's quip and he grabbed her hand tightly. 'I was only joking, love.'

'I should think so as well. You ever raise your hand to me, Georgio, and you'll get the shock of your life. Go on – you ask Alan Cox what I'm like these days. I threw a glass of water in his face!'

She was gratified to see Georgio's jaw drop several inches in amazement.

'You what?'

Donna grinned. 'Honestly, we had an argument. Oh Georgio, he can be the most obnoxious man! Anyway, I lost my rag and chucked a glass of water in his face. We were in a restaurant in Scotland; he was soaked.'

Georgio shook his head in amazement. 'My God, if anyone said you would ever do anything like that to me, I'd refuse to believe it. But to Alan Cox! What did he do?'

375

Donna bit on her lip for a few seconds before answering, 'I thought he was going to hit me, to be honest.' She decided not to tell Georgio that he had threatened to put the glass into her face.

'Fucking hell, Donna, what's come over you?'

She stubbed out her cigarette in the tiny foil ashtray and shrugged.

'I don't know, Georgio. I've changed. I think it's all this – it's bound to have an effect, eh?'

He nodded. 'Don't worry, darlin', I'll be home soon and I'll take over the reins again. As for what you did to Alan, I wish I could have been there, I really do.'

They laughed together then, an easy laughter.

'As for the hotel in Sri Lanka, just tell Davey to deal with it. He knows the score. Now then, how about I get us another cuppa and then you can tell me exactly what the score is on the jump?'

As he stood up a small girl came over to their table and grinned at them.

'Hello, Donna.'

She held out her arms. 'Hello, Chivonne. Where's Micky?'

Chivonne settled on to Donna's lap. 'He's with me mum and dad. Is this your dad?'

She looked up at Georgio while Donna laughed at her words. 'Where's your little boy gone?'

Georgio licked his lips and frowned. 'You've got the wrong bloke, little girl. Whose kid's this, Donna?'

'This is my friend Caroline's daughter,' she said. 'You go and get that tea and I'll take her back to her mum.'

Georgio went off and Donna walked Chivonne back to Caroline and her husband. She laughed as she said hello and told Caroline that Chivonne had thought Georgio was her dad!

'Oh sorry, Donna, I thought she was in the wendy house.'

'Where's that man's little boy gone, Mum?'

Donna frowned. 'She just said that to Georgio. What's she on about?'

Caroline shrugged. 'I dunno. Look, your old man's back with your tea. Don't waste your visit. I'll see you outside, OK?'

'All right, then.' Smiling her goodbyes, she walked back to Georgio.

'What a weird little kid!' he said. 'How did you say you know them?'

'Oh her mum is the ice cream's wife – remember? I give her a lift now and then. They're gorgeous children, not weird at all. I wonder why she thought you had a little boy?'

376

Georgio shrugged. Sipping his tea, he said, 'So what's the rest of the news on the jump then?'

Donna sucked deeply on her cigarette and said, 'Once the jump's over with, you're going to be moved to the North of England. You'll be overnight in Liverpool, and then moved on to Scotland. There's a safe house there if we need it, but we're hoping you can be out of the country within thirty-six hours. You're going to Southern Ireland from there, and then on to wherever you want to go. I told Alan it would be somewhere hot.'

Georgio grinned at her, his handsome face shining in anticipation.

'You know me so well, darlin', and now you also know me secret. Me and you will be off to Sri Lanka. After this dump I could do with a bit of currant bun.'

Donna nodded. 'Well, you don't have to make up your mind just yet, there's provision for up to six weeks in Eire. You're to be kept on a smallholding, and it's as safe as houses according to Eric and Alan.' She smiled once more. 'Then we can make up our minds where we're going. After all, I've got to live there too, haven't I?'

Georgio nodded. 'Anything you want, Donna, you've got.' He grasped her small hand in his and kissed the long cool fingers. 'I can't wait to get out and give you something I've been dreaming about for months, girl.'

He leered at her and Donna felt once more the old longings and stirrings he always created inside her when he touched her. But something had happened to them, and although Donna felt she had won something, she also had a terrible feeling she had lost something as well.

Donna dropped Caroline, Micky and 'Vonne outside their block of flats and helped Caroline inside with the pushchair and the carrier bags. Inside the flat Donna put the kettle on and made the coffee while Caroline settled the children in front of the TV.

'So how's everything really?'

Caroline asked the question she always asked when 'Vonne was out of earshot. Chivonne, like most little girls, could repeat back a conversation word for word and it was best not to say too much in front of her.

Donna shrugged. 'The same. Can I ask you something, Caroline? Do you think you've changed at all, since Wayne's been away? Do you feel any different at all?'

Caroline sipped her coffee, her peachy young face breaking into a smile.

'I'll say! When he gets home here, things are going to be different.

377

I have had to sort meself out for so long, I don't think I could handle him coming in here like the big I Am and taking it all over. I even like sleeping on me own now. I hated it at first, but now I like to stretch out in the bed and really relax.'

Donna laughed with her.

Caroline grinned impishly. Shutting the kitchen door, she murmured, 'I've had a bloke and all. Bet you wouldn't have thought that, eh? Met him down the Bingo. Picking up his mum he was, and offered us a life home. Next thing I knew he was round here, only as a friend, like. Anyway, to cut a long story short, me and him had a bottle of wine one night, watched *Basic Instinct* on the old video, and Bob's your uncle.' She looked half-excited and half-ashamed.

'You didn't! How did it feel?'

Caroline shrugged her slim shoulders as if thinking deeply. 'Funny at first, strange. You know, you get used to one bloke, don't you? Then it felt good, really good, because there was no love in it. Nothing but the need of what I was doing, and it sort of got me going somehow. After all this time without the nudger I was ready for something to happen, I suppose. I just never thought about it until the opportunity presented itself. And did it present itself!'

Donna laughed with her and they both felt Caroline's embarrassment and also her need to tell someone what she had done.

'It's funny you know, Donna. We stay faithful, like, but at the end of the day all I had done is scratch an itch. That's all. After being used to a regular sexlife I felt the loss of it deeply. Also I think contact with another person helps you. I like being in bed on me own as I said before, but it's nice to know I can have it warmed up by a tasty bloke with a nice body and a good sense of humour, if I want him. That's the real bonus. It's all up to me. He rings me sometimes and I say, no thanks, not tonight, and I put the phone down and forget about him. Another time I think to meself, "Yes please, Boysie, get your arse round here!" I'm in charge, see? It's all up to me and no one else.'

Donna listened to the younger woman in delight. She was envying her for finding out what life was really all about at such a young age, an age when she could enjoy the discovery and know she still had years to enjoy it.

'I know what you're saying, Caroline. After all those years of living for Wayne and around Wayne, now you're doing things just for you. For no one but yourself. I'm beginning to feel like that too.'

Caroline grasped Donna's hand across the rickety kitchen table and said earnestly, 'I found out that my Wayne was knocking off some bird in Plaistow. It really threw me. Was your old man ever unfaithful to you?'

378

Donna threw back her head and laughed, a deep belly laugh. 'From day one, Caroline. Only for years I didn't let it take root inside me. If I ever mentioned it to him, it would have split us up because once I admitted it to him, I knew I'd have to lose him. In fact there were times over the years when, if I was really honest, I think he wanted me to say something. When he blatantly had affairs. I think on reflection, he wanted me to punish him for them. But being the kind of person I was, I just let him have his head. I wanted him more than I wanted to be without him. I couldn't imagine being without him.'

Caroline smiled and shook Donna's hand gently. 'And now?'

'Now?' Donna closed her eyes and looked deep inside herself for the answer. 'Now, I think I just want to please myself as well. I have done things lately that I would never have dreamed of even a year ago, and though they are bad, they have been good for me. Does that make sense? The years of deeply buried resentment are over and I am finding it hard to carry on as if nothing has happened. I realise that I am the only one in my marriage who gave anything emotionally. Georgio only ever gave me *things*. In twenty odd years together he never once gave me even a small part of himself.'

She opened her eyes and looked into the shining eyes of her young friend.

'I could never have talked to anyone like this before today. Funny, isn't it, really? I always kept everything inside. Because that's what Georgio wanted me to do, and being a right stupid cow I did whatever he wanted. And that included giving up the real me. Yet, even saying all that, I still want him. I still love him. But on my terms now. I want him on my terms.'

Chivonne walked into the room clutching a teddy bear. 'Night, Donna.'

Donna kissed the child's soft cheek. 'Goodnight, 'Vonne.'

'Hang on, Donna. Put the kettle on again and I'll settle the kids down.'

Ten minutes later they were both drinking fresh coffee, and smoking fresh cigarettes.

'I wonder what made her think Georgio had a little boy?' Donna mused.

Caroline shrugged. 'I've got no idea. Kids get strange notions all the time.'

'She seemed so sure, though. The way she was looking at him.'

Caroline pulled deeply on her cigarette and smiled. 'How did your visit go? Wayne was his usual scintillating self!'

Donna laughed with her. 'Not bad. He was like the old Georgio

379

today, the man I fell in love with. I think what you said earlier was right. It does change you, being out on your own. I want more now than before. I want something for me.'

Caroline shrugged her slim shoulders expressively.

'Don't we all?'

Alan looked over the Ordnance Survey map again and retraced the route with his finger. If everything went to plan the jump could be over in under seven minutes and Georgio could be well on his way to Liverpool before the road blocks were even in place. He grinned to himself.

The police and the prison service would not know what the hell had hit them. It would be a national security job, and would receive national press and TV coverage. They had to make sure that everything went exactly to plan in Liverpool and in Scotland.

He tossed back his scotch as the phone rang and let his answering machine pick up the message.

He heard his own voice telling the caller he wasn't available and then frowned as he heard Jonnie H.

'Alan, ring me back soon. I've some news for you.'

He picked up the phone and said, 'Jonnie? What's going on?'

Jonnie's voice was agitated. 'To be honest, Alan, I don't know, mate. But I've heard a whisper that Georgio is being put up for another robbery. The word on the street is that he's also into something deep.'

Alan's voice was heavy with sarcasm. 'With respect, Jonnie, we hear these rumours all the time. I've heard them about me—'

Jonnie interrupted. '*What?* You've heard that you're supposed to be into beasting then, have you? Only that's the word on Georgio.'

Alan's voice was incredulous. 'Beasting! Are you off your trolley, man?'

Jonnie H. laughed. 'I know it sounds mad, but I'm only telling you what I heard, Alan, no more.'

Alan's voice was dismissive. 'You tell whoever is putting these lies about that I have known Georgio Brunos since childhood and he would no more be involved with beasting than he would be a grass. Who told you, Jonnie? Let me sort them out myself.'

Jonnie's voice came over the line so low Alan thought he had not heard him correctly.

'Say that again, Jonnie. Who?'

'Nick Carvello, and you know Nick. He wants to know the score.'

Alan put the phone down, convinced the whole world had gone mad. Nick Carvello was not a man to cross at any time, but his thoughts on beasting were legendary. If he thought Georgio was

380

involved in anything like that, Georgio could kiss goodbye to his jump and probably the use of his legs.

Picking up the phone again, he dialled a number and realised that his hands were shaking.

He was in for an even bigger shock.

Donna picked up the phone only after the policewoman nodded at her to do so.

'Hello.' Her voice was small, frightened.

She listened to Alan's voice and cut him off. 'I can't talk, Mum, the police are here, searching the house.'

She put the phone down and looked once more at the policewoman, who stared back at her as if she found her offensive. Donna dropped her eyes in confusion. She could hear Dolly's strident voice coming from the small office.

'You've got a bleedin' nerve, coming round here and turning over law-abiding people! What are you doing? I've only just cleaned that place up! I hope you're going to tidy up when you go!'

Donna sank down on a chair in her lounge and listened to the noise and confusion around her. The lounge looked like a bomb had dropped on it. Drawers were turned out, the carpet had been pulled up, the glassware in the cabinets was scattered all over the place. They were taking up the bedroom floorboards now and she could hear the dull thump of tools and the muted voices of the police officers as they laughed and joked their way through their job.

Standing, she walked towards the door. The policewoman immediately stood in front of her.

'You're not going anywhere, lady.'

The voice was deep, manly, and Donna saw as well as heard the contempt in the woman before her. A rush of annoyance came over her and she shoved the woman out of her way roughly.

'You got the "lady" bit right anyway. Now I want to talk to whoever is in charge, and I want to know what bloody grounds they have for tearing apart my home!'

She stormed out into the hallway and stood uncertainly for a few moments, not sure exactly what to do. Picking up the onyx hall phone she dialled Harry and Bunty's number. Harry answered himself.

'Hello, Harry? The police are turning over my home and you said if I needed any help, I only had to ask. Well, I am asking now. Georgio is already doing eighteen years. What more do these bloody people want, eh? What else is he supposed to have done?' She asked Harry the questions as if he could answer them and this wasn't lost on him.

'Stay put, Donna. I'll see what I can do.'

381

She smiled grimly into the mouthpiece. 'You do that, Harry. You do that.'

Slamming down the phone, she stormed up the stairs and walked into her bedroom. A male CID officer was holding up a sheer black bra; he had obviously just made a joke and Donna felt the rage build inside.

'Well, as you can see, young man, they're hardly big enough to hide anything inside, so why don't you put my underwear back in the drawer like a good little boy and then get the hell out of my house!'

Frank Laughton was standing in the doorway of the ensuite bathroom and he felt a moment's sympathy for the woman in front of him. He could see the hurt, fear and confusion in her face.

'We're only doing our job, love,' he told her steadily. 'We have had information relating to a series of crimes we believe your husband was involved in. We have to follow it up.'

Donna looked into the man's face and said through clenched teeth, 'Well, I hope you can prove it, because I have never even had so much as a parking ticket. This is my home, I own it lock, stock and barrel, and I know my rights. I'll haul your arses into court over this, boy, for harassment, whatever. But I'll see that you pay for this day's work. If it's the last thing I ever do, I will make you smirk on the other side of your face. My husband is doing eighteen years – isn't that enough for you, Mr Laughton? What have we ever done to you, eh? What is all this really about?'

Laughton couldn't look her in the face. Instead he walked to her dressing table and pushed her underwear back into the drawers.

'Your husband is a violent criminal, whether you like to admit to that or not, love. He was tried by a jury and put away in accordance with the laws of this land. We have gained information, as I said earlier, that your husband, Georgio Brunos, was involved in other activities. A man who was arrested on charges of manslaughter and robbery has put your husband's name forward, and we are honour bound to check out the accusations he made.'

Donna clenched her fists and said to Laughton, 'So you think I have money hidden under the floorboards, do you?'

He laughed. 'Not you, love. Maybe your husband hid something there. It has been known before.'

'You turned this house upside down after you arrested him the first time. If anything is there now, Mr Laughton, you must think that I put it there. Surely that follows, doesn't it. So *are* you accusing me of anything today?'

Laughton sighed heavily and looked around him at the younger policemen. His look said Donna was a foolish woman and this was not

382

lost on her. Turning, she stormed from the room. At the bottom of the stairs the policewoman was standing with her arms folded. Donna ignored her and slipped past into the kitchen.

This room was also a shambles. Dolly sat at the kitchen table, her face a tight mask of anger.

'Bloody real, ain't it, eh? Have you seen what they've done to his office? Like a shithouse it is. I hope to Christ they're going to clear up behind them.'

As she spoke the phone rang and Donna picked it up, pushing another police officer out of her way as she did so and glaring at him until he walked away from her.

'Hello?' She smiled and held out the phone. 'Tell Mr Laughton it's his superior on the phone, would you?'

Ten minutes later Donna shut the front door behind Laughton and his officers. She watched from her lounge window as the police cars all moved off her drive, shame at what had happened vying with rage inside her. As soon as the last car departed she ran into Georgio's office. The desk drawer had been forced open and she felt afraid, even though she wasn't sure why. Dolly stood in the doorway and held out the fax and another bundle of letters.

'Are these what you're looking for, Donna?'

She took the papers from Dolly's outstretched hand. Taking the floppy disc from her own pocket, she held the whole bundle to her chest.

'Oh, Dolly, thank you.'

Dolly looked into her eyes. Then, shaking her head, she turned away.

'You're in over your head, lovie. I've seen it coming for weeks.' Her voice was sad. 'I'll make us both a cuppa and then we can get cleared up. Maeve will be here before you know it, and probably Stephen, so be prepared.'

Donna looked down at the papers and the disc. She didn't know why these were important, but instinctively she felt they were. Sitting on the office chair, she wondered what had happened to her over the last year to make her change so much. Was it because of Georgio or was he just a symptom, not the cause? Whatever had happened she knew one thing now for sure. She was indeed in over her head, and even if she wanted to get out of it all, she couldn't.

That was the worst of it. She was in for the duration now.

The days of choices were over.

Alan listened to the policeman's voice and fought down the urge to tell him to shut the fuck up. Instead he murmured the right words.

383

Putting down the phone, he poured himself another scotch and sat by his window, watching the world of Soho coming to life. It seemed a young man by the name of Danny Kilbride had put Georgio's name up for three robberies in Essex. Alan knew that the boy was lying. What he needed to find out was who the boy was lying *for* – and why.

His bell rang and he pressed the intercom gingerly, not sure what other surprises the night might hold for him. It was Stephen Brunos and Alan let him in, relieved it wasn't the police, wondering why he was so sure they would be coming for him.

Stephen looked as suave as ever, only a few tell-tale worry lines across his forehead to show what he really felt.

'I suppose you've heard?' Alan said. 'It seems a young feller by the name of Danny Kilbride has put Georgio's face in the frame. I heard from Jonnie H. tonight that Georgio was to be fitted up but I didn't think it would happen so fast.'

Stephen shrugged. 'It's all bullshit. Probably another of Lewis's games.'

Alan saw the logic of this and nodded. 'I also heard today that Georgio is involved with beasting,' he went on. 'Is there any truth in that?'

He watched Stephen's eyes widen to their utmost.

'What the fuck do you think, Alan? Can *you* see Georgio involved in anything like that? I mean, you know him as well as anyone does, don't you? It's another bloody load of shite. I bet Lewis is having a field day. Can you imagine what it will be like for Georgio inside if that mud ever sticks?'

Alan sipped his scotch again, his mind reeling from all the shocks of the day.

'Georgio has made some bad enemies, Alan,' Stephen went on, 'and I think you know exactly what the score is with him and Lewis. But that aside, we want him out. We all want him out, don't we? When is the jump, Alan, tell me that.'

He shrugged. 'I don't know – early in the New Year, I should think. What has Georgio said to you about it all?'

Alan watched Stephen battle it out with himself. He knew that Stephen knew nothing, and that's how Georgio wanted it. Why Stephen should think Alan would tell him remained to be seen . . .

'How much do you know, Stephen? Only Georgio is keeping a very close mouth about everything to me. In fact, I think only Donna really knows what is going on.'

He watched Stephen's reaction.

'I don't know any more than you do, Alan,' Brunos admitted bitterly. 'Donna and me aren't exactly friends these days. She sticks her nose into everything – the bitch is a pain in the arse. Once Georgio is out I hope to Christ he drops her like last week's news. Do you want to know what really makes me laugh? She's seen more of him since he's been banged up than she did in all their years of marriage. You know Georgio, he was always off gallivanting somewhere.'

Stephen laughed delightedly. 'That woman is like a fucking leech, do you know that? She has hung on to him for the last twenty years by her fingernails. Well, I could blow her world wide open but I won't. Not just yet. I'm waiting till I can do her the most damage. Then I'll open my mouth and I'll enjoy watching her squirm.'

Alan was shocked at the hatred in Stephen's voice as he spoke about Donna. He hadn't realised just how bad Stephen's animosity towards her had grown.

'What's Donna ever done to you, Stephen?' He was genuinely curious.

Stephen looked into Alan's eyes and said seriously, 'She's tried to push her way into my businesses, and I can tell you now, Alan, no one, but no one, does that. Even Georgio didn't ask me what I was doing. She could cause everyone so much trouble if she wanted to. If she got arrested she'd be singing her little heart out before they'd finished cautioning her. Think about that the next time you have any dealings with her. She is unreliable and she is a woman. The two go hand in hand. I wouldn't trust any woman, but her less than any of them. She is dangerous, very dangerous, and my brother can't see that.'

'Your brother loves his wife very much.'

Stephen sniggered. 'Oh he does, does he? We'll see about that, Alan. Donna Brunos has got a short sharp shock coming to her, and I can't wait to see her face when she finds out exactly what it is.'

He glanced at his watch. 'I'd better make my way over to her. The police should be long gone by now and I have to play the dutiful brother.' He sneered again. 'But I'll have me day with her. If you only knew the half of it!'

He laughed, but it was a hollow sound. 'Beasting? Georgio? Now I've heard everything!'

Alan let him out and went over everything that Stephen had said in his mind.

Why did he hate Donna so much? What was the real cause of it? And what could Stephen possibly know that could harm her so much? The two questions lingered in his mind, even as he picked up the phone to find out all he could about Danny Kilbride and Donald Lewis.

385

Chapter Thirty-Four

Bunty's face was a picture. In spite of his fear, Harry was enjoying her discomfiture.

'That woman could inadvertently blow the lot of us out of the water. Can't we do anything?' she whined.

Stephen yawned behind his hand. He had never liked Bunty; he cared for her even less than he did Donna.

'We need to keep calm, Bunty,' he told her now. 'I'm going out to Sri Lanka tomorrow, and I'll sort everything out when I get there. Once this little lot is over, things can go back to normal again. We're all making a lot of money, you two especially. Georgio's money is being banked for him. Stop worrying! It was a fright, but it's over.'

Bunty looked at him with open animosity. 'What do you know about it all? My Harry had to lay his arse on the line tonight to stop that bitch down the road from being hassled. She knows a lot more than she's letting on, Stephen. You'd better find out just how much she does know. Ask Georgio what he's told her. She has us all over a barrel at the moment.'

Stephen stood up. 'I'll sort it all out, OK? I just said I would, didn't I?' His teeth were gritted. 'Once I have seen Candy and the man I'll have everything sorted and we can get back to normal. By the New Year most of the operation will be in Germany and France anyway. Relax, stop worrying, and most of all, play the game. No one would suspect you two. As for this Danny Kilbride, he's working for Lewis or my name's Jack Nicholson. It's just another fright for Georgio, that's all. Lewis is trying it on to make Georgio pay him the money. If we keep cool heads, we'll be home and dry in no time at all. Now I'd better get round to Donna and do my concerned brother-in-law bit.'

Harry watched Stephen as he left the house.

'What do you think, Bunty? Should we take a dive now? Pass it all over to Georgio and Stephen?'

Bunty made a very unladylike snorting noise with her lips.

386

'Don't talk out of your rectum, Harry, you know it annoys me. We could make a blasted fortune in the next twelve months. Look how much we've already earned.' She flopped down on to the sofa beside her husband and laughed gently.

'We'll give it one more year, then me and you can retire with Daddy and do all the things we ever wanted to do without ever having to worry where the money's coming from.'

Harry closed his eyes.

After tonight, the prospect of the money didn't seem so appealing to him. They were involved in something so big, the very thought of it scared him, and caused him sleepless nights. His wife, who as a woman should have been against what they were doing, was getting greedier and greedier by the day. He wished he had never met Georgio Brunos, wished he had never been tempted to get involved in any of it.

In fact, he wished he had never met Bunty, her father, or any of them.

'What are you thinking about, Harry?'

Bunty's voice was harsh. The nasal twang grated on Harry's ears.

'What am I thinking about? You actually, darling.'

He saw the absurd look of pleasure on her face and sighed again.

He was trapped, and he knew it.

Donna watched as Stephen nailed down the floorboards and relaid the carpets. He tutted loudly.

'You'll have to get a proper carpet-fitter in to replace this lot. They've just ripped it away from its tracks. Bloody bastards they are. I bet you got a shock when you came home from the visit and found them in your house, didn't you?'

His voice was neutral and Donna nodded in agreement. The emerald-green suit was crumpled now, and her make-up smudged. She caught a glimpse of herself in the mirror and sighed. The house was still upside down. Maeve and Dolly were clearing up downstairs and Donna was supposed to be doing the bedrooms.

'That's the understatement of the year. Still, at least they didn't find anything. That's the main thing.'

Stephen was amazed at her words. For Donna to openly admit that there could have been something *to* find shocked him. It seemed that she had finally grown up. Georgio had always been like some kind of god to her. It pleased Stephen to see the once too-good-to-be-true Donna Brunos finally embroiled in things that were not legal. He smiled to himself as he stood up.

'Georgio is a survivor, Donna. He'll get over this lot the same as

387

he's always gotten away with everything else.'

Donna looked at him quizzically. 'I hardly call doing eighteen years getting away with anything, do you?'

Stephen pursed his lips and thought before he answered her. 'It depends on what he was supposed to be getting away with, doesn't it? You have obviously realised that your golden boy is involved in some pretty heavy stuff. If the half of it were known he'd still be locked up, but they'd throw away the key. But there, that's nothing to do with me, is it?'

He smiled at her superciliously and Donna felt an urge to take back her fist and slam it into his insufferable face.

She was saved from answering by Maeve bustling into the room with two mugs of coffee.

'Oh, look at the state of this place, would you! What the hell were they looking for, I ask meself?' She glanced around the room and shook her head. 'Here, drink this.' She gave them both a mug of coffee. 'What time is your flight tomorrow, Stephen?'

'At two-thirty. I'm going to shoot off in a minute, I haven't even packed yet.'

Donna sipped the thick aromatic coffee, grateful for its warmth and fragrance.

'Off to Rhodes again, are you?' she asked. 'When's Mario going?'

Maeve picked some clothes off the floor and placed them on the bed. 'Stephen's not off to Rhodes, he's going on a short holiday to Sri Lanka. Booked it a few days ago.'

Donna felt the icy sensation at the back of her neck that denoted trouble. She said nonchalantly, 'You lucky thing. I'd love to visit Sri Lanka. Georgio and I were planning to go before . . .' she paused. '. . . before all this happened.'

Stephen had the grace not to look at her. 'I just thought I'd go out for a break, that's all. I've always liked it round there. I was in Goa last year if you remember?'

Donna nodded, watching him warily. 'Whereabouts are you going to?'

Stephen lifted his shoulders in a gesture of forgetfulness. 'Can't remember the name.'

Maeve turned from hanging up the clothes and said, 'Hikkadoa, isn't it? Something like that anyway. I heard you telling Mario about it the other day and the name stuck in me mind.'

Donna smiled. 'Never heard of it. Sounds nice though.'

Stephen put down the coffee mug with a clatter. 'I wonder if they've interviewed Georgio tonight?' he said suddenly. 'If they turned this place over, you can bet they've dragged him off to be interviewed. What on earth could they have been looking for? Any ideas, Donna?'

Maeve watched them look at each other and sighed inwardly at the open animosity on their faces.

'No idea whatsoever. Do you really think they'll be questioning my Georgio?'

Stephen nodded. 'I'd lay money on it, love. They don't do all this on a whim. They must have something pretty good to get the warrant for this lot. You want to be careful now, they might be watching you.'

'Why would they watch me?' Donna's voice was on the defensive.

'I don't know. All I can think is that they must believe you're involved, to do all this. You said yourself they'd already turned the house over when they arrested him the first time round. Why do it again now?'

Stephen enjoyed Donna's worried expression. Pleased he had finally taken her mind off Sri Lanka, he turned towards his mother and kissed her on the cheek.

'I'd better be off, girls, I have a long journey tomorrow.'

After he left the room Maeve said gently, 'He's me son, Donna, but I'm finding it increasingly hard to like him these days. He's gotten a slimy feel to him, do you know what I mean?'

Donna nodded into Maeve's strained face and said, 'Funnily enough, I know *exactly* what you mean.'

Georgio was put back on the Wing just as breakfast was being served. He walked straight to Lewis's cell and strode in without the usual knock. Donald Lewis was eating a bowl of thin porridge, the *Guardian* spread out over the table in front of him. Without looking up, he said. 'Hello, Georgio, I've been expecting you.'

Georgio ripped the paper off the table and screwed it into a ball.

'What the hell was all that about last night, Donald? Don't pretend you know nothing about it because I have sussed you right out, mate. Fucking right out!'

Lewis laughed. His small even white teeth looked yellow in the light of the cell.

'Getting brave all of a sudden, aren't we?' He pushed his bowl of porridge away and said nastily, 'Sit down, Brunos, and shut the fuck up. When I want your opinion, I'll ask for it.'

Ricky stood inside the doorway. 'Do you need anything, Mr Lewis?'

Donald shook his head. 'If I need you, Ricky, I'll call. Stand outside and keep nosy parkers at bay.'

389

Georgio sat down because he knew he had no choice.

'Now, Georgio, me and you have been getting on very well since I've been out of hospital but there's still the outstanding matter of my dosh. I have decided that I want it, and I want it soon. If I don't get what I want then I'll see that you never walk out of here again. I can fit you up as easy as I can eat my breakfast.

'A young man called Danny Kilbride is on a murder charge. I've already arranged for him to co-operate with the police and now they're talking manslaughter. I have got word to Kilbride to put all the blame on you for three robberies in the North of England. You might get off them, but it won't do your appeal much good, will it?

'I want me fucking money, Georgio, and I want it as soon as possible. The ball is well and truly in your court. By the way, your house was turned over last night – floorboards up, the lot, turned over by Laughton, your old friend and mentor.

'I'll give you so much grief, boy, you won't know whether you're coming or fucking going by the time I'm finished! I'll have your parents' restaurant razed to the fucking ground and I'll have your sister Mary and her kids go on the missing list. I swear before God now, either me and you make an arrangement and become bosom pals again, or I'll make you into my biggest enemy – and you know what that'll mean in here, don't you?'

Georgio felt the dryness in his throat. He didn't need this now. In another two weeks he'd be out of this place, home and dry. Lewis would be just a bad memory . . .

Lewis watched Georgio battle it out with himself, then he played his trump card.

'Don't give me all that old fanny about if I kill you I'll never get the money. I ain't doing this because of the money any more, Brunos. This has become personal now. I'll kill you if I don't get it, and Timmy's death will seem like a joy after what I've dreamt up for you, boy.'

Georgio knew that Lewis was telling the truth. After the attack on him, he had to come back bigger and stronger than ever. Georgio knew that people on the Wing had heard the rumours about him owing Lewis money and now Lewis had to push the issue to save face. To show his strength. Georgio didn't even hold this against him. It was prison law, far more binding than the law of the land.

'So what's it to be, Georgio?'

He bowed to the inevitable; after a swift planning session in his mind, he smiled in a defeated manner.

'I'll have the money for you within twenty-eight days. I'll have to get someone to fetch it for me, but that won't be a problem. I want

390

your word, however, that this will be the end of it all. Me and you trundle along nicely, I don't want us to fall out after this.'

Lewis held out his hand. He had won the game and could afford to be magnanimous.

'No hard feelings, Georgio. I'll call the Old Bill off your back and me and you can get down to planning what we're going to do on this Wing. It needs a shake-up and between us I think we could do the job perfectly adequately.'

Georgio grinned. 'You won, fair and square, Donald. Now about those two nonces . . . Can I have your word that you'll let me have them? I've been racking me brains for a way to do them and I think I could really liven this place up at the same time. In your name, of course.'

Donald picked his teeth with his fingernail. 'Of course.'

Georgio and Lewis grinned at one another and Georgio winked. He could afford to be as friendly as he liked. All in all, it couldn't have worked out better for him.

From now on Lewis would be like his Siamese twin. He wanted his money and Georgio wanted to cause a disturbance the like of which Parkhurst had never seen before.

'Shall I get us both a nice cup of tea?' he offered.

Lewis nodded happily.

'Why not?'

Alan saw Donna before she saw him. He studied her sitting by the window table of his restaurant, sipping mineral water and watching the world go by. He smiled to himself in pleasure. She really was a very good-looking woman. She was as usual, dressed immaculately, her plain black dress cut high at the neck, tailored and smart. She wore sheer black tights and high black shoes. She looked businesslike yet painfully vulnerable at the same time. She wore a deep red lipstick and the slash of colour gave her a childlike appearance.

He walked over to her, smiling in welcome and waiting to inhale the fragrance of her perfume. The Chloë smell had become uniquely hers to him. Flowery, cool and crisp. That summed up Donna Brunos.

'Hello, Donna. I didn't expect to see you here today.'

Donna looked up into his face and he saw the worry in her eyes.

'They busted me, Alan.' Her voice was low. Taking the seat opposite, he signalled to the waiter.

'I heard. But it's all sorted now. According to a friend of mine, Lewis set it up for Georgio. He owes Lewis a large amount of money.'

Donna nodded.

391

A tall dark-haired girl came over to the table, dressed in the regulation black skirt and white blouse. Donna saw the smile for Alan and felt a moment's jealousy at the girl's easy way with men.

'Bring us a bottle of red wine – a half decent one, Charlotte, if you don't mind. And the menu, OK?'

The girl was exquisite. Her perfect skin glowed and Donna knew it was not thanks to foundation.

'Certainly, Mr Cox.'

Donna closed her eyes. To add insult to injury the girl had a very attractive French accent.

'Pretty girl.'

Alan nodded in agreement. 'Very pretty. Only twenty, but she's as clever as Einstein. Should do well.'

Donna sipped at her mineral water again. 'Do you know why Georgio owes Lewis money?'

Alan shrugged, not committing himself. 'I've heard a few rumours, of course. Nothing concrete.'

The girl came back with the wine and Donna caught a subtle hint of Coco perfume. Charlotte expertly opened the wine and poured it into the glasses. She placed a menu before each of them and, smiling once more, walked away.

Alan sipped the Mouton Cadet and licked his lips.

'So what's the score with Lewis and your old man?' he asked.

'Georgio went into business with him in Sri Lanka and Thailand. They were to build hotels and jump on the tourist bandwagon, Georgio after all was a builder, as you know. It was to be legal, all legal, he explained it to me.

'Well, the rub is, Alan, the man out on site tucked him up. It turned out that he had no permission for the sites, no government agreement, nothing. Georgio lost a small fortune, and unfortunately so did Lewis. That's why Georgio got involved with the robbery. He had been stripping the other businesses for capital and nearly ruined himself, Alan. Well, you know the rest.'

He didn't speak for a while but allowed the information to sink in, wondering how much was true and how much was Georgio's idea of a good story.

'What do you know about Sri Lanka and Thailand? Have you any documentation, anything that can corroborate this story?'

Donna shook her head. 'Nothing much, just a few letters and brochures. I received a fax the other day saying they were in trouble. Then last night after the police left, Stephen turned up and I find out that he is off to Sri Lanka. That seemed very suspicious to me. I don't trust him.'

392

She gulped at her wine as if it would give her some kind of help, and finished: 'If Stephen is involved I would bet my last halfpenny that something illegal is going down. The fax also had another message on it. It said "stopped shipping until further notice".'

Alan grabbed her hand. 'Cheer up, girl, we'll find out the score, especially once Georgio's home. I admit that Stephen can be a pain in the arse, but for all that he's shrewd. Maybe Georgio wants him to sort it all out, especially if Lewis is on his back. I must admit if you were my wife, I wouldn't want Lewis coming after you, whereas I wouldn't worry too much about Stephen. You concentrate on the jump. It's not long now and then we'll all know what the score is.'

The waitress came back again and asked them if they were ready to order.

'Give us two house specials and have Julio set a table in my office. Open another bottle of wine and then leave us in peace, love, OK?'

The girl's face was a picture and Donna felt a moment's pity for her. Alan picked up the wine glasses and the bottle and Donna followed him up the stairs to his office.

He sat her on the small sofa and she watched as he directed Julio where to put the table. When he finally sat beside her she was smiling.

'You're a real busybody, Alan Cox – has anyone ever told you that before?'

He chuckled. 'My wife used to say that. I've always been an organiser. It's in my nature.'

'Would you ever marry again, Alan?'

He was surprised by the question and she saw it.

He shook his head negatively. 'Not on your nelly, girl. I'd never get tied to anyone again. Would you?'

Donna frowned. 'Would I what?'

'Ever get married again?'

Donna sat back on the chair, amazed that she even had to think about the question.

'But I'm not divorced, am I? I'm still married!'

Alan stared into his glass as if it had become the most interesting thing in the world.

'Of course; I'd forgotten that!'

They laughed easily together, both aware that she had got out of answering the question.

'What do *you* think is going on in Sri Lanka?' Alan asked her.

Donna shrugged. 'I really don't know. I was a bit sceptical about Thailand, I must admit. Especially now with Stephen being involved. I wouldn't put it past him to have a brothel out there to be honest.

393

But not Georgio. I know he was involved in Talkto but that was only on a sponsorship level. He is a sleeping partner.'

Alan grinned, displaying his large white teeth.

'You mean, *you're* a sleeping partner. Remember, that's all yours now. Even the hotels are in your name if I know Georgio.'

Donna stared at him from under her eyelids.

'They are. In fact, I'm quite a rich woman on paper.'

'Should I make a play for you then, before all the toyboys arrive?'

He looked at the door as if expecting them to rush through it and Donna grinned.

'Toyboys? Do I look that old?'

Alan placed a hand gently on her cheek.

'You look lovely, Donna, you always do to me.'

He stood up abruptly and refilled their glasses. Both were aware that he had stepped over the boundary line. Neither was sure how to react now that he had. Alan returned to his seat and lit himself a cigar.

'So Stephen's off to Sri Lanka then? I wonder what they were shipping? Stephen's into so much it'd be hard even to guess what he's doing out there, wouldn't it?'

Donna nodded. 'If it's Stephen, it's bound to be something disgusting. It always is with him. In fact, I was thinking of going out there myself. I own the properties along with Lewis so I have a right to see what's going on. But Georgio wants me to leave it until he's on the outside, so that's what I'd better do.'

Alan nodded vigorously. 'That's what I'd do – leave it all. Let Georgio clear up any mess that's left. It's about time he pulled his bleedin' weight!'

They laughed together.

'This wine's gone to my head, Alan. I haven't eaten anything today.'

She lay back against the sofa once more and closed her eyes. Her face in repose was so achingly lovely in the lamplight that Alan felt a constriction in his chest. Leaning across her, he brushed her lips with his. Donna's eyes flew open and as she looked into his deep blue gaze she opened her mouth to accept another kiss. A real kiss, a deeply sensuous one.

Losing herself in the sensation of being touched by a man who wasn't her husband, she allowed him to begin caressing her, feeling the fullness of her body rise up to greet his. She felt his hand pushing between her legs and opened them involuntarily, wanting the touch of him. As his fingers explored her thighs there was a knock at the door.

394

Donna pushed him off her as if he was a rapist and jumped up from the sofa, knocking over her glass of wine. She straightened her clothes and tried to control the trembling inside her body, in her hands. Not trusting herself to speak, she walked into his bathroom and shut the door quietly behind her. Leaning against it, she placed her forehead on the cold painted wood and took deep breaths. She could hear Alan directing the waiter about the food. Splashing cold water on to her face, she stared at herself in the small mirror. Her eyes were bright, her skin pleasantly flushed. Her lipstick was gone, kissed away by Alan Cox.

She knew that if the waiter had not knocked she would have been unable to refuse Alan. She had been too long without a man, too long without the company of her husband. The drink and the circumstances had proved too much for her and she swallowed deeply as she realised just what she had been willing to do. And God Himself knew, she *had* been willing! In her mind's eye she played out the scene, allowing it to reach a conclusion, and no matter how much she tried to deny it, she still wanted it to happen.

She realised she had wanted Alan for a long time. The shock to her was the fact that he felt the same way about her. He wasn't a man who would take her lightly Not Georgio's wife.

For him to want her, it had to run deeper than that and even as the thought thrilled her, she was frightened because she felt out of her depth. Never a woman to encourage men, she wondered how she had encouraged Alan Cox. She must have done, because he wouldn't touch his friend's wife without thinking he had the right. Her permission and Georgio nearly home! She took a few deep breaths to steady herself.

Opening the door, she walked back into the room. Alan was sitting at the table eating a steak as if nothing had happened.

'All right, girl? Come and eat your meal. You're right, the wine went to both our heads, I think.'

Donna picked up her bag and walked to the door.

'I'm sorry, Alan, but I think it's best if I go now. Let's forget about tonight, it was just a moment's madness brought on by too much wine.' She kept her voice light.

Alan cut another piece of steak and shrugged. 'Whatever you say, love. You're in charge.'

Donna walked from the room, her heart heavy in her chest because more than anything, she wanted to stay there. Stay and re-enact the scenario that had played in her mind minutes before.

She knew one thing. She had to get away now, and she had to keep away.

She had enough problems as it was.

395

★ ★ ★

Donna and Dolly sat together drinking hot chocolate and eating toast and Marmite.

'We haven't done this for ages, Donna, have we?'

She shook her head and munched on her toast.

'Why have you taken the house off the market, love? I phoned the estate agent because that other couple was supposed to be here today and they told me about it.'

Donna wiped her mouth with a napkin and said, 'I've decided not to sell, that's all. Georgio's not too happy about it, he wanted it all sold, the lot.' She looked around her at the furniture, carefully picked over the years, and tended with love and care.

'You're doing the right thing, love,' Dolly told her sincerely. 'Donna I need to ask you something and I want a truthful answer.'

Donna looked at her quizzically.

'What, Dolly?'

'I know that Georgio is getting out.' She held up her hand to stop Donna either denying or confirming what she said. 'What I want to know is, do you stand by everything he's done?'

Donna took a deep breath. 'It would seem that way, wouldn't it?'

Dolly looked into the face she loved so much it distressed her at times because the owner of that face was a grown woman with a streak of naivety it pained her to see.

Donna put down her piece of toast and looked back at Dolly properly. The two women stared into each other's eyes for long moments before Donna answered.

'Let's just say I accept what he's done, Dolly. I can't say I agree with any of it. Why are you asking me all this?'

Dolly looked away, concentrating on the table as if it held the answer to the world's problems, then she began to speak.

'A while ago I found some things that I guessed could have caused serious trouble, Donna. It was just after Georgio was arrested. I put them away, I don't know why. I just knew they could cause bother and I didn't want that. Not for me, you, or Georgio. Especially not for Georgio. You know how I've always loved him like my own son? I love the both of you.

'But something has been puzzling me, and I think I had better tell you everything now. I know how much we have grown apart and I take the blame for it. You see, Donna, I trusted Paddy with all this. He was working for Georgio, you see? Can you understand! I thought it was all for the best . . .'

Donna looked at the woman's bent grey head.

'Dolly,' she said gently, but perplexed and anxious now, 'I don't

396

know what you're talking about love. Tell me what this is all about.'

Dolly stood up and went to her large leather-look handbag that had caused many jocular comments from Georgio over the years. It was a shabby affair with worn plastic handles and Dolly took it everywhere with her. She often joked that her whole life was in that bag, from her birth certificate to her Post Office savings books. Opening it, she took out two magazines. Walking back to Donna, she placed them on the table before her.

One cover showed a girl of about twelve. Her face had the bland complacency that is the mistaken stereotype of Oriental womanhood. A man stood behind her, his hand clasping a barely formed breast. The girl's face was covered in thick make-up, making her look like a parody of a woman; her vagina, in perfect pink and olive colours, was devoid of pubic hair.

Donna looked down at the picture and felt the revulsion inside herself. Dolly placed the other magazine on top of it and Donna shook her head in bewilderment.

This one showed a small boy, Asian-looking, with large liquid black eyes staring into the camera. His fear was evident, as was his thin naked body. Two men were beside him, two large-bellied men whose faces were obscured by the camera. From the angle of the photograph it was quite clear what they intended to do to him.

'Where the hell did these come from?' Donna's voice was a whisper, because without being told she knew the answer.

'Both these mags were in the garage. There were stacks of them in boxes, along with two boxes of computer discs. Paddy picked the boxes up but not before I had slipped out one of each magazine. I don't know why I did it, but I did. Oh, let me explain. Paddy rang me and told me to go into the garage and place the boxes outside for him. He told me I wasn't to let on to you – well, we all knew that. Georgio always kept everything from you so that wasn't unusual. It was only that the boxes weren't sealed, you see. That's what made me look inside. I wish to hell I'd never been near or by them.

'Anyway,' Dolly went on, 'I put them out of my mind, convinced myself that it was something to do with Paddy and nothing to do with Georgio. I couldn't bring myself to believe that he could be a party to this . . .' she waved her hands at the magazines . . . 'this filth. If you look inside those magazines it would turn your stomach. Little children, Donna, they're all little children . . .' Her voice cracked and Donna grabbed at her arm.

'But what has this to do with Georgio?' she asked frantically. 'Why are you showing them to me now?'

'Because, Donna, the boxes I moved outside for Paddy to pick up were addressed to Georgio Brunos. They had a Liverpool postmark.'

'That doesn't mean anything . . .'

'If they were addressed to him, then he must have known about them. He had visited Sri Lanka just before, Donna. If you look through these books, all the children are foreign – either Indian-looking or Thai. Now Stephen's going out there, isn't he, after you get a fax saying they're stopping the shipping?'

Donna stared at Dolly, trying to take in what the older woman was saying. As the meaning hit her she began to shake her head.

'Never, not in a million years, no way. Not my Georgio. It's that piece of slime, Stephen. Stephen the woman-seller, the pimp, that's who's behind this little lot, Dolly. My Georgio hates anything to do with sex-offenders. Remember how he used to carry on about them, and rapists as well? He wouldn't be caught up in all this, I know he wouldn't. He never even so much as had a blue film in our home. I can't, won't believe he knew anything about this.'

Dolly sighed and lit herself another cigarette from the butt of her previous one.

'Well, Donna, it came from somewhere. If the police had found these . . .' She left the sentence unfinished.

Donna stood up and paced the kitchen floor.

'That's it! Maybe Georgio knew nothing. Perhaps Big Paddy was just using this place as a pick-up point. The dirty bastard! Bringing that filth into my home!'

Dolly watched Donna for a few moments before she said, 'But Paddy has no interests in Sri Lanka or in Thailand, as far as we know anyway. Lewis and Georgio were in that partnership, and knowing Lewis like I do, this doesn't surprise me about him at all. To be honest, I'm not so sure it surprises me about Georgio either. Not now.'

Donna turned on Dolly like a vixen.

'Don't you dare cast aspersions on my husband like that, Dolly. I will not have it, do you hear me? Georgio is a sod, God knows I've had to accept that myself over the last year, but this! Never. I'd stake the next ten years of my life on that.'

She stopped her pacing and lit a cigarette.

'Did you say computer discs earlier? There were boxes of discs?'

Dolly nodded.

Donna closed her eyes.

'They're still at it, Dolly,' she said in a voice that shook. 'It *is* Stephen.'

She ran from the room to Georgio's office and grabbed the floppy disc she had slipped out of the box in the car lot.

'They're still at it, even now, and Davey Jackson is involved as well.'

She laughed with relief.

'It's not my Georgio. I knew it couldn't be. I knew even he would never stoop that low.'

Then she cried.

Chapter Thirty-Five

Donna sat in front of Georgio's computer. It was a large Gateway 2000, and over the past few months she had begun to use it occasionally for letters and invoices to do with the businesses. Now, it had taken on a sinister feel. The office too had a dark quality she had never noticed before. She turned the computer on and put in the start-up disc, listening to the familiar whirrs and scrapes with heightened awareness as the computer read the disc's information.

Dolly stood behind her, her breathing loud in the room. Once the index was displayed, Donna took the disc from her and loaded it.

'Get us a large scotch, Dolly, I think we might both need one.'

Dolly slipped from the room and Donna stared at the computer screen, flickering eerily in the dim office.

The disc menu was on display and Donna studied it intently.

> MESSAGES
> GIRLS AND BOYS COME OUT TO PLAY
> BABIES IN THE WOODS
> BOYS ONLY
> GIRLS ONLY

Donna felt a sick sensation in her stomach. Directing the mouse to MESSAGES she pressed Enter. The screen cleared and a letter appeared before her, just as Dolly trotted back into the room.

'Here's your drink, love.'

Donna stared at the screen as Dolly placed the whisky beside her on the desk.

'What's that all about?' She read the letter out loud.

Greetings,

All work's on time and ahead of schedule. Germany is ready, Maldives have received modem line. Can soon distribute to Liverpool, and bypass London altogether.

This new batch is probably best ever.
Getting hang of it all now. New bloke working out fine.
Give my regards to everyone at The Black Dog and tell them I'll be
over soon.

Candy.

Dolly and Donna stared at the screen intently, as if it was going to talk and answer their unasked questions. Donna exited from the letter and the index returned to the screen.

Dolly's voice was high as she said, 'BOYS AND GIRLS COME OUT TO PLAY? What the fuck kind of message is that?'

Donna placed the mouse beside the message and pressed Enter. 'Well, we'll soon find out, won't we?'

The screen cleared. The few seconds of whirring as the machine read its memory were agonising and then a large message appeared on screen:

BOYS AND GIRLS COME OUT TO PLAY!

Donna pressed the page-turner and immediately a picture appeared before them. It was in full colour and was also strikingly clear.

It showed a girl of around ten years old in a school uniform, a tight, short-skirted school uniform. The girl was Asian, with thick dark hair in pigtails and grotesque make-up: red lips and heavy blue eye-shadow. She held up the hem of the skirt to display her vagina and belly button. She was smiling out at them and Dolly took a step backwards in shock.

'Holy Mary, Mother of Christ. I didn't know you could put pictures on these things!'

Donna turned the pages. Little boys were displayed, then girls and boys together, in disgusting poses with one another. Girls with girls and boys with boys. It wasn't until the twentieth page that men appeared on the screen, and always their faces were not visible. It was either the back of their head, or else their face was obscured by a child's leg or arm.

Dolly picked up Donna's drink and placed it in her hands. 'How do they do this, Donna? I never knew they could do this.'

Donna took a large gulp of her scotch and sighed. 'The technology now is amazing, Dolly. If my guess is right, they're sending this down a phone line. It's just the next step from a phone call, really. The keyboard is the dial and the telephone receiver is the screen. It's like making a visual phonecall. The graphics are brilliant nowadays, as you can see.'

401

'So Georgio was using this computer to bring the stuff into the country?'

Donna shook her head. 'You can do this anywhere, Dolly, on any compatible PC.'

'Well, I think there's something fishy going on here with all of them,' Dolly said fiercely. 'Davey Jackson, Georgio, the lot of 'em.'

Donna gulped at her scotch. 'That's what I have to find out, isn't it?' she said bitterly.

Dolly sighed. 'How are you going to do that, girl? Ask your man himself?'

Donna pushed her hair back off her face and said seriously, 'No, Dolly, I wouldn't accuse Georgio of this unless I had the proof and I haven't any proof at all he was involved in any of it.'

Dolly snorted through pursed lips. 'What the hell more do you want, my girl? You're blinkered where he's concerned, do you know that?'

'The Message file on here said "Give my regards to everyone at The Black Dog". Well, The Black Dog is one of the holdings I own with Stephen through Talkto. I will pull the address from the files and go and find out what I can from there.'

Dolly was annoyed. 'You won't have anything said against him, will you, Donna? Can't you see that he has to be in on all this, eh? Are you telling me it was going on behind his back then?'

'I don't know, Dolly, but I can find out,' Donna said desperately. 'And until I know for certain then I'll take it my husband, the man you supposedly love like a son, is innocent. I can't accept that Georgio would have anything to do with this lot. I know him better than anybody, Dolly. Better than you or Stephen or anyone.'

'Yeah, you knew him so well he was masterminding bank robberies behind your back—'

Donna interrupted. 'No, Dolly, you don't understand. I know his *heart* better than anyone, and he would no more have anything to do with all this than you or I would. It's Stephen and Davey Jackson who are the culprits here.'

Dolly's belly laugh surprised her. Turning the chair away from the screen Donna said vehemently, 'My God, Dolly, you've changed your tune.'

Dolly's face was grey in the muted light of the computer screen, and suddenly Donna saw how old she really was, the deep lines around her eyes and mouth emphasised by the pale light.

'Maybe I have, Donna, but I've a terrible presentiment in me bones that you're going to find out things you never dreamt of before, couldn't have imagined in your wildest dreams in fact, and they'll all

402

boil down to one person – Georgio.'

Donna turned the computer off and the room was dark. Opening the curtains, she turned on Dolly and said, clearly and heavily, 'You watch your mouth, lady, before your find yourself out of a home and a job.'

Then she walked from the room, leaving Dolly staring behind her.

Edna McVee was a big girl, a very big buxom girl, and she knew her worth. She made that quite apparent as she took a toke on her joint and said loudly, 'Bollocks, Henry. I get a tenner a time or I go somewhere else.'

Henry, a small-boned Maltese man with a pencil-thin moustache and handmade shoes, weighed up in his mind his chances against Edna without a blade. He sighed deeply as he realised she would probably kill him.

'Fair enough, you fat slag,' he said nastily. 'But I want a good show, right, and the touchers pay me first. Deal?'

Edna smiled and it transformed her face magically. Under the thick make-up and backcombed blonde hair you could see her youth and prettiness shine through for a few short seconds.

'The touchers pay *me*, Henry, remember?' she sneered.

'I ain't being funny, mate, but you're getting greedy, and if you get too greedy we'll all leave eventually. This ain't the only shithole in London, you know.'

Henry bowed in the face of adversity and sixteen stone of young womanhood before him and smiled craftily.

'Get your fat arse in the booth then, we've got customers waiting.'

Edna stood up in all her heavy glory, the silk basque she was wearing straining to keep her size forty-six double D breasts in place, and waltzed from the small office and out to her booth. Edna knew she was popular. The men liked the big girls, with big breasts and thighs and rounded white arses. She knew her worth and she made sure she got it. It was as if the bigger she was, the more they felt they were getting for their money.

Henry watched her swagger out and grinned to himself. He had to hand it to Edna. She was one of the few toms he knew who could actually look after herself. She never touched hard drugs, just a bit of puff, and never drank alcohol while performing. In reality, he wished he had a few more like her, but Edna McVees were rare in the peeping game. Most were smacked out of their heads, otherwise they couldn't do the job, and he admitted to himself that he would have to

403

be in a fucking coma himself before he could do anything even remotely like it.

Whistling now, he left the office and went downstairs to the small bar area. The bar was illegal really, they had no licence, but as it was only for members he didn't worry too much about it. The men and the occasional woman who used The Black Dog were after that little bit extra and he supplied it. Or tried to anyway.

The smoke hit him as he walked into the bar and he coughed slightly.

'Put the fan on, Carrie, for fuck's sake. What you trying to do, choke the fucking punters!'

Carrie laughed as she flicked the ancient switch to the ceiling fan and said loudly, 'No, Henry, they pay to choke me normally!'

He laughed good-humouredly at the joke and his astute eyes roamed around the small cellar room. As usual it was filled with City gents, with the odd working man here and there. Early evening, which in Soho was until eleven o'clock, always saw the same clientèle. Men who had homes to go to, and wives and kids to see.

He walked through the bar and into another cellar room. Here were the brocade curtains that separated the small pallets that passed for beds. During the evening the beds, twenty-six in all, would be in full use over and over again. He smiled as he thought of the money and rubbed his hands together unconsciously. He wrinkled his nose at the sour smell and went back into the bar area, leaving the door open as a signal to the people working there that the night was beginning.

Immediately a man stood up with a transvestite boy of about sixteen and slipped through the open doorway.

Carrie ticked a small X on a chalk board behind the counter. The evening was on its way and she knew that she had to keep a keen eye out from now on. The number of workers who tried to slip one in without paying the house was getting ridiculous.

Whistling once more, Henry went back upstairs to the peep booths. He walked into a small booth and put his hanky up to his mouth to stop the smell of semen and sweat making him gag. Treading warily, so as not to ruin his good suede shoes, he popped a fifty-pence piece into the small opening before him.

A grid went up and looking through he saw Stella, an old professional at the peepshow game, gyrating around on a stool. She was tall, thin, and wearing nothing but a small G-string. Satisfied that she was doing her job, he opened the money box with a key and emptied out the fifty pences into a bag he kept in his pocket.

The smell was disgusting and as he locked the money box once

404

more, he walked out, crying at the top of his voice, 'Sid, wash this fucking place down. It smells like a Turkish wrestler's jockstrap!'

Sid, an old man in his seventies, wheezed towards him, smiling, with mop and bucket.

'I'm going as fast as I can, Henry. It's been really busy today.'

Henry laughed. 'Don't give me that, Siddy, you dirty old git. If you spent as much time washing the booths as you did wanking in them, we'd have a clean bill of health in no time. Now this is your last warning, old man. Keep the booths clean, right, or you're out!'

Siddy pulled out the mop and washed over the small wooden seat in the booth, then he mopped the floor. Unlike Henry, the smell didn't bother him. He had lived with that smell day and night for nearly thirty-five years.

Wiping his shoes with a clean white handkerchief, Henry's eyes widened in amazement as he saw a small striking-looking woman standing in the doorway. Turning on all his oily charm he said in his best imitation of Bob Hoskins, 'Can I help you, love?'

Donna looked at the small man's white teeth and Armani suit and smiled widely.

'Henry Pratt, I presume?'

He grinned again and said, 'Well, I ain't Doctor fucking Livingstone, love. What are you after?'

Donna walked towards him and said gently, 'I am after you actually. I'm Donna Brunos. Stephen asked me to keep an eye on things while he's on vacation.' Henry liked the vacation part of her answer, to him it spoke of sophistication and poise, but he still didn't trust her. Henry didn't trust his own mother; it was inbred in him not to trust anyone.

'Well, he never said nothing to me, love.'

Donna forced her smile to remain in place as she answered him. 'As I own twenty-five percent of this business I don't think he need tell you anything, Mr Pratt. Now I want a drink and a looksee and then I'll tell you what I'm here for, shall I?'

Henry wiped his tongue around his teeth and then shrugged. 'Suit yourself, but I need proof of who you are, darling. I can't let any Tom, Dick or Harry mooch around the place. You could be Old Bill, darling, though you ain't got their usual smell if you'll excuse the personal remark.'

Donna opened her briefcase and took out a file from her Talkto portfolio, handing it to him along with her driving licence.

Henry glanced at them perfunctorily and then said, 'Should have brought along a wedding photo, only in all the years I've been here I ain't never seen you before, lady.'

405

Donna snatched back the file and said, 'My husband was never doing an eighteen-stretch before. Now if you want to phone Big Paddy, I'm sure he'll verify who I am.'

Donna's heart was beating in her chest for fear that Henry might decide to do just that. Then on an inspiration she said, 'Or I'll tell you what. Suppose I nip round the corner and get Alan Cox? Will that be enough proof of who I am for you?'

She saw his face blanch and smiled gently to herself.

'It's no trouble, I can easily bring him here,' she went on. 'I run all Georgio's businesses now, even his businesses with Alan Cox, so don't worry about putting him out. He'll understand.'

Henry shook his head and smiled graciously.

'There's no need for that, love, but you must understand that I have to be a bit circumspect, what with the filth crawling all over us. Come through and I'll take you down to the bar for a drink.'

Donna replaced the files in her briefcase and walked through the booths with Henry. The music was louder inside the building and Donna felt the throb of heavy rock vibrating through her temples.

'These are the booths where the peeping goes on, love. Want a shufti?'

Donna nodded, dreading what she was about to do.

Taking one of the fifty pences from the bag in his hands, Henry walked into the nearest booth and put it in the slot, grateful that Siddy had wiped the semen from the walls, seat and floor. That was all he needed, Georgio's wife covered in some wanker's cum.

Donna watched as the grid rose up. Wrinkling her nose at the sour smell, she put her eyes gingerly to the slit. It was the size of a letterbox in length, but was wide enough to get a hand inside, or a face. She watched a huge girl gyrate to loud music, her face blank. Her hand disappeared between her heavy thighs and Donna straightened up, nausea assailing her as she swallowed deeply. But she was grateful at least to see a woman in the booth. She realised she had half-expected to see a child.

'What's the average age here?'

Henry laughed. 'They lie about their age. Toms lie about everything, even what they had to eat – it's a part of their lives, see? But the average age here is from seventeen to about forty-five. We have one woman in her fifties who we use on Wednesdays because it's quite slack then, if you'll excuse the pun!'

He roared at his own joke and Donna followed him along the corridor and down into the bar itself.

As they walked down the narrow stairs she heard the chattering and clinking of glasses that was the trademark of bars everywhere.

406

Unlike the upstairs, this bar had softer music being played from a large stack unit behind the bar. Pink Floyd's *Welcome to the Machine* was playing, and Donna saw in the dimness a few people dancing.

As they approached the bar, Henry said, 'This is where the real money is, as you know. The peep's a good front, it's legal and smelly enough to keep out most of the Vice Squad. They want the bigger fish, always have done, though they've closed us down a couple of times because of the filth up top. The booths get rotten with the punters, you know. In the height of summer the smell would knock down an elephant. Some of the girls stink like pole cats, the dirty whores. What can I get you to drink?'

'White wine and soda, please.' Donna sat on a tall stool at the bar and looked around the room. It was decorated with pictures of women and men in the nude. Some were the everyday kind of thing you could pick up in Woolworth's, others were blown up from hardcore magazines. Women touching themselves, men with women; but no children visible anywhere, thank God.

At a corner table, Donna saw a girl of about fifteen talking to a man in his sixties. The girl had on a small crop top and a tight leather skirt.

As Henry handed Donna her drink she flicked her head and said, 'She looks a bit young. Surely that's asking for trouble, employing jailbait?' Her voice came out hard and neutral and she was amazed at herself.

Henry shrugged. 'She's sixteen, love. Looks younger, but that won't last. A few years tomming and they age overnight. One day you see them and you're shocked, you know. But she's a real pro, worked the Cross for two years before she came to us. Hard as nails she is, and an excellent little worker. With respect, Mrs Brunos, this is the rough end of a rough trade. That's where our money comes from. All the men in here are regulars or are brought by regulars. We have live shows here on a Friday and Saturday, we cater for all sorts. All the whores here, women and men, are specially recruited and they work here because they want to. It's like I said to Stephen a while ago. If we don't employ them, someone else will. He's a bit greedy, your brother-in-law, and these people know their worth. They have to, to survive.'

Donna nodded. The hopeless despair around her from both clientèle and workforce hit her hard. The place was squalid and dirty and until that moment she had never realised such hellholes existed. Two men stood up and slipped from the room. Henry watched Donna as she watched the two men.

'Follow me, love.'

407

Donna followed him across the bar itself and then through the doorway. In the light from the naked bulbs she saw the partitioned room, but it took a few seconds before she realised what was going on. As she walked along the middle of the room, she saw the two men embracing each other intimately. The curtain was barely closed and the younger man looked over the older one's shoulder and winked at her saucily.

Henry laughed at her green-tinged face.

'This is what we're dealing with. They're animals, love. Now, have you seen enough?'

Donna nodded and walked quickly back to the bar. She gulped at her white wine and swallowed it heavily.

Taking pity on her, Henry said, 'I'm sorry, love, I shouldn't have done that.'

Donna pulled herself together and said nastily, 'It's the queers I hate, that's all. It sickens me.'

Her voice was so hard he believed her straight off. It affected a lot of people like that. Lesbians never bothered anyone, but two men could be like a red rag to a bull.

'Drink up and then I'll take you through to the office, OK?'

Donna nodded. Glad her lie had been believed. As she followed him from the bar and up the stairs her hatred for Stephen Brunos rose inside her like a wave.

This place was a sewer, the people in it like rats. Rats caught up in something they couldn't get out of.

In the office she regained her equilibrium and said, 'Has Stephen been in touch from Sri Lanka?'

Henry shook his head. 'Never gets in touch when he's overseas. Not with me anyway. I heard though that the hotel's doing well. Candy comes here to see me when she's in the Smoke, but I don't hear much from her otherwise. She stays in the flats in Wardour Street. Likes the Chinese girls does old Candy, and there's plenty of them round there!'

He chuckled to himself and Donna nodded in agreement, wondering what the hell he was talking about.

'Do you use the flats there, Henry?'

He shook his head, his face hard as a rock as he answered stiffly, 'Too pricey for me, love. Not only that, the youngsters ain't my forte. I have a nice wife and nice kids. I'm happy with that.'

Realising her faux pas, Donna smiled.

'Sorry, I should have thought before I asked you that.'

'That's all right, Mrs Brunos, but Stephen will tell you I ain't never been involved in all that stuff, and I don't want to know about it, to

408

be honest. I leave all that to the coons round at The Heartbreaker. You want to see Christopher round there. He'll give you the keys and the low down.

'Now, do you want to see the books? Only I'm a busy man. No disrespect to you, Mrs Brunos, but that lot downstairs will have me over if I don't keep me boat right in front of their faces.'

Donna shook her head. 'That's OK. I just wanted a working knowledge really. I can look over the books another time. Thanks for all your help, I appreciate it.'

Henry smiled gently. 'Will you be taking this place over then, when Stephen goes to Germany?'

Hiding her surprise, Donna answered him on a laugh.

'That, Henry, remains to be seen.'

He stood up and held out his hand. 'Nice meeting you at last. Give Georgio my best. I'll see you again?'

Donna nodded and shook his hand heartily. He walked back down to the bar and Donna made her way towards the exit, the heavy stench of human bodies deep in her throat. As she passed the peep-booth at the entrance, a man walked out zipping up his flies. Donna could see the flush of excitement on his face and the trembling of his hands.

He looked into Donna's eyes, and seeing the revulsion there, his face went from a pink flush to a deep embarrassed red.

He stumbled out of the doorway into the cold of the evening, Donna following closely behind him.

The Heartbreaker was a small club just off Wardour Street. As Donna walked through the double doors, a large West Indian man approached her. He was big, shiny black, and handsome. He smiled at her easily, showing large pristine white teeth.

'Yes?' His voice sounded amused.

Donna looked steadily into his face before she said: 'Christopher?'

The man licked thick lips and shook his head. 'No, woman, I ain't Christopher. Who wants him?'

'Tell him Georgio Brunos's wife wants him, would you? Stephen asked me to call.'

She saw the man's eyebrows rise and would have smiled if she hadn't been so terrified. But forcing a hard look into her eyes she said belligerently, 'I haven't got all night, you know.'

The man turned from her, his sheer size slowing his progress as he sashayed over to the reception desk. A redheaded woman looked at him askance as he picked up a phone and dialled a number.

'Hello, Chrissy? I have a woman out here, says she's Georgio's

409

wife, wants to see you. Shall I send her through?'

He replaced the receiver.

'Wait here, he'll be out in a while.'

Donna stood in the small reception area and took in her surroundings as she waited. The redhead was in her fifties and painfully thin. Her eyes were cleverly made-up, and Donna admired her expertise. On closer inspection she realised with a shock that the woman was at least sixty. She smiled faintly at Donna, and when the doorman went into the club itself she said, 'What brings you here, Mrs Brunos?'

Donna smiled in a friendly fashion. 'Just a bit of business, why?'

The woman shrugged daintily. 'Just wondered. How's that handsome old man of yours, eh? Haven't seen him for a while. Then, I don't expect you see much of him, do you?'

Donna's eyes glittered as she threw back: 'I see enough of him, love.'

The woman smirked. 'Don't get your knickers in a twist, I was only stating a fact. He was unlucky there.' She looked through the doorway into the club and then bending forward said softly, 'A word of advice. Be careful of Chrissy. He's a dangerous fucker and he looks like butter wouldn't melt, OK?'

Donna nodded, wondering what the hell the woman was being so nice for. In her small forays into the underworld of Soho she had already established that people only gave you what you bought from them. Money was the order of the day and its voice was loud and crystal clear.

'I'll bear that in mind.'

As she spoke a tall handsome black man came out of the club doorway.

'Can I help you?'

Donna was stunned by his upper-class English accent.

'I am here because I need the keys to the flats in Wardour Street. Stephen asked me to keep an eye open for him while he was away. I'm Donna Brunos, by the way, Georgio's wife.'

She held out a hand which was ignored.

Christopher smiled widely. Then he said in a thick West Indian dialect, 'Listen, lady, I don't give a fuck who you are or what you want. Stephen Brunos has no right telling you anything, OK? Now you go back to wherever it is you come from and don't you ever come near me or mine again, OK? You taking that on board or shall I have someone embed the message in your brain?'

Donna looked into cold black eyes, and realised that she was actually in mortal danger. When she didn't answer, the man grabbed hold of her arm.

410

'Listening to me or what, woman? Georgio don't scare me, the man ain't been born yet who can scare me, but I scare plenty of people – your old man and his brother included. Now fuck off, lady, before I lose my temper.'

The redhead walked out from behind the counter and said gently, 'Leave it now, Christopher, I'll deal with this. You go back inside and leave it all to me. I'll see Mrs Brunos off the premises.'

The man turned, opening his mouth as if to disagree, then stormed away, the bouncer following him after a swift movement of the redhead's arm.

'Come on, love, I'll see you to your car.'

Donna allowed herself to be led from the foyer of The Heartbreaker, her chest tight with fear and shock. Outside in the cold night air the woman walked her along Wardour Street and into a small café.

'I'm fine, really.'

The redhead made her sit down. 'Have a coffee, you'll feel better.'

She ordered two coffees. Sugaring her own, she said to Donna, 'What brought you to The Heartbreaker? Not Stephen Brunos, love. He hates your guts. What do you really want?'

Donna lit a cigarette with trembling hands. 'Who are you?'

The redhead grinned. 'Answer my questions first and then we'll see about introductions.'

Donna sighed heavily. 'I just want to know what's in the flats here, that's all.'

The woman lit herself a cigarette from Donna's packet.

'Why? Why are you so interested?'

Donna stared down into her coffee cup without answering.

The woman pulled her face up and looked into her eyes.

'I asked you a question – what's the big interest? Now if I don't find out, Christopher will. And I know him, love, better than anyone. He'll want to know what the score is. I'm trying to help you here if you could only see it.'

'I want to know who the girls are, working them, and where they come from. That's all.' Donna looked steadily into the older woman's face and saw her relax.

'Let me give you a small piece of valuable advice. Where Christopher Scott is concerned, don't ever try and find out anything. Even the filth leave him in peace. Now, Mrs Brunos, you get yourself home and forget tonight, OK? I'll tell Chrissy it was all a misunderstanding. He'll believe me, and then we'll all forget this ever happened, OK?'

Donna didn't answer.

'I don't think your old man would thank you for aggravating

411

Christopher – in fact I know he wouldn't. Neither would Stephen. He's in Chrissy's bad books as it is.'

'Does my husband work with Christopher, in those flats, I mean?'

The woman shook her head and laughed. 'Nah. Georgio is nothing to do with the flats, love. That's between Christopher and Stephen.' She saw Donna's relief and smiled again. 'Happy now?'

Donna didn't answer.

'Forget about tonight and the flats,' the woman urged again. 'Believe me when I say that I am giving you sound advice. Christopher Scott is not a man to cross.'

Feeling better now, Donna said pointedly. 'How come you know so much about Christopher, Stephen and my husband?'

The redhead lit another cigarette with the butt of her old one. 'Christopher is my son, love. I'm Violet Scott.'

She saw Donna's eyes widen in shock and laughed. 'I own The Heartbreaker. Christopher works from there, but it's my club. I had five sons, and Chrissy is the eldest. I was a tom for years, didn't know who any of their fathers were, but I ain't telling you anything you wouldn't hear around the West so don't think this is a confessional. I'm well-known, love, very well-known. Now you look like a nice little body and I don't want to see you get hurt. Ask Stephen about the flats, but don't you ever come near or by me or my son again. I can't be responsible for what he would do to you, OK?'

Donna stared at the woman, but didn't answer.

Violet Scott sighed heavily. 'You're a foolish girl. There are certain people you just don't cross, right, and my son's one of them. Leave it. Just leave it.'

Standing up she left the café but Donna remained there, cold and tired and drinking coffee, as she tried to sort out exactly what she was going to do next.

Chapter Thirty-Six

Donna arrived home at four-fifteen in the morning, to find Dolly still awake and waiting up for her.

The older woman's face was a picture of tragedy and Donna, remembering her cruel words earlier, felt shame wash over her. Dolly had always been there for her over the years, had been like a surrogate mother, and she had repaid her lately with harsh words and threats.

Dolly poured out a cup of coffee for her and then sat at the kitchen table.

'What happened, love?'

Donna stared into the strained, lined face and felt the futility of it all mount up inside her. Swallowing back tears, she said, 'I went to a club called The Black Dog. It was a peepshow place, full of dirty old men, prostitutes and transvestites, to name but a few. I wanted to see if there was any connection to Sri Lanka there, but I struck out. All I saw there was human degradation – the result of men's needs, Dolly, not women's. The only need the women there had was for money. Anyway, from there I moved on to a club called The Heartbreaker, where I was threatened by a large black man called Christopher Scott, and given coffee and more threats, nice ones, this time, from his mother, Violet.'

'I know her, or should say I know *of* her. She ain't a bad old stick really. It's her sons who are the maniacs.'

'Well, nice old stick or not, she warned me off, Dolly. There's some flats in Wardour Street with Chinese kids in. I know it's kids, I have a feeling on me that it is, you know. One thing I did find out from this woman is that Georgio has nothing to do with them anyway. The flats, I mean. It's Stephen. It's always bloody Stephen.'

Dolly bowed her head and sighed.

'What really gets up my nose, Dolly, is the fact that Georgio is doing eighteen years and that prat is out and about in Sri Lanka. Probably setting up more little kids. Maybe he even gets his rocks off with them, I don't know. But I can tell you this much. As soon as I

413

can get a flight, I'm off out there to find out the truth for myself.'

'You're not seriously going over there?' Dolly exclaimed, rattled.

Donna nodded vigorously. 'I certainly am, Dolly. I am going to see just what the hell is going on over there, in this so-called Bay View Hotel, find out once and for all if Georgio is involved. I'll tell you something else for free. If he *is*, I'll see him rot in that place, with his brother beside him. Stephen the Wonderboy is about to get a surprise visit.'

Dolly stood up and said sternly, 'You are not going out there alone. No way. Are you bloody stupid or something!'

Donna laughed heavily. 'Oh sit down, Dolly, for Christ's sake. I have to go. Who else can do this, eh? Are you going to go? Big Paddy? Who else would do this except me?' Her voice softened. 'Don't you understand, Doll, I *have* to go. I need to know exactly what's going on and who the hell is behind it all.'

Tears in her eyes, Dolly said sadly, 'You're making a big mistake. Take this lot to the police, Donna, let them sort it out.'

'I can't, not yet.'

Dolly sat back down, her old bones protesting at being up all night. 'What you mean is, you have to know if your man is involved?'

Donna looked into her eyes and nodded sadly. 'I have to know one way or another, Dolly. I have to see for myself.'

Dolly was silent for a while and then she said, 'I remember you when I first came to work here – a pretty, quiet little thing, madly in love with her husband and trying to be a good wife. You wouldn't say boo to a goose. I saw you overcome your natural shyness to be a good hostess for Georgio, saw you grieve over your babies, saw you keep your head held high, saw you keep your self-respect. Lately, I wonder where that little girl has gone.'

Donna replied in a voice filled with pain, 'That girl grew up, Dolly, the day her old man got eighteen years and she was forced to live in the real world. Shall I tell you something? If nothing else good comes out of all this trouble with Georgio, at least I grew up, Dolly. And not before time! Now I have to find out what's going on. I have to know the score, and to do that I have to go out to Sri Lanka in person.'

'And what if you find out something you don't want to know? What if you find out something that'll break your heart?'

Donna swallowed and said, 'I'll cross that bridge when I come to it.'

Dolly walked from the kitchen. Looking back from the doorway she said, 'Well, I hope it keeps fine for you.'

Donna watched her walk away and felt the familiar lurch of fear in her chest.

414

She opened her bag and looked at the photo of Georgio she always kept with her; as her eyes travelled over his handsome features she told herself, over and over, that Stephen Brunos was behind everything . . . not her Georgio, who would soon be home with her. Then everything would be all right once more.

At Heathrow, Donna boarded the plane alone. She had bought the seat beside her as well to ensure she was not troubled with conversation on the flight. She was bone weary, tired and irritable. As she took her seat she placed a small briefcase on the seat beside her and settled herself for the long flight.

No matter what Dolly said or insinuated, Donna would never believe that Georgio was involved in anything to do with child pornography – even though common sense told her that Dolly not denying it was strange in itself. Dolly thought the sun shone out of Georgio Brunos, she always had. It was Maeve who had always harboured suspicions about her son. Maeve with whom Donna would never have discussed this present crisis. Because she would probably have agreed with Dolly.

A man sitting in the aisle seat opposite smiled at her briefly. Donna ignored him and looked out of the window once more. She sensed his discomfiture and found herself enjoying it. It was men who bought the filth she had seen displayed on her kitchen table. Without men, there would be no demand for it. You never heard of women buying child pornography.

The discs had been at the car lot, so that meant Davey at least knew something about it. Whether he knew the contents was a different matter. Computer porn was big business these days. It was what the newspapers were always shouting about. From what she had read over the last two days, there was no actual legislation concerning it. It came down the phone line to be reproduced in stunning colour at the other end. Men could even use a mouse and change the look of the pictures. There had been a case in America where one man was sending the stuff to over thirty different countries.

Child porn was big money, because unlike *Penthouse* or *Mayfair*, you had to pay for its very illegality as well as the product. But it was hardly a furtive business any more, more of a worldwide market.

In her heart of hearts, Donna knew that this was the business for Stephen Brunos. Technology was his forte. Women were also his forte, whether for telephone sex or his escort agency. He would have no qualms about selling these children worldwide. Corrupting them, using them.

All she had to find out was whether or not her husband was a part

415

of it. Find out for definite, because until she knew, she couldn't even look him in the face again. The worst of it all was knowing that someone like Christopher Scott, a complete psychopath, was involved. But she would find out what was going on and then blow the whistle on it all, no matter who she brought down.

The plane taxied down the runway and Donna lay back in her seat, watching as it rose into the air and the lights of Heathrow spread out below her like fairy-lights on a Christmas tree.

Opening her briefcase, she took out the artist's impression of the Bay View Hotel. It was drawn in beautiful living colour, making it look more like a photograph than a pencil drawing. The building had the most stunning façade: rounded windows, adorned with teak shutters; immense double doors leading into a foyer that held a fountain, surrounded by plush seating.

It really looked beautiful, and Donna was planning to base herself in one of the palatial rooms while she tried to find out what Stephen Brunos was doing there. The hotel was in Hikkadoa. Stephen would be using it as a blind. Taking their investment and tainting it as he did everything he touched.

Holding the picture to her breast, she pictured herself and Georgio lying in one of the larger bedrooms overlooking the sea. Both tanned and fit. Both enjoying the sea breezes and the easy life in Sri Lanka.

She remembered Georgio telling her it was stunning, the women incredibly beautiful and the island itself green and lush, with temples and elephants everywhere.

In her heart of hearts, she knew that Georgio might have been involved in the robbery, and she had accepted that. After meeting people he had mixed with, she acknowledged she would have to be a complete fool, *not* to accept it. But so far as the child pornography went, she wouldn't believe her husband was involved in a million years. What was really worrying her was the fact that Stephen could have involved both her husband and herself without their knowledge. If he was using another subsidiary of Talkto . . . Christ Himself knew there were enough of them.

Her name as well as Georgio's could well be on the filth she now carried in her bag.

Ricky was sitting in his cell reading the paper when Georgio tapped on his door.

'All right, Ricky? Don't tell me you can read and all?'

Ricky laughed loudly. 'I can count as well, Georgio, when I have to. Now what can I do for you? You don't come scratching on my door for a friendly chat.'

Georgio sat on the small plastic-backed chair and grinned. 'I need a weapon, old son. I'm willing to pay for it.'

Ricky folded up his *Guardian* neatly and placed it on the bunk beside him.

'What kind of weapon?'

'Something dangerous. Something small, that can maim.'

Ricky relaxed back on his bunk his thick dreadlocks obscuring his face. Georgio saw the thirty-inch biceps and the flat stomach and shook his head. The man was huge.

'What do you want it for? Or, more precisely, *who* do you want it for?'

'That's for me to know and you to find out, ain't it? As long as it ain't for you, what you worried about?'

Ricky smiled, displaying large white teeth. 'Is it for Lewis?'

Georgio shook his head furiously. 'No, it bleeding well ain't for Donald. Me and him have come to an understanding—'

Ricky interrupted, 'I know the chat on the Wing, boy. You have to pay him his money. Well, it occurred to me that maybe you don't want to pay him. He's weak, he's not that well-protected really, is he? You could harm him now. He's vulnerable.'

Georgio saw the light and laughed. 'You black ponce! You want some, don't you?'

Ricky uncurled a dreadlock slowly and removed a joint. He lit it with a silver Zippo. Taking a deep draw, he held the smoke in his lungs for a few moments before he spoke.

'I'll concede the black part, Georgio, but I ain't a ponce.' He laughed and passed the joint to Georgio who took it. 'The thing is, I think you are up to something, and I would very much like to know what it is. Tell me your story, Greek boy, and maybe, just maybe, we can do a deal here.'

Georgio smoked the joint for a while before passing it back to Ricky. His brain was working overtime. Eventually, he said. 'You must not repeat any of this. We'll be in on it together, OK?'

Ricky nodded, leaning forward on his bunk to listen better.

'You know the two blokes brought in the other week, Tweedledum and his mate. The Olds?'

Ricky nodded.

'Well, they're nonces. Not just perverts, but real honest-to-goodness nonces. They are part of that paedophile ring that got sent down recently. They're the two who made the deal. Sadie knows of them, and she tipped me the wink. Apparently, they done her over when she was a kid. I want to make sure they never forget what they did. Ever. I want to hear them screaming this fucking Wing down.'

417

Ricky's face was hard. 'The dirty bastards!' His thick cockney accent was to the fore now, all pretence at a West Indian timbre forgotten. 'The filthy dirty bastards! They killed those little kids, didn't they?'

Georgio nodded. 'Amongst other things. The big one, Hall, he's been at it for years by all accounts. He's the main man, like. They torture the kids first, video it and all. They made a fortune out of selling the gear. The other one, Denning, is a bit of a dimbo though. Thick as shit. But still as bad. He's the one that lured them away.'

Ricky shook his head at what he was hearing. 'And they're sitting down to eat with us? I fucking accepted a fag off that Denning yesterday. Fucking hell! There'll be murder done once this gets out.'

Georgio sighed. 'That's why it mustn't get out, see? I want to do them meself. That's why I need a weapon. Now I am willing to bring you in on it, Ricky, because I trust you. Lewis knows I want them, and he's happy for me to do the honours. And if you decide to do Lewis on the same day . . . there's nothing I can do about that, is there?'

Ricky smiled again. 'So you wouldn't feel you had to do anything to help old Donald, like?'

Georgio shook his head. 'I wouldn't have thought a big boy like you would have needed help with a runt like him. But his minders now, that's a different ball game . . .'

Ricky pinched out the joint with his finger and thumb and put the roach into his tobacco tin.

'I get what you're saying, Georgio, and I think between us we can work something out. When's it to be?'

'In ten days' time, OK?'

'We can do it sooner. I can have a weapon in three, maybe four days.'

Georgio shook his head. 'In ten days' time. That's the plan for me and I don't want it changed. I've trusted you on this, Ricky. Just bear with me, OK?'

The black guy nodded. 'Fair enough. You must have your reasons. Now, about a weapon. I can get you a blade, a dangerous blade. Will that do you?'

Georgio nodded happily. 'We can really have the place jumping over this.'

Ricky laughed. 'Just watch out for that big Scouser. He's out to assert himself soon, I'll lay money on that.'

'Chopper's the least of our worries – we can do him with Lewis if we want.'

418

'That sounds just right to me, Georgio. After all, we don't want to overdo it, do we?'

The two men laughed together.

Georgio looked serious as he said, 'One last thing, Ricky. Don't let on to anyone by thought or deed what Hall or his mate are. We want this to come as a complete surprise to all concerned. You can bring your posse in on it on the day, not before, OK? If the screws get wind we've sussed them out, they'll be moved off here like lightning.'

'You know what young Benjy calls them, don't you? Beavis and Butthead.'

Georgio sniggered. 'That sounds about right to me. But promise me you won't call the shots till the day?'

Ricky smiled nastily. 'Don't worry, Greek boy, no one will know a thing until I deem it necessary.'

Maeve, Pa and Mario were setting tables in the restaurant for the evening's business. They worked in companionable silence. Pa had put the finishing touches to the linen napkins and stepped back to survey his work. Even though by daylight the restaurant looked shabby, in the muted light of evening it felt cosy, the deep red lampshades on the wall lights giving it a feeling of warmth.

'In the New Year, we ought to think about a redec.'

Pa nodded slightly.

'What do you say, Mum?'

Maeve stretched upwards, her back creaking painfully. 'Jaysus, I could do with one of those meself! But you're right, Mario. The place is getting a bit too shabby, even for us!' She laughed as she spoke. A thick, false laugh.

Mario and Pa stared at one another for a few seconds and she watched them, watching her. Pa sighed and led his wife to a chair by the small bar area.

'Come on, Maeve, out with it. What's wrong with you?'

She shrugged. 'Everything. Honestly, Pa, you know what I'm like. Ignore me. I'm up to ninety today what with one thing and another.'

She looked into his broad, honest face and felt a wave of love wash over her. Pa Brunos was a good man, a basically honest and kind individual. How had he sired Georgio and Stephen? Stephen especially. Mary was all right, even if she was a bit of a snob, Nuala was a mouthy bitch, but she was a good girl all the same. Even Mario, the apple of her eye and as queer as a two-bob clock, was all right in his own way. Patrick was as honest and boring as the day was long, so where did they get Stephen and Georgio?

'Come on, Maeve, we've been together too long for a charade like

419

this to continue. There's something worrying you. Tell me, woman. Tell me what it is.'

'Oh, it's everything. Georgio is in prison, Stephen is getting me down. I don't trust the bugger. Then those bloody big galoots the other week, trying to put the frighteners on us, all over fecking Georgio again. And I'm worried about Donna. She went to Scotland that time. Now I find out off Dolly that she's pissed off on holiday! Holiday, if you don't mind. Her husband's doing eighteen Christing years and she's off on her hols while we haven't even the money to put a bit of paper on the walls in here. That's what's making me down, Pa. Just that. Oh, and the fact that Stephen is a whoremaster, Georgio is not as white as he likes everyone to think, and Nuala is still seeing that fecking villain of hers. It seems we brought the lot of them up wrong.'

Pa put a thick muscled arm across her shoulders.

'We brought them up, but they're adults now. They make up their own minds. We can only pick up the pieces and help them when it goes wrong. This ain't like you, my fiery little Irishwoman! Where's the fighter gone, the woman who could take on the world, eh?' He was smiling at her, trying to cheer her up, she knew that. She appreciated the effort he was making but nothing could cheer her. Nothing.

She answered him in a flat voice. 'She got old Pa. As old as the hills.'

Mario and Pa watched her walk from the restaurant, her back stooped, her feet barely leaving the floor. She looked defeated.

Pa stared at Mario, tears gleaming in his eyes. He shook his head slowly.

'She'll get over it, Pa.'

He wiped a tear from his eye. 'Will she? Will any of us?'

Mario didn't answer, because he didn't know what to say. Instead he followed his mother up into the flat. Maeve was sipping a cup of tea and smoking a cigarette.

'Where's Donna gone on holiday then?'

Maeve lifted her shoulders and shook her head.

'I don't know. Dolly said she hadn't told her, but she knows all right. There's not much slips past that nosy old bitch.'

Mario sat at the small kitchen table and poured himself out a cup of tea.

'You know, Mario, it's funny, but I was just thinking about you all, when you were kids. I tried to decide if there was any way I could have foreseen how you'd all turn out.'

'Mum, you brought us up, but as me dad says, we're grown now

420

and we make our own decisions, lead our own lives. It's nothing to do with you or Pa. Like me, for instance, I'm sorry that I can't like girls.' He smiled gently. 'I'll rephrase that, shall I? I do like girls, but only as friends.

'I know my being gay breaks your heart and I'm sorry, Mum. Sorry to the core of me, but I am what I am. Do you know, there's married men who come to a club I go to. They have lived a lie for years. There's women out there with husbands, having no idea that their men are gay. I am your son, Mum, but I am what I am. I'm not going to make excuses for myself and I certainly don't want you to make them for me. If only I had done this, or if only I had done that . . . All that talk is shite, as you would say. I am what I am and Georgio is what he is because it's the paths we chose.'

'And what about Stephen?'

Mario took a deep breath before he answered her.

'Stephen? Well, while we're being so honest I'll tell you what I think about him, shall I? I think that out of all of us, he's the one you should be worrying about because he's bad, Mum, rotten bad. Inside and out.'

Maeve looked into Mario's handsome face and for the first time in months his sexual preferences didn't cloud her judgement of him. Instead she saw him as another woman or man might see him: good-looking, accomplished, intelligent.

She grabbed his hand and held it tightly between her own. 'You're right – he *is* bad. Putrid, rotten.' She closed her eyes for a second, to pull herself together. Then she said brightly, 'But you know, you're a son a woman could be proud of. Even if you are a nancy boy!'

It was said in jest and Mario smiled widely at his mother, the biggest love of his life.

'I'm sorry, Mum. Truly I am.'

Maeve stroked his cheek with a workworn finger. 'Don't be, Mario. You do what you feel you must. Whatever you want to do, I'll back you to the hilt.'

Mario felt as if his chest would explode with the love he felt for the tiny woman before him. Standing up, he left the room, unable to trust himself not to cry. Maeve watched him go, feeling much more settled inside herself at their open admission of his sexuality.

In his room, Mario opened his briefcase and took out a telephone book. He dialled a number on his mobile and when it answered, he said, 'Hello, Pierre? Could you do me a favour, mate? I need to know a destination address, please, on an airline. I think the holiday would have been booked with a credit card. Find out for me, would you?'

As he gave out Donna's details he hoped against hope that his hunch was wrong, but somehow he didn't think it was.

Donna stood with her case outside Colombo airport. The heat was stifling, heavy and damp. She pulled out the neck of her suit and blew down on to her breasts. The blouse she was wearing was already sticking to her with perspiration. A porter came towards her and loaded her case on to a small trolley.

'Where is your tour bus, Madam?' He smiled at her with crooked brown teeth.

Donna explained. 'I have no tour bus. I need a taxi to Hikkadoa. To the Bay View Hotel. Where can I get a taxi?'

The man smiled again, his dark green boiler suit giving out a faint odour of old sweat and grease as he leant towards her.

'I know very good taxi, Madam. I will take you to him personally.'

Donna followed the little man out into the brilliant sunshine. Everywhere she looked flowers abounded, deep reds and mauves. Jasmine filled the air with its scent, and the sky was a deep clear blue. Even in her agitated state she couldn't help but appreciate the beauty around her.

The porter took her to a line of taxis and started talking to a driver. After a while he spoke to Donna.

'This is my very good friend Raj, and he will take you to your hotel.' He loaded her case into the boot of a very old dilapidated Nissan and Donna slipped him a hundred-rupee note. Two minutes later they were on their way to Hikkadoa.

After half an hour they entered the city of Colombo itself. Donna watched the people in amazement. The women's saris were all the colours of the rainbow, people were selling their wares from the roadside, children ran about dangerously amongst the traffic. The cars were jampacked together, along with bicycles, tour coaches and buses.

The dust was everywhere, and street vendors stood selling their wares without a thought for the dirt covering everything from samosas to painted gourds.

In spite of her worries and her troubles, Donna found herself fascinated by the small city and its inhabitants. The sheer heat and excitement were enough to take her mind off her mission. As the car was gridlocked in the traffic and the incessant shouting and horn-blowing went on around her, Donna relaxed against the faded cloth seat of the Nissan and smiled grimly. In all her married life she had always shared every new experience with Georgio. Never once had she travelled abroad without him. If he had been with her now, he would have been making funny quips about the people, the taxi and the surroundings. He would have been relaxed, sure of himself, would have read up on his subject and pointed things out to her.

The hot steamy day seemed suddenly chilly to her, the scenes before her eyes less bright. Thinking of Georgio had reminded her of why she was here. Of why she was alone.

In another twenty minutes the car had taken the coast road and they were travelling along narrow dirt tracks towards Moratuwa, on the first leg of their journey to Hikkadoa.

Raj, relaxed now and happy to have a customer, started chatting to Donna in his near perfect English.

'How long you stay in Hikkadoa?'

Donna flicked her cigarette out of the car window before replying. 'I'm not sure.'

Raj looked dangerously over his shoulder as he drove. 'Are you meeting with someone?'

'I'm here on business actually.' Donna hoped this answer would shut him up, hoped that when she said she wasn't a tourist he would leave her in peace.

'What kind of a business would a nice lady like you have in Hikkadoa?' His voice sounded doubtful.

Donna sighed heavily. 'Just business, that's all.'

Raj shrugged. He knew the British well enough to realise when to shut up.

Donna watched the perfect coastline and relaxed once more in her seat, half-afraid of what she'd find in Hikkadoa and half-relieved to be on her way there.

Mario walked into Amigo's and smiled at the waiter who walked forward.

'Have you a booking, sir?'

Mario took in the dark eyes and the slightly too long look and knew that each had recognised the other as his own type. He smiled sexily as he answered.

'Can I see Alan Cox, please? Tell him it's Mario Brunos, he'll see me.'

The waiter nodded, offered him a seat at the bar and disappeared up the stairs to Alan's office. Five minutes later Mario was being led up the stairs by the young man, who took a drinks order from him before he left him with Alan.

Alan looked at Mario, a faint smile on his face, but his eyes were guarded. He knew Mario's reputation, and wondered which side of the family war he stood on: Donna's or Stephen's. Then he noted the

423

way Mario crossed his legs delicately and half-smiled to himself. At least he knew which side of the bed he slept on anyway.

'Mario, what can I do you for?'

Mario stared into Alan's face for a few seconds before replying. 'I am here to ask your advice, and also to ask for your help.'

Alan spread his arms wide. 'Ask away, son. I can't promise you anything, but I can listen.'

Mario lit a small cheroot and said slowly, 'Donna has gone to Sri Lanka; she left this morning. Stephen is also out in Sri Lanka. Now I don't know how much you know, Mr Cox, but from the amount of time you've spent with my sister-in-law, I'd say it's a lot more than I do. I do not trust my brother Stephen as far as I can throw him. I don't like the idea of her being out there while he's there either. If I go, it'll be all over the Smoke in no time. Now if you could send someone out there, not only would I be grateful, but Georgio would be as well.'

Mario was gratified to see the look of utter astonishment on Alan Cox's face. From it he could tell that Donna's so-called 'holiday' was as much news to Cox as it had been to Mario and his mother.

'She's gone out to Sri Lanka, you say?'

Mario nodded, saved from answering by the young waiter arriving with their drinks. Once the door was shut Alan spoke again.

'Listen, Mario, I want to know what you know, and I want to know what you suspect. Then we'll try and make some sense out of it all, and see what needs to be done.'

Mario sipped his white wine daintily and nodded.

'All I know, Mr Cox, is this. If Stephen's out there it means trouble. I know Georgio has dealings out there, and in Thailand as well. Now between you and me, Georgio is as crooked as a London financier, always has been. I think he was into something very big before he went down. That's why he stripped his businesses. Knowing my brother like I do, he will still be involved, and whatever it is he is involved in will be dangerous to Donna. She is not equipped to deal with people like Stephen. Oh, she thinks she is, but then usually she has Georgio behind her here. Out there anything could happen to her, and no one would ever be any the wiser. You do get my drift, don't you?'

Alan nodded. 'Before I say anything else, can I ask you something, Mario? What do *you* think is going on out there, yourself like? What do you think the score is?'

Mario took a sip of his wine before answering. 'Off the record?'

Alan nodded once more, afraid of what he was going to hear, but needing to hear it anyway.

424

Mario took a deep breath. 'If Stephen's involved it must be women or porn or both. That's his forte, his business. Talkto is a slut-line. He also runs hostesses and rent boys. I know all this for a fact, have known it for a long time, actually. He deals with both ends of the market, the rough trade and the high-class ladies. He is a forty-two-carat pimp.'

Alan lit one of his large cigars before he asked his next question. 'Do you think Georgio is involved in the same things?'

Mario laughed outright. 'Never! I'd lay money on that one. I know that Georgio wanted into the hotel industry, I think everyone knew about that. But porn, no way. Whatever Stephen's doing out there, it won't be to do with Georgio. For all my brother's faults he ain't a beast. No, I think Stephen has a few games up his sleeve and he's using Georgio and his contacts as a blind. According to Donna, the hotel businesses were fucked ages ago, which is why Lewis is on his back. Stephen's using Sri Lanka and Georgio as a front.'

'So why do you think Donna is in trouble?'

Mario raised his eyebrows and said deliberately and forcefully, 'Because Donna owns what's out there, Alan, and she'll go in with her usual breakneck speed laying down the law. If Stephen's setting up a deal, then the last thing he'll want is her on his back in front of his contacts. I shouldn't say this, I know, but Stephen is capable of killing her, he hates her so much. He always did.'

Alan shook his head. 'But why? *Why* does he hate her?'

Mario shrugged. 'Who knows what goes on in someone else's mind? Stephen's always been strange, even when we were all kids. He takes against people, it's in his nature.'

'So what do you think Stephen's setting up then? What's the score with him?'

'I suppose it can only be a brothel or some kind of porn. I know he's brought girls over from China. They work from flats in Bayswater and Wardour Street. They come over ostensibly as part of a household and stay on supposedly working for a particular family. In effect they're locked up all day and night until they can be trusted to go out alone. You must remember, most of these girls worked in small-time brothels at home. Over here they feel like they've come upmarket. And you know the Chinks – once they own the girl, that girl is theirs for life. It's as simple as that.'

Alan laughed grimly. 'Oh, I know what the Chinks are capable of, mate, none better. As for Stephen, do you think he'd be involved in beasting, real beasting, kids and that?'

Mario looked at the desk and said sadly, 'Without a shadow of a

425

doubt. Stephen has no qualms about anything. People are commodities to him. A girl of twelve on the game isn't much different to one of sixteen, in his eyes. He does the baby phone lines as well, where the girls pretend to be little kids. I don't think Stephen gives a flying fuck what he does or who he does it to. That's why I'm so concerned about Donna.'

Alan nodded thoughtfully. 'I think you have every reason to worry about her if all you say is true.'

Mario looked anxious. 'So you'll send someone out there then, to keep an eye on her?'

Alan took a large puff on his cigar.

'I'll do that all right, Mario, my son. In fact, I think I'll go myself.' He saw Mario's look of surprise and pretended not to.

'There's a flight tonight from Gatwick at eight-fifteen. I can get you on it.'

'Then I think you'd better do it.'

'A friend of mine works at Gatwick on the bookings, see. It was how I found out where Donna had gone. I just hope she doesn't get there and antagonise Stephen because there's something else I found out as well . . .'

Alan frowned. 'What's that then?'

'Stephen has been working for, and with, Donald Lewis for the last five years.'

'*What!*' Alan's face was incredulous. 'How the fuck did you find that one out?'

'From one of Lewis's friends – a man called Greg Gordon. He was Lewis's right-hand man in more ways than one for years. When he got too old for Lewis he was dropped as a boyfriend but kept on in the business. He runs a club called The Pink Paradise in North London. It's a gay club obviously and I met him there. I was amazed when he knew my brother Stephen. Even more amazed to find out he had had dealings with him in a work capacity. They even collaborated putting together the deal through for Lewis and Georgio.'

'But Stephen had nothing to do with that. Georgio worked that one by himself, didn't he?'

'Precisely. I nipped over to Donna's today and against poor old Dolly's wishes went through the papers in Georgio's office. There's nothing there linking Stephen with the hotels from Georgio's end anyway, so something much more sinister is going on.'

'This is getting a little too deep for me, Mario. What you're saying is, when Georgio went into the hotel business, Stephen was working against him?'

Mario shrugged. 'You know as much as I do. Maybe before it all

426

fell out of line he was working with Lewis for Georgio. I don't know, the possibilities are endless, ain't they? Maybe he was Lewis's ears. All I know is, Stephen isn't a man to trust and if Lewis has sent him out there then you bet he will not want Donna breathing down his neck. Whatever he's there for, it's trouble for Donna Brunos. She will steam in and cause him hag, and he'll retaliate.'

'That much is certain, son. You book me the flight and I'll be off tonight.'

Mario stood up. 'One thing, Mr Cox. Why are you going out there yourself?'

Alan got to his feet and peered down at the slight young man before him. 'Let's get something straight here, shall we? My name is Alan or Al, take your choice. As for me going out there, I think my face will be just about the only thing that will stop your brother doing something silly, don't you? Stephen knows me, my reputation, and he also has a small inkling of what I'm capable of. Plus, me and Georgio are like that.' He crossed his fingers. 'Everyone knows that much. Stephen will be very wary of starting anything while I'm there. I only hope I get there in time.'

'If only we knew exactly what was going on?'

'Believe me, son, we will know. Because I am going to make it my business to find everything out. No good having a dog and barking yourself, is there?'

Mario smiled. 'Well, that's true enough anyway.'

He walked to the door and turned back slowly. 'Look after her, won't you? For all her newfound independence, she'll be like a fish out of water on her own.'

Alan smiled gently. 'Don't worry, son, I'll look after her, I promise you that much.'

The two men stared at one another for a few seconds.

'I'm glad she's got you, Mr Cox. Whatever happens, I know you'll do your best for her.'

Then Mario was gone.

Alan sat back in his chair and sighed.

He wished he could look after her properly, every day, every night. But she was Georgio's wife, and Georgio was his friend. Alan was getting sick and tired of telling himself that.

Throwing his cigar into the ashtray, he pulled himself from his seat. He had to get home and get packed.

He had under six hours before his flight.

427

Chapter Thirty-Seven

Night was drawing in and Donna was busy watching the toddy tappers as the car sped into Hikkadoa. Raj, noticing her interest, slowed down and explained their role. He told her how the workers spent their days moving along ropes placed between one palm tree and the next, tapping the juice from the middle of the plants to make a brandy-type drink called Arrack. Donna smiled as the man warned her against drinking it, as it was very strong.

'How far now to the hotel?'

Raj shrugged inside his off-white clothes. 'I am not sure. This is Hikkadoa, now we have to find your destination.'

A woman walked past and he began talking to her in a fast heavy dialect. Donna saw the woman look at her and heard the incredulity in her reply. Then she walked off, pulling her sari around herself protectively.

The night was coming in fast and Donna felt a prickle of fear in this unknown place, with unknown people. The beautiful day was now turning into dark and threatening night. All the thrill of being there, seeing the sights and sounds, was overshadowed by fear of what she would find at the end of it all. In the bright daylight she had felt she could cope with anything. Now, in the deepening twilight, she was afraid, deeply afraid.

Taking a long breath, she lit another cigarette and smiled at Raj. 'What did she say?'

He looked at her, perplexed. 'Is Madam sure she wants the Bay View? Only there is very good hotels here that I could take you to.'

'Really, I need to find the Bay View, and I need to find it soon.'

Raj didn't move, just sat in his seat looking at her steadily.

'And you are sure this is where your booking is for?'

Donna nodded again, harder this time.

'Madam, I am not trying to call you anything bad like a liar, but I must tell you that Bay View is not a hotel at all. I don't think you want to go there, Madam. Not at all.'

Donna looked into the rheumy eyes, took in the grimy face, dirty

428

neck and none-too-clean clothes, and sighed once more. He was a nice old man, but was probably paid commission to send people like herself to other hotels. He was trying to make a few pounds. Opening her purse, she took out a thousand rupees, then another thousand.

'These are for you if you take me to the Bay View, OK?'

Raj took the money and shook his head sadly.

'I will take you, Madam, but you will not want to stay there, I know this.'

Opening her briefcase, Donna took out the brochure of the Bay View Hotel and pushed it across the seat to him.

'See? It's a very beautiful hotel.'

Raj looked down at the picture and shrugged. 'I do not know of this hotel, Madam. I have never heard of this place.'

Donna smiled gently. 'It's not open to the public yet. It has not long been finished. I own it, you see. As least, my husband and I own it.'

Raj frowned and nodded at her. 'Very well, Madam, I will take you there. But I have never been hearing of a new hotel in Hikkadoa.'

With that he restarted the car.

He drove slowly through the tiny village to the outskirts. As they approached a narrow dirt track there was a faded board proclaiming *The Bay View Hotel*, with a black arrow pointing towards the roadway.

Donna smiled in happy relief. 'See? I told you it was here!'

As they drove up the unsurfaced track, avoiding the potholes, Donna saw a family of monkeys feeding. Instead of enjoying the sight, she felt it was somehow sinister.

Her brain was asking why there was no real road yet. The other hotels she had passed mostly had concrete driveways, with beautiful flower-borders. Oh well, she told herself, the hotel was only just finished. Maybe the roads were made last? But then, her mind reasoned, how had they got all the plant out here to do the actual construction work?

'Be careful of the monkeys, Madam. They bite and can carry the rabies.'

Raj's words brought Donna back to reality.

He carried on a slow descent of the dirt road, finally pulling up about fifty yards from a dilapidated building.

'This is the Bay View, Madam.'

Donna stared at the place, stunned. 'No, Raj, it can't be!' She looked at the photograph before her of the palatial hotel complex.

'This is it, Madam – look at the sign.'

Donna saw a sign above the entrance. It did indeed say *Bay*

View Hotel in faded black lettering.

The building itself was wide, built from breeze blocks that were obviously supposed to have been rendered at some time. The windows were devoid of glass, having only mosquito nets covering them.

What really caught her eye was the verandah that surrounded the building. Here white men were sitting, some on rattan chairs and others on the wooden steps, and beside them were children, little girls.

Some looked to be as young as only eight or nine.

The music was getting louder, as if the coming of night had turned up the volume. A foul smell was rife – cooking fat and heavy male sweat vying with each other for supremacy.

As Donna sat in the dusky night, the sound of insects loud in her ears, harsh music and laughter taunting her, she saw a man come out of the big double doors carrying a young boy on his shoulders.

The man was big, heavyset, with a swaggering beer belly and heavy jowls. He was calling something out in German and all the men were laughing at him. But the little boy was neither laughing nor crying. In the lights from the house Donna saw that his small face was set in resignation.

It was this sight that hit her harder than the others. In those few seconds she saw everything with a stunning clarity.

There was no big fancy hotel here, there never had been.

This was a building that had been knocked up to serve a purpose, bringing male tourists together with the children who abounded here.

Raj watched her shocked countenance and felt sorry for her. 'We should go maybe, eh?'

In her state of shock, Donna only half-heard him.

But she acknowledged that he was right.

There was nothing she could do now. Not while it was dark, while the Bay View was open for business. She had to come here armed with knowledge and also armed with daylight.

'Take me away from here, Raj. Now.'

He drove off quickly. No one seemed to have noticed them.

'I told you, Madam, you would not like to stay there. It is very bad place for ladies.'

Donna leant forward in her seat and tapped him on his shoulder. 'What did the woman say earlier, Raj? What were her exact words?'

He looked at Donna in the mirror.

'She said it was a brothel, Madam. A brothel for the children.' He saw Donna's stunned look. 'Madam, you are in Hikkadoa. This is what is here. It is not the only one, you know. Sri Lankans come from

430

all over to sell their children. It is a good way of making the money and the people who come here know this.

'During the day Hikkadoa is a good place, the beaches are nice and clean, the turtles have laid their eggs, and everyone is happy. But in the night, the work begins for the children.'

'That is disgusting.' All Donna's feelings were in those few low words and Raj grinned sadly.

'Madam, this is Sri Lanka. I have cousins in England, nurses, they have a very good life there. Here you have nothing, and no one gives you anything. To some people the only thing they have of value is their children. They may have many of those. The men come here to buy them, it is very simple. Some of them come here with their wives, and in the evening they go out for a little walk, maybe after their dinner. On the outskirts of Hikkadoa these kind of places are becoming very popular. Some Sri Lankans work from their own homes. Women walk the beaches in the evening with their children, offering them to anyone who comes along. I hear it is the same now in Goa.

'Don't judge them too harshly. However much it sickens you, as it sickens me, you must remember that poverty is the driving force. One child's work can feed the rest of the family. It is a great sadness to do that, I know, but it is maybe necessary, eh? I know many English people have never experienced real poverty or hunger. Here they are everyday occurrences for a big part of the population.'

Donna acknowledged the truth of what Raj said, but she could not in any way allow herself to accept it as a justification for child abuse. The beauty of the island was gone for her now, her few hours of forgetting her troubles in the face of its natural attractions vanished. The momentary joy of watching the toddy tappers was a forgotten pleasure. All that remained were bitter-sweet memories of a land full of beautiful women, smiling men, and tiny children sold into a life most people could only guess at, let alone comprehend. Having yearned for a child for so many years, so many lonely years, Donna found it harder than ever to understand the mentality of a woman who could sell off a childhood, a child's life and body, for a few pennies.

'Just get me to a proper hotel, Raj. One away from here, please.'

He smiled comfortingly. 'I will take you to the big new one in Ambalamgoda. It is only one half hour away and I will escort you inside personally; they know me there. Raj is known everywhere in Sri Lanka for his goodness, and tomorrow, if you want, I shall take you to the elephant sanctuary.'

Donna gave him a smile she didn't think she had inside herself.

431

'No elephant sanctuary, Raj, I have work to do tomorrow.'

He shrugged good-naturedly. 'Put the Bay View out of your head, Madam. Hikkadoa is not for a lovely lady like yourself. You must see the real Sri Lanka: the turtles on the beaches, the magnificent countryside and our Buddhist temples. Now they are a thing to see! Kandy is a wonderful city, and you know, they say the most beautiful women come from there. And Sigiriya, The rock temple is astounding, you would enjoy that very much . . .'

Donna let the man talk, strangely warmed by his voice and the singsong inflections in it. She felt a need to listen to him talk of beauty and gentleness, the side of the country she had enjoyed before coming to Hikkadoa.

Yet in a small part of her brain, Donna acknowledged that she had already suspected what she was going to find. She just hadn't prepared herself for the full horror of it.

Where Stephen was, filth reigned supreme. She had known that all along, too. The only thing she had to find out now was whether Georgio was involved, and if so how deeply.

Because her name was on so many documents already, she had a sinking feeling in her guts that along with the house, the building businesses, the car lot, the peep shows and other interests, she was about to find herself the part-owner of a brothel. Not any old brothel either, but one that dealt in children.

Closing her eyes tightly to stem the tears of frustration and heartbreak, she prayed.

She prayed harder than she had when she had lost the boy. Because now she was praying not only for herself and her dead son, but for nameless children and their brothers and sisters after them.

Donald Lewis grinned at Georgio as they played chess.

'You're very good at this, Georgio. But then you would be, wouldn't you? You are far more intelligent than you make out. It's a good scam but one I saw through from day one.'

Lewis moved his bishop and sat back happily knowing he had Georgio in the next two moves. He had not, however, taken proper account of Georgio's rook, and as his bishop disappeared off the table Lewis's face set accordingly. Most people who played with him blatantly allowed him to win, with a great deal of old flannel about how clever he was. His eyes hardened to pieces of grey flint and Georgio smirked.

'Get out of that one without moving then!'

Lewis picked up his king and threw it on to the board.

Like a child, Lewis found it difficult to lose at anything. He was a

432

man with a competitive nature that made him want to win, either by superiority or by cheating.

'Fuck you, Brunos, you Greek ponce.'

Georgio sniggered. 'You just can't lose, can you, Donald?' This was said seriously.

He stared at Georgio with a hard expression in his eyes. 'No, I can't. I hate losers, Georgio.'

'Then you should love me, Donald, old chap, because I just won, and I didn't cheat either. Want a cup of Rosie Lee?'

Lewis nodded slowly.

As Georgio walked away to get the teas Lewis watched him through half-closed eyes.

Georgio Brunos was getting too big for his boots. There was something about the way he was acting, like a kid with a big secret. It was almost as if Georgio knew Lewis was on his way out. Knew that he was going to be usurped in some way. And the only way he would know that, was if he was to be the usurper. He seemed to spend a lot of time with big Ricky and Chopper just lately. Donald Lewis smiled to himself.

He would keep his eyes and ears open and at the first hint of a mutiny, the three of them would be wiped off the face of the earth. His money was important to him, but not as important as his reputation. That was of the utmost importance to him.

It was what kept him alive.

He decided to arm himself and his henchmen well. Insurance was always worth taking out, especially in these troubled times.

Little Dicky sat with his usual white rum and sipped it slowly before answering Nick's questions.

'Come on, Dicky, spit it out. I ain't paying you for fuck all.'

'The word on the street down south is that an Irishman called Paddy is asking around about the jump you're organising. It seems he has a personal interest in it. He also asks a lot about Alan Cox and his association with a certain Donna Brunos. I get the impression he thinks Cox is knocking around with her. I know he isn't. She is being used as a go-between, I sussed that one from the off.

'I also hear that Donald Lewis is making waves about Georgio Brunos, saying he's a beast. He's making sure this gets out to all quarters. It has a grain of truth in it, but not anything I can give specifically. I know his brother is a whoremaster, but that's beasting on a respectable level as you know yourself. The said Donna Brunos has disappeared, and I now find out that this Paddy is hunting high and low for her. The word is she is on holiday somewhere. Now it

433

doesn't take me long to get to the bottom of all this. Can I speak frankly to you, Nick?'

He nodded, respect and admiration for the old man welling inside him.

'Of course you can. I own you, so to speak; you can say what you want, Dicky.'

Dicky swallowed down his white rum nervously and poured himself another before resuming his talk.

'You're organising the jump of Georgio Brunos, Georgio owes a lot of money to Lewis, and Lewis is putting out the word that Brunos is beasting.

'Think about it, Nick. If you want a man's life fucked in the criminal fraternity, what's the best way? Lay a nonsense claim on him. No one likes a nonce. It's the unwritten law, right? So, as to what you wanted to know, for some reason best known to Paddy, he wants to find out what his boss is planning. Why Brunos doesn't want him involved I can't find out. It's maybe a case of the fewer people in the know the better. That is sound business sense for a jump.

'As for the beasting claim, I think Lewis is accusing Georgio of that to put pressure on him to pay the money over for the blag he's doing the eighteen for. Got that so far? Once Georgio jumps it's his business whether or not he pays over the money, not ours, so all in all I think you have nothing to worry about either way.

'As for Jonnie H., he has recruited the McAnultys, but they're as tight-arsed as a duck in water. No one knows the score there. No one seems to want to know anyway. Alan Cox is dealing with Eric the Lunatic, the mad mercenary. I assume that's for the jump. I found this out by deduction and by greasing a few strategically placed palms. Don't worry about your security, OK? It's tight, man. Real tight.

'So, as I said before, everything this end is hunky-dory. Jack Coyne and JoJo O'Neil are keeping their heads down and their traps shut. No one else is interested and that's my job finished.'

'What about Paddy. Do you think he'll be trouble?'

Dicky shook his head. 'Nah, man. He's on Georgio's side anyway, on his payroll. Once Georgio's out he'll be brought back into the fold, is my guess. It's just a pain in the arse to have him sniffing about as well as me. He has muscle but no real contacts, except one of Georgio's business partners, Davey Jackson. This Jackson is either without any knowledge or he's keeping the big man at arm's length. That's the strength of it all.'

Nick smiled. 'Thanks, Dicky. You've put me mind at rest. You know how I feel about nonces. But for all you've said, there's still

434

something bothering me about Brunos. I just can't put my finger on it . . .'

Dicky smiled, his large white friendly smile.

'Call it jump nerves, man – everyone gets them. Think how Brunos must be feeling, eh? He's the one who's got to do the jump. He's the reason for it all. And on top of everything he's got Lewis riding his back.'

'True, Dicky, true. I'll see you get your dosh, but keep your ear to the ground anyway for the next few weeks. I want to hear everything you hear.'

'It's as good as done.'

After Dicky left Albie brought in Nick's afternoon coffee and placed it gently on the kitchen table. Nick smiled at him.

'All right, Albie?'

Albie nodded, happy to be noticed by the man he worshipped, the man who had been his champion for years.

'I found out that Georgio ain't beasting, Albie, so all the good little boys can sleep easy in their beds.'

Albie smiled once more. His moon face so trusting, so adoring, that Nick experienced the all-too familiar feeling of horror tinged with pity that only Albie could summon up in him.

'I would never deal with anyone who was beasting, you know that, don't you? Now I can carry on with my plans in good faith, can't I?'

Albie nodded his head vigorously.

'Sit down, Albie me old china, and relax for fuck's sake. Why do you always have to be near me, eh? What possessed me to take you on in the first place? I'm as soft as shit me, that's my trouble, ain't it?' He talked as always by asking and answering his own questions; it was a habit acquired over the years because of Albie's inability to talk.

He looked sad and frightened now and Nick sighed.

'Don't worry, Alb, you're like me own child. In fact, you're more than me own child, because you're there all the time, whether I want you or not. I'll never dump you, mate, so cheer up. Me and you are a team – a bit like Lenny and his mate in that novel, *Of Mice and Men*. I'll look after you, son. I'll never be without you, all right. That's a promise.'

Happier now, Albie relaxed into his seat.

Drinking his coffee, Nick contemplated his life, Albie's life, and whether or not he believed all he had heard from Little Dicky. Nick had always prided himself on the fact that he could smell a rat before it was stinking.

And there was a stink coming into his nose now, only he couldn't be sure where the source of it was. Only time would tell.

435

He had four days till the jump and Jack Coyne was on his mind as was JoJo O'Neil, and somewhere, tacked on the end of the list, was Donald Lewis. There was a connection somewhere, and he would find out what it was if it killed him.

Nick smiled to himself ruefully because he knew that where Lewis was involved, the chances of being killed were a distinct possibility. But Nick was a betting man. He knew that with forethought and a little inside knowledge, he could at least lengthen the odds.

Donna sat in a small hotel in Hikkadoa sipping a glass of iced tea. She watched the holidaymakers relaxing in the brilliant sunshine, and was once more amazed at what this idyllic spot was hiding. She corrected herself. It wasn't in fact hiding anything. It was all done blatantly, under cover of the warm tropical nights, though most of the people near her now knew nothing of what was happening under their noses. An elderly couple sat at the table beside her and Donna smiled a greeting to them.

She watched the lane leading up to the Bay View. So far, four cars had come out of the lane, only one had gone inside, and she'd been sitting watching since ten in the morning. Picking up her sun hat, she left a few rupees on the table and began the long walk towards the hotel. Her heart was beating a tattoo in her chest, her legs felt shaky with fear, but she forced herself to carry on walking.

The trees were alive with birds. As she walked, a monkey hugging her baby to her chest crossed the lane, taking no notice of her, and disappeared into the dense undergrowth. Donna wiped her face and neck with a large white handkerchief, the sweat both nervous and from the dense heat. As she turned the corner that brought the hotel into view she stopped and watched for a moment.

The place looked deserted, but Donna saw a movement from inside the front entrance. A heavy-set white woman with thick blonde hair was standing in the doorway, a child of about seven by her side. Donna knew the woman could see her and, plucking up her courage, she walked towards her. Donna's mouth was dry with nerves and dust. The wide-brimmed hat she wore gave her eyes protection from the burning glare of the sun.

The woman walked to the top of the verandah steps and looked down at her. 'Who are you and what do you want?'

Donna stood at the bottom of the steps. The woman's thick cockney accent was a culture shock in these luscious tropical surroundings. On closer inspection, Donna realised that the blonde was a lot older than she had first thought. Her skin was tanned to a

436

deep mahogany and had a leathery appearance, especially around the eyes. Deep wrinkles were etched there, and at either side of her nose. It was the thick blonde hair that gave her the appearance of youthfulness from a distance.

Before Donna could answer the child opened the verandah door and said in broken English, 'Miss Candy, I go to wash now.'

The woman waved an arm in agreement, her eyes staying firmly fixed on Donna.

Pulling herself up to her full height, Donna took a deep breath and walked up the steps. She sailed past Candy and pushed through the verandah doors as if she was meant to be there.

Candy turned on her heel. 'Oi, you! Where the hell do you think you're going? Who the fucking hell are you, lady?'

Donna faced the woman in the coolness of the building and said in her best imitation of Carol Jackson, 'I'm Mrs Georgio Brunos, love. I've come in answer to your fax. Now am I going to get a drink and a seat or do I have to whistle for them?'

Candy's face was instantly friendlier.

'Why didn't you say? Come through to my office, love, and we'll get sorted. I'm sorry about the welcome, but with all the hag at the moment I have to be very careful, you know.'

She led Donna into a large office at the back of the building. Donna felt the cool breeze from the electric fans and sighed with relief. The heat of the day was so overpowering, coming into the cool had caused her to sweat even more.

Candy grinned. 'You get used to it, love, after a while anyway. Now can I get you a cup of tea?'

Donna shook her head. 'Just a glass of water, thanks. Then you can tell me exactly what's going on here.'

Candy poured out two long glasses of bottled water and settled herself behind the desk. Donna sat facing her in a rattan armchair. In the distance she could hear the shrill cry of a bird, and closer the sound of a child's quiet crying. The traffic from the main road was a dull buzz underlying all the other noises.

'So what exactly has happened?'

Candy looked at Donna for a long moment before speaking. 'Have you seen Stephen? I missed him, he's gone up into the mountains on a pussy hunt with my brother Jake. We need more girls here – without their mothers, to be honest. Now that Thailand is run with kiddies, and with the threat of AIDs out there, we've knocked the Thai hotel on the head. The place in Goa will be up and running soon. Stephen said Georgio's pleased as punch about it. How is he, by the way? I don't get much info from Davey Jackson because we always fax each

437

other. You know what that Carol's like. Mother Theresa in a Next bodystocking!'

Donna laughed with Candy, a hard hollow sound that rang false even to her own ears.

'I am my husband's representative here. I have say over Stephen and Davey. Now, will you tell me exactly what the trouble is? My husband is interested in protecting his investments, and so am I.'

Candy lit a small cheroot and shrugged. 'The computer in Colombo went down a few weeks ago. We couldn't get anything through to Liverpool at all. Stephen's going to take back the merchandise with him. We need to keep up the momentum, see. Once we're up and running in Germany, we won't have any need of JoJo or Jack Coyne, but at the moment they're our bread and butter, and we're making a fortune. Jack Coyne got us the printers and the contacts so we have to tread warily with him, though as you probably know, Stephen wants to dump him once we hit Europe in favour of a bloke in Amsterdam.'

Donna interrupted. 'Look, Candy, can you just tell me what the merchandise is that we haven't been able to receive and why, please?'

Donna was nonplussed at Candy's talk of Germany, Europe, JoJo O'Neil and Jack Coyne. She wanted to know exactly what was going down.

Candy frowned at her in consternation. 'It's the same as it's always been, love – the pictures of the kiddies. You do know what I'm talking about, don't you?' Her eyes were slits as she watched the elegant woman before her.

Donna sighed heavily. 'I know what you're talking about all right, I just want to know why the hell it hasn't come through?'

'The modem's no good any more. We had someone hacking into us. We had to stop. Sending the stuff down the phone line is great, but we realised that some of it was going astray. Whoever it is has made a point of hacking into our system. Now it could be the government, but I don't think so. It could be Interpol, they're shit hot on child porn these days. Myself I think we have a nonce hacker! Anyway, as you know, we've stopped for a while. But Jake is going to set up another route from the Maldives. It should be operational in a few weeks. He's also going to set this one up with so many passwords, it'll take fucking Einstein to get into it!

'I think the trouble was with the Internet. We sometimes got it up on the main computer ourselves; some of our contacts are on there. We need to make the contacts more difficult, and that is what is being done. The Maldives system will send everything straight to Germany. We'll completely bypass London, which can only be for the best. We'll leave it all in the hands of the Krauts; and just take the money.'

'When is Stephen back?'

'Today, tomorrow. Depends really. I hate them going on the hunts, it sickens me to be honest. I hated it when I was out in Thailand. But the men like it. They're up in the mountains looking for girls, and the tea plantations have plenty of dirts waiting to be bought for a few quid. We'll keep them a year then their fathers come and renegotiate or else take the girls home. They're weird these Asians, you know. They'd sell their fucking grannies for a few rupees. I thought I'd seen it all in Thailand, and the Philippines took some beating, but it's been going on there for years. Here it's quite new, and the people are falling over themselves to give us their kids. Ugly little fuckers, a lot of them. At least in Thailand the little girls are cute, and cuteness makes money. Here they all look half-starved and their eyes are pused over. I spend more money on fucking Golden Eye ointment than I do on their food!' Candy laughed raucously.

Donna felt an urge to slap the woman before her. She watched as a fit of coughing overcame Candy, and saw her spit into a yellow-tinged hanky.

'How's this place doing?'

Candy's coughing fit abated and she took a long swallow of her water.

'All right. We had a few visits from the local Old Bill, but we soon sweetened them up. A couple of the older girls and a thousand rupees a week saw them off lovely. But you must understand, love. Here, a lot of things are ignored. The caste system is similar to the setup in Thailand. The poor are to be used and abused. That's the bottom line. They all believe in reincarnation anyway, and are all convinced they'll come back as the rich cunt next time, so they accept their fate without a second thought. Ignorant as shit, most of them.'

'Quite.' The one word conveyed to Candy that Donna put her on a similar level and her face hardened.

'Listen here, Mrs High and Mighty Brunos. Your old man couldn't wait to come in with us, and he's had a good bit of bunce off us since. I assume you shared in it, so don't you dare sit there and fucking look down your hooter at me, lady. I do what I do because it's all I know. But I ain't justifying myself to you or anyone else. You're here now because it all fell out of bed for a while and your money is drying up. So don't you dare put yourself above me and mine, I wont have it. You should have let fucking Stephen or Paddy sort this out, love, if you couldn't handle it.'

'Or Davey Jackson.' Donna had regained her equilibrium. 'With respect, Candy, I don't have to like what we're doing, do I?'

The other woman relaxed into her seat again and sighed.

439

'No, you don't. No more than I do, I suppose. But it's like Jake says: if we weren't doing it someone else would be, and at least I see the kids are looked after for the most part. I don't have no bondage or nothing for the little ones. In Thailand, you know, there's brothels where the kids are chained all the time to a bed and have ten or more men a day. When I was in Bangkok a few years ago, a brothel near us caught fire and all the little girls died, burnt alive they were, because they were chained to the beds. Broke my heart it did. No, they don't have too bad a time of it here. I never keep them more than eighteen months or two years. Even the really young ones look shagged out by then.'

Donna nodded, unable to trust herself to speak.

The phone rang, sending a shrill shock through the quiet of the room.

Candy picked it up with an abrupt: 'Yes?'

Donna watched the changing expressions on her face.

'What do you mean? Listen, Stephen, your brother's wife's here with me now.'

Donna rose in consternation. As she stood up, Candy waved her back to her seat, fear in her eyes now. Donna walked from the room and out towards the back of the house. She stood in a wide doorway watching the children as they sat in the shade. They were all different shapes and sizes, different shades of brown. All had large expressive eyes, and unsmiling mouths.

She was still watching them when Candy walked out to her and said, 'I think me and you had better have a little talk, Mrs Brunos, don't you?'

Chapter Thirty-Eight

Candy took her firmly by the arm and led her back into the office. Donna slumped in the chair once more. She looked frightened; she *was* frightened.

'What really brought you out here, lady?'

Donna lit herself a cigarette and took a deep draw on it.

'What do you think? I had no idea what was going on – oh, I admit I had had my suspicions, but I thought that if I came out here and found out the score then I could decide what I was going to do. I had to know if my husband was involved, you see.'

Candy grinned. 'Oh, he's involved all right, up to his neck. This was all his idea, love. Georgio was the brains behind it all. But you can discuss that with Stephen. He'll be here later today.'

She saw Donna's fleeting look of fear and half-smiled.

'You should look frightened, my dear, because Stephen is livid. I opened me big trap, didn't I? But as I said to him, I didn't realise I was doing anything wrong. You looked the part and acted the part. Now you're going to get in a lot of shit, and it's my job to keep an eye on you until he arrives. So let's get one thing straight, shall we? If you attempt to leave I'll break your fucking legs, and that's no idle threat. I am quite capable of doing it. That was my forte in the girlie houses in Bangkok. I was a head girl with a difference, you see. To me they're all scum.'

'What happened to all your talk earlier, then? About how you look after the kiddies?'

Candy looked shocked.

'But I do. That's the point, see? I do look after them, but they're all the same, love. In these countries you find out what life is really all about. Now in Bangkok I worked with the teenagers. Fucking pain in the arse most of them. But, you see, I'm quite partial to girls myself. Not kids, never. But the older girls are always willing to lighten their burden. They're clever, shrewd. We're not talking kids like the ones back home. The children out here are born fucking old. They adapt to their lives, they're pliable, don't cry that much either. I used to

441

find that weird at first. But not any more. It's like I said earlier, they were never kids in our sense of the word.

'In some of these villages the seven year olds have been working on the tea plantations since two or three. They do a full day's collar. In Thailand they work the paddyfields or making baskets. They're not kids. Not in their minds. We've got mothers and fathers queueing up to sell their kids to us, accept it as a part of life. That's the difference, see? Once you get over your Englishness and start looking on it all from their point of view, you find life becomes a lot easier.'

Donna looked down at the floor. 'My husband would have nothing to do with anything like this, I know that better than you. When he finds out there will be murder done here.'

Candy laughed gently and lit a cheroot. 'Your precious husband was out in Thailand a few years ago, love. I supplied him with thirteen and fourteen year olds. He liked the three-headed blow job best.'

She watched Donna's look of shock and disgust and smiled sadly.

'I know it's hard to admit to these things. But there, the truth hurts, don't it? Your husband is as much a part of all this as I am. It was his idea not to bother decorating the place. The men who come here don't give a flying fuck what the surroundings are. In fact, I think the more sordid it is the better they like it. The stench of the place turns them on. Degradation is a heady drug, love, that's why we make so much dosh. In Phuket, you can pick up a little boy or girl on the beach, lay with them all afternoon – if you want in broad daylight. It'll be the same here in a few years. It's the Asian black economy. Goa is just opening up now, as is this place.

'Your husband had the foresight to see all this, along with his brother. We make films here, do anything we want to do, and no one can stop us. It's a bit hairy at the moment, granted, but once we get ourselves off to Krautland we'll be laughing. I don't know why you're looking so green around the gills. It's all this that'll get your old man home, and keep you in luxury for the rest of your days.'

Donna stood up. 'Oh no it won't, lady. I'm leaving.'

She made to walk towards the door, but Candy grabbed her arm in a vice-like grip.

'You ain't going nowhere, and if I have to belt you one right across the boat, I will. Stephen wants a word, and by the sound of it you've annoyed him. If I was you I'd sit yourself down and think what you're going to say to him when he arrives. He ain't a bloke to cross. Believe me, I know.'

Donna saw the determined glint in Candy's eyes, and the taut muscles in her heavy arms. Eyes shining with tears, she pulled herself free.

442

'This is all disgusting, all of it! You're scum, do you know that? Fucking scum! And I'll see you lot blown wide open, you just see if I don't.'

A high-pitched scream echoed through the house and Candy opened the office door instinctively, Donna hot on her heels. Outside was a young Sri Lankan male of about eighteen.

'Keep hold of this lady, Kassim. Make sure she doesn't leave here.'

The boy nodded, staring at Donna with a mixture of awe at her whiteness and adolescent lust. The three went along the corridor to the right of them. The child's voice was a low moan now. Candy opened a heavy wooden door and entered a large room, Donna and Kassim hot on her heels.

The room was dirty. A stale odour assailed Donna's nostrils. On the bed was a girl of about ten. Her long hair was tied to a heavy piece of wood across the end of the bed. Standing by it in just a white shirt was a tall thin white man. He had sandy hair and his face and body were red raw from too much sun. He looked frightened, and on closer inspection of the child Donna could see why.

The little body was lying awkwardly against the end of the bed. He had tried to turn her over on to her stomach and her hair had stopped the procedure. The little girl's head was at an odd angle and blood was seeping from her mouth and nostrils. She was naked, and blood was smeared on the tops of her legs.

The man was pulling on his shorts, his breathing harsh in the still room.

'What the fuck's going on here?'

Candy swiftly examined the child. Then, taking Kassim's hunting knife from his belt, she began cutting the girl's hair to release her from her bonds, all the while talking.

'Who let you in here, Mr Gainsborough?'

The man was standing staring at the child, whose moans were becoming less and less coherent.

Donna rushed to her side. Taking a hankie from her pocket, she wiped the child's brow and face. The blood was lessening now.

'It wasn't my fault, Candy. She was struggling . . . She just kept struggling.'

Candy looked at the man in annoyance and said distinctly, 'Well, so would you if someone had you tied by the hair. You shouldn't even be here during the day. Who gave the say-so, eh?'

Mr Gainsborough, assistant manager in a Surrey bank and a married man, stood on his dignity.

'I arranged it with Jake, actually. I prefer the daylight. I don't like coming when it's busy.'

The child free now, Candy laid her on her back. She stood up to her full height and said loudly, 'I don't give a monkey's what you like and what you don't like. No one ties up my girls – *no one*. It's something I will not tolerate. Now my advice to you is to get yourself down the beach or to your hotel and come back tonight. Otherwise keep away, Mister. These kids only work nights while I'm here. Not all bloody day as well. Now piss off.'

She turned from him and said to Donna, 'Help me get her into bed. He's pulled the muscle, that's all. Could have broken the poor little whore's neck.'

Donna shook her head in consternation. The child was semi-conscious.

'She needs hospital treatment, Candy. Take her to hospital.'

Candy stared into Donna's eyes. 'She'll be all right. Now help me get her into bed.'

Donna's voice shocked even herself as she bellowed: 'This child is dying, you stupid bitch. He's crushed her fucking windpipe! Jesus Christ, will you get her to a fucking hospital!'

Donna could feel hysteria rising up inside her like a dam. She had opened her mouth to scream once more when Candy punched her in the face. The next thing she knew, she was careering across the room, an explosion of lights in her eyes and a black haze of pain running through her cheekbone.

Candy stood over her, and the menace in her face and voice were not lost on Donna or Kassim.

'Don't you dare tell me what to do, lady. You come sneaking in here, causing hag with me and Stephen. Then you tell me what's best for my girls. Well, the buck stops here. Kassim, take her to one of the rooms and lock her inside until Mr Stephen gets here. I don't want to hear one word out of her, OK? And put Asheem outside the window in case she decides to try and escape that way. Mr Stephen wants her later, you understand! She goes nowhere.'

Kassim nodded, and helping Donna to her feet, he half-dragged, half-carried her from the room.

Donna's face was on fire with pain and her mind was screaming with fear: fear for the child and fear for herself. Whatever she had walked into, it was far more serious than she had anticipated. She knew that her life was in danger, and the knowledge gave her fear a physical quality that overshadowed the pain in her face.

She knew that Stephen hated her, and now she had found out what was really going on, seen it with her own eyes, the thought of confronting him frightened her more than anything.

★ ★ ★

444

Big Paddy and Davey Jackson were both drinking tea in Donna's kitchen, Dolly chatting away with her usual cheerfulness.

'I told you the other night, I have no idea where Donna's gone. I think it was Marbella, but I'm not sure. The girl needed to get away for a bit. Would you two like a slice of cake with your tea? I only made it yesterday, it's lovely and moist.'

The two men shook their heads.

Paddy sighed. 'Listen to me, Dolly love. Donna could be in a lot of trouble and we need to help her, so why don't you just tell us where she's gone?'

His voice was heavy with innuendo and Dolly feigned ignorance.

'I just told you, I don't know. Don't be an arsehole, Paddy. What kind of danger could that girl be in anyway?'

She decided to turn the questioning around.

Paddy stood up, and for a few seconds his sheer size frightened her. She had to shake herself mentally and tell herself that this was Big Paddy whom she'd known for years, not some stranger out to mug her. He walked purposefully towards her.

'I'm losing me fecking patience, Dolly. Now tell me where she is!'

She pushed him away with both her hands. 'Are you threatening me, Paddy Donovon?'

Davey stood up, his open face troubled. 'Come away from her, Paddy, there's a good man.'

Paddy turned his head to face, him. 'Keep out of this, Davey, right?' He whipped round to Dolly and with one large meaty hand, grabbed her hair at the nape of her neck and pulled her head back painfully.

'Tell me where she's gone, old lady, or I swear before God I'll beat the shite out of you.'

Davey's voice was shocked. 'Paddy, for fuck's sake!'

'Enough! Now tell me what I want to know. I told you – I'm losing me fecking patience.'

Dolly stared up at Paddy with terrified eyes. This was a man she had never seen before, a brute who frightened her witless. Her voice was frail as she said weakly, 'She's gone to Liverpool, that's all I know. Where she went before.'

Her mind was working overtime to find a destination and now she had found one, she hoped against hope he'd believe her.

Paddy's face screwed up in consternation. 'Liverpool? What on earth for?'

Dolly began to cry softly, her voice drenched with tears as she said, 'I don't know, I swear to you. She told me not to tell a soul about it. She tells me nothing and now you know why. I can't be trusted, I

445

can't be trusted! Oh Paddy, please let me go, you're hurting me.'

He released his hold on her hair and snarled into her face, 'If you're lying to me, you old cunt, you'll regret it.'

He stormed from the kitchen and Dolly slumped against the worksurface, holding her hand to her bruised neck.

'I'm sorry, Dolly love, I didn't think he'd—'

Dolly cut him off. 'Go away, Davey. Whatever this is all about, I hope to Christ you both lose out by it, I really do. There's something rotten going on and I hope to Christ you get your comeuppance. That'll be me prayer from this day on.'

She turned away from him. Davey looked at the bent old back for a few moments before hurrying out of the house and to the car.

Paddy was already behind the wheel, his face like thunder. 'If she's gone to Liverpool, she's gone to JoJo or Coyne.'

Davey nodded imperceptibly.

Paddy's eyes were slits as he barked out, 'Or she's gone to Nick the queer. Either way, she could land the lot of us right in it. The stupid interfering bitch! Cox is missing too.'

'Maybe they're just sorting out the final details on the jump?'

Paddy nodded as he acknowledged this. 'Could be – but I don't trust him and I don't trust her. There's been too many rumours on the street. And that Donna, she's been asking about too much. Stephen told me she's into everything. Who knows what she's sussed out, eh? And if she susses out about her big fine husband, she'll sell him down the river like that!' He clicked his finger and thumb. 'And we'll all go along with him.'

He thumped the steering wheel in temper.

'We have to find out where she is, and we have to find out soon. Even Georgio would agree with that.'

Davey sat beside Paddy as they drove towards London. His heart was heavy in his chest; he wished he'd never got involved in any of it.

If Carol ever found out . . . he felt a rush of fear so acute he could almost taste it.

He hated it, hated all of it. It was greed, nothing but greed. Now Georgio was banged up, the merchandise was on the streets and he was in charge of distribution through mail order. Davey was in it up to his neck and knew he couldn't get out.

Stephen arrived at eight in the evening, hot, dusty and angry. The hotel was just picking up and he walked through the front door with a fixed smile on his face. The sight of the children affected him not at all. He nodded pleasantly at the men and made his way to Candy's office.

446

She was sitting drinking a large brandy and Seven Up. Her face was hard. Stephen closed the door gently behind him then said, 'How much does she know?'

'Too bloody much. She walked in here as if she knew everything, Stephen. Told me that she was out here looking over Georgio's interests. Told me he had sent her.'

Stephen laughed nastily. 'Oh, she did, did she?'

Candy nodded. 'There was a bit of trouble and all while she was here. That geek Gainsborough tied up the little girl from Colombo. The stupid prat tied her to the end of the bed by her hair, if you don't mind. Somehow, during his games, probably as he turned her over, her hair got wrapped around her neck. He crushed her fucking windpipe.'

Stephen frowned. 'Is she all right?'

Candy shook her head. 'She's dying slowly. She'll be gone by the morning, I'd say. She's stronger than I thought, to be honest. I think he damaged her inside as well. She's bringing up blood, and bleeding from the nose. I've locked her in one of the rooms in the roof.'

Stephen sat down heavily. 'And Donna saw all this?'

Candy nodded. She watched as he ran his hands through his thick dark hair.

'Where's Jake?' she asked.

'He's still in Colombo. I left him there to sort out the other business. The police tried to close down the bar again.'

Candy closed her eyes. 'It never rains but it pours, eh? I heard they've been shutting down a lot of the gay bars there. Give it a couple of weeks and we can reopen. It's always the same. It's just a show, nothing serious.'

Stephen shook his head. 'Fuck that anyway, I'm more interested in what's happening with that stupid bitch.'

He poured himself a large brandy. Then he said, 'She'll just have to be an accident, won't she? Let's face it, she won't be the first British tourist to die through drinking and swimming. It happens all the time. Arrack is lethal out here with the tourists. There's a heavy undertow on a few of the beaches, it'll look all right. I saw it done myself years ago, in Phuket. I felt more sorry for the tour rep to be honest, she had to sort out all the details.'

Stephen laughed and Candy smiled grimly at him. 'But that's murder.'

He opened his eyes wide and said in a childish voice, 'No! I never would have known! What do you think Gainsborough did today then? Had a little accident? Don't go soft on me, Candy, I ain't in the mood.'

447

She shook her head in amazement. 'You're as hard as nails, aren't you?'

As she took a gulp of her drink and lit a cigarette, Stephen said, 'I'm harder than that, Candy, and at the moment it's just as well one of us is, ain't it?'

'What about Georgio then? Have you thought about him, what he might have to say about you topping his old woman?'

Stephen laughed nastily. 'Fuck Georgio. Me and Lewis are rowing him out only he doesn't know that yet. So just take me to Donna, will you?'

Candy opened the office door, her face a picture of disbelief at what she had just heard.

'You're a snidey bastard, Stephen.' Her voice held genuine admiration.

'That's me, Candy – always a step ahead of the competition. Now, where the hell is she?'

'I stuck her into one of the back bedrooms. Kassim's outside the door and there's another lad outside the window. She's slippery. She is also traumatised at what she saw. Very vestal virgin, is our Georgio's wife. Where the fuck he got her from I don't know.'

Stephen grinned. 'The Roman Road.'

Candy laughed in delight.

'Amazing what you can pick up on the markets, ain't it?'

Donna sat in the deepening twilight, her feet curled under her. She could smell the bedding and an odour of heavy greasy food. The kitchen must be nearby. Voices wafted into the room from the grounds and she guessed the hotel was open for business. All she could see in her mind was the child, and the blood. She had a raging thirst, but no appetite. Fear had made her bowels loose and she had had an uncomfortable time trying to hold everything inside her. There was no sanitation nearby. What was supposed to have been an ensuite bathroom was a dust-filled hole.

She could hear the movements of insects in the deepening gloom and had to stifle the urge to scream. As the doorhandle turned, she felt a wave of panic wash over her.

Stephen stood outlined in the glare of the corridor. As he switched on the light, Donna shielded her eyes with her hand.

Candy followed him into the room and said loudly, 'Why didn't you put the lights on, you stupid cow? Do you want anything to eat or drink?'

She sounded so normal, Donna felt for a split second that she was losing her mind.

'How's the child?' Her voice felt rusty, as if she hadn't used it for years.

Candy rolled her eyes. 'I got one of the men to take her to the hospital. She'll be fine.'

Donna licked dry lips. 'No cars have left since I've been here, I've been listening out.'

Candy looked at Stephen in a 'See what I mean?' kind of way and shrugged.

'I'll get you a drink, all right?'

When she had left the room, Stephen walked over and sat on the bed.

'Why did you come, Donna – eh? Why didn't you keep your big nose out of it? You realise that I can't let you leave now, don't you? There's too much at stake here. You saw and you heard too much. You're like a fucking leech, do you know that? Like the spear in Christ's side.'

His low sing song voice frightened Donna more than if he had struck her or shouted at her.

'I see you've had a right-hander.' He touched her swollen cheek softly with his fingers. Donna pulled her head away abruptly. It was almost a sexual act, a caress, and it made her feel sick.

'Still the ice lady, eh? My God, you make me laugh. Georgio's little virgin to the last. Do you know something, Donna? He fucked everything that walked. It was common knowledge to all and sundry. Alan Cox could have enlightened you, Georgio took enough of them to Amigo's. Tall, blonde bimbos were his forte. Oh, don't look so shocked. You must have known, must have guessed.'

Donna watched him with fearful eyes. Stephen was thoroughly enjoying himself, relishing seeing Miss High and Mighty brought so low.

'Georgio masterminded all this.' He lifted his arms to encompass the room. 'It was after he visited Thailand with me the first time. I took him all over. As you know I love the place, always did. He loved it as well. Loved the girls. "They're like pieces of meat," he said. "Faceless, nameless, you can just do what you like and they don't mind." He bought bar girls at a dollar a time, three and four in bed at once. He loved all that, old Georgio, it appealed to him. Some were only twelve or thirteen. He drew the line at the really young ones. Always had that Victorian streak, did our Georgio.'

Donna put her hands over her ears. 'Shut up! Shut up. Stephen!'

He dragged her hands down and held them firmly on her lap.

'You know it's true, Donna. You were the best front he could have for years, and you never realised it. He used to laugh at you behind

449

your back. We all did, even Big Paddy. He's in on all this as well as Davey Jackson. You thought they were all protecting you from me and the likes of me, and all the time they were protecting me and Georgio from you. Funny when you think about it, eh?'

Candy came back into the room with three glasses on a tray. She passed one to Stephen and one to Donna. Donna took hers but didn't drink from it.

Stephen sipped his and then gave it to Donna.

'Don't worry, we're not going to poison you.' He laughed and shook his head. 'You read too many fucking books.'

Donna sipped the Arrack and Coke then gulped at it, her throat swollen and sore, needing the coolness of the drink.

'You must get that child to a hospital, Stephen, otherwise she'll die.'

He laughed again and Donna saw the insane glint in his eyes. She realised that Stephen was over the edge.

'Oh, I must, must I? You have no authority here, Donna. You are in deep shit, lady. It's you who'll be going to the hospital, love. Not the kid. You'll be in the mortuary by morning!'

He saw the fear in her eyes and savoured the sensation it gave him. To see her brought low was like balm to his ego.

'You're like my mother, do you know that? All good outside, and wind and water inside. All the mouth and the talk. Oh, yes, it's like you modelled yourself on old Maeve. Maeve the mother figure, Maeve who talked to us all as if we were kids even when we were grown men and women. I hate her, Donna, almost as much as I hate you. Do you know the funny thing? When the word gets back that you're dead, I'll have to identify you, won't I?'

He laughed again.

'I'll enjoy that. It will give me a real good laugh.'

Donna was terrified. 'You're mad. Georgio will know what happened.'

Stephen rubbed her face with his hand, caressing the swollen cheek once more.

'Georgio will be grateful, darling. He wasn't going to stay with you, you stupid bitch.'

As he spoke Donna launched herself at him, hands and nails flying. It was so unexpected it took him and Candy by surprise but as she reached the door, Stephen caught hold of her hair, dragging her painfully back to the bed.

'You're not going anywhere, woman. Not yet anyway.'

Just then the door opened and Alan Cox walked into the room with two heavyset men behind him.

450

'Hello, all. Entertaining the family, Stephen?'

Donna catapulted from the bed as if on a spring and ran to Alan, her face alight with relief at seeing him.

Stephen looked stunned.

'Surprised to see me, Stephen?' Alan put his arm around Donna and smiled down at her. Then, pushing her away gently, he walked towards Stephen.

He was still looking stunned as Candy, realising what was happening, went for Alan with her glass. Donna shouted to warn him and Alan turned around and slammed his fist into Candy's abdomen. The glass flew out of her hand as she dropped to her knees.

Alan Cox stared at Stephen as he sat on the bed, his face a mask of surprise and fear. As Stephen went to rise, Alan began to lay into him, punching him with the full force of his considerable weight behind each blow.

Donna watched in shock as Stephen attempted to crawl across the bed, trying to avoid the rain of blows descending on him with premeditated regularity, battering his head and his face with a ferocity Donna would never have believed possible. As Stephen hit the floor, Alan was kicking him, kicking him so hard he was being shoved across the concrete, and all the time Alan was talking.

'Hurts does it, Brunos? Frightened, are you? The big whoremaster is frightened, is he?'

In her mind's eye Donna saw Alan kicking to death a Chinese man in Soho. In her heart she knew it was about to be re-enacted in a squalid hotel-cum-brothel in Sri Lanka.

Grabbing him, she began pulling him away. 'You'll kill him, Alan, you'll kill him!'

He shrugged her off as if she was a fly.

She looked at the two heavies for help. They stood watching, stony-faced.

'Stop him, someone, for Christ's sake!'

But no one moved. Even Candy was watching in fascinated silence.

Pushing her way in front of Alan, Donna put her hands up to his face, cupping his chin.

'He's not worth going to prison for, Alan, especially not out here. Leave him. It's over. Leave him alone.'

Alan looked down at her as if in a trance. Then his shoulders slumped inside his jacket, and his body seemed to relax.

His eyes moved to the bloody face below him, and his mind registered that Stephen was still breathing. Inside he was sorry for that fact; he wished him dead. Never had he wanted anyone dead so much.

451

He glanced over at the two men waiting by the door. Their faces remained devoid of expression or thought.

Donna pulled him away from Stephen's inert form.

'There's an injured child here, a girl, in a lot of pain. Her windpipe's crushed. We have to find out what happened to her, Alan.'

Candy pulled herself up with the help of the bed. 'I told you, she's gone to the hospital.'

Donna looked into the hard face. 'What hospital is she in then, and we'll go there?'

Alan looked at the woman and said through clenched teeth, 'I'm going to raze this fucking place to the ground. My advice to you is to tell the lady what she wants to know or else I'll kick the truth out of you.'

Candy looked from Alan to Stephen and then to the men by the doorway. She sighed.

'She's up in one of the rooms in the roof.'

Donna's face paled. 'But she was dying, the child was dying!'

Candy nodded. 'I'm quite well aware of that fact, Mrs Brunos.'

'Then you'd better lead the way, hadn't you?' Alan's voice was loud in the room.

He looked at the men by the door and said, 'You know what to do.'

They nodded and left the room quietly.

'Come on then, we haven't got all night.'

Candy led them to the attic room, and as the door was opened, the heat hit them. It was like opening an oven.

The child was on an old blanket on the floor. Her eyes were closed, her mouth slightly open. As Donna ran to her, there was the sound of shouting and Candy made a move for the doorway.

'Stay where you are, lady, I haven't finished with you. There's another few men down there with my two. I came well-prepared. You ain't going fucking nowhere.'

Alan picked up the child gently and ran with her from the room, Donna and Candy following. He took her to the room he had found Donna in and she saw Kassim inside with a large cut over his forehead, talking to himself in an Indian dialect.

Inside the room, Alan placed the child gently on the bed, but Donna knew as soon as she looked at her that she was dead. Her tongue was swollen, it was noticeable in the bright light, and her lips were blue. Her large brown eyes were half-open.

Donna stared at the broken body for a few moments and then she became aware of a high-pitched keening noise. For a while she wondered where it was coming from, maybe from the child, then she

452

felt Alan's arms around her and she realised that it was coming from inside her, and out of her mouth.

Alan stared down into the strained dirty face of Donna Brunos and felt his heart move inside his chest. All her longing and need was written in her eyes, every defeat etched into her face. Yet also, in the back of her eyes, there was an inner light, strength that hadn't been there before. He had glimpsed it once or twice, but now it was the making of her. Donna Brunos, wife of Georgio, was gone.

Donna Brunos, Woman, had taken her place.

Holding her tight, he let her cry herself out. The child's broken body was an outlet for everything that had ever befallen her and instinctively Alan Cox knew that.

It was this underlying softness, the capacity Donna had for caring deeply, that attracted him to her.

As he held her, he heard the destruction of the hotel all around them and felt whole once more, cleansed of every wrongdoing ever attributed to him. He likened the feeling to one the soldiers must have felt at the end of the war, when they opened up the gates of the death camps.

He was wiping out all his past misdeeds and writing a new page in his life.

A life he wanted to share with the woman in his arms.

She had become like a drug to him, and now he knew that he needed her more than he had ever needed anyone or anything in his life.

And with the destruction of Georgio Brunos's memory, there was a chance he just might get her.

Chapter Thirty-Nine

Donna was sipping a glass of lemonade, while Alan and his henchmen were sorting out the last of the Bay View Hotel. One of the men, a bull-necked heavyset individual with deep brown eyes and thick wavy hair, was speaking rapidly into the phone in Urdu.

Alan smiled at Donna grimly. They both looked towards Stephen who lay slumped in a chair staring ahead as if in a trance. His face was blue and swollen, and he was covered in his own blood. Donna felt nothing as she looked at him.

'He must have been off his head, Donna, to think he could get away with murder. Did Georgio know you were going to top his wife if needs be?' Alan dragged Stephen's face around to look at him.

The wounded man smiled, wincing as the move made his lips crack open once more.

'He was going to leave her high and dry, mate. Even the money from the house, he planned to take that. He was going to leave you with nothing, darlin'. All this was his baby, he loved it out here.'

'Shut the fuck up, Stephen!' Alan's voice was harsh and Donna, leaning forward in her seat, said, 'No, let him finish, I want to know.'

Stephen shook his head as if she was a recalcitrant child. 'You're a stupid cunt, Donna, you always was. Even now you want to know the truth, don't you? You're like my mum; tell the truth and shame the devil.' He laughed hysterically. 'She didn't know the devil was living in her house, the devil and his cohorts.

'Lewis was unaware that his money was being used for all this. That's where I was going to sort it all out, see – once Georgio was on the trot. Lewis really believed that I was investing his money, and he was getting a good return on it. I was shitting meself for a while, in case he and Georgio ever got to nattering. That line Georgio spun you about Lewis losing money on the hotels was shite – just a lucky guess. I involved Lewis, and then I was going to row Georgio out, see. Because I set all this up. All I needed was his money, but Georgio being Georgio wanted to run the whole fucking shebang. He even wanted the palatial hotel as well. It was me who fucked all that up. I know my market, see, something Georgio never gave me credit for.'

'You're a piece of fucking shite!'

This from Joey, the leader of Alan's posse. It was delivered in a thick Geordie accent.

Stephen sniggered. 'So what does that make you lot then, eh? It was the people on this island that made all this possible. They fought hammer and tongs for us to take their kids, buy them off them. Rent them for a year, and then renegotiate. Supply and demand, mate, the British way of doing business.'

Alan shook his head and said half to himself, 'I still can't believe what we stumbled on here. Are there any other operations going on? What about in the Smoke?'

Stephen shrugged. 'What do I get for my information?'

Alan looked into the battered and swollen face and finally, after long moments, answered him.

'You get out of here, that's what you get. Then you disappear off the face of the earth, mate, because I'm going to put the word all over the streets about you, Brunos. About all this, about your wonderful achievements in Asia with little kids.'

Stephen had the grace to look away, knowing he was caught up in something that was now beyond his control.

'So how are Jack and JoJo involved?'

Stephen dabbed at a trickle of blood and swallowed heavily before answering.

'Jack wanted out pretty much from the start, but you know Jack and JoJo. Where JoJo leads, Jack inevitably follows. They sort out the printing of the merchandise over in England. The books are big money, you'd be surprised the number of men who want what we supply. Georgio's brainchild was the modem. You know what he's like with computers. It was one step on from what we were doing here, see? We videoed the kids, took photos, and then we marketed them. Georgio thought up the first batch of titles. Now we're worldwide, thanks to a contact we found in a northern university. He marketed the stuff for us over the Internet, then we just decided to do it for ourselves.'

'And what about the children, Stephen?' Donna's voice was empty.

'What about them? Like I said earlier, they were bought and paid for, Donna.'

He grinned at her then, knowing it was killing her hearing all the gory details.

'Some of the kids are quite good at it, you know,' he went on conversationally. 'In fact, with these Asian kids, it's a kind of knack they've got. They're scum, and we have a permanent supply.'

455

Alan's fist hit Stephen on the side of the head with such force it split his ear open, nearly tearing it off.

'I'll fucking kill you, Brunos, do you hear me?' he snarled.

Donna watched, expressionlessly.

Joey topped up her glass of lemonade and said in a low voice, 'I was offered into all this like, but I knocked it back. I'm glad I did and all. Every time I look at my own kids, I'll think of these poor little fuckers. Some of the kids here don't even know where they're from. We'll have to take them to one of the Catholic missions, I think. Let them sort it out. When the parents finally arrive the locals will explain what's happened. The trouble is, a lot of the time the parents sell the kids and then forget about them.' He ran his hands nervously through his thick wiry hair.

Joey noticed the green tinge to Donna's face and said gently, 'Get the lass away, Alan, we'll finish up here. It's better if you disappear now anyway. Leave it to me and the local filth to clear this lot up.'

Alan held out a meaty fist. 'Thanks, Joey, I appreciate it.'

He grinned now, displaying pristine white teeth.

'You're paying well, but in all honesty I'd have come here for nowt. I don't know, Alan. There's shite in the world these days, and yet it's the armed robbers that everyone seems to hate. Property or other people's money is sacred. Human life is a different ballgame altogether, eh?'

Alan nodded, and taking Donna by the arm, he led her from the room.

As they walked through the hotel, she looked at all the children. They were sitting quietly, their faces devoid of expression, no real feeling evident anywhere, accepting this latest development in their fate as they had everything else.

'What'll happen to them, Alan? What will be the end result?'

He opened the car door. 'I can't answer that one, darling. It was their parents who brought them here. Let Joey sort it out now. We've done all we can, haven't we?'

She looked up into his face and said softly, 'Have we? Then why aren't I feeling any better?'

Alan sighed heavily and Donna looked at him properly. She saw the lines around his eyes and mouth, the deep hollows across his face through lack of sleep, and she shook her head in despair.

'Who cares about them though? Who really cares?'

'I don't know, love. Now get into the car, will you? God only worked one day at a time, remember, and even He ended up having a day off.'

If Donna had had a chuckle inside her, she would have given it. As it was, she couldn't even cry any more.

456

★ ★ ★

Jack Coyne looked worried and JoJo O'Neil was getting annoyed. 'So you can't get through. Big deal. You know what the situation's like out there. Sometimes they can't use the phones for days.'

Jack shook his head. 'I don't care, JoJo, there's something not right. I can feel it in my water.'

JoJo laughed loudly. 'Are you sure? You can feel it in your water! Now I've heard everything. Knowing Stephen, he's on a pussy hunt with that piss-head Jake. Only knowing Stephen's little foibles, Jake's shagging the kids and Stephen's after their grannies!' He laughed uproariously at his own wit.

Jack was silent for a while, until JoJo said heavily, 'Will you go home? I can't stand you sitting there with a face like a wet weekend in Blackpool. I've got a little bird coming round soon, and I want to get her in the mood for shagging, not hanging herself.'

Jack wiped his large hand across his face.

'I still think there's something not right. I couldn't even get a fax through to them. They're supposed to be letting us know when the next lot of merchandise is coming through, and we've heard nothing. Even the modem line is dead.'

JoJo lost his patience. 'Jack, fuck off home, will you? Play with the kids, play with yourself if you have to, but please, go home.'

Jack stared at JoJo's bandaged hand. The stumps looked swollen and he knew JoJo was eating painkillers like sweets, on top of his usual bucketful of alcohol a day.

'He might as well have shot you in the head,' he said spitefully, 'because since Nick blew your fingers off, you've been half-mad.'

JoJo's face was dark with temper as he bellowed, 'I'll see me day with him!' He looked down at his fingerless hand and said through gritted teeth, 'Once the jump's over, he's mine. I promised that to meself. He's mine and I'll have that bastard screaming for mercy.'

Jack interrupted him, saying levelly, 'The way you're treating the businesses, you won't be able to sort out your dirty washing, let alone Nick Carvello. Drink and drugs, drugs and birds, drink and birds. That's all you do.'

JoJo looked at his business partner and only friend and said jovially, 'So what else is new?'

Jack sighed. He knew in his heart that something was wrong in Sri Lanka, and also knew that until he could prove it, his friend and mentor just wouldn't want to know.

Five minutes later a young girl with tits like rugby balls and a mouth like the Toxteth sewers arrived.

Jack went home then.

457

All he was interested in was his wife, his kids, and keeping out of prison. With JoJo going over the top like this since the run-in with Nick, he knew that everything he held dear was in danger, and he would cut his partner's throat with a blunt razor before he let him destroy everything.

Alan sat on the splendid verandah of the hotel sipping a large scotch. The room was actually on the beach itself, about twenty yards from the sea. The sound of the waves coming in was reassuring. The sea was constant, dangerous, and commanded respect. He could identify with that. He loved to listen to it at times like this, with the only other sounds the high peeping noise of the insects, and with the reflection of the moon on the shimmering water.

Donna's hotel was discreet and classy. It was for people who enjoyed solitude and were willing to pay for it. It was a far cry from the Bay View in Hikkadoa.

There was a small pathway leading to the water itself, and a freshwater shower. Following the pathway, Alan slipped into the sea, letting the cold water envelop him and cleanse him of the sights and sounds of the day. He wanted it to wash away the feeling of dirtiness Stephen had left upon him.

He closed his eyes tightly as he pictured the small body of the little girl. He tried to blot out the picture, and the unwanted memories it evoked. They didn't even know her name.

He swam for ten minutes then came out of the water. As he walked up the pathway he saw Donna on the verandah in a thin wrapper, fresh from the shower, the outline of her body revealed against the lights.

As he reached her she sat down on one of the padded chairs and picked up her glass of scotch.

Alan rubbed himself dry then settled beside her. 'How are you feeling now, love?' he asked tenderly.

Donna shook her glistening wet hair. 'I don't know. It's all been too much to take in, I think.'

'It's the little girl that's the horror, eh?' He grasped Donna's hand as he spoke and she was grateful to him. She nodded her head, eyes shimmering with tears.

'She was so small, Alan, so vulnerable. Like a little doll. I wish we could go to the authorities.'

He wagged her hand up and down as he spoke.

'Listen, Donna, we went through all that earlier. They would bang us all up, you included, and believe me when I say a lesbian wing on Holloway would be preferable to being banged up here. Let Joey sort it out.'

Donna took a deep breath and watched the moon.

'We always seem to be letting other people sort things out, don't we? Shall I tell you something, Alan? When I first met Jonnie H. and Nick and all the others, I was terrified inside. I had to pretend that I was in control, you see. For Georgio. If you knew how frightened I was! Even when I met you. I didn't like you very much, a convicted murderer.

'No matter what I found out about Georgio, I never cared. Nothing could be that bad, see, because I loved him so very much. I was grateful to him, because until I met Georgio I was little Orphan Annie, Donna Fenland, nobody. He made me into somebody. He gave me a family, and a life. As the years went on, I was grateful if he made love to me. Really grateful. Pathetically grateful, in fact, because I knew he was seeing other women. Yet that was preferable to not having him. I needed him desperately.

'How could I have let him, or anyone for that matter, do that to me? How did it happen, Alan?' She looked into his face then. 'How did I allow myself to get caught up in all this?'

Alan put a heavy hand up to her face and cupped her cheek. 'As you said, Donna. You loved him.'

'But is that really any excuse – for all this?' She pulled his hand away from her face. 'It was weakness, Alan. I was weak inside. I've always been weak inside. Deep down I wanted the house and the cars and the big brash husband. I'd never done a day's work. Forty years old and never, ever done a real day's work.' She laughed gently. 'That's shocking really, isn't it? I judged those mothers today, who took their kids to the Bay View Hotel, and I've never been without money once in all my life. Without love, without affection, yes, but never without money. Georgio always gave me plenty of that. Who am I to judge them when I can't even produce a child?'

Alan was quiet beside her, knowing that she had to get it all out of her system before she could get on once more with her life.

'You're a nice man, do you know that? Why didn't I ever realise it before?'

He shrugged, embarrassed. 'After what you just found out about your old man, the Yorkshire Ripper would be classed a nice man.'

Donna laughed then, a tired sound. Standing up, she looked down into Alan's face. Then she knelt in front of him, resting her head in his lap. Instinctively, he placed a large hand on her hair, rubbing the nape of her neck gently. Wanting to make her feel better, knowing that she needed someone to make it all all right.

As she pushed her face into his groin, he felt the first stirrings of arousal. Closing his eyes, he begged his body not to embarrass him

459

further. It was only when he felt her hand slipping into the front of his boxer shorts that he realised what she was doing.

As she slipped his erect penis into her mouth, he lay back in the armchair with shock. Easing back on his foreskin, she took his whole member down the back of her throat, pulling gently on his balls as she did so. Then drawing her lips along the length of him, she released it and looked up into his face.

Burying his face in her hair, he whispered her name over and over.

An hour later they lay on the beach together, letting the waves wash over them. Donna snuggled in the crook of his arm, smelling the saltiness of the sea on his skin and the everpresent scent of his Cuban cigars.

'Fucking hell, Donna, I can't believe this.'

His voice was quiet, full of pent-up emotion. 'If you knew the number of times I've thought of us like this . . .'

His voice trailed off. She was better than his wildest fantasy, and as far as he was concerned, Georgio Brunos must have been stark staring mad to let her go. But then, Georgio never did have any real taste.

Donna leaned up on her elbow and looked down into his face. 'I think we both needed it. After today, it was the natural conclusion really.'

Her words hurt him, cut him to the quick.

'It meant more than that to me Donna. Much more.'

She lay down again and let the cool water run over her body. She couldn't answer him.

'Tell me why you murdered that man, Alan. I really want to know.'

He sighed painfully. 'Are you sure?'

She snuggled tighter into him, feeling the pull of the man beside her.

'I'm sure,' she whispered. 'After the last few weeks, I don't think anything could ever really affect me again.'

Finally, after what seemed an age, Alan began to talk.

'Years ago when I was in the West End, before the restaurants and all that, I used to do a lot of ducking and diving. Me and the wife weren't hitting it off and I spent a lot of time in the clubs and that. I was the typical villain in those days, out all night, asleep all day, poncing around making a bit of bunce. I'd had me day with the bare knuckle and I was investing in all sorts of places. That's when I met Joey's father.

'You see, Donna, we sorted out the Chinks. They were everywhere then, and we all realised that if we weren't careful, they'd take the place over. There weren't any real big villains about then, the Krays were the only ones who ever really had an empire of sorts and by

460

today's standards that was penny ante. But anyway, back to the story.

'I first met up with Jack Coyne and JoJo in a house in Fulham. They were all down: the Liverpudlians, the Geordies, the Birmingham boys, even the fucking Scots. They were everywhere, see, and they were running women. Now the Asians, or Pakis as we called them all in them days, were like us. They felt there was room for everyone. The rinky dink dinks, however, had different ideas. They wanted the lot – gambling, women, everything. Well, the Chinks are renowned for kids. You only have to look at Thailand and that. And they were catering to that market. We was all up in arms, see.

'Anyway, one day we went to see this Hep Keng or whatever his name is, and walked into serious aggravation. Jack Coyne shot him, he shot him in the face. It was fucking pandemonium. There was shooters going off all over the show.' Alan was quiet for a moment, remembering.

'Well, the rub is, we were all right. The only real casualty was a Scottish bloke who was shot in the back. We all scooted off before the Old Bill arrived. Then as we were all mustering up for the next round, I go in a club in Soho.

'There was a little bird I used to see called Minerva of all things. A right funny little bird she was and all. She really made me laugh. Anyway, I'm looking for her, and the next thing is I see her mate Jacqueline something or other – last names ain't a must in Soho, as you know. It turned out that a Chinese guy had cut Minerva's throat with a Stanley knife – beat the shit out of her first, like. I heard that every time her heart beat, the blood shot three foot into the air. He stood and watched her die. All over me, because she was my little bird and I was one of the men treading on his toes.

'Minerva was seventeen, full of life, a great little kid. I found out who he was and, well, you know the rest.'

Donna was quiet, drinking in all he had told her. 'What happened then?'

Alan shrugged gently. 'I was nicked, got sent down, and the others sorted it out. JoJo O'Neil done a deal with them, the ponce! That's why I never liked him. He's always dealt with them. And that was it. I never regretted one day what I did for her. It was the least I could do really. If it wasn't for me she'd probably be married now with a load of kids somewhere. Worrying about paying the mortgage like everyone else.'

Donna kissed him gently on the lips, and he whispered, 'Rough justice, that's what we call it.'

She kissed him again. 'I wish I could tell a story like that about Georgio. You're worth ten of him.'

461

Alan didn't answer; he didn't want to break the spell. Instead he gathered her into his arms and kissed her properly.

Pulling away, she looked over the sea and said to him, 'I feel as if a veil has been lifted from in front of my eyes, as if I can really see the world properly for the first time in years. I hate him now.'

The words were like music to Alan's ears.

Sadie came into Georgio's cell in full sail. After being told by Lewis that she was once more a free agent, she had gone to town.

She was wearing her best clothes and her hair was freshly dyed and backcombed to within an inch of its life. Her make-up had been applied with exaggerated care.

Georgio grinned. 'I take it you've seen the new bloke then?'

Sadie grinned impishly. 'Isn't he a darlin'? And I hear he's as queer as a fish.'

Georgio laughed. 'What's the word on the Wing, Sade?'

She sat down sedately on a chair. 'You'd better be careful, Georgio. From what I've read off Lewis's lips, he's really arming his blokes up. Is there going to be a showdown, do you know? Only I've seen the way Big Ricky looks at him sometimes. He's also taken to staring at Beavis and Butthead as well. What's going on?'

'Nothing is going on as far as I know. Just you keep your eyes peeled and read any info you can. That's all you need to do, love.'

'So what's happening with Beavis and Butthead then? I'm telling you now, Georgio, if something ain't done about them soon, I'm going to do something myself.'

Georgio closed his eyes in annoyance. 'It will all be sorted soon, all right? Fucking hell, Sadie, what's got into you, eh? Fuck me, I feel sorry for the bloke you finally take up with, you're worse than a woman!'

Sadie grinned. 'I'll take that as a compliment.'

'Take it any way you like, just give me a break from all this. I've got a lot on me mind.'

Sadie knew when to change the subject. 'I love the way your wife dresses,' she confided. 'Very understated, but sexy.'

Georgio laughed in delight. 'That's Donna all right. The understated bit anyway. The sexy bit I ain't so sure of at times.'

'You're a right slag, Brunos, but then you know that.'

Georgio laughed again, coarsely. 'Listen, Sadie, I ain't a man who can be tied down, my old woman knows that. She keeps her mouth shut and her head down. That's how I like my wife. Now my girlfriends are a different ballgame . . . I like 'em to be a bit sassy, like. Have a bit of a spark, you know. But me wife, I like her to be "understated".'

'Who was the girl who visited today?'

Georgio rolled his eyes to the ceiling. 'Fucking hell's bells! It didn't take you long to find out about that, did it? What is this? Top security or Gossips' Corner? That, my little munchkin, is my future wife. Only don't mention it to the old one, as she don't know yet!'

Georgio laughed at his own wit and Sadie tutted in distress.

'You've been on the prison hooch, ain't you? It takes the lining off the stomach, you know.'

'Sadie love, it could take the lining out of me overcoat and I couldn't give a toss. Today, I needed something and so I had it. By the way, where's the heroin coming from? How's Lewis getting it in?'

Sadie hunched slim shoulders. 'That's a state secret, mate. No one knows. But I think it's coming in through the kitchens meself. Black Dessie brings it to Lewis, I know that much, and he's in the kitchen, so I just put two and two together.'

'Do you know where Lewis keeps his stash?'

Sadie looked worried for a moment and said slowly. 'What if I do?'

Georgio grinned then. 'If you do, Sadie, I'll give you a good bit of bunce for the information. I'll also make sure you get first choice with the new boy, how's that?'

Sadie smiled, making herself look very young and pretty.

'He keeps it in his clock radio. But for Gawd's sake don't let on I told you!'

Georgio rubbed his hands together in glee. Then, lifting his mattress, he took out a bottle of Famous Grouse whisky.

'How'd you get that?' Sadie asked.

Georgio took a long pull and then said, 'There's a friendly little screw I know. Want a pull on it?'

Sadie nodded and he handed her the bottle. 'And don't get fucking lipstick all around the top.'

Sadie rolled her eyes and took a long drink. Then passing the bottle back to Georgio, she took a joint out of her pocket. Lighting it, she said, 'Might as well have a bit of a party, eh?'

Their laughter could be heard all over the Wing.

The sun was rising and Donna and Alan sat side by side, watching its brilliant ascent.

'I'm going to book a flight as soon as possible.' Alan nodded his agreement. 'The sooner we get back the better. There's still a lot to be done.'

Donna pulled on her cigarette and blew out a long stream of smoke. 'I can't wait to see Georgio and tell him he's going to have to sit it out for years. I'm really looking forward to it.'

Alan stared at her in the dappled red of the sunrise and said seriously, 'You can't tell him that, Donna.'

'What! What are you talking about?'

He took a deep breath. 'There's too much been done. The jump is due in three days, Donna, there's no way we can stop it now. No way. Too much has already been set in motion.'

She shook her head in denial at what she was hearing. 'You're joking! Tell me you're joking!'

'I wish I could,' Alan groaned, 'but the jump's out of our hands now. It's in the hands of Eric and the others. It's Georgio's jump, only he can cancel it. That's the law of the criminal world. If we went and called it off now, Georgio would know about it in a matter of hours and he would have the jump rearranged in another few hours. We did all the collar, love. Now Georgio gets to name the fucking day.'

Donna was flabbergasted.

'You're telling me that after all you've seen here, he is still going to get out? The jump will still be on?'

Alan nodded.

Donna got up abruptly.

'Well, that's just where you're wrong, Alan Cox! My husband will rot in that jail for this little lot, if I have to turn Queen's evidence myself! He isn't going anywhere. Especially not over to Ireland. I'll see to that personally!'

She walked back into the hotel room and poured herself a large scotch. Her whole body was shaking with indignation, and her temper was on a short leash.

Alan followed her inside.

'Listen to me, Donna. By the time we get back, the jump will be only two days away right? Now Georgio will have already lined up his disturbance. That will happen no matter what. And Eric will have Jonnie H., and the whole caboodle already in place down south waiting for the jump. We can't stop that. Only Georgio could, and he'll make sure it goes ahead. At this point only he can stop the men from doing what they're paid for.'

Donna threw back the drink and pulled her dressing gown tight around her body as if hiding herself from him.

'You're not seriously going to tell me that you want him out still, are you?'

Alan said quietly, 'Of course not. But what I can do is see that he has no real help. In fact, it would be better to let the jump go ahead, because if we play our cards right, he'll be left high and dry and it won't be down to us, not directly anyway.'

464

Donna looked at him as if he had developed horns in front of her eyes.

'What are you talking about?'

He barked at her in growing anger, 'Listen to me, Donna. I have a lot of clout in the criminal world, but in case it escaped your notice, so does your old man. The truth of the matter is, if we fuck him up, we'd never be able to sleep easy in our beds again. You know yourself, Paddy, everyone, is in on this. When it all comes out, there's going to be a lot of red faces, and not with embarrassment – but with rage. We can't even let this be handed over to the police, it's gone too deep for that now. We have to do it in such a way as to fuck him up, but he can't point the finger at us. Do you understand what I'm saying?'

Donna shook her head in stunned silence.

Alan stared into her strained face and said sadly, 'The trouble is, at this moment in time, neither do I. But I'll think of something, love, don't worry about that.'

She poured herself another drink and said waspishly, 'And what about Stephen Brunos, eh? He knows more than enough about everything. What if he tells Georgio me and you came out here like Batman and Wonderwoman and fucked up his plans? What then, eh?'

Alan closed his eyes and said sadly, 'Donna, Stephen Brunos is dead.'

She frowned in consternation. 'What do you mean, dead?'

He said slowly, 'As in doornail. He knew as well as I did that he was dead the minute I walked into that hotel room. With all that was going on, I couldn't ever let him open his mouth. There are too many dangerous people involved, Donna, that's what you seem to be forgetting, what you can't seem to take into your pretty little head.

'I can't stop the jump, Donna,' he said again. 'I wouldn't dare. Only your husband can do that now, and that's the last thing he wants. The jump will go ahead, and you and I will let it, whether we like it or not.'

Donna dropped on to the bed as if someone had punched her in the solar plexus.

'The jump must be stopped!' Her voice was hysterical.

'Leave it to me, love, just leave it to me. Your life's in as much danger as mine at the moment. More even, because Georgio won't take any of this lying down. If he finds out, we're in deep shit.'

She looked into Alan's face and said through her tears, 'How the hell did I get involved in all this?'

465

Alan glanced out of the door at the brilliant sunshine and answered her softly.

'You were involved from the day you married him, love, you just didn't realise it.'

BOOK THREE

'Should all despair;
That have revolted wives,
The tenth of mankind
Would hang themselves'—

William Shakespeare, 1564–1616 *The Winters Tale*

'I'll be revenged on the whole pack of you'—

William Shakespeare, *Twelfth Night*

Chapter Forty

Colombo airport was stiflingly hot; the sweat poured out of Donna's body as they sat waiting for their flight.

She watched as Alan walked towards her with two glasses of iced tea and then dropped her eyes; she still couldn't bring herself to actually talk to him. He gave her the tea without a word and sat beside her once more.

The airport was busy with voices, smells and people. The hard bucket seats were making Donna feel more and more uncomfortable, and her eyes kept scanning the monitor for their flight. Alan lit a cigarette and handed it to her. She mumbled her thanks.

'Look, Donna, this silent treatment ain't going to do anyone any favours, is it?'

She remained silent.

'Will you at least answer me, Donna? You're acting like all this is my fault.'

She turned slightly to look at him. 'What do you want me to say, Alan? Thanks for all your help in getting my husband out?'

Annoyed now he snapped, 'It'd be a start anyway. You did ask me to do it, didn't you? Only if I remember rightly you came to my restaurant and practically begged me to help you.'

Donna made an impatient movement with her head.

'You just don't get it, do you, Alan? You just don't understand anything. I knew nothing about him then, nothing worth knowing anyway – nothing I couldn't forgive. Now, after all this, you tell me you're still going ahead with the jump—'

He interrupted her. 'So what you're saying is, you'd see Jonnie H., Eric, Nick Carvello, me and you all in clink, would you? You'd prefer that, than to let me sort it all out with the minimum of damage?'

Donna shook her head in disbelief.

'And just how are you going to do that, eh? Once Georgio's out, that'll be it, mate. He won't go back. They'd have to kill him first.'

'Well, that just might happen yet, Donna, you never know your luck. Fancy yourself as a widow, do you?'

469

She lapsed back into silence.

'The trouble with you, Donna Brunos, is you still haven't adjusted to the real world, the world of your husband's livelihood.'

She faced him and said in a low voice, 'You knew what he was and you never told me, never even gave me a hint. I must have been stark staring mad to believe all I did over the years! When I think of all the people who were in the know, and I had no idea about any of it. He used me, Alan – you all did in one way or another. Now I have to face my mother-in-law, and tell her that her son is not coming home and her other son is going to be on the run all his life. And it's all my fault, my fault . . .'

Alan stared at her in disbelief. 'How the fuck is it all your fault?'

'Because if I hadn't gone to you,' she wailed, 'Georgio would still be hoping for an appeal. As soon as I gave him the message to say you were willing to help, everything started to go wrong.'

Alan laughed bitterly.

'So it's all *my* fault now, is it?'

'Alan, go away. Just go away. I need to think this thing through and then decide what I'm going to do.'

He stood up abruptly. Bending over he said to her, 'I'll go away, love, if that's what you want, but first let me give you a word of warning. Think long and hard about who you're going to grass up to keep that geek locked in jail. Because I am telling you now, your life will be worth shit if you grass. No one likes grasses and this little lot affects more people than even you know about. So think on that one, Mrs Squeaky Clean.'

She watched him walk away from her. She could see the anger in him, in the straightness of his back, in the tilt of his head.

And on top of all her other feelings another one was telling her to call him back.

But she didn't.

Eric was running through the jump once more with Jonnie H. and the McAnultys.

'You've made sure the skip lorry is running properly?'

Jonnie H. nodded happily. 'I went over it myself this morning, Eric. It's running as sweet as a nut. It will be reported stolen after the jump from a site in Kent owned by an old mate of mine. Stop worrying.

'The Merc is in pristine condition enginewise, but it's battered to fuck outwardly. No one would take a second glance at it. The bikes are in the back, ready and waiting. Two Kawasaki 250 trail bikes, and a 125 in case we have to ride over the fields. The car for the chop is

470

already in Kent as we speak, waiting to be driven to its destination. Machinery wise, we're all set.'

Eric smiled. He was only really content when he was working, then he became almost light-hearted, whether it was a pull, a jump or a kidnapping.

He opened a large crate and took out the weapons. Jonnie H. was impressed with them and showed it. The Armalite was handled and admired by them all.

'What a piece of equipment, eh? I'd fucking love to see the faces in Tesco's if you went in there with this.'

Danny McAnulty's voice was almost reverent. 'You'd certainly cause a bit of a stir, laddie. But these go back after the jump. They're leasehire, boys, only leasehire.'

He took out three sawn-off shotguns and they were checked over. The men carefully gauged the weight of the guns before choosing one each.

'These are brand new!'

Eric laughed again. 'Nothing but the best for us, eh?' Then he added seriously, 'I meant what I said. All this equipment goes back after the jump. There's two small handguns. One is to be given to Georgio and the other is for me. If we have to shoot for anything other than fear, then I'll use the handgun. Georgio is the jumper so it's his job to shoot anyone interfering, all right? You lot just shoot to frighten. Now, Danny, you're all sure of your jobs, aren't you?'

'I take the keys out of the cars behind the Merc. Cyril will do the same behind the earthmover. We'll just throw them into the fields. Once the public see the guns they'll be all right. Iain here will be the man to set up the bikes while you get the driver from the sweatbox. Jonnie H. will take out the police once the doors are opened. We're all relaxed and ready to go.'

'Good, good. Now once we're past the chop, you lot fuck off as quick as you can, right?'

The three men nodded.

'We'll be back in Scotland the night and no one will even know we've been gone,' Danny assured him, grinning.

'Remember to shout,' Eric reminded them, 'it distorts the voice, and keep your hands and faces covered all the time. Especially you, Iain. Your tattoos could give the game away immediately.'

Iain looked down at his hands. He had *hate* tattooed across his knuckles and ACAB on each wrist. ACAB stood for All Coppers Are Bastards; it was a standard Borstal tattoo from the seventies. He also had a broken line around his neck with 'Cut Here' written above it, like an advert in a magazine.

471

Iain put his hands behind his back like a naughty child and Eric, watching him, smiled. Iain McAnulty had the brain capacity of a flea and the physical strength of a rogue elephant, exactly the kind of person Eric liked to deal with.

'Cheer up, sonny, you'll be covered up, but keep your faces and hands away from people until the jump's over OK? Witnesses always remember things after an event. There'll be some old lady telling the police about the Scottish man with the tattoos buying fags in her little village shop. We're not taking any chances, right?'

Everyone nodded their agreement, acknowledging the truth of what he said.

'You do not talk to anyone, you do not leave your vehicles, and you definitely do not drive above the speed limit until after the jump. You do not bring any attention to yourselves whatsoever, that includes bibbing up women, cunting other drivers if they cut you up, and especially not taking any interest in police vehicles if they pass you on the road. Do I make myself clear?'

Everyone nodded once more.

'And most important thing of all: you DO NOT go in any pubs or shops, and you DO NOT smoke dope or drink anything until you're well out of the way. Even then I would advise you to keep well away from any hostelries on the route home. You're strangers wherever you go, bear that in mind, and strangers are news to the majority of the populace, OK? Even Happy Eaters are out of bounds.'

Jonnie H. said, 'What about if we want a piss, Eric?'

They all laughed.

'You piss down a country lane, and even then you make sure you're out of sight, because a man pissing sticks in people's minds. You'd be surprised what's got people captured in the past. Believe me, I know what I'm talking about. An accent, a brief description of a car or a person, and you could find yourself arranging your own jump in a couple of years, so bear that in mind.'

The men all sobered at his words.

'Now then,' he said patiently. 'Let's go over the timing once more. What time are you setting out with the skip lorry in the morning, Jonnie?'

Nick Carvello was going over the movements of Georgio once he left Liverpool. The safe house in Liverpool was in fact a lock-up garage; the car to take him from Liverpool to Scotland was a diamond white Cosworth driven by a Scot called Baldy McIntyre. Baldy was a respectable businessman with perfect credentials. Georgio would

472

travel beside him, and be provided with a driving licence and a business suit, in case of emergencies.

Once in Scotland, it was Nick's job to ferret him over to Eire. This was the most difficult job of all. Traffic on the water was hardly as dense as traffic on the M1, and the boat had to look half-legal at least. If it was a fishing vessel it had to keep clear of coastguards, both Irish and British, once in Irish waters. The Scottish safe house was a council flat on the Clyde where new faces were ignored because everyone was too busy watching their own backs to take any notice of anyone else. It was designated a no go area for the police so the Cosworth would not be too noticeable, and would only drop Georgio off in any case. There was no way it could be left unattended outside. It would be stolen within five minutes.

Nick sipped at his drink and watched Albie washing up the dishes, his movements deliberately careful, frightened even to chip a cup or a mug. He forced his eyes back to the map on the table. Once over to Ireland it was all in the hands of an old comrade of his, now living in Southern Ireland breeding fighting dogs and arranging bareknuckle fights. He had only helped out once he knew Alan Cox was involved.

Alan should have been in touch before now. Nick would try him at his restaurant later. It was strange that so near the jump he had gone on the missing list.

Poring over the map, Nick felt the familiar mix of adrenaline and fear that accompanied any job of this magnitude. If it fell out of bed they could all be doing long sentences before the year was out.

It was partly the thought of getting one over on the Old Bill, and partly the excitement of carrying out such a huge-scale jump that attracted him, as it attracted Eric and the others. Villains of their calibre needed the rush achieved by daring exploits.

It was this rush that always got them caught in the end.

'Get in the car, Donna, before I drag you into it.'

Alan's voice was rising and the other occupants of the multi-storey car park at Gatwick looked over at them.

'You can't make me do anything!'

Alan grimaced. 'That's just where you're wrong, lady. Now get in the car!'

Donna got in and Alan slipped into the driving seat, his face set in anger. As he reversed out of the space he said through gritted teeth, 'Believe me when I say you are the most stroppy cow I have ever come across! Georgio must have been off his fucking rocker to have ever asked you to do anything for him! So now you know what I really think.'

473

Donna turned her face away from his.

'Well, he did ask me, didn't he? And now look where we all are. It's keeping things from people that brought all this on, like your keeping from me the fact you knew a lot more about my husband than you let on.'

As they left the car park, Alan pulled the car to a halt. He turned and glared at her, his face screwed up in anger.

'I knew enough to blow your life wide open, I admit that, but it wasn't any of my business, was it? You preferred to believe that your husband was a mixture of the Pope and the fucking Apostles. If I had told you the score you wouldn't have believed me – and why should I have said anything to you anyway? Why the fucking hell should I, eh? What were you to me? Nothing, that's what. You were just a mate's old woman out to help him. I'm a villain, lady, not fucking Marje Proops! If your old man was batting away from home all those years, what reason would I have had to tell you all about it? Answer me that one if you can. Why would I have got involved in all that, eh?'

Donna looked into his face, her own eyes glittering in anger. 'Get me home, Alan. I just want to go home.'

'Oh, you want to go home, do you? Shall I tell you something? If you were my wife I'd slap your face for you. Because I have never, ever come across such a bolshie bitch in all my life. Just because you think you're so fucking squeaky clean, you expect everyone else just to put their lives on hold, all for you. You think that Eric and me, and Jonnie H. and all the others, should all go: "Oh, dearie me, Georgio's been a naughty boy. Let's leave him in clink, shall we, chaps?" Well, I have the germ of an idea of how to fuck up the jump, and that's all we can do now. Fuck the jump up. I think I can do that through Nick Carvello. But as for the rest of it, it goes ahead whether you like it or you don't. Get that into your thick skull.

'And another thing while we're on it. There's an old adage that you should have tattooed on your arse. "If you can't do the time, don't do the crime." You was quite happy to put us all on the line when you thought your old man was the dog's bollocks. Now you find out you're dealing with the scum of the earth, your old man included there, lady, you want to stop it all here and now. Well, as I just said, *you can't* – and if they get a capture and grass you up, you'll be looking at a good eight or nine years for your part in all this. So think on that one, darlin'!'

He started the car up and wheelspinned out of the airport.

Donna sat beside him, her ears ringing.

'I never wanted any part of murder, Alan.'

Hearing the tightness of her voice, he could only laugh in disbelief.

474

'If I hadn't arrived in Sri fucking Lanka, the murdered person would have been you, love. When you get involved with big boys' games, you have to take the big boys' consequences. That's why I never wanted you as my number two. If you cast your mind back, I tried to get someone else, but oh, no. Mrs Villain's Wife wanted to be in on it all – and look where the fuck it's got us, eh? You know what's really your trouble, don't you? You're trying to blame everyone else for this lot except yourself. Well, you're as much to blame as anyone. More so in fact, because you took on something you was ill-prepared for. Now someone's dead. Big deal!

'Don't you realise that if anyone tries it on while the jump's in motion, they'll be shot at? Use your fucking loaf! You were there when we bought the hardware. Now you're shitting it, and rightly so. You'd have more chance of pulling off the Second Coming, love, than stopping this jump. The only way to stop it would be to grass to the filth and the moment you did that, we'd all be out for your blood. Me included. Bear that in mind, Donna, and keep your trap shut and your arse behind closed doors until it's all over. Right?

'You've already caused one murder, I'm sure you don't want to be the instrument of another, least of all your own! Jonnie H. would see you tortured and killed if you were the means of separating him from his wife and kids. And that would seem like heaven to what the others would cook up for you!'

Donna's heart was in her boots. She stared out of the car window, fighting back tears of frustration and fear because she knew that what Alan said was true. She could no more grass up any of the men than she could take an active part in the jump.

She had started the ball rolling; now she could only wait patiently until it stopped.

And it would only stop with Georgio in Ireland.

Alan's voice broke into her thoughts.

'And what do you think Georgio's going to say when he finds out that his brother's dead, eh? And his hotel's been razed to the ground? Talk yourself out of that one, Big mouth! Because he'll find out all right, don't worry yourself on that score.'

Donna still didn't answer. Looking at her out of the corner of his eye, Alan felt a great sorrow for her. She was too naive for her own good. That had been the trouble from the very beginning.

Now he had to frighten her into keeping a low profile while he sorted out Georgio's demise.

Because, now that Stephen Brunos was dead, they were all in big trouble.

The only hope he had was through Nick Carvello. Nick, whose

475

hatred of beasts was legendary. Only he could save the day.

For the first time in years Alan Cox was frightened, deeply afraid.

And all thanks to the woman sitting beside him. If he was a different kind of man, he reflected, he would have slapped her across the chops before now.

As he looked at her set face, he told himself there was a first time for everything.

Dolly heard the key in the lock and her body froze in terror. Ever since Paddy's visit she had lived in mortal fear of him coming back after he found out she was lying.

Donna walked into the warmth of the house and Dolly's tearful embrace.

'Oh Donna, Donna! Am I pleased to see you, lovie!'

Donna pulled herself gently away.

'Calm down, Dolly. I tried to ring from Sri Lanka but the phones out there are so erratic. You have to book the calls hours in advance. I'd have been home before I could have called, if you see what I mean.' She tried to lighten the woman's mood.

Dolly walked into the kitchen and put the kettle on with shaking hands.

'There's been trouble here, Donna. Paddy came over with Davey Jackson, looking for you. He . . . he threatened me, Donna. Paddy threatened me. He grabbed my hair . . .'

Her voice broke and Donna watched her dissolve into tears once more. She tried to comprehend what Dolly was telling her.

'Paddy? Paddy attacked you?'

Dolly nodded in agitation. 'He wanted to know where you were, Donna. And who you were with, like. I told him you'd gone to Liverpool with Alan Cox, I didn't know what else to say. They wanted to know where he was and all. He was livid, Donna. Paddy looked capable of murder.'

Donna sank down on to a kitchen chair, her mind racing. What the hell had happened? It seemed the world was going mad. If she hadn't gone out to Sri Lanka, none of the last few days' events would have occurred. Alan was right to say that anyway. She had caused a lot of problems by rooting around and finding so much out. But what else could she have done? Little children were involved. Babies.

She had had to sort all that out, no woman could have left that to chance. No woman in the world.

Except a woman like Candy, she reminded herself. Except the women who sold their children off like so much dirt.

476

Myra Hindley wasn't as unique as people made out. There were many others like her, cold-blooded enough to harm a child, whether they did it purposely, with their own hands, or handed them over to someone else to harm. The child was still damaged, and at their instigation.

'And Davey Jackson was with him, you say?'

Dolly nodded. 'He tried to stop Paddy. In fairness to him, he did try to stop him, Donna.'

'That was big of him, I must say! Pity he wasn't so concerned for the children he employs!'

Dolly's face screwed up in bewilderment. 'What are you talking about?'

'I'm talking about a brothel out in Sri Lanka. I am talking about pornographic pictures of children coming down phone lines from Asia to England. I am talking about taking the porn and putting it on to floppy discs and making the pictures into porno mags for paedophiles, sold all over the British Isles by mail order. I am talking about Georgio, Paddy, Davey, and all the others being involved in it. That, Dolly, is what I'm talking about. You were right all along.'

Dolly's face dropped. 'So it *was* Georgio then. He was behind it all.'

Donna nodded.

'I had a feeling on me it was him,' Dolly admitted shakily. 'I don't know why, but I just knew it. That's big business. No wonder Paddy wanted to find out what was going on.'

'It's big business all right, and Georgio wanted to make it so big he stripped all the businesses here to do it. I must have been half-blind over the years, blind and deaf. Dolly, how could I have lived with a man all these years and not realised he was just scum. A piece of scum!'

Dolly sighed, her own fear forgotten now as she looked at the broken-hearted woman before her.

'He wasn't always scum, Donna. Georgio's trouble was greed. He was always greedy – and greedy people do terrible things. Remember him years ago? Before the building business got big? He was a good man in them days.'

Donna snorted. 'Was he? He was so good he was shagging anything that moved and wasn't nailed down, that's how good he was. Do you know how I feel, Dolly? Can you even guess what I'm feeling now? I find out that twenty years of my life were completely wasted on a piece of scum. A piece of shit. A Greek ponce! I feel as if everyone must have been laughing up their sleeves at me over the years. Stupid Donna, the idiot in the Mercedes. The well-dressed, well-spoken wife

477

of the biggest slag God ever put on the earth.

'And do you know the worst of it all? she admitted bitterly. 'I looked down on people like Carol Jackson. I thought she was common! Because I had my degree, I assumed I was far more intelligent than them. Yet Carol Jackson has more savvy, as she would call it, in her little finger than I have in my whole body! I'm a useless prat and Georgio used me for this jump, knowing that. Knowing I was silly enough to believe whatever he told me.

'Oh, sod the tea,' Donna decided. 'Let's get out the scotch, Dolly. There's a lot more I still have to tell you.'

Carol Jackson watched Davey as she put the children's tea on the table. He was gnawing at his thumbnail, always a sign of agitation, and she wondered what was bothering him.

'Are you all right, Davey?'

He stared out of the window and ignored her.

'Davey! I said, are you all right?'

He looked at her then, his blue eyes shadowed with fear, and Carol dropped to her knees by his chair.

'What's the matter, Davey? You haven't been right for a while. Is there something wrong? Can I help you with it? Is there anything I can do?'

Davey looked down into his wife's face. Her blonde hair was as usual backcombed into a tangle, her make-up expertly overdone. One of her false eyelashes had come unstuck in the corner and it gave her eyes an oddly pleasing appearance. As if she was oriental. Her lipstick was gone, but the pencil outline remained.

He saw her as she had been on their wedding day, belly nearly down to her knees but her face alight with happiness. For over twenty years she had stood beside him. He knew that if she had even an inkling as to what he was involved in, really involved in, she would be disgusted. As he was disgusted. And for the first time ever, he wondered what he would do if he lost her. Really lost her. For so long she had wanted him, had made all the running. All their married life he had been virtually single. She had been the married one for them both.

He wondered how he would feel if she wasn't there, waiting for him to come home, waiting with his meals, waiting to listen to him. He wondered what it would be like to open a drawer and not find any clean underclothes, socks or shirts miraculously folded up there by his wife's hands. He wondered how he would feel if he had to visit his children at weekends instead of playing the big-time father as and when it suited him. Normally Christmas and birthdays.

He wondered what Carol's reaction would be to hearing what he was involved in from a third party.

But he knew the answer to that one. She would pick up the bread-knife and stab him through the heart.

Carol was a child-lover; she was decent in her own way. She would never countenance paedophiles or their merchandise. She thought that the floppy discs had grown women on them, and even then she hadn't been too happy about it.

If she knew there were children on them, that the children were being abused to satisfy his greed and a pervert's lust . . .

His eyes went to the bread-knife on the table again. Carol would be capable of murder.

But worse than the thought of her anger, was the thought of her contempt. Her complete disgust and hatred for him, because he knew that was exactly what she would feel. He felt that way himself.

It was Georgio again. He always went along with Georgio and Georgio had got him involved with talk of riches and all they could bring. The children would be used anyway, he'd maintained. Whether it was by them or by someone else. It was different out there, acceptable even. He had told Davey that in China the old men slept with young children because it was considered lucky. It was supposed to bring back their virility.

To Georgio it had all been one big joke, nothing to worry about, and Davey had believed him. As he'd always believed him. Georgio had smoothtalked him into it all, and now with every day that passed he felt the noose tightening around his neck. He was getting in deeper and deeper and didn't know how to get out.

'Have you seen anything of Donna, or heard from her?' he asked quietly.

Carol shook her head. 'Why are you so worried about Donna, love? Is she in trouble?'

He saw the worry in her eyes, the concern written all over her face. Carol had never really liked Donna over the years, yet she had rallied round for her when Georgio had been put away.

How could he have wanted Donna, or any woman, when he had all he really needed right here? Inside his home, the mother of his children, his wife. His Carol, whom he had never, ever appreciated.

She would stand by him through prison, debt, anything. Except what he was involved in now. If she knew about that, she would drop him like so much dirty laundry. Why did you have to be on the verge of losing someone before you realised how much they meant to you?

479

'Oh, Carol darlin', I love you more than you'll ever know, more than you could even guess.'

She looked at Davey as if she had never seen him before. In all their years together, never once had he spoken to her like that. Not even in the dead of night when he took her body. Never once had he offered an insight into his mind, except when he was in prison. Then he loved her in his letters. Wrote her poems, and told her he couldn't live without her.

But never had he spoken the words out loud before, and they caught her offguard and made her want to cry.

Because she knew that, to speak them, Davey had to be in big trouble.

Donna told Dolly everything, leaving out only the fact that she had slept with Alan Cox.

Dolly had listened in shocked silence, and when Donna told her about Stephen Brunos, she shook her head sadly and said, 'Poor Maeve. It'll break her heart.'

It was while they were talking over what could be done, what should be done, that the knock came on Donna's front door.

Dolly stood up, her arms and legs trembling. 'Jesus! It might be Big Paddy back again!'

Donna stood by the kitchen door, her heart in her mouth. But it was only Carol Jackson calling through the letter box. Sighing with relief, Donna opened the front door to her.

Carol walked into the house, bringing with her the smell of Estée Lauder and her own sound common sense.

She looked at Donna and said seriously: 'I want to know where you disappeared to, what you're up to, and finally, what it's got to do with my old man.'

480

Chapter Forty-One

Donna stared into Carol's strained face and felt her heart go out to the woman. Knowing Carol as she did, Donna was aware that the knowledge she had inside her could wreck Carol's life – because here was a decent woman who would never, ever countenance what Georgio, Paddy and her husband were doing.

'I think you'd better come into the kitchen and have a large drink, Carol.'

Carol looked fearfully at Donna's tired face, the dark smudges under her eyes and the hard edge to her lips, and instinctively knew that what she was about to hear would only hurt her.

'Do I need a large drink then, to hear what you've got to say?'

Donna walked towards the kitchen and said over her shoulder, 'Carol, love, you'll need more than one drink before this day's out, believe me when I tell you that.'

Carol sat nervously at the table, Dolly's bowed head bothering her more than anything. If it upset Dolly then it was serious.

Donna seated herself and poured Carol a scotch. 'Before I start, how much do you know about Georgio and Davey's dealings in Sri Lanka?'

Carol felt her insides turning to ice water as Donna spoke.

'I know enough,' she said. 'The point is, how much do *you* know?'

At this point, Dolly looked over at Carol with distaste – a look Carol didn't understand; was unsure how to take.

'I expect you've found out it was porn, have you?' she said defensively. 'Well, my advice to you is to come down to the real world with everyone else, Donna. Porn is a part of our daily life, whether it's a blue film or a page three girl. Soft porn never hurt anyone. So if you're running round like a cat with a scalded arse over a bit of old bluey, I'm here to tell you that you're wrong, Donna. Dead wrong.'

When Donna and Dolly still remained silent, Carol sighed heavily.

'Listen, I know porn probably gives you the heebie-jeebies, it does me to be honest, but it's like Georgio said: if we don't do it, someone else will. Whatever happens it'll be made and we might as well be

481

making it. Can't you see that? It's just economics, sound economics.'

Donna sipped her scotch and looked into Carol's heavily made-up face.

'Have you ever *seen* any of the books or the contents of the floppy discs? Have you ever *seen* any of the so-called soft porn my husband and yours are peddling to all and sundry? Only I have, and believe me, Carol, it's bloody disgusting.'

Carol spread her hands. 'What are they, hardcore porn? Stag movies? Look – my sister used to make them for a living in the seventies. They've been around since the silent movies, love . . .'

Donna interrupted her. 'The films and photographs aren't of women, you fool, they're of children! The hotel in Sri Lanka deals in children. Little ones, Carol, like your own kids. I've been there, seen it, done it, got the bloody T shirt, for Christ's sake!

'Stephen Brunos was out there,' Donna said into the shocked silence, 'sorting out the next shipment. That meant making sure the stuff went down the phone lines, to be retrieved this end and put on to disc after disc after disc. I found a projection table a while ago. It started in pounds, single pounds. Then it ran into millions. I thought it was just something Georgio was working out for the building business. It was the floppy discs, Carol. And Davey knows all about it, everything. So does Big Paddy.'

Carol couldn't, wouldn't believe what she was hearing. Her face was drained of colour; only her eyes were burning bright.

'Not my Davey, no way! Georgio, yes, he'd sell his own little boy for a few quid but not my old man. *No way.* You've got this all wrong. No way, I tell you! The hotel in Sri Lanka is just that, a fucking hotel. I don't know where you get your information from, lady—'

Donna interrupted her again. 'I have just come back from Sri Lanka, Carol. Listen to me, woman! I know what I saw out there, all right? I know the score.'

Carol was still shaking her head.

'You're off your trolley. Davey was right in what he said. You've been like a fucking Jonah ever since Georgio got banged up, always sticking your nose into everything . . .'

Donna nodded. 'That's why Paddy had to keep an eye on me, ain't it? That's why Davey kept an eye on me as well. To stop me finding out about this little lot.'

Carol bellowed. 'What little lot? I've only your word for any of this. I've been with Davey for donkey's years. He hates anything like that. Hates the nonces and the beasts . . .' Her strident voice broke.

482

Donna wiped a shaking hand across her forehead. 'Show her the books Dolly.'

Dolly got up. Going to her large handbag, she removed the books and placed them in front of Carol.

Carol stared down through tear-filled eyes at the faces of the children. She shuddered.

'This still doesn't mean my Davey's involved . . .'

Dolly said quietly, 'Paddy and Davey turned up here to collect some boxes. I secretly took these out of the boxes before they arrived. Your Davey's involved, all right. They all are. Scum, the whole lot of them.'

Carol looked down at the books once more. Leaning over the table, Donna turned the pages.

Carol stared at the children arrayed before her, saw the blank faces, the small bodies opened up to the camera, saw the huge hands of faceless men touching them, abusing them . . . and felt the bile rise inside her. All along, she had dreaded something like this. It had always been lurking in the back of her mind.

Georgio Brunos was capable of anything. Once he had talked about Thailand while visiting her house, had described to Davey how the women could be used. She had been in her kitchen listening. Unable to stop listening to the things Georgio was saying, was describing. She could still hear Davey's excited voice, egging him on for more details, more stories. And she could hear Georgio's voice, getting louder as he described the brothels, the bar girls, the absolute abuse possible in a country where willing bodies were cheap.

She had gone to bed, half-ashamed at eavesdropping, half-ashamed at not saying anything. When Davey had gone out there to look at the proposed hotel sites with Georgio, she had known exactly what was on the agenda. But she hadn't said anything, because if she had voiced an opinion, she would have had to admit it was true, and that was the last thing she wanted. Once she admitted that, Davey and she would be over. Her marriage would be over. It was over now, she realised. It had been over from the moment she had walked into this house.

'Do you know something, Donna? Inside, I knew about all this. I even knew when I was driving over here, only I didn't admit it openly. It was more a subconscious thought. But there all the same. I just couldn't admit to myself that Davey was involved in it. Oh, Georgio being involved don't surprise me. He always was a slag. Always. He even tried it on with me when I was pregnant with Jamie. Said pregnant women turned him on.'

She saw the look of horror on Donna's face and sighed.

483

'You know something, Donna? I thought I was blinkered where Davey was concerned. But you with Georgio . . . Jesus wept, you were blind as a fucking bat!'

Because she was hurting so much she wanted someone else to hurt, too. Wanted Donna, the person who had blown her world wide open, to hurt more than she did.

'Do you know what makes all this worse? Georgio's got a child himself, a son.'

Dolly shook her head in disbelief.

'Be quiet now, Carol. Leave it. This isn't the time or the place . . .'

'Oh fuck off, Dolly! Still protecting your Golden Boy, are you? She has a right to know. Once he's out that's where he's going. Shall I tell you something else, Donna? You turned up there once, at Parkhurst, and she was there too, going in for a visit with the child. She'd come all the way from Marbella with Georgio junior. You even spoke to her. Davey told me. He said Georgio nearly fainted when you walked in instead of her.

'He's going to leave you high and dry, love. That's why he wanted the house sold. He wanted it all, everything, and he would have left you with nothing!

'Even you, Dolly, his surrogate mother, were going to be fucked off out of it. He is evil, *evil* – and he has brought my old man as low as him. He was in this with Harry and Bunty. Oh, you may well look surprised. Why do you think Harry come up trumps the night you was turned over, eh? Loyalty to Georgio, my arse! He couldn't drop you lot quick enough when Georgio got the capture, and this is why, love. These little children are their road to riches. Untold riches, as my Davey put it. The dirty, weasel-faced, little bastard!'

Donna stared down at her hands in distress. Of all the things she had found out, the fact that Georgio had a child, a living child, was the worst of all. In her mind's eye she could see the tall blonde girl with the handsome dark-eyed child. As Donna walked into the prison, the girl had walked out. Donna had admired the child. She felt a scream spiralling up inside her, and fought bravely to keep it inside her head, not let it come barrelling out into the faces of the two women before her.

'What a mess, eh? What a godawful dirty mess.'

Donna was amazed that her voice sounded so normal, when inside she was screaming.

Screaming at the injustice of a God who allowed Georgio to beget a child and left her barren. Allowed things like child prostitution to flourish, to be easily available to debauched men. Who allowed her to love someone, to trust someone who was a nothing. A dirty filthy NOTHING.

The thought of Georgio's hands on her made her want to gag. The knowledge that she had lain in bed longing for his touch made her insides rise up as her mind rebelled.

Carol, her anger spent, sorry now for what she had said, grasped Donna's hand in hers and said softly, 'What we have to decide now is what we are going to do?'

Donna's face finally crumpled, her strength finally gave out and the three women cried together.

Each betrayed in her own way, each reliant on the others now to make something good come out of it all.

Wiping her eyes, Donna said in a voice stronger than she would have believed possible: 'What we do now is blow this thing wide open.'

Georgio stood in the rec room watching a game of pool. Big Ricky was playing the new man on the Wing, Alfie Heartland. He was a well-known face in Parkhurst and other maximum security nicks; he was respected, handsome and violent. An armed robber, Alfie was now doing a fifteen for a raid on a local building society where he had pistol-whipped a have-a-go artist. Alfie was known for his sense of humour and his knowledge of horses. An avid gambler, he had already sorted himself a screw to put his bets on, and had established a book.

As Georgio watched them play, he saw Beavis and Butthead having a conversation in a corner. They were supposed to be playing cards but were deep in conversation, and Georgio noticed that they looked over at him now and again.

Nervous already, because of the jump planned for the next day, he began to feel paranoid. They knew a lot about him, and if they opened their mouths he could find himself in big trouble. He sauntered over to their table and sat with them for a few moments. No one noticed, everyone was too busy watching either TV or the game of pool. Only Sadie observed this and she kept an eye on Georgio from her chair by the TV, her face set in a frown. Georgio spoke to the men, then stood up and stretched languidly before going back to the pool table.

Sadie watched him for a few more seconds then slipped from the room unobtrusively.

Georgio didn't see her go.

Alan Cox sat in his office nursing a brandy and smoking a cigar. All

485

he wanted to do was crawl away somewhere and come back in forty-eight hours, when it would all be over. But he knew he couldn't do that. He knew he was too involved with Donna Brunos to do that.

If it hadn't been for her, he told himself, he would have blind-eyed the whole bleedin' affair. Then he shrugged mentally, telling himself that was a lie.

He was blaming her because he *was* involved, and he wanted a scapegoat. Donna, with her airs and graces, her clean-living good looks, was perfect for the part.

What was really bothering him was the fact that he'd thought he knew Georgio Brunos, when he hadn't. He hadn't even scratched the surface.

He recalled Georgio as he had been when they were young, when Pa Brunos had taken them boxing. Once they had gone their separate ways, they had both changed. But the boyhood friendship had lasted. Look at what Georgio had done for him when he had been put away . . .

Now, Stephen was dead, Georgio was for the out . . . and Alan had to try and prevent it.

The knock on his door disturbed his thinking and he said loudly: 'Enter!'

The door opened and he was amazed to see Donna walk into the room.

'Hello, Alan.'

He looked at her as if she had just appeared out of a glass bottle.

'Donna?' It was a question and she smiled slightly as she took a seat opposite him.

'Surprised to see me, are you? Well, I had to come. Carol Jackson knows everything now, and thanks to her, so do I. It wasn't just Georgio and Davey and Paddy involved, it was also Harry and that horse-faced bitch he's married to. Donald Lewis was ripped off and he hasn't an inkling why. He thinks Stephen is just a greedy bastard. Carol has told us all she knows. She also told me that JoJo O'Neil and Jack Coyne are in this up to their armpits, and that Georgio got JoJo a hiding from Nick Carvello to teach him a lesson because he was getting greedy. The more I find out, the more involved it gets and the more I hate Georgio Brunos. But then I expect you guessed most of this, or even knew about it?'

Alan blinked for a few seconds as if digesting what she'd said, and Donna, looking at him, felt the full masculine force of him, and the memory of him unclothed rose up in her mind. As if reading her mind, he reddened. A flush crept up from his neck and enveloped his handsome face.

486

Donna noticed he was the first to look away and felt a momentary euphoria. She was growing up at last. She was a woman in her own right. And, she added to herself, not before time.

'Yes, I had guessed most of what you said, Donna, but something I don't understand is why, if Paddy was involved in everything, he was not to know about the jump? There's skulduggery everywhere we look, and your husband seems to be the main instigator of it all.'

Donna bridled in her chair. 'Don't call him that! He's not my husband any more. I spent the best part of twenty years with that man, and the truth is I know you better than I ever knew him. Physically *and* mentally.'

Alan placed his hand on hers, leaning towards her. She could smell the cigar on his breath as he said gently, 'Donna . . .'

She pulled her hand from his and said quickly, 'I want the jump stopped, Alan, and this time I will not take no for an answer. Tomorrow Georgio Brunos is once more let loose on to the world, and I can't allow that. I will not allow that to happen. I want him locked up for so long, his brain, his cock and his legs will have long been useless to him.'

Alan's eyes widened at her terminology and she smiled, a hard, brittle smile.

'Have I shocked you, Alan? It's a pity I didn't spend more of my life saying what I really thought, doing what I wanted to do, instead of saying and doing what Georgio wanted. Well, that's all over now. One good thing has come out of all this. I am a person in my own right, and I've found out that I am a fighter. I'll fight anyone who tries to stand in my way over this. Anyone at all.'

Alan looked at her, really looked at her, and what he saw was a woman of potential. The woman she would have been, had she been married to anyone but Georgio. Her whole world had disintegrated around her, and like the phoenix, she was rising from the ashes – and rising with a vengeance. He felt privileged to know this woman. Felt the pull of her, the want of her. Georgio Brunos must have been stark staring mad ever to have looked at another woman with her waiting in his bed.

'I can't stop the jump, Donna . . .'

She made a deep guttural sighing noise in the back of her throat and Alan held up his hand to stop her from talking. 'Hear me out, darling, just hear me out. *I can't stop the jump* – but I can make sure that Georgio is on his own. That's the best I can do. Make sure he doesn't make it to Ireland.'

Donna frowned. 'What do you mean?'

487

Alan stood up and poured them both a cup of coffee before he answered her.

'What I mean is this. Eric will only stop the jump on the say-so of Georgio now. If I go to him and try to call it off he'll need Georgio's confirmation. That would come through Anthony Calder or someone closer. That's the law of the criminal world. I mean – think about it. I could be setting Georgio up for a number of reasons. The worst thing of all is this: Stephen Brunos is dead, and that shit hasn't hit the fan yet. When it does Georgio will suspect a lot more than he does now. He'll know we've tumbled him. As it stands now, Stephen's death will be a holiday accident. It happens all the time: it nearly happened to you, love. But Georgio, unlike the authorities, will know it's more of a hit. If we fuck Georgio now, he'll come after us with everything he's got. Because he will put two and two together. No, the jump has to go ahead. We have to fuck him up *after* the jump. Then, when he's back inside, when he's finally putting everything together, we'll have to sort him out from there.'

Donna looked into Alan's eyes and took a deep breath.

'You don't mean . . . you're not saying . . .' Her expression was one of utter confusion.

Alan nodded, his face hard now. The face Donna had seen when he had attacked Stephen Brunos.

'That's the only way out for any of us, Donna. While Georgio is breathing we're in mortal danger. He'll hear the whisper about us, and believe me, we will be gossiped about. Especially to Georgio. He's shrewd, he'll have sussed everything out before anyone else does. I know him, he's got someone waiting for him in Ireland, someone who will be amazed and then frightened when he doesn't arrive, someone who knows a lot more about what's going on than you ever did.'

Donna nodded. 'You mean Vida, the mother of his child?'

Her voice was bitter as she spoke and Alan's eyes opened wide in amazement.

'I know everything now,' she whispered. 'I told you that. Carol filled me in about her, along with everything else.'

'Well, you'll know that Vida is the one setting up the final stage of the jump from Ireland. I suspect you were to be left high and dry. I sussed that out at the beginning of all this.'

'Well, thanks for letting me know,' she cried. 'I was under the impression we were friends!'

He shook his head. 'While you were still all over that Greek ponce I had to keep me peace, didn't I? He could have fucked Vida off out of it. I didn't think he would, but that could have been the scenario. I

488

was doing a mate a favour. And with respect, Donna, look where the fuck it's got me.

'I now have to make sure the mate – and believe me when I say, for all his faults, Georgio *was* a mate to me when I needed him – I have to make sure that this mate, this good old mate, stops breathing at the first available opportunity! So don't sit there like fucking Britannia, all knowing and womanly strength. Remember I am also in this up to my neck and I still have to live in the criminal world afterwards.'

Donna acknowledged that what he said was true.

'So what is your plan, Alan. What do you want to do?'

'Nick Carvello is well-known for his hatred of beasts and nonces,' Alan began. 'A while ago, Lewis put it about that Georgio was beasting. He obviously knew that it was true because, with Stephen, he was going to try and take the lot from Georgio. Now Nick believed it all: he wanted out of the jump. I was the one who talked him into staying with it, gave him my word it was all bullshit. You see – I thought it *was* at the time. Everyone did. Georgio the nonce-hater, Georgio the man's man.

'Anyway, all that aside, I'll tell Nick on the quiet that it's true. I'll tell him everything, and that will be for our good as well because Nick will go after JoJo and Jack Coyne like a maniac. He hates them. He will hate Georgio for putting him in the position he is in. Helping him, knowing he's a nonsense – that will send Nick into a mental the likes of which you couldn't even imagine. Consequently, when Georgio reaches Liverpool, Nick will either be waiting for him with a twelve-bore sawn-off shotgun, or your hubby will arrive up there to fuck-all help. No safe house, no safe passage, nothing.

'If I was you I'd pin your hopes on the former. Because one thing you must understand: Georgio will have to die. If he doesn't, me and you are in more trouble than you realise. Especially you, because he'll find out you went to Sri Lanka and he'll know you put the fuck on him.'

Donna listened to Alan in wonderment. Everything was like a nightmare. Her life was in danger, her whole world was collapsing around her, and instead of running from it all, running from Georgio, she still wanted to fight him.

'Ring Nick Carvello now. I'll wait until the jump's over. But I warn you, Alan, if he gets to Ireland, I go to the Old Bill and I tell them everything I know. And I don't care if they lock us all up and throw away the key, I'll see my day with that bastard I married.'

Alan nodded, stifling an urge to throttle the woman before him, without whom none of this would be happening. Yet even as he

489

raged, he had to admire her. Donna Brunos had more scruples than anyone he had ever met in his life.

She would fight for what she wanted.

He hoped to Christ she finally got it.

Lewis smiled at Sadie as she sipped at her small scotch and water.

'So, Sadie, what's this big story you want to tell me?'

Sadie looked at Donald Lewis and took a deep breath.

'Did you know I was deaf until I was sixteen, Mr Lewis?'

Donald shook his head. 'How the fuck would I know that? Why would I be interested in that?'

Sadie licked her lips nervously.

'Well, I lipread till then – you know the life I had, Donald, everyone does. I suffered from what's known as glue ear. I was as deaf as a post. Anyway, I still lipread, even now.'

She saw Donald's eyes narrow and sipped once more at her whisky before finishing what she had to say.

'I lipread something tonight I think you ought to know about, Mr Lewis.'

Donald Lewis looked through slitted eyes at Sadie and said gently, 'Go ahead, love, tell me what's on your mind.'

He refilled her glass with scotch and sat waiting for her to talk again.

'It concerns Georgio, Mr Lewis. Georgio, and Beavis and Butt-head.'

He nodded. 'Go on.'

Sadie gulped at the drink now, needing Dutch courage. 'In the reccy room, a while ago, Georgio went and sat with them. I watched them, out of curiosity, you know. I often do it. I know a lot of what goes on, but I keep me own counsel. It doesn't pay to get involved in other people's troubles and I just want to do me time in peace. I ain't out to get on anyone's tits, like.'

Lewis sighed heavily. 'All right, Sadie, we've established you're not a grass. Now will you tell me what the fuck this is all about?'

She pushed her hands through her hair nervously.

'Georgio sat down and said to them: "You open your traps about me, the kids, Sri Lanka or the merchandise and I'll rip your hearts out." I couldn't get the answer from them as their faces were obscured but then Georgio said, "Our business was just that, our business," and then he said that no one would believe them anyway, because he was the last person anyone would take for a beast.'

Sadie saw the blank look on Lewis's face and said quickly, 'I know what I read, Mr Lewis. I wouldn't have come to you if it was about

490

anything else. But from the look on his face, he was involved with them all right. He was warning them off. He's supposed to be fucking them up in the morning to get on a laydown. You'd be surprised what I read around this nick. Now, you'd better believe me, Mr Lewis, because I am laying my life on the line here.'

Lewis looked at her and said expressionlessly, 'And why are you doing that, Sadie? What's in it for you?'

She laughed mirthlessly.

'What's ever in anything for the likes of me, Mr Lewis? But I had dealings with them two, years ago when I was a kid. They're filth, Mr Lewis. They murdered little kids – raped, tortured and murdered them. I was the one who told Georgio who they were. I wanted to come straight to you, but he stopped me. Now I know why. Also I know Georgio has a hotel in Sri Lanka, or at least business dealings there.

'Their case involved international paedophile rings, Mr Lewis. They turned Queen's evidence against the others in their ring. That's why they're in here. No one saw their faces before or after the trial. Now Georgio is frightened they're going to blow his cover, I don't know what made him think that, or what they might have said to him. All I know is what I read off his lips, and you have to do something about it. You're the only person I can trust with this. And now, Mr Lewis, my life is in your hands. My gift is also now at your disposal, I realise that.'

Lewis nodded at the logic of what Sadie said. Her gift, as she put it, would be very handy, very handy indeed.

'But why are you telling me all this *really*? Come on, Sadie, I know you. What's really behind this? You was stuck up Brunos's arse for ages, I thought you was his best mate.'

Sadie threw back the scotch and coughed heartily, her eyes watering at the unaccustomed alcohol.

'I was fucked rigid by them when I was twelve. They hurt me and they hurt me bad. I wouldn't wish what happened to me on anyone, Mr Lewis. Especially not a small child – say a three year old. Even you couldn't countenance that, surely?'

Donald Lewis, psychopath, sociopath, cruel-minded and evil as he could be, mass of contradictions and twisted in his perceptions of right and wrong, could not, under any circumstances, countenance that. Not in prison anyway. The other men would never allow it, no matter who it was. It was this fact that Sadie was relying on.

'You did well, Sadie love,' he told her now. 'And as you point out, your little gift will be an asset to me. I'll look after you now, you're

491

under my protection. I'll sort this out, don't you fret your little head any more over any of it.'

Sadie smiled. 'Thanks, Mr Lewis.'

She went back to the rec room and Georgio winked at her as she sat down to watch *Emmerdale*. She smiled gently at him and then turned her face to the screen. But she wasn't seeing the pictures before her, she was seeing two men, a dark smelly room, could smell faeces and blood mixed with sweat, the men's breath laden with brandy and cigarette smoke, and she was hearing a child's crying, a child's terror.

The child was herself.

Davey walked into his house at eleven-thirty. He was half-drunk and tired. He slipped off his leather jacket and placed it on the banister at the bottom of the stairs. Yawning slightly, he walked into the front room.

Carol was waiting for him. She had on no make-up, a shock in itself to Davey, who rarely saw her thus, and she was wearing a towelling dressing gown. On the floor by the coffee table were two cases.

'What? You leaving me again, Carol?' His voice was half-jocular, half-bored.

Carol stood up. Folding her arms, she smiled. 'No, Davey, I'm not leaving you. I'm throwing you out.'

She watched with pleasure the look of absolute shock on his face. Then she saw him grit his teeth.

'Listen, Carol, I ain't in the mood for all this tonight, love. In fact, I am that far,' he put his finger and thumb together to make a perfect O, 'from smacking you one. And if you persist with this load of old crap, I will not only smack you one, I'll slap you black and fucking blue!'

Carol faced him. 'Oh you will, will you? Well, Davey Jackson, I am that far,' she made the same perfect O at him, 'from putting a knife right through your dirty stinking nonceing heart! Now take your bags and fuck off before I do just that. And another thing while we're at it: I think you had better see a solicitor, mate, about access to Jamie and the other kids, because knowing what I know now, I don't think I can allow you to see them without me or someone else present.'

She was hurting him, and she was enjoying it. As she saw the dawning of realisation hit his face, she smiled wickedly, even though her heart was breaking inside her chest.

'Carol . . . Carol love, listen to me.'

He took a step towards her but she backed away.

'No, Davey, I ain't ever listening to you again. You dragged me into something that I would never, ever have dreamt you capable of.

"A bit of old bluey", you said. "Nothing too near the mark", remember? "We even supply the Old Bill with the merchandise", you said. You lying fucking scumbag! Now take your gear and get out. We're over, Davey, finished. I put up with your abuse, your temper, your whoring and your prison sentences, but this little lot . . . That is the finish, mate, and I mean it. I take a fucking oath on it. Get out whoring again, go back to one of your silly little birds, do what the fuck you like – but *get out of my house!*'

Davey looked at the woman he had been forced into marrying, a woman he had loved in his own haphazard way over the years. The woman who had brought up his children, washed his clothes, cooked his food and visited him in prison. The thoughts of earlier in the day came back to him in a wave of fear.

'Carol, darling, listen to me, love . . . Please – let me explain.'

Hearing the whine in his voice, observing the complete shock on his face, Carol snapped. She launched herself at him, seeing the pictures in the books in her mind's eye, knowing that he'd made those books possible. As she attacked him the venom spewed out of her. She felt a strength born of hatred and resentment spill out and move into her arms. She dragged him, shouting and hollering, along the passageway and opening the front door, she slung him over the step on to the pathway.

She could hear Jamie crying in the background, could hear the lonely sobs of her child as she stood at the top of the stairs, watching all that was going on, woken by the raised voices and frightened of what was happening. But Carol ignored her daughter.

Stalking back into the front room, she picked up the cases and threw them out on to the lawn; Davey's leather jacket followed suit. Then, with one last look, she slammed the door in his beseeching face and walked steadily up the stairs, where she picked up her youngest daughter and held her tightly.

The child she had had at forty-one to keep Davey at home.

The child she loved more than any of the others.

And sitting at the top of the stairs with Jamie on her lap, she cried bitter tears.

493

Chapter Forty-Two

Georgio was awake long before the rest of the prison stirred.

He lay in his bunk thinking over the events of the day. Twenty-four hours from now, he would be on his way over to Ireland. Vida would be waiting for him, and he would disappear off the face of the earth, his money with him. He smiled in the dimness of the morning light that was trying to force weak tendrils through the curtains on his window. He felt the rush inside himself at the thought of what he was going to do; felt the fear and the excitement welling up inside him.

He heard the clanging of doors that denoted the changeover from night staff to day staff, then the early-morning calls from different cells, the laughter and the coughing fits. The sounds of a prison — sounds he would never forget, and never experience again after today. Knowing this, he almost savoured the noises, capturing them in his memory to keep with him and replay when he was lying on a warm, sun-drenched beach.

He was ready and waiting with his toothbrush when his cell door was opened, and as he ambled along to the shower he grinned pleasantly at Big Ricky, who grinned back, a wide, blank-eyed grin that gave Georgio a feeling of fear which he suppressed. In less than two hours, the day would be turned into a nightmare for screws and nonces alike. He couldn't wait.

Sadie watched him walk past her cell and pushed her face into the pillow to stem her breathing. She had half-loved Georgio, trusted him through all her grief over Timmy, allowed him the use of her lipreading gift. Now she would be used by Lewis, and knowing him he would use her to the utmost. But she was willing to take that chance to get her own back on a man who could use children, use his wife, use everyone around him. Even Timmy had been used. Sadie would avoid Georgio like the plague this morning. She would stay in her cell and wait the day out. In the shower, Georgio was singing at the top of his voice. He soaped himself liberally and washed his hair, scrubbing himself hard,

494

wanting to wash off the stink of the prison. A stink he would not have to put up with for much longer. He was even looking forward to his breakfast. After rinsing himself off, he put a clean dry towel around his waist and strolled into the toilet cubicles. At the far end was a cupboard used by the prisoners who cleaned the floors. Opening it, the stench of urine and faeces hit him, making his eyes water. He smiled, and using a piece of wood, stirred the contents of the black bucket, grinning as he pictured the contents hitting the Governor full in the face.

Closing the door, he strolled back towards his cell, smiling a greeting here and there. Young Benjy was standing outside his door and Georgio hailed him heartily.

'Fuck off, Brunos, I ain't in no mood for you!'

Georgio watched him, a smile on his face as the boy stalked away. 'Who rattled his cage then?'

Ricky stuck his head out of his own cell and said in a low voice, 'Who knows, Brunos? Maybe it was you.'

Georgio looked puzzled and Ricky smiled that smile of his again, showing immaculate teeth.

Georgio laughed. The day was his, there was nothing that could phase him. Not today, the day he jumped.

Whistling, he strode into his cell to dress before going for his breakfast.

Nick's eyes were bright with malice as he spoke to Albie over a breakfast of coffee and doughnuts.

'Can you believe it, eh? Georgio Brunos a beast. A seller of children. A beast in all ways. I hate the nonces, God knows I hate them, but it's the beasts, the people who supply the filth, that I really hate. Remember when I found you, Albie? How I looked after you? Took you to the hospital, visited you, brought you back to live with me? How old was you then?'

Albie put up his hand, fingers outstretched, three times.

'Fifteen, eh? Fifteen and abused and used. Hard to believe that in a country like this, a so-called democracy, there's still that black economy, children for sale. Young men for sale, arses for sale!'

Albie flinched at his words and Nick smiled sadly.

'I always get upset about it, you know that, Albie. Now I have to decide what I'm going to do to Georgio Brunos. How best to fuck him up. I would call off Eric if I could, but as Alan Cox said, Eric doesn't give a flying fuck either way. He'd jump Georgio if he was a rapist as well as a beast. He wants his dosh and he'll only get that off Georgio once the jump's over. No, it'll be much better to see Mr Brunos for

495

myself. Face to face like. In a knife-to-cheek situation, know what I mean?'

Albie smiled knowingly.

'You'd like that, Albie, wouldn't you?'

He made a noise in his throat, causing crumbs to spray across the table. Nick looked at him with distaste. 'Wipe your mouth, Albie, you know I can't bear bad table manners.'

Albie wiped his mouth with a Kleenex and smiled again.

Nick put another doughnut on his plate and wondered aloud, once more, what was the best way to pay back Georgio Brunos.

Eric felt the calm excitement he always experienced when a job was in progress. He sat in the skip lorry waiting patiently for the other men to do their jobs. He wasn't worried about them, they were good men, well-briefed and frightened of him. One thing he had learned in the Army: frighten the hell out of the men and they'll respect you. The majority were in the forces because they needed the order and discipline. They wanted to be told when to eat, sleep, shit and do their overtime. He smiled as he thought it, checking his watch once more.

A police car cruised past and he stared ahead of him at the paper perched on the steering wheel. He would not leave the yard with the skip lorry until he knew the sweatbox was on the ferry. Then he would move it to the spot at Devil's Bridge. It was planned out perfectly. There were roadworks on the slip road near where the jump was to take place; Jonnie H. and the others would be following him in the Mercedes van, all dressed as workmen. A council logo painted on the side of their vehicle would ensure their passage without hindrance.

All they needed was Brunos to do his job and they'd be on their way.

He thought of what Alan had told him that morning. So Georgio was a beast. Big deal. What the fuck did he care about that? Alan Cox should have done a stint in Viet Nam, where the children were used to carry weapons and messages, and blow up fucking roads. They weren't just used for sex out there, mate. They weren't children in the European sense of the word, they were tiny old men and women, advanced enough at seven to barter their services. Old enough at eight to sell a sibling.

He shook his head in wonderment at the world and the people in it. Alan Cox was like a big tart. Imagine expecting him to give up the chance of forty grand over a few kids! It was laughable. And as for insinuating that maybe Georgio wasn't such a good payer of debts,

496

maybe he wasn't, but he'd pay Eric out all right. Because if he didn't Eric would haunt him until he did, and Georgio knew that. Anyone who knew Eric knew that.

He'd slit a throat for the price of a pack of fags if he was skint enough. That's why he was where he was; that's why he was called on by villains, terrorists and the like. He had no scruples and didn't see the sense in gaining any at this late stage. Let Brunos carry on beasting when he got out, that was none of *his* business. All Eric knew was that once Georgio was out, he would be paid out in full. He would see to that himself.

His mobile phone rang and he answered it.

'Yeah?'

He listened for a few seconds.

'OK, Jonnie, make the break. See that the vehicles are ready and able in one hour from now. I'll ring when I'm on my way.'

He turned off the phone and went back to his contemplation of what he would do with his forty grand.

First on the agenda was a little Somali woman he'd had his eye on for a while. With forty grand tucked away, he could buy her, her sisters, and the whole village if he wanted to. But she would do for starters.

He needed a holiday, and had always liked the anonymity of Africa. It was like his second home. He smiled as he thought that. In reality, it was his only home.

You could get lost in Africa. You could buy anything and live out there for a pittance, and live well. He had worked for most juntas, been involved in enough coups to write a handbook about them, and he had enjoyed every second of it.

Yes, Somalia would be his first stop, then he might even take a trip to see one of his wives.

South America was always good for a laugh.

As he daydreamed, his eyes were taking in everything around him. Even while asleep Eric listened to the world around him. It was a habit that had kept him alive longer than any of his contemporaries.

Maeve was reading the *Sun*'s problem page and drinking a cup of strong tea when the doorbell rang. Sighing, she went down the stairs to answer it, annoyed at the interruption to her morning break. The doorbell rang again and she shouted, 'All right, all right, I'm coming.'

Flinging open the door she was confronted by two policemen.

'Mrs Brunos?'

Maeve felt the fear a policemen at the door brings to all mothers.

'Yes. What can I do for you?'

The older policeman smiled sympathetically.

'Can we come inside, love? We need to talk to you.'

They followed Maeve up the stairs, their heavy boots making a loud noise on each step. Inside her small front room, Maeve faced them fearfully.

'Is it one of my children . . .'

The older man spoke again, his face regretful, his whole body language telling her that something bad had happened.

'It's about your son, Stephen Brunos. I'm afraid he met with an accident in Sri Lanka.'

Maeve's mouth moved a few times, but at first she couldn't get any sound out of it.

'What kind of accident?'

The younger man put his hand on her arm. 'Why don't you sit down and I'll make us all a nice cup of tea, eh? Is your husband around, love?'

Maeve shook her head, allowing the policeman to sit her down on one of the worn armchairs.

'What's happened to my boy? Tell me what's happened?'

A small voice in the back of her mind was relieved it was Stephen they'd come about, and not one of the girls, Mario, or Patrick. Patrick the womaniser, Patrick who came and went like a ghost. The policeman was talking once more, but Maeve couldn't take in what he was saying.

'The British consulate has established that it was indeed your son's body. His passport was in his hotel room and the photograph was his. It seems he had rather a lot to drink, and then went swimming. There's quite an undertow apparently. A terrible tragedy . . .'

Maeve wasn't listening any more. She had heard all she needed or wanted to hear.

The front door opened and Pa Brunos's heavy tread could be heard on the stairs. The tears came then, because she felt so sorry for him, because she now knew what the police were going to say, and once Pa heard it as well it would be true.

She'd lost a child of her body, he was never coming home again. Stephen, the least loved of her children, the one she found it difficult to love, had always found it difficult to love, was lying somewhere on a tropical island, alone, dead a cold. His handsome features never to age, his mother never to get over the loss of him, even though she was telling herself that she was pleased it was him and not one of the others.

498

Pa took one look at his wife, and the police, and knew that death was stalking his family.

Taking Maeve's hand in his, he listened silently and without tears to what the older policeman was telling him.

Jonnie H. was nervous. Sweat trickled down his back, even though the van was freezing.

'You checked the bikes over?' he asked yet again.

The oldest McAnulty brother sighed heavily.

'Will ye fucking calm down, Jonnie? Everything's ready to go.'

Jonnie lit a cigarette and drew on it heavily.

'I hate the waiting. Never was any good at waiting, know what I mean?'

Danny nodded. 'It doesnae bother me. In Scotland waiting is a national pastime.' He laughed loudly. 'Especially on the Clyde. I've had to wait all my life.'

Jonnie stared at him for a while and said, 'Just my fucking luck, stuck on a jump with a Scottish philosopher! Here, you didn't marry a social worker, did you? I hear they do your brain in and there's load of them hanging around in Scottish nicks, just waiting to marry a con and write a book about it.'

Danny smiled wryly. 'You Cockneys have a weird sense of humour, Jonnie.'

Jonnie grinned, showing his extensive teeth. 'It ain't that we've got a weird sense of humour, Danny, me old mate, it's more a case of the Scottish ain't got one!'

One of the younger brothers, Iain, said loudly, 'What about Billy Connolly then?'

Jonnie nodded and said soberly, 'All right, I'll concede the Big Yin, but I reckon he's got an English granny somewhere along the line. He was a bleedin' throwback!'

They all laughed, nervous laughter that was too high and too long.

Jonnie pulled on his cigarette again.

'I hate the waiting, I can't stand the waiting.'

'You should get yourself a ten-stretch, Jonnie, you'd soon get used to waiting then. There's nothing like a big one to give you patience.'

'Well, mate, if everything goes wrong today, I might just find that out for myself.'

The van was quiet then, the men all contemplating getting caught.

Danny's voice was low as he said, 'Calm down, everyone. It's nerves that make people do things wrong, that get someone shot or killed. We'll be in and out in no time. So stop worrying and let's put the radio on. Maybe we'll find a good play on Radio Four.'

499

'A fucking play on Radio Four?' Jonnie H. sneered. 'Now I've heard everything.'

Iain's voice was dry as he said, 'They might be doing *The Great Escape*, eh?'

The men all laughed again, loud and long.

Jump nerves had got to all of them.

Donna was lying on the settee in her lounge, still in her dressing gown, a pot of tea on the small Japanese table beside her. The room was in disarray, and she looked around it as if for the first time. She had lain awake all night, and at some point a cigarette had dropped from the side of the ashtray and burnt through the lacquered top of the table. Far from distressing her, she found it slightly amusing.

She would love Georgio to walk in now. Never, in all their years in the house, had he seen the rooms looking less than perfect. Both Dolly and she had made sure of that because that was what he wanted.

Donna had spent the best part of her life in the conservatory, rarely using the lounges because the white leather furniture showed every speck. She had been frightened to crumple a cushion in case the lord and master came home and wanted to sit and watch TV. Then the room would be used, but Donna had never felt at home in there.

It was strange, she reflected, just how much Georgio had dominated her life, even down to subconsciously keeping her out of her own home, parts of it anyway. Like the French windows on the landing. They opened out on to a small balcony with wrought-iron table and chairs. If Georgio wanted to, they took their breakfast coffee out there in the summer and looked over the garden and the fields beyond. But only if he suggested it.

Once, she had gone out there alone, and Georgio had woken up and found her there. And in his own inimitable way, had made her feel a fool.

'What are you doing out here all on your own?'

She could still hear the incredulity in his voice, as if she had done something sneaky, underhand. She had pointed to the second cup and he had shook his head, as if the thought of him, Georgio Big Man Brunos, sitting on a small balcony in his own house with his wife, was something distasteful. Lowering even. He had walked down the stairs and she could hear him greeting Dolly in the kitchen, leaving her up there alone, feeling a trifle foolish.

The memory hurt her – yet another suppressed slight that had resurfaced in the last few days. Small things that over the years she had ignored. Could you really love someone so much, you allowed

500

them to dominate even the most trivial parts of your life? He had told her what to wear, and how to wear it. He had told her what she should be, how she should talk, how she should act, and she had gone along with it all. Never daring to question anything, because if you questioned Georgio he had a knack of making you regret it, making you feel a fool.

If you wanted Georgio, you did what he said, and if you didn't then you knew you would lose him. Now, after all that had happened, she wondered why the thought of losing him had been so very frightening. She looked around the room again and smiled once more.

It was a shambles. But she was actually enjoying it. Enjoying living in her home – and it was her home now. Georgio had signed the lot over to her. Home, business and brothels. She laughed gently, covering her hand with her mouth.

She was the proud owner of a building business, a car lot and a brothel. Not any old brothel either, a brothel for children. Georgio had always promised her he would see her all right, look after her, and he had. Oh yes, he had looked after her all right.

Picking up the ashtray, she hurled it across the room, sending ash and cigarette ends all over the place.

She felt better for the action.

On the verge now of wrecking the house, feeling the urge rising inside her, she took a deep breath.

'Get a grip,' she whispered to herself.

'Get a grip on yourself, woman.

'Everything you survey is yours and Georgio Brunos can't take any of it.'

What was the old adage she had heard from Carol Jackson? That was it. If you wanted to hurt a man, hit him in the pocket. Well, Georgio would never get a cent from her, or from this house, ever again. She would burn the lot first and enjoy herself while she did it.

Lying back on the settee she closed her eyes.

Would today never end?

She had to hear something soon or she would lose what little remained of her mind.

Carol called through her door in a strident voice: 'Go away, Davey, I'm warning you!'

He stood on his own doorstep, aware of the stares of women coming home from taking their children to school.

'Carol love, open the door. I just want to talk to you. We have to sort out what's going to happen.'

She laughed delightedly. 'Up yours, Jackson. You have more

501

chance of getting a dose off the Bishop of Durham than you've got of ever getting back in this house again. Now piss off before I call the Old Bill.'

'If you don't open this door, I swear to Christ I'll kick it in.'

She pulled her dressing gown tightly around her breasts. 'Kick away, you prat, and I'll have you arrested. Go on, kick the door in. I have enough on you to put you away till doomsday, mate.'

Davey could hear the taunting in her voice and he closed his eyes in distress.

'Listen, Carol love,' his voice was calmer, sweeter now, 'I want a few bits from the house. Just a few bits, that's all.'

Carol was wary. 'Such as?'

'There's some keys in the bedroom, up on top of the wardrobe. I need them, Carol, they're important.'

Her eyes narrowed. 'I've already got rid of them, Davey.'

'You *what!*' His voice was incredulous.

'I gave them to Big Paddy. Why – didn't he give them to you?'

Davey wiped his hand across his face.

'Tell me you're fucking joking, Carol. If you've really given them keys to Big Paddy, I'll break your fucking neck!'

Carol's laugh came through the door, maddening him.

'You'll have to catch me first, Jackson, and I have a feeling I know a little too much about you to worry about you hurting me. So do Donna Brunos and old Dolly. Enjoy threatening her, did you, with Paddy? Oh, he was as pleased as punch when I gave him the keys, Davey, over the fucking moon he was.'

She watched him storm down the pathway and slam the gate behind him. A part of her wanted to open the door and call him back; the other half of her saw the books her husband had peddled, had conned her into peddling, and her heart hardened.

Running up the stairs, she placed her hand on top of the wardrobe and felt around for the keys she hadn't known were there until her husband mentioned them.

Looking at them, she realised she had the keys to the lock-ups in her hands. That's where the merchandise would be stored and that's what he wanted. She weighed the keys, moving her arm up and down, juggling them. Trying to decide what to do with them.

Dressing quickly, she left the house, with no make-up, no backcombed hair, no nothing.

Her next-door neighbour watched her with a slight frown on her face. The Jacksons should not have been living in a respectable residential street as far as she was concerned. They should have stayed in their privatised council house where they belonged. The woman's disgraceful language was bad enough, as were the skintight clothes on her ample frame and that shocking bleached blonde mass of tangles on her head, but Carol Jackson's choice of car was what really got her down. A shocking pink Golf Gti was hardly the kind of car one welcomed in Runnymead Close.

Georgio ate his breakfast in silence. He could feel the electric atmosphere around him as the men all waited for the off.

Lewis was nowhere to be seen, but this didn't worry Georgio. He knew Lewis would be taking a leisurely breakfast in his cell, a full cooked breakfast, as he did every morning, consisting of eggs, bacon, fried slice and button mushrooms. Georgio couldn't help smiling as he thought of Lewis's face when he found out Georgio had jumped, right away from him and the prison . . . taking Lewis's money with him.

He looked up from his breakfast and saw Ricky watching him. He winked and Ricky winked back. But he didn't smile and Georgio carried on eating, knowing that it might be the only food he got for a good few hours.

Beavis and Butthead, *aka* Harvey Hall and Bernard Denning, watched everyone surreptitiously. Since arriving in Parkhurst they had realised exactly how much danger they were in. Listening to the men talk was a terrifying experience, and both being convicted child-molesters and paedophiles who had accidentally murdered some of their victims, they had become wary, terrified of ever being unmasked for what they were. The average person on the street would feel no compunction in attacking them. Outside the court, women had screamed abuse at them, had tried to attack them, and they were normal housewives. What would these hard-faced, violent men do if they guessed who these two really were? And both Hall and Denning knew that eventually the men would find out.

The waiting was worse than anything. They had listened to the men's opinion of nonces. Transvestites and homosexuals were accepted in this environment, as long as they were consenting adults. But rapists, child-molesters and especially beasts, were hated, despised. Yet Georgio was a beast, he was a supplier. But no one in here was aware of that apparently. To them he was just one of the lads, a blagger, a villain.

Harvey Hall watched Georgio eating, saw him pushing the food into his mouth as if frightened someone was going to take it away from him. Unlike Denning, Hall could feel the tension in the air. He had made a shrewd guess that the men were all waiting for something, and he had a nasty feeling that the thing they were waiting for concerned him and Bernard.

503

He felt the fear loosen his bowels and shifted uneasily in his chair.

Eros, the young black man who had come on to the Wing with them, started singing. Everyone had already put him down as a religious nut, which he was. Inside for murder, he was a paranoid schizophrenic who believed that certain people were asking to be killed. That they gave him subliminal signals which he acted upon, on the say-so of none other than Christ Himself. Eros was waiting to be assessed and then transferred to a top-security mental hospital. The men were used to lunatics like him and left him in peace. Unlike the public, they were capable of handling him if he became aggressive. There were plenty like him in the Wing who were left to their own devices.

'Jesus is waiting for you! Jesus just wants you to love him.'

There was no real tune and Benjy, the joker, began singing with him.

'And if Arsenal wins the cup, I'll be singing on the other side of my arse!'

Everyone laughed except Eros. He answered in a deep brown rich-timbred voice: 'You can't mock God, boy. Jesus is watching over you all. He is here now while I am speaking!'

'Well, tell Him to go and get me another cup of Rosie Lee then!'

The laughter was louder. Even the screws joined in, keeping their distance though because any altercation in here could turn into a war.

Benjy walked over to Eros and said loudly, 'What punishment would Jesus give out to people who murdered and raped little children, eh? What's the score for all that then?'

Hall and Denning stiffened in their seats.

Eros stared up at Benjy and said seriously, 'The wages of sin is death. Suffer not the little children, He said. The bad men will scream in Hell, and their bodies will be burnt on the Day of Reckoning. For all eternity they'll be tortured in fires of brimstone!'

Benjy pretended to wipe the sweat from his brow and said, 'Is that all? I thought they might be forced to listen to reggae for all eternity. Now that's what I call a punishment!'

Ricky laughed good-naturedly. 'Your trouble is, you don't know good music when you hear it, boy. Gregory Isaacs is a god, a musical genius.'

Benjy made a face. 'With respect, Ricky, I've heard better tunes form a cat with a banger up its arse! He sings like Gazza plays football – badly!'

While the bantering was going on Georgio looked at the clock on the wall. It was just after nine-thirty.

Another half an hour till the off.

504

Eros began singing again, one of his own peculiar songs, and Georgio looked over at Hall and Denning, a slight grin on his face. He couldn't wait to get started.

Then Eros stood up and began to dance with an invisible partner.

Ricky shook his head in wonderment. 'The man's as mad as a hatter.'

Benjy tut-tutted loudly, like a motor mechanic assessing the damage to a car.

'It could be worse, Ricky mate. It could be you!'

Everyone laughed again, a friendly, contagious sound.

Georgio joined in, feeling euphoric at the thought of his planned escape. At the thought of getting one over on Lewis. At the thought of never having to listen to any of them again. Especially Eros.

It was coming up to a quarter to ten when Lewis made his entrance into the rec room. Everyone was there, the air was alight with tension and the screws had picked up on it. Lewis still limped slightly, and was still on medication, but there was a burning brightness in his eyes that denoted his inner strength. His easy smile made the prison warders nervous. There was something going down but they couldn't even hope to guess what it was. Since open visiting and the new Governor, they felt they had lost a lot of their authority and credibility with the prisoners.

But it was always the same on the violent wings: these were men who would kill their own grannies if they annoyed them enough, and they were men it was hard to police. You could only watch and wait and see what was going to happen, and hope against hope that you weren't going to be caught in the crossfire. Most of the warders were in the pay of Lewis anyway. They had a job to do for him as well as the Home Office.

The screw in charge today was a Mr Hollingsworth. He had been deliberately chosen because he was quiet and on the verge of retirement – exactly what Lewis needed on a day when the Wing was to be pulled apart.

Hollingsworth called the two screws out of the rec room at one minute to ten exactly.

It was what Lewis had told him to do, and Mr Hollingsworth, being used to taking orders, did precisely what he was asked of him.

505

Chapter Forty-Three

Donna parked the Astra van outside the lock-up garages in Pitsea and turned off the engine. She looked at Carol, who was watching the road to see if Davey had arrived before her, and was maybe waiting for them. At the moment the two women trusted no one. If Paddy had been found, and the chances were that he hadn't, then the men could arrive at any minute.

'Do you think we're doing the right thing, Carol?'

She shrugged, helplessly. 'I really don't know, Donna. All I do know is that we have to get out the merchandise and burn it. Burn the bloody lot. If that arsehole of an old man of mine thinks I'm going to sit back and let him carry on with this lot, he's got another think coming!'

She slipped out of the van and Donna watched her with apprehension as she approached the garage doors.

What she was supposed to do if Big Paddy or Davey jumped on them, she wasn't sure. Donna picked up her mobile and turned it on in case she had to phone for help.

Carol unlocked two padlocks and two mortice locks on the wooden door of the garage. The door opened fully to allow access for a vehicle, and it also had a small inset doorway. Carol opened the doorway first and Donna watched as she stepped inside, her heart in her mouth.

Carol popped her head out and gestured to Donna to back the van up.

Five minutes later the two women had opened the door fully and were packing the boxes of books and discs into the back of the Astra.

'Oh, please hurry up, Donna, for fuck's sake. If we get caught by the Old Bill it'll be bad enough, but if Paddy comes we'll be in deep shit.'

Donna was moving the last of the boxes from the back of the lock-up. The Astra van was nearly full and the last few boxes would be difficult to cram inside it. As she moved them she called out, 'Carol, come and look at this!'

506

Carol walked over to her and frowned. The concrete had been taken up at some time and now, after the removal of all the boxes, they could clearly see that a hole had been dug in the floor of the lock-up.

'What do you reckon this is then?

'I don't know,' Donna said. 'Maybe something's buried here.'

Carol stepped back in fright.

'You don't think it's a grave, do you?' Her voice was hesitant, fearful.

Donna laughed nervously. 'Well, if it is, then the person was buried standing up! Look at the size of it.'

Carol lit a cigarette and pulled on it deeply.

'That's what I'm frightened of. Maybe it's a little kid. After what we've found out the last few days, I wouldn't put nothing past that lot.'

Donna felt her face blanch. 'Oh, leave it out, Carol, that's stupid.'

The other woman shook her head.

'Listen, Donna, that lot are capable of anything, especially your Georgio. I ain't being funny but I wouldn't put fuck all past him. I mean, would you have believed that Big Paddy, that nice bloke, could rough up old Dolly, eh? Maybe they branched out into British kids, who can tell? For all we know, Georgio and Davey could have been nonceing.'

Donna shook her head impatiently. 'I can't believe that, Carol.'

She pulled Donna round to face her.

'Well, they were peddling all this filth, weren't they? What makes you so sure they weren't getting their rocks off on it? They must have had contacts or they'd never sell the stuff, would they? They had to know men who wanted this stuff. This ain't a bit of ordinary porn, love, a bit of old bluey. This is babies, little kids.'

Donna acknowledged the truth of what Carol was saying, but everything inside her rebelled at the thought of Georgio, even knowing what she knew about him, actually touching the children. His baby son came to mind, and she felt a wave of pure hatred rush over her body. Then she heard Candy's voice talking about Georgio in Thailand with the twelve- and thirteen-year-old girls. 'The three-headed blow job' she had called it.

'Pack the last few boxes into the car, Carol, and I'll start digging this lot up.'

Carol stared at her as if she were mad.

'You're going to dig this place up? Are you out of your mind! Paddy, Davey, anyone could turn up!'

'At this moment in time, Carol,' Donna told her, 'I couldn't give a flying fuck, as you would say. I will never sleep again unless I know what the hell is under this floor.'

507

Carol was stunned. She shook her head in distress, her flattened, bleached hair waving with the motion.

'Oh Donna, please. I don't think I want to know.'

'That's the trouble, love. That's why people can buy all this stuff – because no one wants to know. No one likes to think about it. It's too horrible to contemplate. Well, if you want, you go ahead and take the books and discs. Go on home. I'll stay here alone and sort this lot out.'

'You're mad, Donna, stark staring mad. Get the Old Bill. Let them sort it out.'

Donna wiped her hand across her face.

'And what if there's nothing here? What then? They will question you, me, the lot of us. We'll be in it up to our necks, and I hate to remind you but you and I are as guilty as the men in this. Or at least, that's how it will look. We'll be arrested, your kids will be without you *and* Davey. Think about it, Carol. Until we know what's under this floor we can't decide anything.'

Carol blanched with fright.

'Oh, for Christ's sake, Donna. How the hell did this happen to us?'

She shook her head sadly. 'It happened, Carol, because we let it. My mother used to say, "People only do to you what you let them," and that's true. Now pass me that crowbar and let's get started. You shut the van up and lock it, then close the main doors. I'll start pulling up the concrete.'

Carol passed her the crowbar and walked from the lock-up, her heart in her mouth.

Whatever they found, even if it was nothing, Carol knew it would be the final nail in her marriage to Davey, because she would never, ever forgive him for putting her through all this.

As she shut the door of the lock-up, all her fear of Paddy and Davey evaporated . . . overshadowed by the fear of finding the remains of a child.

Georgio watched the minute hand of the clock reach ten. Then Big Ricky went to the camera in the corner of the room and, standing on a chair, he placed a sweatshirt over the lens.

Georgio watched and then Lewis walked towards him and he smiled. Lewis didn't smile back.

All eyes were on Denning and Hall, and the two men sensed that their lives were in grave danger. The rec room was ominously quiet as the men waited for the first blow to fall.

Ricky took out of the waistband of his trousers a long-handled knife. It was made from the remains of a broom-handle, and fixed into the end of it was the blade of a steak knife stolen from the kitchens. He waved it in front of his face with a deep laugh.

Denning grabbed Hall's hand as if the action could save them and the men in the room sniggered.

Ricky and Georgio walked towards them. Georgio pulled out his own blade, a smaller, scaled-down version of Big Ricky's.

'Thought we didn't know who you were, didn't you?' Georgio's voice was low.

Then Ricky stabbed Hall in his stomach, pulling the blade across the beer belly, a deep red gash appearing as if by magic. Hall grabbed his stomach in both hands, mortal fear on his face. Denning watched in fascinated silence as did the rest of the men in the rec room. First blood had been drawn, and it seemed as if that caused the men watching to go mad.

Chopper picked up a chair and smashed it against the pool table. Grasping a chair leg, he began to lay into Denning, putting all his considerable strength into the blows he rained down on the man's body. Denning dropped to the floor at the first assault and then the men were all over him and Hall.

Lewis walked calmly over to Georgio, who was watching the spectacle, fascinated.

'Aren't you going to help your friends out?' Lewis said.

The words were lost in the shouts and the screams of the two men being attacked.

Georgio stared into Lewis's face and then, smiling, he pushed the knife he held into Lewis's chest until it was buried right up to its crudely-fashioned handle. He watched Lewis's eyes widen with shock and pain, and as Lewis's minder came towards him, he tried to pull the knife free. But Lewis was falling to the ground and this made it difficult. As the minder reached him with upraised fist, Georgio watched with pleasure as Big Ricky dragged the man backwards by putting his arm across his throat, and then he watched the man's throat being cut, slowly and deliberately, with the long-bladed knife.

Georgio pulled the knife out of Lewis and smiled at Ricky, who was pleased to see his enemy on the floor, writhing in agony. Georgio wiped the blade of the knife across Lewis's throat, as if cutting through butter, and the blood pumped up into the air, catching Georgio's denim shirt and trousers.

Turning from Lewis, Georgio and Ricky joined in the fray around the beasts.

The language was ripe, the men frenzied in their attack. The rec room was demolished within minutes.

Looking around at the carnage, Georgio laughed in delight. It

509

couldn't have gone better. Everything was exactly as he wanted it.

Standing back, he wiped his face and was surprised to find he was sweating. He watched in shocked silence as Hall's head was hacked from his body. The men were going wild with bloodlust and hatred. He saw the head being thrown around the room, from man to man, saw it kicked across the floor and thanked God he wasn't on the receiving end of it. Denning was still alive. Georgio watched as he tried to crawl under the pool table.

'Oi! Watch out, Denning's trying to get away!'

Georgio's voice was jovial, loud. He ran across the room and dragged the man out from under the table by his legs. Denning was unrecognisable, his face just a bloody pulp. In the distance, Georgio could hear the alarm bells going off all over the prison – the noise he had been waiting for. Throwing Denning's legs back to the ground, he watched as the man began jumping on the nonce's body, on his chest, head and legs; falling over and picking themselves up once more to attack the men again. All laughing hysterically, eyes bright, some with bloodlust, some with the buzz of cocaine or heroin.

Georgio looked around him and felt an urge to roar with laughter. All his life he had manipulated people and this, to him, was proof of what he could achieve if he wanted to.

Eros, still singing, had somehow picked up on the atmosphere in the room and Georgio watched as he lifted Hall's decapitated head and cradled it in his arms. Singing to it in a loud voice, an old hymn that seemed to make the scene more surreal as his voice rose over the other men's, who all stopped what they were doing and watched him in a fascinated, spent silence. It was as if only now were they fully aware of what they had done.

The men looked around them at the four mutilated bodies and the blood everywhere, and most felt as if they were awakening from a nightmare.

Fifteen minutes after the first blood had been drawn, the guards came into the rec room and what they saw astounded them. All the man were standing around in silence, drenched in blood, and in the centre of the room was Eros, a man's head in his arms, singing 'Jerusalem'.

Mr Hollingsworth took in the scene – Lewis's body mangled and twisted, and said in a shocked voice: 'Get the fuck out of here, men.'

Two minutes later the wardens were on the other side of the Wing doors, and Mr Hollingsworth was on the blower to the Governor's office. One of the younger screws was shocked to hear him shouting: 'Get the fuck down here, man, they've all gone fucking barmy!'

Slamming down the phone the older screw said sadly, 'I thought

510

I'd seen everything in this job, son, everything.'

The younger man spoke for all the screws when he said, 'What do we do now, Mr Hollingsworth?'

The older man lit himself a cigarette and said in a tired voice, 'We have a cup of tea and wait for Dopey Bollocks to get here. Now you'll find out why the Governor gets paid such a hefty wedge. This is his baby, Sunny Jim, nothing to do with us. Let him sort it out.'

Donna was sweating and tired. The concrete had been easy to prise up, it was the dirt underneath that was giving her the trouble. With only a piece of wood to dig with, it was a slow and laborious job.

'Come on, Donna. Get a move on, will you?' Carol was keeping lookout at the garage doors.

'I'm nearly there. Will you stop keeping on at me!' Donna's voice was loud and irritable in the empty garage. Tugging at the dirt now with her bare hands, she said, 'There's something down here, Carol. Give me a hand.'

Carol walked over to her on wobbly legs.

'What is it?'

Donna was too tired now and too involved with what she was doing to be frightened any more.

'How the hell do I know? Give me a hand, girl, there's something solid under the earth.'

Carol looked into the hole that Donna had dug. It was about eighteen inches deep, and as Donna went on, tossing more dirt out with her bare hands, Carol saw pieces of a red blanket.

Donna heaved at the blanket, putting all her weight behind her arms. The blanket started to come free from the dirt around it and both women realised that it contained something. Putting her hand over her mouth, Carol ran to the garage door, bile rising up inside her as she retched outside in the thin daylight.

Holding her stomach she heard Donna give a high-pitched laugh, then she heard: 'Oh my good God!'

Taking her courage into her hands, Carol stepped back inside the doorway and walked towards Donna.

Davey Jackson and Big Paddy pulled into the garage block just as Carol walked across the garage floor.

Mr Justice Hanningfield, Acting Governor of Parkhurst while a permanent Governor was being chosen, walked on to the SSB unit with his two assistants.

'What is going on here?'

Mr Hollingsworth said quietly, 'There's been a bit of trouble, Mr

511

Hanningfield. It seems the men got wind of Hall and Denning's identity. They slaughtered them just before morning tea was served. They also slaughtered Donald Lewis and one of his cronies. At this particular moment the men are in post-attack trauma, quiet but still dangerous. I've seen it before. There's been something brewing here for months and today is the upshot. I don't like to cause trouble, sir, but I did advise against putting two sex-offenders in with the blaggers. I told you they wouldn't swallow it.'

Hanningfield looked at the man before him, and his lip, covered with a pencil moustache, twitched in agitation.

'So what do we do now?' Hanningfield's voice was clipped.

Mr Hollingsworth shrugged maddeningly and said, 'Well, forgive me for speaking out of turn, but I was under the impression that it was your job to tell us that.' He hesitated for a few seconds before adding, 'Sir.'

Inside the rec room the men were high on blood and revolution. Georgio knew that he now had to talk them into letting the Governor in to negotiate.

'Go down to the latrines, Benjy, and bring me back the shit in the cupboard. I am going to shit up this Governor.'

Ricky looked at him in amazement. 'You're really going to shit up the Governor?'

Georgio looked around the room. 'After this little lot, I think it is about the only thing left we can do, ain't it? Might as well get hung for a sheep as a lamb. Anyway, I want to get my own back on that supercilious cunt. I hate him!'

Georgio's strong voice was loud in the quiet room and he bellowed, 'What's the matter with you lot? They were scum, shite, they were child-killers. We done the country a fucking favour, saved the taxpayers millions looking after them. The papers will know who they are within hours. We'll be fucking heroes! The average person on the street will be right behind us! What's the fucking matter with you lot? I'll take the blame, and I'll be proud to take the fucking blame. They were a pair of shitstabbers. The same with Lewis. He frightened the shit out of everyone. Now me and Ricky will be in charge, things can loosen up a bit.'

Benjy came back in the room with the bucket of faeces and Georgio laughed delightedly.

'I can't wait to see the bastard's face, can you? This'll teach him to put nonces and beasts in with the real men, won't it! Someone take down the sweatshirt. Let the governor see what he's caused.'

★ ★ ★

512

Hanningfield looked at the wardens around him.

'How is that no one noticed that the interior camera was not in use?'

The wardens all looked down at their feet.

'Sometimes we lose contact for a few minutes. It's an old system, Mr Hanningfield. We have our little hitches.'

'Little hitches! Is that what you call them? Four men dead, as far as we know, and you talk about bloody hitches!'

'With respect, sir, the perimeter fences aren't exactly the greatest either. The cameras there are sometimes in completely the wrong direction. That's how the other three went walkabout last year, remember, so don't blame us because the money ain't being spent on this place. Our job's hard enough as it is. You should try looking after that lot!'

Hanningfield said in a tightly controlled voice, 'You have more experience than I in these matters. Please let's save all this for later, shall we?'

Mr Hollingsworth said calmly, 'We have to separate the ringleaders, that's the first stage. We have to get them off the Island. Bring into the force the GOAD.' He glanced at the Governor and said snidely: 'To you that's the Good Order And Discipline rule. Once the others know they're gone, we'll soon sort them out. We'll get the leaders off on a laydown. It's Section 43. We can remove them from the prison without escort in times of crisis – and I think this is a crisis, don't you?'

A loud shout came from the wing gates and a warden came into the main office, saying, 'They're calling for you, Mr Hanningfield. They want you, sir.'

Hanningfield looked at the monitor screen showing the carnage in the rec room and Hollingsworth smiled as he saw the man's face go pale. Then he said jovially, 'Well, best not to keep them waiting, eh?'

Hanningfield marched from the room and the wardens all followed him sheepishly. Standing outside the Wing gates, the Acting Governor saw the bloodsoaked men and nearly lost the use of his voice.

Georgio stood to the fore of the men and shouted: 'You had no right to put that scum in with us, no fucking right, man. We're not nonces. You insulted us by putting that scum in with us. You're to blame for this, mate, and you know it!'

The wardens, carrying guns, stood watching the performance with glee.

Hanningfield shouted: 'Give this up now and I'll try to get everything sorted out quietly. You must give up on what you're doing.'

Georgio laughed. 'Oh, we've stopped what we're doing, Mr Hanningfield, sir. You can come in and clean up. In fact, we'll help you if you like.'

All the men laughed derisively.

'Open the gates, we'll all go back to the rec room and you can take the weapons and deal with us there. We were trying to prove a point. Scum we might be, to the likes of you anyway, but there is no way we will countenance nonces on the Wing, no way at all.'

He put down his knife in full view of the Governor and the wardens and all the other men followed suit, even Big Ricky. Now the job was out of the way, Ricky had what he wanted and so did Georgio. All that remained was to get the trouble over with as soon as possible.

Back inside the rec room, the men all stood about waiting for the armed screws to arrive. They were there within two minutes. The men were all lined up against the far wall, and Georgio stood with the bucket behind him waiting for Mr Hanningfield to make his grand entrance.

He didn't have to wait long. With the reassurance of armed men, and the quietness of the prisoners, Mr Hanningfield felt safe enough to walk into the room and assert his full authority. In the back of his mind were thoughts of how he would dwell on this part of the morning in his final report.

He looked around the room, his heart beating a tattoo as he saw Eros sitting in a corner of the room with Hall's head still in his arms.

It was like walking into a waking nightmare, and he realised just how badly he had underestimated the people before him. They were capable of so much more than he could ever have guessed. He realised that despite the pamphlets he had read, and the books on the prison service he had pored over, he had no real idea of what to do with violent criminals like these. Nobody had. That was the trouble with the prison service. If someone had told him this would happen he would have laughed in their faces. He dined out on his stories of the criminals he had in his care, and now he would be ridiculed and vilified in the national press on top of everything else.

No one would take into account that Eros should have been in Broadmoor, that Brunos and the black man laBrett were intelligent and manipulative, that the men were bored out of their skulls with nothing to do and too much time to do it in. That the cons in here were basically the top echelon of the criminal world, looked up to by everyone in prison as real villains, blaggers and the like. That the men here were doing sentences longer than most marriages lasted and should in reality be treated with respect and asked to help in the running of the Wing, instead of being treated like animals with no

514

privacy whatsoever – even the act of opening their bowels done in a toilet devoid of doors and while reading a paper, to give them a semblance of privacy. That they were sexually active and the only way open to them was with one another, which led to self-hatred, disease and deviance. That wives left them, divorced them, and stopped bringing their children in to visit. That the drugs which were growing more and more rife were their only escape from the boredom of the day, and their way of coping in a system which locked them up and threw away the key.

Rapists had their own prisons where people tried to help them; young offenders were helped. These men were just left. A whole sub-class of society left to rot away and gradually grow more bitter and more explosive as time went on.

No, no one would think of that aspect.

They locked them up, left them to stew and this was the upshot.

Hanningfield walked towards the men, brave now it seemed that everything was under control. And as he opened his mouth to speak, Georgio walked through the crush of men and threw the contents of the bucket into his face.

Hanningfield smelt the stench before he tasted the contents of the shit-bucket. His stomach seemed to rise up inside him as it rebelled against what he knew was inside his mouth, in his eyes, and covering his good suit.

All he could hear was the roar of mocking laughter as the men called out in jeering voices:

'Shit up the Governor!'

'Shit up the Governor!'

Over and over again.

Davey and Paddy walked into the lock-up and were amazed to see the two women kneeling on the floor.

'What the fuck's going on here?'

Paddy's voice was loud in the empty garage and both Donna and Carol nearly passed out with fright.

The men walked over to where the two women knelt looking down at a red blanket.

'Jesus Christ!' Paddy's voice was low, incredulous. 'Did that little lot come out of there?' He pointed to the hole before him.

Donna nodded and her eyes strayed to the bundles of money before her.

'The dirty bastard, the filthy bastard! Did you know about this, Jackson?' Paddy turned on Davey who was staring at the bundles of money in shock.

515

'How the fuck would I know about this little lot? Do you think it would still have been here if I had?'

Carol said testily, 'Where's it come from, that's what I'd like to know?'

Davey laughed softly. 'I wondered what Georgio had done with Lewis's blag money. He had to have taken it nearby, because he couldn't have gone too far away. See, he didn't have the time.'

'The broken concrete was covered by the boxes. It was only as we moved them out that we saw it.'

Paddy was fuming. 'We always moved the merchandise by night, he knew that. We never chanced moving it during the day. Georgio was going to come back for this, wasn't he? And we'd none of us have been any the wiser.'

He shook his head in temper and with a sneaking respect for the man who had tucked him up in more ways than one.

'When's he due out, Donna? I really need to know the answer, right?'

She nodded, all the fight and the fear gone now because it was only money, nothing but money, under the concrete floor.

'Today, Paddy. The jump's today.' She saw both Davey's and Paddy's look of shock and laughed loudly. 'You realise what's going to happen, don't you? Georgio is going to leave the lot of us high and dry. He's laughing up his sleeve at the lot of us.'

She roared with mirth, big tears rolling down her face at the stunned expression on their faces.

'He has had the lot of us over, you as well as me. I wonder when he would have come for his money, eh? Knowing Georgio like I do, he wouldn't have left this here for long. Maybe he was going to send his darling girlfriend Vida over, eh? Maybe that was the plan.' She was laughing so hard, it was hurting her.

Carol placed an arm around her shoulders and helped her to her feet.

'Come on, Donna, give over, will you?'

Paddy nodded. 'Get her away from here, Carol. Me and Davey will sort this lot out.'

Carol sniggered hysterically. 'You fools. We phoned the Old Bill – we thought this was a body. They'll be here any second now!'

Donna started to laugh again, too. She was in stitches at the sight of the two men's consternation.

Paddy and Davey were stunned.

'You're joking!'

Donna stopped laughing long enough to say, 'Afraid not. I wish I was, Paddy. I wish to Christ I was.'

516

Paddy and Davey walked slowly away from the two women as if they were mad, then hearing the sounds of police sirens, ran from the lock-up leaving the two women there alone.

Donna and Carol heard the men's car pull away. Looking at one another, they stepped closer together and, placing dirty hands around each other's waists, hugged each other as if they were dancing.

Chapter Forty-Four

Dessie Brooks was bored; he was bored with looking at the women, and he was bored with sitting still. Every few minutes he fingered the small mobile phone in his pocket.

A woman walked past him, and he smiled at her. She ignored him as Dessie had expected, but it didn't deter him from trying it on with every woman who took his fancy. That covered over eighty percent of the female population. Dessie smiled at them, from fifteen to fifty-five. He was a great believer in safety in numbers and the old adage: You don't look at the mantelpiece when you're stoking the fire. Dessie liked them married if possible, then you always had an out. Married women were less likely to complain if he was a bit rough with them, because they shouldn't have been out with him in the first place.

Dessie liked this job, but it was boring. Even watching women became boring after a while.

Five minutes later Dessie struck pure gold. A woman of indeterminate age, wearing a black leather coat and high heels, sat beside him and actually smiled at him.

Their conversation took the usual course.

'Never seen you here before.'

Dessie hadn't sat near the ferry terminal before, not out of choice anyway, and never in the open. He usually travelled in the back of a meat wagon to prisons.

'I'm here visiting the prison actually. A friend is in Albany.'

Dessie smiled widely. The friend was in fact her old man and they both knew it.

'Too bad, love. What's he in for?'

The woman pursed her lips and looked into Dessie's face before answering, 'He's doing seven years for malicious wounding. But it wasn't his fault.'

Dessie nodded.

'The ferry should be in soon.'

As she spoke Dessie saw the sweatbox come into the ferry terminal and, turning to the woman, he said heartily, 'Fancy a drink in the pub? The ferry won't go for a while yet.'

The woman nodded. 'My name's Cathy, what's yours?'

Dessie put his arm around her and walked her over to the pub. 'My name's Eugene, Eugene O'Doughall.'

The woman exclaimed loudly, 'That's a bleedin' mouthful!'

Dessie, always hopeful, said, 'We'll see about that later, eh? Now you sit yourself down and order a drink while I go for a Jimmy Riddle.'

Dessie slipped outside the pub and made the call he was getting five hundred pounds to make. He dialled Eric's mobile and said, 'The box is in place. It's five past one.'

Eric grunted and Dessie shut off the phone and went back to the lovely Cathy and the *Sporting Life*.

All in all, it hadn't been a bad day.

Eric began the laborious drive to Devil's Bridge in the skip lorry. He drove in the slow lane, allowing plenty of room for people to overtake him, even going so far as to wave them past as a good plant-driver was apt to do. His balaclava was rolled up like a bobble hat and pulled down over his brow and he was wearing the dark overalls.

He felt under the front seat for the Armalite and smiled to himself. He loved jumps best of all. He enjoyed the snatching of children being brought up by arsehole foreigners in arsehole countries, but it came a poor second.

It was excitement he craved, he adored. It was like being in the Falklands again or the Gulf. Not that he was in the Gulf with the British Army, or not officially anyway. A mercenary was called on by all sorts and the British government were not averse to a bit of a tickle now and again themselves. It was a habit they'd got from the Yanks. Something he had learned in Korea, something that had stood him in good stead and filled his pockets for over thirty years.

Behind him drove Jonnie H. and the McAnultys. The bikes were primed and ready to go, the weaponry all accounted for and within arm's reach.

All they had to do now was arrive at the destination and wait.

And the waiting was the hard part.

The police were aware that a top security prisoner was on his way, and as usual in these cases they sat at roundabouts and crossroads along the route. The vehicle was not to stop at any time. On the sweatbox's arrival at Portsmouth, it was allowed off the ferry and watched closely by a large traffic vehicle which followed the sweatbox to the next destination where it was handed over to a small Panda car.

From there the sweatbox picked up speed as it hit the A1 and the panda car followed at a distance of three vehicles. Unless you were in the know it looked like a normal police vehicle that could have been carrying C-grade prisoners to an open jail.

Only the police and the prison service knew who it was carrying. The two policemen in the Panda car were enjoying the drive and speculating on different things, matters that had nothing to do with the sweatbox before them.

Wives and kids, DIY and rugby were the talk for the two PCs, who were unaware that the sweatbox was to be jumped in less than thirty minutes.

Parking the skip lorry in the small slip road, Eric lit a cigar and sat back reading the *Guardian*, every so often looking into the mirror beside him to gauge the traffic. Jonnie H. had parked the Mercedes twenty yards away behind the bushes on a grass verge. It was practically invisible from the road.

They waited, the tension in the Mercedes mounting and the men getting jump sweat in their thick boilersuits and knitted hats.

Harry Hutchins and Freddie Carver sat in an L-reg Cosworth by the footbridge two miles down from Devil's Bridge. Both were calm, not to say bored. Harry was to drive the Cosworth and Freddie was to drive the Granada. Both were experienced drivers, both had their creds and both were used to the pressure.

Harry was one of the best drivers in the business; he was also a good friend of Eric's so consequently had worked all over the world on snatches, from Turkey and Egypt to Dubai. He had taken weeks driving the different roads around this area to find the route he wanted. To the casual eye he looked nondescript; with his sandy hair and eyebrows, and regular features, he looked like everyone's dad or brother.

Freddie was small and dark. Like Harry he was a good driver and didn't panic easily. And like Harry, he took the job seriously and was well-prepared for it; even though it was only his task to remove the McAnultys, not Georgio, he had arranged for them to pick up their car within five miles of the jump. The police wouldn't know what had hit them.

All the men would disappear off the face of the earth.

The drivers included.

Peter Jones was singing as he drove the sweatbox along the A1. Even though it was against regulations, he always brought a small cassette-player with him and sang his heart out to country and western music,

520

ignoring the shouts from the back of the van and the banging on the wall behind him.

'Fuck 'em' was his attitude. He was the main man in these cases. He knew it and the screws knew it.

He locked them in and he let them out. He was the Big Cheese and he loved every second of it.

Dolly Parton was next, singing *I Will Always Love You*. It was one of his favourites so he turned it up even louder, distorting Dolly's voice to drown out the shouts from the box behind him.

Contemplating Dolly's three biggest assets, one of them her voice, he sang his little heart out.

The three wardens and the prisoner all groaned as the first waves of music wafted through the grille.

Jones was still singing at the top of his voice when he saw the skip lorry crossing the road ahead of him and put his foot instinctively on the brakes. The skip lorry was parked across both lanes of the road, stopping all traffic.

He was too late to see the Mercedes van skid across the road behind him.

Closing his eyes, he realised he was caught up in a jump. Opening the grille behind him, he shouted through to the warders: 'Keep your cool, we're being jumped.'

He heard three voices shout out: 'Turn that fucking cassette off!'

Jonnie H. was on the Panda car before they could call in. Thrusting the sawn-off shotgun in through the window, he shouted, 'Out! Fucking out! Out!'

The constant shouting frightened the police officers. Getting out of the car, they watched as Eric ripped out their radio. He then removed their walkie-talkie radios and told them to follow him to the sweatbox.

A woman wearing a fur coat and driving a Mercedes Sports handed her keys over to Jonnie H. with the plea, 'Please give them back to me. I really have to be home for the children.'

Jonnie laughed outright and threw the keys into the field beside them.

No one refused their car keys and everyone was quiet, watching the excitement around them.

In the sweatbox Peter Jones was feeling frightened but protected. He knew that the windscreen was bullet-proof and he sat with his arms folded, waiting for the jumpers' next move.

His face soon took on a different expression when Eric walked towards him with the Armalite.

The three wardens in the back of the van heard the sound of the shot as it hit the windscreen, closely followed by two more. They were terrified.

Peter Jones pushed himself down in the driver's seat, and the shots whistled past his head. He stayed down there, praying that the men would just go away and leave him alone. Suddenly, he smelt the petrol. Sitting bolt upright, he saw it being poured inside the hole in the windscreen, its fumes making him gag.

The wardens smelt it through the metal grille and one of them blurted out: 'It's fucking petrol! They're going to burn us out!'

David Harker, the oldest and most intelligent there, said, 'Then they burn him out as well, don't they?'

The wardens looked over at the prisoner, who was laughing at them. Once more pandemonium ensued.

Eric was standing on the wheel arch of the sweatbox now and he had lit a piece of rag. He shouted out as loud as he could, his face screwed up in hatred behind the balaclava: 'Get out of the van, or I'll burn you where you fucking sit! I'll burn you alive! Now GET THE FUCK OUT!'

Peter Jones opened the door of the van in double quick time. Dragging him out, Eric was now all reassurance and friendliness, the screaming hatred gone from his voice.

'You just open the back of the van, mate, and you'll be home tonight eating your dinner with the wife and kids, all right? Now take it easy, just do what we ask, OK?'

Fumbling with the keys, Jones began to open the back of the van. His hands were stiff with fright and he was having trouble remembering the combination of movements that opened the doors.

'It's a combi lock, mate. I have to remember the combination, the movements that open the lock, otherwise it'll just jam.'

Eric, expecting this, said gently in his ear, 'Just relax, mate, and open the door. No one will get hurt, all right? I give you my word.'

While Eric was handling the driver, the McAnultys had finished taking the car keys and were getting out the bikes ready for the off.

All they kept repeating, over and over, was: 'Come on, come on,' under their breath like a mantra.

The two policemen were lying on the ground by the sweatbox, their arms cuffed behind their backs. Listening out with all their might for names, accents, anything that might be of help.

Jonnie H. spotted a man getting out of his car. He was parked behind the Mercedes van and trying to see what was going on. He had a mobile phone in his hand. Walking over to him, Jonnie H. slammed the butt of the shotgun into his face. The man crumpled and Jonnie stood looking at the line of cars, daring anyone else to get out and have a look. The woman in the Mercedes Sports was crying.

Jonnie H. turned away and went back to the bikes, saying in an incredulous voice, 'You always fucking get one, don't you? Can't people keep their fucking noses out of nothing?'

The man dragged himself back to his car, his face bleeding profusely.

The lock popped and the double doors sprang open. Inside the dimness of the sweatbox four faces were looking out.

Eric shook his head in amazement. 'Who the fuck are you?'

Big Ricky, grinning widely, said, 'Who the fuck are *you*? Come on, man, gimme a break. Let me out of here.'

'Unlock him.'

The screw nearest Ricky unlocked both feet and hand chains and Ricky, standing with difficulty, made his way over to the doors. Outside, the men all looked at him in shock.

'Who the fucking hell's that? Where's Georgio?'

Ricky sighed heavily. 'Give me a lift, man. I'll make my own way after that, OK?'

Eric, not sure what to do for the first time in his life, heard Jonnie H. say to the black man: 'Was you the only one taken out? Was anyone else to go?'

Ricky shook his head. 'Let's get going, man. I'll tell you all about it once it's quiet, OK? The filth won't be long coming, you can bet your bottom dollar one of this lot's got a car phone.'

He pointed at the lines of cars and next thing he knew he was on the back of a motorbike and they were bumping over the ploughed field that took them past the Devil's Bridge and to the chop. Just as the police arrived on the scene, sirens wailing and faces red with embarrassment.

As they approached the footbridge for the chop, the police gained on them. Jumping off the bikes, the men pulled out handguns and shot at the police cars' tyres. All the policemen dropped down in their seats, fearful of the consequences if they got out. They watched as the six men ran over the footbridge, and called in on their car radios for more assistance and to give as much information as they could. They could not even see what cars the villains were getting into because of the position of the bridge itself.

Freddie Carver took one look at the man with Eric and said: 'Who the fucking hell is that?' Rolling his eyes heavenwards, Eric was removing his overalls and jumper and trying to get changed quick enough to

523

get away and find out what the hell was going on. The men were throwing the overalls into the boots of the cars.

Jonnie H. shouted across at Eric: 'What are you going to do with him?'

He shook his head. 'I don't know yet. You'd better come with me.' He pushed Ricky into the front seat of a motor, and down into the footrest out of the way, then he got in the back of the Cosworth with Jonnie H. Harry pulled away and they drove sedately along the country road so as not to bring any attention to themselves.

Tidying up his shirt, Eric put on a tie and slipped on a suit jacket. Without the balaclava and overalls, both men looked like normal businessmen on their way home from work. Jonnie H., shrugging on a tweed jacket and a red tie, looked at the huge black man crouched in the footrest and shook his head sagely.

'This is going to cause untold hag, Eric – you do realise that, don't you?'

Eric laughed. 'What a fucking turn-out! Who are you, mate – and where the fuck is Georgio Brunos?'

Ricky, smiling widely at his piece of good luck, said: 'Let's get on our way and then I'll tell you what happened.'

Donna and Carol were still chuckling when they pulled away from the garages in the Astra van.

'Did you see them two run? I'd have thought my Davey would have had more sense than to fall for that one. There's always Old Bill round there. It's a shithole of a place.'

Donna smirked. 'I loved seeing that Paddy shitting himself though. I hate him now. To think I was going to give him a percentage of the building for all his help! God, I must have been so naive, so stupid!' Her voice trailed off.

Carol, placing a hand over hers on the steering wheel, said lightly: 'We're all stupid where blokes are concerned. It just takes us a while to suss that out.'

Then she laughed.

'What are we going to do with all that dosh, eh? What I couldn't do with a few grand of that now I ain't got Davey hanging round my neck!'

Donna looked at Carol seriously and said, 'Are you really finished with him, Carol? Really, truly finished with him?'

Carol nodded. 'Oh, yes. I put up with a lot from him over the years. Well, you already know that. But those books . . . they killed anything I felt for him. I could never look at him again without seeing those kids.'

524

'You should have seen them in Sri Lanka. It made me feel sick to think that they were there, being abused and used, and I was living off the proceeds.'

Carol bit on her lip. 'We all were, darlin',' she said. 'Not just you. I should have guessed something like that was going on, but you don't, do you? You trust people, and you trust them completely. I knew my Davey ducked and dived, I just didn't think he ducked and dived like that. Makes you wonder what else the fuckers were up to.'

Donna turned off the A13 towards her house.

'I should have known, too. Look at Talkto. Stephen was in over his head there.'

'Is he really dead, Donna?'

She nodded vigorously.

'Oh yes, he's dead all right, or should be by now – and do you know something, Carol? I don't really care. I know that sounds terrible but it's the truth. He didn't deserve to live, none of them do really. Georgio included. Once he's back in nick, me and Alan Cox will be hounded. I might use my half of that money to go somewhere. What will you do with yours?'

Carol's face was a picture of shock and astonishment.

'Are you serious?'

'Of course I am. That wasn't Georgio's to take anyway. And let's face it, we can't give it back, can we? So you might as well have half and I'll use mine to get away from here. From everything.'

'How much is there?'

'Nearly three-quarters of a million pounds.'

'Jesus wept! Are you sure about this?'

Donna smiled grimly. 'Sure as I've ever been. Take it, start up another business, Carol. The notes are untraceable – that's why Georgio wanted it. You can spend it where the hell you like, love.'

Carol grinned, showing off her white teeth. 'You're getting to be a right villain!'

Donna shrugged. 'Well, I had a good teacher, didn't I?'

Bunty was sitting in her lounge reading a magazine when she heard the sound of a car on her drive.

She carried on reading, waiting for the inevitable knock. Bunty never opened a door before it was knocked on at least twice – it was part of her so-called image. People felt as if she was too busy to see them when she did that. It made her trivial little life worth leading to give the impression of busy-ness and authority, as if the world would stop turning without her.

When the knock didn't come, she put down her magazine and went over to the window. Her scream brought Harry from the kitchen, sandwich still in hand and linen napkin still tucked under his ample chin.

'What the hell's the matter, woman? Mrs Jenkins nearly sliced off her bleeding hand!'

'Look, Harry! Look what they're doing!'

He went to the window and what he saw gave him such a shock that he dropped his sandwich on to the damask covering of the chair beside him.

Then they were both rushing to the front door, fighting one another to get there first.

Flinging it open, Bunty shouted, 'What the bloody hell do you think you're doing?'

Donna gave her a big smile. 'I'm making a delivery, Bunty. Sorry it's not a Porsche. But this lot is where it should have been from day one!'

Piled on the drive were the books and magazines from the lock-up garage. Tipped out of their cardboard boxes, they were strewn everywhere, the wind picking up the magazines and distributing them haphazardly around the garden.

'By the way, I'm burning the floppy discs, Harry. I think that's the best thing, don't you? Oh, and before I go, you two had better get cleared up here. I've phoned the *Standard*, *Recorder* and *Sun*. They'll be here in no time. Child porn is big news, isn't it? Especially for the tabloids. And think what the local papers will make of it, you a magistrate and all!'

Carol and Donna got into the Astra van and watched Bunty as she began laying into Harry with her tongue.

Carol grinned. 'Be the first time Bunty ever did manual work in her life, eh?'

Donna watched the two of them in the van's mirror as she drove away.

'I enjoyed that,' she said. 'Now let's get home and see what else the day brings us, shall we?'

Eric and Jonnie H. were with Alan Cox and Anthony Calder at Eric's safe house in Ilford. The four men were listening in silence to the huge black man sitting before them.

'Listen, before I speak, I have to have some kind of assurance that what I tell you won't come back on me?'

Anthony Calder said levelly, 'Just tell us the truth. We can get the buzz from inside so don't worry about lying to us, all right?'

He poured Ricky out another large white rum and the four men sat back to listen.

526

'Georgio came to me to set up the nonces, right? I went along with him on the proviso that I could take out Donald Lewis at the same time. I wanted the big spot, I was sick of Lewis and his henchmen. I was doing a big one and didn't want to do it with Lewis hanging round my neck, you understand that?'

The men nodded.

'Well, this morning it all went off at ten a.m. We done two paedophiles, Hall and Denning. They were the two who turned Queen's evidence in that big trial a few months ago. You know, killing all the kids and that? So anyway, Georgio found out who they were and that was what he asked me to get him a weapon for. I asked why he wanted the weapon and he told me. That's when we cooked up the scam between us. I knew he was having hassle off of Lewis over money, the whole Wing knew that, so it seemed logical for the two of us to team up. We did. Well, four men died this morning.'

There ain't been a dicky bird on the News yet, but there wouldn't be, would there? They'll keep a lid on it until they can announce that they've sorted it all out. There's been nothing about the jump either. If there was I'd have had a call by now.'

Ricky nodded at Alan and continued. 'It was pandemonium, man. The Wing went crazy. Like, one guy was decapitated. There's this nutter, a schiz called Eros. He's had to have this guy's head forcibly removed from his arms. It was fucking weird man, really weird. Like it wasn't really happening. It was like we all got caught up in the violence, you know? You had to be there to see it.

'Georgio took out Lewis and I took out Lewis's minder, and then it all seemed to die down. The screws were in, we had made our point: No nonces in with the lifers. And then it was all quiet again. We were in a state of shock really at what we had done. I mean, you never seen blood like it. We were like animals, man. Like we all caught everyone else's excitement.'

He looked at the men as he spoke and Eric nodded in agreement. 'I know what you mean, I've seen it happen before in wartime.'

'Anyway, when we were all cornered by the screws in the rec room, in comes the Governor, Hanningfield. A prize prick if ever there was one. He was surrounded by his armed men and thought he was fucking something else, you know? Looking down his nose at us. We could see that the dead men had frightened him, shocked him, but he acted like he was the big king pin.

'Well, Georgio shit him up, man, Georgio shit up the Governor! You should have seen Hanningfield's face when the bucket of slops hit him. It was a picture, it was pure genius. I realise now this was to get on the laydown and meet with you lot. And that's what would

527

have happened, except it all went wrong for him.'

Alan sipped at his brandy and demanded, 'How? What went wrong?'

'There's a TV called Sadie. Georgio was friendly with her – nothing funny, I think Sadie had stayed in her cell throughout the riot. No one even realised that she wasn't there, to be honest. It all happened so fast, you know? Anyway, as I was saying, as we were all being led out, they were locking us up in our cells – I expect they were sorting out who were the ringleaders and whether to remove them – when Sadie shouts out: 'Georgio was in with Hall and Denning! He's part of their business!'

'No one took any notice. If Georgio had had any sense he would have ignored it. Instead he went crazy, man! And Sadie, this little queer Sadie, she fucking stabbed him, man, right through the heart! She went fucking loopy. I ran to help Georgio but they thought I was going to start the riot again and the armed screws nabbed me. I was off on a GOAD, and well, you know the rest. I think Sadie was put under sedation, she was off her head. There's no way they could have moved her with me.'

The four men were silent then Alan said, 'Is he dead?'

Ricky shrugged enormous shoulders. 'Your guess is as good as mine. They put the others in the cells at gunpoint, and then I was removed and blamed for being the leader, I suppose because Brunos was out of the way.'

He nodded at Eric and said, 'Thanks for taking me, man. I appreciate it.'

Eric shook his head in wonderment.

'You're welcome. We'd come for a jump and you were there. Call it fate! Now, who wants another drink while we sort out what the fuck happened here, and more importantly, who's going to pay all our bills?'

Donna and Carol arrived home to find Mario waiting with Dolly in the kitchen.

'Hello, Mario, what brings you here?'

He took in their dirty hands and clothes and Carol's flushed face and said, 'Stephen died on holiday, Donna. He drowned. My mum sent me over to give you the news.'

Donna stared at Mario for a few seconds before saying, 'Make a pot of tea for Mario, Dolly. Me and Carol are going up to shower and change, OK? We won't be long.'

Upstairs Donna listened to Carol on the phone to her elder daughter, asking her to look after Jamie until she got home. Then they looked at one another and shook their heads.

'Let's get showered and listen to the News on the radio, Carol. I need to know what the hell is going on with Georgio before I can make my next move. I've been frightened to listen to the news today. Once I find out the score, I can make my decision.'

Carol began to take off her clothes.

'What about Alan Cox?' she suggested. 'Why don't you ring him?'

Donna grimaced. 'Alan Cox is the *last* person I want to talk to at the moment.'

Already feeling better at the thought of a hot shower, Carol said saucily, 'I wouldn't want to talk to that one either love. I'd be too busy doing other things with him!'

Donna laughed gently. 'That's the trouble, Carol, I already have.'

She walked into the bathroom naked and Carol slumped down on the bed and said incredulously: 'Well, well, well. You *are* a dark horse, ain't you?'

Donna looked over her shoulder and said in a low voice, 'There's lots of things you don't know about me, Carol. There's an awful lot I don't know about myself.' She hesitated for a moment and then said, 'Yet.'

Epilogue

Donna watched as the bodies of Stephen and Georgio were lowered into the ground. She knew she should be crying, but she was dry-eyed. She could see Maeve being held up by Pa Brunos, the rest of her children around her, waiting for her lead as to what to do next.

It was funny, Donna reflected, how she seemed to have no feelings any more. Her husband, the big love of her life, was being buried and she felt nothing at all.

She saw Big Paddy trying to catch her eye and she looked away from him, swallowing down a half-smile. He didn't frighten her any more, none of them did. She wondered why.

Davey was trying to attract Carol's attention. Out of the corner of her mouth, she hissed to Donna: 'If that ponce don't leave me alone I'll knock him into the grave along with your Georgio.'

Donna felt hysterical laughter well up in her throat; she swallowed it down. Then her attention was drawn towards Milton Hardcastle, the liar of the building sites. He was crying like a baby over Georgio and she wondered at how her husband could have been so loved, yet been so bad. Was he really that good an actor, or was he just caught up in the love of money?

She instinctively turned her face away from the TV cameras. This was still a big news story. The man murdered by the transvestite, instigator of one of the most violent riots in prison history, was being buried alongside his brother who had died on holiday. She had nearly laughed out loud on seeing Stephen described as a 'young up-and-coming businessman' in the tabloids. They were making the two brothers out to be like Cain and Abel. One too good to be true and the other rotten to the core. They even had Maeve believing it. She had sold her story to the *News of the World*, giving them photos of the two men as children, describing their childhood.

Donna shrugged inside her black coat. Good luck to Maeve; let her make some money from them. It seemed fitting somehow.

The priest was still talking, making the most of his television fame. The Chase cemetery had never been so popular. People had come from all over the East End, hoping for a glimpse of the dead men's family and friends.

The worst of it all was, Donna was now a very rich woman; yet she didn't really want the money. Even the pay-outs from the insurance seemed dirty to her.

Maeve had refused to allow her to pay for Georgio's funeral, insisting that it would be paid for by her and Pa. They would bury their two sons together.

Donna heard the priest's '*Amen*' and sighed inwardly.

Carol stood beside her, together with Dolly, and the three women moved away from the graveside towards the black limousine as if of one mind.

Alan watched Donna from the other side of the graveyard and his heart went out to her. He walked to his car and climbed in beside Nick and Albie.

'Well, the dirty deed is done.'

Nick nodded and watched the mourners as they made their way back to the black limousines.

'Georgio lost out every way in the end, eh?' Alan said heavily.

Nick said softly: 'Poetic justice, really. You can drop me off in Soho, Alan I have a few people to see before I make my way home.'

Alan started the car and drove away before the three-ring circus started. Already the camera crews were taking shots of everyone, hoping against hope to see a few well-known villains to add colour to their stories.

As Donna walked to the funeral car, Detective Inspector Frank Laughton placed a gentle hand on her arm.

'I'm sorry, Mrs Brunos. I never meant you any harm, you know that.'

Donna faced him and said: 'I know that, Mr Laughton. You were just doing your job. Now it's all over, for everyone.'

Laughton was nonplussed at her words and Donna grinned up at him as she added, 'I really thought you had fitted him up, I really believed that.'

Looking down into her face, he said honestly, 'I did – but you see, Mrs Brunos, I had the edge. Because I knew what your husband was. I just wanted him off the streets, that's all.'

Donna nodded sagely, then squeezed the bigger man's arm.

'You were a wise man, Mr Laughton,' she murmured, 'and I didn't see that for a long time.'

Detective Inspector Frank Laughton watched in silence as she moved away from him. He knew in his heart there was a story to be told; he also knew that it was one story he wouldn't even begin to

531

understand. Because Donna Brunos had been far too good for her husband – and he had a feeling that even she was aware of that fact now.

Maeve and Pa Brunos were waiting for her on the small pathway between rows of graves.

'There's a lot of me here now, Donna. I'll not be buried in the Old Country after this.'

Donna hugged Maeve to her, both women feeling the enormity of what had happened. 'You knew what Georgio was, didn't you?'

'I knew, I always knew, but he was my son.' Maeve stared back to the open graves and whispered brokenly, 'They were my sons, and in me own way, I loved them.'

Donna nodded, and linking arms the two women made their way back to the funeral cars.

Pa Brunos's sad voice broke through the air. 'What a day, eh? Two sons buried. Two sons.'

He shook his head, tears rolling down his face and for the first time that day Donna wanted to really cry. Not for Georgio, or for Stephen, but for the two people who had created them. Turning, Donna looked into Pa's face.

'My Georgio, he loved you, Donna. Don't you ever forget that.'

She felt the tears on her tongue, tasted the saltiness of them. They reminded her of the tears she had shed when Georgio had first been taken from her, when she had cried out for him.

Pa wiped his eyes with a crumpled handkerchief. 'I'll see you back at the house then, eh?'

Donna nodded, watching as he led Maeve away, towards their funeral car.

Carol's voice broke into her thoughts. 'Do you want us to come back with you?'

'If you don't mind. I don't think I could stand it there alone.'

Carol hugged her. 'That's what friends are for, ain't it, Doll?'

Dolly pursed her lips and blew out the air with an unladylike snort. 'Have you seen who's over there?' she said viciously.

Donna nodded wearily. 'Leave it, Dolly love,' she said. 'Please, just leave it.'

'Look at her standing there, bold as brass, all tits, teeth and fucking tan!'

Carol's voice was envious and Donna giggled despite herself. 'Funny how it doesn't hurt any more. All I feel is relieved it's all over.'

As they climbed into the limousine, Donna glanced once more at Vida, standing alone with the child beside her. Her long, streaked

532

hair was backcombed to its full height and her face was covered in make-up. She looked down, unable to meet Donna's eyes. As they drove past, Donna searched the child's face for any sign of his father there. He was Georgio's child all right; he even had the long thick eyelashes more suited to a girl than a boy.

Then closing her mind on the scene, Donna pushed the woman and the child from her mind.

It was time to move on.

For all of them.

Maeve sat on her bed. She could hear the sounds of the family coming through the thin walls. She looked down at the photographs in her hands and felt the sting of tears again. Georgio looking at the camera with his huge dark eyes, Stephen making his First Holy Communion, looking serious and proud all at the same time. His face, like Georgio's, full of childish innocence.

Then she thought of the child at the cemetery, Georgio's child, her flesh and blood . . . and she knew exactly what she had to do. The child was the living image of him.

She stood up unsteadily and went back to the wake.

A lot of the relatives from Ireland had flown over, but the family from Rhodes had not bothered. Only Pa's younger sister Patrina had come, and she had travelled down from Manchester where she lived with her eldest daughter, having been widowed two years previously.

Patrina took her arm and squeezed it.

'What a day. Who would have thought any of us would be burying our children? It's the wrong order. They should be burying us.'

Maeve pulled away from her and walked over to where Donna sat sipping whisky and nibbling a ham sandwich.

'Hello, darlin'.'

Donna looked into the strained, tired face of her mother-in-law. 'Hello, Maeve,' she said tenderly.

Opening her arms wide, Maeve pulled Donna into them and the two women cried together publicly. The rest of the family stood back watching, pleased at this turn of events. It reinforced in all their minds that Georgio couldn't have been all bad to have held the love of these two women.

Maeve was crying for what could have been, and Donna was crying for all the children in Sri Lanka and the rest of the world who had been harmed by the two men buried earlier in the day.

Maeve whispered into Donna's ear, 'I'll see to the child, Donna. You're a good woman to have told me everything.'

Donna smiled through her tears. She sincerely hoped that

Georgio's son gave Maeve more happiness than his father ever had.

Donna was saved from answering by Uncle Jimmy beginning to sing 'Kevin Barry'. From long experience Donna knew that once the Irish rebel songs began, the wake was about to turn into a party. Tears and laughter would be the order of the day, then the reminiscences.

Maeve turned from her and began to sing with him:

> *In Mountjoy jail, one Monday morning*
> *High above the gallows tree*
> *Kevin Barry gave his young life*
> *For the cause of liberty.*

Donna knew she had to sit the wake out, and she would do that. But only for Maeve and Pa and the family.

Not for Georgio or Stephen Brunos.

She was a free woman now and a wealthy one, who owned a building business, a car lot, and Talkto Enterprises, as well as two plots of barren land abroad, all of which she was selling to the highest bidder.

She was free, free and clear, with stolen money in her possession, as well as a house worth in excess of a million pounds. She was as free as a bird now.

Yet she still wasn't happy.

There were too many loose ends to tie up.

Alan Cox arrived at Donna's house at eleven-thirty in the morning the day after the funeral. Dolly opened the door to him.

'What do you want?' she snapped.

Alan smiled. A charming smile. 'I'd like to see Donna, please.'

Dolly bridled. 'Well, you can't. She's prostrate with grief and she can't see anyone.'

Alan laughed. 'I'm sure she is.'

He pushed past Dolly and walked into the house, calling Donna's name.

Dolly shut the door and said, 'She ain't here.'

Alan looked at her. 'Well, her car's in the drive,' he said loudly. 'Don't tell me she's walked off somewhere. This house is in the back of beyond. Now where is she please, love? I have to see her, Dolly.'

Dolly shook her head in resignation. 'She's gardening. Sit in the kitchen and I'll fetch her.'

Alan followed her through and said, 'I'll find her, while you get the kettle on, all right?'

He was past her and out into the garden before Dolly could answer.

He followed the pathway towards the tennis court. Turning a corner, he came across Donna dressed in tight jeans, a thick cable jumper and Wellingtons, looking far too elegant to be burning rubbish in a small brazier.

He walked up to her and said, 'My mum used to do the gardening. Said it relaxed her.'

Donna looked over her shoulder at him. 'What brings you here, Alan?' she answered.

He watched as she threw a small bundle on to the fire. 'I've come to see how you are and to tell you something.'

Donna threw more rubbish on the fire and laughed gently. 'What have you come to tell me, Alan? Say it and go away.'

He bit on his cigar then he said, 'I've come, Donna, to see if you need any more help.'

'No, actually, I don't. So you had a wasted journey.'

He bit once more on the unlit cigar and burst out: 'You're not making this easy for me, you know, Donna. I'm trying to tell you that—' He looked at Donna's gloved hands and said incredulously, 'What the fuck are you burning there?'

He walked towards her and when he saw what was on the fire he nearly choked on the cigar in his mouth.

'Where the fuck did you get that money from!'

Donna laughed gaily. 'It was Lewis's money, from the robbery. I gave half to Carol Jackson, and as you can see, I'm burning my half.'

Alan pulled her round to face him. 'Are you mad, woman? There's a fortune there!'

Donna nodded. 'I'm not mad, Alan. In fact, I have never felt better in my life. And I'm enjoying this, really enjoying it.' She took a fifty-pound note from a bundle and lit it in the fire.

'Here, light your cigar.'

Alan looked at the burning money for a second, watching the Queen's face crumple and burn, and then he bent his head and lit his cigar, puffing on the huge brown Havana between laughing and coughing.

Finally he held the lit cigar in his hand and grinned at her. 'You're a wealth of surprises, do you know that?'

Donna looked up into his face and, feeling the pull of him, her need of him, she said, 'You had to come to me, Alan. You realise that, don't you? You will always have to come to me. My days of running after anyone are long gone. Georgio knocked all that out of me. Now what you see is what you get, and what we had in Sri Lanka was the best I have ever had in my life. But we had things to do, both

535

of us, before we could be together.

'Now the only thing I ask is that you always come to me, that's all I want from you. That you will always do the running.'

Pulling her into his arms, Alan said gently, 'I'll always follow you, Donna, wherever you want to go. I have never in my life loved before, not really, not until the day you walked into my office. You're in my mind all the time, and you're in my heart. I will follow you, Donna, every day of my life, because I know now I can't live without you.'

When she still didn't answer, he whispered, 'You do love me a little bit, don't you?'

Donna smiled at the hesitation in his voice and then, grinning, she pulled him to her, hugging him tightly.

'That, Alan Cox, is about the only thing I am really sure of.'

Then she kissed him.

When she had finished, he looked down into her eyes and said, 'Come to bed with me.'

Donna laughed, her blush accentuating her creamy skin.

'What, now? What about Dolly?'

Alan grinned and said craftily, 'I'm sorry, Donna, but I can't accommodate her and all. One woman at a time is more than enough for me.'

Throwing the last of the money on the fire, Donna linked arms with him and said: 'I'll make sure you never want another woman again.'

Her voice was strong and he laughed gently.

'Actually, that's just what I was hoping you'd say.'

Together they walked into the house, the fire sending up thick black smoke behind them.